The Girl From East Berlin
a romantic docu-drama of the East-West divide

Robert Corfe is a journalist and writer who for many years has worked in international commerce and engaged his energies on social issues. He is also the author of *My Conflict With A Soviet Spy* *the story of the Ron Evans spy case* (originally published under the pseudonym of Eddie Miller) recording his adventures in Finland in the mid-1960s; and some twenty years later, *Death In Riyadh dark secrets in hidden Arabia* (originally published under the name of Geoff Carter), describing his experiences as a businessman in the Gulf States. He is also the author of several specialised political science titles.

The Girl
From East Berlin

a romantic docu-drama of the
East-West divide

Robert Corfe

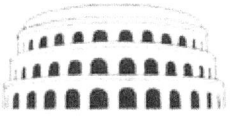

Arena Books

Second edition 2021
First published by Arena Books in 2007 under the pseudonym of James Furner.

Arena Books
6 Southgate Green
Bury St. Edmunds
IP33 2BL

www.arenabooks.co.uk

Distributed in America by Ingram International, One Ingram Blvd., PO Box 3006,
LaVergne, TN 37086-1986, USA.

Corfe, Robert- 1935
  The Girl From East Berlin *a romantic docu-drama of the East-West divide*
  1.   Cold War – Fiction 2.Berlin (Germany) – Fiction 3.Love stories
  I.   Title
  823.9'2[F]

ISBN-13 978-1-914390-08-1

BIC classification: FSR

Printed & bound by Lightningsource UK

Cover design
By Jon Baxter

Typeset in Times New Roman

This is a historical narrative of a people divided against itself through the accident of political events.

The story of Berlin may stand as a metaphor for the political division, strife, and despondency of peoples worldwide.

In retrospect, and in a changed world, sixty years after the events, it is therefore now possible to

Dedicate this book

to the cause of universal amity and unity amongst peoples and races in what is now referred to as our "global village."

Contents

List of Illustrations
Between pages 286 and 287

a) Entrance hall of Martin Schutz's apartment block
b) Site of the former Eierschale night club as it appears today
c) Strausberger Platz today
d) Site of the former Art Shop as it exists today
e) View of Stalin Allee in 1959
f) Street scene in the grotty end of Stalin Allee as described early in the book
g) Karpfen pond, Treptower Park, where Dagmar often walked with her father
h) The Renot family home as it appears today
i) View of the ground floor flat shared by Dagmar and her grandmother as it appears today
j) View of Graetz Strasse in 2006
k) The grim former barracks barracks of the Volkspolizei in Bouche Strasse
l) Puschkin Allee today
m) Karl Marx Strasse (West Berlin) where Papa Renot liked to window-shop, as it appears today
n) Beach at Langer See where Dagmar and Dietrich first met
o) Humboldt University as it appears today
p) Window display of FDJ HQ in Unter den Linden (1959)
q) View of Max Möller's flat in Zehlendorf
r) Site of the crash after the car chase, off Gertrauden Strasse (picture taken two years after the event)
s) The notorious Stasi prison in Hohenschönhausen, now a memorial site and museum (See Chapter 63)
t) - w) Berlin Wall in 1963
x)   Souvenirs on sale of a dreaded past, central Berlin 2006

All illustrations © by the author, Robert Corfe

Prologue

"But each day brings its petty dust
Our soon-chok'd souls to fill,
And we forget because we must,
And not because we will."

Matthew Arnold, *Absence*

Time is an emollient which erases the memory of past pain and events, or casts a new and false perception on the truth of experience. Eventually, the memory of a past age takes on the reflected ambience of the present as the former is absorbed and only seen through the values of the latter, and in this way *original* memory or *original* experience is lost forever. This explains the apparent impossibility of re-creating the true thought-patterns of the past, or accurately re-creating history as it was actually felt at the moment of impact.

But forgetfulness and a sweeter cast of thought in distorting the recollection of long-ago events is often not only a blessing but a necessity, for how else could we adapt and derive strength to face the present and plan for the future? If we are to live in a good and meaningful sense we must reject the past with its shame or disappointments, or at least create a new kind of consciousness which soothes the pain of unwanted memory. In this way sanity is preserved and strength is summoned for a constructive life ahead.

The city of Berlin has experienced many vicissitudes during its relatively short history as a major capital. Its people, and indeed, those throughout the diverse regions of the country, have long been adept in turning their backs on the past, not purely out of free choice or the will to do so, but rather through the necessity of survival. The subjectivity of the German temperament has placed the race amongst the most a-historical of peoples, and these characteristics have arisen in all probability through the frequent, sudden, and violent changes of political circumstances through the past four hundred years of its tumultuous history.

These changes have not so much been due to the internal politics of the country, for it never achieved a unified autonomy as a nation-state until 1870-71, but rather as a victim of external European power politics over so long a period. This explains both an underlying resentment against the threat of foreign aggression which tortured the German psyche for so long a period, and the compensatory militarism and an ultra-nationalism which developed as a logical consequence in the last quarter of the 19th century. Germany defined as a geographical term comprising a wide variety of princely and other states, at one time partly held together by the loose federation of the Holy Roman Empire, which Voltaire once famously described as neither Holy, Roman, nor an Empire, was rarely powerful in itself and of little significance in influencing the politics of Europe.

For centuries its people were rather the pawns of French or Austrian or Swedish high politics, and when this culminated in the bloodiest of all civil conflicts, the Thirty Years War, it was a Richelieu, a Hapsburg, or a Gustavus Adolphus who "called the shots" in sustaining the interests of their own countries, but it was Germany which unwittingly remained the battleground and victim in a complex struggle supposedly between the forces of Catholicism and Protestantism. It was inevitable that all this would lead to deep feelings of resentment and injustice, which passed from one generation to another; and even when Prussia, the most dominant state, achieved an honourable role in helping regain the peace and stability of Europe in 1815, she felt cheated of her rightful recognition by perfidious Albion and the suave diplomacy of Wellington who was so well-received in the courts of Europe.

A prominent historian of a later generation, Hermann von Treitschke, made much play of this episode in the years leading up to the First World War, in stirring the pot against Britain as the power intent on frustrating the German desire for a place in the sun. It was, perhaps, an unfair and unfortunate stance to adopt, since the elderly Blücher's late arrival on the field of Waterloo in no way diminished the subsequent heroism and contribution to the final victory of the allied forces, and so it may be asked, what was there to prevent the two countries remembering the event in a spirit of mutual cooperation and warm friendship? But then political alliances, or even comradeship in war, are not in themselves sufficient to generate a genuine feeling of amity between peoples. There has to be something more.

International friendship between peoples is not to be achieved through the pronouncements of political leaders, or those meaningless agreements with their saccharine clauses to which we became so accustomed in the immediate post-War period, but rather through a consciousness which penetrates the majority population, and this is only achieved through the passing of generations. It has been acknowledged that the people of Germany today are not only amongst the most liberal and democratic in Europe and throughout the world, but also amongst those who are most intent on international friendship as a *practical* realisation, and partly for this reason they have been most keen on promoting the ideals of the EU. And Berlin is the recently restored capital whose citizenry are most keen in promoting these ideals.

But these changes could not have come about without a forgetfulness of the past and a determination to build a new world, and adopt new ideals or a new mindset to enable such a future. The past needed to be forgotten since in the eyes of the world it was shameful, and new ideas needed to be sought as the foundation for confidence and self-worth in the task of reconstruction. The resentments referred to above are not only long forgotten, but to contemporaries, belongs to a past which is "incomprehensible." Nonetheless, they are mentioned as facts of existence since there are occasional passages in the book which follows when characters seem to betray the expression of resentments long-forgotten or even of unknown origin. This reflects the underlying reality that although we may be successful in suppressing the consciousness of past events, we can never erase the subconscious and escape entirely from the consequences of the past.

The present book was written more than forty-five years ago, and describes events which took place some two or three years previously, and so were still fresh in the author's memory. The manuscript had lain boxed-up and undisturbed in an attic amongst a jumble of ageing documents for four decades, and on its re-discovery, it was dusted down and re-read, and suddenly a world from a past and different age was revealed again in all the pristine clarity of its immediate occurrence. The book had been written in the light of both personal memory and with the correcting aid of detailed diary entries, and because of this the following docu-drama may more accurately be described by the ugly (and possibly confusing) word of *faction* than as a proper work of fiction.

It takes on the form of a true historical record, not only because of the accuracy with which people, things, and events are described, but because impressions and feelings are recorded with the immediacy of their occurrence without the reflection or false perception which accumulates with the passing of time. Drama or irony is often added to the description of historical events because we often know the dénouement of a significant episode, and can smile at the remarks of personalities in realising their ignorance of impending disaster. A more true account of history needs to be stripped of this intervening or covert commentary, for in real life we can never predict the future, and when we attempt to do so, our conclusions usually swerve to the wrong side of optimism or pessimism. And so it is with the characters in this book. We live in an unpredictable world where all certainties are illusion. At most we can only dream and hope for the best.

Therefore, the characters in this book are not presented as figures within a structured tragedy, acting out their parts along an anticipated path. Their remarks, and attitudes and actions are recorded exactly as people thought and behaved at the time, without any attempt to give a 21st century gloss to the things described. Many will find such a literary approach shocking and anachronistic, and will ask themselves, can such people really have existed? The answer is, yes they did!

But we live in such an anodyne world, where we have become used to presentations of history dressed up in all the colourful external trappings of the past but without the thought patterns or opinions of the age; or when an attempt is made to re-create the feelings or opinions of a past age, it becomes a mere pastiche of reality, or an exaggeration, or a stereotypical representation distorting actuality. This is made evident to those on reaching a certain age when they see films or read books of fiction about well-known events which took place in their youth, and they realise that such representations bear little resemblance to the facts, feelings, or ambience surrounding an episode.

To re-create a popular impression of the past as it really existed is considered too confusing, or too jarring, or too unreal, for the majority to accept, and so history needs to be nicely wrapped-up in the ideas of our own time. The events of the present book took place between 1957-1961 – scarcely fifty years ago – and yet the world presented seems so different from our own, that the younger generation may hardly believe that such a world ever existed. And if this is the case with events of only fifty years ago, how much more false must be those elaborate and appalling costume dramas of the 19th century and before which have entertained us on our screens over the past three decades! There is nothing more unreal or pretentious or anachronistic than presenting dramas of the past expressing the mindset of the present.

And this situation is compounded by the fact, as argued at the start of these paragraphs, that time is an emollient which erases the memory of past pain and events. But why should this be so? It is not that the recollection of the past is unpleasant in itself, or that a new light needs invariably to be cast on old events. It is *only* because of the transformation of values that memory is falsified so that a new interpretation may be given for explaining or justifying the thinking and actions of the past.

If we return to recent German history over the past one hundred and thirty years, we can immediately identify six revolutionary events necessitating an up-ending in political and moral thinking: viz., the formation of the Empire or Second Reich in 1871, and the move from particularism to nationalism; the defeat of 1918 and the change from cultural-imperial pride to the levelling-down of the Weimar Republic; the ascension of National Socialism and the Third Reich in 1933; the defeat of 1945 and the emergence of social democracy in West Germany; the

Russian victory in East Germany and the imposition of Communist rule; and lastly, the collapse of the East bloc and the Berlin Wall in 1989, and the difficult absorption of the so-called German Democratic Republic into the Federal Republic of the West.

With all these violent twists and turns, and the need to adapt both attitudes and behaviour to fit the expectations of such contrasting regimes, is it any wonder that the Germans are amongst the most a-historical of peoples? Fate has denied the Germans the privilege of enjoying the pride of an easily comprehensible political history with its centralised state and apparently steady progress, as with France, or Britain, or Spain, or Sweden or Denmark, with their notable (and sometimes not-so-notable) kings and queens. Because of the messiness of German history, and the division of the country into hundreds of competing and sometimes federated nation states from middling-sized kingdoms and electorates, to bishoprics and oligarchic city republics, down to miniscule principalities, it is difficult to trace the political development of the country; and until its unification in the third quarter of the 19th century, even more difficult to identify national heroes. Internal political or religious division within a country does not easily make for heroes, or create a spirit of glory, for a victor in one part of the country may be disdained in another. And when a country is used as a pawn in a game of international power politics between competing foreign monarchies, this can only cast shame on the posterity of a people.

For all these reasons the Germans have tended to rely on legendary or semi-mythical figures for their heroic or political inspiration to a greater degree than other peoples. A Herrmann (Arminius), a Henry the Fowler, or a Frederick Barbarossa, although historical figures, have been mythologised through tales of uplifting fantasy, whilst even more distant figures have been evoked for the world of music drama. In the realms of literature, philosophy, science, or music, the Germans may be rated as second to none, and it is in these fields that their *real* heroes and heroines may be found and cherished, and indeed, in the history of civilisation, the truth of culture and science will always enjoy a higher and more honourable place than the mere exertion of naked power which constitutes the stuff and vanity of politics.

If one takes the shorter time-span contrasted with the longer term, say decades or generations rather than centuries, it will soon be revealed that Germans have a quicker ability to turn their backs on the past, and adapt their mindset to the changes of the contemporary age than any of their neighbours. There are both good and bad aspects to such adaptability: for whilst they avoid the Austrian's romanticism of a past and decadent epoch, or the Briton's unhealthy obsession with the Second World War as an essential prop for his self-esteem; the forgetfulness which such adaptability brings tends to hide the possible rationale for guilt or the recollection of the causes of past disaster.

The characters in the present book, and especially those described in student circles, reflect the opinions and feelings of those at the end of the 1950s and start of the 60s. If one was to return to Berlin twenty years later, as I did in 1980, the milieu of student life had been totally transformed. The students of 1980 would not have recognised those of 1960. Of course life is changing in all societies, and this is universally recognised, but in Germany or Berlin there is this difference: because of the will to forget and an a-historical attitude, the present becomes so implanted in the mind as an essential fact of existence, that the past is denied its recognition of reality.

It is not only rejected as anachronistic but as somehow "unacceptable" or immoral. Succeeding generations are therefore loathed to acknowledge that such people ever existed. In the same way the students of 1960 would have found those of 1930 totally incomprehensible. Not only would they not be understood, but there would be no wish to comprehend the historical circumstances which gave rise to such a mindset.

It is life-experience, of course, which moulds the characteristics of a generation. The young people of the 1950s and early 60s had experienced the direct effects of war. The author of this book was brought up in a city exposed to bombing night after night, week after week, month after month, year after year. He was accustomed as a child to trudging, or being carried down, six flights of stairs into a musty cellar, and resting in deck chairs for an hour or so until the siren signalled the all-clear. In the morning he would look for or collect pieces or schrapnel from the London streets to exchange with schoolfriends for other souvenirs of war damage. When the war ended his generation became imbued with a feeling of hope and optimism which they tended to carry throughout their lives.

The young people of the 1980s, however, and irrespective of whether they were from Britain, Germany or elsewhere, developed a quite different mentality. They grew up in the shadow of the Cold War and the constant threat of nuclear annihilation, and because of this, they were marked by a particular sense of hopelessness in the face of danger, and a long-lasting pessimism. The young people of Germany and Berlin, who were students in the 1930s, grew up in the shadow of the Peace of Versailles, experiencing the collapse of the currency and the impoverishment of the middle class, and hence it is no wonder that in their despondency, they were driven to resentment, and eventually, to a vengeful militarism.

As each generation forms characteristics which are typical of the age, so the young people at the start of the 21st century will prove to be different from those of the 1980s. The present generation are marked by fears quite different from those of the previous generation: viz., by the fear of uncertainty over career potential, irrespective of qualifications; by corporate dominance overriding democratic power; by the unpredictable nature of globalisation and the instability of employment; by the excessive costs of home-ownership, or by the fear of poverty in a pensionless old age.

The characters and episodes described in the book which follows will therefore appear no less startling to German readers than to those of any other nationality. The matter-of-factness of the narrator may be reminiscent of a memoir or diary record, and this gives greater credibililty to everything which appears in the book. When we reach the heroine's tale, i.e. Dagmar's Story, and that of her former lover, Dietrich Liebermann, who is the central hero of the book, the authenticity of the account may perhaps be questioned. But the factual basis of the story is true on so many counts that it is difficult to question the veracity of Dagmar's report to the narrator - and then everything we know about her personality confirms her integrity to the factual truth.

For example, the story opens with the chance meeting with the striking veterinary students by the shore of the Langer See, and the occurrence of the strike was widely circulated by the German press. Then again there are descriptions of political pressures and threats placed on schoolchildren; of university life; of primitive agricultural methods – not to mention the bloodbath during the Uprising of the 17th June 1953. All these things have been documented in detail. Then it may be asked, why should Dagmar be motivated to invent such a story? And in any case, her drawer of mysterious objects provides definitive proof of those happenings in the story which affected her life most closely. Hence we are forced to accept the conclusion that all the events described in the book are facts *in actuality* and not merely fiction based on fact.

The story related in this book not only holds a personal and political significance for the people of Berlin and the people of Germany, but also for the people of the world. This is because it is about oppression and its effect in debasing people, and the constant need to confront it in fighting for freedom. The Berlin Wall was brought down in 1989, and that day must have been the happiest in that city of tribulations, and soon after, the power bases of the East bloc collapsed in ruin and disgrace, and none apart from criminals and the demented mourned its passing.

But the end of the East bloc has not spelt the end of oppression or injustice throughout the world, for as we now all know, new and unexpected evils have sprung up to replace the old. And that is why the story of Berlin, may be seen in its historical context as an apt metaphor for the political division, strife, and despondency of peoples worldwide. And that is why in retrospect, and in a changed world, almost fifty years after the events described, it is now possible to append a dedication to the yellowing pages of an ageing manuscript to the cause of amity and unity amongst peoples and races in what is now curiously referred to as our "global village."

Robert Corfe
April 2007

BOOK I

In Stalin Allee

"Who ever loved that loved not at first sight?"
As You Like It, Act III, Sc. 5, 1, 81.

September 1959

Chapter 1

It was quite by chance that I first met Martin Schultz. It was at a dinner held for foreign students at the Café Royal. The meeting seemed so insignificant at the time that I could hardly have guessed our brief London acquaintance would lead to such far-reaching results. And yet it was through the particular course of our friendship which led directly, and it seemed, inevitably, to what occurred in East Berlin, and all that followed.

This train of events and what subsequently occurred in Stalin Allee – so many years ago – seemed no mere accident. That, surely, it never could have been. The affairs of the heart – especially those of great passion – always leave the impression of having sprung from a special destiny. The explanation of mere chance seems somehow to diminish the memory of the happiest experiences in life, and so fate takes on a particular value of its own. So Martin was to blame!

But how? We were firm friends and he was an inspiring guide in that divided city, but even if we were good companions, enjoying the company of the other, as the days passed, it became apparent there emerged a parting in our perception of the world around us. In our obsession with material things, in our intellectual interests, and in our pleasures in the night life, possibly this parting was hardly recognised by either at the time, even though there were differences which surfaced, calling for the resolution of conflicting views.

To Martin I was indebted as a guide, but in his role as an "all-knowing" cicerone he was in fact not entirely the perfect mentor I desired. For one thing, there was a certain aspect in which his sympathy was deficient. For another, it transpired he was not the all-knowing guide, and we encountered strangely unexpected incidents when his knowledge lapsed severely. For another, there were occasions when he met obstacles and was rudely intercepted, and I would stand aside, stupefied and astonished. These were circumstances when German found himself against German. I was not so disadvantaged in any of these situations. In East Berlin Martin did not belong – and did not want to belong. Berlin was a Free City with free communications, but an invisible as well as a visible line divided the East or Russian or "Democratic" Sector, from the British, American and French Sectors of the West.

I could forgive Martin his lapses of knowledge in the sights and antiquities of old Berlin in the East sector of the city; I could sympathise with him in the face of non-cooperation or rudeness at the hands of East sector officialdom exerting some petty authority; but I had little understanding for his coldness and lack of practical sympathy for the people of the East. An abstract sympathy, in the political sphere, he had, but that is a far thing from the direct human contact of practical sympathy. What were his feelings for these people of the East? The East sector dividing line he seldom crossed. The people were little understood – avoided even. Were they despised – looked upon as pariahs? Certainly there was an element of fear and mistrust which divided the two halves of the city, and certainly this made for a situation whereby East Berliners were perceived – even if only unconsciously – as second-rate beings – as unfortunate underdogs.

These things awoke in me a dissatisfaction with Martin Schultz as the guide and mentor of his native city. He was evasive on my urging we explore the East sector, and dismissive as to what was to be seen or done there. As the days passed, his company became oppressive even, and yet I was forced to appreciate the dilemma he experienced in living in the city of his birth and upbringing. He was a victim no less than a participant in the existence and re-making of the city, and his attitude had been stamped by historical circumstances beyond his making.

This myopia, this stubbornness, this lack of sympathy, aroused in me a desire to learn more about the unknown – to pierce beneath the surface of the superficial in finding a sharper reality – to search out a profounder truth. Unbeknown at the time, thoughts and feelings were to stir on a deeper level, beneath the immediacy of superficial events and everyday conscious perception. These, then, were the circumstances through which I was led, unknowingly, by a chain of events, into an emotional relationship in which I was hopelessly enmeshed.

How different were my feelings those many years ago, when I first wrote off to Martin Schultz, informing him of my intention of visiting his native city – and how unsuspecting I was of the consequences of such a visit. Unexpectedly the opportunity for a trip occurred, and it was then that the "odd" notion first struck me of a visit to Berlin. I had met Martin the year before. I searched through my belongings for last year's pocketbook – remembering his promise to be my guide – and found his address, scrawled down in pencil. If the address had been lost, how different life's course and perception of the world might then have been!

I hurriedly wrote off to Martin Schulz, who lived in the suburb of Friedenau, saying I intended arriving in Berlin within the next seven to ten days, and begging for an early reply.

So were taken the initial steps towards my first visit to Berlin. Much has happened since that far off day those many years ago, when I wrote off to my Berliner friend. So much joy and pain, doubt and questing, was the outcome of this visit and all that followed. But it was a personal relationship which secured my lasting attachment to Berlin – a relationship found not in the Western half of the city, but in the grimly desolate East sector. It was through this relationship that I came to know Berlin intimately – beneath the surface – its darker and unknown aspects – its secrets, and the unspeakable. It was through this relationship, and the recollections of the past, that the streets, squares, lakes, woodlands, and the hidden gems and corners of the city, will evoke forever haunting memories of one whose name and being may never be forgotten – a fair Berlinerin, who seemingly epitomised the destiny of her city.

When therefore the events of August 1961 shook the world, their significance for me was more than merely a political crisis. Those critical days in August were of heartrending meaning. August 13th – unlucky thirteen! – was a personal trauma, and the days which followed of deep anxiety; just as for many Berliners, those days brought anguish and despair. Friends were divided from one another, families broken up, and even husbands separated from wives.

Those fearful, tearful days in August prompted many questions, most of which remained unanswered. What had happened to the girl I had come to know so well? Was she safe – in good health? Was she still in the same unhappy plight as when I left her – vexed by the terrible secret she carried within her heart? Then I asked myself, had I wronged her? I could not answer that. More signicifant, perhaps, would be the question, had I wronged myself? It seemed during those days as if she was becoming buried in the past by the course of events which had changed the life of Berlin. There was one thing only I knew for certain. Tanks, armoured cars, and truckloads of bricks and mortar had passed down the street where she lived – a street I had come to know so well – and a barricade had been erected at one end of the street across the Wiener bridge and alongside the Landwehr canal. Never had bricks and mortar been so cruelly used!

How different were my feelings and attitude towards Berlin during those days which shook the world back in August 1961, compared with that happy day, so long ago, when I received a reply from my friend Martin Schultz. It was less than a week since I had written, and here was his reply already! I was delighted at receiving so soon a letter – so unexpectedly soon. I tore open the envelope and quickly read its contents.

He rebuked me for not having written for so long, adding he was overjoyed I had brought such news. So at last I was coming to Berlin! He told me to write or cable him the time of my arrival in Berlin Zoo station, when he would be waiting on the platform to welcome me to his city. Meanwhile, he would work out a plan for our tour of the city. We would see the sights of the town and visit the finest night spots. He regretted being unable to put me up in his apartment, as the spare room was at present being decorated, but promised to find a cheap Pension nearby. He told me to prepare for a riotous time, begging me facetiously not to arrive wearing a bowler or pin-striped trousers – in which monstrous accoutrements I had never bedecked myself. He warned me not to fall asleep or otherwise forget to leave the train at Zoo station, as I would then be driven to the East sector where I might find myself having to answer some awkward questions, and he concluded by reiterating his pleasure at my decision.

I replied to his letter by return post, thanking him for everything, and telling him the time of my arrival. Then, I finalised arrangements for the journey. I was filled with a sense of increasing anticipation at the pleasure and interest of the trip. Three days later, I left for Berlin.

Long was the journey through the Continent that day to the old German capital – twelve hours in the great express as it sped, steaming, to the heart of Eastern Europe. Thirty minutes we stopped at Helmstedt, the West German check point between the two Germanys, then slowly we steamed the few kilometres by fields, through a wooded area, passed ploughed land stretching into the distance, on which could be seen a frail look-out tower on spindly legs; by a barbed wire fence, another stretch of ploughed soil, before coming to a halt in Marienborn, the little frontier station of the German Democratic Republic. We had just pierced the Iron Curtain, in reaching the furthest Western limits of the Soviet empire! Here we waited an hour, were issued with transit visas, and handed propaganda newssheets, before moving off again on the last hundred and ten mile lap of the journey to Berlin. At Griebnitz-See, just before the Zonal frontier of the city, the train drew to a halt for completing formalities. Our entry visas were torn away from the little folders with which we had been issued at the East German frontier, and at last we moved off to enter the heart of the great city.

Evening was drawing in. An atmosphere of relief filled the compartment as the train moved forward. No more officialdom and no more questions! West Berlin lay ahead. A sense of expectation and mutual goodwill was felt amongst passengers in the compartment as they reached for coats and assisted one another in lifting down heavy cases from the racks. The shared companionship of travellers was coming to an end as each would go their separate ways. As the train sped forward through the forested landscape, suddenly a glimmering expanse of water showed through the trees.

"That's beautiful," I remarked in awe.

"For sailing, it's fine," said someone.

"And in Summer you can swim, and sunbathe on the warm sandy beaches," put in another.

The train sped through a station: Berlin-Wannsee! It was moving faster now. I gathered together my luggage. Another station passed by the window: Berlin-Nikolasee! An endless stretch of forest and sandy soil, and sometime later, another station: Berlin-Grunewald!

"I had no idea Berlin was so big," I said.

"Not big enough," came the response. "It's still an island."

We left the forest; and buildings emerged in all directions. The train slowed now, and the tracks broadened out alongside. On the far rails, an old grubby *Stadt-Bahn* (City train) passed by, full, with standing passengers pressed against the doors. We passed through a junction with many and crowded platforms: Westkreuz! It was darkening now, and then we crossed atop a high embankment, close by a massive black roofless edifice, an empty shell, its hollow windows only open to the sky. The ruin passed, we looked down upon the spectacle of a million lights, and a dim-red crescent of light lit up the dome of the sky. This was West Berlin! The train passed slowly through yet another station: Charlottenburg! Now farewells were exchanged, as passengers moved towards the corridor sliding back the compartment door.

I pulled down the window as we passed through another station, Savigny Platz, and as we slowly clattered over a bridge, below which ran a broad highway, filled with fast moving traffic, a passenger remarked, "That's Kant Strasse." A moment later we steamed under a high arched steel and glass roof, and with a high-pitched screeching, the train jogged to a halt. This was Bahnhof Zoologischer Garten! There was a great bustling and noise of doors and whistles, the hooting of luggage carriers, the puffing of locomotives, and the loudspeaker announcements of arrivals and departures.

"Hullo, James,!" cried someone stepping up to the window.

"Martin! How are you,?" I replied as we shook hands.

"Welcome to Berlin! Come, hand out your luggage, and again, welcome!"

I passed my suitcase through the window. With a nervous excitement and impatience, that any traveller might feel after so long a journey and cramped confinement, I pushed down the corridor towards the exit.

"It's good to see you," exclaimed Martin as I stepped down from the train onto the confused and noisy platform.

"It was good of you to reply to my letter so promptly," I responded.

Again we shook hands, and as we pushed through the crowded groups assembled on the platform, I had to insist on taking the suitcase from him. It was almost with a feeling of trepidation that I walked through the crowded station with its green high arched roof, after the intimate shelter which the little railway compartment had afforded for so long, and I glanced back at the train stationed motionless along the length of the platform before disappearing with my companion down the steps to the tunnel below.

"I expect you're tired," said Martin.

"Not after a bite to eat."

"Well, first things first," began Martin. "I've found you a room. Quite a good room! It's only about fifteen minutes walk from my place, and it costs five marks a night. That's cheap for anywhere in Berlin. But before that, I suggest we eat. There's a place just near here – not very good – but they give you plenty."

"Lead the way."

We emerged into the open street. Now only the sky was our roof. New office and shopping blocks stood across the wide and complex junction: functional in design and strong in structure, their height rising perpendicular to the stars. On each shone neon lights, tasteful in arrangement, with plain typographical text, contrasting sharply with the more decorative styles of my own homeland. Vast towers of steel scaffolding and half built walls, and piles of concrete girders, and mountains of sand were also there; and behind a wooden partition came the scream and rattle of pneumatic drills, and the heavy metallic thud of pile-driving.

The roar of traffic rushed by, and the trams rolled inevitably along the tracks of the broad roadway. We stood by the kerbside waiting for the green pedestrian light, and when it flashed to *Geh*! We pushed across the street with the rest of the surging throng.

"This is Hardenburg Strasse," said Martin. "They're extending the Underground. The restaurant is just across here."

We pushed through the swing doors of Aschinger's, its front chequered blue and white, and inside, we bumped passed some patrons just departing, and squeezed between tables and the backs of chairs in searching for a place in the noisy crowded room.

"It's pretty full," I ventured.

"That's your fault for not coming on a weekday," replied Martin. "Everyone in Berlin dines out on a Saturday night."

We found seats, sharing a table with two elderly women, in a restaurant crowded with the middle-aged and elderly. Within minutes we were served ice cold beer, by one of the hurrying waitresses bearing trays carrying a dozen glasses of the frothy overflowing liquid.

"Did anything eventful happen on the journey,?" asked Martin.

"The police removed one chap from our compartment at Helmstedt," I replied, "just before the East German frontier. He intended travelling to Berlin on a Bundeswehr pass."

"Clot,!" said Martin. "If he'd reached the frontier, he'd have been arrested. West German soldiers are forbidden to use the land route to Berlin. It's interpreted as an act of aggression."

"We passed through Magdeburg," I said. "I've never seen such desctruction. Just a wilderness of ruins, and the cathedral standing there, magnificent, aloof and boarded up. I've never seen the like in West Germany."

"You'll see ruins enough in Berlin," replied Martin taking a draught. "I think you'll be shocked. Berlin was the worst hit of all."

The waitress took our order. We settled for deutsches beefsteak, *Rotkohl* (red cabbage) and boiled potatoes. The old women opposite were already tucking into mountainous portions of *Eisbein* – all fat, I called it – washed down by what looked like rosebowls filled with red beer.

"That's *Berliner Weisse*, the national drink of Berlin," confided Martin. "A raspberry flavoured beer."

Soon our sentences ran into each other, as we excitedly expressed the thoughts which raced through our minds. The train journey was a past memory now, and after a filled stomach and several more glasses of beer, there would be no more looking back! Now, only to look forward to the pleasures of Berlin and all that the city had to offer.

"How's London?"

"The same – as always."

"You know, I really liked London. I had a fantastic time there. So international – and the girls! We had some fabulous times, and I have to thank you for taking me to the right places. Do you remember that French club we went to – where was it now? I've forgotten – the memory plays such tricks. Yes, I liked London!"

"And what are the girls like in Berlin?"

"They're wonderful! But then girls everywhere are wonderful. But you, James, you went for the blondes. Not so many, perhaps, as in Hamburg. They're not as vivacious as some of those Italian and French girls we met in London. The Berliner girls are different."

"Tell me."

"It's their temperament. You must understand them first. A famous Berliner once compared the girls of this city with those of Vienna. He said that the girls of Vienna are happiest talking to men whilst those of Berlin prefer to talk about them. The Viennese girls are full of life; those of Berlin of rules for life. When a Wienerin is in love she declares, 'I love you,' but with a Berlinerin, she can only say, 'I will not deny that I feel an inclination for your company.'"

"What am I to think of that,?" I said laughing.

"As I see it, that puts the Berlinerin on a higher level. She doesn't wear her heart on her sleeve. When she loves, it really means something."

"I'm already beginning to like the Berlinerin. I can't wait to meet her," I laughed.

"You'll like the girls here, and I'll take you to the best night spots. But now I suggest we speak English," he said switching languages. "It's best not to be overheard sometimes, and these Berliners, if they're not content with listening to your conversation, then they want to join in. We don't want to appear unsociable, but at present a little privacy would be preferable."

Indeed, the women opposite, who had finished eating and were sitting with half-filled glasses, had been eyeing us for the past few minutes with rising interest, as if waiting for a cue to put in a comment, inopportune as the interruption might be.

"Now here's the programme for your visit," said Martin flourishing some sheets he pulled from his pocket as if suddenly revealing a great surprise.

He placed the notepaper with spiky handwriting on the table, pressing them flat.

"And now we must discuss the programme and see that everything's to your liking," he said officiously.

A napkin was flapped across the table in removing remaining crumbs, and a moment later, a large steaming hot dish of potatoes was placed before us, followed by a dish of *Rotkohl*, a small plate of sliced gherkins, and lastly, the two portions of beefsteak.

"Are we supposed to eat all that,?" I exclaimed, overawed by the quantity.

"You said you were hungry. We Germans couldn't survive on your sparrow portions," laughed Martin in response.

As we ate, Martin outlined the programme, asking for my assent on the main proposals. Everything had been considered: visits to the museums and galleries, a tour of the Hansa quarter, a boat trip down the lakes, and a visit to Pfaueninsel, a half-day in the East sector, and alternative programmes for good or bad weather; and for the nights, a concert, an evening at the Berlin State Opera, a film, and of course, the inevitable night clubs, a party, and introductions to friends with whom we would dine or accompany us on our tours around the city. The programme was neatly divided into paragraphs, and the names of the days and most important places of interest had been underlined in ink. All had been laid out with Teutonic thoroughness.

"But tomorrow I must leave you to your own devices," said Martin replacing the programme into his pocket. "But only tomorrow! I have to lunch with one of my professors with several other students from our faculty. I suggest you just wander around the city centre and accustom yourself to the atmosphere of the place."

At last we paid our bill, emptied our glasses, and made for the great outside.

"We can address each other as *du*," said Martin as we went through the swing doors, after I had already reverted back to German. "*Sie* is too formal between friends."

We boarded one of the cream-coloured double-decker buses and it crossed the great junction through a confusion of torn-up streets and buildings works diversions.

"That's the Kurfürstendamm – the Piccadilly of Berlin," exclaimed Martin, as we crossed a wide pavement-crowded street with a multi-coloured spectacle of neon lights and rows of pavement cafés and top-grade restaurants. "And there's the Kaiser Wilhelm Memorial Church," he added pointing out of the other side of the bus to a ruined gothic structure encased in wooden boarding at one end of the street. "They're going to clean it up, and preserve it as a kind of monument to the horrors of war."

The bus drove at speed down a broad long roadway, passed endless stretches of cleared rubble and level land ready for rebuilding. In the distance beyond – a dark reminder – in severe black outline against the glow of the city lights behind, stood huge blocks of jagged masonry, seemingly immovable and indestructible – eternal as the pyramids – mere gutted shells – a memorial of the past. In lonely isolation they stood – empty – and abandoned to the sky.

The bus was driving down Bundes Allee and we left the area of total desolation, passing buildings which had suffered a lesser misfortune, but still the gods had taken their toll, as occasionally great gaps divided one apartment block from another. Martin pointed out the high square tower of Schöneberg, the City Hall of West Berlin, with its illuminated clock and the world-famed Freedom Bell. How broad straight and endless seemed the street – how huge the city!

We alighted from the bus at Mainauer Strasse and walked to a little Pension situated on the first floor of a house in a street with the unusual sounding name of Stubenrauch Strasse. Martin pushed the bell at the side of the massive double doors. The cracked paintwork had peeled from the dry and ancient wood, and the heavy framework of the door had warped away from the wall where plaster had crumbled to the ground. A handsome but over-sized black and white enamel plate announced the name, PENSION DUBROWSKI. We waited.

A light appeared under the door. As it was opened and we peered into the hallway inside, momentarily we saw no one, until we lowered our sights, and there stood a little woman hardly four foot six inches, as dumpy as a barrel, about fifty-six years of age, with straight jet-black hair cut in a fringe and plastered around her head and ears as if with candle-wax.

"This is the Enghlishman, Herr Furner," explained Martin.

"An Englishman, good,!" shouted the little lady glancing at me with her sharp black eyes which stared out of her square face with its pallid sagging complexion. "Come in!"

On entering, we closed the heavy door behind us, passed through another pair of doors which were glass-panelled, and stood in a small hallway. I felt apprehensive in this musty, dusty, darkened, high-ceilinged apartment, with its seedy uninviting atmosphere of decay and an ancient past. But here, suddenly, surprisingly, we were met by a little dog, which jumped up in welcome, and its appearance was almost as outlandish as that of its mistress, with its pointed ears, a long wiry beard and whiskers, and black spindly legs supporting a grey square-shaped body.

The little lady began rushing around with frantic gestures to arrange the booking-in of the new guest. She disappeared into an office, and re-appeared a moment later with a bundle of forms, all the while shouting in a high pitched guttural voice as if she thought my friend and I were little less than stone deaf.

Although I made it plain to her I spoke German, she still preferred addressing her remarks to me through Martin, perhaps because he had arranged the reservation. Since I was to be the paying guest, this slight might have given rise to some small cause for offence, but this was a negligible matter compared to what followed.

Not content with using Martin as a go-between, she insisted he repeat all her instructions to me in her presence. If she did this to lend an emphasis to what was said, her piercing voice and use of repetition was in itself a sufficient indication of that. Much time was taken in discussing how breakfast should be arranged. Normally she did not serve breakfast, but she could buy the necessary and heat up a jug of water for tea or coffee. Also, she was painfully aware that breakfast for an Englishman might pose a rather special problem.

"So! A German style breakfast would be in order,?" she exclaimed, her eyes bulging with surprise.

Then of course I would have tea, being an Englishman, and lastly, there was the problem of what bread I should prefer.

"Or would he prefer rolls, or a portion of each?"

The latter arrangement sounded best.

"And what sort of rolls should they be: *Milchbrötchen, Knüppel* or the *Schrippen* variety?"

I replied it didn't matter as I couldn't be expected to tell the difference. Martin, however, insisted that we settle for the latter, as to leave the matter open would only put the considerate lady into a further quandary.

Then came the question of the choice of bread. By this time the absurd complexity which seemed to have taken hold of this discussion which should have been so simple a matter was leading me to an outburst of impatience. Knowing the name of one type of German bread, I exclaimed the word *"Pumpernickel,!"* in as clear a voice as matched that of the little lady.

This done, I expected the entire matter to be finished with. I was mistaken. Next came the question of the proportion of rolls to bread. We finally settled for two rolls to three parts bread – subject to any alteration I should subsequently make according to the whim of choice. Lastly, the little lady fired a number of questions, one after the other in ready succession, requiring only a "yes" or "No" answer: sugar, milk, cream, butter or margarine, one boiled egg or two?

The forms she had thrust into her apron pocket were now pulled out and laid on the little table, and banging her fist on the forms and shouting in my face, she gave specific instructions as to how they should be correctly filled in. Whilst I was so engaged, the good lady spoke with Martin, reminding him of how necessary were the strict rules for security, and of how she was so often bothered by police enquiries as to whether she had seen a man of a certain description who might be posing under any number of possible aliases, and of how Berlin was full of spies and counter-spies working for authorities of every political persuasion. Then she spoke about all and everything – her mouth a perpetual noise machine.

The forms completed and checked, we went to the end of the little red-carpeted hallway, opened a door, switched on the light, and before us was dimly illuminated a room, capacious enough, it seemed, to house a platoon of troops.

Following my guides, I walked through the doorway with a sense of foreboding at the size and heaviness of the furnishings, placing my suitcase on the middle of the floor. The little lady rushed round the room assuring us that everything was in order, placing her hand on the bed to show that it was in fact as firm and level as it appeared.

Then came the question of cost. The room would not cost five but six marks a night as there was a double bed – not that that would afford me any privileges – and the bed was a monstrous piece of brown timber, the posts of which had been carved with Egyptian motifs whilst the feet were a kind of inverted Corinthian columns – an article of furniture which might comfortably have slept four in a row. The lady told us that in Summer this room was let out for ten marks a night, and she pointed to an official notice on the wall bearing witness to the fact. We raised no objection to the price change, and if she had originally quoted five marks, well, that was just a mistake on her part we would have to overlook.

Would I have hot water brought into the room for washing,? and she pointed to a marble-topped wash-stand, with a red-brown earthenware bowl and jug and shaving mug, supported on legs which were also carved into the shape of inverted Corinthian columns. I replied tentatively that if there was a bathroom, I'd prefer to use that.

"Ach so,!" and the little lady rushed from the room, leading us into an antiquated washroom.

Here the instructions were elaborate. The exact spot was indicated where I should hang or place every toilet article. I was taught how to handle the temperamental aspects of the ancient geyser, and it was forbidden to wash blades in the bath, and I was shown scratches left by previous erring guests. If I required a bath, twelve hours notice was to be given to allow time to heat the green-tiled stove which stood beside the basin. The geyser, apparently, which stood over the bath, was only sufficient for supplying hot water for morning washing, which water was to be poured into a jug and thence to the basin.

At what time would I wash every morning and how long was needed? This question was important because the other occupant of the flat, Herr Thürauf, who had been her tenant for two years now - he worked for the Deutsches Bank and was a real gentleman (*ein Herrliches Mann!*) – always occupied the bathroom at seven-thirty for fifteen minutes. We settled this question and the following as to how long after vacating the bathroom breakfast was to be served in my room.

In the hall again, the quaint lady disappeared into her office, reappearing with a bunch of enormous keys which she thrust into my hand. The uses of the different keys were explained: one for the front door of the building (which was locked at eleven o'clock every night), one for my room, and two for the front door of the Pension. One of the locks in this latter door was temperamental, and gripping me by the wrist, she led me to the front door for a demonstration. The key was not to be inserted too far and the lock was to be turned twice but not thrice, or else it would be locked again, and she demonstrated the incorrect procedure of attempting to gain entry in addition to the proper way, in further elucidating her exacting instructions.

After this, all had been settled, and the gruelling experience came to an end, and amidst good wishes for my stay and *viel Spass* (much fun) in Berlin, and profuse thanks for arranging everything so nicely, Martin and I slowly backed our way towards the exit and left the Pension. That was my first encounter with the officious exactitude of German landladies – such precision – such consideration – only made possible through the fastidiousness of the German mind!

Relieved, we ran down the wide stone staircase and out into the street.

We sat in a quiet bar, thoughtfully leaning over the table passing our fingers over the condensation which had settled on the glasses of our ice-cold beer. A well-deserved drink and glorious silence! The dropping of coins into a slot machine, the whirr of a disk and the occasional clinking of falling winnings into a metal tray was the only sound to be heard, as the other patron of the bar stood by a one-armed bandit trying his luck.

I was tired and contemplative after the long day, and the recent experience at Frau Dubrowski's had been particularly fatiguing. I was curious to gain Martin's impression of this outlandish lady but not wishing to cause offence by too blunt a question, I decided on a discursive remark by suggesting that hers was hardly a German name.

"No, I expect it's Polish or Russian," replied Martin. "Or perhaps she comes from East Prussia – half the Prussians have Polish sounding names. They like to imagine they're pure Germans, but actually, half of them are of Slav descent. Berlin's a mixed city; we have all nationalities here. During our brief history we've had incoming floods of Czech and Austrian Protestant refugees; Dutch craftsmen; French Huguenots; Jews from both East and West; Polish Catholic immigrants, and even a handful of Swiss, and for all I know, even English as well – they all came to Berlin. You can see name plates representing all nationalities everywhere in Berlin. You know, it's ironic," he continued thoughtfully in a melancholy tone, turning his glass, "in the good old days of the Great Elector and of Old Fritz, Berlin was a haven of freedom for the persecuted religions of the world. A man was free to say or believe what he liked. 'Let every man go to heaven in his own fashion' – that was Old Fritz's motto. But Berlin today! It's been turned from a city 'for' the persecuted into a city 'of' the persecuted. But that's history for you – just brute force with no sense. There's little justice in brute force."

I felt that weariness was leading Martin astray into morbid reveries, and not wishing to become involved in a discussion on the metaphysics of history at that late hour, I decided to distract his attention away from the topic by the direct question as to what he "thought" of Frau Dubrowski.

"I think she's pleasant," he replied meditatively as if curious as to why I asked the question.

I felt like responding with the remark that I thought she was "pretty grotesque" but I withheld the comment.

"She tries to be helpful," he added.

"But does she have to shout all the time in that deafening guttural voice?"

"She's a cockney Berlinerin – it's part of her dialect."

"It's a very hard dialect."

"I admit, it's not good German," and then after a pause he added suddenly, "she's a typical Berliner," and took a deep draught of beer and banged the glass onto the table.

"How do you mean?"

"She's got a big mouth. She talks too much. That's got a lot of Berliners in this city into trouble – a big mouth – when they talk too much, to the wrong people, at the wrong time, and about the wrong things. They can't keep their mouths shut. Maybe it's all right for us in the West, but it can be a dangerous thing to be a Berliner in the East sector. And when they've learned their lesson, it's often too late."

Chapter 2

As I lay in bed staring up at the high ceiling, with its elaborate baroque moulding, it occurred to me that the room was so high that an imaginative developer might have divided the room into two floors. I was struck by the ugly heaviness of the furnishings and the atmosphere of decay which pervaded the flat. This apartment had clearly seen better days, I mused, perhaps as the home of a well-to-do trader during the Imperial Wilhelmine era.

The sun already shone through the windows. I had lain awake quite some time, since being awoken before six o'clock by the shouting of workmen and the rattle of a cement mixer and other building noises.

Breakfast was brought in and I went to open the large double framed windows. The little lady immediately went into a fluster, explaining that the windows were *kaput*, that only she understood them, and that only she must be allowed to open or close them. She gently opened the frames, propping them onto a wooden wedge. The hinges were falling apart, and the casement was too old and rotten to allow for proper repairs.

Whilst seated in the great armchair bending over the low table from which I took breakfast from delicate chinaware neatly laid out on a tray, the quaint lady fussed about the room adjusting things which were only just out of place, talking incessantly to my embarrassment and irritation. She asked if everything was in order and I refrained from telling her I disliked the way tea was served.

I continued breakfast in silence after she had left the room, but only for a moment, for she returned again, apologising for not having brought in the tea strainer. The dog followed her, and having run round the room in a circle, it jumped onto the bed, and stood there wagging its tail, looking mischievously at its mistress as she apologised to the new guest.

The lady turned round angrily, and without advancing towards the bed, waved her arms, shook her fists, swearing violently at the little creature in demanding it instantly makes its departure. The dog wagged its tail all the while, not at all put out by this tirade, which considering the open windows might have been heard across the street. The lady at last pushed the dog from the bed and chased it once round the room and out through the door.

"Was everything satisfactory,?" asked the lady as I was about to leave the Pension.

"Yes, but could I have coffee instead of tea,?" I requested.

Her eyes bulged in astonishment.

"Coffee instead of tea, for an Englishman,?" she exclaimed. "Don't you like tea?"

It's just that an Englishman isn't used to drinking tea out of a jug and pre-sweetened," I replied.

What was a stranger to do on his first day in a great and unknown city? For the diffidently curious, for the pressed-for-time, for the know-everything-in-three-hours – then *Stadtrundfahrt's* the word! To do the obligatory, if the city's to be "done," then it's to Tauentzien Strasse, by the Kaiser Wilhelm Memorial Church. To know all – or all that's "worth knowing" – but safely, in comfort, in the innocuous ambience of a steel and Perspex box, then the *Stadtrundfahrt's* the thing! Waiting, sitting in upholstered ease, came a high soprano voice from across the aisle, "We come from Wisconsin."

"Is that so! Why, we're neighbours," came the friendly response. "We're from Minnesota."

"Does any guy here speak English,?" said a middle aged joker, weighed down with photographic equipment, as he struggled aboard the bus.

The talk was all of hotel meals, of eccentric plumbing, of intractable bathroom taps, of past flights and destinations, and those to come. All was the distraction of new sensory experience – all was surprise and wonder at the trivial.

Cameras at the ready, at last we moved off, gazing through the tinted Perspex. We drove down the Kurfürstendamm, the show-place of West Berlin, with its hotels and street cafés; we were shown the famous gas flame in the centre of Reichskanzler Platz,* situated in a bronze bowl on a high concrete plinth, erected to the memory of those who fell in the cause of freedom on 17th June 1953 during the East German Uprising; and then we saw Hitler's stadium built for the 1936 Olympic games – impressive for its massive proportions and severe post-classical style.

We stopped outside the St. Canisius Catholic church, an example of modern architecture set in a peaceful environment on the banks of the Lietzensee, and we admired its bell-tower set apart from the main building. We stopped outside the baroque Palace of Charlottenburg, fronted by the magnificent equestrian statue of the Great Elector; and we drove through the newly reconstructed area of Ernst Reuter Platz and the Hansa quarter with its diverse apartment blocks designed by architects of international repute. We came to a spacious circus and arterial junction of the city, the Grosser Stern, in the centre of which rose a high column, surmounted by a winged golden figure – the Goddess of Victory – a major landmark, for this commemorated the victories not only of the Franco-Prussian War of 1870-71, but also those against Denmark in 1864 and Austria in 1866. Around the monument, beyond the broad roadway of fast-moving traffic, were three statuesque figures, of Roon, Moltke and Bismarck – heroes of the victorious Imperial era.

The coach moved into the broad straight long avenue of the Street of the 17th June, and on either side was the Tiergarten, the great park of the city centre. Now we were accelerating. Far in front, almost a speck in the distance, stood a grey stone gate, severe in classical simplicity. This was our first glimpse of the Brandenburg Gate – symbol of the city, and all it meant in the past and future. The guide announced that in a few minutes we should be entering the East sector, and that our route there was controlled by the East German authorities. Momentarily, there was a movement of unease amongst the sightseers.

"Say, will you be staying on the bus with us,?" said a man apprehensively to the guide. "'cause there's no way I'm staying in here if they change the guide," he continued to others in the nearby seats.

Far over on the left was the Congress Hall, or the "Pregnant Oyster," as it had been irreverently named by the wit of the Berliners; and

---

* Now known as Theodor Heuss Platz.

beyond that, far to the front, on the border between East and West, stood the ruined Reichstag (the Parliament building of the old Germany) which had been destroyed by fire in mysterious but criminally tragic circumstances in 1933, prior to further bomb damage during the War.

The coach pulled to a stop in front of the Brandenburg Gate. To the right, over the guard house, flew a red flag. Surmounting the Gate was the magnificent copper statuary group of Gottfried Schadow, representing a quadriga; the Goddess of victory in her chariot drawn by four chargers. The restored group had been re-orientated towards the East, and the Goddess no longer bore the eagle aloft her banner, for this, as with the Iron Cross, had been removed on the insistence of the Russian authorities.

A green uniformed *Vopo* with an open-necked shirt – a *Volkspolizist* or People's policeman – boarded the vehicle. A few words were exchanged with the guide, and then the Vopo left the bus, waving it forward. We drove through the Gate into the Pariser Platz on the other side. Across the roadway, a queue of traffic was waiting to go through the sector boundary control in the opposite direction – Western vehicles these were, for East Germans were forbidden to drive into the West sector without special authority.

The bus drove down the Unter den Linden – most famous street in the city's history, leading to the old centre – passing on either side huge starkly severe buildings in grey and yellow stone, and behind them, an endless waste of ruins, No colourful hoardings here, or sign of neon lights, a few pedestrians moved along the pavements, and vehicles, fewer still, drove along the wide streets in their depressing dream-like emptiness. Across the huge edifices on either side, hung long red banners, on which in white lettering, bore such slogans as, SOCIALISM AGAINST FASCISM AND WESTERN AGGRESSION,! and, WORKERS OF THE WORLD UNITE IN PEACE AND FRIENDSHIP! We passed the massive Russian embassy, and then the headquarters of the Young Pioneers and then the Marx-Engels museum. The sightseers on the coach were more subdued with their cameras now.

On the left we passed the Humboldt University, and on the right, the German State Opera, restored to its former 18th century glory, and then into the spacious Marx-Engels Platz, where had once stood the Royal Palace and Berlin residence of the Hohenzollerns – a bombed ruin which the masters of the new Germany were not prepared to restore. We drove into the great square of Alexander Platz where was situated East Berlin's largest department store, the Warenhaus, on which were suspended giant portraits of Nikita Krushchev and his grim visaged henchman, goat-bearded and bespeckled, Walter Ulbricht, premier of the

German Democratic Republic, and at that time, surely, the most hated man in Eastern Europe.

Then we drove through streets of desolation – a lunar landscape of jagged ruins – towards the mighty Moscow-style shopping and apartments blocks in the far distance in Stalin Allee. This, we were told, was the show-street in East Berlin. Two tall towers rose from the ruins to the sky, on either side of the street, as we approached the reconstructed area. Slowly we drove down the wide street, divided by a strip of well kept lawn, passing the vast ten storey blocks, the facades covered with millions of beige coloured bathroom type tiles. The street was empty and the show-shops which were open, emptier still, and the guide pointed to dark patches on the great edifices, where tiles had worked loose, falling onto the street below – and even two of the ornamental balconies had collapsed onto the pavement in similar circumstances. The flats above the ground floor shops had been let to Communist officials and amenable workers at attractively low rents.

There was a gaudy air about the street – only size was impressive – and a soullessness and seeming irrelevance to all things living. On the left, as the buildings gave way to an open space, the huge figure of Joseph Stalin, looked down in smiling benevolence on the street below, a mass of colourful flowers beneath the plinth of the statue. At Strausberger Platz, at the far end of the reconstructed area, the bus reversed, and drove back down the other side of the street. We were told that a stop would be made for a fifteen minute break in the middle of Stalin Allee, and that the East German authorities had kindly arranged for us to spend our West marks on drinks and refreshments in the famous Budapest restaurant. Again, there was a stir of uneasiness in the coach.

"Is that guy going to turn us out the bus,?" came a plaintive cry behind.

The enquiry was met with an unknowing shrug of the shoulders.

The bus pulled to a halt, and all descended from the vehicle, standing dazed, in a huddled self-protective group on the pavement, clearly taken aback by this unexpected extrusion from the bus, for they stood naked and helpless on East German soil – on land which in political reality even if not according to the written agreement of the great powers, formed part of the Soviet empire. The paradox lay in that this was outside the Russian zone of Germany in being within the Free City of Berlin, but that nonetheless this was in the East sector of Berlin, and that sector was the capital of that Russian satellite, the East zone of Germany, or more politely, the German Democratic Republic.

The empty bus was driven away from the pavement.

"Hey! Where's the driver taking that bus,?" called out a male member of the group.

"Don't worry, Sir," replied the guide, "the bus'll be back to fetch us in fifteen minutes."

"I guess Dudley's afraid they're goin' to leave him behind," laughed a female companion.

"I tell you, I'm not going to let my eye off that guide," came the response.

The group moved towards the restaurant, which we entered. It was spacious – class One by East German standards, and there were white table cloths, and thick hangings by the windows, but ironically the décor would be judged dowdy, old-fashioned and "bourgeois" by contemporary Western standards. Knowing from Martin that West or Deutsch marks could be exchanged for East or Reich marks at the Zoo station at a rate of five to one, I was disinclined to make any expenditure.

Strolling from the restaurant to an open-air area at the side of the building, I encountered one of those extraordinary sights so telling of the strange aberrations found in a Socialist state. On a low stage, under an ornately designed canopy sat a twenty man orchestra, immaculately dressed in dinner jackets, playing in full form. As the music resounded against the walls of the bleak surroundings, the sole audience in this lonely garden were two men huddled miserably over a glass of beer.

At last we left the grim grandeur of Stallin Allee, crossed the river Spree, eventually arriving in Treptower Park, to see the Soviet War memorial. For the second time in the East sector we were turned out of the bus. We strolled along a paved avenue, the Grove of Honour, between birches and memorials and the five thousand Russian dead, towards the towering figure of a soviet soldier, a child in one arm, a sword in the other, and at his feet, a broken Swastika. This was the memorial to the Soviet troops who had died during the battle of Berlin during the final days of the War. We climbed the steps of the Hill of Honour and entered the domed chamber of the cylindrical mausoleum, beneath the statue, and saw the mosaics of the Soviet painter, Gorpenko, depicting representatives of the Soviet Republics mourning their dead, and we passed wreathe carrying parties of Russians laying their offerings in different parts of the shrine.

There was a cheerful murmur, some laughter and friendly banter. We were back in Tauentzien Strasse. Relieved, still in one piece, arms and legs intact, infused with a suggestion of fatigue, and self-congratulation that we had done the obligatory – not seen merely, but actually been to the "other side" – we bravely emerged from the bus to face the open elements, self-satisfied and enlightened. Soon all would be a fading memory – crowded out by sensory perceptions of a more transitory kind – but anyway, Berlin had been "done!"

Martin lived in an imposing apartment block in Menzel Strasse, not many minutes walk away from Frau Dubrowski's. I arrived there early the following morning. High wrought iron railings safely fended the garden from intruders, half hiding the great front of the house from the view of the street. I pushed open the heavy iron gate which crashed shut behind me. The garden was unkempt – long grass overgrown with weeds. Impressive caryatids stood above ornate balconies at the sides of the windows supporting Florentine window porches. Chunks of plaster had fallen away from the walls revealing ugly brickwork beneath, unmasking the pretentiousness of the building, and the tall dark windows looked forbidding, set deep into the masonry and guarded by the plaster Valkyrie-like goddesses which the caryatids represented.

Entering the house, I climbed the broad staircase, my footsteps echoing against the spacious vaulted stonework. The hallway was a pale green and on every landing the motif of a cherub in blissful flight entwined in olive branches was moulded onto the wall in white plaster. I reached the third floor and pulled the brass bell knob at the side of the door, and the name *Schultz* in gothic letters, was inscribed on a metal plate. Martin answered and after an exchange of greetings, I left my coat in the narrow passageway, and followed him into the end room. His study and bedroom was a lofty chamber overlooking the front of the street, and he possessed the largest and most ornate desk I had ever seen.

There was much I had to tell him about my first day's experiences in Berlin, and once he had ascertained that my interest was more than merely superficial, he took down a heavy calf bound tome printed in small gothic type, profusely illustrated with woodcuts. It was the first of a six volume history of Berlin published at the start of the century. Martin enthused that the books were a constant source of fascination, and he explained how in 1880 Berlin had been a city of a mere one and a quarter million, and of its subsequent mushroom growth. By 1910 it had a population of three and three quarter million and by 1939, on reaching the apex of its development, almost five million. At one time the authorities were contemplating a Berlin with a population of twenty million, and in a gesture of Neroesque megalomania, Hitler had contemplated rebuilding the city after the War to his own plans, and re-naming it, Germania.

"And so you see, most people in our city today are only Berliners of the third or fourth generation," concluded Martin. "Despite that, Berlin hasn't lost its unique character. Our city quickly absorbs new immigrants, in say, just one generation."

He told of his own great grandfather, who had come from Memel in East Prussia, settling in Potsdam ninety years ago. It was his grandfather who was invalided out of the army after an accident during manoeuvres who had settled in Berlin some sixty years ago, setting up in business on his savings and an army pension.

We glanced at pictures of Berlin as it had been at the beginning of the previous century. How small and modest a city it was then: attractively proportioned houses with plain fronts, and public buildings unassuming in their classic simplicity. The Unter den Linden in 1810! A phaeton, a military gentleman and his lady in a loose Regency dress, and a small boy chasing a hoop! It might have served as an illustration for a Jane Austin novel.

He turned to the back of the volume showing me pictures of the more famous landmarks, explaining they were situated in the East sector which held the heart of the old city, and that it was better to see the pictures before going to the East as these buildings were now either in ruins of non-existent.

That day we made the first of our tours, closely examining the sights, arts and antiquities of the city, together with their literary and political associations.

Time passed quickly and they were warm sunny days. Frau Dubrowski continued to fuss nervously about the room every morning and I found no effective way of assuaging her fastidious temperament. Every morning I had to describe what I had done the day before and relate what I intended doing during the day ahead, and when I complained to Martin about all the "busy-bodying," he merely laughed, exclaiming that, "Berlin is so full of elderly and lonely widows who never have a chance to talk to a man from one month to another."

We visited Tempelhof airport, seeing the Airlift monument; made a boat trip down the Havel from Spandau, and as the weather was remarkably fine, we swam in the broad river and lay on the warm sands, as the gentle breeze swayed the branches of the trees in the forest behind and the water lapped peacefully at our feet. Another day, we toured the new American built Free University in Dahlem, met several of Martin's friends, and were shown the generous libraries and magnificent lecture halls, before dining in the canteen.

After lunch, we made our way towards the botanical garden and as we stood on the kerb of Thiel Allee, waiting to cross the street, a long convoy of American tanks thundered by, their guns pointing forward, a helmeted soldier standing erect in the turret of each.

"It's a joy to see these tanks sometimes in the streets," cried Martin above the din. "They make you feel you can sleep safely at night. But it would be good to have more. All round Berlin are a hundred times more Russian tanks – all with their guns aimed at the city."

On other days we visited the Dahlem museum, seeing the original Queen Nofertete head – a work of all-absorbing beauty; and Pfaueninsel (Peacocks' Island) with Frederick William II's gothic mock ruin palace in its idyllic surroundings, and his aviary, and an ancient farm; and then a great industrial exhibition in the fair grounds of the Funkturm.

It was here we encountered one of those strange sights in Berlin – so telling of the city, but symptomatic of psychological rather than political significance. On leaving an exhibition hall we saw a queue of thousands, predominantly middle aged and elderly people waiting patiently for we knew not what. Curious to know the attraction, we followed our way around to three new railway carriages, a First and Second class and a Restaurant car. So these were the objects of intense curiosity! This was how Berliners compensated for the land-locked status of their city: a few pensive moments of imaginative fancy into the pleasures of railway travel!

"Most of those people are from the East sector," remarked Martin. "You can see by their clothes."

I was eager to make a second visit to the East sector. Quite apart from its being the historical centre of Berlin its atmosphere had worked in me a curious fascination. Here were two Berlins, existing cheek by jowl, yet living widely divergent lives. West Berliners were entitled to visit the East sector, and East Berliners the West, and I understood the latter took full advantage of this facility and the accompanying privileges, as permission to use East marks in patronising concert and exhibition halls, and certain cinemas showing quality films, etc.

As many as a quarter of all students of the Free and Technical Universities in West Berlin came from the East sector, and many workers living in the East came daily to their work in the West sectors. The *S-Bahn* was staffed by East Germans, for the most important junctions of the network lay in the East sector, and its tracks extended beyond the zonal frontiers in all directions of the city. Then building workers connected with the maintenance or expansion of the city and Underground networks also came from the East.

The attitude and feelings of the West Berliner towards his compatriot in the East aroused my interest. The West Berliner, in his natural apprehension of anything from the East, tended to see the East Berliner in a light amounting almost to disdain, for there seemed little place for sympathy in regarding the unfortunate lot of his less fortunate citizen. Perhaps this arose from a feeling of cynicism at the inevitably tragic circumstances in which the city had come to find itself. Perhaps the Berliner had finally lost all hope in the eventual re-unification of his city after a division of so long a period.

The East Berliner was a stranger – a foreigner even, in the eyes of his compatriot from the West. The East Berliner was dismissed even as a "non-person" since he came from a different world; because social contact might lead to unhappy compromise in the nature of relationships; and because his tragic political status seemed fixed, if not for all time, then at least for the conceivable future. Although the East Berliner enjoyed defined privileges in the West sectors, as an East German, he was legally disenfranchised in the Western half of his own city to a degree which virtually made him a stranger in his own land. The East Berliner was not diplomatically represented in the West; the likelihood of business contacts were remote; and there was everything against the development of spontaneous friendship because of the many hindrances which existed. The fact that both had freedom to perambulate the city and call themselves *Germans* was of little relevance in view of current political circumstances. Only Berliners with relatives on "the other side" could maintain genuine contact with their "foreign compatriots."

I recollected that during the journey to Berlin how a self-effacing East German of sickly and penurious appearance had come into our compartment, and how he had been cold-shouldered by the other passengers, and of the relief at his departure from the train at Magdeburg. But the East German, too, had kept his distance. Neither wished to embarrass the other – not even by a simple gesture of human recognition. I recollected Frau Dubrowski's fear of "the Man from the East;" and Martin's awkwardness, even, in discussing any aspect of the lives of East sector citizens. I wondered what the East Berliner thought of his compatriot in the West, and indeed, as to his impression of everything that the West presented, where standards differed so and freedom was a greater reality. Was the soul of the East Berliner warped with envy against his compatriot in the West? Did he regard the West Berliner as somehow a better being since he was not ground down by the repressive tyranny of a totalitarian state? Did he despise himself for his passive subjection; or did he merely ignore or forget what he saw in the West, burying his soul in the profound cynicism that even the last shred of hope for freedom was gone? What thoughts – what aspirations, if any, lay in the heart of the East Berliner? I was not to find the answers to these questions until some time later, and then only through experiences of a uniquely personal nature.

After some days it struck me that Martin was purposely delaying our visit to the East sector. Having aroused my historical interest in visiting the East sector, on that first Monday on calling at his apartment, he had subsequently come up with an assortment of excuses – the good weather and this or that priority – for not making a visit on any particular day. Now was never the time, it seemed!

"Martin, I believe you're resolved against our visiting the East," I burst out at last.

He was taken aback by the accusation, and throwing up his arms towards the window, he replied half facetiously: "Not at all James – but look how fine the weather is! It's not like this every year at the beginning of Autumn. We want to take advantage of the beautiful nature of Berlin with its lush green forests and calm blue lakes during the last few days of this – well – Indian Summer as you say in England."

"If we visit the East sector we'll be outside for most of the time – so what's the difference?"

"The difference,?" he replied disdainfully. "Why waste sunshine days in the East sector? There's no beauty in East Berlin, I can assure you!"

"Days,!" I retorted. "Why talk of days? We haven't been in the East sector for an hour. And as for your beautiful nature, much as I admire it, I didn't come to Berlin just to appreciate that."

"Okay,!" he relented, "but we can't do it today – we've already arranged to meet Anne and Fritz and spend the day at the Krela's villa in Schlachtensee. On Monday it'll be the East sector."

We pushed through the congested corridor of noisy merrymakers and from the hallway beyond the steps came the heavy beat of a percussion band striking up a Viennese waltz.

"It's better in the Monks' Cellar for several reasons," shouted Martin above the din. "Firstly, it's darker, and when you've had a few drinks you're not so particular as to what the girls look like. Also, the atmosphere's more informal – not so many tourists – the people come to enjoy themselves, not merely to gape."

As we made our way through a crowd of dancers, by a line of tables under the vaulted ceiling of the Cellar, we were hailed by two of Martin's student friends, and after introductions, we were beckoned by Helmut and Detlef to join their company.

"Welcome to Resi's," exclaimed Helmut. "We were keeping the seats for some girls but I don't think they'll show up now. They were a little annoyed last time we met them – Detlef had had too much to drink, and when we saw them home, he collapsed in the hallway of their apartment block. Detlef's a bad man," added Helmut playfully punching his friend in the shoulder.

Telephones stood on the tables, together with little printed charts illustrating the lay-out and seating arrangements. Martin explained how the phones were operated.

"I think I'd rather ask in person for a dance," I said, overcome with apprehension at the unusual procedure in chatting-up a prospective partner.

"Impossible,!" laughed Helmut. "The fun of this place is making a gallant invitation over the phone, and then remaining incognito until you have the girl on the floor."

"You can phone any girl you wish and say what you like to her," said Detlef. "You can ask for a date, for her phone number, for her measurements – or even discuss Hegelian metaphysics if you're so inclined."

"The girls appreciate a little fun and mystery," said Helmut. "If you ask them personally for a dance they'll turn you down anyway."

"That's why Helmut always comes here: he knows the girls won't like his looks, so he charms them over the phone first," laughed Martin.

"But if you're afraid the girls won't like your voice, you can always send a letter through the pneumatic tubes," said Detlef.

"Ach, letters,!" exclaimed Helmut contemptuously. "Who's got time to compose letters? Besides, letters are old-fashioned – you can't get off with a girl that way nowadays."

Much later, Martin and I left the club with attractive company that night, for another destination. The white light of dawn had already broken over the Eastern sky, when in the early hours of the morning, we left a large tenement block in the suburb of Wedding, and our footsteps clattered in the empty street as we made our ways towards home.

"Moment mal! Cameras in the East sector are strictly forbidden," cried a guttural voice as I made for the exit of the Pension. My heart fell! Another act of interference was upon me. I had already put up with enough of Frau Dubrowski's frantic behaviour for one morning, and it was still only just after ten o'clock.

At seven-thirty I had been awoken by her noisy complaining as she vented her indignation at my late home-coming to Herr Thürauf who was trying to shave in the bathroom: "Half-past five in the morning it was – half-past five, Herr Thürauf! Now what can a young man be doing out at that hour in the morning? And an Englishman too – you'd expect better from an Englishman, wouldn't you, Herr Thürauf – such supposedly respectable people!" The dull heavy voice of Herr Thürauf, of the Deutsches Bank, punctuated her remarks with a deep and affirmative *"Ja!"*

"It's quite in order to take photographs in the East," I insisted clutching onto my camera for fear she would charm it away.

My protests were of no avail. She threatened destruction of the film, confiscation of the camera, and finally, internment.

"Listen, Frau Dubrowski," I said at last, "if you went to the East sector to see for yourself, you'd know that everyone carries cameras. The only thing is, you mustn't take pictures of uniformed officials and sensitive government buildings. I've been there – I know!"

"What were you doing last night,?" asked Frau Schultz almost as soon as she opened the door to me. "Martin's still in bed – the lazy boy – you'll have to pull him out yourself."

I burst into Martin's room, greeting him loudly, and shook his limp hand as he lay sleepily in bed. A tray of used breakfast things lay on a chair beside him.

"Come, it's half-past ten already. What's wrong with you,?" I exclaimed snatching the bedclothes away.

"I'm kaput,!" he responded yawning, stretching his limbs.

"You're behaving like a desiccated old man," I said standing akimbo, laughing at his sleepy appearance.

"That girl I had – she was terrible,!" he replied sitting up at last.

"She was your choice," I said settling into the armchair and stretching out my legs.

"When is it we're supposed to be meeting those girls again?"

"On Wednesday," I answered.

"Ach! We'll forget it," cried Martin. "Next time we'll go to a better place. Resi's is too well known – too many tourists. Next time we'll go to a student place I know. At present it has one of the best jazz bands in Germany. The Eierschale!"

Soon Martin was ready for our East Berlin outing, and having transacted our favourable currency exchange at the Berlin Zoo station (legal in West German law but strictly illegal in the eyes of the East German authorities) we made our way by Underground to Potsdamer Platz, just within the East sector, the walls of the station of which were paved by great marble blocks redeemed from the ruins of Hitler's Reichs Chancellery. We made our way down Ebert Strasse to the Brandenburg Gate, before strolling along the Unter den Linden towards the heart of the old city.

Martin was diffident and unsure of his bearings. Clearly his visits to this part of the city were rare. Perhaps the Vopos with their machine guns, lolling at many of the street corners, made him uneasy. I tentatively fumbled with my camera with the idea of getting a street view.

"Just to be safe, it's best to ask if it's allowed," said Martin.

We went up to a Vopo – he might hardly have been more than sixteen years of age – and Martin put the question.

"You may photograph anything," replied the police official with bland aloofness, not deigning to glance in our direction. Two worlds divided these Germans from one another. There was no affinity between them, and not even a simple question and answer served as an excuse for a momentary gesture of human recognition. "But not that building – the Russian embassy,!" added the official as an afterthought.

So everything might be photographed: the desolation, the grim and empty streets, but the brand new Russian embassy in all its magnificence was off limits – forbidden to be flattered by the camera! There was something profoundly comic in such a proscription.

Martin explained that the ancient lime trees, from which the street took its name, which formerly lined the avenue, had been cut down in the severely cold Winter of 1951 to serve as firewood, and that now only saplings stood in their place. He pointed out the spot where had formerly stood one of Berlin's most famous equestrian statues, that of Frederick the Great. It had mysteriously disappeared one night several years ago, never to be seen again, after some Russian diplomats had objected to its view from their embassy windows.* We peered into the windows of the Communist Youth headquarters of the Young Pioneers, noting the military-style bias of the sporting equipment offered for sale, and were especially surprised by the price of a football at a hundred and twenty marks – approximately five times the price of a similar product in the West.

"It's real leather," remarked Martin. "It's a luxury here. Even a small ladies purse is a treasured item – if it's made of leather. Consumer goods of all kinds are few, or poor quality, and atrociously expensive. People this side of the city, if they want something decent – or just something – go to the West sectors and get it there; even though they have to pay five times the price when they've changed their money."

We admired the restored interior of the State Opera, originally designed by von Knobelsdorff, with its gilt furnishings; the unusual St. Hedwig's church, modelled on the Pantheon in Rome; and the magnificent baroque ruins of the French and German Cathedrals, standing in close proximity – to remain forever in their existing condition as a memorial to the horrors of war. The French Cathedral had been built by Cayart and Quesnay, at the beginning of the 18th century, for the French Huguenot refugees, who had been so cruelly expelled, following the Revocation of the Edict of Nantes. Prussia had so often opened its doors to the oppressed and persecuted of Europe!

On returning the Unter den Linden, we stopped in front of the East Berlin University, before which was the seated statue of its founder Wilhelm von Humboldt.

---

* The 46 ft. statue cast by Christian Daniel Rauch in 1851 of Frederick riding his favourite horse Condé, was re-erected in 1980, a quarter of a century following its disappearance, but it was re-orientated towards the West as opposed to its original setting towards the East.

"This is the Friedrich Wilhelm University, at one time one of the greatest universities in Germany, but now, spiritually a ruin," mused Martin. "The Soviet authorities re-named it after its founder, but we in the West prefer to disregard the change, calling it by its first and correct name. You know, history's ironic: this University was founded at a time when all Germany was oppressed by a conqueror. The German states had fallen to France, and through the treaty of Tilsit, we lost the great University of Halle. It was in 1810 that Humboldt and the Prussian authorities founded our first university here in Berlin, so that the culture and learning of Germany might develop and flourish in freedom. The early history of this University was illuminated by some of the greatest intellects of the nineteenth century: Hegel, Fichte, Schleiermacher, Barthold Georg Niebuhr, Schelling, Schopenhauer, and the Grimm brothers – some amongst the most provocative thinkers of their time! Today, it's little more than a factory for functionaries of the Communist party. Russian is compulsory and all students have to take examinations in Marxism-Leninism. That's why we in the West refuse even to recognise it as a university."

Martin was perceptibly becoming more reflective and downcast as we approached the heart of the old city, and at last we found ourselves standing in the "Red Square" of Berlin. On this spot had stood Berlin's most famous palace, the Roman baroque masterpiece of Andreas Schlüter, one of the greatest architects of northern Germany. For two and a half centuries, it had perhaps been the most prized architectural monument of the city. Then, in 1951, the authorities had decided to extend the area of the Lustgarten (Pleasure Garden) by obliterating the last remains of the old palace in creating the Marx-Engels Platz. We entered the partial ruin of the huge Berlin Cathedral, closed to worshippers, but the crypt housing a theological college.

We looked at the great town hall, its clock tower a prominent landmark as viewed from the Brandenburg Gate. This massive Neo-Renaissance building was formerly the town hall of greater Berlin, and from the 1860s until 1933, had housed one of the most socially advanced civic authorities in the world. Even in the 19th century it had been named the Red Town Hall, not primarily because of the Social Democratic affiliations of its council members, but because of its distinctive red brick. Today it housed the municipality of East Berlin.

Walking had induced hunger. We had passed few restaurants, but decided to re-trace our steps to the Unter den Linden, where an acceptable eating place had caught our eye, but it was to culminate in an unpleasant experience. Its appearance was exclusive and formal. On passing through the swing doors, we were obliged to leave our cloaks with the attendant, before pocketing the little disks he had given us, and passing through to the dining hall. We were directed by the head waiter to a table, and sat down before a clean table cloth and heavy silver cutlery. A white-coated waiter with napkin across arm and carrying a silver dish and casserole quickly passed by. There were heavy ornate hangings by the windows and massive brass chandeliers suspended from the ceiling. Most patrons were in uniform: either Volksarmee (People's Army) officers in steel grey, or a few Vopo officers, including women, in their green military outfits.

"Passes, please,!" requested a waiter who had come to take our order.

I took out my British passport, which was glanced through and examined officiously.

"We can only take West marks," he said, but before I could answer affirmatively, he had taken Martin's green West German passport. "I'm sorry, but we only serve citizens of the Democratic Republic," he continued apologetically returning the document.

"My friend's not a citizen," responded Martin.

"I'm sorry, but this restaurant is only for citizens and party members," said the waiter. "Unless you have a meeting or official business in the DDR."

"My friend's neither a citizen nor a party member – and neither is he on official business," protested Martin.

"This is not your part of the city," said the waiter after a pause with cutting irony. "Your friend's a foreigner and hence a guest in the Democratic sector."

"Yes, my guest, I'd say," said Martin.

"Come on, let's go," I said rising from the table.

As soon as we were outside, Martin suggested we go to a smaller privately owned restaurant, as the H.O.* managed concerns were over-strict on regulations. Soon we were settled in a dark little beer house, in the oldest part of the city, sitting on hard black benches with high backs, chewing tough salted beef, toying with bad potatoes, only satisfied with the *Sauerkraut* and tepid beer. I had taken the initiative by flashing my passport in the face of the Fräulein, whilst Martin remained aloof. Clearly I was to receive more gratuitous service than any West German could hope for. Martin was by this time depressed and irritable. I hazarded to remark that he was not as at home here as in the Western half of the city, and on my expressing surprise at his answer to my question that this was only his third time in East Berlin, he burst out: "But why should I come here? What's the pleasure in being treated like a pariah in your own city? Insulted at every street corner! We can't spend money

---

* *Handels Organization* (Trade Organisation) controlling the production and sale of consumer goods.

here, except on books and prints and tram fares, and perhaps, a bite to eat."

"East Berlin's too important to ignore," I responded. "All the old city is here. All the history is here – and the greatest museums, the Pergamon, the National Gallery – the lot."

"We West Berliners prefer to keep out of here on principle. There are things going on here, in this half of the city, that you, I, and anybody else, could never imagine."

"But Berlin's a Free City," I protested. "Anyone's entitled to go wherever he chooses within the zonal limits. Freedom of movement was clearly stipulated at the Potsdam Conference of 1946, and since then, the four occupying powers have confirmed this again and again."

"What about the Berlin blockade? For eleven months all land communications to West Berlin were cut off. All food, fuel, and even coal had to be brought in by the Airlift. The Russians tried to starve us into submission."

"But that was in 1948-49. Much has happened since then."

"It's only ten years ago," said Martin. "There's nothing to stop them closing the frontiers any time. They could even close the sector crossing points if they wanted to."

"Those things happened in Stalin's time. That's a thing of the past. Stalinism's way out!"

"I can assure you," said Martin with quiet intensity, "that the East sector's not a Free City. Not when you have the Volkspolizei with sub-machine guns standing on every street corner, and the secret police, and political kidnappings."

"Isn't that dramatising,?" I suggested.

"The Volkspolizei are not there for nothing. It's not just a big show."

"Isn't it just part of their style – to complement the totalitarian image?"

"I can assure you, my friend, that in that respect, you're wrong," said Martin with earnestness. "You don't know what goes on in East Berlin. No one knows what goes on in East Berlin. They have no telephone directories, no address books – nothing by which groups can easily keep contact and guarantee safety. But in the offices of the security police are filed the addresses and data on everyone. The police know everything: they tap the telephones and censor the post. Let one person in this city take a false step, and he'll disappear in the early hours, never to be seen again, and no one will even make a peep. There'll be no outcry, no petition, no complaint – nothing, and the life of the city will carry on just as on the day before."

"And the relatives?"

"The authorities have strange ways of ensuring silence from relatives, or friends and colleagues."

"It's hardly credible," I exclaimed meditatively.

"We in the West will never know what happens here day-to-day, but we know enough to keep clear of trouble. We still have refugees from the East – between two and three hundred come over the border daily – it's only a trickle compared with the numbers a few years ago – but they bring their stories with them. But you have nothing to worry about – not you foreign tourists. The authorities won't harm a hair of your precious heads. After all, the East sector is a tourist city as well. It's a propaganda centre, as the capital of the Westernmost satellite of the great Communist empire. If it doesn't look very pretty, well, they've just fallen down on their presentation skills. It was for people like you that Stalin Allee was built. The authorities will lay down the red carpet for you foreigners, and if they could, they'd lick your arses as well. But for us West Germans, it's a different story. We know too much – we've lived through it all before, and the authorities know that – totalitarianism, I mean."

I was taken aback by the intensity of his feelings, but they helped explain the dichotomy between the two halves of the city.

That afternoon, we slowly made our way to the Karl Marx bookshop in Stalin Allee, and browsed along the shelves in the great sepulchral store, with its parquet flooring, acres of beige carpeting and upholstered chairs in matching leather. There was a hushed reverential silence in the great interior, and we espied only two other prospective customers on the several floors of the shop. After browsing through the finely bound sets of the great classics and the party ideologists, and noting that the works of Marx, Engels, Lenin and Stalin were available in many languages, we went upstairs to the art section, finally buying some attractive Chinese prints.

Our hunger was returning as we continued along the Moscow-style street, and on reaching a confectioners, I bought an attractively packaged box of assorted biscuits for a street snack, but they were so unpalatable, with their powdery soapy taste, being without salt or sweetening, that we decided to abandon them. We were about to deposit the box into a bin, when instead we gave it to an elderly dosser lounging at a street corner, who received the biscuits with gratitude.

Fritz laughed at his joke and banged his fist on the table – "Have you heard anything like it,?" he exclaimed; and then he drew on his cigar and puffed out a great cloud of smoke as he sat beneath the large black and white notice: DANGER – SMOKING STRICTLY PROHIBITED! Martin and Inge had just taken their places at the end of a Cha-cha, sitting in the other corner beneath a red board announcing, ATTENTION! ROAD WORKS AHEAD!

An attractively costumed waitress placed another six glasses of cognac for each of us. The location was crowded and noisy. Opposite, on the wall was a sign, BEWARE OF THE DOG, and above that, WARNING – BRIDGE UNDER REPAIRS! For two hours now, we had been listening to Fritz Krela's jokes, and occasionally dancing. We were in the Eierschale (the Eggshell) night club, and the walls of the room were covered with signs – startling in their diversity – which had been salvaged from the ruins of the city.

This was yet another hectic night out. Martin was still filled with cheer and vigour, but I was becoming enervated by the smoke and noise, and my feelings of sociableness had begun to pall. Still, I listened politely and laughed dutifully at Fritz's jokes. Much as I admired his wit, I wished he could have relaxed as a patient listener – if only for a few minutes. I could respect the energetic overweight Fritz as the hard-working civil engineer, who was putting in twelve hours a day as the norm, but I hardly thought that his leisure hours need likewise have been complemented by such an expenditure of activity.

My thoughts began to wander, as I pondered on other aspects of the life and fate of this extraordinary city, which seemed to epitomise not merely a country's destiny, but rather, the ideological conflict which split the world into two, for it was here – and here alone – that those worlds came into physical contact on the human level – albeit unsatisfactorily. In Berlin alone was the Iron Curtain pierced, but it seemed to leave a festering wound rather than the alleviation of concord. It was just two o'clock when we climbed the narrow staircase and emerged into the fresh night air of Breitenbach Platz.

"I have only two more days in Berlin – two days only and that's why I want to make just one more visit to the East sector," I insisted. We were in the middle of a heated argument, and Martin was again being stubborn. "After two days I must be back in London."

"All right, but just this morning," relented Martin at last. "This afternoon I've arranged to pick up some text books from a friend."

"Don't worry about me. I'm capable of taking good care of myself in the East sector," I laughed.

"Well, you should be able to look after yourself by now," chuckled Martin. "Just don't do anything I wouldn't. But remember, this evening we're going to this private dance in the Grunewald. Be here by seven – and don't be late. We'll be eating first."

And so, with this brief altercation was decided the course of that fateful day.

It was warm and sunny. It was decided we should visit the Warenhaus department store in Alexander Platz, and so we took the *S-Bahn* from the Zoo station for a direct connection. On the journey, as the train wound its way around the Tiergarten and through the Hansa quarter, on its raised track, our attention was alerted by a crazed dosser, shouting violently and seemingly to threaten now one passenger, then another. As always on such occasions, he was ignored, in so far as discretion allowed, and out of sight, passengers touched their heads to those across the carriage. A recurring word distinguished from the incoherent jumble of his speech was, "*Spitzel!*"

"What's that mean,?" I whispered to Martin.

"Snooper – police informer," came the reply. "It seems he's an East German building worker. Another East sector citizen driven crazy by the system. There are plenty of those around."

Complaints must have gone on ahead, for at the Lehrter station, just before the crossing point, two police officers boarded the train and took him off.

"They wouldn't see the humour of it on the other side," chuckled Martin. "Here, they'll let him cool off. There, they'd lock him up, and then put him on a charge for slandering the state."

The carriage had emptied, except for a dozen or so drably dressed middle-aged people, before we left the Lehrter Bahnhof – one of the great main stations of pre-War Berlin and now a partially deserted ruin of lonely weed-infested platforms – and the train clattered towards the East side of the city. We crossed a bridge over a broad stretch of water, the Humboldt harbour, passed the ruins of the Reichstag, well over to the right, and then drove into Friedrich Strasse station. A large red and white placard suspended above the platform proclaimed: SOCIALISM FOR PEACE AND FREEDOM! A metallic voice over the platform speaker announced we had entered, "the German Democratic sector." The carriage filled up again: elderly people with shopping and the ubiquitous uniformed officials. Martin and I stayed on for two more stops.

The Warenhaus was a large grey building of steel and concrete constructed in the 1930s. We intended spending the rest of our East marks here exchanged some days previously. We could find no lifts in use , and so walked up the bare concrete staircase to the top floor, before browsing through the store. Soon we were overcome with a feeling of impatience and ennui, for not only did the merchandise appear shoddy and thirty years behind the times, but display or arrangement was rough or non-existent. Finally we became absorbed in the book and record department. Martin found a set of Russian operatic records with which he began to wax enthusiastic, and after my suggesting they'd hardly be likely to accept East marks for such a high value purchase, he nonetheless shut himself away in a booth, to hear them through and check for faults. I, meanwhile, browsed through the books.

A plump male assistant, pranced up to me with a friendly gesture, asking how best he could "serve" me. I responded in an off-hand manner by insisting I was merely browsing. He asked the inevitable question.

"Oh, we do like Englishmen," he replied smarming back his hair.

He followed this up with other inoffensive questions.

"I should like to be able to do something for you," he concluded.

He was being difficult to throw off. I was overcome with a feeling of sudden nausea for the environment of the store was oppressive. I decided to leave forthwith. I excused myself from the "nuisance."

"Remember, the English are always welcome to the Warenhaus," he called after me.

I decided to window shop in Stalin Allee for the last time, as possibly offering the best opportunity for parting with my remaining East marks. I would leave Martin to sit with his records here in the Warenhaus. As I opened the door of the little booth in which he had enclosed himself, I was met by the stirring sounds of *Boris Gudunov*.

"Listen to the deep tones of the Kremlin bells. The police with thonged whips are driving the starving populace of Moscow into the Red Square, to force them to ask for the return of Tsar Boris," was his only response to my interruption.

"Russian democracy,!" I only commented, and slammed the door, shutting him into his little box again.

Chapter 3

Relieved to be alone, I left the Warenhaus. I was glad to meet the breeze in the open street, and striding, releasing pent-up energy after idle gazing at rotten merchandise, I made rapidly towards the distant towers of Strausberger Platz, being the start of the rebuilt section of Stalin Allee.

Cutting through the narrow streets, I came to an area of awesome desolation – of jagged masonry stretching far ahead. I passed down a narrow roadway – and buildings there were none on either side – frightening by the very emptiness of its deathly silence. I wondered what ghosts and memories of the past this street must surely summon. Had there been tenement blocks, or small businesses, or apartment houses for the well-to-do? What memories were cherished in this street of the dead? As I entered Stalin Allee, I saw the street sign of the narrow roadway in place – fixed to the summit of a wooden post – the only thing that lived: a name!

With quick footsteps I advanced along the pavement of the great roadway, and slowly the vast superstructure and towers of the distant buildings came closer into view. The sky was blue and a gentle breeze blew the long grass and weeds which had grown atop the great cliffs of rubble on either side of the road. One day, this land will be another Pompeii, I reflected, an excavation ground! Archaeologists from a hundred lands will flock here in their fervent search for the "wonders" of the Third Reich!

How strangely isolated were the huge edifices of Stalin Allee as they rose in their grandeur to their great height out of the oceanic wilderness of wrecked buildings and hopeless rubble! A strange phoenix from a foreign soil had come to relegate that which had stood here before.

As I passed under the high corner wall of the building into the uterine form of Strausberger Platz, I felt relieved at having come alone. Martin's absence – without his presence as a hanger-on, allowed me greater latitude, or so I felt. Now I had the freedom of a tiger and the vigour too. I came to a little Art Shop and stopped to look in the window. Here I might be able to spend the rest of my East marks.

Quickly, my interest was absorbed by the display. It differed from most shops in the East sector in that its wares were attractively displayed, and its window was a glare of colourful patterns. There were fine prints and behind them, some textile and batik works and cleverly made straw tapestries. On the window display stands stood wooden carvings of African origin and some brass statuettes of oriental design. On a little red cloth mat fringed with yellow tassels stood porcelain and glass art works from China. There were small soup bowls together with porcelain spoons – painted in lively colours – circular ashtrays with exotic green dragon figures, and a horse and mythical beast cut from emerald green glass. On a black lacquer tray inlaid with mother of pearl, surmounted on a little pedestal, stood ivory figures – exquisitely carved, representing characters from an old Chinese village. Then again, on the centre display stand, stood a delicate Chinese tea set in translucent porcelain and finely painted with a delicate design in turquoise blue. Then on a shelf to the right stood a chess board with a set of finely wrought figures.

It was a delightful display. Peering into the interior, there were original oils and a collection of picture frames of varying shapes and sizes, some gilded and some elaborately decorated with plaster moulding into floral designs, and some were plain or painted a pale grey or beige.

Only two customers stood inside the shop, quietly by the counter, as they were helped by the assistants. I saw a slim girl with fair silky hair hanging to the nape of her neck – straight hair, falling in a wave from the crown of her head, above a pale, slim and shapely neck. She handed a wrapped parcel to a customer, and as she nodded in polite acknowledgement, her golden hair shimmered in the sunlight. The customer left the shop. The girl was indeed pretty, and how politely and with what a gentle gesture she had served the customer. With a few momentary movements she revealed all I had desired to know about her, and yet I yearned to know more. All was sweetness and light – kindness and charity. My heart stopped as I felt rooted to the pavement.

I would buy some prints and spend my East marks here, I concluded with a rising heart beat. They are fine prints – and inexpensive – worthy of framing. The slim girl with the fair hair would serve me, and perhaps she could show me a larger range of prints, and perhaps we could see and talk about the Chinese figurines, and the tapestries and the African art works and the oriental statuettes. After all, a stranger and customer so suddenly and unexpectedly finding himself in so exotic a shop could hardly be expected to decide so suddenly on a purchase until he had browsed and taken the good advice of the assistants whose purpose was there to help him!

How patient and helpful was the manner of the slim fair haired girl, and how comely her figure! Perhaps she is fond of the cinema or music! I wondered if she had seen the current art exhibition in the Palace of Charlottenburg. Surely she must enjoy art exhibitions! Then, sobering thought, I recollected that in forty-eight hours, I should no longer be in Berlin. What was the use of such idle thoughts? Then again, I had forgotten she was from the "other side" and the idea of a flirtation could not be considered – should be repressed even – but still I could spend my East marks here, and still she could serve me, and perhaps we might talk awhile. There could hardly be harm in that. She had a rare and touching beauty. She was a gem – isolated – living in a world of ugliness.

I entered the shop and looked at the framed prints and original oils which stood on the floor against the raised platform beneath the window. Over the back part of the window hung a large portrait of Karl Marx, bearded and patriarchal, clutching a leather bound tome of *Das Kapital*.

Still I was undecided what to say to the fair girl in the event of her offering to serve me. On entering the shop, she had disappeared into a little exit at the back, and my heart dropped in fear I might be approached by the other assistant, who was quickly tying a parcel for a customer. I wanted to will myself into a state of invisibility, or to leave the shop and re-enter later when the fair girl was perhaps alone but this I could not do as it would attract unwonted suspicion.

I turned away from the back of the shop and looked at the Karl Marx portrait, trying to absorb all my concentration in its symbolic meaning. It was an oil, either copied from an earlier painting, or more probably, reproduced from an old photograph, which the painter had had to enlarge using imagination to fill in the detail. The colours were garish and the technical detail clumsy. The modern copyists lacked the fine technique of the older painters. The portrait was mounted in a richly gilded frame decorated with olive leaves and dancing cupids – a baroque extravagance hardly representing the severe scientific method of the personality it enclosed.

"Can I help you,?" came a voice behind me.

I turned. The fair girl was standing in front of me, and she nodded her head just perceptibly with a deferential gesture, her golden hair glimmering in the sunlight. I was taken aback by her sudden re-entry, and unexpectedly, my heart pounded.

"You display many beautiful things," I began awkwardly, trying to seem and feel like any casual customer. "I was admiring this portrait here. It's very fine, isn't it,?" I said attempting to be mildly sarcastic, wondering what kind of response this might elicit from the fair one.

"Original," she only replied without showing any emotion. My throat felt constricted.

"How much is it,?" I managed at last. She had given the lead to some kind of interlocution and I thought it apt to feign taking an interest in the object under view.

"Five hundred marks," she replied.

"I'm afraid that's too much," I said slowly shaking my head sideways in a thoughtful tone as if somewhat dejected at the high price of the painting. "Let me see; that would be about forty-five pounds in English money. No, I can't afford it – it's too expensive."

"We have a reproduction."

"I wouldn't be interested in a reproduction of that. Only an original! Is that original,?" I said pointing to a landscape.

"Yes."

"How much?"

"Three hundred marks."

"Still too much. Is that original,?" I said indicating cut flowers in a vase.

"Yes."

"It's beautiful! How much?"

"A hundred and fifty marks.

She was so quiet and patient in response to my time-wasting questions.

"Do you sell prints – reproductions?"

"Naturally," she replied. "What prints would you like to see/"

"How about the Dutch School,?" I suggested.

"Yes," she replied gently nodding her head again in a polite bow. "We have the prints over here," she continued, indicating with a graceful sweep of her arm towards a large cabinet at the side of the shop.

I followed her to the cabinet, her slippered feet pattering on the floor. How neat was her figure, and how attractive the movement of her hips and the shapely slimness of her legs. She wore grey felt slippers and a woollen spun skirt of a dark green brown, and a white blouse over which was worn a loose long-sleeved grey cardigan – and she had fine features and a beautifully pale complexion.

We stood close together beside the cabinet in a secluded part of the shop – hopefully out of earshot from the counter and other customers. She paused momentarily in deciding which drawer to open, and then she pulled open a drawer – and I helped her – they were long drawers of the kind used for storing maps.

She began to lift the prints, passing them through her fingers, and sometimes she recommended one and I immediately replied, "Yes," for it was inconceivable to question any choice which the fair one had made. Sometimes I asked her opinion of a print and always she gave a little affirmative nod, and took out the print and put it aside. How similar were our tastes – or so it seemed. She was just a few inches shorter than I – a perfect match in height and size!

Her pale slim fingers moved gracefully – such sensitive artistic fingers – and sometimes she gently raised an arm, smoothing back her silky hair which fell over her forehead and cheek.

There were many prints placed aside – all were beautiful, and the problem would become one of exclusion rather than choice. Here was a Vermeer, and there a Rembrandt, a van der Velde ships at sea scene, another Rembrandt, a van Maes conversation piece, a van Dycke group, and a Metsu landscape. How would it be possible to narrow down the choice to the purchase of several only?

"Do you like that,?" she said pausing at a Ruben's plump Venus.

"I prefer paintings of slim girls," I returned significantly.

She refrained from taking the print from the cabinet.

We came to the bottom of the drawer. There were no more Dutch masters, and above the cabinet lay an imposing pile of prints recommended and chosen. Momentarily, we glanced at it with uncertainty. Were we to undergo the tiresome process of glancing through them again? No, that would not be a good idea, since by so doing I should be led inescapably into making a too sudden purchase. Something more provocative must be attempted in creating a longer time-span to achieve a secretly desired purpose.

"Do you like the French Impressionists,?" I enquired.

"Yes," she answered softly. "Would you like to see them.?"

"I would," I replied. "I think they reproduce better."

We both took down the heavy pile of prints from above the cabinet, and our hands met, and we put the prints into the drawer – such a pleasing act of successful and perfect cooperation! How very patient and how resigned she seemed!

The drawer was closed and we opened a lower drawer and began searching through the prints of a later period. Now we were crouching near the floor and I was afforded the pleasurable opportunity of admiring the shapeliness of her limbs. The same procedure was re-enacted as before except that we less frequently stopped at a print to lay it aside above the cabinet. As the Renoirs, Manets, Cezannes, Lautrecs and Gauguins were carefully lifted by the slim gentle fingers and disappeared from view before I had had time to register them, my mind was otherwise distracted.

I became absorbed by the beautiful rhythm of her every movement. Her patience, her toleration, even, seemed infinite. Never for a moment did she betray the slightest perturbation. Her urbanity together with the pale complexion and frail sensitive features were those of a Madonna from a Medieval painting. These characteristics seemed to shroud her in an inexplicable mystery. Her serenity reflected a patience exceeding that of ordinary mortals – it suggested a fatalistic resignation in life. In this lay the attraction of her being. Again and again I asked myself, What is the secret – the reason for your resignation in life?

I wanted to unbalance the serenity of her manner – this most provocative aspect of her being. From the moment of my entering the shop I had wanted to disturb her resignation if only to draw any response for good or ill.

Time was passing and opportunity too. If we came to the end of this pile, and I had said nothing of consequence – had failed to provoke the fair one, my chances would be lost forever. I couldn't ask to be shown another School of painting – the procedure would be tiresomeness reaching to absurdity – even for this angel of patient fortitude. I resolved on asking her some personal question – no matter what. But what question? Her name? No, that would be too soon. Where she lived? No, that would be too audacious. Her interests? No, that might only embarrass – needing too long an answer and too much thought. Did she like music? No, that would be too banal – of course she liked music – how otherwise could she be so rhythmical in her movements? Did she like going to the West sector? No, the purpose of such a question might be misconstrued, and besides, it was silly.

"Do you speak English,?" I ventured at last, mustering all the courage I could. "I speak so little German, and so badly."

"No," she only replied, and just perceptibly turning her head to indicate a negative answer.

"Do you speak French,?" I enquired softly.

"No."

"Do you speak Latin?"

"No."

"Do you speak Russian?"

"No."

I only spoke about three words of the language myself and had she given an affirmative answer, I might have found myself sorely vexed, but it was the only question which came to mind with the present train of thought.

"Do you speak Polish?"

The question was ridiculous but nonetheless harmless.

I had exhausted my repertoire of questions for the moment, but the fact I had succeeded in putting them, enhanced my feeling of well-being. I had achieved a degree of self-confidence and could now go on.

My own feelings of optimism, however, did not stem from any signs of success from these unorthodox tactics. She never smiled and she never turned her eyes, and she never made any significant movement. She gave a short monosyllabic answer to each question – a quiet "No!" As I had spoken to her she listened patiently; her fingers ceasing to move for a moment and her eyes seeming suddenly to stay still, fixed on the print which lay in front of her.

I had exhausted my questions.

I helped her to sort through the prints, lifting each one in turn so that we could see that which lay beneath, and often our hands touched. Sometimes a set of thin gold jingling bracelets fell over her wrists, and with a gentle movement, she brushed them back with the fingers of the other hand, and how graceful was the sweep of her arm and the slight turn of her head as she smoothed back her fair silky hair when it fell over her cheek. Sweet gentle, sensitive creature, how beautiful you are – what lies in the mystery of your resignation in life?

And what lay in the secret of her beauty? The answer was her frailty, for only could such sensibility and beauty shine through a body so slim and frail. She had the frailty of a flower, and immediately, I thought of a bluebell on its slim green stalk, its neck curved, its head bowed modestly to the ground. I thought of the delicacy and lonesomeness of the bluebell, plucked from the damp soil in the darkness of the forest where the sun rarely shone. In the presence of her frailty I felt a renewed strength, and suddenly I was overcome with an urge to dominate and conquer. Involuntarily, I was driven to just that. It was now no longer necessary to call into doubt the line of my questioning. As if without thinking, I said: "Have you been to England?" (It was an absurd question.)

"No," she only replied.

"You must come to England. It's an interesting country."

"That would be difficult for me," she replied modestly.

My feelings of elation knew no bounds. This was the first full sentence she made in reply to anything I had ventured.

We were standing very close, and I spoke quietly to her as I faced the prints, only glancing at her from the corner of an eye. She remained still – we both remained still – only our hands moving as they turned the prints – for we were fearful of attracting untoward attention. She was a working assistant here in the shop and perhaps it was improper I should be so taking up her time, and wasting the time of her employer.

"You must come to London," I said.

"I would like to," she answered.

"You wouldn't be lonely there. It's very large and international."

"It would be difficult to get permission."

"You could fly from Tempelhof in the West sector and then nobody would know."

"That would be expensive. And I don't speak English."

"But I could teach you. In no time you would learn."

"That would be kind of you," she exclaimed softly after a momentary thoughtful pause.

"It would be a pleasure for me."

"That's a nice one," she said recommending a lively Renoir café scene.

She had brought me back to reality with a bump. Of course, we had been considering the choice of some prints – prints I should purchase. My purpose in entering the shop had only been to spend my remaining East marks. Suddenly I was struck by the silliness of the flirtation.

Ten or so prints had been taken out of the drawer and laid above the cabinet. They were priced between five and ten marks each. I said I would take two, but first I'd walk along the street and think about which to take, returning later to make my purchase.

The fair girl promised to keep the reproductions aside for me, and I thanked her, and lowering her eyes, she nodded her head in a polite bow, and I left the shop.

Chapter 4

As I strolled along the street I felt ashamed and foolish at my passing flirtation with the pretty Berlinerin. It was amusing but hardly kind perhaps. She had remained motionless, betraying no feelings as I made these advances, and indeed, there seemed no reason as to why she should be flattered by them, as the chances of such a flirtation turning to anything of consequence was unlikely in the extreme. Perhaps such advances had been made in bad taste – were cruel even.

Could she have seen them merely as the bumptious teasing gestures of a young tourist from the West who had come to spend a half day in the East sector to see how the "other side" lived? Could she have seen them as the empty gesture of a young man who after a morning's sightseeing had suddenly become elated with senseless self-satisfaction – who wanted only to say, "Come to the West," without sense of responsibility in what was entailed in such an invitation? The idea that the fair girl might have thought that, or worse still, that it might in fact contain a grain of truth – that the subconscious springs for such a flirtation had emerged from a vain desire to express an advantage because of more fortunate circumstances, disgusted me. Or, worse still, perhaps she had seen my flirtation as something which was meant to be patronising. Had she thought that I wanted to act like the fairy tale prince carrying off the beautiful maiden imprisoned in the giant's castle? A flirtation on any such terms – such trivialising sentimentality – was obscene.

No, the flirtation was in bad taste! It was meaningless and foolish. In less than forty eight hours I would have departed from Berlin – perhaps forever, never to return.

Quickly I strode down the street stopping sometimes to glance in a window. At a crossing I saw a horse and cart carrying scrap, turn into Stalin Allee. An old man sat above the cart, its wheels grinding loudly as the panting animal pulled round the vehicle. The man slouched liked a corpse, holding a whip above the horse's back. I was suddenly filled with a feeling of impatience and ennui by the grimly depressing environment. I could no longer respond to the sights and sounds around me.

On reaching the end of the Moscow-style section of Stalin Allee, I returned to the grimy tenement blocks – their plaster facades crumbling to the ground. Washing was hanging from several windows from lines fixed to the end of sticks so that the newly cleaned linen would not be blown against the dirt of the walls. From one of the ugly balconies hung a long carpet which a woman beat violently, her head swathed in a scarf. Again I thought of the fair girl from the Art Shop. What sort of house did she live in,? I wondered. Could she live in such a tenement block with its dirt and cramped confinement?

I returned along Stalin Allee by the other side of the street. I was struck by the soul destroying grimness of its architecture, and now, even its fine proportions seemed monstrous through their banal pomposity. Some penurious looking people, perhaps elderly unemployed were window gazing to satisfy an idle imagination, for they were hardly prospective purchasers of anything.

Stopping by a clothing store, I glanced at the hideous displays. No "art" had been used in arranging the stands or hanging the drapes. I imagined the fair girl in the Art Shop might have made a better job in arranging the merchandise. Somehow, strangely, suddenly, unwarrantably, her presence was intruding on thoughts in which she had no business or reason to intrude. What business had she with clothes shops or anything else? But still her presence would not go away. Her existence was pushed more and more to the forefront of my mind. I tried to distract my obsession by this thought or that, but still she retained my consciousness, as she began to take on an omniscient quality in the world of reality. As I walked ahead, thinking of her strange beauty, I was forced to speculate on the pattern of her life, but could draw no satisfactory conclusions. Her presence seemed somehow incongruous in the surroundings of the East. How delicate was her beauty! I was resolved to visit the Art Shop again. I had not flirted with her merely out of amusement. Of that self-accusation my conscience was clear. I would ask her out to lunch – perhaps to the Budapest restaurant.

I arrived at the Karl Marx bookshop and went in. As before the atmosphere was stuffy and claustral. There were two customers – a couple of thickly set middle aged women with cropped grey hair. They stood together, speaking quietly and officiously with an assistant. Perhaps they were Communist officials up from the East zone visiting Berlin to stock up the library of a provincial branch of a trades union or other "cultural" centre. I browsed through the shop but quickly went to the English section in the foreign department. I bought a three volume edition of Gorky's memoirs and Pushkin's novelette, *The Queen of Spades*.

With rapid steps, I returned towards the Art Shop, nervous yet in happy anticipation. I thought of the ten or so prints lying above the cabinet and of the choice which would need to be made. I realised the need to invent a suitable pretext for prolonging my stay in the shop.

On reaching the shop I glanced inside. It was crowded, and the fair girl stood behind the counter – and how politely she served her customers and with what graceful movements she passed to and fro between the exit and the counter. Again, her hair shimmered in the sunlight. Her beauty now seemed greater than it had appeared in my mind's eye as I had strolled down Stalin Allee. I glanced at the different art works in the window. I would ask for a specific painting – preferably a painting necessitating a protracted search, or better still, one which was unlikely to be in stock.

I went into the shop and stood by the Karl Marx portrait, admiring it, as if confronted by it for the first time. I waited patiently for *my* girl to be free of her customer. She came out from behind the counter and stood close beside me.

"Have you got Monet's *The Woman On The Terrace*,?" I said only, feeling a tremor run down my spine. I now felt greater trepidation than I had done previously. Was I actually afraid of the fair Berlinerin or only of my own audacity?

She nodded, and we went over to the cabinet, and together, we opened the drawer of French Impressionists. We began to look busily through them as before. Of course it would have been more sensible had we first looked through the small pile of ten or so prints above the cabinet – it might conceivably have been there – but we were not sensible. How quickly our hands moved – almost too quickly! This was becoming a purely mechanical process. We were hardly glancing at the pictures – but I prayed that time and courage would stand by me in successfully advancing the crucial question.

How pure, how provocative was her beauty when her hair fell over her cheek, concealing half her face from view, and how smooth and silky was her hair as it fell from the high rounded crown of her head. Such a smooth and beautifully rounded head to stroke! How calm and aloof she was. Again I asked myself, What is the mystery of your resignation in life? Was she burdened by a great sorrow or had she lived in fear?

Suddenly, I realised my self-confidence had gone as I was filled with a tremor of diffidence. I was overcome with shame at the audacity of my advances and at the guile of the little ruse required for attaining the sweet object. My mouth dried up, and my tongue clove to my palate. Perhaps it would be better to give up the idea of the flirtation and choose two prints, leaving the shop forthwith. By that course I should avoid the risk of losing face should she decline my invitation. I would never again have cause to visit the East sector.

Outwardly I feared betraying such feelings of diffidence – to tremble or be lost for words. I helped her shift through the prints – helped her with such deftness that she need hardly have touched them. Often our hands met, and I noticed the two artistic rings she wore on the fingers of each – silver rings mounted with a dull orange stone.

"What's it like,?" she enquired at last.

"It's sort of full of an orangey-red-yellow," I replied.

"It doesn't seem to be here," she said a little later as we came towards the bottom of the drawer.

"Ah, that's a great pity," I exclaimed, shaking my head despondently. "I especially wanted this picture."

"Perhaps another might do as well."

"I'm especially looking for this picture. Perhaps we could make quite sure it's not here."

"What's the picture of?"

"A woman on a terrace, sitting in a deck chair."

"We don't have many Monets."

"That's a great pity. You see, I don't want this picture for myself. It's for an elderly aunt."

"Yes,?" replied the fair girl doubtfully.

"She's a collector of fine prints – and everyone knows what beautiful pictures can be found in East Berlin."

"Really,?" she exclaimed sceptically.

The invention of this fabulous fiction was helping to restore confidence. I had grasped onto something which was bringing us (I hoped) into closer union.

"It doesn't seem to be here," she said when we reached the bottom of the pile.

"I suppose it's unobtainable anywhere in Berlin," I sighed.

"We have more prints at the back of the shop. I could look there for you."

"I don't want to cause you any more trouble – you've been so patient."

"It's no trouble. It would only take a few minutes."

"Please don't bother," I insisted gently.

She glanced at me curiously.

"I'll choose two of the prints we laid aside earlier.

The prints in question were taken down from above the cabinet and we glanced at them again, slowly and carefully, expressing views, and finally choosing two which she recommended. She took the prints to wrap them in the little exit at the back of the shop. They would be my possessions, and she had chosen them, and forever, they would remain part of her, for they had reflected the feelings of her own heart.

I stood by the counter, and the shop was full, and my heart throbbed with apprehension. In the next half minute all would be decided. Instinctively I felt I should forget the idea of inviting her for lunch, although such a decision touched me with a pang of regret.

She returned from the exit and handed me the wrapped prints, and I gave her a twenty mark note. She wrote out a bill, and pressed down the buttons on the cash register and the till slid open. The twenty mark note was placed under a clip and my change was handed to me.

"Will you lunch with me,?" I said only as I took my change.

"Yes," she replied nodding her head affirmatively without looking up.

"In an hour – outside the shop – at one o'clock?"

"At two," she said. "I'm free then."

I pushed my way through the crowd behind and left the shop. My feelings of elation were boundless! In two hours I should be dining with the most beautiful girl in all Berlin!

I left Stalin Allee, taking a short cut across the rubble towards the distant built-up area far over on the right. The sun shone brightly, and I jumped over the broken blocks of masonry and climbed over the boulders which were overgrown with weeds and grass. The further I moved from Stalin Allee, the faster I walked and ran, and as I sprinted over the rocks and boulders, the more invigorated I became in mind and body. The greenery of the plants and wild blooms seemed to wave in greeting and share in the joy of the sunshine day. What artistic and peaceful ruins they were – how finely contrasted were the colours of the grey masonry topped with the green and violet yellow hues of the year's remaining flowers!

On reaching the built-up area, I passed through some narrow streets filled with the yellow light of the sun, where the poor people lived, and sought a modest beer house to sit and read in for the next two hours. I found a small bar whose entrance lay in a narrow alley, ordered a large beer, and sat in a dark corner of the saloon. I read the entire Puskin novelette about a wretch who sacrificed love and threw away a beautiful maiden for the sordid sake of winning a promised fortune at cards. How could such a depraved being have ever existed?

At ten to two, I left the bar returning to Stalin Allee and punctually at two, I was standing nearby the little Art Shop, but not directly outside it, for fear that my immediate presence might attract attention and embarrass the fair girl, or draw teasing comments from one or several of the other assistants. I waited five minutes, but still she did not arrive. I waited ten minutes, and still no one entered or left the shop.

Perhaps she had only nodded her acknowledgement and accepted my invitation to lunch as a gesture of civility in preventing my losing face, or more probably, to save herself from embarrassment which might have arisen from my further advances across the counter – and in public view. Or perhaps she had had second thoughts and had realised the complications which could arise from going out with a boy from the West. I decided to enter the shop, but it was rather in a spirit of reluctance and uncertainty, and on finding it empty, I hesitated, as if there for a dubious purpose (which in fact I was) and again stopped by the Karl Marx portrait and momentarily looked at the pictures nearby. I glanced towards the counter. If asked my business I should truthfully reply I had come to meet the fair girl for lunch.

The sole person in the shop was a large bespectacled man of about fifty. He stood by the exit behind the counter bending over some picture frames he was wrapping in thick paper. He did not look up although he must have noticed my presence. Evidently he was the proprietor - or manager, if it was a state owned shop.

Suddenly, from behind a curtained annexe at the other end of the counter came a short plump girl with straight black hair, and she walked from behind the counter and made towards me. I turned hesitantly and craned my neck forward, glancing at her curiously and then looked towards the curtained annexe. She gave a significant look, smiled just perceptibly, turned on her heel, and quickly disappeared from where she had emerged. Momentarily I was nonplussed. A second later, the fair girl emerged from the exit, carrying a large raffia basket, and with quick footsteps, came out from behind the counter, went to the far end of the shop, and stood before me. I leaned forward momentarily with a questioning gesture.

She stood in that part of the shop which was out of view of the back exit, and the proprietor who had tied up the picture frames, disappeared into this exit.

I was about to ask why she was not yet ready for our tryst, when smiling and turning her eyes towards the exit, she put a finger to her lips; then beckoned me to approach with a little stabbing gesture towards the floor.

"Aren't you ready,?" I whispered as we stood close together. "Haven't you a coat?"

"I can't come," she replied turning her head sideways and then glancing in my face as if enquiring as to my next gesture.

"Yes, you can," I said resolutely. "We'll go to the best restaurant."

"I haven't time."

"You have time," I insisted. "We'll dine in the Budapest or Warsaw restaurants here in Stalin Allee. You'll be back here within the hour."

"I have food with me," she said pointing into her shapeless raffia basket, filled with knitting, a small handbag, and other oddments.

"You can leave that," I replied.

"See, I have sandwiches with me," she said lifting the basket a little and pointing to some small bundles wrapped in silver foil and grease-proof paper.

"You can eat them at home tonight – or at any other time, but now we'll eat properly – at a first class restaurant." I was possessed by the strange enchantment of her demurring manner and the provocation it aroused. I spoke louder in my determination to persuade. "It's not good you should dine only on sandwiches. You need more – you work so hard. In an hour you'll be hungry again."

She put a finger to her lips, and smiling, turned her eyes towards the exit again, indicating we should not be overheard by the proprietor.

"Why can't you eat these sandwiches at home this evening,?" I continued in a lower tone. "They'll still be fresh."

"My mother prepares hot food for the evening," she replied.

"Then you can give the sandwiches to me and I'll eat them this evening, but now we'll go to the Budapest restaurant."

"I cannot leave the shop. I must stay here."

I had run out of words. What more could I say? How else could I bolster my argument? I had been insistent but she remained obdurate. There was a pause. My high spirits subsided. I decided to make a dignified exit and wondered how best to accomplish this, when suddenly, the fair girl looked up at me, her green eyes fixing mine, with a significant expression. It was only a momentary gesture but filled with meaning, for her eyes only seemed to say: "I am yours, I am yours!" My spirits were renewed.

"Then come out with me in the evening," I exclaimed. "Tomorrow night! Saturday!"

"Where,?" she asked.

"Meet me in the West sector."

"Where in the West sector?"

"At the Zoo station – by the entrance to the *S-Bahn*."

"At what time?"

"At four o'clock."

"That's too early."

"At six then."

"At seven o'clock," she said.

"You won't be late?"

"No."

"Then, at seven o'clock by the *S-Bahn* entrance to Zoo station," I repeated with emphasis, and turned to go. "Till then! *Auf wiedersehen!*"

"Yes," she replied, and smiling at my apparent concern as to whether she would remember the appointment "*Auf wiedersehen*, and thank you."

As I left the shop I noticed the plump girl had been standing nearby, just behind me, and she grinned broadly, evidently entertained by the scene she had witnessed. The fair girl waved her arm as a parting gesture, and her colleague strode beside her as I stepped through the door.

Emerging into the sunlight of the open street, I was elated and supremely happy, and to free the excess of pent-up energy, I walked quickly towards the old centre of the great city. All the world was friendly and well-wishing, and not an object, living or inanimate, could create for me an ugly or unpleasant association. She was mine, she was mine – the most perfect creature in all Berlin!

I walked the entire distance from the little Art Shop in Stalin Allee to the station of Unter den Linden just behind the Brandenburg Gate. In my present mood the tenement blocks and even the great ruins and fields of rubble seemed to have become endued with a strangely poetic beauty.

In the Unter den Linden I saw a group of Young Pioneers, singing merrily and waving red flags, as they marched in a file towards the Marx-Engels museum. Their singing lent a happiness to the day. Just across Schadow Strasse, a small party of laughing bumptious officers of the Volkspolizei, climbed into a large staff car, and slamming the doors, drove away from the kerb. In their laughter and merriment, they seemed to share in the elation of my happiness.

Chapter 5

That evening, I arrived at the Schultz's flat some minutes later than the time specified by Martin earlier in the day. I was in high spirits. I carried a bunch of violets for Frau Schultz, for this would be the last occasion of our meeting during my present stay in Berlin, and I had to express my indebtedness and thanks for her kind hospitality on the numerous occasions I had eaten there.

Before arriving at the house I already had the words for my double-apology clearly in mind – that is, for my lateness, and for my having walked off from Martin earlier in the day in the East sector. I hoped Martin would answer the door, and was eager to express my apologies, and anxious that he should listen patiently and in silence, so I could use the opportunity as a natural prelude to the story of my little adventure that morning. As yet I had been denied the opportunity of telling anyone the story (and this was a tale which Frau Dubrowski would not draw from my lips) and for most of the afternoon I had looked forward in eager anticipation in relating to Martin how I had lost my heart to the fair East Berlinerin. I had pondered long and formulated with care the sentences with which I should break the news to Martin, and had even anticipated his response and the precise words of his reply. I anticipated his encouragement of the affair, his amusement at the story and his laughing congratulations at the audacity of the initial conquest. In response, in projecting a calmer saner attitude to the episode – in pre-empting the reproach that I was somehow engaged in a wild escapade – I would adopt a dismissive stance, explaining that my interest in the girl was "merely as an amusing pastime" for my final hours in Berlin, so refuting any suggestion that more serious intentions were involved.

Martin opened the door. He was dressed in a fine jet black suit, a white tie covered with glittering silver stars, and a modest buttonhole. He was in high spirits. I tried to begin my apology, but before I could say a word, he shook my hand, slapping me on the shoulder with the other, and ordered me inside. As he took my coat and hung it in the hallway, he spoke loudly and excitedly about the eventful evening before us. He slapped me on the shoulders again, directing me into his large room at the end of the hallway. I could see it would be difficult to draw his patient attention. Not only had I hardly had an opportunity to open my mouth but he had failed even to notice the small bouquet I carried for his mother.

"Come – sit down – make yourself at home," he exclaimed waving his arm with an airy gesture towards the armchair. "Take the most comfortable chair – you won't have much time to rest later tonight. Well, how are you?"

"I'm certainly looking forward to tonight," I only replied.

"Good."

"I've brought your mother some flowers," I said raising the small bunch.

"You shouldn't have done it," he said with gratitude advancing to take them. "It was too kind of you. My mother loves violets."

Frau Schultz entered the room, bearing a tray of cutlery, two bottles of beer and glasses and other things for laying a table.

"Herr Furner's brought you some flowers, mother," said Martin. "Isn't it kind of him.!"

Martin took the beer from the tray which had been laid on the large centre table, and two glasses were poured. We sat in armchairs opposite one another.

"*Prost,!*" he exclaimed, and took a deep draught from his glass and laid it on the small coffee table in front of us. "We'll have a great time tonight. You'll like this house in the Grunewald. It's a large inn – quite an old place – mostly hired out to clubs and associations and to people who want to hold a great party. There are wonderful surroundings, and it's very exclusive. Our club had to wait quite some time till it could get a free Friday night. And all round there is nothing but the darkness of the thick forest," he said indicating great space with a slow sweep of the arm. "Can you imagine? And the girls,!" he continued and clicking his tongue, "and the opportunities which can arise! Of course, in Summer with the long warm evenings it's better – but still, I think we'll have a great time."

I became restless during this monologue and the incessant chatter of his exuberance. I was barely listening to his final words, for again, I was considering how best to present my account of events earlier that day. I was only waiting for Martin to exhaust the greater part of his pent-up excitement, and for a suitable break, and then I would ask for his careful attention before telling my story.

Frau Schultz re-entered, bearing the flowers in a vase. She placed them on the centre of the table which she began to lay with cutlery, mats and plates. Martin continued his monologue in a quieter vein, the presence of his mother seeming to diminish the display of his excitement, and I was thankful for this.

As soon as she left the room and the door was closed, I said: "I'm afraid I have a double apology to make."

He was all ears.

"Firstly," I said, "I think I was a few moments late, and –"

"No – that was nothing," he interrupted. "you weren't a minute too late. I was only just ready myself."

"Secondly, I'm sorry about missing you this morning. It was entirely my fault. Something happened," I said significantly in a modest attempt to gain his interested attention.

He failed to catch my last phrase – or at least, saw no significance in it, and I felt disconcerted that my attempt in provoking his curiosity had failed yet again. Instead, he replied: "Please don't mention it. It caused no inconvenience. I remained in the gramophone kiosk for over an hour. They wouldn't let me buy the records for East marks, but still, I enjoyed listening. I didn't bother to look for you afterwards – I guessed you had gone off alone to seek a closer contact with the 'Spirit of the East' as you call it. Besides, I didn't want to cramp your style. You're better dealing with the East Germans alone – you know what I mean. Have some more beer," he added bending forward to pour some into my glass.

"In fact, after I left you I had quite an interesting little adventure in the East sector," I said raising my glass.

"Yes? Tell me," replied Martin slowly, and I saw that I had at last captured his attention.

He sank back into his armchair fixing me intently with his blue eyes waiting patiently for my story.

"Martin, this morning I met such a girl as you have never seen. The most beautiful Berlinerin in the East sector. You have never seen a girl like her. She's a darling. The sweetest girl you could imagine – gentle, kind – long silky blonde hair – and the neatest little figure you ever saw."

"Your're in love,!" exclaimed Martin, and a broad smile broke over his face.

I had overstepped the mark in expressing my enthusiasm. I had not intended saying that much. I had not planned nor even contemplated saying such things. How then had I come to express such thoughts? Something inside me – outside my control – had suddenly snapped, and all was out. My feelings had welled up – could no longer be contained –

and my heart poured out. My rational faculties – all that I intended saying and doing – were thrown into disarray. Still, although I felt that Martin's taunt was merely a teasing gesture – not really meant as anything serious – I was embarrassed by it.

"Nonsense – nothing like that," I replied waving my hand dismissively. "But still, she's the sweetest creature."

"Where did you meet her?"

"In an art shop, in Stalin Allee."

"So, she's a shop girl."

"She works in an art shop, yes, but she's no ordinary shop girl," I said defensively. "She's so petite – so delicate – and such a nice girl as you've ever met. Martin, you could never imagine finding such a prize in such a place."

"And when are you meeting her again?"

"Tomorrow night."

I told Martin the story, from the time I left him in the Warenhaus to the final parting with the East Berlinerin in the little Art Shop, and of the arrangement we had made. I spoke with an enthusiasm I had not originally intended. Martin remained silent, sitting back comfortably in his chair, watching me intently. He made no interruption, but sometimes a quizzical expression passed over his face, and sometimes he looked meditative, and only when I made a humorous reference did he laugh or try to be facetious. As I spoke I tried to construe his thoughts, but could not. When I finished my account there was a pause of some moments.

"Good,!" exclaimed Martin, but he was not over-effusive. "I'm sure you'll have a fine time with her tomorrow."

That was his only comment. He attempted to make it sound like a congratulation on my gallant piece of flirtation, but his voice was flat and his tone betrayed a sceptical frame of mind. What was he thinking? He was surprised, yes, and seemed to accept the story as if only just credible, but perhaps he doubted the rightness of my conduct.

My reason for telling him the events of that morning was not merely to elicit encouragement in pursuing the adventure, or for the pleasure of telling the story, or as a youthful boast, but to discuss with him the curious enigma which surrounded the fair girl. What was the strange mystery lurking behind those pale features expressing a fatalistic resignation in life? I tried to describe the strange attraction of the girl, and hoped this would lead to a discussion which would at least succeed in uncovering some interesting clues.

"She's a very different girl," I said. "She has a strangely mysterious quality."

"I've heard that said before," chuckled Martin.

"But I mean something quite different," I countered. "I don't mean only a fascination in her being different from other girls, or that contrived fascination in attracting admirers. She was so passive. Neither am I suggesting she's mysterious in the sense of possessing an enigmatic quality of character. I mean something quite different."

"Then if her mystery is not 'exactly' enigmatic, as you say, you must be able to describe it," replied Martin after a thoughtful pause. "After all, mystery is enigmatic."

"Naturally."

"You say it is not a quality of character to be read in her expression."

"It's something deeper than that. It's in her soul."

"Then it must be something emotional – some quality you perceived – something reflected perhaps in her bearing and manner."

"That's exactly it," I replied.

"Then what is this particular quality?"

"I can only describe it as a sort of fatalistic resignation in life."

"How do you mean?"

"Her bearing and countenance is so resigned and passive – as if strangely separate from her surroundings. She seemed unaffected – out of place even in her immediate environment."

"As if living in a dream-world?"

"No, not quite a dream-world, but as if living in a kind of trance. It seemed as if some strange concentration of thought was hidden in her mind."

"As if carrying a great sorrow?"

"That could be it – but I cannot say. There was nothing in her countenance which was sorrowful. There was only this fatalistic resignation in life."

"Perhaps she's burdened by a tragedy, or perhaps she's experienced great suffering. She may be oppressed by fear, or live under threat, or perhaps she's attempting to repress the memory of some unfortunate personal event."

"I cannot say," I replied. "It could be any of those things – or others. For half the afternoon I've thought about it, but she remains inexplicable."

"You can only hope to cultivate an intimate friendship with the girl, before beginning to uncover the mystery."

"I'll try."

"But what lies in the attraction of this fatalistic resignation in life?"

"Her passivity, and the provocation of this – her modesty – and the beautiful rhythm of her body and the coordination of her movements – such polite, formal yet spontaneous movements; and she has an attractively slim figure, and such finely proportioned features. Martin, I assure you, there's not a girl like her in all Berlin."

Martin looked at me thoughtfully but said nothing, then he lowered his head, as if pondering deeply.

Frau Schultz came into the room carrying a tray of food which was laid on the centre table. Martin and I rose from our chairs and helped remove the things from the tray; a large tureen of soup, several dishes and casseroles, cruets and more bottles of beer. We settled down at the table, and after some final reassurances as to the table service, Frau Schultz left the room. Martin ladled out the ample portions of soup and passed the rolls.

Eating silently, we occasionally exchanged remarks about unimportant matters, but Martin remained thoughtful and solemn. My story about the Easter Berlinerin had seemed suddenly to deflate his exuberance. Again, I wondered what he thought of the affair. He asked no further questions, but sometimes we remarked as to where I might take her the following night, and as to the type of house she probably lived in, and so forth.

"I hope she turns up – you never know with girls," I said with a smile.

"I think she'll come," replied Martin reassuringly. "It's quite an event for an East Berlinerin to be taken out by a boy from the West. It doesn't happen every day, and when it does, it's an appointment not to be missed."

"You think it means as much as that, do you?"

"I expect she'll be wearing her best party frock."

"It's quite an adventure then."

"For both of you. That's something I've never done – been out with an East Berlinerin. In fact, I don't know anyone who's done that."

He said these words not in a tone of enthusiasm, but as if his thoughts were wandering. Martin had listened sympathetically to my story, but to me, his pondering silence indicated a secret disapproval of the flirtation.

We began to talk again about the evening in front of us in the Grunewald, and Martin described a distinguished guest expected – a young French violinist – making a name for himself internationally, who was visiting Berlin for a week to perform in a couple of concerts at a well known hall.

"They think in a few years he'll be world famous," said Martin. "Already he's played in Great Britain, Italy and Holland, and as the object of our club is to further understanding between the European countries and to work for a Federal Europe, of course, he's very welcome."

"Why hadn't I thought of it before,?" I suddenly exclaimed clicking my fingers.

"What?"

"I could have invited her to this dance this evening – the East Berlinerin, I mean. It's not exactly an exclusive private affair."

Martin dropped his knife and fork onto the plate, a startled expression crossing his face.

"Bring an East Berlinerin to a dance like that,?" he exclaimed indignantly.

"Why not,?" I said surprised at his reaction.

"It would be impossible to bring an East Berlinerin into a circle of West Berliners like that – not socially, anyway," he replied waving his arms.

I was perplexed by the abruptness of his reply, and was about to answer that an East Berlinerin was as "good" as any girl from the West, when I checked the silly retort.

"Of what use would she be – I mean, how would she fit in,?" continued Martin in agitation at his own thoughts. "And what would she feel herself? People would talk – they'd invent suspicions – think she was a spy from the East or something, especially if she's pretty. You know how nasty girls can be to each other. It'd be cruel."

I said nothing.

And so that's what Martin thought about my flirtation: that it was cruel! That day we didn't speak about the Easter Berlinerin again.

Chapter 6

There was dull drizzly weather the following morning, and my feelings were a mixture of anxiety and impatience, as I lived only for the evening to arrive all the sooner that day. I had not enjoyed the previous night's festivities in the Grunewald. They had been noisy and meaningless, leaving me with a feeling of emptiness and boredom.

Now only the fair Berlinerin had any place in my thoughts, and all sensations – all sights, all sounds – seemed somehow to refer back to her existence. What would she have thought? What would she like? What would she have chosen,? were the only thoughts of significance passing through my mind. I had wished to wish her into existence on the seat beside me at the Grunewald dance, so that I might squeeze her hand, comfort her, and press her shoulder towards mine. I had wished to make her the guest of the evening, despite anything Martin had suggested – for was she not the sweetest, the dearest, the most beautiful – the most perfect creature at the dance that night? How dared Martin say it was "impossible" to bring along my fair East Berlinerin! What had any of those girls – those plain Janes – on her! Here was the most perfect creature in all Berlin!

How slowly time passed by that day – that day for our tryst – and for the first time I was struck by the meaning of the phrase to "kill time," and sought to do just that. I revisited the Dahlem museum, and saw once again the famed Queen Nefertite head, but she left me cold on this occasion – her neck and features did not quite have the delicacy and beauty of the fair Berlinerin. She was now the measure by which all things, earthly and heavenly should be judged! It was still overcast and drizzly when I left the museum, and I dined lonely and depressed in a small bar, before making my way to the 16th century hunting lodge at the edge of the Grunewald, where I saw a collection of fine old masters. When I emerged from the Jagdschloss and reached Clay Allee for the journey back to my room, the clouds had parted to reveal a blue patch of sky and the sun shone through, a mild white night, in hopeful anticipation of a fine evening. This was the first indication, in preparation for the happiness, for the hours which lay ahead. I hurried home, changing into my best attire, carefully choosing an appropriate tie.

I reached Zoo station a few minutes before seven, and waited for the Easter Berlinerin below the steps leading up to the *S-Bahn* trains. It was seven o'clock and still she had not arrived. Never mind! What girl is ever punctual,? I consoled myself. I watched the crowds surge hurriedly down the steps – people from the suburbs come to spend an evening's entertainment in the heart of the great metropolis – all kinds of people; young and old, groups of schoolchildren, concert goers, pairs of happy lovers, regular diners-out, a couple of artists come to paint the city by night, some loud-boys in leather jackets, and a musician in evening dress with a cello. They were all coming to add their own bit of individuality to the city, and to bring colour and atmosphere to a Berlin Saturday night.

It was eight minutes past seven and still no girl. I waited impatiently. I watched another crowd surge through the barriers and move quickly down the steps. My eyes were alert for the faintest recognition. I saw a girl with silky blonde hair and the outline of a slim figure. I took a step forward – but no, it was not her. The girl had turned her head – it was a girl far less attractive than the girl I was waiting for. The crowd disappeared into the noisy brightly lit streets of the city, and only a trickle of people came down the steps – a few elderly ladies supporting one another, and an elderly gentleman moving stiffly with a stick. I glanced at my watch again. Ten past seven. She'll be coming by the next train, I told myself – she must!

I climbed the steps and stood by the barrier to watch the trains arriving and leaving the station. A train came from the East for Potsdam – thundering into the station and screeching to a halt. The doors opened, and in a moment, the platform was crowded. I looked intently for any sign of the East Berlinerin. The platforms cleared again – and she had not arrived on that train. Perhaps something had delayed her. Time was passing. I watched several trains from the East arrive and leave the station – trains to Wannsee, Staaken, Westkreuz – and Potsdam again. My impatience subsided as I watched their arrival and departure, for every train came directly from the East, and every train might be carrying my East Berlinerin – but still she did not arrive.

It was with a shock that my eye caught the time of the great black and white enamel clock suspended between the platforms. Eighteen minutes past already! Momentarily, I felt upset and angry – angry at myself. Why should she come, I asked? I had been so insistent on meeting the girl. I had hardly given the poor thing a fair chance to refuse. Then I asked myself, why should she go out with a boy from the West? What were her prospects from such a friendship? Did she suppose I held serious thoughts about her? After all, my advances in the Art Shop might only have been made in a mood of light-hearted frivolity. What need had she to be shown the bright lights of West Berlin, to be taken to a restaurant or dance place, or even to enjoy herself in the company of a boy from the West, when finally, "When the clock struck twelve," she had to return to the dingy squalor and depressing poverty and ruins of the East sector – to forget forever, the boy and the evening she had once enjoyed in West Berlin? A memorable evening it might remain, but at best, two memories of a different sort: for the boy, the day he took out a girl from behind the Iron Curtain – a fine date she was! – and for the girl, the day she saw a world that perhaps might be and yet might never be hers. No, I couldn't blame her if she didn't turn up.

I decided to look for other exits to the city train platforms, and went down the steps into the main hall of the station. Perhaps she could have left by another exit, or perhaps she could be waiting somewhere in the great hall – perhaps I had missed her in the surging throng which had moved down the steps where I stood. There were no other exits. I walked through the main hallway, but she was not to be seen.

I returned to where I stood before – below the steps – and waited again. I glanced at my watch. Nearly twenty-five minutes past seven already! Bitter and angry thoughts crossed my mind. I had never waited for a girl so long. This waiting was ridiculous! Why did I stand here like this? She wouldn't come now – I was resigned to that. Still, I would wait for three more trains to pass from the East. The entire flirtation was a foolish episode. I should never have begun those advances in the Art

Shop. I could not understand the uncanny force which had made me make them – I had not done the like before.

I would go dancing at the Palais am Funkturm and meet a girl there – a type more amenable and friendly than this difficult girl from the East who had already cost so much time and trouble, and several times, near embarrassment. What did she take me for, a medieval troubadour, sighing and waiting eternally for the "Lady" he could never possess? She had kept me waiting outside the Art Shop, and I remembered all her little ways and wiles by which she had led me on. Did she think she was a fairy tale princess? No girl would treat me like that and get away with it! My evening would not be spoilt by her absence. This was to be my last night in Berlin, and somehow, it would be a night to remember. There would be hundreds of attractive girls at the Palais am Funkturm, I thought, and the prospects would be better and more immediate there than waiting for this girl from the East. Who did she think she was – a princess? A princess indeed!

A crowd surged through the barriers, and down the steps – a great throng of hundreds of pushing and hurrying people – hurrying to reach their destinations and favourite spots in the city's night life! A group of laughing young people brushed quickly by, and down the next flight of steps they went into Jebens Strasse, and into the bright lights.

The crowd dispersed, and I glimpsed a slim figure in a blue coat and long fair hair, moving quickly down the steps. Could it be her, or not? The hair was combed over one side of her forehead, and she moved as if in a hurry. A gust of wind blew open the folds of her light coat, and momentarily revealed the many white petticoats she wore beneath. Yes, it was her, but what a transformation – now she was truly a princess! Her slim legs moved quickly as she carefully trod down the steps on black high-heeled shoes. She carried a small beige handbag under her arm, and another gust of wind blew against her fine silky hair, which tremored in the wind, and she adjusted it slightly with a graceful movement of her fingers. She moved quickly and cautiously down the stairs turning a little to one side, so as not to trip on the steps. She was too long a time in reaching me. I was impatient to meet her, and have done with introductions.

Stepping towards her I raised my hat, and she smiled – her eyes twinkling. I put my arm across her shoulders and directed her down the next flight of steps into Jebens Strasse.

"How are you,?" I asked.

"Please excuse that I'm late," she replied smiling, her eyes turning towards me, twinkling.

"That's nothing," I said holding her shoulder. "I was a little late myself."

I was too elated and happy at that moment to feel or even remember any impatient or unpleasant thoughts. The noise of the station and of the busy metropolis drowned our voices.

"I have kept you waiting too long,?" she said.

"No. Only two or three minutes," I fibbed.

The East Berlinerin pressed closer towards me and said something, but I could not catch her words because of the traffic. After several steps, we turned the corner into the great highway of Hardenburg Strasse. We were infected by the excitement of the city, and she was all smiles, her eyes twinkling with happiness and joy which the environment of the city seemed to exude.

As we crossed the junction of Hardenburg Strasse amidst the great throng, she tightened her grip on my arm, and spoke again but I missed her meaning. I understood it to be some pleasant observation, for she pointed towards a certain direction and I merely replied, "Yes," and laughed. The bright lights and neon signs shone from all directions – from every building, and the sky was clear, and a thousand stars looked down from the dome of the sky onto this city of Berlin.

We were together – completely together – alone together in the centre of this mighty surging metropolis. We were on the pavement again and she glanced up at the bright lights and flickering neon signs as they flashed their colours, patterns and shapes – joyous lights attracting the attention of all.

We arrived at Aschinger's restaurant, and it was crowded again, as always on a Saturday night. Jokingly, I asked if she would like to eat there.

She turned her head towards me, smiling, and squeezing up her nose, she replied, "*Nein, hier es ist nicht schön* (it's not beautiful) – too many people."

"You don't like many people,?" I remarked jokingly.

"No," she answered smiling and turning her head.

We walked several more steps.

"Kurfürstendamm,!" she exclaimed.

"Is the Kurfürstendamm beautiful,?" I asked.

"Yes," she replied, her face breaking into a broad smile.

We crossed Kant Strasse.

On approaching the Ku'damm, she pressed closer towards me and gripped tighter my arm. Her hair was against my shoulder, and we walked closer together, in even step. I lifted my arm taking hold of her hand, slipping my fingers into hers, holding her hand firmly, as our arms were linked in one another's. She turned her head slightly and looked at me smiling, her eyes peeping from behind the hair which almost covered one half of her face. She seemed all twinkles and sparkles – and how rhythmically her feet trod the paving stones.

We turned a corner into a wide brightly lit street, and hundreds of neon signs along its length gave it an atmosphere of liveliness and gaiety. The pavements on both sides were very wide, and illuminated glass cases displaying luxury goods stood at regular intervals, and numerous pavement cafés and restaurants fronted the handsome buildings. Hundreds crowded the pavements: casual sightseers; Saturday night diners making for their usual haunts; young people laughing and talking in high spirits; and tourists with cameras and flash guns to record forever this particular Saturday night.

The East Berlinerin tightened her fingers in mine.

"Here it is beautiful," she exclaimed, "Kurfürstendamm!"

Suddenly, she pulled on my arm, pointing out an artists' equipment shop. We went up to the window, and she turned her head looking with interest at the wares inside. The window was illuminated by spotlights, and she pointed out several articles, and some she criticised, as prints of pictures by third rate artists. What do you think of that, and what do you think of this,?" she asked.

"Do you paint,?" I queried.

"No," she replied. "I just like to look at paintings."

There were several books in the window, and in one of them she showed especial interest, *Knaur's Lexikon of Modern Art*.

"But we can't get that book in the East sector," she said a little sadly.

It was apparent she had window-gazed there before, since her familiarity was clearly more than accidental.

"Do you like dancing,?" I enquired as we passed a restaurant from which came the strains of a palm court orchestra.

"No," she replied smiling and screwing up her nose again.

We came to a quiet pavement restaurant, and I glanced enquiringly at her, and she tightened her arm and said, "Yes."

The restaurant was almost empty. We occupied a table with a clear view of the street, and I took her coat and a glamorous green party frock was revealed beneath. Her slim pale arms were bare and a low cut dress revealed a tall shapely neck and handsome shoulders. The menu was brought and as we leaned forward our heads were close together, and her slim finger passed slowly down the card. She looked critically at the menu, and her fingers still wore the same curiously artistic rings she had previously worn in the Art Shop.

We chose veal omelette with boiled potatoes and vegetables, and as we awaited the order I complimented her on the beauty of her dress.

"My sister made it for me," she replied. "She's a tailor's apprentice."

"Is she older or younger than you,?" I enquired.

"She's four years younger," replied the East Berlinerin.

"Does she work in the East sector?"

"Yes."

"Do most of your clothes come from the East sector?"

"My best clothes come from the West, naturally," she replied. "My shoes and stockings all come from the West sector. But it's so expensive to buy from the West – although for shoes perhaps the cost comes to the same in the end because the quality of shoes in the East sector is so terrible – terrible,!" she said shaking her head with emphasis. "They just fall to pieces after a few months."

I asked her name.

"Dagmar Renot," she replied.

"Dagmar! That's a beautiful name," I said.

"Thank you," she replied modestly.

"Renot! Isn't that an unusual name? It sounds French."

"But I'm not French, I'm German," she said defensively.

"Perhaps you're descended from French ancestry."

"That was many years ago," she only added.

The wine waiter approached. Dagmar, the fair Berlinerin, would only drink lemonade, as alcohol made her head go round, or so she claimed, and I chose a beer.

"Is the little Art Shop where you work an H.O. concern,?" I asked.

"No, private," she replied.

When the meal was served, she ate very slowly, taking small portions onto her fork and assisting every other mouthful with a gulp of lemonade. She assured me she enjoyed the meal but my feelings were sceptical, and finally, she left much on the side of her plate.

"It was tasty," she said after taking another draught of lemonade, "but such a lot – and so rich."

I was surprised. She had eaten so little, and the portions had been modest – plain and simple fare.

"Do you often come to the West sector,?" I asked.

"Yes," she replied with a nod. "Sometimes twice a week."

"That's very often. Isn't it expensive?"

"I can spend East marks on nearly all entertainment I want."

"That's kind of the West Berlin government to make it possible."

"Last week I saw a wonderful play in the Schiller theatre with my girl friend," she said with enthusiasm. "It was the second part of *Faust*."

"That's a difficult play."

"But it was beautiful. And the acting was marvellous. You know the actor Gustaf Gründgens? He was Mephisto. Next week I'll go with my girl friend to hear a Mozart concert with the New York Phiharmonic orchestra. They're playing in the Konzertsaal in Hardenburg Strasse."

"Do you prefer the East sector or the West sectors,?" I asked facetiously in an attempt to elicit her political views.

"The West sectors, naturally," she replied, amused at such a question.

"Then why don't you come to live in the West,?" I ventured.

"I cannot," she replied in a serious tone. "My work."

"I think there must be many art shops in the West sectors. Couldn't you find work here first, and then move here to live?"

"It's not as easy as that. There'd be many complications."

A thoughtful expression passed over her face.

"But here in West Berlin there are so many benefits," I argued intently. "There's such an artistic and cultural life – and of course, it's more free."

"I know," she replied, "but my parents."

"Wouldn't they like to come to the West?"

"They'd never leave the East sector," she replied in a resigned tone.

"But you must come to the West," I insisted taking her hands in mine. "And then perhaps one day you could come to England. There are many things you would like there."

"I should like to, but unfortunately, I cannot leave the East sector," she said thoughtfully. "Perhaps it's difficult for you to understand," she added smiling.

I formed the impression she was somehow haunted by a fatalistic conviction of being bound to the East. I was glad to be alone with her here in the privacy of the quiet restaurant, but was careful not to probe too deeply into the apparent mystery of her being. From what she already said it appeared she had little sympathy for the ideals of the East, and so I thought it no indiscretion when I asked her if she was a member of the Communist party.

"No," she answered with an amused smile.

"Have you belonged to the Young Pioneers,?" I ventured. "I saw a group of them yesterday walking and singing in the Unter den Linden."

"No," she replied in a solemn tone.

"I was under the impression that all young people are obliged to join the Young Pioneers or a similar youth group."

"Not all," she only answered.

I thought it best to change the topic and asked where she lived.

"In Treptow," she answered. "I can show you on the map," she added pointing to the city atlas I carried. She seemed relieved I had changed the subject, and I decided not to touch on politics again.

She took the atlas and her delicate fingers ran through the index pages, and then she turned to the appropriate map. She pointed out the *S-Bahn* station nearest her home – Treptower Park – and then, with her slim forefinger, she traced the route to the exact spot where she lived: Graetz Strasse.* On the large and confusing map of innumerable landmarks it seemed a small and unremarkable street, but as it was her street, it took on a special significance. I tried to conjure up an image of the place where she lived. The East Berlinerin was silent awhile. One end of the street led to a canal and a purple line was drawn along the length of the latter.

"What's that signify,?" I asked.

"The sector boundary," she only answered.

So she lived almost on the boundary of the East sector! I looked more closely at the map, and saw that her district comprised a small tongue of land jutting out into the West sector into the suburbs of Kreuzberg and Neukölln. How cruel fate had been! If only the great powers seated at the conference table had perchance made one small slip of the pen, then her entire life and those of many like her might have been destined towards a different future.

"Do you live in a nice flat,?" I asked.

"Yes," she replied, but she didn't sound quite sure. "I can give you my address," she added smiling, opening her little handbag.

She took out some paper and wrote down her address in a neat hand, and I took it, placing it safely in my wallet.

"What are you doing in Berlin,?" she said.

"I'm studying your beautiful city," I answered evasively.

"Berlin's not beautiful," she answered smiling.

"The West sectors have many attractions."

"They're so new. Not like East Berlin. How long will you stay here?"

"I cannot answer that," I replied humorously.

"Then you do not know," she said failing to apprehend the truth behind my facetiousness.

I had no intention of telling her about my imminent departure from the city – not yet anyway. Only twelve more hours in Berlin, I reflected. I was glad she had misconstrued the hidden meaning of my last sentence so that I was spared exposing her to the conflict of feelings that might have followed.

---

* Long since re-named Karl Kunger Strasse.

"Have you been in the Grunewald and on the Wannsee,?" she asked.

"Yes," I said, relieved that she had changed the subject.

"There it is wonderful!"

"Do you like walking,?" I asked.

"Yes. I like to walk in the forests and where there is beautiful nature. It is so peaceful and refreshing in the Grunewald – like being in the heart of the countryside – so still and quiet. There you can forget the world."

"I should like to take you to the Grunewald," I said softly.

"That would be nice," she said, her eyes brightening. "Do you know Pfaueninsel? I could show you a beautiful old farmstead there. It's hundreds of years old, and there are some pretty cottages – thatched and timber built – so delightful!"

I cursed myself for having not met her before. The prospect of having to return to London was heartrending indeed. It was a wretched fate having to leave Berlin in such circumstances as these.

I settled the bill, and before we left, the East Berlinerin took a little souvenir of the evening: the tissue folder from around the stem of her lemonade glass, and on which were written the words, Roxy Hôtel.

Chapter 7

It was too late now for a concert or the theatre, and at her behest we strolled along the Ku'damm window gazing. She held tightly onto my arm pressing closely to me. We looked into one of the square glass pavement stands, displaying jewellery and ladies gloves. She pointed at the articles with her finger, exclaiming how attractive they were and inviting my comments. Our heads were close, and when we walked on again, some golden hairs had settled on the shoulder of my coat.

She tugged on my arm and we approached a music shop. Photos of great operatic singers were displayed and she pointed to each in turn, asking humorously if I had heard of this or that singer. Laughing and joking, we walked a little further – in even step, and the city was ours. We came to a dress shop. She was particularly struck by an attractive costume and she arched her shapely neck as she eyed it critically from different angles, and became lost in its contemplation.

On reaching the corner of Fasanen Strasse opposite the great Kempinski Hotel, we crossed the Ku'damm to return down the other side of the street, and as we crossed the broad road, I tightened my arm around her shoulder. We came to a shoe shop, and pointing her finger to the delightful things in the window, she inclined her head closer to mine in appraising the items of her choice. We came to a shop of Objets d'Arts and she was entranced by the multitude of exotic and ancient wares, illuminated by the spotlights within. There were mother-of-pearl jewel caskets, old coins, argand lamps, ornately designed brass and marble clocks, Dresden figurines, crystal chandeliers and other objects of miscellaneous interest. I was enchanted by the slimness of her figure! I threw my arm around her waist and dragged her reluctantly from the window. She stepped close to me as we walked, pressing her head against my shoulder until I sensed the warmth and sweet scent of her silky hair. Time was passing and I experienced a rising sense of perturbation as I wondered as to how far I should pursue the physical aspect of our friendship during these last hours together. Again, we found ourselves at a dress and textile shop, and again she pulled at my arm as we moved close to the window.

"Do you like that dress,?" she asked pointing to a model.

"Yes, it's pretty," I replied.

"But the colour is a little sad don't you think – mauve,?" she said turning her head critically. "But that dress is very chic," she added, pointing to another.

"It's a glamorous party frock. But I think blue would suit you best – it would show off your figure," I said pointing to another.

"Do you really think it would suit me,?" she asked with interest.

"Would you like me to buy it for you,?" I added.

"That would be too generous," she replied laughing and resting her cheek against my shoulder for a moment.

It was a department store, and I pulled on her waist, and we strolled into an arcade away from the crowds. The soles of her shoes resounded on the tiled floor, and it was quieter here and we were quite alone. On display were dressers' dummies in skimpy lingerie set in the erotic ambience of soft bedroom furnishings. The East Berlinerin stood silent, her warm body pressed against my side.

"Those are beautiful," I remarked.

"Yes," she only replied dreamily.

I brushed back her long silky hair and kissed the nape of her neck. She remained quite still. I held her shoulders with one hand and held her thigh with the other, until facing one another we were pressed together. She stood relaxed and meek, her head lowered towards her breast. I stroked the rounded crown of her head and chin. Her eyes were closed, and I kissed her forehead several times. Her eyelids flickered gently. I kissed her temples, and the bridge of her nose, and I kissed her eyes and cheeks – so endearingly pale they were. Again, I kissed her forehead, and again the shapely proportions of her nose.

"Please don't – we hardly know each other," she only pleaded.

But it was too late. Her eyes were closed, and I pressed my lips onto hers, and held them firmly there. I felt her lips dilate, and she kissed my mouth, and gently, slowly, she covered my chin with kisses. I was enraptured by the beauty and rhythm of her being. She remained still for some few moments, and she lowered her head again, and I lifted it as before, and once again, I showered kisses upon her face, and then again, we fell into a long embrace and our lips were pressed together. With one hand I clasped her neck, and with the other I stroked her back and felt the neatness of her figure.

"*Du bist so schön,*!" I exclaimed.

"I didn't say you could call me *du*," she answered smiling. "You should ask a girl first before you can call her *du*. That's only polite."

"Can I,?" I said smiling down at her.

"I want to know you better first," she replied. "I think *du* means so much. I don't like those boys who call every girl *du*. It makes a relationship seem cheap and insincere. I don't think a boy and girl should use *du* until they know each other well, because then the word can mean so much more."

"Then, I'll ask you another time," I said, and I kissed her again on the forehead and bridge of the nose.

At last she pulled herself away.

"I hardly know you," she exclaimed.

"I hardly know you," I responded, "but I know what I feel."

"We don't know each other. You know so little about me."

"But time is on our side."

Again, I threw my arm around her shoulder.

"We mustn't! Someone might come," she said. "It's not proper to kiss in the street when we may be seen."

"We're quite alone."

"I'd rather we just talk," she said slipping her arm into mine. "To kiss too soon is not good. Please tell me more about yourself. What are you doing in Berlin?"

"I've told you," I replied laughing. "Studying your beautiful city."

"What are you really studying – architecture?"

I laughed.

"Or are you working here?"

"No, I'm not working in Berlin."

"How long will you stay here?"

"I won't tell you," I said laughing.

"Why not,?" she exclaimed pulling on my arm. "Do you like Berlin?"

"I've told you: I like it very much."

"Will you stay here a long time – some years perhaps?"

I said nothing, only remained silent for a moment as I reflected on my sad, and now it seemed, tragic departure from the city. Only eleven hours more, I reflected! I must tell her sometime, I thought, but not yet. Again, I cursed myself for not having met her before. Perhaps she read the tendency of my thoughts, for the next moment she asked: "When do we meet again?"

I said nothing. The question was sudden and unexpected. I was unready to give an answer.

"When,?" she said again, tugging on my arm.

She was insistent. I could no longer evade her question. I had to reveal the truth.

"I must tell you," I began, and I swallowed and felt a choking sensation. "I leave Berlin tomorrow – tomorrow morning. I must return to London."

She only exclaimed a long drawn-out "*Ja-a,!*" and looked thoughtful for a moment. We turned towards another window and she pointed to some textile fabrics for curtain hangings.

"That one is nice," she said evasively pointing to a colourful cotton fabric with a floral design, but her voice sounded flat and the words were meaningless.

Arm in arm we left the arcade, and continued down the Ku'damm. We looked in the square glass show cases and other windows and approached the Kaiser Wilhelm Memorial Church at the end of the street.

It was still early in the evening and with a spasm of anxiety about the future I wondered how we might spend the next few hours – the last hours we would be together for a long time to come. Return to Frau Dubrowski's with a bottle of wine and lemon squash and talk about literature and music for the rest of the evening? No, we couldn't do that – Frau Dubrowski might – or rather, very possibly would become curious and disturb us. Perhaps we might visit a news theatre, or better, just stroll through the Tiergarten towards the Brandenburg Gate. Approaching the corner of Ranke Strasse as I held my arm across her shoulder, I was about to suggest the latter, when she suddenly stopped in her path, and looking vexed, she turned to me and said: "I must go home now."

"But it's still early," I replied taken aback. "It's only just gone ten. We have all the evening in front of us."

"But really, James, I must go home."

I caressed her shoulder and held her neck, and tried to draw her closer, but she was unyielding.

"Are you tired,?" I asked, for suddenly she looked so pale.

"A little tired," she replied. "I had so much to eat."

"Then we could go to a news theatre and rest awhile," I suggested.

"No, I must go home," she insisted.

"Does your mother say you must be home by eleven o'clock,?" I teased, laughing.

"No, but I'm a little tired, that's all. I've been over-excited."

I saw by the sudden change of her demeanour that the revelation of my home-going had altered her attitude. I could see she was adamant, and I realised I had to accept her decision. My only hope now was to convince her of the sincerity of my feelings so that a meaningful correspondence could be maintained between us.

"I shall see you to your home," I said.

"No," she replied resolutely, "just to the *S-Bahn* – where you met me."

"You must let me see you home," I said with emphasis. A vexed expression crossed her face and I tried to construe her thoughts. "That's the least I can do at the end of an evening."

"Not to my home – please not," she pleaded.

I could see she was adamant and not wishing to push the matter or ask any possibly awkward questions, I relented.

"Very well then," I said. "We'll walk through the Tiergarten to the Brandenburg Gate. It's such a beautiful night."

I was flattered by the idea of exchanging final farewells in front of the Brandenburg Gate – it seemed so aptly symbolic.

"But the Brandenburg Gate's four or five kilometres from here. It would be impossible to walk so far."

"There's no hurry."

"We'll return to the Zoo station, and return home by *S-Bahn*," she said gripping my arm. "Where are you staying?"

"In Friedenau."

"Then we'll go as far as Friedrich Strasse together, where you can change for the other line."

We made our way towards Zoo station. I tried to lighten the atmosphere between us, and thought we might go possibly into the little photographic kiosk in the main hallway of Zoo station to have our photos taken as a memento of the evening. I was seized with uneasiness about the emotional turn our friendship had taken. Was the fair Berlinerin self-reproachful at her having given herself away so soon? Was she resentful at my having not told her earlier of my impending departure from Berlin, or had it mistakenly occurred to her that I had been frivolously flirtatious all along, or had she simply decided that nothing could possibly come of such an affair because of the distance dividing us?

On entering the hallway of Zoo station, I decided against the idea of a photograph as inapt and childish. I bought tickets for the city trains and we climbed the steps onto the *S-Bahn* platforms.

We sat together in the back of the carriage on our way to the East sector, and Dagmar wore a contemplative expression, as I held my arm around her trying to lighten her downcast countenance.

The train passed through the Hansa quarter, passed the new Protestant church with its floodlit skeletal tower, just fifty metres from the line, and passed the more distant and towering blocks of residential flats, their hundreds of windows lighting up the darkness, and passed the parkland of Bellevue and the Tiergarten, and passed the distant floodlit golden winged figure standing aloft, the Victory monument.

"I hope to return to Berlin soon," I said thoughtfully, but the words suggested an intonation of sadness as if I knew that the chance of returning "soon" was an unlikely possibility. She said nothing and perhaps the tone of my pronouncement said more than the words themselves.

"Do you read much,?" I said in a brighter tone of voice. I wanted to break the silence which had come between us, and to arouse her interest in at least something – anything – in a final attempt to provide a connecting link for the future.

"I like to read good books – modern novels," she replied. "That's when I can get them."

"When you can get them?"

"I only like novels from the West – but they're not available in the East sector – or very few."

"Then you buy such books in the West?"

"Yes, but they're expensive – even pocket books. We can't use East marks for books."

"Then let me send you some books from the West – some English novels in German."

"Do you have books in German in English bookshops?"

"In London we do."

"That would be very kind of you to think of me like that."

"It would be a pleasure. What would you like me to send?"

"I've enjoyed Cronin but I'd be pleased with any book."

"I promise as soon as I'm back in London, I'll search out come books for you."

"You're very kind and considerate," she replied thoughtfully. "You shouldn't do it."

The train was approaching the East sector and time was running out. Only three or four minutes, I reflected, and then we'd be parted from one another – for how long,? and suddenly the question took on the proportions of an intractable problem. Opposite stood a drunk, who aroused our attention with his prurient stare, and I felt constrained in the expression of any feelings. Dagmar put her hand to her temple, wincing, as if in pain.

"What's the matter,?" I asked.

She shook her head as if to say that everything was all right.

"What's wrong,?" I persisted, "migraine?"

"No."

"Let me take you home."

"No, I'll be all right – after a few moments," she replied. "I'm just a little tired and over-excited – that's all."

When the train drove into Friedrich Strasse, the drunk was still hovering over us and I felt that a physical gesture of parting affection would be unsuitable in the circumstances. As the train halted and the doors opened we shook hands and exchanged a formal farewell, before I hurriedly left and the doors crashed shut together. As the train moved out of the station, we waved and our faces were lit with friendly smiles, but as I ran down the steps and moved along the corridors to the other platform, my feelings were clouded with scepticism.

As I lay in bed that night I thought long over the events of the evening, and it was not until after several hours that I finally fell asleep. As I walked briskly through the fresh night air from Friedenau station to Frau Dubrowski's I was happy and optimistic about the little adventure, but as I lay thoughtfully in bed, in the quiet claustral atmosphere of the room, I was hurt by doubts. If only I had been remaining in Berlin a few days longer, I would conquer – and then she would be mine forever and I would be hers! I pondered on what might be the outcome of our friendship. I hardly knew the girl or anything about her background. When and in what circumstances would fate next bring us together? – for intuitively, somehow, I felt we would meet again – but then possibly, such an intuition only sprung from a deep overpowering desire that we *must* meet again. Then again, all speculation and hope seemed futile. Who could really claim to predict the future?

BOOK II

The Mysterious One

Mysterious love, uncertain treasure,
Hast thou more of pain or pleasure. …
Endless torments dwell about thee:
Yet who would live, and live without thee!

Joseph Addison, *Rosamund*, Act III, Sc. 2.

Chapter 8

Did you ever hear from that girl you picked up in Berlin,?" asked Phil turning to me.

"I haven't heard from her yet," I said evasively.

"I thought you wouldn't," he replied.

Three of us were sitting on high stools at the lunch time bar of Mooney's Old Irish House in the Strand, which was crowded as always midday on a weekday.

"I didn't say I wouldn't hear from her – just that I hadn't," I retorted sharply.

"I don't think you'll hear from her now," added Chris.

"I don't think about it much myself," I lied. "It doesn't make much difference if she writes or not. Still, it was amusing whilst it lasted."

"Life can't be easy in East Berlin," mused Phil. "I mean they can go over to the West sectors and see for themselves how the other half live. It must be bitter to experience such a contrast between two worlds."

"You can't guess how they feel," said Chris. "The authorities must keep close tabs on everyone. After all, East Berlin's the only hole in the Iron Curtain, and the Commies must know they can never finally succeed in the propaganda war for their own people until they've somehow, someday closed that hole."

"Which they'd never be able to do, because the Western powers wouldn't let them," interjected Phil.

"So I think it not improbable her parents persuaded her not to write because of all the complications which might arise. It's not exactly a promising basis for a romantic friendship," continued Chris. "Or perhaps the East German postal authorities have just intercepted your correspondence as 'undesirable.'"

"There's no knowing," I said resignedly, "but as I've said, I don't think about the matter. It was just a flirtation to while away the time."

Some minutes later I was walking up Southampton street through Covent Garden towards the University. I had been back in England a month now, and it was more than three weeks since I had written to Dagmar, and still I had no reply. For more than a week I had been daily expecting a letter, waiting feverishly – but no – nothing had arrived. Every day, I had been the first to collect the small bundle of post dropped through the letter box in the early morning. I had picked up the several letters from the mat expectantly, turning them over, but there had been nothing with my name.

On rushing downstairs on one occasion I had seen the outline of the postman through the coloured panes of the front door, and had opened it, confronting him before he had had time to drop the letters through the slot. He had stood, momentarily startled by my gesture.

"Anything from Berlin – for Furner,?" I had asked him as he sorted through the mail.

"Sorry, not this time guv," came the reply, and I saw the suggestion of a faint smile.

"Thanks all the same," I answered, taking the letters, and closed the door. Impatiently, I flung the letters onto the little hall table and ran back to my room.

Sometimes I encountered another lodger in the hallway as I stood feverishly glancing through the mail and I could not avoid catching glances of bemusement. How much might they know?

"Expecting a letter, Mr. Furner,?" they would ask.

"I thought there'd might be one for me," I replied off-handedly.

"You're up early today, aren't you,?" exclaimed another of the middle-aged nosey parkers clearly sensing the unusual.

"Early lecture this morning. See – here's a letter for you, Mrs, Craddock. Have you got relatives in Brighton,?" I responded giving like for like.

Often I was the first to return in the evening, and eagerly I snatched up the letters from the mat, left by the second and third deliveries.

The days were made longer by this eternal waiting for the expected letter. Only four more hours and I would be home to meet the afternoon post, I often told myself. Only three and a half hours now. How time dragged! Only ten minutes now, I consoled myself as I alighted from the bus at the top of the hill, and as I turned the latch key I wondered who'd been the first at home and if the letters had already been placed on the hall table.

On searching through the post and finding none addressed to me, I was somehow consoled in knowing that there was another day ahead – a day of hope and happy anticipation. I lived only from one postal delivery to the next – blessing each delivery with respectful handling as every envelope passed nervously through my fingers. One such hope inspiring envelope might yet contain a letter with a world of meaning and a symphony of feeling, and for the arrival of that anticipated experience hung my happiness.

I recollected how oppressive life might otherwise be if no mail arrived after days of endless succession. Then truly a dread depression would enter into this sense of waiting – or if perhaps by some weird and supernatural happening, the existence of the house had been lost to the postal authorities; or if like the radio comedy character, the postman had simply decided, in his eccentricity, to "tear up the letters," then all would be lost. But the daily satisfaction of fingering and searching through the small packet of correspondence remained a warm assurance that the system was still intact, and a welcoming confirmation that hope might thrive.

On crossing Long Acre, which was still littered with cabbage leaves and vegetable matter from the day's uncleaned refuse, and passing down Endell street, I became concerned at Chris's suggestion that perhaps my letter to Dagmar, or possibly her reply, might have been intercepted by the East German authorities. Innately, I felt that any correspondence between us was necessarily clandestine. The things I wanted to tell her – but implicitly – about life in the West; and all I wanted to persuade her to do – to fly from the world which was hers – all these things were forbidden matters.

In the eyes of the rulers of the People's German Democratic Republic – in the eyes of a police state – they were illicit things designed to turn a young girl's head in drawing her away from a sense of communal obligation to the "great Communist ideal." They were things which amounted to "lies and blasphemies;" false propaganda from someone from a prospective enemy state. In the eyes of the ideologues such letter writing could not be dismissed as motivated by simple romantic attachment. A more serious aspect was involved – the inescapable political dimension.

Perhaps her parents had urged her to ignore my letter because of the distance dividing us, or out of political expediency which drew them to the East. I knew nothing about her parents, except that the fair Berlinerin had told me they would never leave the East sector. Perhaps her parents were sympathetic to the regime, or perhaps, even implicated in its ugly administration. Was her father possibly a Communist official – perhaps even a green uniformed jack-booted officer? I thought long about this, and concluded it could not be. Her joy in things Western was too explicit, and her tone of sad resignation with which she told me her parents would never leave the East indicated that advanced age or financial limitations were the more probable reasons for their wishing to stay put.

Or perhaps she had herself decided to ignore the letter. Perhaps, after our final parting, she had resolved it would be senseless – a stupid thing to enter into such a correspondence. And perhaps too, she had considered the fact of my withholding the news of my imminent departure from Berlin until the end of the evening, after I had stolen kisses from her lips, as a meanness and deceit – that I had been playing with and exploiting her feelings. She had a right to such indignation – that I could not deny.

In my letter to her I had tried to counter such feelings she might have harboured. I had written with care. More than a week had elapsed since I had written and destroyed the first draft before finally sending the completed letter. Could anything have caused offence? Could anything have been left amiss?

I had asked after her health and what concerts she had attended. I expressed my sorrow on having to leave Berlin so soon – how three weeks was too short a time to see and absorb the sights and pleasures of the city. I begged her sincerely to believe me that I missed her company, expressing deep regret on not having met her earlier. I said I had not yet had time to send her a novel from the West and would wait until she asked for a special choice. I described something about my own routine, and finally, I asked after the little Art Shop in Stalin Allee. In a p.s. I asked if I might use *du* in my next letter, remarking that I felt the *Sie* form to be too restraining.

No, on reflection I didn't think anything in my letter had gone awry. Perhaps before its arrival she had already resolved not to enter into a correspondence and so my letter would have fallen on deaf ears. If this was so, or if for any other reason she had declined to respond to my courtship, I was resolved not to fall under the prejudice that these things had in fact occurred until after I had received a confirmation of their truth.

I would wait till Saturday – for three more days, and if still I had not heard, then I should write again – a little humorous reminder, enclosing a copy of my earlier letter. Then I recollected I had told myself this before – I had already given her five more days before sending a reminder, rationalising that girls are sometimes dilatory and awkward in responding to any amatory approach. But then, I would certainly write to her on Saturday if I had still heard nothing.

On returning home that evening, filled with a sense of anticipation, I turned the key in the lock, pushing open the heavy front door with its loose hinges and cracked frame. There were no letters on the mat. I had not been the first home that evening. I closed the door, walking briskly to the little table at the end of the hallway beneath the staircase. There had been a large post that afternoon. I passed the letters through my fingers.

Almost disbelieving I saw an envelope addressed to me – the words Herrn James Furner written in careful block capitals on a large white envelope with a foreign stamp. My heart throbbed as I was overwhelmed with a feeling of elation, and a crowd of wild thoughts rushed through my mind. She had written! Slowly – calmly, I took up the letter – my mind a storm of excitement, then dazed with a feeling of doubt and half-belief that the letter had in fact arrived – that it did exist, I pressed the letter between my fingers, and it was real, and I heard the crackle of the envelope lining and the pages of the letter within. It was a thick envelope and I sensed with pleasure the mottled texture between my fingers.

Beneath the letter I saw a card also addressed to Herrn James Furner in the same hand, also bearing a foreign stamp. I took that up also. A letter and a card, both addressed to me, and from the same sweet creature, and received together on the same day! I glanced at the post mark of each. They had been posted together some ten days earlier – Berlin, N.4! Curious, I thought, and my letters shall be sent from the postal district of London, N.6. The most trivial associations touching the fair Berlinerin only enhanced my feelings of joy.

I ran upstairs, unlocked the door of my room, entered, threw down the letter and card onto the centre table, placing my bulging briefcase on a chair. I would read the letters after eating – not before – when relaxed and comfortable and with time to study carefully and ruminate over every word and sentence she had written. It's a skill to read such letters, I told myself. It's not the text itself: it's between the lines which really matter – it's that which really reveals the heart.

I lit the decrepit gas fire, carefully – very carefully, replaced a broken element which had somehow fallen onto the hearth during my absence in the day – perhaps a sudden gust of wind had blown down the flue. It was a large room, and very cold in the Autumn and Winter months, for there were two ill-fitting casement windows at either end facing north and south respectively.

Removing my coat, I hung it in the wardrobe, unpacked the shopping from the briefcase, and prepared supper in the adjoining kitchenette. She had written, I kept telling myself, and I tried to conjecture the mood of her reply.

The table was laid, and I moved it by the fire, emptying the saucepan containing my modest fare onto a plate, and as I felt this to be a particularly auspicious occasion, I opened a cheap bottle of Hock, which had been stored away for just such a celebration, pouring out half a tumbler full of wine. I raised the glass and drank an ample toast to Dagmar, the fair Berlinerin, before tucking into the meal before me.

After eating I pushed the plate aside, and took up the letter and card. The p.c. was a picture post card with soft brown and yellow colours and a splash of green and red, from Vermeer's painting, *The Street*. It illustrated a peaceful scene, the rooftops and cobbled streets of a quiet mews with a single figure of an old woman through a doorway in a wall leading to the back yard of a house.   The original hung in the Rijksmuseum, I noted, but the card itself had clearly come from that little Art Shop in Stalin Allee.

Alongside the postmarks of each item was stamped a curious slogan: *Der Kampfgegen Erkültungskrankheiten geht Alle an,!* Which meant something like: "All in the struggle against catarrhal disease!" The slogan seemed refreshingly different from the usual run of slogans emanating from the East bloc and I could not forebear a smile. I thought of the coldness of the room in which I sat and the insufficient heat given out by a gas fire, and momentarily, I felt a current of cold air pass behind my neck.   I wondered how long I could bear up against the inclement draughts and temperature of the room before ailing to a common cold and "Catarrhal disease."

I read the card which was written in block letters in a neat spiky hand. The entire section reserved for correspondence was filled with writing, and as I read the card, always hurrying towards the end of each sentence to reach the verb elucidating the final sense, I was diverted by the complex formality of the German grammar – with such exactitude had the sentences been constructed!

Dear James!

I received your letter of 8.10 which I gladly received, and thank you. Perhaps I have been long in replying and trust you are not angry, but much work has kept me busy these last weeks. I could not exactly read your address. Is it Hornsey Lawe or Hornsey Lane? On the card I have written Lawe and on the letter Lane. It is to be hoped you receive them both. - Greetings, Dagmar.

p.s. Please write more clearly.

I smiled, and laid the card aside, and opened the letter, which was written on thick fine quality deckle edged notepaper.

Dear James!

For your letter which I received fourteen days ago I thank you. It pleases me that you enjoyed your last days in Germany here in our city of Berlin. It must have been interesting for you to have travelled here. Berlin is a city of two worlds with much to be seen, and perhaps for this reason you enjoyed your days in Germany, but in order to get acquainted with a country, or even with our city of

Berlin, some few weeks are too short. Perhaps you have seen many things, but I think there must be much which still remains unknown to you. Next time you must stay longer in Berlin.

According to your letter you like very much to amuse yourself (*vergnügen Sie sich gern*) and you very much miss Berlin for this reason!

Shortly after you left Berlin I saw in the West sector the play *Epitaph For George Dillon*, at the Berliner Theatre, by an English writer. It was very good. Last week I saw with my girl friend an exhibition of the graphic works of Eduard Munch in the Congress Hall. He was a new artist for me and I liked very much the strong feelings he portrayed.

It is very kind that you will send me a book. I know so few modern English writers because they are rarely available in the East. I have read Cronin and like him, but I have heard that the writers Graham Greene and Somerset Maugham are also very good. I should be grateful to receive any book by a good English writer.

Now in Autumn we have much more to do in the business than in Summer. Foreigners are only allowed to buy books and reproductions from our shop, unless they have first changed their money in the Issuing Bank of the DDR and produced the receipt thereof. If we sold Artworks this would be punished, although these are very much sought for by foreigners – especially preferred are batik and animal works.

It was kind that you should be so interested in how I am. I have been somewhat weak and ill during the past few weeks and have had to visit the doctor and have special treatment.

Here in Berlin the Autumn cold has come very early this year, although it remains dry and sunny. Please write me how the weather is in London. I believe you have much fog and damp in London throughout the Winter months.

Again, I must thank you for taking such an interest in me – in a girl who lives so far away from your native city.

With heartfelt Greetings, Yours, Dagmar.

p.s. Please send the book to an address in the West sector, which is written on the next page. I'll go and fetch it there.

On the back page of the letter was written an address in the suburb of Britz of a certain gentleman with the impressive un-contemporary sounding name of Friedrich-Wilhelm Brüning. Brüning! I recollected having seen the name before, and on turning to the back of the envelope and the address of the fair Berlinerin, I noted the words, *bei* (c/o) Brüning. This meant that the address in the West sector was of a relative, but it also pointed to the possibility that she was not living with her parents, but another relative, or perhaps she had a stepfather with the name of Brüning. I thought about this.

Yes, she had a stepfather, I concluded after a while, and suddenly the entire mystery of her being and her resignation in life became clear as the facts fell into place. She had a beautiful mother who had been married to a handsome husband (Dagmar's father) who had been a cultured intellectual with a taste for art and music. He had been a writer or critic until deprived of his livelihood by the Communist regime and condemned to menial work – a clerical post in an unimportant government office, perhaps. But still he continued to promote his views, and despite oppression and humiliation, he continued to bear up against "the slings and arrows of outrageous fortune," and to educate his daughters to think as he did. And then he had died in mysterious circumstances. And then some years passed, and the family felt the loss of the father and the strength he had given them until one day the mother met another man – charming and handsome again – and they were married, but it transpired he was a bully – tyrannical – and a dictatorial official employed by the state. He had made their lives intolerable by an overbearing manner and political tirades to which he forced his family to listen. But Dagmar had borne against it all through her stoicism and resignation in life.

Then I had doubts as to the authenticity of such a story. The other Brüning came from the West sector, and he was unlikely to be a "sympathiser," and he must have been a friend of the family too. That seemed to upset the neatness and credibility of my little explanation. Dagmar's fatalistic resignation in life remained an insoluble mystery.

Again I took up the letter, re-reading and pondering over each sentence with care. It had been carefully written without the sign of a blot or correction, in a blue violet ink, but I perceived no warmth in the letter. On the contrary, it was cold and matter of fact – lacking sparkle or feeling. Was it that the complex grammar stood in the way of feelings she might otherwise have expressed, or was it that she consciously made use of this style to conceal true feelings?

Those few feelings which did push their way to the surface had a suggestion of bitterness, such as her platitudinous remark describing Berlin as the city of two worlds; that it must have been "interesting" for me to have travelled there; and her remark that it had pleased her I had enjoyed my last days in Germany might have contained a hidden sarcasm. Her statement that three weeks were too short a time to get to know a country and that there was still much for me to learn, although factually true, was hardly a happy expression of benign consideration. Her short paragraph saying that according to my letter I missed Berlin merely because I liked to amuse myself was unquestionably the most striking sentence. It may have expressed all her justifiable feelings of resentment at my misusing her. I had indeed said I missed the life and pleasures of Berlin, but I had not anticipated she would seize on those remarks as having sprung from egotistical motives, still less, that she would have thrown them back in my face. My innocent intention had been to compliment her city, but through a subtleness, often used by the fair sex, she had ingeniously turned round my meaning to use it as a mild rebuke.

The final paragraphs of the letter expressed a better frame of mind, and her thanking me for taking such an interest in her – in a girl who lived so far away, expressed a bemused tolerance at my bothering to write, together with a hidden suggestion that my intentions could hardly be taken as serious.

I was amused by the little passage about the Art Shop, solemnly explaining the regulatory formalities under which foreigners might buy Artworks from her shop. It reflected a consciousness of duty to bureaucratic formulae! How beautifully it illustrated the observance of the German mind for the Kantian principle of duty for duty's sake. Her reference to her health aroused my curiosity. What could this mean? Was there something which threatened her long-term health, or was she merely hypochondriacal and interested in using this as a pretext to attract sympathetic attention? I decided to ignore the reference as insignificant.

It seemed that the assumption I had made in Berlin after parting from her, that she considered the friendship as not worth prolonging as little was likely to come of it, had probably been correct. Such an explanation could be read throughout the letter, but despite that, she nonetheless left the way open for further correspondence. She thanked me for my interest in her, inviting me to send her a book. In no way did the letter discourage my hopes or diminish my feelings for her. I was resolved to win a warmer more positive response from my letters. If only I had not left Berlin so soon! If only fate could bring us together, then we should surely belong to one another forever!

I realised the inadequacy of building a relationship such as ours (on which personal friendship was merely based on a period of two days) by means of correspondence. Even under the best circumstances a relationship maintained through correspondence could never be fully satisfactory, for the feelings of one or both might change, and furthermore, polite and warm sentiments might degenerate into the insincerity of meaningless form. I felt the start of our correspondence was not entirely satisfactory; that it might end as suddenly as it had begun, through a carelessly written or misread sentence - and I specially felt this in view of the hypersensitive feelings of the fair Berlinerin.

Nonetheless, I was now determined to use all my efforts in cultivating our friendship by this only means available at the present time.

Chapter 9

That night studies were pushed aside, as I settled down at my desk, attending to the more urgent task of writing to Dagmar.

After thanking her for her letter I expressed the hope her health had now improved, saying I expected the treatment would be of benefit, and hoped she wasn't overworking at the little Art Shop. I promised that on the morrow I should choose a book. I said I missed Berlin because of its culture, the beauty of its surroundings, the liveliness of its people, and most of all, because I missed the company of the East Berlinerin. I pleaded with her again that we might use the *du* term, and asked her to tell me more about her interests. I ended by saying I often thought of her, and asked for her photograph. As a p.s. I enclosed a five Reich mark note as I had been unable to change it in any English bank.

I folded the completed letter, sealing it into an envelope, and ventured into the cold night air to ensure it would be transported by the next collection. The following day I bought a copy of Joyce Cary's, *The Horses Mouth*, sending it to the address she had given in the West sector.

The subsequent days passed more quickly and having replied to her letter by return, I anticipated a shorter waiting interval until the receipt of her next epistle. Sure enough, within a fortnight I received her second letter – a little longer than the first – surely a hopeful omen.

Dear James!

Your letter of 4.11 I have received and thank you. For the five East mark note I also thank you, and it is already known to me that banks in the West do not normally change currencies of East European countries. Western people can only change East German currency in the money exchange of Berlin Zoo station. Perhaps it was a pity you did not keep the note and change it yourself when you next come to Berlin – that is, if you ever want to come to Berlin again!

I have received the book also and very many thanks for it. Uncle Willy, who lives in the West sector, brought your parcel over to me when he came to visit us last Saturday. I have already started reading the book and find it most amusing.

It is very kind that you should wish to send me another book. I know so little about contemporary Western literature that it is difficult for me to make a choice. Perhaps you could tell me something in your next letter about modern English writers. I am fond of all books providing they are good. I have heard that all the following writers are particularly good: Pearl S. Buck, Collette, Cronin, Greene and Galsworthy. If you should wish to send me another book I should be very pleased to receive any by the above writers, as well as many others of course.

You ask for my interests. I like serious music very much, good books and nature. Now in Winter I like to visit concerts, plays and the opera. Later this month I shall visit the German State Opera and see a performance of Mozart's *Don Giovanni*. I saw this opera once before but I shall go again because of the beautiful music. Which composer I like best I could not tell you.

Last Sunday I went with my girl friend to an exhibition in the Palace of Charlottenburg. There I saw paintings by Schmidt-Rottlof, Derain, Matisse, Vlaminck, Munch, Kirchner, Hechel, Dufy, Friesz, Mondrian, Nolde and Kandinsky. You can imagine that this exhibition was very interesting for me.

My health is still a little weak and so far the treatment has not been of great use. Now with the approach of Christmas we have a lot to do in the business and it is often tiring.

You ask if we should write *du*, and you say that young people in the West use this term every day. We in East Germany also use *du* but only if we are very well known to each other, or are equal colleagues in a business, or students, or equal members in some kind of club or organisation. We do not yet know each other well enough to use *du*, and if you remember, I told you once before that some people misuse the correct meaning of this form.

Unfortunately, I do not at the moment possess a suitable photo of myself, which I could send you. Should I have one you would receive it.

Again, many thanks for your kind letter and the book. Please tell me something about your life in London in your next letter. When we met I don't think you exactly told me what you did – is it work, or are you a student?

            With heartfelt Greetings, Yours, Dagmar.

How beautifully precise sounded the German words – how rhythmical and finely formed the sentences! On recovering from my reverie in the music of the language, I turned to the contents of the letter. The tone was reserved as in the earlier, but she had told me something about her interests with a tantalising glimpse into her family life. Also, she had asked me to describe my life in London and had shown a curiosity in my interests.

So Friedrich-Wilhelm was known as Uncle Willy! I assumed he was a close relative and friend who often visited the family in the East sector. The little passage describing the delivery of the book with such intimate side references to "Uncle Willy" and "when he visited us last Saturday" seemed to infer she was close to her family.

Apart from this I felt the letter lacked an intimate spontaneity which would have been desirable. It was padded with lists of names of writers and painters and an unnecessarily long paragraph about the five East mark note. The description of her interests revealed little about her inner-self. Nonetheless, the letter was pleasing for it expressed a better frame of mind than its predecessor.

It was not for two days that I answered her letter, sending a packet containing a Cronin novel to Uncle Willy in the West sector. I thanked her for her letter complimenting her on her wide range of interests. I followed this with a description of London attempting to describe it in terms of her own interests – as if London had been designed for her. I enclosed idyllic photographic views of the neighbourhood where I then lived, including pictures of Highgate village high street; of Coleridge's house; of Kenwood; and Highgate and Hampstead ponds, which I described with some exaggeration as the Wannsee of north London, and I pointed out that London was hilly in contrast to Berlin which was built on the flat march of Brandenburg. As requested, I wrote several paragraphs on contemporary English writers, and repeated my request for her photo, bluntly requesting that if she didn't possess a suitable picture, to visit a photographer and "get one done." I told her I was a student and said something about college life and my eventual aspirations, and I returned to the London theme, urging that she visit England.

It was more than two weeks before I next heard from the fair Berlinerin, and meanwhile, I had begun to feel apprehensive as to the possible effect of my previously hurried letter. I arrived home early one evening and took up the letter with others from the doormat. The postman had pencilled a circle round the street number and re-written the number more clearly. As with all Continentals she had written the 1s with long tails from their heads so that they were easily mistaken for 7s. I shall have to explain to her, I reflected, as I ran upstairs, that in England we write our 1s with a single stroke and refrain from crossing our 7s.

I tore open the envelope and took out the letter. It was shorter than the previous one and the writing more evenly spaced.

Dear James!

I have your letter of 19.11 and thank you. You are always impatient that I should l reply to your letters impossibly quickly. Your letter before the last one took nine days to reach me but I replied to it after only three days. Your last letter I have already had for twelve days but as a punishment for your impatience I have purposely delayed writing to you. You must be punished, you see, because impatience in impolite!!

Tomorrow I shall go to Uncle Willy's and fetch the book you sent me. It was very kind of you to send me one so soon. Although I gave you a list of writers in whom I was interested I did not want you to spend a lot of money on me.

Your description of London was most interesting. Please tell me more about your wonderful city. I believe you that I would like London and I have no doubt that you should think that. Unfortunately, as a result of the political and economic situation in which Germany now exists fourteen years after the War, it would be impossible for me to visit and get to know your country in the near future. As I live in East Berlin I could never obtain a passport for a Western country.

I was most interested also to hear about modern English writers. The coloured photos you sent were very beautiful and had they been black and white I would have made prints from them.

On Saturday I was in the City Opera and saw Bizet's *Carmen* and on Monday I was in the German State Opera and saw Puccini's *Tosca.* Both performances were beautiful and good. The leading role in *Tosca* was sung by Christel Goltz who was also a guest artist in the Bayreuth Festival.

Last Sunday I was walking with my father in Trepower Park, and there was sunshine and it was quite warm and the Winter nature was very beautiful with the yellow and red leaves and many different trees. By the side of a pond we found a lame pigeon. It was very young and could not fly and seemed deserted by its mother. Papa and I brought it home and we are feeding it with milk and bread until it is well and can fly again. Already after a few days it seems much better.

Now at Christmas time we have a great deal to do in the business. It is always different and interesting to meet people of all professions: artists, doctors, scientists, etc.

It is very kind that you should pay so much attention to me. I live so far and you know so little about me.

With heartfelt Greetings, Yours, Dagmar.

I was more pleased with the temperament of this letter than either of the former. Slowly but surely I was drawing her out of her reserve. I had caught yet another glimpse of her intimate life when momentarily she let slip the guard which concealed her feelings, and either inadvertently or inevitably she had yet shown another small facet of her personality. To me, the most telling part of the letter was the description of the little incident in Treptower Park. How beautifully it was written – with what simplicity and warmth of heart, and how nicely it reflected the purity of her character – the simple joy of life through her love of nature, and her harmonious identity with the purer values of the world.

The rest of the letter paled into insignificance by comparison with this one paragraph. All scepticism as to the successful outcome of the friendship which had tempered my earlier feelings – the great distance which lay between us, or political factors – fell aside, as I only experienced an overpowering sensation of longing for her affection. What a perfect being she seemed! Her mild reproach for my impatience was made in good humour, and only the final paragraph, thanking me for my kind attention, saying I knew so little about her, aroused my curiosity, and was to remain inexplicable for a long time into the future. I was pleased with the letter and eager she should receive my reply at the earliest opportunity, for despite her mild reproach at my impatience, I now felt confident of a better hope in speeding our correspondence.

That evening I wrote and posted a long reply – written in a passion of enthusiasm, with little foresight as to its outcome. As requested, I told her about the London into which I came into daily contact, describing the student life and clubs and night spots, and cultural associations to which I belonged. The letter was marked with intentional exaggeration to ensure effect, and filled with a facetious sense of humour aimed to provoke, but not hopefully to shock or arouse a sense of bewilderment. I asked her to tell me something about her family, and enquired how she intended celebrating Christmas. I said I intended returning to my home in the country from where I would send her a card, and that shortly after the new year I hoped to spend a fortnight skiing in the Austrian Alps with student friends.

Each letter received enlivened my hopes as to the outcome of the friendship although an intolerable distance of time stood between the possible and portentous occasion of our next meeting. When would this be and under what circumstances? I did not know. I had no plans for visiting Berlin in the conceivable future, and indeed, if and when a second visit was possible its purpose was only likely to be for abducting Dagmar from that free island surrounded by a sea of oppression.

As the correspondence progressed and my fondness grew, I became increasingly fascinated and obsessed by her being, and sometimes, under unexpected circumstances I was reminded of her existence, as when a tune or motif would evoke her presence, or when a few bars from a pop number would conjure a picture of the rhythmical movement of her body, and I would see her slim legs dancing a tango – brisk lively movements – her feet tapping the floor; and at other times, when seated in a concert hall, I would alarmingly – touchingly – be reminded of her by the gentlest or most beautiful passage in a symphony or concerto.

There was only an interval of some ten days between my reply and the arrival of her next letter – a hopeful sign, it seemed of the acceleration of our correspondence. It was shorter and the handwriting more crowded, and there were overwritten mistakes – a change from the usual neatness of her letters that might have been copied from a first draft. The content, too, was more striking for it expressed a conflicting series of moods.

Dear James!

I have your last letter and thank you. It was interesting what you told me about your life in London. It seems you very much like to amuse yourself, but I think you misunderstand me when you write about such things. Such things as you write of do not form part of my interests – although I like concerts, opera and the theatre.

Please explain to me what you mean by the word *Vergnügen*. For me this means to dance often, to flirt, and to amuse oneself and such similar things. I like if I have time enough to go to those places where I can cultivate my interests and where I can relax at the same time and find inner strength. The word *Vergnügen* is in this sense misused!

I shall gladly tell you about my family. My mummy is a housewife and has much work to do with a family of five of us. My father is a *Korrektor* for a newspaper. Gisela my younger sister is a dressmaker by trade, but is also employed as a photographer's model. She has already appeared on two front covers of a leading East German fashion magazine. Our eighty years old grandmother, the head of the family, is still living, and we all love her very much.

It is very fine that you possess the means to be able to go to the Austrian Alps after Christmas. I shall spend Christmas in the family circle. If I am able to go to the Baltic once a year for three weeks it is already a great pleasure for me to be able to afford this financially. I found it not very tactful of you to let me feel how well you have it. This made me sad as I read it. You have no idea of the economic situation as it exists here in East Germany, and for this reason I will excuse you.

The sentiments you express in your letters are very kind, but a great distance separates us, and for this reason I would plead that you only regard me as a pen-friend. I think that in the present circumstances, if we were to regard each other as more than this, it would cause disappointment for us both. As you must know, there are tragic political circumstances which separate East Germany from the Western countries. Also, you know so little about me that it would be wrong to allow our friendship to become too intimate until you know me better.

With heartfelt Greetings, Yours, Dagmar.

On having read the letter I was taken aback by its conflicting moods, and then, perplexed and frustrated by the desire to possess her. I wanted to laugh. Her own feelings of resentment could not escape the invitation of ridicule. Perhaps in my letter I had been cruel in describing London life with verve and facetiousness, and perhaps this had justified a suggestion of petulance in her reply, but had it been necessary for her to drag in the paragraph about the definition of the word *Vergnügen*? Could she really have been serious when she wrote that? I smiled curiously as I read the sentence where she had solemnly written that she liked to go to those places where she could cultivate her interests and at the same time relax and find "inner strength," and yet, at the same time I loved her for it. My feelings were a storm of conflicting emotions.

I had written but one sentence suggesting the possibility of visiting the Austrian Alps depending on financial circumstances. To me it had seemed an insignificant little sentence, detached from anything else I had written, hidden in a long paragraph about my return home to the country during the Christmas break, and yet she had taken out this sentence and used it as a reproach as if I had boasted of affluence, gloating over her more modest circumstances. I had certainly not intended creating such an impression and I abhorred the idea she could have so misinterpreted my meaning. I was irritated by her self-pity and annoyed by the accusation that I had been "tactless," but the final sentence excusing me for this tactlessness, on the assumption of ignorance I thought presumptuous if it was not absurd. I wanted to tease and gently deride her for her self-pity, but as I subsequently learnt, perhaps it was fortunate I deferred my teasing until a later occasion.

The impression she gave of her family, of this closely knit circle, was almost Victorian in its bonds of simple affection and fidelity. I loved her for the simplicity of her soul. So her father was a *Korrektor* for a newspaper! A *Korrektor* was a proof-reader but could not the word also imply some kind of censor? And for what kind of paper was he a proof-reader? Were not all East German papers directly under Communist control? My earlier suspicions that he might possibly be employed by the Communist authorities were revived. I imagined him as tall, reserved, and good-looking, with thick horn-framed spectacles. I saw him in his green uniform and peaked cap, arriving home on a wet day carrying a fat briefcase full of official documents, and I saw him seated in a comfortable armchair as Dagmar pulled off his jack boots laying them to dry by the warmth of the tiled stove!

Then I concluded that the Brüning to whom I addressed her letters was in fact the grandmother, but why was it necessary to write *bei* Brüning? Was it that the flat in which the family lived was in the grandmother's name or was it that Dagmar lived in an adjoining flat with the grandmother, or was there some other more complex explanation?

The last paragraph of her letter, pleading that our feelings for one another be restrained, seemed somehow odd. Particularly striking was the final sentence arguing that our feelings be held in check as I yet knew so little about her. She had written a similar sentence in a previous letter. For the first time I suspected she might be withholding intentionally some factor about herself which innately she thought I might have a right to know. These passages read like a hidden code that something was amiss – that possibly on some future occasion, she might refer back to passages in these letters saying, "Well, you remember what I wrote long ago ...,"etc. She had given me no lead for specific doubts, and because of this, it was impossible for me to augment any vague anticipations.

This letter with its conflicting moods, terseness and enigmatic references, somewhat cooled my passion, but my curiosity in her life and circumstances were sharpened, and perhaps thereby, my determination to further the strange yet unstable friendship which had progressed to the present point in time.

It was not until after a week when I replied to the letter, and then it was in the form of a short note with the seasons greetings, together with a card of a Dickensian-like scene and a micro-reproduction of a daily paper announcing the recent general election victory. The following day I sent her another translation of an English novel by airmail to her uncle, so she would receive it in time for the great festive day, and then I left for my home in the West country.

Chapter 10

During the restful days spent in the country, far from the bustle of town, I had plenty of time to ponder over the progress of my friendship with the fair Berlinerin.

I perused over our correspondence and recollected those too few hours in the heart of West Berlin, remembering the happy aspirations and doubts I had on parting from her at Friedrich Strasse station. At that time I had not imagined that such a coolly detached correspondence would develop in view of the warmth and friendliness we had mutually expressed. I had indeed felt uncertain if a correspondence would result from our single Berlin outing, but if it did, I anticipated a more intimate exchange, unsoiled by the expression of unhappy or resentful feelings. I thought back to that fateful night when we parted at Friedrich Strasse station, asking myself if I would have bothered to write to her at all if it had been possible to predict the outcome of such a stilted correspondence. I thought perhaps I might have refrained writing to her. I might have interpreted her letters as a polite brush-off – and perhaps in fact, this had been their real intent. There was no way of discovering the truth behind such lingering suspicions.

Despite the terseness, suggestions of resentment, and curious references, there was a quality in those letters nonetheless arousing a greater determination to win her heart – a motivation even towards some heroic gesture. How surprising was the effect of those letters – those offhand, cool, to me unnatural letters – and sometimes I suspected the girl to be a harpy! What was it which provoked heroic feelings and a will to conquer? A kind of witchcraft? I read through the letters again, pondering over the possibility of their hidden meaning, and it was then I saw them in a different light. They were not the letters of an ice-cold girl – they were highly-charged – packed with repressed feelings – written by a hypersensitive creature. They were alive – throbbing like a pulse and nowhere had she lapsed into the expression of formal compliments or pedantic sentiments.

In her directness; her sincerity, her cool irony and provocative impudence, lay the secret of her sexuality. They were letters full of restlessness and changes of mood, reflecting confusion and conflict. She was concerned with concealing her feelings; she was proud, fearful of self-betrayal. In matters of personal relationships she had the reticence and modesty of the Berlinerin, and I recollected what Martin had told me when we first dined in Aschingers.

She was hemmed-in by the constraining limits of Berlin – perhaps she experienced a claustrophobic oppression. She had suggested it was impossible for her to leave Berlin for the Federal Republic, and it was apparent from several references that she considered my letters as bordering on the callous in mocking her predicament. Then there were references of a terse of ironic or more usually of a self-pitying kind, expressing a different state of mind. These were provocative references calling attention directly to her, which seemed to express a secret invitation to conquest. Her self-pity was a plaintive cry for the patient sympathy of a friendly listener.

She loved the lights of the West, and yet unhappily, was fate-bound to the East. She lived on the frontier of a world apart – a world of freedom and greater justice – and yet a world the benefits of which she might never share. I felt the only way of finally winning the heart of the fair Berlinerin was by carrying the friendship through to its only logical conclusion – by a heroic abduction – Siegfried-like from the fire-girt rock. I realised the almost insuperable difficulties lying ahead: her penurious situation; the probability that she might never again visit her parents in the East without fear of arrest; and the risk of punishment which might hang over the parents themselves after I had abducted their lovely daughter.

There was also another aspect in these letters arousing my interest in the Berlinerin. Her letters were strangely incomplete. There was a curious self-restraint – a holding back as if concealing some important factor about her existence. Was it the fear of interception of our correspondence? Perhaps, but although her letters reached me after varying intervals following their despatch I never saw evidence that her letters had been tampered with. I pondered long over these questions, but she remained an enigma. Would I ever discover the mystery of the fair Berlinerin?

A few days before Christmas I received an Xmas card, a photo of a snow-laden conifer with an Alpine background, with best Christmas greetings and all good tidings for the New Year. She thanked me for the card and for the little newspaper which she said was "simply delightful."

Some ten days later I received a thick envelope from her containing a short letter and three delightful post card reproductions of old masters: Altdorfer's *Repose During the Flight*, a curiously enchanting picture of the Holy Family; a self-portrait of Dürer in the guise of John the Baptist; and Liotard's *The Chocolate Girl*. I was elated by the letter which was written in a happy frame of mind.

Dear James!

On the Holy Evening I received your book from my relatives when they came to visit us from the West sector. Many thanks for it. I have begun to read it, and it is delightful.

I received it from you just as I received my other Christmas presents. I put it with all the other presents on the Christmas table. How did you spend Christmas? On the Holy Evening we had a small party in our home when our relatives came to visit, and we opened all our presents together, and then we had a very wonderful dinner. Uncle Willy and my aunt brought us some very fine things to eat from the West sector, and real French wine. After dinner we sang carols round the Christmas tree, and later we all went to the church here in Treptow – except for my granny who is now very old and finds it difficult to walk.

What presents did you get? I got from my parents an Indian silk scarf and an art book, a dress from my sister, Gisela, some shoes, and chocolates from my aunt and uncle, and some handkerchiefs from my granny, and very many sweets and things to eat from my other friends.

Please excuse what I wrote to you in my last letter. I was overworked and nervous before Christmas, and I believe that my letter would have had another style had I been more relaxed. Now I have a few days free for recreation.

The weather here is not Christmas-like. It is rainy and very mild like in Autumn. It is a pity there is no snow.

Please write and tell me how you spent Christmas.

With heartfelt Greetings, Yours, Dagmar.

I was in no hurry to reply to the letter after its receipt. My mind was occupied by another matter – on something more imminent – the planning of a trip to the Austrian Alps. I should be going for two weeks with friends in the second week of January, and decided to surprise Dagmar from Badgastein with the largest and most colourful card she had ever received. During the hectic activity following the first days at the resort – fatiguing days and late nights – I had forgotten the fair Berlinerin until some time had passed. Then one evening, tired, thoughtless yet carefree, but complacent in a hedonistic mood, and impatient with the harder realities of the world beyond the snow-laden resort, I strolled down to the town centre and chose the largest card I could find.

Pressed for time in the crowded little shop and only wanting to write hurriedly and despatch my latest communication to the fair one, I was suddenly lost for words. Thoughts, there came none! Berlin seemed a remote and faraway place as I stood by the counter in that little souvenir shop in Badgastein. Then, for want of anything better to say, tactlessly – with unforgivable stupidity – I thought I should tease her for her self-pity. At last I wrote the following little note:-

Many thanks for your Christmas card and last letter with the three beautiful post card reproductions. Had a very nice Christmas. I shall not tell you how I'm enjoying myself here in Badgastein, as I do not want to make you feel "very sad"!!! Shall write a longer letter to you later.

With kindest greetings, Yours, James.

I placed a stamp on the card and popped it into the letter box. I walked back towards the Pension, feeling I had performed a duty, but then, at once, doubts flooded my mind. Was this an occasion when irony had been carried too far?

On returning to England I wrote a long letter to Dagmar but received no reply. The first weeks of the new term passed quickly, and it was with shock I realised it had been more than three weeks since I had written to the fair Berlinerin. No such waiting period had elapsed before. I wrote again. I waited. Still nothing! I sent her a card for St.

Valentine's day together with a humorous little note. Ten days later I wrote yet another letter – this time copying the first – trusting that my intervening letters had not gone astray. I requested that if she wanted to break off the correspondence to tell me just that, so that I was not left under any misapprehension. The days passed.

It was almost the middle of March and yet another term was drawing to a close. I had heard nothing from Dagmar for more than two months. I regretted the card I had sent from Austria. I was already resigned to the idea of the friendship ending if she wished it, but was resolved on first receiving some kind of communication from her for there remained a remote possibility that the East German authorities had in fact at last intercepted our post. I was about to write to Martin requesting he visit Dagmar personally at the Art Shop in Stalin Allee delivering a letter by hand and perhaps bringing back a message, when I unexpectedly received a letter from East Berlin. I took the letter up from the hall table, late one afternoon, but not with pleasurable anticipation. I was curious as to its contents but sensed that the tidings could not be good. The letter read as follows:-

Dear James!

I have received your letters of 23.1, 16.2 and 26.2 and your card for St. Valentine's day for which I thank you.

Please excuse me that I haven't answered your letters before, but after having received your card from Austria I have not had the intention of writing to you any more. Because I did not give you an answer to your long letter of 23.1 I thought you would feel that I wanted to break off the correspondence.

You wrote in your letter of 26.2 that a pen-friendship must be founded on the basis of mutual understanding. I am fully in agreement with you on this.

In your long letter you put questions and expressed opinions (which were very strange for me) about many things. As to a further correspondence, I think the differences between your opinions and mine would be too great for a mutual understanding. The differences of our outlook could be caused by the different nationalities, but I don't entirely believe this as concerns us.

With friendly Greetings, Yours, Dagmar.

I put down the letter with a mixture of sadness, relief, and disappointment. I had already resigned myself to the fact that our strange friendship had come to an end. I now felt indifferent. Now I am free at last,! I sighed. I have neither ties nor anxieties to vex my mind. It's a pity things have turned out as they have after so much letter writing and high hopes, but then perhaps the friendship was doomed to fail from the moment we met. There was an absurdity in the hope of its materialising in a permanent happy outcome.

It was perhaps a long letter for one intended to break off the friendship – one and a half pages of big spiky handwriting written with a thick nibbed pen – and if I had written a tearful letter of apology asking for forgiveness, there might have remained a slim chance of pouring oil on troubled waters and reviving some kind of correspondence between us, but I felt no inclination to repair the harm I had done. Firstly, I had been worn-down by her strange changeable temperament, and secondly, I was unwilling to renew a correspondence marked by such reserve and ambiguity.

I sat down and thought over the entire course of our friendship which now seemed to have reached its end. Had I remained in Berlin for a longer period after meeting her I felt things might have turned out differently, but it now appeared she had never had any intention of allowing our friendship to become serious after my departure from the city. I had been stupid in nurturing high hopes as to the outcome of our relationship. There was nothing more to be said between either of us, and I decided for forget Dagmar, the fair Berlinerin, allowing her memory to sink into that oblivion of all such sadly broken friendships.

Some days passed, and although I experienced a freedom from care, still I was haunted by her memory. Less than a week after receiving her letter an idea occurred that took the form of a stratagem. It was a last ditch attempt by a roundabout route to save the friendship. It was a letter which read as follows:-

Dear Dagmar!

I have received your letter of 5.3, and am sorry you should have felt obliged to write it. Naturally, I fully realise our short pen-friendship has ended, and I am disappointed that this has happened. I did not intend my post card from Austria to hurt you.

I can understand that perhaps my long letter of 23.1 was not entirely correct in that I put so many personal questions, but the reason for this is perhaps different from that which you might suppose. When I said I hoped our relationship might continue on the basis of a pen-friendship I did sincerely mean this and nothing more, but at the same time I realised (and I am sure you can also understand this) that despite any such mutual agreements between a boy and girl as to the nature of their friendship, there always exists the possibility that an alteration might be experienced in the feelings by one or both which changes the nature of that friendship.

Had this by chance arisen in our case I think that certain difficulties might have occurred that could have had unhappy consequences.

In several of your letters you plainly emphasised the frail state of your health, explaining that you had to undergo special treatment. Naturally this aroused a curiosity (which I suspect you half intended) and it also seemed to me you were trying to conceal some unhappy fact about your health which you know is important to yourself and to a relationship you might sometime enter into in later life.

Under these circumstances (which I suspected but did not wish entirely to believe) I did not want to compromise my own feelings, and neither did I wish one day to discover that you should see differently in me – i.e. as a pen-friend.

In view of this it seemed only natural I should question you as to your health, your family and your education. I am sorry you should have taken these questions so badly to heart. You must believe me when I say I did certainly not ask them out of idle curiosity.

As for the Iron Curtain which divides the two worlds in which we live, as far as we were concerned, I never regarded this as anything more than a superficial barrier. I am only very sorry about your poor state of health, and I hope that one day you will become stronger and well.

If it should be possible for me, I should be glad to grant you any special favour at any time.

Heartfelt Greetings, Yours, James.

Within ten days of its posting I received the following strangely pitiful reply:-

Dear James!

I have received your letter and thank you.

I do not want you to have a false picture of me because of any misconception you may have concerning my illness. To avoid this, therefore, I must write briefly concerning this.

I am unfortunately on a vegetarian diet. My illness is connected with an exhaustion-state, mild excitability, poor blood circulation and being run-down. Unfortunately, many young people suffer from this illness. It is an after-the-War illness (*Nachkriegserscheinung*) due to lack of vitamins, as a result of the situation forced upon us in the East. I hope you are satisfied with this explanation.

I do not wish this correspondence to continue. The reasons for this I wrote to you in my last letter.

With friendly Greetings, Dagmar.

I was shocked by this simple little epistle – as curt and straightforward as a doctor's bulletin. She had at last bared the truth on one aspect of her existence. It seemed even as if she had thrown the truth at me defiantly as a gesture of contempt in response to the reproachful implication of my last letter suggesting she had in fact been concealing the truth. Later I thought that possibly if the letter had been written as a gesture of contempt, the note about her health need not necessarily have been an explanation of all which lay behind the truth, but written rather to simulate the truth – to achieve a desired effect.

But the friendship had now been ended, and there was little to be gained by pondering over the motives of her letter – and it if came to that, there was little purpose in thinking about all those other little mysteries and ambiguities surrounding her existence. I now had no further intention of attempting to renew the friendship – of writing to her, or even of thinking about her. She was through!

BOOK III

Premonitions of Misfortune

Love has no thought of self!
Love buys not with the ruthless usurer's gold
The loathsome prostitution of a hand
Without a heart? Love sacrifices all things
To bless the thing it loves!

Bulwer-Lytton, *The Lady of Lyons*, Act V, Sc. 2, 1, 23.

July – August 1960

Chapter 11

Early one sunny afternoon towards the end of Summer as I crossed the crowded Prinzipalmarkt from opposite the fine gothic gable-end of the City Hall, hurriedly returning to my room in the Stubengasse, I was unexpectedly beckoned from across the street.

As I had spent the morning in research in the cavernous enclaves of a nearby museum, I was still lost in contemplation and surprised to see Horst signalling to me from across the street. He had stopped beneath one of the pillars of the City Hall and was waving a newspaper.

He was casually dressed and as I crossed the busy narrow main street towards him I saw he was visibly perturbed.

"Have you heard the news,?" he cried without responding to my greeting.

"What news,?" I returned.

"Everyone's talking about it," he said waving his paper.

We began strolling along the pavement beneath the fronts of the ancient houses.

"Has the world come to an end,?" I hazarded, putting him in his place for his uncalled for excitability.

"You always told me, James, you read the papers every day," he returned.

I smiled to myself. It was true I read the papers daily but I remembered that Horst had a mild contempt for the press and had on more than one occasion reproached me for "time wasting newspaper reading."

"Today there is *big* news," he continued, flourishing his copy of the *Westfälische Rundschau*.

"It must be for you to buy a newspaper," I returned ironically.

"You must have hidden yourself in some godforsaken place if you haven't heard yet."

"I got up later than I wanted, and rushed to the museum of Art and Culture-History to get there at opening time. They've thrown me out for the lunch hour. What's the great sensation?"

"It's Berlin!"

Berlin! My heart jumped to my mouth. Berlin! I had not anticipated hearing that word. For months past I had forgotten the existence of the city and my recollections were a distant memory. And now, suddenly again to be reminded of Berlin.

"What's happened in Berlin?"

"They've closed the frontier. It's in all the papers."

"Impossible! The Western powers wouldn't let them – surely not," I replied involuntarily.

"Read it for yourself," said Horst pushing his paper into my hand. "There! Early this morning the East German police closed the frontier to all West Germans. – Come, lunch round the corner, and let's talk about it."

I hesitated momentarily. I had intended rushing back to my room to file the notes I had taken in preparation for an article which was already long overdue.

"I expect we'll meet some of the others there," added Horst.

That was exactly what I feared – some of the others! If I joined them I knew the chances were I would be tied down for the afternoon – in one place – in endless conversation and drinking. But then, this about Berlin gave rise to an exceptional excuse, and I knew I couldn't rest until I heard more.

"I'll lunch with you," I agreed.

"Good," exclaimed Horst, and we turned the street corner into Klemens Strasse.

We came to our regular haunt, a quaint old beer house nearby, opened the heavy timbered wrought iron door, and entered. The parlour was crowded with diners and drinkers, and the light was dim, for it came through the misty yellow glass of the narrow high-arched latticed windows, and the adjoining building was only divided by a narrow passageway. An accordionist, in the green military uniform of a *Schütze*, was playing a stirring march tune, lending a liveliness to the environment, and his interested listeners were watching him intently and clapped vigorously at the end of the number, banging their glasses on the table.

Horst and I passed by the dark wooden tables, and made for our corner at the back of the L-shaped parlour. We joined a group of friends, seated at their usual table, peering through a pile of newspapers in wooden holders. There was Günther and his brother, Kurt, and Luciano, a student from Italy. We were in Münster, and for different reasons, some of us students were domiciled in the city during the vacation period, but we made up a *gemütlich* group, meeting often, discussing the arts and politics. When Horst and I joined the others, there was a hubbub of excitement.

"What's behind all this,?" I asked. By this time I was impatient to hear more, and tense with a feeling of foreboding. Recollections of Dagmar were already welling up in my mind.

"The East German police closed the Russian sector frontier between the two halves of Berlin early this morning," said Günther. "And they've threatened a total blockade of West Berlin."

"It looks as if there could be another Berlin Airlift," said Kurt.

"That's only a threat," said Luciano calmly. "I don't think they'd dare blockade the Berlin corridors to West Germany.

"But why have they done this? What are their given reasons for blockading Berlin,?" I exclaimed. "The East German government have made no warning threats. There's been nothing in the news to anticipate that such a thing might happen."

"That's exactly it. Without warning, the East German authorities have suddenly struck out a blow in severing the communications of the city," said Horst.

"The reason they've given for the blockade is objection to the rallies of two refugee organisations to be held in West Berlin next month," explained Günther.

"And their reasons are absurd," said Luciano throwing up his hands. "Merely a diplomatic pretext to test the reaction of the Western powers."

"The East German government describes the rallies as militaristic and revanchist," continued Günther.

"And the claims are nonsense," retorted Horst. "The allies must stand firm and then the East Germans will be forced to retract their measures. These rallies were planned months back. They're recognised and supported by every reputable political organisation in West Germany – as well as by the church."

"Then on what grounds could the East German government claim the meetings are militaristic or revanchist,?" I asked.

"On none,!" replied Horst. "it's just an excuse to try out their strength on the Western powers."

"There's something written in here about the aims of the rallies," said Kurt turning over the pages of the *Westdeutsches Tageblatt*. "Here," he said pointing his finger on the place: "Firstly, to look after the material interests of ex-prisoners of war, to secure adequate pensions, and to help their members establish themselves in new jobs, and so on. Secondly, to campaign for the return of those still in camps behind the Iron Curtain."

Günther let out a short sardonic laugh. Kurt glanced up from the paper smiling, and Horst thumped the table with his fist.

"That's what offends the Eastern powers," said Luciano. "The Russians are behind it."

"With thousands of prisoners of war still in Siberian camps," said Horst. "They don't want this kind of publicity on their doorstep reminding them of the fact."

"And so to spite the West, they get their henchman, Ulbricht to blockade the city, and invent a fantastic fiction about the rallies being militaristic and revanchist," said Günther.

"To seek an amnesty for German war criminals still serving sentences," said Kurt continuing to read. "Thirdly, to keep alive the lessons learnt behind bars concerning liberty and democracy, and fourthly and lastly, to give old friends a chance to meet again and express their common feeling."

"The Russians are sensitive to any kind of political demonstration in West Berlin," said Luciano.

"Not merely political," added Horst. "They're sensitive to anything which happens in West Berlin, be it a religious demonstration, a cultural conference, or an international exhibition or festival. They're sensitive to anything which shows up the East bloc in a bad light."

"In fact," continued Luciano, "anything that draws East Berliners into the West sectors is going to give the Russians a headache. West Berlin has become the seismometer of differences between East and West. Every tremor is felt in West Berlin – even if it sometimes doesn't go further than that."

"And in that lies the threat to the freedom of West Berlin," said Horst reflectively. "The Free City just can't be made to fit into the scheme of things in the Communist bloc. It's the only hole in the impregnable Iron Curtain! As long as West Berlin exists as a Free City it will remain, in the eyes of the Warsaw Pact countries, a putrid sore on the map of Eastern Europe. It has to be!"

"But I don't think these rallies in West Berlin are the real reason for blockading the city," said Günther. "I don't think the Russians care a sausage for what goes on at a couple of rallies held over a four day period. I think there's something deeper behind it."

"Such as what,?" I asked.

"Well," began Günther tentatively, "it could even be a dress rehearsal for a permanent closure of the Russian sector frontier."

"Impossible,!" cried several outraged voices.

"The Western powers could never allow it," said Horst.

"But how could they stop it,?" said Günther.

Dumbstruck, no one hazarded to answer the question.

"Has the blockade been imposed on conditions,?" I asked.

"The East German authorities have closed the sector frontier for a period of five days," replied Günther. "The rallies start tomorrow and so it's just for their duration. No West Germans will be allowed to cross into the East sector."

"But East Berliners will be allowed to cross into the West?"

"Apparently. They haven't extended the ban in that direction. It's only West to East traffic that's affected."

"Then perhaps it's not all so bad," I said with a sigh of relief.

"It would be difficult to extend the ban from the East to the West sectors," remarked Horst in a sullen tone. "There are too many workers in the East who have to go to the West sectors daily – workers on the Underground and building projects, for instance, as well as the City railways. The East German government couldn't very well stop them from working just because of a couple of rallies in the West sectors."

"I don't think it's anything to panic about," said Luciano. "It'll all blow over after five days."

"Let's hope it's only bluff – just a big scare," I said.

"Nothing the Communists do is ever bluff," said Günther leaning forward. "What seems like bluff is always a trial of strength towards a longer term goal."

"Is there any threat to the Berlin corridors,?" I asked.

"The situation is summed up here, in a statement by the East German News Agency, the AND," said Kurt taking up a paper. "It says that 'the territory of East Germany including East Berlin'" –

"Which legally is not part of East Germany," interrupted Horst.

" 'Must not be misused for the organisation and demands of the militaristic and revanchist meetings which are to take place in West Berlin during the above mentioned dates. Only persons with valid residents visas will be allowed to cross into the East sector. Anybody who attempts to contravene this order will be liable to penalties under the East German criminal code.' And here's about the corridors: 'they must not be misused for the transport of militaristic and revanchist elements, but only for supplying allied needs.' That seems to sum up the situation as the East Germans have created it."

"That's not the whole story," exclaimed Horst in anger. "Look here in the *Bild Zeitung* - under big headlines! It reports that early this morning a Pan American airliner from Berlin to Bonn was buzzed by an unidentified fighter. According to a passenger, the fighter came within a hundred and fifty metres, before flying off." He threw the paper across the table.

"What's the reaction of the Western powers in Berlin,?" I asked.

The mayor, Dr. Brandt, will see the three Western Commandants tomorrow," replied Kurt. "There's no suggestion here of any counter-measures to be taken. It only says they'll discuss the threat to West Berlin's communications. And in a report from London it's stated that a British spokesman says that 'the government views with concern any action likely to increase tension in Berlin.'"

"The buzzing of one allied plane in the Berlin corridor within a few hours of the start of the blockade, isn't very promising that things are going to pass over lightly," said Luciano.

"It's so easy to blockade Berlin," said Kurt, "and there's so little the Western powers can do by way of counter-measures."

It was late in the afternoon when I arrived back at my room in the Stuben-gasse. I was saddened by the situation in Berlin and recollections of Dagmar rushed to the forefront of my mind – memories of her letters, memories of the little Art Shop in Stalin Allee, and memories of those few blissful hours in the Kurfürstendamm. Then I remembered Martin, and the enjoyable days we had spent together. I had forgotten Berlin and now suddenly, memories surged forward as vividly as if I had been there only yesterday. I remembered its broad streets and vast crumbling apartment blocks, Frau Dubrowski's, the parks and the boat trips on the Wannsee, and the strange taste of its national drink, the *Berliner Weisser*. They were happy memories that returned – Berlin, with its friendly inhabitants and their sardonic wit, and the grotesque mock classical ornamentation, fronting the massive 19th century apartment blocks beside cleared bomb sites, and the fine linear forms of great towers of steel and concrete constructed only yesterday.

It had been less than a year since I stayed in Berlin. This time one year ago I had never even dreamed of visiting the city. Berlin had meant nothing. But so much had happened during the intervening period. I had travelled often, and now I had been some months in Münster, studying at the University on a students' exchange programme. The candidature for applicants to study there had occurred suddenly, and without special reason or deliberation I had jumped at the opportunity. The absorbing interest offered by my studies and life in Münster, and the busy activity over the previous twelve months, made those days in Berlin seem very distant.

I thought of the long discussion which had taken place in the beer house – of Horst's agitated state of mind, of Kurt's sense of anticipation and his brother's cooler more analytical attitude, and of Luciano's calm although concerned interest. Horst and his two compatriots had reason to be vexed over the matter – it was their country which was implicated, but

Luciano and I, the two foreigners present nonetheless felt similarly concerned.

We had all expressed views on the crisis, but nothing enlightening had come out of the discussion. Would the Communists attempt to blockade the corridors leading to West Germany? Would they interfere or hinder rail passengers or road transport from the Federal Republic to Berlin? Would they extend the blockade beyond the stated period? Was this a first trial attempt at raising an Iron Curtain between the East and West sectors of the city? I felt how helpless we were in averting any crisis which might occur.

I began filing notes I had compiled in the museum earlier in the day, intending to start on the article I had vowed to write, but concern over the Berlin situation weighed heavily. For the first time I began to experience an involvement with the city which had a deeply emotional basis.

It would be simple for the Communists to raise an Iron Curtain between East and West Berlin. The prospect of them doing so filled me with such alarm – of the consequent despair which would be experienced – that I tried to push the awareness of this possibility to the back of my mind. Again I thought of Dagmar – and yet again. Did I still love her? I did not know.

Chapter 12

As we strolled casually along the grassy bank of the lakeside, our mood a mixture of misapprehension and vexation, we kicked our feet through the tufts of long grass. The conversation had stalled. There wasn't more to be said, it seemed, and for some moments our heads were bent forward in thought, as we saw only the tufts of bright green grass, and occasionally, where the ground almost met the level of the water's edge, the tall sharp reeds rose from the muddy earth. Sometimes we jumped over a hillock or a patch of marshy soil, or across a small stream leading into the lake.

There were three of us. Horst carried a small branch and with a swishing motion, he cut off the head of a dandelion or the white top of a hogweed, and trampled a cluster of buttercups underfoot.

Pierre was more silently meditative. He was the eldest student in our group who frequented the vacation-time discussions. He was an idealist, with a vivid imagination and an original turn of thought, provoking lively discussion, and for this reason, and because of his good humour, he was one of the most popular members of our group.

It was a hot day and the sun burned down on the ground, so that crickets chirped and leaped out of our path, and bees passed from flower to flower by the bank; and the water's edge was alive with humming insects. And people, too, were round about, and the shrill yells and laughing of children and the sound of toddling feet on the gravel, and the admonishing voices of elders were to be heard. To our right, we heard the gentle lapping of water against the side of the bank. The As-See was a large lake, and on this day, it was a blue expanse of broad and peaceful water. Away from the bank several yachts sailed slowly by, their white sails flapping in a gentle breeze, and the voices of the yachtsmen calling to one another came from across the water.

My two companions and I were oblivious to most of this, for we were absorbed by something which did not touch our immediate environment. We had been out walking for more than an hour, after lunching in town, and had been engaged in animated discussion. And now the conversation had stalled.

"But why – why these vicious lies,?" exclaimed Horst in incredulous anger at last. "What can be their object? What can anyone gain by them?"

"There isn't a purely political explanation for the lies," replied Pierre in his strangely accented German.

"Exactly,!" exclaimed Horst. "There can be nothing political. Then why? Who can be satisfied by these fantastic fictions.?"

"They satisfy the craving for national hatred. You know, Horst, there are many who thrive on hate."

"But the press! The self-appointed guardians of justice and liberty! Newspapers which command millions of readers! How can it be, Pierre?"

"There's nothing infallible about the press."

"Our own allies attacking us! That's what these lies amount to – a broadside attack on the integrity of our country."

"The wounds of war take long to heal."

"I can accept that. I can even accept the re-opening of old wounds – sometimes it's good for a country to be reminded of its past. Terrible things have happened in Germany. It's right we should be made to feel something of our past guilt – to see that these things may never happen again. But this, Pierre, is something different."

"It's the resentment which thrives in the little-man of the former enemy."

"If it were merely a reminder of the evils of the past, I could understand that," continued Horst. "But this is slander without a grain of truth. And the motivation for this attack lies in what you have called resentment – nothing more!"

"That seems to be it."

"How do the facts lie? In Berlin we have the organisation of two refugee rallies. Their object? To improve the material lot of their members. And who are attending these rallies? The majority are elderly men and women and a lot of down and outs with hardly a pfennig to their names. Many own hardly more than the shirts on their backs, and many are crippled by disease or war injuries."

"I know, I know," replied Pierre anticipating Horst's rising anger.

"And what do great sections of the Western press do,?" continued Horst. "Firstly, they swallow the bait of the East German propagandists, hook, line and sinker, and in the words of the Communists, condemn the rallies as militaristic and revanchist. Secondly, certain sections of the press go even further – especially the British press – implying that these rallies are not only neo-Nazi inspired but para-military. They compare them to the Nuremburg rallies of the 1930s. Have you ever heard such rubbish?"

"I agree with you Horst," said Pierre.

"Half the people attending these rallies wouldn't be capable of holding a rifle let alone firing one, and many can hardly walk let alone march. To think that the press is capable of such calculated malice! Why, I don't believe that half the journalists who've written these reports have attended the rallies or been within a thousand kilometres of Berlin!"

"In so far as editors twist reports of their correspondents, in adding their own comment, you're probably right."

"If these rallies are to be compared with anything, it's with a demonstration of the unemployed or a mass meeting of old age pensioners petitioning for better state aid. James, if a few thousand unemployed or old age pensioners met together in a great hall in a large city in England, and the national press began slinging mud at them, calling them fascists, militarists and revenge seekers, what would those unemployed or old age pensioners do?"

I could not withhold a smile at the curious turn of thought which must have provoked such a question.

"They'd be most indignant," I only replied.

"And so would these refugees who are now in Berlin likewise be indignant, at the mud-slinging by various parts of the press. And what can they do by way of defence or retaliation? Nothing! They are helpless. They're the poor and the under-privileged. They can only be indignant and bewildered."

"Refugees are always helpless – especially when they're poor and elderly," said Pierre. "They're without property and so without rights – or at least effective rights. Many are at the end of their tether – exhausted –

given up the struggle for life. It's easy then for the press, if it so chooses – to fling mud at them."

"These lies of the press can only feed the craving for hatred and create new hatred," said Horst after a pause.

"It's one of the tragedies of our time: there are so many powerful men in Europe today, who would use their powers for dividing Europe rather than uniting her," said Pierre. "They are the little resentful men – the small-minded provincials – those who feel strangers and lost – culturally and politically, as soon as they leave the frontiers of their own lands. They are the parochial chauvinists of the Europe which is dead and gone."

"Can it be that these lies are only spread for hatred's sake,?" said Horst.

"More probably out of jealousy for Germany's economic resurgence," replied Pierre.

"But how can the spirit for the new Europe hope to take root and flourish, if such men control the presses of Europe,?" cried Horst.

"It can't," responded Pierre. "We must wait for the emergence of the new men and women of Europe. For men and women who not merely believe in fraternity between peoples, but who are actually prepared to live it. We must work together to unite Europe into a new cultural identity. We must build on those common elements in our past – for a future where war and conflict between the peoples of Europe becomes an impossibility. Everything must be done not merely to strengthen the bonds between country and country, but between individual and individual."

There were some moments of silence, and we crossed a wooden footbridge, jumping down onto the bank at the other side, and continuing our stroll along the lake.

"Did you know, Pierre, that James has done his little bit for international fraternity by 'individual to individual,'?" said Horst suddenly.

"How do you mean,?" said Pierre.

"He had a girl friend in Berlin."

"Excellent – in the heart of Europe – he couldn't do better for the cause of international understanding," said Pierre turning to me.

"But that was in East Berlin," I said dismissively.

"Now that's going a step too fast," responded Pierre facetiously. "First we must work for the unification of Western Europe, and then we can turn to the East and forge our bonds of friendship there."

Pierre may have momentarily perceived a reflection of sadness cross my brow, for his curiosity was sufficiently aroused to ask about this friendship. He had somehow sensed it was more than just a casual flirtation. I told him the story.

"You were mad – mad,!" he cried in anger. "You should never have left Berlin."

"But we have other obligations in life – schedules to be met," I responded.

"Such things only happen once or twice in a lifetime," he continued. "It may never happen again. You loved the girl! You should have taken her. What does it matter about some stupid job, or studies – or whatever you were doing? That was unimportant! But a girl you loved. Real love is not an everyday occurrence. You'll learn that, my friend. You'll regret what you've done. You'll meet another girl, I know. One day you may have all the women you want. That's easy enough. But to meet the girl you love, and she loves you – that's different. It's seldom. And you let her slip through your fingers – such a gem! Mad! My friend, you may end up like the humdrum majority with second best, and second best is nothing. And it will have been your fault."

"Why don't you write to her again, James,?" suggested Horst. "There's still a chance she may respond."

"If she loves you, she will," said Pierre categorically.

"Why don't you go to Berlin in the weeks before the new term,?" said Horst. "Make the Berlin Festival the excuse for a visit. There, that's what you can write to her, and so you won't seem to be pressing your attentions too hard."

"Write to her," said Pierre. "Don't start doubting. Swallow your pride. You've nothing to lose but a twenty pfennig stamp."

What Pierre had said struck me to the heart. I had wronged myself. I had wronged Dagmar. I had wronged the eternal cause of love. If the relationship had been destroyed, then I alone was to blame. Only pride stood between me and the attempt to renew the friendship. I should brush it aside. If I failed, I stood to lose a twenty pfennig stamp; and if I succeeded, I had the world before me.

The following morning, I sat for a long time at a table spread with writing paper and envelopes, pen in hand, wondering how best to express my feelings to the fair one. At last I wrote the following little note:-

Dear Dagmar!

I am now living in Germany – studying in Münster. I like it very much here and am studying hard although the new term has not yet begun.

I may come to Berlin sometime but I don't know when. May I visit you then?

Are you well and enjoying the fine Summer in the beautiful nature of Berlin's lakes and forests?

With heartfelt Greetings, Yours, James.

It was a short letter but contained the gist of what Pierre had advised. I held little hope of its eliciting any response.

After posting the letter, I felt my writing to her had been silly, even childishly absurd. How would she receive it? Perhaps only smile, and drop it into a receptacle without having opened the envelope. I felt I had exposed myself to humiliation by writing to her. Nonetheless, I waited in anticipation, and tried to forget the waiting. This had been absurdity carried too far!

Chapter 13

For ten minutes Eberhard's angry voice had filled the beer hall, insisting on silence from us all, as his big figure leant backwards and forwards on his chair as he hammered the sharp edge of his hand onto the table with a force which made the beer swirl in our glasses. The clear logic of his thought as one argument followed up behind another only seemed to increase the anger of his rhetorical outburst. Several of us had attempted to interrupt him with a point, intended to mediate between him and the object of his anger, if only to pacify the violence of the discussion for we were all in agreement, but he seized on these interruptions – which were as oil poured on fire – and continued to press his case.

Eberhard was no idealist and had few illusions. He was a Bremer of well-to-do Burger stock with a practical common sense outlook. His healthy scepticism countered anything which defied the realistic. Often he was engaged in friendly argument with Pierre, and at different times each had dominated the conversation at our beer house debates. On this particular night Eberhard's anger had been aroused by the nonsensical situation stemming from the lies over the Berlin rallies which had earlier been published by sections of the West European press.

It was a Saturday night and the beer hall was full and noisy, and at some distance from our table played a military brass band from the local *Schutzverein* (voluntary defence corps), but despite this general hubbub, Eberhard's voice had attracted the uncertain attention of others at nearby tables.

Nine of us were seated around the long table. There were, besides Eberhard, Günther and Kurt, who were listening quietly, and Pierre, who for the past fifteen minutes had been waiting for a lull in the conversation and raising his hand in pleading for calm, so that he might elucidate a point of view, and there was Horst who was quietly sitting back in his chair nodding in assent to every point Eberhard made. Then there was Olav, a bearded Norwegian and ex-seaman, and Lee, an American, and lastly, a fellow countryman, Mike.

In concluding his speech Eberhard picked up the folded edition of *Neues Deutschland* which lay in front of him and was the official mouthpiece of the East German state, and from which he had earlier been quoting long passages to the company assembled, waved it defiantly in the air and threw it contemptuously onto the table.

"We all agree – there's no need for such anger," exclaimed Kurt trying to pacify his countryman.

"But was there a situation more ridiculous than this,?" exclaimed Eberhard.

"We're all intelligent. We can see the situation without your having to hammer the points," said Günther.

"Then why is everyone so docile,?" cried Eberhard.

"Docile? Who's docile,?" exclaimed Pierre. "We're not docile – everyone in Germany is either angry or concerned about it."

"I mean the Western allies. Why don't they react? Why don't the Western powers protest against this infringement of the right of free access from the Federal Republic to West Berlin – deliver a protest to Moscow?"

Eberhard was referring to a television broadcast of Dr. Brandt which several of our group had seen the previous night.

"They haven't had time yet," said Günther.

"And more urgent, why don't the Western governments publish a declaration refuting that these Berlin rallies are provocative? No time should be lost in achieving that."

"Governments don't control the press," said Mike.

"At least the governments could publish such a declaration – a form of bulletin," said Eberhard.

"I don't know if it would serve much purpose," said Mike. "The press would soon find a way of making such a declaration sound insignificant. The big boys in the editors' offices just say what they like and go hang the rest of us. There's no stopping the press!"

"But Eberhard, the main thing is that the rallies have been held as planned, and that the attempts of the East Germans to prevent them have failed," said Olav.

"Yes," added Lee.

"And the only disadvantaged, ironically, have been a bus load of Baptists held up at Helmstedt a couple of days ago, plus some Baptists in East Germany, who were refused rail tickets to Berlin – East or West," added Olav smiling. "It's *their* rally which has been spoilt not the refugee rallies."

"Yesterday, two hundred people were held up at the Helmstedt frontier," said Eberhard, "and if the Western governments used their authority in reacting against these incidents, their occurrence would have been impossible."

" 'Authority!' That's a difficult thing to define," said Mike.

"And these slanders in the press. Of course they encourage the Communists to do as they please," said Eberhard, his anger rising again. "What kind of a situation is this, when this mouthpiece of the East can quote long passages from the Western press? Of course the East Germans have reason to be very satisfied now. Half the Western press have helped support their own case. Look how the Communists can gloat over the isolation of West Berlin: - 'See, your Western allies have deserted you,' they cry, 'and soon we shall cut the corridors and absorb you into the Democratic Republic.'"

"You can rest assured that America will *never* abandon her obligations to the people of Free Berlin," exclaimed Lee with emotion.

"What sort of a Western press is it in Europe which can publish these obscenities,?" said Eberhard. He picked up one of the newspapers on the centre of the table. "And the British press is the worst. It publishes nothing but defamation and hate."

"Not the entire British press," said Mike. "Not the *Times*! It's published fair reports all along on the Berlin rallies. See here," and he unfolded his copy of the paper. "This is from their own correspondent reporting on one of the rallies: 'If anyone today had tried to label it as militarisitic, revanchist, or anything else in the tired vocabulary of East German propaganda he would have been laughed out of the building..'"

"But take this paper, for example," said Eberhard, and he waved it in the air.

"That's an anti-European paper," I replied, "not merely anti-German. That paper has lashed out hate propaganda against every country in Europe – even against poor little Denmark, about a year back."

"James is right," said Mike. "That paper belongs to the gutter – even though its proprietor is the most famous press baron in Britain."

"What does it hope to gain,?" continued Eberhard as if I and Mike had not spoken. "And a right wing paper too, by all accounts. A strange kind of right wing press they have in that country which licks the arses of the Kremlin bosses. Who are the scum behind this paper?"

"Just cool it," said Kurt. "We're attracting attention."

"Let him say what he wants," snapped Lee.

"I apologise if I went too far," said Eberhard glancing round at us each in turn. "I didn't want to seem offensive. I don't really care if the foreign press lashes out anti-German propaganda if it really wants to. I'm only concerned that the Western press refrains from jeopardising the present status of the freedom of the city of Berlin."

"I don't think you'd need worry on that score," replied Mike. "I don't think the East Germans would dare attempt a total blockade of the sector frontiers between East and West Berlin, if that's what you mean. The resulting outcry would be too great."

Some days later I received a card from Berlin, illustrating the floodlit Brandenburg Gate by night with a view from the East looking through the handsome proportions of the Doric columns into the West sectors. Momentarily, I wondered from whom the card could have been sent. Was it from Martin? I had written to Martin some few days previously. No, the card could not be from Martin – he would have replied by letter. Then I recollected having written to Dagmar. That was less than a week previously. I turned the card over, and sure enough, it was from her. I was overjoyed at this unexpected surprise. I had forgotten even my having written to her. The card which was written in large bold letters with a thick nib, read as follows:-

Dear James!

I have received your letter and thank you.

I am astonished to hear that you are now studying in Münster. I am glad you like it there, and I hope you are settling in well to your new way of life. My health is somewhat better.

With heartfelt Greetings, Yours, Dagmar.

In view of Dagmar's previous letters, the card was surprisingly friendly. It was an invitation to renew the friendship, and the reference to her health put further emphasis on this as if she was saying, "See, I am fit now, so the gate is open for your return."

I replied to the card the following day, describing something of my life in Münster, and saying how glad I was for the renewal of the correspondence between us. I asked how she was enjoying herself in Berlin, and as to the little Art Shop in Stalin Allee.

Meanwhile, the political situation in Berlin took a turn for the better: the traffic between the corridors returned to normal, and restrictions on West Germans entering the East sector were withdrawn. Everywhere was a feeling of relief, and our small discussion group did not think it worthwhile again raising the question of Berlin after that Saturday night when Eberhard had become so perturbed. We concluded we had become over-excited by an apparently minor crisis, and that the temporary blockade had only been another scare and propaganda tactic without further significance. Such was our complacency! The only reminder of the five day crisis in Berlin was an unusual situation of minor importance: the West German barge crews delivering oil from Hamburg down the Elbe to the great inland port of Magdeburg had been forbidden from landing on East German soil.

Early one morning, however, about a week after the last beer house discussion on Berlin, whilst two of us were sitting peacefully in the back garden of a little café breakfasting on a glass of red wine and chocolate cake, as we watched and listened to the water of a fountain bubbling over into a lily pond, Eberhard excitedly came through the open French windows of the café into the garden, waving a copy of the *Bild Zeitung.*

I smiled across the table at Luciano on seeing Eberhard again in this flustered state, for since the start of the last Berlin crisis it was becoming his accustomed role. Luciano contorted his lips and with a wave of the hand indicated that it was probably nothing of consequence.

"Take a look at this," cried Eberhard brandishing the paper.

"Have the Russians dropped the bomb,?" exclaimed Luciano.

"I told you it would happen," cried Eberhard furiously. "All a result of the slanders in the Western press."

"Come, sit down Eberhard. It's too early in the morning to be getting angry," I said.

"Have a glass of wine to cool your nerves," said Luciano.

"That blockade of Berlin last week was merely a trial tactic," exclaimed Eberhard sitting himself between us. "Something to test the reaction of the allies. It was exactly as I said – and you all agreed – remember? Well, we can assume the trial was well-planned in advance and went off as scheduled, and as far as the Communists were concerned, it was a total success. The Western press swallowed their propaganda as if it were the tastiest morsel ever offered."

"What's happened? Have the Communists raised an Iron Curtain between the two sides of the city,?" said Luciano facetiously.

"Not so far wrong," replied Eberhard. "The East Germans have enforced an entry by permit regulation on West Germans desirous of entering the East sector."

"For what reason,?" I enquired astonished.

"They've given no reason," replied Eberhard.

"How will such permits be obtained,?" I asked. I now imagined insuperable difficulties should I go to Berlin to visit Dagmar in the East.

"From the appropriate offices of the Volkspolizei at the sector crossings, or else, relatives and friends may obtain permits for West Germans themselves."

"Will East Berliners be freely allowed into the West sectors,?" asked Luciano.

"The measures aren't meant to touch them, it seems."

"It sounds serious," I replied.

"It's a second move in a pre-planned strategy," said Eberhard. "What if this too is successful?"

"Only an outcry from the world press can save Berlin now," said Luciano. "That and the strength of the three Western powers controlling the city."

Chapter 14

O n returning to my room later that morning I found two letters from Berlin. The first was from Martin, a long letter thanking me for having written to him again after so long and describing something of the present mood in West Berlin. It seemed that Berliners were filled with gloomy apprehension.

What would be the next move of the Communists in the East? How would the Western allies counteract another attempt to blockade the city? Martin said the only consolation of the West Berliners for the safety of their city lay in the blissful sight of American tanks rumbling through the streets, and in the sight of American bombers, flying to and away from the city, supplying the essential needs of the armed forces. Small as these forces were in comparison with the vast armies of Russia surrounding the zonal frontiers of the city, they nonetheless helped to sustain the morale of ordinary citizens. The second half of Martin's letter dealt with a happier subject. In ten days he was leaving for France where he had secured a teaching post for six months in a school in Lyons.

The second letter was from Dagmar. It read as follows:-
Dear James!

I have your last letter and thank you. I am glad to hear you are so happy and well settled in Münster. It is well known that this is a very good and famous University city in north west Germany.

I no longer work in the little Art Shop in Stalin Allee. I am now working in East Berlin's biggest art shop. There is much work for me there and it is very interesting. Every month we have a new exhibition of art works and paintings. At present we have an exhibition of cartoons by the Dane Herluf Bidstrup.

In the theatre I have recently seen Sartre's play, *The Vicious Circle*. Do you go to the theatre or concerts in Münster?

At the end of this month I have a holiday. I do not yet know where to go. Perhaps I shall go to a quiet little village in Thüring. We say that Thüring is the green heart of Germany.

My health is better. Last Sunday I was in the East Berlin Zoo.
With heartfelt Greetings, Yours, Dagmar.

In the envelope had been inserted a photographic card illustrating a flock of flamingos trooping past the Lenné Tempel in the East Berlin Zoo.

I was immensely pleased with this encouraging letter. I replied by return post, saying I had heard several good concerts in Münster and seen several fine open air productions of the travelling Detmold theatrical company and that I was glad to hear she would be having a holiday shortly. I said that my vacation lasted until about the first or second week of next month and suggested it would be nice if we could meet sometime during that time. I asked if she could get a visa to visit West Germany, and that if this was possible I could meet her in Hanover (a large city not far from the East German frontier) when I could take her to Bavaria or Baden-Baden where we could enjoy a pleasant holiday in a little village among mountains in the heart of the Black Forest, or perhaps visit relatives she might have in the West. I asked her to reply speedily as arrangements would need time and planning.

My hopes with regard to our friendship were higher now than at any time, but the political situation in Berlin was critically unstable, and although I did not, and somehow, dared not refer to that factor, I felt that at any time all hopes might be dashed should the Communists for any reason (or none) decide to erect an Iron Curtain between the two halves of the city.

On walking to the post office to despatch the letter I passed a group of elderly men discussing the Berlin Situation. If the Red forces attempted an attack on the Free City, would the British attempt a sell-out of West Berlin to the Reds? That day, everywhere in Münster, people were alive to the grave situation facing the old capital of their country. Since the start of the five day blockade of West Berlin at the beginning of the month, the British had not been popular – and understandably so. The reticence of the British government over the Berlin crisis had the effect of provoking the kind of apprehension which springs from weakness. Would there be a Munich-style sell-out?

The following day, to the relief of most, counter-measures were introduced by the three powers in West Berlin. East German officials were refused travel visas to Western Europe. The situation was tense. Also, eighty businessmen, comprising the heart of Chicago industry, cancelled visits to the Leipzig Fair after consultation with the US mission in Berlin. This was a noble gesture – refuting all-powerful mammon, demonstrating that even the opportunity for gain may be subordinated to the ideals of democracy. Leading circles in America were advocating a total boycott of trade with East Germany. The British, as so often, were wavering, expressing a wish to see only selected sanctions. A few days later, an event occurred in Münster which both helped to revive the credibility and restore the popularity of the British in the eyes of the German people. At a rally of ten thousand veterans of the Afrika Korps, the association's Chairman read out a letter from a British ex-sergeant in the Eighth Army. In the letter, the sergeant said he had written the letter as a pledge to a dying young German soldier during the North Africa Campaign. He praised Rommel, the popular Commander of the Afrika Korps, and despite having lost relatives in air raids on Britain, he wrote, "but in spite of this, I want to have one of your boys as my true friend." Perhaps partly because of this touching gesture of international friendship the unpleasantness aroused during the previous two weeks through the insensitivity of certain sectors of the press was dissipated.

After several days I received another letter from Dagmar. She must have replied to mine by return post. Her letter ran as follows:-

Dear James!

I have received your letter and thank you. I feel obliged to reply to your letter quickly so that neither of us may make arrangements to upset the plans of the other.

At present we have wonderfully beautiful weather in Berlin.

For my holiday I shall travel to a quiet village in Thüring. The surroundings will be beautiful, with much forest and not too high mountains. I shall stay with a farmer's family and this holiday will bring me much joy. I need for my health the pure forest air where I can relax in the peace of the countryside. That you can understand.

I could not come to West Germany. I have no relatives there. Also, I could not obtain a visa, and then it would be far too expensive for me.

Today I send you a card of the Virgin's bridge. You have no doubt heard of this bridge which is situated in old Berlin.

With heartfelt Greetings, Yours, Dagmar.

The card was a photographic illustration of the old iron lifting-bridge (the only drawbridge out of the 957 bridges in the city) crossing a narrow section of the Spree, situated in a small back street. I interpreted Dagmar's letter as an invitation to make a hurried initiative in proposing arrangements to visit Berlin. The reference to the Thüring holiday was clearly an indication that little time would be left me for decision-making.

Therefore, I left my room in the Stuben-gasse hurriedly making my way to the travel bureau in Salz Strasse. I made some detailed enquiries and then hurried back to the Stuben-gasse and wrote the following letter:-

Dear Dagmar!

Many thanks for your last letter.

I am sorry you would be unable to visit West Germany but then I can well understand the difficulties preventing this.

I do not know the dates of your own holiday which you say is towards the end of this month. I hope the dates for your Thüring holiday are not yet definitive.

On Saturday 24th of this month I shall be coming to Berlin to attend the Festival. I already have the programme and am greatly looking forward to it. This will be the tenth year of the Festival. I hope you will be in Berlin at this time.

I shall arrive by train at Berlin Zoo at 19.12 hours. It would be nice if you could meet me then. If you cannot, then please meet me the following day (Sunday) at 18.00 below the steps to the S-Bahn platforms in Zoo station where we last met.

I do not know where I shall stay in Berlin. My West Berliner friend will not be in the city at this time. I understand it would be rather difficult to find an inexpensive room in the West sectors during the Festival.

Please write very soon so that all necessary arrangements may be made.

With heartfelt Greetings, Yours, James.

I posted the letter immediately, hoping its results would be fruitful.

I had crossed the Rubicon and decided to go to Berlin come what may. I prayed for Dagmar's early response and bought the rail ticket for the journey. Nearly a week passed, and still nothing from Dagmar. Had one of our letters been lost or intercepted, or more probably, had my last letter put her into such a quandary that she was unable to make a decision? Nine days passed, and still no reply. I wrote her a short reminder with the time and day of my arrival and trusting she had received my last letter. Several more days passed by.

Then one Tuesday afternoon on returning from lunch to my room in the Stuben-gasse, my landlady excitedly met me in the hallway exclaiming that a telegram awaited me. It had been lying on the table for more than an hour, and she had visited the beer house where I usually ate to see if I was there. I explained I had been dining with the family of a friend. The landlady said she hoped the news wasn't terrible and that no close relative had died. I replied that I didn't anticipate such an event, and rushed upstairs to my room.

I tore open the yellow envelope and read its contents:- I AWAIT YOU ON SATURDAY AT THE OSTBAHNHOF (East Station) = Dagmar +.

I was overjoyed. My letters had been effective and all plans for visiting Berlin had not been made in vain.

Nonetheless, I had not contemplated travelling direct to the East sector. The idea touched me with apprehension. I had no visitor's visa to stay in the East, and certainly one could not be obtained at such short notice. I had heard that it often took two or three months to obtain a visa for East Germany (and the East sector of Berlin came under East German law) and I naturally assumed from Dagmar's telegram that either she was inviting me to stay with her family or in some kind of a Pension in the East. But then I realised that a visitor's visa was a secondary concern. Would I have difficulty in obtaining a permit to enter the East sector, and such a permit would presumably be issued on the train after it had left the Zoo station?

Would the Pass control allow me such an entrance permit seeing that I was carrying luggage? They might well be suspicious of my intention of staying in the East sector and might even hold my luggage in the East station (Ostbahnhof) to ensure that I did not do this. Would they accept the explanation that I had a tryst with a girl and intended returning to the West sector with my baggage as soon as we had met? I felt reluctant to travel direct to the East sector, and carrying luggage, especially after the recent crisis in Berlin. There was the possibility of arrest, and even the chance of facing charges for contravening visa or passport regulations. In view of the present mood of the authorities it seemed as if no possibility could be excluded entirely.

Finally, I concluded that despite these doubts, I should have to keep my tryst as arranged as there was now no more time for altering arrangements. If necessary, I should need to bluff my way into the East sector. I decided to take a minimum amount of luggage, and that packed tightly into a hold-all which if necessary could be hidden inconspicuously under the seat of the train. I decided in advance what to say and how to react in the case of several eventualities when faced by the Pass control and the East German police. My fondness for Dagmar and optimism in the progress of the friendship increased almost hourly as the great day approached. My curiosity as to her family circumstances was intense, and I tried to visualise the flat where she lived, and I thought about her father (wondering again about his occupation) trying to reconstruct the life of her family.

During the nights too, my sleeping hours must have been obsessed by thoughts of Dagmar, but these were reflected in strange and unpleasant dreams, expressing the deeper subconscious mind. One night I found myself before Dagmar's home, and her mother opened the door and I was ushered into a large old-fashioned flat. Dagmar was not to be seen, although I tried to search her out. I was directed along a hallway into a spacious living room. The blinds and curtains were drawn to, and the room was lit by dim yellow lights. On the walls were many pictures and ornaments, and the furniture and hangings were of an ornate 19th century kind. There was a strange sad atmosphere of decay and dust in the dark flat, as if time had long since ceased to exist. I was impatient to meet

Dagmar, and wondered why the curtains had been drawn over to exclude the light of day. The family – the father, the grandmother and the sister – were seated on several sofas and chairs, and they rose to greet me, formally and with friendly interest.

There was a sickly degenerate environment of lost fortunes and I experienced a feeling of apprehension. I received no clear impression of those in the room other than the sister whom I noticed was attractive and in good health. My eyes searched eagerly out for Dagmar, and the parents, as if to distract me, motioned me with a hurried gesture to be seated, and a tray with cakes and coffee was placed on a little centre table. I saw Dagmar in one corner of the room, and I rose and advanced towards her, and the parents expressed alarm, beckoning me to be seated again. Ignoring them I approached Dagmar, and she was apprehensive, glancing at me with a diffident expression. Her features had changed from the time I had seen her last. She looked plain and ill, having lost the beauty of her sensitive features. I was disappointed and realised that the friendship was doomed.

I awoke and found the bright sun shining through the window. Another day had begun. I was glad to be rid of such a horrid dream, contenting myself it had no basis in reality, but only in strange diseased imaginings. I wondered why I had dreamt such a dream, and if it foretold the future, recollecting how sometimes I had found answers to problems through the revelations of dreams. I decided its portents had little meaning, and so I pushed it from my memory.

The following night – more hours of disturbed sleep – I dreamt yet again about Dagmar. I found myself in a London pub, where student friends approached, saying a girl unable to speak English was looking for me. I was gladdened, knowing that the girl was Dagmar, and was astonished she should be in England. Impatiently, I ask for her whereabouts and was told she was "downstairs." I descended some dirty wooden steps leading into a damp musty passageway. I walked quickly along the passageway, hurriedly searching through dusty, half-furnished rooms, with cheap kitchen furniture. She was nowhere to be seen. The place was deserted. I returned upstairs and enquired from my student friends for more specific directions. They replied she *must* be downstairs, that she's looking for me, that they saw her a moment ago. I had to find her within the next few minutes or else she would be lost forever in the midst of the vast population of the world. I searched frantically, running through a maze of rooms and passageways, through dark streets and through crowds of people.

At last I found her. She was in an empty room with bare grey stone walls and an earthen floor. As I came into the room she failed to see me and was glancing into a pink plastic mirror decorated with green stars. I stood by silently – expectantly – ready to surprise her with my sudden arrival. But as I watched her I noticed her features were changed. Her face wore a strange pained expression – and somehow I was reminded of that expression of resignation in life – the enigmatic expression as when I had first seen her in the Art Shop. She looked at herself strangely in the mirror – and I asked myself, what does she see there? Her slim fingers clutched tensely round the handle of the mirror and she turned her head, glancing at the mirror's image, but it was not as if she did this to reflect a clearer impression of her own features but as if to get a clearer impression of some fixed image in the mirror, for her eyes were wide open with a searching expression and not as if she was lost in the aesthetic contemplation of herself. Despite my disillusion at her deterioration, I advanced gladly towards her, but on seeing me, she lowered the mirror as if to hide it. Her face lit up with gladness, but I pointed to the mirror and she tried to hide it behind her, but I took hold of her wrist and we struggled and her face became pained again and angry and more pallid, and finally she grasped my wrist with her free hand.

I awoke and saw the bright sunshine gleaming through the thin cotton curtains.

"You must awake, Herr Furner."

I heard the shrill voice of my landlady.

"You've a long journey today, and you haven't finished packing."

She was shaking my wrist.

"What's the time, Frau Feldmann,?" I asked alarmed.

"Nine o'clock," she replied.

"Thank you for waking me," I said. "There's plenty of time – over one and a half hours before I catch my train."

She left the room, and I jumped out of bed. I was optimistic and elated. Today was the great day! The dream though was curious, and I wondered what had been reflected in the mirror. A pity I had been awoken a moment too soon to find out. Was the dream a portent or did it try to reveal something of the mystery which surrounded the girl from East Berlin?

BOOK IV

The Family In Treptow

Love is ever the beginning of knowledge as fire is of light.

Thomas Carlyle, *Essays: Death of Goethe.*

August 1960

Chapter 15

As the international express moved out of Zoo station I was seized with a feeling of apprehension. My hold-all lay on the rack opposite. I decided not to put it under the seat. For one thing, it was bulky and the bright tartan of its canvas cover made it conspicuous, and for another, I thought it better policy to be as candid as possible in my dealings with the East German Pass control. I would adopt a cheery manner and stick to my story of having to meet a friend at the Ostbahnhof before returning to book into a hotel in the West sector.

It had been a long journey, my return to Berlin, and now as the train was pulling out of Zoo station I realised that in a few minutes the journey would come to its end. Many different thoughts had passed through my mind. As I waited on the station in Osnabrück earlier that day for my connection to Berlin I knew my return to this city would be an event of some significance involving the consummation of a strange and curious friendship, or else disappointment of high-held hopes, but in either eventuality, the sojourn in Berlin would be memorable in the light of experiencing heartfelt feelings. I was resolved, though, not to be influenced by anything other than my own intuition, for already, I felt instinctively the probability that inducements of a kind could be brought to bear that might attempt to interfere with the natural course of our relationship.

I was the sole occupant in the compartment, for the train had emptied in Zoo station before continuing on its final destination to Warsaw. Outside, the fine new buildings of the Hansa quarter, illuminated by the thousands of lights from their windows and the street lights below, passed slowly by, in the twilight.

"Pass control,!" snapped a voice in the corridor from the other end of the carriage.

Three green-uniformed officials appeared outside the compartment. I casually took out the passport from my breast pocket and handed it to the first official who entered the compartment. His second colleague looked over his shoulder and together, they examined the passport. The third official remained in the corridor, blocking the passageway, his hand held over his holster. I waited anxiously. It seemed they were interested in every stamp in the passport.

"Why are you visiting Berlin,?" asked the first official.

"I'm a tourist," I replied evasively.

"Where's your visa,?" asked the second.

"At the back of the passport."

"That's a transit visa allowing you to cross by rail through the DDR from Marienborn to West Berlin," said the first official after carefully glancing at the visa.

"What do you intend doing in Berlin,?" enquired the second official.

"I've come to attend the Festival."

"That's in the West sectors."

"Do you intend staying in the East sector,?" asked the first official.

"No," I lied.

"Why are you travelling to the Ostbahnhof?"

"Is that your baggage up there,?" asked the second official before I had time to answer his colleague.

"Yes, it's my baggage. I'm meeting a friend at the Ostbahnhof and then I'm returning to the West sector," I replied reddening a little in anticipating difficulty.

"An East Berliner?"

"Yes."

"Take down your bag," ordered the first official.

I lifted the bag from the rack onto the seat. The official pressed his hands round the hold-all but made no attempt to open it.

"Any arms or munitions,?" he asked glancing up.

"No," I replied, unable to suppress a smile.

The second official filled in a form, pressing on the large binder he carried. This formality completed, the passport was returned together with another document.

"You may enter the East sector providing you don't remain overnight," said the second official.

Ten minutes later the train drew into the Ostbahnhof and pulled to a halt. I grabbed the hold-all and went into the corridor, filled with anticipation and hoping that the platform would not be overcrowded in searching for Dagmar, and hoping also, that I would be able to recognise her after almost a year's absence.

The station was noisy but not overcrowded, and as I came onto the platform, I saw a fair haired girl in a blue coat arching her neck from side to side a few metres away, standing above a subway exit leading below the platforms. I advanced quickly towards her. She was dressed exactly as when I had last seen her.

"Dagmar,!" I exclaimed, and she turned towards me and we fell into an embrace.

"Hullo! How are you,?" she replied with happiness in her voice.

"It's so long since we last met. I was afraid I might not recognise you," I said. "But you look just the same," I hastened to add.

"It's only a year since you were last in Berlin."

"Eleven months – but so long."

I placed my arm around her shoulder and we went down the subway beneath the platform. Several ill-dressed persons carrying luggage passed us by on the steps.

"You travel too much," replied Dagmar.

"You are wearing just the same clothes as when we parted last."

"That was so you'd recognise me."

"You didn't really think I'd forgotten how you looked?"

"You were always asking for my photograph in your letters. I thought you might forget."

"I would never forget you," I laughed, pressing her shoulder.

We were happy and elated during those first few moments of our renewed friendship, and oblivious to the surroundings. I thought of the dreams of the two previous nights, and with self-satisfaction I concluded they could have had little meaning for the future.

As we came to the bottom of the steps, a tall man of about forty in a smart grey uniform came from behind us, and asked apologetically for a light. Dagmar took a step back, and as I took out the matches, the man glanced curiously at my bag and then at Dagmar.

"You're new in Berlin,?" he asked.

"Yes," I returned.

I gave him a light. Dagmar put her arm through mine but held me back when we were about to follow in the same direction.

"Wait a minute," she said. "Do you think he recognised you were a foreigner?"

"He obviously knew I wasn't from here. But then perhaps it's better he should think I'm a foreigner rather than a West German."

"But we must be careful," exclaimed Dagmar. "You haven't a residence visa. He could have followed you from the train."

"Was he one of the station police?"

"I don't think so. He was wearing the uniform of an officer in the People's Army. But you can never be sure. This station's full of police."

We walked along the passageway.

"We must get out of the main station as soon as we can," said Dagmar. "I'll ask for the tickets at the S-Bahn kiosk."

We walked through the station to the main hall, and as Dagmar insisted, I stood in a corner against the wall of the station by some telephone kiosks, whilst covertly she went across the hall to purchase tickets.

Two large portraits, of Ulbricht and Kruschchev, were placed over the main exit of the station. Somehow, I still could not accustom myself to the idea of a girl as beautiful as Dagmar living in such a drab environment – but then, there must be beautiful girls the world over, I reflected. Queues stood by several food kiosks and a number of dossers sat half reclining on the long benches in the centre of the hall. Dagmar returned with the tickets.

"I haven't asked yet," I said hesitantly, "but where are we going?"

"You can come home and stay with us, yes,?" she replied. "Is that all right?" We began walking towards the S-Bahn platforms. "You must understand that we live quite modestly. I hope you don't mind sleeping in our sitting room."

"Of course not," I responded.

"My mother can make up a bed for you there."

"It's very kind of your parents inviting me to stay with them when they know so little about me."

"Did you have a good journey from Münster,?" asked Dagmar as we stood on the S-Bahn platform.

"Yes," I replied.

"Did you have any trouble getting into the East sector?"

"No," I said compromising with the truth. I wasn't going to tell Dagmar about the incident with the Pass control after the train left the Zoo station, as this would have only given her another cause for concern.

"Didn't they ask about your luggage?"

"I don't think they noticed it," I said evasively.

"They wouldn't have let you into the East sector if they knew you intended staying here. They're very strict. If anyone stops us between here and Treptow asking questions, just say you're a foreign tourist going to the West sector."

"Don't worry," I replied. "I'll see you won't get into trouble."

A train rumbled into the station and we climbed in. It was crowded and we stood between the seats. As the train moved out of the station I held Dagmar's hand and looked at her contemplatively, tired after the long journey from Münster.

"Were you surprised when I wrote to you after your return to Germany,?" she asked smiling softly.

"I was very happy you replied to my letter."

"I didn't expect you to return," said Dagmar, and she pulled out a newspaper from under my arm and unfolding it began to peruse it. "It's a very big newspaper."

"It's the *Times*," I replied, "England's most famous paper."

"Do you read this every day?"

"Not all of it. It would take all day."

She opened the newspaper and began reading a column aloud, with a pronunciation making the words unrecognisable. I laughed at her courageous effort. She stood closely by me now, her fair hair falling over my shoulder.

"See, I can read English," she exclaimed flirtatiously.

"I think you could learn English very quickly," I said.

"Do you really think so,?" she answered with interest.

"You have an ear for language."

"You come from England,?" exclaimed a man in English just behind me in a friendly tone.

"Yes," I replied and turning a little towards him. I was feeling too happy at that moment to feel any other emotion than goodwill towards the world to be put out by the interruption, or to even regard his question as an intrusion.

"You are a tourist,?" he asked.

"I've come to Berlin on holiday, but I'm studying at a university in West Germany."

"And how do you like Berlin?"

"I like it," I replied abruptly, not wishing to be drawn into a conversation.

"There's plenty to see in Berlin – especially in the East sector," he said. "We have the finest museums and galleries in the East."

"I know – I've been in Berlin before," I replied.

The train stopped at a station and the doors opened

"You're staying in the East sector?"

"No."

"I thought – as only you had a bag."

"I had to meet a friend here. I'm booked into a Pension in the West."

"And where are you going now?"

After a momentary hesitation I replied, "To Treptow."

I felt Dagmar tug on my arm.

"So am I. Perhaps we can travel together."

"As you see, I'm with a friend. We have a schedule to keep."

Dagmar tugged on my arm, looking up indicating we should move towards the doors. We pushed our way through the crowd.

"We get out at the next station," she said. "We must change. This train goes on to Karlshorst. – Who was that man?"

"Just an over-friendly Berliner," I replied.

"He knows we're going to Treptow. We must dodge him at the next station. You remember, he pointed at your bag. Strangers can't be trusted. We mustn't be followed."

"Then we mustn't make it too obvious we're running away. It could rouse his suspicion."

The train moved into Ostkreuz station and stopped. I opened the doors and Dagmar and I hurriedly made our way to the other platforms.

Treptower Park was only one station from Ostkreuz, and we came down the steps of the station into a short side street, and then into the wide avenue of Puschkin Allee. At once I was overcome by the pungent smell of East bloc petrol, a distinctive odour found in any street in any country behind the Iron Curtain. The streets were dark now, lit by dim old fashioned lamps. We crossed Puschkin Allee and went along the broad sandy unpaved sidewalk. Large houses with long front gardens behind high railings lined the avenue. On my enquiring, Dagmar explained that several were embassies, and others, headquarters of various political bodies. High trees divided the pavement from the roadway, along which moved some trucks, and occasionally, a car or two. We turned left down another street, a great stretch of which was lined by vast red brick barrack like buildings, red and white propaganda hoardings hanging from below their roofs.

"Is this an army headquarters,?" I enquired curiously.

"The local HQ of the Treptower Volkspolizei," replied Dagmar.

"It's large enough to house a division of troops," I said surprised.

Dagmar said nothing. We came to a residential section – vast crumbling tenement blocks, a few bombs sites, and then shops lining the pavements. An atmosphere of dirt and decay pervaded the district. Little traffic disturbed the silence of the evening and a few dark figures moved slowly in the street or emerged from dark entrances. We passed a small beer house from which came the sound of noisy voices and raucous singing.

"This is Graetz Strasse – the street where we live," exclaimed Dagmar.

We crossed the street to the opposite corner on the right. Graetz Strasse was different to what I had expected. On the map it had looked a small narrow insignificant street, but in fact it was broad, with a double row of tram lines running down the centre, and vast old tenement blocks on both sides.

"We shall go to number sixteen," said Dagmar.

"I thought you lived in number fifty-five."

"Yes, I live there with my grandmother, but my parents and sister live in number sixteen and that's where you'll be staying."

A dusty almost empty tram rumbled slowly by and down to the far end of the street where it stopped.

"That's the sector frontier at the end of the street," said Dagmar in a faintly sad tone.

The conductor alighted from the back of the tram and the driver came to the front of the vehicle carrying a long metal rod, and began changing the points.

"Nowadays, the trams can't go any further, and so they just turn back and go the other way," continued Dagmar. "There's a bridge at the end of the street, but now of course, it's closed to vehicles. It's guarded night and day by the East German police and only pedestrians use it."

"I suppose it's nice in a way to feel you live so near the West," I said.

"It makes no difference to our lives," she replied. "The East is the East."

" 'And the West is West, and never the twain shall meet,'" I recited.

"This is the house," said Dagmar.

I pulled open a massive double-door, and we walked into a cavernous hallway. Dagmar turned on a light – a single small bare bulb hanging from the high ceiling. The walls had been painted a dark green and patches of white showed where plaster had crumbled away. Several doors with different kinds of name plates led off the hall, and a large board on the right listed the occupants of the building. A broad wooden staircase with decorative cast iron banisters was at the far end. I was awed by the huge size of the interior.

"We walk through," said Dagmar.

I followed her through the hallway and our shoes clattered on the chequered black and white tiled floor. We walked through a smaller door and into a large concrete paved courtyard. As we crossed the courtyard I glanced up and noted the great height of the buildings, and the sounds of our shoes echoed off the stonework around. We passed through a hallway similar to the first, and began climbing the staircase.

"Not much further now," said Dagmar turning to me with a smile. "Only on the second floor."

We stood outside a large brown varnished door. A brass plaque bearing the name *Renot* was fixed a few centimetres above the letter slot. Dagmar fumbled in her bag and then, explaining that she had left her key at home, knocked twice gently on the door with the great iron knocker cast to represent a mermaid. The bell at the side of the door above which was a little white enamel plate with the word "Ring" in gothic letters must have been out of order.

In a few moments the door was opened by a little lady with brown greying hair, with a thin almost pinched complexion, wearing a colourful apron over a plain dark dress. Her hair was set in a style reminiscent of the 1930s.

"Welcome,!" she exclaimed smiling broadly and glancing at me with cordiality.

"This is my mother," said Dagmar softly.

"Welcome, welcome,!" repeated the little lady quite excitedly as I extended my hand. "Please come inside."

She curtsied as we shook hands and I bowed in return.

Dagmar and I entered the little hallway of the flat.

"Please make yourself quite at home," said her mother as I took Dagmar's coat. "What would you like to drink? You must be tired after so long a journey. Do you prefer coffee or tea?"

"I expect he'd like tea Mamma," said Dagmar.

"That would be fine," I replied.

Frau Renot disappeared into the kitchen on the left, and Dagmar showed me into the sitting room opposite. It was furnished with old heavy dark wood items with floral decoration. A faded worn red carpet lay on the floor, and at the other end of the room by the high windows stood a spacious dining table. Comfortable armchairs were by the door at the left, and beyond them a tall glass-fronted cabinet full of bric-a-brac, and a bookcase. Against the right wall stood an antiquated combined radiogram-sideboard. Beyond this, extending to the windows stood a chaise longue. Around the walls were reproductions of modern art works, coloured prints, lithographs and several silhouettes of Negro and other African subjects, crudely pinned onto the walls.

"You will sleep on the couch over there. Let's have some music," she added turning to the radio.

"Have you records too?"

"The gramophone's broken. We just keep linen in it now."

"You have a nice flat," I said still finding my bearings.

"It's rather old, and we have many difficulties in these buildings because of the need for repairs. Often we must wait months for the builders to put things right. But at least we're not over-crowded like many people."

"It must be quiet living away from the street at the back of the building."

"The courtyard's noisy."

"Are these pictures from the Art Shop where you work?"

"Most. Look, here's my sister Gisela," she added drawing me to a framed photograph hanging on the wall over the couch. "This picture is one of the two front covers she's appeared on in one of our leading fashion magazines."

The picture illustrated an attractive girl with dark hair in a colourful dress.

"And here's the other picture," continued Dagmar, drawing me proudly to another coloured photograph which was a head and shoulders portrait. "Do you think she looks like me."

"I think she's very different," I replied.

"Now she's in the country with her boy friend, Franz. He's an engineering student. They return tomorrow night and you'll meet them then."

Dagmar pointed out other favourite pictures, and we went to her bookcase and glanced through her collection – mostly classical works, and those I had sent her stood on the top shelf.

Frau Renot returned with a tray of cakes and open sandwiches and tea. The three of us sat down at the table and as we conversed, I wondered as to the whereabouts of her father but felt it might be improper to remark on his absence.

Frau Renot was indulgent in her hospitality, reminding me there was plenty of food in the house, but the meat sandwiches containing thick cold slices of bacon were fatty and after having eaten one of these, I confined myself to cakes and biscuits, by way of apology explaining I had lunched on the train. She glanced constantly from Dagmar to me with an expression of pleasure and appreciation as we talked to one another, as if trying to satisfy herself as to the degree of our friendship, and the daughter spoke in a tone of affection to her mother, as she helped carry in more cakes and re-fill the tea pot.

Despite the indulgent hospitality, I experienced an inexplicable feeling of unease, which I tried to conceal, as the mother with friendly gestures pried into the details of my personal circumstances in Münster, but outwardly our conversation was marked by fluency and frequent laughter and the desire to show consideration through every gesture and word.

Dagmar told her mother about the man who approached me on the city train.

"I hope he didn't know where you were going," exclaimed her mother alarmed.

"No, Mamma," replied Dagmar. "We lost him in the crowd when changing trains at Ostkreuz."

"You must always be careful whom you speak to in public places in the East sector," said Frau Renot. "Berlin is full of Stasi informers."

"He couldn't have followed us, Mamma," said Dagmar.

"Informers stop at nothing," said Frau Renot excitedly. "They're ruthless. They don't have to have proof – they use the slightest pretext."

"Mother speaks from experience," said Dagmar.

I was curious to ask more, but as I sensed the matter was painful, I said nothing. Frau Renot changed the topic by saying I should eat all meals with the family since as a student I could not afford to eat out every day. I told her I had brought sufficient resources with me and had anyway anticipated staying in a Pension.

"And when you want to take out Dagmar for the day just tell me beforehand and I'll make up lunch packs for you both," added Frau Renot.

"You're very kind," I responded.

"Dagmar will be working for the first few days of next week, and so you can spend the time with us, and then meet Dagmar at her shop after work."

I felt apprehensive at the suggestion but could not very well object. At last Dagmar said she was tired as it had been a busy day, and asked if I could see her across the road. We put on our coats and left the flat whilst Frau Renot began to make up a bed in the sitting room.

I was relieved we were at last alone and as we came onto the staircase, I put my arm around her waist and she moved close beside me.

"I hope you'll be comfortable there," she said.

"I will be," I said.

"Are you pleased you came to Berlin again,?" she asked coquettishly.

"I'm very happy to be with you. There is nothing more I could have wished for."

As we crossed the street I kissed her forehead. At that moment it seemed as if all my expectations were to be fulfilled, and I wondered for how long such blissful happiness could last.

"I live just here," said Dagmar. "We walk through to the back – it's on the ground floor."

We passed through an archway beneath another massive tenement block. Doors on both sides led into flats, and then we came into a spacious courtyard which we crossed, where a pair of massive doors led to another communal entrance. A few steps further, on the left, was the entrance to her grandmother's flat.

We fell into a long embrace and kissed with passion and I felt loathed to part from her even though it would only be for a few hours.

"Why do I do this,?" she murmured to herself. "I feel I shouldn't."

"You're the most beautiful creature I've ever seen," I said stroking her hair back from her temple.

"You have travelled much. You have been to so many places. I'm not the first girl."

"Please don't speak like that."

"You're free to go where you will. You're not destined to live always in Berlin."

"Don't say that. You too will one day be free."

"You know so little about me."

"I know all I want to know about you."

"But there are things you don't understand."

"Let's talk about them another day. Now you're tired."

She opened her bag and took out a key. I stepped forward with a furtive gesture.

"You can't come in now," she added holding me back. "Granny's asleep! Until tomorrow, James. I'll come and waken you."

She blew a kiss as she opened the door and I returned the gesture and tip-toed out of the dark building.

That night I lay awake for some hours before finally falling asleep. In my excitement and conflict of feelings, which wavered between certainty and doubt, I asked myself how long could this ideal of the "perfect creature" last, and how secure now was the friendship which had been renewed between us? I sensed that this was only the beginning of our relationship and that many difficulties might lie ahead.

Chapter 16

The previous night I had spoken too soon on suggesting it must be so very quiet living away from the street. It was not yet six o'clock when I was awoken by the clattering of feet and voices in the courtyard. I soon learnt that the faintest sound was magnified many times, and the innumerable windows looking down onto this darkened space seldom pierced by the rays of the sun, served not only as lookouts on the movements of the occupants of the vast tenement block, but as ears as well. A whisper became an audible hiss, a voice or conversation sufficient to alert the casual eavesdropper, and a shout, an argument or a hearty early morning greeting, enough to awaken the deepest sleeper from nocturnal slumber. And so as this was early in the morning, and as neighbours here customarily recognised each other with hearty greetings I was awoken shortly after dawn – and on a Sunday too.

Every person left his or her distinctively audible mark: now was to be heard the light pattering of short quick footsteps, and then the long strides of heavy boots, and then a shuffling of feet and the sound of a walking stick, accompanied by coughing and wheezing. Shortly after seven o'clock loud laughter and noisy men's rough voices filled the courtyard followed by a great crashing of metal bins and banging of lids and the sound of heavy containers being dragged across the surface of the yard. I pulled the duvet over my head, but all to no purpose for it continued for ten minutes. Surely they could not be emptying the dustbins on a Sunday, I thought. This was followed by shouting from one of the windows, and a lively exchange between two hoarse women across the courtyard, by which time I finally considered myself irreversibly awoken for the day.

In this way my first night behind the Iron Curtain (if at that time the East sector could strictly be described as that) came to its eventful close. Certainly the row which filled this courtyard was more disturbing to sleep than the nearby presence of a heavy traffic roar.

I lay in bed impatient to arise, but no sound emanated from within the flat. I felt awkward but dared not leave the room for fear of embarrassing partially dressed occupants moving to or from the washroom. I regretted not having obtained more specific instructions the night before. At last there was a tap on the door, and Frau Renot peeped in to announce there was now hot water for me in the "bathroom". I climbed out of bed and gathering my washing kit, I recollected there wasn't what could really be described as a "proper" bathroom.

As I crossed the narrow hall to the washroom I caught a faint glimpse through the end doorway of a bulky sleeping figure well covered with a mountain of bedclothes, a tuft of grey hair at one end and a pair of exposed feet sticking out at the other. On the floor lay sheets and pillows, and the room was in a state of early morning disarray. That must be the father, I mused. He must be accustomed to sleeping in late!

I entered the washroom which had really been built for use as a toilet and consisted of a narrow passage of great length and wasted space. The pan itself had apparently long since been broken, for the tank was partly dismantled and several buckets of water stood nearby for flushing the drain. A table stood at the other end of the passageway and on this was placed a wash bowl and a hot jug of water in preparation for my ablutions. On a makeshift shelf above were kept the washing utensils of the household plus bottles and jars of cosmetics and haircreams, etc. On nearby shelves stood a collection of mysterious bottles of various colours, representing the family medicine cabinet, and nails had been hammered into the dark green wall, to the latter's grief exposing plaster which had fallen away, and onto these nails had been suspended towels, dressing gowns and an assortment of other articles. The room was crowded and dark, for the window was a small opening above reachable height, and in this environment, I began to wash, adapting myself to the cramped conditions and lack of running water.

Having dressed in my Sunday best, I ventured into the kitchen, a large airy room with French windows leading out into a balcony at the far end, and was greeted by Frau Renot, who took me to the washroom and allotted an exact space for each of my toilet articles. This in order, I was led to the sitting room, where in silence and unanticipated, I breakfasted quite alone on open sandwiches, a pot of tea, and a couple of apples which were brought in as an afterthought. In this situation I could not quite decide whether my lonesome repast was intended as a special privilege or intentional exclusion from the family circle. What was the attitude towards me of the other male whom I knew was then present in the flat? Was I really welcome, or had I given rise to a conflict of attitudes within the family?

It was with relief when Dagmar appeared at 10 o'clock, and the atmosphere was lightened with cheerful greetings; and the mother's suggestion that Dagmar and I take a stroll in Trepower Park on account of the fine weather was a welcome proposal. As we left the flat it was apparent that Herr Renot remained in bed and asleep. He must be a troglodyte, I thought, and on a fine morning like this, but I felt unable as yet to remark on his existence. In good time, I assured myself, he would make his appearance. After visiting the Soviet War memorial, we admired the other open air sculptures, and then slowly strolled around the Karpfen pond and sat down on a bench. We were attuned to one another's mood, experiencing a quiet sense of happiness, but strangely, our conversation did not touch on her home or family, or personal relationships, as if dark or secret recollections constrained her openness.

On returning for lunch it was to the grandmother's flat at number fifty-five that we made our way.

"We always take our main meals here," said Dagmar as she opened the door of the flat. "Granny is too old to cross the road. She can hardly walk."

As soon as we entered the passageway Frau Renot, wearing an apron and with wooden spoon in hand, emerged from the kitchen and greeted us with warmth.

"Lunch is nearly ready. Please, Herr Furner, take a seat in the dining room, and in a few minutes we'll all be together," she continued with a bow, indicating the room at the end of the passage with her wooden spoon, and the daughter was taken aside to help with final preparations.

I began walking down the passage but before reaching the end room, Frau Renot overtook me, and with some fastidiousness, led me into the dining area, directing me to sit on a particular chair at the end of the table. She then departed as hurriedly as she had entered, but I was left embarrassed, for she had made no attempt to introduce me to a second person who was seated at the other end of the table.

Feeling awkward and not knowing whether to ignore the presence of this second person, or being so bold   as   to   make   my   own introduction, I momentarily hesitated by the chair before slowly and stiffly taking a seat. There was a loud munching, and I looked across at the figure wondering if he would condescend to introduce himself. I thought that if introductions were to be made, then surely it was for the assumed host to make the first move – but no, he said nothing, and so silence reigned. I was overcome with a feeling of claustrophobia, and nervously, I cleared my throat, and tried to adopt a pose of nonchalance.

Glancing across the room at the furniture and windows beyond, I discreetly observed the figure opposite.   There was a banging and scraping of cutlery on plates and dishes, and a slapping of lips, and a great activity of facial muscles as the jaws masticated the food which came between them, and a stretching of arms in several directions over the dishes which lay before him.

The figure belonged to a man of some corpulence, with a large head and thinning grey and white hair receding at the temples and forehead, and a pale yellowish skin. He wore a white linen business shirt with a blue line, and the fabric was darkened and made course by age and repeated laundering. He was collarless and tie-less, and the open-necked shirt made just visible a patch of grey hair on his chest. A pair of thick-strapped braces crossed his shoulders harnessing the tops of his trousers well above the waist line. His jacket hung on the back of the chair on which he sat.

His skin was fleshy and face deeply lined, and his large pale blue eyes, which were set deeply, stared out from grey almost black eye sockets.   I returned his intense glance and hoped my gesture was not intrusive, and I sensed a suggestion of suspicion in his look. Everything about him was untidy; the only neatness being the hair combed flat over his skull, perhaps to conceal an advancing baldness. His age might have been anything between sixty and seventy.

Frau Renot quickly entered the room, smiled hospitably at me, and deposited a dish of sliced beetroot before the hungry man, which service went unacknowledged by its recipient, for he thrust his fork into the dish as if it had been there all along with the others. Still no introductions had been attempted. I began to wonder who or what this man might be and as to why he was being so handsomely fed at the dining table. Could it possibly be … ? … but no, surely that was impossible – the man was too old and unseemly to be that. Perhaps he was a neighbour who had kindly consented to carry out an urgent household repair, and was being rewarded with lunch in lieu of cash. In any event I concluded he was unlikely to be anyone of consequence as otherwise, he would surely have condescended to make himself known.

Dagmar came quickly into the room, placed a pile of plates and cutlery onto the table, and with a sense of momentary shock, I witnessed her place her arm around the old man and lightly kiss his forehead.

"Good morning, Papa," she exclaimed. "James, this is my father."

I rose from the table stretching my hand across it.

"Good afternoon, Herr Renot," I said.

We shook hands, but he made no attempt to rise, only looked up and nodded, and I took my place again on the chair; experiencing a different sense of awkwardness. Dagmar hovered over us, wondering perhaps how the two of us would relate, and then hurriedly left.

Instinctively, I realised that sociableness called for conversation, and that the initiative for this was now an obligation falling on my own shoulders. Possibly he was more afraid of me than I of him. Did my smart and formal attire shame him in the light of his collarless, open-necked appearance? The quandary between us was resolved when he exclaimed: "I hope you slept well with us last night."

"Thank you, I slept very well," I answered.

"The bed's only makeshift."

"It was kind of you to invite me here," I said after a pause, but the compliment was only met by another nod, and I realised was a poor attempt at generating a conversation.

Herr Renot continued to look at me as he ate his food and I was pained by the thought of the impression I must have made.

"The weather is remarkably warm," I exclaimed helplessly at last, but in desperation.

"Continental climate," replied Herr Renot cheerfully, giving full accent to the words. At least his demeanour was now friendly.

"Berlin is a beautiful city," I said lamely.

He only nodded again, as if doubting the sincerity of my statement.

"I believe you work for a newspaper," I ventured at last, having summoned up my courage.

He only nodded but said nothing.

"Journalism's a subject which interests me," I said brightly. "Are you a reporter?"

"*Korrektor,*" he replied.

"That must be interesting work. Does it entail deciding on ideological values or merely a legal knowledge of what can and what cannot be printed,?" I said in a slow thoughtful tone so as not to put the question in too blunt a manner.

He glared at me suspiciously across the table.

"I mean," I continued, "does the work of a *Korrektor* mean censorship? Is it a governmental job?"

"No," he replied. "Reader – simple proof reader!"

"I understand. Do you work for *Neues Deutschland,*?" I asked, it being the only East German paper I knew by name.

"No," he replied pushing his plate aside after stuffing in the last mouthful of gravy soaked potato.

He picked up a paper on the centre of the table, opened it up, and threw it across to me, proudly pointing to the heading.

I read aloud the title of the paper: *Neue Zeit*: Central Organ of the Christian Democratic Union of Germany." I opened it, peering through the pages, and Herr Renot leaned forward with an expression of pride in his tabloid newssheet which comprised no more than six to eight pages.

"This isn't a Communist paper," I remarked.

"CDU – Christian Democratic Union," he replied, clearly accenting the words and showing his teeth.

"I thought you had a one-party political system in Communist countries," I said.

"We have eight political parties in East Germany," he answered.

"That's many," I exclaimed in polite surprise.

I could see the old man was itching to make me better informed on the topic of East German politics, and keen to encourage him, I asked him to elucidate.

"The eight political parties represented in the *Volkskammer*, the People's Assembly, are the SED, the Socialist Unity Party; the CDU; the LDPD, the Liberal Democratic Party of Germany," he began listing the organisations on his chubby fingers, "the NDPD, the National Democratic Party of Germany; the DBD, the Democratic Peasant Party of Germany; the FDGD, the Free Association of Trade Unions; the FDJ, the Free German Youth; and the DFD, the Democratic Women's Association of Germany."

By the time he had finished listing these "Free" and "Democratic" associations, I foolishly remarked that it looked as if the people were "spoilt for choice." He made no comment at this remark.

"But what about the Communist party – where does that fit in,?" I exclaimed, realising he hadn't mentioned the most important association of all.

"That's the SED. The SED's a combination of the KPD, the Communist Party, and the SPD, the Social Democratic Party," he explained.

"Why was that?"

"Result of a law passed in 1945."

"By the People's Assembly,?" I asked.

"No. An order of the Soviet Kommandatura in the East sector. The SPD members voted against the referendum of merging the two parties," he said thoughtfully. "But of course they couldn't do anything about it," he added throwing up his hand with a suggestion of irritability at the memory of the event. He spoke in a staccato almost monosyllabic fashion.

He took out a cigar from the breast pocket of his jacket, lit it, and glanced at it thoughtfully for some moments with a sad expression.

"And these parties, do they really differ from each other?"

"The NDPD, that's perhaps the equivalent of your right wing Conservative party in England," he began hesitantly. "The CDU, well, you have that in West Germany, although it's not quite the same. The LDPD's the same as your Liberal party."

He stopped speaking suddenly and began puffing at his cigar.

"And what about the other parties?"

"Well, they have connections with – sort of affiliated to the SED," he said reluctantly.

"And how many seats does the SED have in the People's Assembly,?" I enquired.

"A hundred and seventeen out of four hundred members."

I refrained from asking further questions on the peculiarities of East German parliamentary life as I noted the old man had betrayed a slight impatience at my last few questions, but the ice between us had been broken, and it looked as if I had elicited a friendly attitude towards me.

He leant across the table and was about to speak again when Frau Renot placed a dish of stew on the table, expressing her pleasure that we had made each other's acquaintance.

Herr Renot, speaking loudly and accenting his words so that he displayed his teeth, said he'd been explaining to me about "democratic reform," facetiously adding, that now I knew as much about East German politics as he did, and he laughed at his little joke.

Dagmar and her mother began to lay the table after the used plates of Herr Renot had been cleared away onto a sideboard.

"He was late in bed today and didn't have breakfast – that's why he's had lunch before us," said Frau Renot with an affectionate gesture towards her husband.

"He needs the sleep – that's why he has to lie in," added Dagmar.

I said nothing but only felt it unnecessary that such an apology should be made.

Dagmar laid an ashtray before her father – he had previously deposited his ash in the empty dish of gherkins – and he began to glance from Dagmar to me with an almost prurient curiosity. We both noticed this unwelcome attention, and she kept her eyes averted as she laid out the cutlery.

"I trust you had a nice walk this morning," exclaimed Herr Renot suggestively to his daughter.

"Naturally," she replied in a tone of slight annoyance, laying a knife and fork with a clatter.

"Beautiful weather for a young couple today in Treptower Park," he exclaimed blowing out a cloud of smoke.

No comment was made in reply to this, but I caught a glimpse of Frau Renot glancing across at her husband with an expression of approval.

At that moment came a slow shuffling of feet and the sound of a stick being thrust onto the floor from the passageway outside.

"It's Granny. She's come in by herself," exclaimed Frau Renot startled. "Dagmar, go and help her."

Dagmar left the room, re-emerging with a tall bent figure whom she gently supported, wearing an ankle-length black dress and brown cardigan.

"We thought you were still asleep and didn't want to wake you," exclaimed Frau Renot.

"I felt hungry and I knew you had something good to eat," replied the old lady with a broad smile and a cracked voice.

"Of course we would have put something by for you," replied Frau Renot cheerfully, "but you shouldn't have come in all by yourself, all the way from the courtyard."

"You have a guest – an Englishman," said the grandmother, her eyes lighting up, and stretching forward her hand as she hobbled towards me with Dagmar's aid.

"This is Herr Furner, Granny," said Frau Renot.

"I know – Dagmar's told me all about him," replied the grandmother. "So you're the young man who sent Dagmar all those urgent love letters."

"Really Granny! You needn't say that," said Dagmar.

"I don't know about *urgent*," I replied blushing.

Frau Brüning laughed, enjoying my embarrassment.

"You can't tell me about life," she exclaimed. "I've had my young days too. I remember those thick envelopes from England which fell through the letter box."

"Granny, you're not being tactful," protested Dagmar.

"Dagmar, go and fetch Granny's chair for her," said Frau Renot, relieving her daughter from her grandmother's teasing.

"She used to hide those letters from me at first, but I caught her out at last," confided Frau Brüning. "And I remember those presents you sent her, to my son in the West sector. And so now the 'English gentleman' has come to stay with us!"

I blushed, and the more my awkwardness, the greater seemed the old lady's pleasure.

"Oh yes, the English are 'Gentlemen,'" she continued. "It's a long time since I last met an Englishman. It was at a little hotel on the Rhine – a big party of English tourists were there. That was during my honeymoon in 1902."

Dagmar returned, wheeling in an antiquated bathchair, upholstered in leather, and she gently lowered her grandmother into the vehicle and wheeled it to the table.

"Ah, my poor legs," exclaimed Frau Brüning rubbing her knees but smiling stoically in face of the pain. "So stiff! Rheumatism,!" she added by way of explanation suddenly turning to me, and she said the word with particular emphasis.

"I'm very sorry," I only returned, for the old lady looked at me as if expecting a sympathetic reply.

"Oh no, you're not really sorry," she replied with a chuckle. "You're only being polite. The English 'Gentleman' again! I sleep so badly."

Chapter 17

We sat down at the table and enjoyed an ample lunch of beef and vegetable stew with plentiful portions of potatoes. There was a high spirited environment, much small-talk, but above all, an intense interest in the English guest who aroused such curiosity, and who by such a strange set of circumstances found himself amongst this East German family.

Herr Renot made his contribution to the circle with occasional witticisms and remarks which I took as tactless rather than facetious, and these were met by Dagmar with such exclamations as, "Oh *quatsch* Papa," or, "Oh, really Papa." Herr Renot continued to smoke his cigar throughout the meal, and when the smoke filled his eyes and made them watery, which was often, he had the unpleasant habit of drawing an enormous handkerchief from his pocket, dabbing it all over his face and finally rubbing the great cloth round his eye sockets, and stretching and pulling down the bags which had formed beneath them. When he did this Dagmar would glance disapprovingly, screwing up her face and slowly moving her head as if to chide him for the unclean habit. Despite his daughter's attempts to prevent the habit, he persisted in using his handkerchief in this way, but Dagmar never dared correct him aloud.

Herr Renot's witticisms, in fact most of what he said, was unpredictable, delivered in a spontaneous fashion with little apparent forethought. Everything about him was immersed in embarrassment, and after a while at the table, the inclination to fix one's glance on the plate or on some other nearby object became a natural response, as soon as it was observed the facetious man was again about to hazard another opening gambit.

At least what he said had the virtue of the unexpected or the original, and avoided repetition; but on the other hand, he seemed quite insensitive to the embarrassment he aroused in both daughter and guest, but perhaps he was incapable of talking in any other fashion. He was so infected by his own high spirits and geniality that he never stopped to think how others might react, and when not making one of his flippant remarks, he would stare at Dagmar or me with an expectant gaze, or puff at his cigar, blowing out clouds of smoke, or look down in front of him introspectively, with a sad expression. He also had the habit of constantly opening and closing the front of his lips and wetting them with the tip of his tongue as soon as he removed the cigar from his mouth.

Frau Brüning's voice was an occasional and relieved interruption during the meal, for it temporarily broke the spell of Herr Renot's ascendancy over the little party and afforded an opportunity to forget the embarrassment occasioned by a previous remark. Frau Brüning's voice was so cracked that sometimes I found it difficult to follow her words. I was the only person who experienced this, and when the old lady directed a remark at me, I had to ask her to repeat herself. She was amused at my failing to understand her, and joked about this, saying that no doubt I understood all the "young girls."

At the end of the meal, Dagmar left a fair amount at the side of her plate, and despite her mother's insistence, she could not be prevailed upon to leave a clean plate.

"A bad eater," exclaimed Herr Renot in a jovial tone. "She's slimming. On a beauty diet,!" and he laughed at the joke.

"Oh *quatsch*, Papa," replied his daughter.

"She reads the fashion magazines. They have comic ideas for the girls of today," continued Herr Renot cheerfully. "She wants to be a beauty queen,!" and he chuckled again.

"Oh Papa, I've never wanted to be anything of the sort," replied Dagmar piling up the plates. "Besides, you've never even looked at those fashion magazines and so you don't understand them."

We all left the table and as Frau Renot and her daughter attended to the washing up, the rest of us settled into nearby easy chairs. Herr Renot began fiddling with an antiquated radio beneath which on the floor lay a confusion of wires and connector plugs and above which hung an aerial nailed half way round the walls of the room, and a diverse range of screeching, whistling and crackling sounds came from the set. Meanwhile, I was attempting to carry on a conversation with Frau Brüning above the crackling of the wireless, but at last Herr Renot switched off the set not seeming surprised at having failed to find a channel.

"Oh really, Papa," exclaimed Dagmar emerging from the kitchen and pushing her father aside, "you don't understand the radio."

After a moment the set was tuned into a concert programme. Herr Renot's face lit up with an expression of naïve pleasure.

"*Schönes* music,!" he exclaimed, and briskly moved his arm to and fro as if conducting an orchestra, before settling down in an armchair and re-lighting a cigar.

Half an hour later a tall slim girl who was introduced to me as Renata arrived at the flat.

"She's my girl friend," explained Dagmar in a confidential tone as the tall girl was curtsying and paying her compliments to others in the flat.

Renata was plain and ungainly, with long untidy hair, and her manner alternated between the domineering and subservient, and I was unattracted by her personality, since her body language indicated clearly that I was an unwelcome distraction between her and her confidante. It was agreed that the three of us visit the East Berlin Zoo in Friedrichsfelde. Dagmar insisted I bring my camera, and after leaving the house we travelled by S-Bahn to Stalin Allee and from there by bus to the Tierpark Friedrichsfelde.

The weather continued warm and great numbers of people swarmed towards the zoo's entrance with its impressive stone gates and palatial Schloss nearby. We pushed our way through the turnstiles coming onto a broad gravel pathway before which lay a spacious garden handsomely laid out in classical style, with fountains, statuettes of goddesses and cherubs, gigantic stone urns on pedestals in which were grown rare or colourful plants, and well kept lawns. We descended a flight of steps and strolled along a broad path dissecting the two halves of the garden. But today it was no longer the garden of Eden of a privileged few. Hundreds strolled along its network of paths, and most prominently, couples speaking a foreign tongue, sometimes with Mongolian features, and groups of Russian soldiers and thickly-dressed children in colourful traditional attire.

On reaching the far end of the garden we came into the park proper. Dagmar held her arm loosely through mine whilst Renata walked gawkily alongside her friend, seemingly unperturbed by the romantic involvement of her friend. Common civility obliged me to engage Renata in conversation, but she was not to be drawn, and her giggling response to my remarks was an irritation.

The Tierpark was impressive in its acreage and far larger than its counterpart in West Berlin, and the ruminants were kept in large enclosures similar to their natural habitat. When we came to some ponies in an enclosure standing serenely against their wire fence, Dagmar stroked their heads affectionately, exclaiming, "How sweet! How sweet they are,!" and when some fawns approached to receive her affection, she rubbed their noses, and laughing, allowed them to lick her hand. I was overwhelmed by the sweetness of her nature, and all the more regretted the restraining presence of a third person in this romantic environment.

When our feet were tired we drank a cordial and ate frankfurters with potato salad, and as we relaxed in the open air restaurant, I learned that Renata was a primary school teacher earning 600 marks a month, whilst Dagmar was content with her lower salary of 400 marks. When the three of us returned to Treptow daylight was already waning, and when we left Treptower station and strolled down Puschkin Allee, I wondered when Renata would make her excuses and depart, but she showed little inclination of understanding the special needs of a romantic friendship. In the warmth of the fragrant evening, I longed to be alone with the sweetest creature.

We came to a small piece of public garden at the junction of Puschkin Allee and Am Treptower, and sat down on a seat, and before us lay grass and neat flower beds, and we laughed and chatted for half an hour or so, when to my relief, Renata rose with the excuse she had exercise books to correct, and had to rise early the following morning. At last Dagmar and I were alone. We spoke softly, and I stroked her neck and held her side, and soon we were enclasped in a firm embrace.

"This is the first time we've really been together today," I said.

"Have you only been waiting for this moment,?" repled Dagmar flirtatiously.

"I could never tire of your company," I returned embracing her shoulder and kissing her forehead.

"How do you like my family.?" She enquired.

"I like them. Your mother's very kind.

"Papa's getting old."

Why does she have to mention her father again,? I asked myself – always explaining him!

"How old is he,?" I asked.

"Sixty-four – an old man," she replied. "He belongs to a different world."

Dagmar took hold of the lapels of my coat and pulling me closer, she kissed my lips. We sat and cuddled for a while, and after an hour, we rose and returned to the flat at number sixteen.

There we met Franz and Gisela who had been in the country. All the family, except for Frau Brüning, were settled in comfy chairs in the sitting room drinking coffee and eating cakes and open sandwiches. Frau Renot made a place for Dagmar and me on the sofa and hurriedly left the room to fetch more plates and cups.

Franz was a handsome slimly built boy with fair hair and a quiet manner. As we entered the room he was talking with Herr Renot, the latter smoking a cigar and brushing off dropped ash from his lapels. Gisela was shorter than her sister but with a larger bone structure, with dark permed hair and blue eyes. She hadn't the gentle poise and slow rhythmical movements of Dagmar, but instead, was more vivacious and energetic. Both had pure white skin, but otherwise had a contrasting beauty, but it was clear that Gisela was the stronger and healthier of the two.

I glanced at old man Renot and wondered how it was possible that such an unprepossessing man could have sired two such beautiful daughters. There seemed to be little resemblance between the father and his children but as I studied their features, I perceived that the setting of Dagmar's eyes had a similarity to those of her father – but then, I mused without the intention of disrespect, that surely it was sacrilege to compare the beauty of those two girls with the features of that unseemly old man.

Frau Renot entered again with cups and plates, and Dagmar and I began to eat, settling into the *gemütlich* atmosphere of the circle. Gisela looked at me with her smiling wide open eyes, reflecting health and energy, with an expression of curiosity which on the one hand seemed to reveal an intense interest in this new boy friend of her sister and what it might portend; and on the other, a curiosity in this strange foreigner who had invaded the family circle in such unusual circumstances.

Franz turned and spoke to me in a confidential tone, as the only other young man in the room, expressing a friendly curiosity. I was surprised to learn he was studying at the Technical University in West Berlin. He said he liked the facilities of the university but was not entirely happy studying there as special circumstances created unpleasant difficulties for him and a doubting conscience. He was quite open, as if entrusting me as a confidant, but just as I was about to probe into what these "unpleasant difficulties" might be, we were interrupted by Frau Renot, and a sudden change of conversation. Frau Renot wanted us to speak together as one friendly group and was jealous that several of the men should withdraw for a tête-à-tête, and frustratingly, that evening I did not have another opportunity of speaking with Franz alone.

After the cups and plates had been cleared away, Frau Renot drew a board and box from the glass-fronted cabinet, and to my dismay, suggested eagerly we play snakes and ladders. This was heartily endorsed by Herr Renot, and in his high spirits he made some flippant remark about the "excitement" of parlour games dependent on chance, and as there was no protest from any of the company present, we rose from our chairs. Whilst Herr and Frau Renot laid out the board and counters, we younger members stretched and yawned, moving aimlessly round the sides of the room as if looking for an invisible exit.

Dagmar picked up the black box containing my electric shaver which was lying on the sideboard. She opened the lid and peeped in, at first almost surreptitiously.

"Oh Mamma, look at this," she exclaimed in delight. "Isn't it chic! I've never seen anything like it," she added stroking the lining of the box.

We sat down at the table and the game commenced but none of us followed the proceedings with keenness or full concentration, and it seemed merely used as an excuse to maintain the *gemütlich* family circle. Herr Renot was silent awhile and looked at the board as he constantly opened and closed his lips, wetting them with the tip of his tongue. He looked thoughtful, wearing a sad expression, and his mind was probably on things which were far removed from the game.

Frau Renot began to enquire about England and the Queen, fascinated by the phenomenon of the monarchy, questioning me with wide open eyes – with almost mystical wonder.

"Do you think the Queen is beautiful?"

"Oh really Mamma, what a stupid question," said Dagmar. "Of course he thinks the queen is beautiful."

"And does she live in the centre of London – in a great palace like *Sans Souci* in Potsdam,?" asked Frau Renot.

"She lives in the centre, yes," I replied, "in a palace, but not like *Sans Souci*."

"And is she loved by the people?"

"She is very popular."

"I know she wears a beautiful red uniform and long red cloak, and rides a white horse, surrounded by many soldiers all in scarlet."

I glanced at Frau Renot taken aback by this fairy tale description.

"Oh Mamma, she doesn't always wear uniform," exclaimed Dagmar shaking and throwing down her dice onto the table. "Mamma once saw a newsreel of the queen in the West sector," explained Dagmar turning to me.

"That must have been Trooping the Colour," I replied. "It's only once a year. Do you read about the Queen in the East German papers,?" I enquired turning to Herr Renot.

"Almost nothing," replied the old man shaking his head. "For the marriage of your Princess Margaret to Mr. Jones earlier this year, perhaps five lines in the East German papers."

I was surprised by the quaintly old fashioned ideas of Frau Renot, and thought that perhaps her conception of the British monarchy was a romanticised picture of the German Imperial system of the Second Reich, as remembered during her childhood, and I asked if she had ever seen the last Kaiser during one of the many parades which had once been held in the city.

"No, I never saw him," she replied in a tone of regret. "The Kaiser abdicated when I was still a schoolgirl."

"Who wants a Kaiser, anyway,?" exclaimed Dagmar with annoyance. "That's such a stupid idea."

Herr Renot rose from the table, saying he was retiring, looking ill and fatigued, and after another half hour the little party broke up for bed.

"It's long past Granny's bedtime and we've quite forgotten her," exclaimed Frau Renot startled by the time. "Dagmar, you must hurry."

I glanced enquiringly at Dagmar.

"I have to help Granny undress and then lift her legs onto the bed," explained Dagmar.

"And Dagmar," said Frau Renot, "give Granny three of those tablets as she slept so badly last night. And see she doesn't keep you awake again. It's so unfortunate for Dagmar, but there's nothing we can do about it," confided Frau Renot to me. "We only have one bed across the road, and she has to share it with Granny."

Chapter 18

The following morning I was awoken by the violent crashing of dustbins and banging of lids in the courtyard outside. This was followed – as had happened the previous day – by the scraping of heavy containers on the concrete surface of the yard. The tenants of this block must have a great deal to throw away, I reflected, but I was soon to learn that the early morning emptying of dustbins with all the unpleasantness of its attendant noise was here as much an accepted part of daily life as is the rattle of the milk deliverer's round in England.

Dagmar arrived at her flat at nine-thirty that morning and I escorted her to Treptower station where she took the train to work. She held my arm as we walked together, and with the other hand she carried the floppy raffia basket which I had not seen since our first encounter in the little Art Shop in Stalin Allee. As we progressed along Graetz Strasse we were acknowledged by several trades people and it was clear that her beauty would attract almost any passer-by.

As we turned the corner of Puschkin Allee, she glanced reprovingly at my coat, brushing off invisible specks of dust from the lapels.

"What's the matter,?" I asked.

"Do you like this coat,?" she only returned.

"I like cavalry twill," I responded defensively.

"I don't like it," she said screwing up her nose. "It's too military."

"But it's not a military coat."

"I think you should buy a new one," she said with good-humoured determination.

Little did I suspect that this brief interlocution was the prologue to a minor drama with disastrous consequences.

As we passed the barrack blocks again, I noted a long red banner hanging across the nearer building proclaiming in white letters, DOWN WITH MIILITARISM,! and across the next building was another announcing, SOCIALISM FOR PEACE AND FREEDOM! The windows of the ground floor of the near building which was divided from the street by high railings were open, and through the dark recesses could be espied the faint outline of figures moving to and fro and a metallic clattering.

"What goes on in there,?" I enquired suspiciously.

"I don't know – it's none of our business," replied Dagmar evasively.

Through another window I saw small arms being piled one on top of another.

"They're dismantling and cleaning rifles," I remarked.

"I told you, it's a police headquarters," said Dagmar. "We're not supposed to look. No one ever does."

On arriving at the station we agreed to meet at her new workplace shortly before it closed at 7.0 p.m., and that meanwhile I should obtain tickets for the opera.

Later that morning I sat hunched up in the front seat of a small mini as it drove at breakneck speed down the broad endlessly long main street of Park Köpenicker Landstrasse towards the outlying districts of East Berlin. There were few cars, but many lorries and trams made the street a busy highway. It was flanked by apartment blocks and the stores and pavements were crowded, and sometimes we passed bomb sites and piles of rubble and empty shells of buildings which must have looked much as they did following the night of their destruction, and everything had a dusty grimy appearance of dilapidation and decay.

Franz rushed the traffic lights, speeding down the centre of the roadway, over tram lines between the narrow strips of pavement on which crowds waited for transport. His recklessness led me to believe he was attempting to escape some unidentifiable ill – and to escape quickly.

The little East German mini already bore evidence of the temperament of its owner with dents and scratches, and it shook and rattled , and the dashboard was so lop-sided it looked as if it might drop to the floor where there already lay screws and an assortment of tools.

Gisela sat at the back, occasionally leaning forward her chin between us to speak, and as the small wheels of the ill-sprung car bumped over the cobble stones she must have been the most uncomfortable of the three, for the back seat was strewn with rubbish and pieces of carpenters' wood.

"You're a fast driver," I shouted at Franz in the hope he would slow down.

"I've been playing about with her for months – changing parts, and buying accessories in the West sector," he responded reading a different interpretation in my words.

"That must cost you a packet," I said.

"It does, but the original car is not so good. You can see what the body is like for yourself."

"I'm surprised you don't refurbish the inside," I remarked.

"I want her to be inconspicuous," said Franz, and he stopped himself suddenly.

I glanced enquiringly but noticed he apparently had no intention of explaining more.

"You see," he continued after a pause, "I, and that is, my family, are an anomaly in this new society of ours. We're some of the few still left who don't exactly fit into the new order of things. In a way we're an embarrassment to the system. But we still go on living as best we can. Of course we face hindrances and lots of red tape, but apart from that, we live contentedly enough. But we don't know when it may all end, and somehow, I don't think it can last much longer. And so that's why I like to enjoy myself while I can – a fast car and fast driving."

I said nothing in answer to this confessional monologue, but became curious as to the circumstances of his background. What made his family so special?

We were driving to the Müggel See for an excursion, where we intended to swim in the great lake, and dine at a restaurant before strolling in the nearby forest. Gisela was on holiday for three more days, and it seemed as if Franz led a relatively free life independent of the constraining limits which bound many of his contemporaries in the East.

Besides this, it was not for another week or so when he returned to the university.

At last we left the Park Köpenicker Landstrasse and its continuation, and drove some kilometres down another road in a south easterly direction. The buildings were smaller and the streets less crowded and we caught a glimpse of the wide expanse of the river Spree as we passed a stretch of parkland, and then to another built-up area before reaching a leafy woodland, with oak maple, plane, lime and chestnut, raising their height to the blue sky. I remarked on the beauty of the surroundings.

"This is the Köllnische heath," said Gisela from the back of the car.

"Are we nearly there,?" I enquired.

"About another six kilometres," replied Franz.

"It's difficult to imagine Berlin's so large," I said.

We passed through a small town, crossed a broad expanse of water and drove down Müggelheimer Strasse through the suburb of Köpenick. The road continued in a straight line, and we left the town behind and drove into the forest.

Finally we came to the end of a pot-holed lane, and the trees gave way to reveal a vast expanse of water. The car stopped and we climbed out. We stretched our limbs and walked forward on the dry wiry tufts of grass and onto the soft powdery yellow sand which we kicked with our feet and down to the water's edge. The expanse of the blue lake reached to the far horizon and apart from the three of us no one was to be seen, and a small tug pulling a barge was crossing the lake in the distance. There was not a sound to be heard other than the lapping of the water on the shore and a gentle murmur of the wind in the trees. We filled our lungs with the scent of the forest and strolled along the lake side.

"It's three kilometres to the other side, and about five across," explained Franz. "This is the Great Müggel See – the most expansive lake in East Berlin. Standing here and forgetting from where we've come, we might be a hundred kilometres from the city."

"We could be in Mecklenburg," said Gisela and she unzipped the hold-all and we took our bathing clothes and went into the woods to change.

On re-emerging we ran down to the shore and dived into the water, and some minutes later, we lay on our towels, drying on the soft sand, before dressing and anticipating the satisfaction of our hunger.

"We go to a restaurant by the Little Müggel See," exclaimed Franz. "There's no straight route but the diversion is pleasant. We pass through some attractive villages."

After a drive of some kilometres, we drove down a narrow lane to an open clearing in the trees where we parked the car and got out, reaching an open air restaurant along the embankment of a small lake. We took our seats and looked at the menu. A little way down the shore a pleasure launch had just docked by a jetty, and a merry holiday group left the boat whilst others waited to board her. Nearby was a picturesque lock where children played in canoes and rowing boats, and others on the opposite shore sat quietly angling, and from the direction of the Spree came a small yacht moving steadily across the water. How peaceful was the environment and what a far cry from the East sector I already knew!

When the waiter came for our order we were again awoken to a sense of reality.

"Passes, please,!" were his words of welcome.

And so even here, far from the city, officialdom still reigned. As Franz took out his pass he looked across at me with an expression of concern as if to say, "I hope you've got some excuse ready – I can't help you now." The waiter glanced at the passes of Franz and Gisela, and then I handed him my blue passport which I opened to reveal the transit visa, and I purposely withdrew the other visa which was an entry permit into the East sector. This latter was a new document, recently issued in a glare of publicity, which might have attracted special attention with unfavourable results – for it was already out of date.

The waiter glanced at the DDR stamp and nodded affirmatively, returning the pass. For the second time I had succeeded in using this document to bluff my way through East German officialdom, although on the first occasion – a long while ago in Stalin Allee – I remembered that the outcome of the bluff had been to little good purpose. That was the occasion when I had bought the biscuits with Martin.

The lunch was not up to expectations: tough over-cooked beef, watery Sauerkraut and an ample portion of potatoes. Gisela and I washed this down with a couple of glasses of sweet Malzbier, whilst Franz insisted on taking a cordial.

An hour later, we were lazily strolling through the forest, and the sun shone from the blue sky onto the yellow sand and patches of green grass and clusters of heather and gorse. Franz and I walked on ahead and Gisela lagged behind, now stopping to pick berries, or to investigate some mysterious rustling which came from a bird or other creature in the undergrowth.

Franz spoke cautiously but was willing to confide his thoughts when I began to probe behind his awkward circumstances. He had one more term at the university, and I remarked it was fortunate that East Germans were permitted to study in West Berlin.

"That depends," said Franz, and then, as if in a sudden change of mood, he added quickly, "There's not enough room in the East German

Humboldt University for all students, and so they have to study in the West."

"I would have thought the East German authorities would be afraid of their nationals becoming 'contaminated' by the West."

"They don't allow anyone to study in West Berlin. But the East German government doesn't lose anything financially by the arrangement because the main burden of cost is born by West Berlin."

He said he was studying to be a civil engineer and I remarked there was a great demand for such skills in West Germany

"That would be difficult at present – or at any time in the near future," he responded. "Someday, I should like to go over to the West, but not now. I'm not even in a position to contemplate it."

"As a civil engineer you'd have greater scope for your talents."

"I know that from my studies," he replied. "Modern methods and techniques, up-to-date design – everything's different in the West."

"Then what's the difficulty?"

"If I felt I had a free choice in the matter, I'd go tomorrow, but there're others I have to consider. Many of us studying in the West are not free. We study there on conditions laid down by the state. If we don't stand by those conditions, then our grants could be withdrawn and our education brought to an end."

"What kind of conditions?"

"We have to make propaganda – just by talking with Western students between lectures. Every day we must talk about the People's 'Paradise' of the DDR; defend Ulbricht; propagate some new policy pursued by the Soviets, or attack the 'Imperialist' powers in the West."

I laughed.

"And do these West Berlin students whom you buttonhole in this way listen?"

"Oh, they listen – they have to. We only speak to them when we're crowded together, in a lecture hall or across a table in the refectory. Of course, they laugh at us, but our aim is to get them into an argument."

"And do you succeed?"

"Sometimes. They prefer to smile and take no notice, or put a finger to their heads."

"But I don't understand how such blackmailing for propaganda can be made to work," I exclaimed at the seeming absurdity. "Who guarantees you make this propaganda, and if you make it, who can judge you're doing it correctly?"

"That's the simplest aspect. West Berlin is full of Stasi agents, and perhaps the Technical and Free Universities are ridden with more and cleverer agents than anywhere else in Berlin. Yes, we East Germans are watched over in the West sectors. If we fail to carry out instructions correctly then we learn soon enough. Sometimes we're summoned to an office in East Berlin and given a pep talk, or if we've displeased the authorities, we're met by threats."

"But not all East German students who attend the West Berlin universities can be blackmailed, surely?"

"Not all. Only some."

"How are these unlucky few selected?"

"Firstly, naturally, come the real Communists – those who've been sold to the movement. The Pioneers and members of the FDJ, the Free German Youth movement. They're out for promotion and advancement, and doubtless a number in the West Berlin universities are *agents provocateurs* disguised as politically apathetic, or even as anti-Communists. They're the most lethal – the people we East Berliners fear most."

"That's frightening."

"We East Berlin students cannot for a moment feel safe in the West. We dare not say anything we really think. We cannot even drink for fear of letting loose our tongues."

"And so political conviction isn't always a priority when you're picked for this work?"

"Not at all. You see, there are so few people in East Germany who are Communists by conviction. We Germans have experienced too much during the past thirty years. We're too cynical to be sold political ideology. That's why the DDR isn't very particular about the convictions of its servants. It just gives orders and they have to be obeyed all down the line. Perhaps that's because the DDR isn't even a real state – only an artificial creation, in reality, a satellite."

"That seems logical enough for entrusting authority to those willing to take it. But forcing people to make propaganda about things which are alien to their sympathies still seems absurd. How are such people chosen – these other students in the West Berlin universities?"

"If the state thinks it can hold a big enough threat over someone, then he's chosen on those grounds."

"Such as?"

"I've told you, James, that our family is an anomaly in this new society of ours," began Franz confidentially. "You see, my father happens to be one of those 'highly undesirable' and 'anti-social beings' known as a capitalist. That is, he owns his own business. It's only a small business, but he employs two or three old hands, and so he's a 'capitalist.'"

"What kind of work is that?"

"He's a carpenter – does general work, makes cabinets and carries out repairs. It's one of those things that's difficult to collectivise. That's why he's still independent. There aren't many trades today where you can still carry on independently, employing a couple of old hands."

"How does your father manage with the state system?"

"With difficulty. He has to deal with an impossible number of forms, account for every pfennig of income and expenditure, and for every piece of material he uses. But he's clever and so he gets along. He even makes a lot of money."

"Haven't you thought of taking over the family business?"

"Me? Never! My father spends all his time playing a wily game of cat and mouse. He enjoys it – but it's not for me. And in the end it's going to be a losing game. And as for his employees, he has to pay them less than they could get under any employment by the state. So he only employs the over-sixties – no one else is interested."

"That must make it difficult."

"It'd be impossible to get young men and train them as apprentices."

"So the business is contracting."

"Fifteen years ago my father had a flourishing builders' decorating business – something which had been passed down for several generations. When the Soviets took over in 1945 all the workers were taken away and employed by a state concern, and so the business collapsed. Then he managed to start a carpenter's business. At first the business made a loss, and more workers were taken away, but the concern has been pretty steady over the past ten years. Of course the state could shut down the business tomorrow if it wished, but at the moment they choose to 'tolerate' it."

"Why doesn't he go over to the West?"

"He's an old man. He wouldn't find employment. At present he has somewhere to live and makes enough money to live comfortably. And so because of those circumstances you can see how the state can afford to regard us as 'reliable' but expendable citizens."

"It's almost macabre. The state holds a threat over your education and your family in the event of your fleeing to the West."

"I was fortunate in getting into the University. The authorities are careful in their selection procedures. Often the sons of we capitalists are precluded altogether from higher education in favour of the sons of the proletariat. But being lower-middle class the authorities judged us nearer the proletariat than the 'bosses, ' and so I scraped through under the net, as it were. Now you can understand how I and many other young people here in East Germany are instruments of the state machine," exclaimed Franz vehemently. "Against our will, we're forced to be efficient instruments of this hated regime. It's something loathsome – it revolts our instinct – but what can we do? Either we obey or our education will be stopped. We'd then be forced into menial employment."

"Have you seen such threats carried out?"

"Certainly! When I was at school, a group of us were picked out – we were sons of professional men, or as I was, sons of that class known as the 'exploiters of the workers,' and we were ordered to undergo the ceremony of consecration required by the Free German Youth. There were eleven of us. Three refused to submit themselves to the ceremony. The rest of us tried to persuade them – we said they were stupid, that their opportunities would be removed – but they were obdurate. They insisted blindly on their stupid principles. Those three were refused entry to High School. Now one of them is a manual worker in a factory. The two others eventually fled to the West. Their families were deprived of privileges until they found it unprofitable to carry on work. They shortly followed their sons to the West."

"It's terrible!"

"All of us living in the DDR hate the regime. Even the consecrated Communists join the party out of cynicism at the fate of Germany. The Communists by conviction in our country are a miniscule minority. The DDR's nothing more than a zombie state created and manipulated by the Soviet Kommandatura."

Gisela came up to us from behind, handing us each a handful of berries, and reproaching us for wasting time talking politics in such a heavenly environment. She began to engage us in light conversation and soon we forgot the problems and worries with which Franz was beset.

After a short while we reached the bank of a small lake. We strolled along the grassy verge and in the still water we saw the reflections of the tall leafy trees and the blue sky. We were awed by the calm beauty of the scene and dared not speak for fear of disturbing the blissful environment. As we approached a tongue of land jutting into the lake we heard a faint splashing from the other side. We strode through some ferns and up a mossy bank between the slim trunks of pines, and on reaching the bank at the other side, we came to an elderly angler by the water's edge, lifting his rod at the end of which was a struggling pike.

The three of us were surprised at suddenly meeting with another human creature so deep in the forest. Gisela gave a shout of delight at seeing the fisherman and with curious interest, moved towards him to see him bring in the catch. With a precocious gesture, she clapped her hands and went over to the old man, congratulating him on his success. He wore a pair of brown boots, leather knickerbockers, a grey jacket and waistcoat and a battered broad-brimmed hat, and was unshaven and smoked a white clay pipe. On engaging him in conversation, we learned he disliked the great city and had not been there for many a year. We asked where he lived.

"Back there," he replied pointing behind him, and through some trees not far from the lakeside stood an old timber and plaster house with a thatched roof and a pile of sawn logs nearby. Round the area was a low wicker fence and a little gate.

"It's sweet," exclaimed Gisela, "like the gingerbread house in Hänsel und Gretel."

I picked up a thick book which lay beside the fishing tackle and quickly glanced through it. The second volume of Schopenhauer's *The World As Will and Idea*!

"It's isolated here," exclaimed Franz.

"Quite alone," replied the old man contentedly. "Not another being to worry about."

"And don't you feel the need for company,?" asked Gisela.

"Why should I,?" responded the old man. "For happiness, all you need is solitude and nature. I'm poor but happy. The state deprived me of much I once had, but they can't take any more. It's a bad fate which faces the young people. But they can't touch me again. They got me into the army in 1914, but never again," he said chuckling, pointing to a crippled leg.

Chapter 19

That evening I arrived at Dagmar's workplace, a large art shop in Friedrich Strasse, some minutes before seven o'clock. I had returned from the country late that afternoon and sped to the West sector to purchase tickets for the opera and East Germany currency at the Zoo station.

In the shop I asked for Fräulein Renot and was directed to the third floor. The shop was quiet and sepulchral, only a few customers browsing in the long showrooms where paintings and other works were tastefully displayed on the walls.   On the second floor were glass showcases containing oriental ornaments, and decorative rugs displayed like tapestries. The shop had the spacious proportions of a gallery, and there were little notices affixed to the stands saying, *Please do not touch*!

I climbed the shallow steps of the broad staircase and reached the third floor. Walking along a light grey strip of carpet in a passageway with parquet flooring and polished panelled walls I reached she showroom. Dagmar sat at a desk by the entrance. She glanced up from her book, rising to greet me, and as no one else was present except for an old man who had his back to us examining a print, we kissed, and

Dagmar directed me to the adjoining hallway which was the start of the exhibition. It was large and empty. The third floor of this huge luxurious art shop was the quietest and least busy of them all. How different was this place from the crowded little shop where we had first met in Stalin Allee.

"Have you been busy,?" I asked.

"Not really," she replied.

"This morning I sold a couple of drawings to a mysterious looking man from a Balkan embassy – I think he was Rumanian."

I laughed.

"Are you ever busy here?"

"Oh yes, we're very busy when we have a new exhibition," said Dagmar defensively. "I must take down all the pictures of the old exhibition and then hang all the pictures of the new. It's hard work, especially deciding where they can best be hung."

"This shop isn't capitalist owned," I said glancing around. "It's too impressive for that. I suppose it's an H.O. concern."

"No," replied Dagmar, and then screwing up her nose and speaking in an undertone, she added, "actually, it's the official art shop of the Communist party. – And now I must change into my new dress. Gisela made it for me, and I'll be wearing it for the first time – just for you. Wait here and look at the cartoons whilst I get ready," and she handed me a little red folder on the cartoons of the Dane Herluf Bidstrup.

On her return several minutes later she was transformed into a beautiful princess, and on leaving the shop, we walked down the broad crowded street, passed pavement cafés where sat groups of foreign students of Eastern and African appearance, to Friedrich Strasse station where we took the train to the West sectors.

As soon as we reached the West I sensed a feeling of escape from an oppressive environment – for this was a different world – and two days alone was sufficient to engender the claustrophobia of a totalitarian regime. No need here to talk in an undertone or to censor one's spoken thoughts. As soon as the train passed within view of the Tiergarten Dagmar became spontaneous and high-spirited.

We left the train at Zoo station, making our way to the City Opera house in Kant Strasse. As we crossed Hardenburg Strasse I pointed out the completed Underground station which was still under construction when we last passed the site.

The foyer was crowded as we pushed our way towards the cloak stands, and there was a crush of hundreds dressed in their finest evening attire, the women in long gowns and fur wraps or mohair stoles, the men in dark suits or dinner jackets. I was about to hire a pair of opera glasses from the cloak room attendant when Dagmar nudged me taking out a small pair of mother of pearl opera glasses from the little handbag she carried. We went towards the auditorium, and I bought a souvenir programme from an usherette.

The last five-minute bells sounded throughout the theatre, as we made our way towards our seats in the stalls, passing by those of many nationalities speaking the tongue of their own countries. The lights dimmed and we were touched by a feeling of anticipation. A spotlight turned onto the conductor's rostrum, and a moment later, Robert Wolf, took his stand and bowed, to a great applause. The evening had begun. The orchestra struck up, and the curtain rose on Ravel's lyrical ballet, *La Valse*, starring Konstanze Vernon and Wolfgang Leistner.

In the first interval we took refreshments in the foyer, and on returning to the auditorium, the lights went down and entranced we watched a performance of Gassmann and Sala's *Paeon*. In the second interval we again strolled through the theatre, and as we passed by the crush of affluent patrons, I knew that the fair East Berlinerin was as attractive and as well-dressed as any other girl in the theatre that night. In her appearance and demeanour there was nothing to differentiate her from any West Berlinerin, and nothing could have betrayed the secret of her status other than the little identity pass concealed in her bag. It was an unfair fate which had destined her for a different world from the majority then present in the theatre that evening. After the second interval, the third ballet proved to be the climax of the evening: Prokofiev's *Romeo and Juliet*, starring Yvette Chauvire, the Prima ballerina of the Grand Opera of Paris.

Our spirits lifted, we left the theatre, and passing by the ruin of the Kaiser Wilhelm Memorial Church, with the recently erected, and irreverently nicknamed, "Lipstick" and "Powderbox", representing a new church tower and prayer hall, we strolled down Budapester Strasse towards the Tiergarten. There was a clear sky and the streets of West Berlin vibrated with life as theatre goers and other pleasure seekers strolled along the wide avenues of the city or sought out the restaurants and cafés of their choice.

"How beautiful is the city by night," exclaimed Dagmar as she clung tightly onto my arm and we walked slowly in even step. "I think modern West Berlin must be more beautiful by night than it could ever have been in earlier times."

"Perhaps because the world's greatest architects have helped rebuild the new Berlin," I answered.

"There's so much space and light," continued Dagmar. "The new buildings are simple and unassuming – so different from the heavy apartment blocks with their grotesque decoration and pomposity."

"Those old buildings have their own kind of charm."

"But the buildings of the new Berlin express a freer spirit. They soar towards the sky, not glaring in a censorious fashion."

Dagmar began humming a tune from the Prokofiev ballet, and I whistled the melody from the dance at the Capulet's ball.

"Don't you feel sometimes, as you're watching in the theatre, you'd like to follow the movements of the dancers,?" exclaimed Dagmar. "I should love to live in this part of Berlin," she continued indicating the buildings of the Hansa quarter.

"Perhaps one day you will," I replied.

"No, I shall never live here – never in the West," said Dagmar sadly.

"Why do you say that?"

"Circumstances will force me to remain in the East."

"I think you're being pessimistic."

"You don't understand the threats held over us."

"I had a long talk with Franz this afternoon when we were in the country."

"Oh, he's been talking to you, has he,?" said Dagmar derisively.

"He told me a lot about himself."

"So he's been telling you his life story – about the threats which hang over his education and his family. It's nothing really!"

"Why do you say that,?" I said stopping in my tracks.

At first she made no reply, just tugged tighter onto my arm and walked stiffly for a few metres and pursed her lips. Either she was temporarily put out by my question or was intentionally avoiding an answer. I was about to repeat the question in a tone of cheery good humour when she herself broke the silence.

"Franz is a coward," she said discreetly screwing up her nose, "and so is his family. If he wanted to, he could leave the East sector tomorrow. He could study in West Germany. He would easily get a grant."

"And what about his family?"

"Many people similar to his parents have gone to the West, and they've started anew and become prosperous too. His parents have money. It's just they don't want to be refugees for a few short weeks."

"I suppose there are lots of people like Franz and his family in the East," I said.

"His father's clever. I think he could manage successfully anywhere."

"Perhaps he's just one of those people who wants something for nothing. You can't have freedom without the effort to grab it."

"That's it. And if they remain in the East, one day they'll lose everything anyway."

"Dagmar, you *must* leave Berlin," I burst out. She looked at me curiously. "If you remain in Berlin – in the East sector, it'll destroy you just as it has destroyed and is destroying thousands. East Berlin is a dead city – people don't live there, they just exist. One day I'll take you away from Berlin, and when we return here to visit, then we'll stay in a great and luxurious hotel – like that one there," I added pointing to a large glass and concrete structure in front of us.

"The Hilton!   Oh, that'd be wonderful," exclaimed Dagmar tightening her grip on my arm. "That'd be so sweet of you – it must be wonderful in there."

I laughed at Dagmar's outburst of naïve excitement.

"Where are we going,?" she asked at last.

"To the Tiergarten," I replied.

"Do we have to go there,?" she said but in a tone which didn't indicate the idea was so disagreeable after all. "It seems so far."

"If you feel you can dance, I'm sure you can walk," I replied.

"Yes, beautiful music gives me much energy," she said. "But why are we going to the Tiergarten?"

"Because it's such a beautiful night, with the clear sky and moon, and because all those twinkling stars want to cast their silvery light on the secret romance of lovers on such a night as this."

On reaching the quiet and isolation of the Tiergarten we became more intimate. Dagmar began to whistle another tune in a careless fashion and I kissed her neck and forehead.

"Nature is so pure here," she exclaimed aimlessly. "So wild – I love wild nature. Look at those bushes. They're so beautiful and excluded as if they had grown there naturally."

"Haven't they grown naturally,?" I asked.

"Not really – nothing in the Tiergarten has grown naturally," said Dagmar. "At the end of the War it was the scene of one of the last defensive battles against the invading Russian troops. All the trees and lawns were destroyed, and the land was pitted with gunfire and bomb craters. Many young soldiers sacrificed their lives here needlessly. And then for some years the Tiergarten was turned into allotments before it was restored again."

"And today it's the most peaceful part of the city centre."

"And in a way the most beautiful."

We strolled a long way onwards until we came to a secluded corner where we sat down on a seat to rest. In the distance behind small trees and thick bushes we saw the lights and heard the steady roar of traffic moving down the Street of the 17th June, and at the end of that street we could just see the Quadriga above the Brandenburg Gate.

"It's so restful here," exclaimed Dagmar leaning her head against my shoulder. "So relaxing to sit in these surroundings and watch the distant lights of the city and hear the surge of traffic."

I caressed her neck and soon we fell into a long and passionate embrace, and having unbuttoned and removed her coat, and embraced her torso, I began to kiss her delicate limbs, and knelt at her feet, and soon we had reached a state of ecstasy, and point of no return, and our only desire was to consummate our mutual affection. At last I lifted her in my arms and carried her to a mossy bank surrounded by thick and friendly flora which hid us from the view of the world. We were exposed to the moon and stars alone as with gentle and nimble fingers I bared her flesh, and she was hardly conscious as I released and cast aside each covering in turn, until I showered her body with a thousand eager kisses, and embracing my neck she writhed in orgasmic pleasure.

Chapter 20

We lay quite still, side by side, close together, in each others arms, our bodies only covered by her coat which lay across our thighs. Her head was supported by my arm which held her torso and my other caressed her thigh, as I gently now and then kissed the delicate features of her face. Her wide open eyes looked skyward with a dreamy expression. The perspiration from our skin ran into one stream as our naked bodies lay pressed together. We were enraptured by a feeling of blissful peace and harmony after the consummation of our love.

Through the undergrowth, beneath the stems of the bushes, we could see the lawn of the Tiergarten and beyond that a path, and at some distance away, the lights from the Street of the 17th of June. The outside world seemed far away as we lay amongst the foliage. Above us, the branch of a tree gave partial protection from the light of the open sky.

"How long have we been lying here,?" enquired Dagmar in a whisper passing her fingers gently through my hair.

"I don't know. I've put my watch away in a pocket," I replied struggling for it with difficulty.

"Sometime we must return," she said fatalistically.

"Yes, I suppose so, to the world where time dictates our fate," I sighed.

"To the world of hard realities and inexorable fate," she added sadly, " – to that fate which controls our lives and is beyond hope of change."

"Not that," I told her. "Why do you have to be so pessimistic in believing in the 'inevitability of fate'?"

"Just because I believe in it – I don't know why, but I do," she replied vaguely.

"I think it springs from the idealism of your national character," I mused, "the 'All or Nothing' attitude to life. If your ideas don't work out as you've first conceived them, then you lose hope. You have little understanding of the need for compromise. The English proverb, 'Half a loaf is better than none,' has little meaning for you because you seem to take it as an unacceptable sacrifice."

"Idealism means so much to us because ideas are the one thing which can never be taken away when all else is lost. You English have always been free. You can do what you want. You just change the world when and how you will. You've no need for idealism."

"It's not quite like that," I replied. "We English could do with a bit more idealism in our lives."

"Don't you think we're like a couple of forest elves lying here,?" said Dagmar changing her tone to express a happier mood.

"I think you're the Fairy Queen of the forest," I replied kissing her on the bridge of the nose, and as I squeezed her shoulders there came the sound of footsteps from the path beyond the bushes. We were startled and Dagmar involuntarily tightened her arms around my body.

"Keep quiet," I whispered. The footsteps came nearer – heavy even footsteps. "We won't be seen!"

"I'm so afraid," she said snatching at one of her garments and holding it over her breasts.

I rose from the coat on which we had been lying and crawled towards the stems of the bushes protecting us from the view of the park. Dagmar sat upright on her haunches, several garments clutched over her front. I peered through the undergrowth and then drew back.

"It's all right," I said. "It's only a policeman on the beat."

We sat upright and silent for some moments, and then the footsteps died away. I rose to my feet, and as I stood buttoning my shirt, in an unexpected gesture, Dagmar threw her arms around my buttocks pressing her breasts into my thighs.

"Promise you'll never say I've been a bad girl," she exclaimed looking into my eyes with a pleading gesture.

"Of course not – why should I,?" I replied consolingly.

"There are some things you may not be able to understand about me."

"Such as?"

"Things beyond my own making which control my life."

"Let's not get back to that," I said straightening my tie.

Dagmar let go her grasp and began to dress, and I pondered on the cause of her strange outburst. At first I explained her traumatic cry as stemming from a spasm of guilt following her compete surrender, but then I suspected it could be something deeper and more complex. What did she mean by her reference to a "fate" which controlled her life? Moments later she began whistling another tune. Again her mind had undergone a change of mood, and I felt it wiser not to probe into the possibly secret import of her words. Why risk spoiling the tranquil frame of mind which had returned?

We were cheerful as we left the park, and then she reverted to that topic which was eventually to lead to such a disastrous episode.

"Your coat is creased and dirty," she remarked with a wicked smile as we approached the Brandenburg Gate. "Not so smart and military as it was this morning," she added with irony.

"Then it was better we lay on my coat and not yours," I responded.

"Yes," she answered, "and I think we'll have to do something about it."

We took the S-Bahn from the Unter den Linden to Treptower Park, and as we strolled down Puschkin Allee I held my arm across her shoulder, and we hummed the waltz from the Ravel ballet.

"Are you good at running,?" she asked, her eyes twinkling with life and laughter.

"I think so," I replied.

"Do you think you can chase me,?" she asked flirtatiously.

"Try me!"

"Then catch me," she said, and she ran ahead as I let go her hand, and no one else was in the deserted street.

She trotted along the sandy sidewalk beneath the high branches of the avenue, affectedly swaying her hips from side to side. I trotted after her, feigning an inability to keep up, and now and again she stopped suddenly in her tracks, arching her shapely neck as an invitation for a kiss.

"See, you can't catch me," she exclaimed, her eyes twinkling with mischief.

She trotted into the little public garden which led to the corner of Am Treptower. Suddenly, I sped forward throwing up a cloud of sandy dust behind me, and clasped her waist between my arms. She gave a little cry as I spun her round, and pressing her to me, I showered a dozen kisses onto her neck and throat.

"Ach! You're such a terribly wild animal," she exclaimed laughing.

"Only you could awaken the wild animal in me," I returned. "Come - to the arbour," I added dragging her across the grass towards a bench which stood within a wooden shelter adjacent to where the great house stood.

"Where are we going,?" she replied startled.

"There – to the arbour," I said nodding towards the seat.

"I don't want to sit again," she said screwing up her nose.

"Not to sit," I returned.

"But if someone should see," she exclaimed.

"They won't," I replied. "We'll use discretion."

"Discretion! Oh, what's discretion,?" she said ironically. "Everyone uses discretion and still gets caught."

Again we surrendered to our passion as I pulled back her coat and kissed her shoulders. The little wooden shelter was a perfect refuge at this late hour of night.

Sometime later we sat flushed but quiet, silently watching whisps of cloud pass across the moon through the branches of the trees.

"Dagmar, I want to ask you a very serious question," I said at last with mock solemnity. "Do you now consider our relationship has reached a stage of intimacy?"

"Why, of course," she replied with a straight face, not knowing what I was driving at.

"I think our relationship has reached a stage of warm and personal intimacy," I continued. "And do you think our relationship is sincere?"

"Yes – I suppose so – but why do you ask?"

"I want to make a very important request," I said taking her hands into mine. "May I now address you as *du*?"

Dagmar laughed again.

"Naturally," she replied with laughing irony and pinching the end of my chin, "although it seems I must have been a terribly proud girl that you've dared not ask before."

BOOK V

A Spy In The Block

Love is nothing else but an insatiate thirst of enjoying a
greedily desired object.

Montaigne, *Essays*, Bk. iii, Ch. 5.

Chapter 21

Had my intuition been sharper, a premonition of at least one of the day's forthcoming events might have been gleaned quite early the following morning before I had dressed.

I had still not accustomed myself to the awkward washing arrangements meticulously prepared for me in the toilet-come-bathroom. A jug of plentiful hot water and soap had daily been laid out for me and my towel had been placed neatly by the washbowl. On this particular day, however, I found myself without the corresponding jug of cold water. I hesitated in momentary confusion over the wash stand, and then put on my dressing gown again and made for the kitchen.

In the hallway I met Gisela in her nightclothes coming out of the kitchen, and we exchanged greetings, and my silky bright-coloured gown caught her eye, and she took hold of it rubbing the fabric between her fingers.

"What a beautiful golden gown," she exclaimed in delight with an impish smile. "You look just like a king."

"That's too much of a compliment," I replied perplexed.

On entering the kitchen in the middle of the room I saw Papa Renot sitting solemnly in his pyjamas on an upright chair resting his feet in a large bowl of mustard water. Momentarily I was put out by the incongruity of the scene, and wondered whether it would have been more proper to have knocked before entering.

Herr Renot put things aright with a hearty, "*Guten morgen*, Herr Furner,!" showing all his teeth and giving a military salute. I returned the greetings. Frau Renot, who had been bathing her husband's legs with a flannel, rose from her knees and greeted me again that morning. Herr Renot sat with one hand on his knee whilst in the other he held a cigar which he was smoking even that early in the morning. Across the chair were a number of male articles of clothing neatly laid out.

He looked so comfortable sitting on his upright chair bathing his lordly feet in a bowl of mustard water, and seemed so much the centre of bustle and activity, that he instantly reminded me of some Royal personage patiently awaiting his courtiers to prepare him for the day, or a Knight who was about to undergo a ritual ceremony of ablutions in preparation for battle or some other great ordeal. As I was subsequently to learn later that morning, my guess was not so far off the mark.

I filled a jug with cold water, wondering what strange reason could have motivated Papa Renot to have arisen so early. Clearly there must have been some good explanation for his early rising, and when I returned to the washroom and closed the door behind me, I reflected that this was yet another little mystery added to those already perplexing my mind.

As it was a warm day I walked Dagmar to the station without my coat that morning.

"James, your coat is really too dirty to be worn," she said speaking in an ironically chiding tone. "You really should be ashamed of such a coat."

"It was sacrificed for a good use yesterday," I replied laughing at her cheek.

"And I've told mamma about your coat and she's going to clean it," continued Dagmar.

"I don't know how she can exactly clean it," I replied apprehensively. "It should be sent to a dry cleaners."

"And that could take eight weeks in the East sector," added Dagmar significantly.

That morning she had to visit her doctor for her twice weekly vitamin injections before going to work.

"Please mind the step," exclaimed the old lady cheerfully as I carefully wheeled her chair through the doorway into the courtyard. "Just here, against the wall by the kitchen window, so I can soak in the sun and speak to Mamma," she continued pointing her finger in the direction where the chair was to be placed.

I carefully adjusted the bath chair and Frau Brüning momentarily pulled up the rug covering her knees so that she could push down the safety brake of the conveyance.

"Many thanks, Herr Furner," said the old lady generously. "Here I'll be comfortable."

"*Bitte schön*! (Don't mention it)," I replied, and hovered by the conveyance not knowing what to do or say next.

I had seen Dagmar off at the station and had returned to Graetz Strasse number fifity-five (where the family spent most of the day) when Frau Renot had gleefully asked if I should like to wheel Granny into the courtyard and talk to her. I willingly assented to carry out the little errand. I was expected to stay with the family throughout the day, rather than wander off and find my own amusements, and I anticipated a dull time. In my awkwardness, I dreaded the hours ahead. How was it to be expected that I should entertain or be entertained by these elderly and middle aged people of East Berlin? Conversationally, it seemed as if we had little in common – and yet I couldn't leave these good people with the excuse of visiting a museum or gallery without betraying an attitude of ingratitude, as they had already half taken possession of me. I only longed for the day to pass quickly, when I should again go to the city centre and meet Dagmar at the art shop.

"I believe you took my granddaughter to the opera last night," said Frau Brüning smiling. "I hope you enjoyed yourselves."

"We saw three ballets – they were very good," I replied off-handedly.

"My granddaughter didn't get home till nearly two o'clock," added the old lady suggestively.

I blushed. She was trying to embarrass me again.

"Good morning, Frau Brüning," said an old man sitting on a bench against the wall of the building, some two or three metres away. He slowly removed the large peaked cap from his head of untidy hair and then replaced it again. He had been sitting silently on the seat with walking stick in hand.

"Good morning, Herr Schomberg. Another warm day," responded the old lady.

The old man sat in the shade of some stunted bushes dividing the courtyard from that of the next block of buildings. He wore old-fashioned gold framed spectacles, a collarless shirt fastened at the neck with a silver stud, a grey jacket, and patched trousers.

"This is an Englishman who's staying with us," said Frau Brüning. "He's after my granddaughter, Dagmar."

"He has good taste," replied the old man. He stretched forward his hand and just rose from his haunches as we exchanged greetings.

"He's the young man Dagmar's been writing to for the past year," explained Frau Brüning.

"A steady affair! Real love then," replied the old man facetiously. "And all the way from England!"

"He's studying in West Germany."

"And how do you like the 'fine life' in the East sector,?" exclaimed the old man ironically, turning to me. "Paradise, eh,?" he chuckled.

I made no answer to this statement inviting a compromising comment, but just then our attention was diverted by another person entering the courtyard from across the other side. An old man with a battered dark blue peaked cap, a pointed well-groomed beard and long blue jacket with brass buttons, shuffled towards us with a walking stick.

"Why, look Herr Schomberg," exclaimed Frau Brüning in a whisper leaning forward towards her companion, "it's Petty Officer Lufner – he's wearing his naval cap and it's not a Sunday."

Herr Schomberg leaned forward on his stick pointing his finger to his head as Frau Brüning spoke. When she had finished, he turned round to glance at the newcomer, grinning derisively. The old lady chuckled towards Herr Schomberg as if sharing a joke and he nodded affirmatively.

The newcomer shuffled towards the centre of the courtyard with slow short steps, looking towards the sky. The sun dazzled his eyes as the light lit up the proud weather beaten features. He was a tall thin figure but bent with age. On reaching the centre of the courtyard he stopped, and looked into the sky moving his head slightly from side to side as if trying to determine some un-resolvable problem. Then he took an old brass compass out of his pocket, looked at it, moved it round, and looked at it again. He slowly shook his head as if he saw a premonition of misfortune in what the compass read.

"We're moving due East," he announced at last in a firm authoritative tone. "A bad change from yesterday, North by North East," he said shaking his head. "It's no good omen we're moving East."

"You're right there," exclaimed Herr Schomberg.

"Petty Officer Lufner, why are you wearing your naval cap today,?" asked Frau Brüning.

"Because, my dear lady, of the fine weather," replied Lufner in a tone arrogantly defensive. "A fine day for watching out for the enemy."

Herr Schomberg glanced at me, and putting his finger to his head again, he nodded towards Lufner.

"We have an Englishman with us today, Petty Officer Lufner," said Frau Brüning.

"Captured,?" exclaimed Lufner drawing himself up to his full height. "Were you at the Battle of Jutland?" he enquired of me.

"That was before my time," I answered.

"I expect you were hardly out of the cradle then," he exclaimed looking me up and down.

"It was about twenty years before I was born," I replied.

"I was in the *Kriegsmarine* twenty-three years – till 1916 – but there was nothing like the Battle of Jutland. The German Navy was never defeated in that War."

"It never risked defeat," I thought, but said nothing.

"Today I'm retired – a Petty Officer – and things are going badly for the country," he said shaking his head. "I no longer see our Zeppelins – just the red banner flying from the masthead. Times will worsen yet!"

"And your gloomy prophesies won't help things," exclaimed Frau Brüning laughing at the old seaman.

"If the sun shines and I can wear my cap on a fine day, then I can keep up my spirits," replied Lufner seating himself on the other end of the bench from Herr Schomberg. "I content myself only with warning others. The ship is unsafe, but I'll gladly be the last to leave her. Don't take me seriously," he chortled after a pause in response to my expression of concern. "If I was treated seriously I'd be locked up by now. Only madmen are really safe in the New Germany!"

"We old ones shall remain on the ship till death divides us," said Schomberg. "We've lived too long within these grey stone walls to be driven out now – come what may!"

"Yes, Herr Schomberg is right," said Frau Brüning.

Lufner sat glancing at his feet, looking dejected and confused.

"How long have you lived in this flat, Frau Brüning,?" I enquired nodding towards the kitchen window.

"Fifty-eight years I've lived here," replied the old lady. "I've seen a lot since then: two world wars have come and gone since I've lived in these rooms."

"Good morning, Frau Brüning, good morning, Herr Schomberg,!" came the voice of an old woman who had just emerged from the doorway of the nearer building in the courtyard. She wore a black shawl across her shoulders and a cotton headscarf.

The greetings were acknowledged, and she was addressed as Frau Hartmann, but from the cursory reception she received and the awkward silence which fell over the company it was apparent her presence was hardly welcome. But the cool reception failed to dampen her spirits and she began to use a ready wit. She failed at first to notice Lufner, who was camouflaged by the bushes which hung over him as he sat shaded on the far end of the seat.

"Good morning, Herr *Kapitän*," exclaimed Frau Hartmann with irony. "I didn't see you hidden there."

"That's not my correct rank," replied Lufner taken aback by the slight he felt had been offered him.

"Why not promote yourself,?" exclaimed Frau Hartmann. "You've been a petty officer for more than forty years. That's long enough for anyone to hold one rank."

Lufner refused to extend his hand for the obligatory greeting.

"Then be off-hand if you choose," remarked Frau Hartmann lightly. "And who is this,?" she added extending her hand to me.

"Herr Furner, an Englishman," replied Frau Brüning. "He's courting my granddaughter, Dagmar."

"She's a pretty girl, Dagmar," said Frau Hartmann reflectively. "And so at last, after all this time, Dagmar's found herself a new admirer. That's good!"

I took an instant dislike to the old lady after this tasteless reference, and it seemed as if the rest of the company disliked her too. I shook hands and bowed stiffly, asking myself what this old woman could know about Dagmar's private life – persuaded that she had no right to know anything about her friendships.

"He's the romantic Englishman," said Frau Brüning laughing.

Frau Hartmann took her place on a second bench and I sat between Schomberg and Lufner.

"How long have you been in East Berlin,?" enquired Frau Hartmann.

"Four days."

"I don't expect he knows," interrupted Frau Brüning, and I detected an abrasive tone in her voice.

I felt Herr Schomberg nudge me in the side, and I sensed an uneasiness, and that Frau Hartmann was someone who should be treated with care. Clearly she was a busybody.

"Would you like to live in the DDR,?" asked the old woman cheerfully, and I took her meaning to be ironical.

"That's a loaded question," I chuckled.

"It's fine for young people but not for us old ones," she said. "For those who have courage to face the truth and learn to understand the system, it's a great world which lies ahead. But it takes time to perfect the good society. People don't understand that."

As our conversation progressed, I realised with a cold sensation running down my back, that Frau Hartmann was an ideological supporter of the regime. She had spoken with earnestness and with no intended irony. I said nothing and the others had already shut up like clams, and there followed a stubborn silence.

"Take my son, for example," she said sometime later. "The state has given him a car, food tickets to the best restaurants, and identity papers facilitating special privileges. He leads a life of security and affluence – but mind you, he's had to work for it. But without the new system his life would have been quite other than it is now."

"He belongs to the lucky minority," I remarked.

"He hasn't got to where he is now without a struggle," she responded as if offended by my reply. "Sacrifices have had to be made along the way. The state has to differentiate between the deserving and the undeserving."

"Herr Furner," came a voice from the kitchen window.

I looked up and saw Frau Renot.

"Papa would like to speak to you," she said with a gleeful expression.

With apprehension I rose from my seat and went over to the kitchen window wondering what on earth was now expected of me. I peered through the window into the darkness of the kitchen where I espied Papa Renot, his face lit up with a cheerful countenance, standing behind the shoulder of his good Frau. Even at that first momentary glance, I noticed he was dressed immaculately: a dark blue suit and clean shirt – and he even sported a tie.

"Herr Furner," he exclaimed brightly, *"Gehen wir mal spazieren* (We go for a walk)" and he displayed all his teeth when he pronounced the word *spazieren*. I must have shown no immediate reaction to this announcement for the words were expressed as an order rather than a request, and so he clarified, *"Wir werden jetzt miteinander einen Spaziergang machen!* (We – both of us – go for a walk)," and he gesticulated with his hand pointing from himself and then to me.

"Would you like to go for a walk with Papa,?" urged Frau Renot cheerfully.

"Why, of course," I replied smartly trying to appear as obliging as I could.

"We'll go alone. Beautiful weather,!" exclaimed Herr Renot joyfully throwing up his hands towards the kitchen ceiling as if towards the blue open sky.

I returned to the kitchen and we immediately left for our walk. We passed through the courtyard of the buildings and out into Graetz Strasse towards the direction of Treptower Park. So that's why he was up so early this morning, I reflected, so he could preen himself and put on his best attire before taking this curious guest outside and sussing him out on a morning stroll.

He was a short man and I towered above him, as he shuffled along beside me on the pavement. Even Dagmar towered above her father but then she was the tallest member of her family. As we passed along the pavement I was painfully lost for words and would have been thankful for any inventive idea to break the silence – but inspiration came there none. What did I have in common with this old man?

We must have looked an incongruous pair shuffling along the street, and undoubtedly we were conspicuous, and the feeling of being an object of attention was not helped by the fact that every few yards along the pavement Herr Renot was recognised and briefly greeted by an acquaintance. On passing these acquaintances Herr Renot merely lifted his cigar in salute and grunted a *"Guten morgen!"*

The old man puffed at his cigar and looked down solemnly in front of him, constantly wetting the front of his lips and twitching them up and down. He took quick short steps of only eight to ten inches a time and so was tiresomely slow, and after some yards I held my hands behind my back so I could more easily reduce my natural walking pace to that of a tortoise, but despite this, the old man still seemed to be hurrying in an effort to keep up with me. I slowly turned my head in several directions, looking across the street, and then to the rooftops, and then down to my feet again, in an attempt to create the impression that I was quite unhurried, and to appear as casual and leisurely as I could.

On closer observation I noticed his suit was not as immaculate as I had originally thought on seeing it from the courtyard with my eyes still dazed by sunlight. It was ill-fitting and bore several – what were apparently – bad tea stains. Nonetheless, he seemed to adopt an air which indicated he was in reality in his best attire, and he made ample evidence of this by constantly brushing his lapels not of dropped cigar ash but of invisible spots of dust. This curious affectation which was kept up periodically for the duration of our walk, gave evidence of a man who was particular about his personal appearance even if about little else. I strolled alongside wearing my best suit, feeling that my wearing it under such circumstances was an impropriety and possibly even a cruelty to the old man.

We crossed the street and went down Wildenbruch Strasse.

"We go to Neukölln," exclaimed the old man breaking the silence at last.

"Yes," I only replied.

"In the West sector. I'll show you where Dagmar was born," he said.

"Was Dagmar borne in the West sector?"

"Before the War."

"Of course."

"We once lived in Neukölln. Bombed out in 1944," he exclaimed cheerfully.

"That was unlucky in more ways than one. And so you moved to Treptow."

Our conversation had a strange staccato quality. We passed a couple of bored looking Vopos lounging in the middle of the roadway, chatting to one another as they glanced at their feet kicking some pebbles, machine guns slung over their shoulders. The road was narrowed by a barbed wire fence to the width of a pedestrian footway, and on the other side of the fence was erected a large wooden hoarding announcing in four languages: YOU ARE NOW ENTERING THE AMERICAN SECTOR!

Chapter 22

We crossed the sector boundary, and on the other side stood new blocks of flats under construction.

"This is Neukölln," said the old man brightly. "We lived here many years before the War."

We went down the long street, over the Schiffahrt canal, across the wide street of Sonnen Allee, until we reached the broad busy highway of Karl Marx Strasse.

"That's the town hall," said the old man pointing to an impressive structure on our right. "A fine building," he added proudly.

I nodded assent. I was un-attracted by Neukölln. It was grubby and run-down, and despite the liveliness of its main street with its new department stores, bargain shops, and flashy chromium-plated stand up cafés, the ugliness of its grey buildings created a depressing environment. But the old man was at home in the surroundings as he puffed away contentedly at his cigar and toddled along beside me.

"Neukölln is changing," he announced loudly showing his teeth. "Very different today from 1945. Much has happened since then. Voolvorts,!" he added suddenly pointing across the street. "American! A very big company."

"I know, we have them in England," I replied.

Occasionally he glanced in a shop window – he seemed to prefer tobacconists and grocers provisions stores – and would stand meditatively awhile puffing out clouds of smoke, glancing at the wares. He never suggested making a purchase, but usually would leave the window with a sad expression without commenting on the attractive goods within.

The street was noisy with heavy traffic, filling the air with dust and fumes, and as we strolled along, the old man looked solemnly down in front of him and began brushing his lapels again. I wondered what he was thinking. What could be on the old man's mind? Perhaps he was thinking back to his younger days when he had lived in Neukölln, to the days when he had lived a different kind of life. Perhaps he had courted and won his Frau in this very suburb, back in the 1930s. I wondered what the old man looked like in the thirties. Undoubtedly younger and fitter than now, but I expect he had the same facetious sense of humour and monosyllabic way of speaking.

"Neukölln was always democratic," he exclaimed suddenly. "A workers' district. No time for charlatans or political glib talk. Demagogues were always laughed at here. Neukölln fought against chauvinism until the end."

Indeed, I remembered that at one time Berlin had been a part of Germany most opposed to Nazism. Once this city had been known as Red Berlin. Then suddenly, I recollected the name of Neukölln. Had not the suburb been the centre of Red Berlin? – Red Neukölln they had called it. In those far off days, the Communists of Berlin had been a different lot from those now ruling in the East bloc states. They had been ordinary workers and intellectuals pursuing an ideology in the hope for a better world, just as had millions of others throughout Europe and America. They were a far cry from the Communists of contemporary Eastern Europe – from that privileged elite of armed and uniformed thugs sitting in lordly pomp over the oppressed masses.

Then I remembered another factor about the suburb of Neukölln. Had not a certain dynamic political leader in far away Munich sent up a brilliant young doctor of philosophy from the Rhineland to smash down the resistance of that Red Berlin, just before the start of the thirties? And was not the mettle of that young doctor of philosophy put to its hardest test in the suburb of Neukölln as his piercing yet "golden" voice resounded through its halls and meeting places? Was not Neukölln to become the centre of demonstrations and clashes between those two conflicting ideologies, and was not that brilliant young doctor to find his greatest inspiration in the challenge it offered?

Then I mused that perhaps the old man himself had led an active political life as a Christian Democrat during his younger days. Perhaps the Neukölln of the 1930s had formed the most challenging and memorable part of his career, and I realised that at that time he would have been in his prime. Perhaps his small part in the struggle during those critical and chaotic times had given him a sense of purpose and civic pride.

"Good morning, Herr Renot," exclaimed an old man with thick lensed spectacles standing by the window of an electrical appliance shop.

"Good morning, Heinz," replied Herr Renot smartly and raising his cigar.

Heinz looked at me.

"This is an Englishman, Herr Furner," explained Herr Renot.

I shook hands with the stranger and he asked where I came from.

"My son was in England for two months, three years ago," said Heinz glancing at me with interest from behind his spectacles. "He was on a technical course in Manchester. He liked it there."

"Does he live in East Berlin?"

"Not for twelve years past," he replied with a laugh. "He lives in Düsseldorf. He has a good job there – sells machinery – British made. The firm have given him his own car – a large Opel, and he travels all over the Ruhrgebiet."

Herr Renot and I took our leave of the old man and we had not walked many more metres before he recognised two more acquaintances standing outside a greengrocers.

"Good morning Fritz, good morning Ernst,!" exclaimed Herr Renot brightly. "So, Ernst, you're buying fruit in the West sector?"

"No – impossible price,!" laughed Ernst with a wave of the hand. "My wife's birthday tomorrow. She used to love peaches in the old days, and I was just passing the shop, when I saw these. I thought I'd only ask the price – there's no harm in that, is there?"

"There's another fruiterers some way further down the street and their prices are cheaper than here," said Herr Renot in a confidential tone.

"But their fruit's not as good as here," interjected Fritz.

We continued our way down the street, and suddenly the old man stopped in his tracks and pointed across the street.

"That's where we lived during the War," he said indicating a cleared bomb site, "when Dagmar and Gisela were very small," and he lowered his hand to show their height. "Bombed out! B-o-o-m,!" and he threw up his hands to imitate the explosion of a bomb. "*Alles weg* (everything gone!)," he added cheerfully with a big grin.

We paused momentarily, and the old man puffed at his cigar, and we saw several building workers with planks over their shoulders walk across the site.

"I wonder what they're going to build there now," I remarked.

"I expect they're going to build a big eight storey department store, all made of glass and concrete," replied the old man brightly.

Soon we reached Hermann Platz, a large square at the end of Karl Marx Strasse. By this time we had walked a considerable distance. I had begun to feel exhausted by the long perambulation, and wondered whether we should ever reach home in time for lunch. We had seemed to be walking further and further away from the East sector. I wondered whether the old man's legs could possibly last out until we reached Graetz Strasse again, but then I realised that possibly I was more fatigued than he as a result of the tiresomely slow pace at which we were strolling.

As we stood at the corner of Hermann Platz the old man asked if I happened to be carrying a West deutschmark ten pfennig piece, and I gave him the coin, and he excused himself, disappearing down a subway into a public convenience. I waited some minutes at the corner of the square, watching the traffic pass by, and when the old men re-appeared again, we returned a little way down Karl Marx Strasse and then left the street and made our way back via some smaller streets.

Almost no conversation ensued between us. The old man continued to puff at his cigar, twitch his lips and look down solemnly at the street in front of him as he toddled along. What was there we had in common that I could discuss with this old man? What could I ask him or say that might ignite an intelligent conversation?   I began to feel increasingly awkward, and asked myself as to the specific purpose of the walk.   We were approaching home again and he had said nothing of consequence which might have justified our being together so long, but clearly he attached some importance to the occasion judging by his early rising and the attempts to spruce up his appearance.

There must be an ulterior purpose behind this walk, I told myself. Was it intended as an opportunity for me to ask for the hand of his daughter and to discuss subsequent arrangements which might result from this? I was alarmed by the thought of such a stratagem. If that was his intention, I was not yet prepared to consider making a formal proposal. During our walk the old man had not attempted to broach the topic of his daughter, and had not mentioned her name except incidentally.

We re-entered the East sector by Lohmühlen Strasse which we walked down to find ourselves at that end of Graetz Strasse where the trams terminated. At the frontier I applied for and was issued with a pass valid for the next thirty days for entering and leaving the East sector.

We began walking up Graetz Strasse, and on reaching a flower shop, the old man nudged me in the side with his elbow suggesting "We" buy some flowers for Dagmar. It was a charming idea although I felt the initiative should have been left to me. On suggesting that the flowers would be more fresh if I bought them in the evening, he countered this by explaining that no purchase in East marks could be made without a pass.

"I'll buy them in the West," I suggested.

"That's unnecessarily extravagant," he responded.

One should think of saving money whenever possible, he continued. He had his pass with him and he patted his bulging breast pocket to prove it. We must have looked an odd pair standing outside the flower shop, as we debated how, when, where, and with what currency to buy a bunch of flowers. At last we went into the shop.

"I'll buy some flowers for Mamma," he murmured.

"No, I'll get them," I insisted. "I'm the guest and it's my prerogative I should buy flowers for the hostess."

The old man had been silent during much of our walk but clearly he had been pondering over its implications, and the certainty of a particular outcome.

From that moment I seized the initiative. The assistant approached us, and I pushed in front of the old man and began the selection, insisting on the biggest, the freshest, and most colourful flowers in the shop, and meanwhile, the old man stood quietly aside.

At last, two huge bouquets were display wrapped: gladioli together with lilies of the valley which I intended presenting to the good Frau (and they would be the larger bunch), and pink, white and red carnations for Dagmar.

Finally we re-emerged into the street, two dark figures hidden behind enormous round expanses of white paper which held the bouquets, and now we were even more conspicuous than before, as we moved slowly along the street, and our vision was impeded as we had to peer over the tops of the great bundles we carried.

As we crossed the large courtyard I thought to myself that surely we were now the centre of attraction to every old gossip and eavesdropper in the block of buildings whose prime interest was to spy on the movements of others, and I wondered what curious suspicions might be aroused by that incongruously odd looking pair crossing the courtyard with two enormous bouquets.

"Now we'll surprise Mamma," whispered Herr Renot in delight. "Many flowers,!" he added by way of exclamation and stretching out his arms to indicate the size of the load we were about to bring into the house. He put the key into the lock and turned it, and the door opened, and we entered the narrow passageway.

"Sh-h-h-h,!" he said putting his fingers to his lips. He drew the key out of the lock and quietly closed the door. Before I had time to realise that the move was of significance, the old man had taken the larger bouquet out of my arms, leaving me with the carnations which were intended for Dagmar.

"I'll present the flowers," I exclaimed in a whisper.

"Yes – naturally – you present them," whispered the old man in an elated fluster.

It was clear there was a misunderstanding between us.

"I'll carry those flowers then," I said pointing at the bouquet the old man carried, trying to clarify my point.

"No, you give her those," he replied pointing to my bouquet.

"No, those are more suitable for your wife," I returned.

"No, those are larger – these are for Dagmar," he insisted. "Dagmar must have the larger bouquet. We were buying flowers for Dagmar, not for my wife. My wife must have the smaller bunch."

"But -," I began, but before I could finish, Frau Renot came out from the kitchen into the little hallway to greet us. Our arguing had betrayed our homecoming, and so the presentation could not be made with the kind of surprise originally intended. Nonetheless, his big face lit up with a happy smile.

"Herr Furner's brought you some flowers, Mamma," he exclaimed.

"Oh, how kind,!" she replied clapping her hands in delight. "But you shouldn't have spent your money like that."

"He insisted on buying them, Mamma," exclaimed Herr Renot cheerfully.

I felt embarrassed and foolish by the old man's intrigue, and resented having fallen a victim of his guile, and being used as a pawn to ingratiate me with the females of his household. What was he trying to achieve? What did he hope to gain by this?

"And Herr Furner's bought these for Dagmar," said the old man delightedly, proffering the larger bouquet. "We must put them on Dagmar's dressing table in Granny's bedroom, so she'll get them as a surprise when she comes home tonight," he added in a confidential tone.

Chapter 23

The flowers were taken into the kitchen, unwrapped and laid out on the table, and as Frau Renot filled a vase at the sink, my eyes were met by an incredible image – by something lying in the centre of the room – and momentarily, I was rooted to the spot, doubting whether what I saw was really what it appeared to be. I must have reacted with an expression of bewilderment, for Frau Renot nervously fumbled with the vase a moment, and smiled at me reassuringly, as if to say, "Yes, I did it just for you!"

What confronted me was not of the supernatural kind, but rather of that category arising from the weird juxtaposition of familiar objects, as in Surrealist painting when melting time-pieces are seen to curve and droop over the edge of table tops.

On the middle of the kitchen floor stood a wooden washing tub – round and hooped – and the foam of white frothy soap-suds rose almost to the top and overflowed to the floor, and the white vapour of hot steam rose from the foam, for the tub held boiling water. Out of the soap-suds and curving and drooping - limply, pitifully – was not a melting time-piece, but some fawn coloured fabric, and in the form of a collar and lapels, and the material was unquestionably cavalry twill. Surely it could not possibly be – but yes – there was no doubt about it – it was my expensive – my stylish – my valued Summer coat. Out of the soap-suds at the other side of the tub rose the top of a washing board, and on the floor lay a scrubbing brush, and nearby, a number of leather buttons which had been removed and laid out.

It seemed a drastic way of cleaning an overcoat – clean it would undoubtedly be for no half measures had been taken – but surely this was German thoroughness carried beyond excess. I asked myself if the coat would ever be fit for wearing again, and could hardly comprehend how anyone could have taken it into their heads in resorting to such an extreme course of action.

Perhaps the good Frau, as with her daughter, had taken a dislike to the style of the coat, and together had conspired to ruin it for me, and perhaps all this was yet another manifestation of Berliner humour; or had she merely cleaned the coat out of the kindness of her heart? If the latter were the case then I should only have to blame the final outcome of this purge on my coat on last night's little escapade, when admittedly it had become soiled.

"You're cleaning my coat,?" I exclaimed at last, pointing my arm to the soap-suds and still incredulous.

"It was very dirty. I don't know what you could have been doing last night," replied Frau Renot cheerfully.

"When do you think it'll be ready for wearing,?" I asked with an apprehension which must have clearly betrayed my thoughts.

"It must first be hung out to dry," said the good Frau, "and then it must be pressed."

"I can see you've worked very hard on it," were the only words I could muster by way of conclusion.

"You must always look your best when you go out with Dagmar," exclaimed the good Frau with significance.

"Br-h-h-h! It's chilly," I exclaimed to myself as we passed along the street, and my mood was far from complacent at that moment and I felt disinclined to start a conversation. My mood was introspective, and I was nursing my own anxieties – or at least a particular big worry disturbing my mind at the time.

"What's wrong,?" asked Dagmar consolingly, tightening her hold on my arm.

"It's cold," I replied brusquely.

"It's soon the end of Summer. We can't always have the warm nights," said Dagmar.

"A pity your mother didn't realise that this morning," I replied sharply.

"Let's not get back to my mother again," said Dagmar irritably.

"I still say it was a ridiculous way to clean a coat," I exclaimed.

We had just come from the City Opera where we had seen a production of Schoenberg's music drama, *Moses and Aaron*, and were walking through the southern area of the Hansa quarter. Despite the magnificence of the production it was not sufficient to induce forgetfulness of the cold night air. I felt justifiably indignant.

"I don't think you're grateful," said Dagmar sulkily.

"I'm only anxious – that's all," I exclaimed. "The object of your original complaint was its military style, and from that moment, in your eyes, the coat was only fit to be thrown away."

"I didn't mean literally about its being thrown away," said Dagmar defensively.

"Let's find a café where we can have a hot drink."

Later, we were seated in a quiet restaurant with coffee and cakes, and the warmth and environment was conducive to improving our disposition. We were silent and thoughtful awhile. My mind went back to the grandmother and this morning's meeting with her neighbours in the courtyard of the tenement block.

"Your grandmother's exceptionally lively and good-humoured considering her incapacity," I remarked.

"She's never down-hearted. Even in the worst of times she keeps up her spirits," said Dagmar. "She's a typical Berliner – it's wonderful to be like that."

"She takes everything lightly. Perhaps that's the secret of her happiness," I said. "Did you know she noticed what time you arrived home last night?"

"Granny doesn't sleep well."

"She was quite light-hearted about it. I met some of her friends this morning, too. Petty Officer Lufner, for example – what a character he is!"

"He makes beautiful model ships," said Dagmar brightly.

"He's crazy!"

"It's mostly pretence," explained Dagmar. "Being sane doesn't get you very far in our society."

"And I met Frau Hartmann."

"She's evil," replied Dagmar with spite. "That's the only word to describe her."

"The others didn't seem to like her either."

"Everyone hates her."

"Why exactly?"

"I prefer not to talk about her," replied Dagmar abruptly, stirring her coffee. "I just hate her – that's all."

"That's strong language to use, 'hate,'" I remarked, and I wondered what must have transpired between Frau Hartmann and Dagmar to have aroused such a feeling.

"What else did you do this morning,?" enquired Dagmar keen to change the topic.

"I went for a long walk with your father in Neukölln," I replied with a smile.

"Papa told me he'd be taking you for a walk," said Dagmar smiling just perceptibly as she lowered her eyes.

"I found it a little awkward. There wasn't much we could speak about."

"Papa's very old, and he's old-fashioned, and has funny ideas," said Dagmar reflectively with a suggestion of melancholy. "He doesn't understand the modern times we live in. He comes from a different world."

"He told me something about Neukölln. You lived there once – before the War."

"Until 1945. Papa's lived there for most of his adult life."

"He seemed to have a sentimental hankering for the place."

"That's his usual walk," said Dagmar softly, "down Wildenbruch Strasse, along Karl Marx Strasse, and back again via Weichsal Strasse."

"I don't know how we came back – we walked down a lot of small side streets. I didn't take to Neukölln – it's dirty," I added after a pause.

"I don't like it either. It's ugly, but Papa likes it."

"Was your father born there?"

"No, he comes from the country. He was born in Mecklenburg. He came to Berlin as a young man to find work."

"Do you remember living in Neukölln?"

"Yes – but just the War, and living in shelters every night, and the bombing, and the next morning finding entire streets blown up. It was terrible! Papa was a warden then."

"He still seems to have a civic pride in the place. Was he interested in local politics at one time?"

"Papa's always worked for newspapers, but he was once very active in politics, in the twenties and at the start of the thirties."

"In what capacity?"

"Oh, just helping to print and deliver circulars in his spare time, sitting on various committees and arranging meetings, and once he was even the assistant editor of a newssheet circulated throughout Berlin. I believe he devoted all his spare energy to politics long ago."

"And when did that 'career' come to an end?"

"Shortly after Hitler came to power. Things became difficult then. People mysteriously disappeared, and the Nazis used to print such terrible lies and nonsense about all opposition groups, and it was impossible to retaliate, so they couldn't go on. Papa didn't feel safe, so he just gave it all up, and got a clerical job working for a publishing firm."

"And so that's how his 'glorious' political career came to its pitiful end," I remarked ironically.

"But Papa fought bravely against the Nazis," said Dagmar defensively, " – and against the Communists too."

I said nothing. Much as I liked the old man for his kindness, hospitality, and good humour, I did not imagine that bravery was one of his attributes. He seemed too passive and easy-going a character for that. He seemed a man of thought rather than a man of action. I could see him sitting on committees, sticking circulars through doors, and cracking jokes before assembled party colleagues, but as a political fighter – demonstrating, marching or heckling, that was not a role I could envisage for him. Then I reflected that perhaps it was men of the type and calibre of Papa Renot who sadly had been the backbone of democratic opposition to Hitler. The idea struck me as amusing if it wasn't so tragic in its outcome.

"Why didn't your father return to Neukölln after the War, and take up his political career where he had left off,?" I enquired at last.

"It would have been impossible for us to have moved back to Neukölln at that time. We were already living in the flat in Treptow, and were lucky to have a roof over our heads. But Papa did do some political work in Neukölln just immediately after the War. In fact, for a few weeks he almost became a leading politician. He worked hard, and was full of enthusiasm, and all his colleagues were keen, and nearly every night, he would bring some of them back to the flat and they'd talk till very late about the new democratic Germany they hoped to build."

"Was he working for the CDU then?"

"No, for an all-party anti-fascist league called the National Committee for Free Germany. It had all kinds of members, from generals down to factory hands, all working in unison with one another. The movement had offices all over Berlin."

"What happened to the association?"

"It was broken up on orders from Ulbricht. Many of its members were so disillusioned – they had worked so hard and done so much – that they gave up politics altogether. Papa was never really active in politics again since those last weeks after the War."

"Why didn't your father subsequently go to the West as a refugee?"

"Papa had found work in the East sector as a proof reader for the Christian Democrat paper."

"But that was in the East."

"At the end of the War the Russians forced all parties to place their headquarters in the East sector. That was before the actual arrival of the other three powers who were to occupy Berlin. At the time the four sector boundaries meant nothing to the people of Berlin – they were just something on paper – theoretical dividing lines. The four sectors were only intended for the military administration of the city and the four Commandants were supposed to work together helping to re-build a free democratic Berlin. But when the other three powers occupied their sectors it was soon found that the Russians wouldn't allow the free development of political parties.

"They infiltrated political offices with spies and agents, used fifth columnists and every method of coercion for ensuring Soviet influence. At the same time, Communists were given all kinds of little privileges. The most discouraging event for the people of Berlin, who wanted to see political freedom, came just a year after the end of the War. The Russians enforced an amalgamation between the Social Democrats and the Communists, forming the Social Unity Party. That spelt the end of political freedom in the East sector."

"Your father told me about that when we first met."

"From that time I think we all began to know there'd be a permanent division between the East and West sectors. Then, one by one, each of the political parties began to set up its own separate political headquarters in the West sectors, so as to be free from Soviet interference. Then in 1948 came the currency reform in West Germany and so in West Berlin. We could no longer use the same money."

"Why didn't your father go over to the West when the political parties were severed? I'm sure he could have found a job then."

"They didn't want him to. You see, Papa was working for the Christain Democrats – he still is in a small way – and they were the last to severe their ties between the East and West sectors. Jakob Kaiser was the Chairman of the movement then, and until the end of 1947 he did everything possible in trying to prevent the political dismemberment of Germany. It was only at the end of that year that the CDU finally severed its links between East and West. In the East sector the elected Committee of the CDU had been twice dismissed by the Soviet Kommandatura, and it was because of this that the movement in the West sectors felt compelled to sever its links. They wanted Papa, as well as others, to stay by their posts and work as best they could."

"But he must have known that things would be hopeless."

"Papa just kept hoping against hope that one day there'd be a change for the better."

"The eternal optimists," I exclaimed with irony.

"What was the alternative? Papa had his work and was proud of it, and he had his newspaper, and he believed that as long as it existed, there might be a chance for better things."

"I understand. So he remains faithful to the party – through thick and thin – so long as it remains a party in name."

"And that's about all it is," said Dagmar quietly, lowering her eyes.

"But everything's changed in Berlin since the time of Jakob Kaiser and the division of the CDU between the East and West sectors. Surely your father must recognise that. Any opposition to the Communists in the East was made impractical long ago."

"Papa still has a vague hope. He believes he's doing some small amount of good by remaining in the East."

"Hasn't he ever been struck by the wretchedness of the political situation? Hasn't he ever been overcome by exasperation and despair?"

"Yes, several times when things have gone really badly for us," said Dagmar thoughtfully. "About three or four times to be exact – when great difficulties afflicted our family."

"And hasn't he thought of moving to the West as a refugee then?"

"Yes, several times. Once Papa took me to the biggest refugee home in the West – it's situated in the factory of the Lorenz firm. We only went to enquire about the chances of Papa finding work in West Germany. It was terrible there! I don't think I could ever live in such a place – not even for a day. It's run by the Red Cross – a vast ugly building. Sometimes a hundred or more people sleep in a room. Can you imagine it? When I went with Papa there were eight thousand refugees there. It was terrible!"

"Perhaps it would be worth living there for a few weeks if you could eventually go to West Germany. There you would start new lives – cherish new hopes, and live in freedom."

"It would have been impossible. For Gisela and I – yes, we would easily find a place in West Germany – in a few days perhaps, but Papa, never! He would have spent the rest of his life in that camp – it would have been dreadful!"

"And so your father just gave up hope of finding a place in the West?"

"Yes, we'll always remain in the East," said Dagmar dolefully, lowering her eyes.

Chapter 24

On entering the washroom the following morning I discovered that several other little favours had been designed and carried out – favours which reflected the imaginative understanding of a considerate hostess. Absurd pieces of pink ribbon had been neatly stitched onto my towel and flannel so that these could be hung on nails in the wall, and further along the wall to my surprise, I discovered my toothbrush also hanging from a nail – suspended from a piece of pink ribbon inserted through the hole at the end of the handle. These bright silky pieces of pink ribbon, I supposed, were the result of yesterday's flowers, and yesterday's flowers were the result of the "Conspirator," Papa Renot!

Dagmar must have been late up that morning for I waited until long passed the time when she usually came to her parents' flat, and so I decided to fetch her from number fifty-five. I hoped she was already dressed and that my calling on her would not be inconvenient, but as she was already late, I concluded my calling on her was permissible.

Dagmar opened the door and on seeing me, although fully dressed, she gave a little cry, raising her hand to her mouth.

"I hope I haven't come to embarrass you," I exclaimed.

"Of course not," she returned smiling. "Please come in. I overslept. I was so tired last night – two nights running in the West sector, and two such very late nights."

She led me down the passageway to the entrance of her bedroom, and I followed tentatively, still conscious that my appearance was an intrusion.

"My hair is terrible. I haven't brushed it."

"Is that why I startled you? Your hair is always beautiful," I said passing my fingers through it, as she seated herself at a dressing table and began to attend to her make-up.

As I stood there silently, I was overcome with a sensation of uncanny apprehension, as if I had been in the room before. It was a small crowded room almost half the space being taken up by the double bed placed against the wall, and the bedclothes were thrown about in a state of disarray. The wooden bedstead was raised quite high from the ground, and I noticed that the side of the heavy piece of furniture was thickly charred, and an end leg was missing and the bed was supported by eight calf bound volumes of *Schiller Werke*.

"Poor Schiller,!" I remarked facetiously, putting my foot against the side of the bed. "He has to take your weight and Granny's too."

A piece of charcoal dropped to the floor.

"Don't do that," said Dagmar sharply. "It's Mamma's and Papa's marriage bed. We carried it all the way from Neukölln. It was one of the few things we salvaged after we were bombed out. It's of sentimental value, only Mamma and Papa couldn't fit it into the flat across the road, and so they exchanged it for a bed of Granny's."

On a small chest of drawers by the window stood medicine bottles and jars and an old fashioned silver backed hairbrush and hand mirror, a brass comb, and an opened leather bound casket full of marble beads and pieces of ancient imitation jewellery, as well as a black woollen cape and other objects. The top of this crowded little chest clearly served as the grandmother's dressing table.

Dagmar had succeeded in appropriating for her own use the best piece of furniture and most intimate corner of the room. She sat at a gilded dressing table on a chair of matching design. A little rug lay at her feet and post card reproductions of art works were pinned on both sides of the wall in that corner of the room which she had made specially hers. The toilet articles on the dressing table were neatly laid out – pink backed brushes, lipsticks in pink containers and a matching toilet box.

She took up the brush and began briskly to straighten her hair. I leaned against the wall by the window watching her, fascinated by her beauty. How enchanting was her hair – millions of silky golden threads – shimmering as they caught the sunlight when she brushed it to one side of her forehead, and I recollected the beautiful lines of Heine's poem on the *Lorelei*, and the terrible fate of those boatmen who had been distracted by the enchanting maidens attending to their hair. Her eyes twinkled as she smiled at me from behind the lock of hair affectedly brushed to one side. Strange how that girls like to be watched by men as they brush their hair! No wonder her hair was finer than silk – so vigorously and long did she brush it.

I watched the pale gentle features of her face – so resigned she looked, and I recollected how I first saw her in the little Art Shop in Stalin Allee. Those seemed distant days, although less than a year had elapsed. I remembered her pale calm countenance – her resignation in life, I had called it, and now she wore the same expression. What lies in the mystery of your resignation in life, I asked myself,? and I knew I had asked the question many times before.

How frail and delicate she looked! Perhaps in her frailty lay the beauty of her person, for the languid rhythmical movements of her body were unlikely to be found in one with a heavier build or a stronger constitution. Perhaps her natural frailty was a bar to that bouncing energy or sudden ungainly movements often found in those of a fitter disposition, and so her frailty gave her an ethereal quality and a strangely transcending beauty by comparison with the more terrestrial beings of her sex – or so I thought.

She took up the two silver rings with the dull orange stones and put them onto her slim sensitive fingers. Those rings had been the first of her possessions I had noticed – long ago, as we had sorted through the prints in the corner of the little Art Shop in Stalin Allee. That was a happy and eventful sunshine day when I had met the fair Berlineren.

"Now you must not look at me," said Dagmar smiling coyly from behind the tresses which fell across her forehead. "I'm going to use my lipstick and if you watch me I'll be nervous and slip."

She lifted her hand mirror from the table, her slim fingers gripping the handle sensitively, and the silver rings glimmered momentarily in the sunlight. Suddenly, I started back in shock, catching my breath, and a twinge of horror ran down my spine. The mirror! It had a pink plastic back and was decorated with green stars – exactly as I had seen in my weirdly unpleasant dream, less than a week ago in Münster. Dagmar noticed my reaction, looking at me curiously with an expression of concern.

"What is it,?" she exclaimed.

"The mirror," I replied.

"What is it about the mirror,?" she responded chuckling.

"Oh, it's nothing," I returned recovering from the uncanny feeling which had seized me. "Only I thought I'd seen it before."

"You couldn't have done," replied Dagmar laughing. "You've never been in here before."

"It was in a dream."

"Do you believe in dreams?"

"Sometimes, yes."

"What was this dream,?" asked Dagmar slowly, her tone changing to one of curious solemnity.

"I prefer not to say. It was one of those inexplicable dreams."

"I'm interested in why you should have dreamt about my mirror. And I think I've a right to know."

"I'd rather forget the dream. It was unpleasant."

"Did you see something terrible – something tragic,?" asked Dagmar in a grave faltering tone.

"Why do you ask that,?" I exclaimed, surprised by her response.

"I feel you should tell me. Are you psychic?"

"Not to my knowledge. – It was only that you refused to let me see the image in the mirror, and I struggled with you," I replied, realising I should have to satisfy the mounting tension of her curiosity.

"Is that all,?" she retorted, as if relieved. "Is that what frightened you."

"Not exactly. It was your telling me not to watch you use your lipstick just now, just as in the dream when you were embarrassed when I found you with that same mirror."

"You shouldn't believe in the premonitions of dreams. It's not healthy," said Dagmar reassuringly.

"Sometimes it may be difficult not to."

"A dream may reveal things greater than ourselves – things we cannot change. That's why we shouldn't believe in the premonitions of dreams," said Dagmar beginning to apply her lipstick.

"It's strange I should have dreamt about this same mirror," I said after a pause.

"There are many mirrors like this," replied Dagmar. "Perhaps you had seen one like this before – in a shop or store – and it just stayed in your head waiting for this dream."

"I expect so," I replied. "Do you mind if I watch your reflection in the mirror,?" I added hesitantly.

"Why not,?" exclaimed Dagmar. "Come, stand behind my chair."

Slowly, almost with trepidation, I approached her dressing table, and she rose and kissed my cheek as a consolation for my fears. I watched her reflection in the mirror, as her slim pale fingers deftly, artistically, applied the lipstick. What more beautiful reflection could a mirror have displayed? Her eyes glanced up and smiled at me.

"Strange you should have wished to hide those fair features from the world," I said smiling and laying my hands gently on her shoulders.

"Beautiful forest,!" exclaimed the old man suddenly, throwing up his hands towards the sky.

"Yes," I only returned.

There was a pause as we continued to make our way slowly along the path. The old man was brushing his lapels again and twitching his lips. I felt painfully awkward. Since we had left Graetz Strasse practically no conversation had ensued between us. The old man was looking solemn and thoughtful today.

"Have you many forests like this in London,?" he enquired.

"No," I answered.

"Hyde Park, that's a big garden, yes,?" he exclaimed after another pause, and stretching out his arms to indicate a great expanse.

"Yes, a very big garden," I replied.

It was early in the afternoon and we had just arrived in the Plänter Wald in Treptow. We had lunched at number fifty-five and then left the flat and taken a long tram journey from Graetz Strasse down the Park Köpenicker Landstrasse to reach the Plänter Wald.

The outing had not already been unmarked by incident. In the tram we had had the misfortune to encounter one of those tipsy persons who latch onto anything out of the ordinary arousing their attention. As Papa Renot and I were conspicuous as a pair, we became a target for this dosser, and I had wished that the old man had had the sense to change seats in keeping well clear of the drunk, but he had not, and worse still, he allowed himself to be inveigled into a verbal exchange. I had become an object of curiosity, and the information was soon out that I was an Englishman, and this interesting fact, aroused the dosser to become more noisy and loquacious.

His lurching to and fro and wild gesticulations attracted the attention of the conductor on an otherwise empty vehicle, and he tapped the man on the shoulder, reminding him to behave. But this was of no avail, and the drunk's increasing irritation at the stubborn reserve of the odd couple facing him, led him to suggest some offensive imputation. What "business" had an old man to be associating with such a "handsome youth?" He should be ashamed of himself! He should look for a man of his own age. After leaving the tram in Bulgarische Strasse, we must both have felt profoundly awkward after such a sickening episode.

We walked silently through the park until we came to a footpath alongside the bank of the river Spree, and for some time not a word was exchanged between us.

"Does the London river – the Thames run alongside Hyde Park,?" enquired the old man at last nudging me in the side.

So he's got Hyde Park on his mind, I mused.

"No," I replied. "We only have a lake in Hyde Park."

"Like the Wannsee in the West sector,?" he enquired with interest.

"No, much smaller," I replied.

I wondered what was on the old man's mind. Yesterday he seemed to have been thinking about Neukölln and today it was London. He looked very solemn, and he puffed at his cigar, thoughtfully blowing out clouds of smoke, and he brushed his lapels and twitched his lips again. On today's walk I felt more awkward even than I had the previous day. In Neukölln there had been the distraction and noise of the streets to help take away my attention from his company. Today there was nothing more than the quiet intimacy of the park and the still breadth of water of the river Spree to bring us closer, and it seemed as if today's walk was intended to do just that, so that confidences might be exchanged between us.

The old man remained solemn and meditative. Was he waiting for me to speak first? Was there something he particularly expected me to say, and had he taken me on that long and unpleasant tram journey and brought me into this restful park so that I could summon up my courage to say this thing? Was I supposed to ask him for the hand of his daughter? If so, I was not yet ready for this ultimate decision, for there were things which still mystified me about her, and I wanted answers to these questions before asking for her hand. And in any case, what was the proper form of words in asking a father for his daughter's hand?

As soon as I asked myself this question I was seized with panic. I suddenly realised the complexity involved in asking a father for the hand of his daughter. It would certainly be more difficult than asking the daughter herself. The relationship between a boy and girl intent on marriage should be marked by mutual feeling and their engagement should follow as a spontaneous consequence of their love, but how to ask a father for the hand of his daughter? What manner to adopt – to be supplicating, to be solemnly intent, to be bold and abrupt, to be dashing, to be suavely self-confident – or what? I was none of these things. All this seemed to present such formidable difficulties as to be insuperable.

We strolled along at a tiresomely slow pace, and I held my hands behind my back, looking down at my feet or glancing across the river at the industrial buildings on the other bank. Papa Renot looked anxious and I felt a tension between us. If only one of us could break the silence.

Suddenly the old man stopped, nudged me in the side with his elbow, and pointed across the river at some tall chimneys belching out black and yellow smoke, large steel tanks and a confusion of metal pipes and twisted steel.

"East Berlin's gas works,!" he exclaimed brightly.

I looked at the scene appreciatively.

"Very fine," I replied lamely, and I felt I had never spoken more meaningless words.

And so our conversation was now to be reduced to pointing out landmarks! A promisingly eventful afternoon confronted us!

At last we left the banks of the Spree and re-entered the forest. We passed an old wooden Chinese pagoda, and there was a verandah and open air café in front of the structure and tables under trees. I was tired, and a coffee would have been welcome by this time, but the old man made no indication of stopping, and so we walked between the little round tables and into the forest again.

There were no longer remarkable landmarks to allow as an excuse for breaking the silence between us and I felt the perspiration on the palms of my hands. My mouth was dry and I was tense and painfully nonplussed. Why has the old man bought me to the depths of the forest – there must be a reason? There has to be an ulterior motive.

At last the old man stopped in the middle of the great silent forest, and nudging me in the side with his elbow, he exclaimed without glancing at me, "*Hat Dagmar sich denn über die Blumen gefreut?* (Was Dagmar pleased with the flowers?)," and he seemed to wait in anticipation for my answer.

I could have burst my sides with laughter. Had he brought me all this way just to ask that question? There was an absurdity in all the rigmarole of his efforts.

"Yes, she was very pleased with the flowers," I said quietly.

He nodded affirmatively, smiling contentedly to himself, and we continued on our little adventure.

On arriving home again, the old man was in a happy frame of mind. In the sitting room he beckoned me to follow him to the escritoire and opened a small drawer and took out an envelope with several photographs.

"This is my son," he exclaimed, showing me a photo of himself standing beside a much taller man, of about thirty years of age. The old man looked self-conscious in the photograph, glancing nonchalantly sideways and holding the omnipresent cigar, and his son who was better looking was smiling broadly at the camera, his arms crossed in a relaxed position.

"I didn't know you had a son," I said.[*]

"Dagmar's half-brother. He's the son by my first wife. She died," he added sadly.

"Where's your son now,?" I asked.

"In Hamburg. He's been more than ten years in West Germany. This photo was taken four years ago, when he came to visit Berlin. And this is my grandson," added the old man showing me a blurred photo of a baby in a cradle. "I've been three months a Grandpapa," he added cheerfully.

"Just look at my coat," I exclaimed as Dagmar came down the steps of Treptower Park station towards me.

"You must buy a new coat," she said kissing me on the cheek.

"It's ruined, and whose fault is that,?" I responded.

"Ah – ah,!" she said with a correcting raised finger. "Let's not speak about Mamma again. Is it dry enough for wearing?"

"I made it imperative the coat should be dry enough by this evening."

"You didn't really need it for the short walk to the station. We're not going out tonight are we?"

"I thought we could go to the cinema in Treptow."

"That wouldn't be nice," said Dagmar screwing up her nose. "Films in the East are all propaganda! But we can go if you really want to for the experience. But don't blame me if I fall asleep. So many nights out have made me fatigued."

We walked briskly along Puschkin Allee and we were silent awhile, and I broached the issue of the awkwardness I had felt during the long walk with her father that afternoon. Perhaps she could find out from him as to his exact intentions.

"Really, James! I think you can ask my father yourself," she answered.

"But you seem to know about these walks before I do."

---

[*] The author has here undergone a slip of memory, for in volume ix of his handwritten *Memoirs*, under the entry date for 27th September 1959, on dining on the first occasion of their meeting in West Berlin at the Roxy Hotel, he records clearly that the girl from East Berlin told him she had a brother aged 37 who lived in Hamburg working as an aircraft engineer.

"That's no reason for me to be an intermediary. My father has his own ideas."

"I don't like being beckoned by his little finger, and then expected to keep him company for hours at a time."

"He just wants to get acquainted with you. There's nothing odd in that."

"Well, I wish he'd have something more specific to say or do. I hope he's going to be more definite next time."

Little did I realise that I had made a wish which was to be over-fulfilled, and that this would culminate in an even more embarrassing situation.

Chapter 25

You know in two days it'll be Dagmar's birthday, don't you,?" said Frau Renot to me in a confidential tone as she laid the soup tureen onto the table. We were all seated except for Frau Brüning who had retired early to bed.

"You shouldn't have told him, Mamma," scolded Dagmar. "It's not tactful."

"Not tactful,!" replied the good Frau in mock astonishment. "Why, I'm sure Herr Furner will be delighted to buy you a small present."

"Of course! I'm grateful you've told me," I agreed.

"See, Herr Furner agrees with me," said Frau Renot ladling soup into little brown bowls.

"You needn't have told him in front of me," added Dagmar. "It would embarrass him."

"Many happy returns for the day after tomorrow," I exclaimed.

"I'm sure Herr Furner's never embarrassed," said the good Frau laying her hand affectionately on my shoulder.

Dagmar smiled across the table at me in amusement and I lowered my eyes, pretending not to notice.

"Besides, a birthday is a family event, and Herr Furner must be told," added Frau Renot in a tone of importance.

"Oh, really Mamma," exclaimed Dagmar.

"She's frightened you'll find out her age," laughed Papa Renot loudly from the head of the table.

"Oh, *quatsch*, Papa!"

"Does Herr Furner know how old you are,?" enquired the old man facetiously.

"I expect he's too polite to ask," answered his wife. "Herr Furner doesn't want to ask a lot of personal questions all the time."

"She'll be seventeen,!" exclaimed the old man. "That's a beautiful age for a girl. Sweet Seventeen! Do you know the American song? They sing it on the West Berlin radio."

"*Quatsch,* Papa!"

"Dagmar will be twenty-three," confided Frau Renot. "Of course we'll be holding a party for her and Unlce Willy and Aunty Caroline will be coming over from the West sector."

"And let's hope this birthday party will be an extra special one," exclaimed the old man pointedly in my direction. "An event of happiness for us all!"

"And Dagmar tells me you're having a birthday soon," said Frau Renot. "And you'll be twenty-five. Such a nice age difference. Just two years between you."

After the meal Dagmar and I glanced through the paper discussing which cinema to visit, and finally we opted for a Russian film in Eastmancolour entitled, *The Four Companions*, as being the least undesitrable of several uninteresting choices. We reached our destination after a tram journey of some distance, and the cinema was dirty and draughty, and the seats hard and uncomfortable, and there were few patrons and those mostly elderly. The film was the most didactic I had ever seen: the story of four Muscovites and one-time childhood friends, being a scientist, an architect, and engineer, and a doctor who embark on a holiday trip down the Moscow-Volga canal.

As they leave the great city, travelling in a barge full of cargo, they each in turn sing to the glories of their respective professions to the scientist's balalaika. The tale recounts their criticism of each other during the trip, describing how through egotism, each with the passing of time, had acquired "anti-social traits," i.e. idiosyncrasies marking them off from the acceptable norm. Through good-humoured lectures, mild practical jokes and a lot of moralising, the three in turn line up against the fourth member of their group in purging him of faults. There were flashbacks to their early childhood – four little boys playing on the muddy banks of the Volga excitedly describing to each other their aspirations in life – and these remind them of the purity of their youthful enthusiasm and long last innocence. These reminiscences strengthen them spiritually for the future, and the film ends as they return to Moscow, happily singing to the balalaika, uplifted and renewed for the tasks which lie ahead.

Immediately in front sat a drunk (we could smell the alcohol) who slept through the film, and was still sleeping after the lights had gone up and we had begun to leave, and some rows in front had sat another perdurable sleeper, but of a more noisome kind. Several times he dropped off into a slumber and shortly afterwards began to snore so loudly that hisses and whistling from several quarters were needed to bring him to consciousness.

As Dagmar and I left the cinema, I saw a notice in the foyer advertising a forthcoming attraction, a revival of Eisenstein's *Strike*. I was amazed that such a film should be shown in a country where strikes were forbidden, but it reminded me that great art was fortunate in transcending even the constraints of state censorship.

We returned to the flat at number fifty-five, left our coats in the hallway, and tip-toed into the sitting room so as not to awaken Frau Brüning. Dagmar was in a thoughtful mood, and she switched on the lamp above the radio, placing it on the little coffee table by the sofa. She beckoned me to sit down saying she had something to show me. Quietly and feeling strangely uneasy, I followed her gesture.

During our return to Graetz Strasse we had spoken little and Dagmar had worn a vexed expression as if worried by some inscrutable problem. Several times she had drawn in her breath as if to speak, but either from loss of words to express her thoughts or from a sudden change of mind, she had refrained. Twice I asked what she was thinking, and on the first occasion she impatiently replied, "I don't know," her tone suggesting a specific anxiety that might have borne her down, and on the second occasion, she replied with almost painful hesitancy, "I don't know how to express myself in words," and this answer heightened my curiosity but I said nothing more during our homecoming.

Dagmar went over to a small cabinet near the window, took out a drawer, and came and sat down beside me, placing the drawer on her knees. It was full of papers, small bundles and all kinds of objects.

"What have you there,?" I enquired softly, leaning back on the sofa, gently placing my hand across her shoulder.

"Souvenirs," she only replied.

"Souvenirs of your travels,?" I enquired smiling, and then I realised with regret the ironic insinuation which could be read into the statement.

"Souvenirs of my life," she replied a little sadly.

"Let's see them," I said encouragingly.

"They aren't very much," she said sharply as if checking herself, and suddenly laying her hands across the top of the drawer. "There's nothing really interesting in here."

"Anything that's part of you is interesting," I replied, "and these souvenirs are a part of your life and must reflect your personality."

"They're only vain empty things – little scribblings, drawings, photos, and all kinds of keepsakes."

"Do you want to show me what's in the drawer or not,?" I said bemused by her hesitation.

"Yes, I'll show you," she said sighing sadly, removing her hands from the top of the drawer.

She began removing the papers and other oddments, quickly passing them between her fingers and only occasionally pausing to explain some object of interest. The items seemed of little significance to me then, and they were of so little intrinsic value that I wondered why she had bothered to hoard them in this way. Nonetheless, she seemed to regard them as of special worth.

There were many sheets of art paper with rough sketches of fashion designs, and faces, and then just scribble and doodles, and then, some political cartoons of a scurrilous kind.

"I didn't know you were an artist," I said.

"I'm not," she returned sharply.

"Then why do you keep these drawings?"

"Because they remind me of long ago."

"I thought you didn't believe in looking back into the past. You said it made you sad."

"But these things are from happier days. From two years ago."

"Then what happened two years ago – or since – to make you unhappy,?" I said encouragingly to draw her out.

"I don't like to think about it, and so you can understand I don't like to talk about it. Let's leave these silly drawings," she added suddenly and hurriedly lifting them and passing them through her fingers.

Beneath the drawings were quarto sheets filled with pencil writing.

"What's this,?" I asked.

"A story," she replied.

"So you're a writer as well as an artist,!" I exclaimed in delight.

"Perhaps a writer but not an artist, but if I'm a writer, I'm not a successful one. Papa typed out the story for me and I sent it to some magazines, but it was never published."

"What's it about?"

"It's a sad story about an unhappy girl."

"Sentimental?"

"It's *Kitsch* really – I ought to throw it away but I don't," she said lifting more things out of the drawer.

A small piece of white paper suddenly caught my eye and I took it out of the box.

"You remember this,?" I exclaimed brightly holding up the paper.

"Yes, it's the souvenir from our first meeting," she replied, a happy smile breaking over her face. "The tissue folder from my lemonade glass.

That was nearly a year ago when we went to the Ku'damm together and ate in that pavement restaurant."

I replaced the tissue folder and Dagmar continued to pass through the objects in the drawer. There were Chinese prints, blank post cards, shrivelled petals and skeleton leaves glued onto white sheets of cardboard - and all kinds of meaningless junk. At the bottom of the drawer I was surprised even to discern some fine strands of cigarette tobacco. Surely there wasn't a box of cigarettes amongst all the other jumble!

Then there were blank picture post cards of Friedrichshafen on Lake Konstanz: coloured photos of the castle, of the lakeside, of pretty streets, of a twin-towered onion topped church, and a general view of the town with the distant white capped Alps in the background across the lake.

"Who did you know in Friedrichshafen,?" I asked.

"I didn't know anyone there," she replied.

"Then how did you get these,?" I asked. "Friedrichshafen must be a thousand kilometres from Berlin, and these cards weren't printed all that while ago."

"I prefer not to say," she replied.

"It seems as if you have a lot of secrets to keep from me tonight."

"I wish you wouldn't speak like a detective."

"Can't I be inquisitive without appearing to you like a detective?"

At last we reached something I recognised – my own letters with their London postmark.

"So you kept them," I exclaimed smiling, "although our little affair had been broken off after I sent you that card from Badgastein."

"Your letters interested me," she replied defensively.

I saw the pink St. Valentine's card I had sent her the previous February, with the little silk heart stuffed with material. After passing through my own correspondence, Dagmar lifted up all the papers and oddments from the top of the drawer which she had supported with her arm, and laid them on the coffee table. Then she took a large envelope from the drawer from which she drew out a bundle of photographs.

She began to show me the photos, rapidly slipping those on top to the back of the pack, but she said nothing and was perceptibly embarrassed when I stopped her, asking for a closer glance at the portraits – for they were mostly of her – dozens of them. She held firmly onto the pack, apparently to ensure I would not snatch it from her out of insatiable curiosity.

The pictures had been taken more than two years ago – mostly during her adolescence, showing a pale introspective girl, who enjoyed simple pleasures. They were portraits of a serious young lady who had not yet developed the poise and seductive charm which comes with maturity.

"These pictures of me are not attractive," she exclaimed, "I look so solemn." I added no comment.

Suddenly she reached a picture which she covered with her hand and she shuffled the pack.

"What's the matter,?" I asked.

"I can't show you any more," she replied.

Jokingly, I leaned forward to snatch the pack away, and we struggled, and she gripped the pack with both hands, trying to rise from the sofa, and so I relented and let go my grasp. She replaced the photos in the envelope. She was in a silly mood.

She took up several more things from the drawer and then I saw a loose cigarette at the bottom. Immediately, I snatched it up and glanced at it, wondering what kind of a souvenir this was, and Dagmar had not seemed to notice. It was a cigarette of average length but then I noted more than one half was filter. I tried to read the name of the brand but realised that the small almost indecipherable letters were in Cyrillic script.

"What are you doing with a Russian cigarette,?" I asked.

"Where did you find it,?" she enquired startled.

"From the bottom of the drawer," I replied calmly.

Frantically, she lifted up everything from the bottom of the drawer, taking up an envelope containing a cigarette packet, and picking up several loose cigarettes she replaced them in the packet.

"They're unusual souvenirs, aren't they,?" I said.

"It would take too long to explain," she replied.

"We're in no hurry – we've got all night."

"You wouldn't be interested. Anyway, I prefer not to talk about them."

She began hurriedly replacing everything in the drawer again, and I watched her with curious fascination, wondering what strange thoughts were passing through her mind.

"Why have you shown me the things in this drawer,?" I asked.

"I thought you'd be interested," she replied sulkily.

"I was, but every time we came to something interesting you dismissed it as unimportant."

"You're too analytical," she said. "You only ask questions about things which interest you – not questions about things which seek a closer sympathy with my feelings. Your questions are too personal – things that might be tactless."

I laughed at the expression of these curious thoughts – so typically feminine, I thought in my prejudice.

"You mean like Russian cigarettes," I replied. "You resent my natural curiosity. Why did you show me the drawer if you had so many things to hide?"

"I've shown you almost everything – only one or two very personal things have I hidden from you."

"Don't blame me for not asking questions you'd prefer to put into my own head. After all, we are separate individuals," I pleaded.

"I like to look through these things sometimes," said Dagmar dreamily, "and I feel I'd like to share them with others, but then I find they're such personal things that I daren't talk about them – not even with closest friends – because of the memories they arouse."

I lay in bed, thinking, for a long time that night. I was now certain – more than at any time before – that Dagmar was concealing from me some important episode about her life – something which may have happened perhaps two years ago. I recollected it was a mysterious fascination which had first drawn me to Dagmar when I saw her in the little Art Shop in Stalin Allee. I had asked myself then, what lay in the mystery of her resignation in life. I remembered the discussion I had had with Martin Schultz about Dagmar on the evening of the day we had met. Martin had suggested that perhaps some sorrow or threat hung over the girl's life. Her letters to me had been enigmatic as if repressing some aspect of her existence.

Perhaps her soul was oppressed by some anxiety or insuperable problem. Why had she been moved to show me the things in the drawer? Had she intended revealing to me something about her past and then suddenly changed her mind? Had she perhaps intended to arouse my curiosity to such a degree that I would force the story from her, thereby lightening her mind in sharing the secret with another, or maybe, even in the hope of finding a solution to her problem? This explanation was plausible for she had acted as if she might have harboured the burden of some dark and terrible event.

She had not opened her heart or expressed her feelings freely, and her reticence and resignation in life suggested she might be repressing her inmost thoughts. But I was too tired that evening to attempt forcing the "real" story from her, or the secret with which her mind was apparently burdened. If she had in fact intended me to force such a story from her, how had she hoped or anticipated I might react to the revelations?

Then there were other things which aroused my curiosity and suspicion. The incident concerning the mirror that morning still haunted my mind. Of course, I might well have first seen the mirror in my dream in some store during my first visit to Berlin, and its visual appearance might have sunk deep into the recesses of the subconscious, only to reappear during that night immediately previous to my second journey to the city, but even so, the phenomenon was uncanny.

Dagmar's awakened interest in my dream and her question as to whether it had been "horrid" was also curious. Then on my relating the dream, she had dismissed it with relief as of no consequence, exclaiming only, "Oh, that's all!" What horrid episode, then, had she suspected I might have dreamt?

To me the only significance of the dream lay in its revelation that Dagmar was concealing some factor about her life she was loathed to reveal. My struggle with her that evening for the possession of the photos as we had sat on the sofa was reminiscent of the struggle in the dream for the possession of the mirror. Most curious of all that evening, had been the discovery of the Russian cigarettes which she mysteriously hoarded amongst her most personal possessions.

Much as I loved Dagmar, the occurrence of these paradoxes prompted me towards a greater caution with regard to developing our relationship.

Chapter 26

P apa, Papa,!" exclaimed Frau Renot excitedly in a confidential undertone, as she hurriedly entered the room, "Frau Hartmann may be trying to cause mischief again."

Herr Renot and I were sitting at either end of the dining table finishing lunch.

"What sort of mischief,?" exclaimed the old man unimpressed by his wife's excitability, and swivelling a spoon around his plate with a movement of the whole arm as he delivered the last of the prunes into his mouth.

"Frau Hartmann knows we have an Englishman with us. Frau Klingberg's just told me she overheard Frau Hartmann talking with Frau Baumann about Herr Furner."

Masticating the prunes, the old man watched his wife with intense interest as she spoke. He spat the stones into his spoon, placing them on the plate.

"I expect it's nothing," he replied waving his hand aside.

"Frau Klingberg said that Hartmann was speaking very confidentially to Frau Baumann – just outside Frau Baumann's flat on the fourth floor – but she couldn't help overhearing."

"I shouldn't worry about it, Mamma," exclaimed the old man trying to console his wife.

"Frau Klingberg came all the way downstairs just to tell me. She seemed concerned. She said Frau Hartmann thought we had no right to have an Englishman staying with us."

"What does Frau Hartmann know about Herr Furner, anyway? Only a lot of rumours, and she can't do anything with them," exclaimed the old man. "In these flats every old woman sees everyone entering and leaving the block. They haven't got anything better to do, and so it's natural for rumours to spread around about Herr Furner."

"But Frau Hartmann does know something about Herr Furner."

"What? Only that he's an Englishman. She doesn't know whether or not he's got a Visitor's visa for the East sector, and she hasn't any way of finding out."

"She suspects Herr Furner's anti-Communist," exclaimed the good Frau excitedly.

"Oh *quatsch*, Mamma! How can she know that? Besides, Herr Furner's not even staying here in these flats. He's staying with us across the road. I bet Frau Hartmann doesn't know that."

"Frau Hartmann's met Herr Furner," exclaimed the good Frau with emphasis.

"*Quatsch*, Mamma,!" said the old man.

"Yes, I met Frau Hartmann a couple of days ago," I interrupted.

"When Herr Furner was out in the courtyard talking to Granny, that morning," said Frau Renot. "Do you remember now, Papa? Just before you went on a walk together."

The old man looked thoughtful awhile, then broke off a piece of bread and began to chew it.

"What's this about Frau Hartmann suspecting Herr Furner's anti-Communist,?" he said at last.

"I've never said I'm anti-Communist," I said defensively. "The old woman asked if I'd like to live in the East sector, and I answered ambiguously, saying that that was a loaded question."

"Frau Klingberg only said she overheard Hartmann say she 'strongly suspected' Herr Furner was anti-Communist." Exclaimed Frau Renot.

"What did you say to Frau Hartmann,?" said the old man turning sharply to me.

"Not much. I was only with her for a few minutes. Herr Schomberg and Lufner were also witnesses in the courtyard. She asked a lot of harmless questions, and I gave straight answers. I couldn't do much else, could I?"

"What did she ask?"

"How long I'd be staying in East Berlin; how long I intended remaining, and where I was staying."

The old man fixed me intently with his eyes.

"And did you tell her?"

"I couldn't do otherwise."

The old man glanced earnestly at his wife as if to ask her, "What shall we do now?" Frau Renot returned an anxious glance.

"Frau Hartmann was going on about bona fide visitors to the DDR having to stay in the appointed international hotels, and so that Herr Furner was unlikely to have a proper Visitor's visa. That's what Frau Klingberg said she heard," continued Frau Renot. "Frau Hartman came to the conclusion that the only reason Herr Furner was in East Berlin was to court Dagmar."

"What does Frau Hartmann know about Herr Furner and Dagmar," exclaimed the old man in angry astonishment. He turned his eyes on me again.

"To that charge I plead not guilty," I said raising my hand. "I'm afraid it was Frau Brüning who told Frau Hartmann about my friendship with Dagmar."

"So Granny's known about this all along – she was witness to it. Why didn't she let us know there'd been a lot of gossiping in the courtyard with Frau Hartmann involved,?" exclaimed the old man to his wife.

"Granny's old. You can't expect her to be on her guard against the Stasi. Old people are naturally careless," replied his wife.

"What is it about Frau Hartmann,?" I asked, overcome by a feeling of guilt at being responsible for this situation.

"She's an informer – a *Spitzel*," replied Frau Renot.

"She's thought to be the official house-spy for this block," said the old man.

"And worse still, her son's a high ranking officer in the SSD – the State Security Service," added Frau Renot.

"In that case I think it's best I left the flat across the road," I said.

"That won't be necessary," said Frau Renot.

"But I think it is," I insisted. "It would be no trouble moving into a small Pension in the West sector."

"But if you go straight to the police and get a Visitor's visa, you could stay here," said Frau Renot.

"They'd never issue it on demand," I replied.

"I'll come along with you. I'll talk with the police," said the old man brightly in a tone of importance.

A few minutes later Papa Renot and I were plodding along Graetz Strasse towards Treptower police station. He had lit up a new cigar before leaving the flat and his mood was optimistic.

"And remember, I'll do the talking," said the old man in a confidential tone nudging me in the side. "I'm resident here. The family are registered with the police."

I smiled to myself at the idea that such "connections" might be of any value. He seemed to regard himself as a "customer" of the police, and therefore entitled to a favour in the same way that a butcher might put aside a special cut for one of his regulars.

We crossed the street and went through the gates fronting one of the red brick barracks, and as we walked up the path to the heavy brown doors, Papa Renot brushed his lapels of invisible specks of dust. As we reached the doors, one was thrown open, and two Vopos quickly ran down the steps to the pathway below, almost knocking over the old man in their path.

"Smoking forbidden in government buildings," exclaimed the elder official pointing to the old man's cigar.

Papa Renot hesitated momentarily, and then made as if to stub it out on the steps.

"Not there – they were swept half an hour ago – out in the street," said the same official, and the two Vopos quickly disappeared, their jackboots resounding on the stonework.

The old man made towards the street again, when I stopped him, exclaiming, "It's all right, they've gone now. You can stub it out on the steps – no one's looking."

He followed my hint, and on entering the doors of the building we climbed a dozen steps and went up to a little window high up in the wall marked *Enquiries*. The old man tapped on the window. It was abruptly opened, and a fat red face appeared, looking down at us officiously.

"I have an Englishman here who's an acquaintance we'd like to stay with us in Treptow," began the old man in a tone of self-confident good humour. "We'd like to apply for a Visitor's visa to take immediate effect."

It was clear the old man had thought out this little speech beforehand, judging by its well-turned phrases and the official style of its terminology. I shared none of the old man's confidence, and was unimpressed by his ingratiating manner which was unsuited to breaking through the stone-hard attitude of bureaucracy.

"This isn't the correct department for issuing visas to foreigners," replied the official bluntly, looking the old man up and down with suspicion.

"This is my pass," said the old man taking a card from his breast pocket, " – I'm registered here."

"That's irrelevant," exclaimed the police official waving his hand aside irritably. "You must apply to the competent office."

"Could you give us the address?"

The official puffed out his lips with a gesture of bored despair at the stupidity of such a request, and with languid movements, he stretched his fat arm across the table and took up a pencil. An address was written on a slip of memo paper.

"I shouldn't be too hopeful," he said with indifference as he handed over the slip.

"*Danke, danke vielmals,*!" exclaimed Papa Renot, "*Auf wiedersehen,*!"

The police official made no acknowledgment as the window was slammed shut.

After a tram journey to the other end of Treptow and a fifteen minute walk, we reached the supposedly competent office for the issuing of Visitors' visas to foreigners. It was a massive red building in Stern Damm, although not half as large as the police station off Graetz Strasse.

We went through the double doors of the building into a spacious hallway with many doors leading off. We knocked on a door marked *Enquiries* and entered, walking up to a counter behind which stood several Vopos sorting through boxes of index cards. Behind them others sat at tables typing out forms and copying data. Papa Renot and I stood expectantly behind the counter.

The old man grinned ingratiatingly with bumptious self-confidence, but the officials did not bother to look up from their index cards to see who had entered, and the typewriters continued to tap loudly. This was a busy office.

At last, one of the officials ceased typing, rose from the table and strolled over to the counter. Again the old man stated his business. The official turned to his colleagues to enquire what department was competent to handle such a matter. One replied he knew nothing – he had never heard of a similar enquiry before. Another said he thought there were no competent authorities in the building to handle the matter, whilst another confirmed this opinion, suggesting nonchalantly we should go to the Administration Police in Neue König Strasse and ask for Department Two, which dealt with foreigners, passes and residence permits. Where was Neue König Strasse? In the city centre, Berlin Mitte.

Yet another official contradicted the fact that this was the competent office, saying all vises for foreigners were only issued at the office in Am Zeughaus. There was momentary confusion and an argument began as each used his specific knowledge of established procedures against the others. Finally it was suggested we should visit a department on the third floor dealing with foreigners in Treptow, and a pass was written out for us to see the appropriate official and a room number was given.

The old man and I climbed the staircase to the third floor, and then we walked along several corridors until we found the door with the correct number. The old man faltered momentarily and then knocked twice. His self-confidence was diminished.

We entered a large typing pool. All around the walls, from floor to ceiling, were stacked hundreds of box files, and between the windows stood metal card index cabinets, and we were deafened by the clatter of typewriters.

"We're looking for Captain Töpper," said the old man to the nearest typist.

"There," answered the typist looking up from his machine pointing to the end of the room.

We walked to the far end of the room where Captain Töpper sat at a large table covered with papers, thick books and binders holding forms. Captain Töpper was a green-uniformed green-skirted official, with black hair tied neatly into a bun, about forty years of age, with a trim figure and a pinched complexion. She sat reading a thick typescript holding a pencil between her fingers as every now and then she jotted down a correction between the lines.

We stood silently in front of the table, and after some moments, she looked up from the typescript and glanced enquiringly at the old man, fixing him intently with her cold dark eyes, as if telling him to come directly to the point. The old man repeated his speech almost verbatim as he had first delivered it in the police station near Graetz Strasse.

"And this is the Englishman,?" replied Captain Töpper speaking quickly with a clear sharp pronunciation.

"Yes," we both replied at once.

"And what's your name,?" she enquired of the old man.

"Renot," he replied.

"And what's the address the Englishman's actually staying at now,?" she said snatching up a piece of paper, holding her pencil at the ready.

The old man hesitated.

"I'll give her the address of my Pension in the West sector – where I stayed last year," I whispered quickly, nudging the old man in the side.

"Sixteen Graetz Strasse," replied the old man.

He should not have said that, I told myself. Captain Töpper scribbled down the address.

"And that's your address, yes,?" she asked sharply.

"Er – yes," replied the old man.

"And how long's he been staying there?"

"Three or four nights," he replied.

"Now, Herr Renot, you're a citizen of this country and you know the laws of the DDR," began Captain Töpper slamming her pencil onto the table. "You know that no foreigner without a visa is permitted to spend the night in the Democratic sector. A foreigner may spend all day in the East sector, if he so chooses, but it's strictly forbidden to remain beyond midnight."

"We'd only like a visa for a few nights – for ten or fourteen days at most," pleaded the old man humbly.

"That's irrelevant," replied the Captain. "It doesn't make any difference if he wants a visa for ten days or ten years. He's not carrying a visa at the moment and that's all that concerns this department."

I was embarrassed and upset at having to watch this castigation of the old man, especially at the hands of someone so much younger than himself.

"Well, we'd like to apply for a visa," said the old man. "That's what we've come for."

"Then I don't know why you've come to this department, We have nothing to do with the issuing of visas. Who sent you to this department?"

"The Enquiry office. They said this was the competent office for dealing with foreigners in Treptow."

"This office is only responsible for filing details on foreigners resident in Treptow. Our responsibility is merely to check on the renewal of labour permits and expiring residents permits. We have no power for issuing visas to foreigners wishing to enter the DDR," exclaimed Captain Töpper throwing up her hands.

"To which department must we go then?"

"There's only one central office in the DDR responsible for issuing visas. That's in the Am Zeughaus."

"Where's that?"

"A long way from here. Behind the Unter den Linden."

"Then we'll go there," said the old man beginning to move away.

"They can't issue it on demand. Visiting the DDR is a privilege," exclaimed Captain Töpper crossing her legs and gesticulating with her hands all the while. "The authorities like to discriminate in issuing tourist visas to foreigners. We have to keep out undesirables. So applying is a timely process because of the checks which have to be made."

"Come, we'll go back to Graetz Strasse," I whispered to the old man.

I could see there was little chance of breaking through the bureaucracy and I noted Captain Töpper was becoming impatient as she rolled the pencil between her fingers.

"Who's the director of the office in Am Zeughaus,?" enquired the old man.

"I know nothing about the office in Am Zeughaus – it's not my department," replied Captain Töpper irritably. "Besides, there isn't a director – it's a government body, coming under the Ministry of Foreign Affairs. All applications must pass through the correct channels. But again, I must point out emphatically, Herr Renot, that a foreigner staying overnight in the Democratic sector is absolutely forbidden."

She fixed the old man with her dark brown eyes and there was a momentary pause.

"*Danke*,!" replied the old man dejectedly, "*Auf wiedersehen*!"

"*Auf wiedersehen*,!" replied Captain Töpper drawling the words, so they had an ironic intonation, and with our tails between our legs we left the building.

As we returned to Graetz Strasse Papa Renot was silent and thoughtful, and seemed depressed. Perhaps he experienced a feeling of humiliation and shame after his castigation from Captain Töpper who had treated him much as an irate schoolmistress would admonish a naughty nine year old. I felt disinclined to break the silence and thought it wiser to leave him to his unhappy ponderings until the police station was far behind us. As we walked through the courtyard of the flats at number fifty-five I told the old man I would immediately gather up my belongings from across the road and move into a Pension in the West sector. He said nothing in reply.

Everything was explained to Frau Renot, and he explained how he had done his best to find a way of bye-passing the red tape.

"It's so absurd," she replied. "I can't understand it. He can stay here all day but can't stay the nights. Why would anyone want to pass a law like that?"

"That's how it is. I tried to get the official to give us the name of the departmental director in the city centre, but she would say nothing. She was acting like the Minister of Police – but she took down our address."

"Our address! Was that necessary,?" exclaimed Frau Renot in horror.

"I had to give it her, Mamma."

"I think I'll have to be leaving immediately," I said. "It's impossible for me to stay here. It would be compromising your safety."

"It's a pity you must go now you're so comfortably settled," bemoaned the good Frau. "Go into the sitting room, both of you, and I'll bring cakes and tea."

As the two of us sat with our refreshments, and Papa Renot looked fatigued after his long ordeal, Frau Renot hurriedly entered the room in excited optimism, followed by Herr Schomberg. The neighbour knew an inexpensive Pension in the American sector not twenty minutes walk away, and it was arranged I should go there and ask for a room.

"But you must still have all your meals with us," insisted Papa Renot. "No breakfast or other meals at the hotel."

Some minutes later I returned to No. 16 with Frau Renot and began packing, and as I took down my toilet articles as they hung on their little pieces of pink ribbon, I felt a pang of sadness at being so suddenly forced to leave my kind and hospitable hosts. It was with a feeling of regret that I left that makeshift and inconvenient old washroom with all its disrepairs for the last time.

BOOK VI

Fate of The Small People

'Tis that delightsome transport we can feel
Which painters cannot paint, nor words reveal,
Nor any art we know of can conceal.

Thomas Paine, *What Is Love?*

Chapter 27

I took up my hold-all and was about to leave the flat when Frau Renot rushed from the kitchen and stopped me. It had suddenly occurred to her that there could be complications if I attempted to leave the East sector on foot carrying an overnight bag. Awkward questions might be asked by the frontier police. "We would all be in trouble then," she exclaimed. It was thought best I should walk to the Pension, book in and pay in advance for the first few nights, and then return to Graetz Strasse to fetch my luggage, leaving the East sector via the circuitous but safer means of the S-Bahn.

I walked to the end of Graetz Strasse to the Wiener bridge, a frontier crossing point into the suburb of Kreuzberg. Four Vopos armed with machine guns stood silently on either side of the road. They made no attempt to intercept me and I passed a notice in four languages: YOU ARE NOW ENTERING THE AMERICAN SECTOR! Just beyond this notice at one side of the bridge was another four language hoarding stating: THE CARRYING OF ARMS OR MUNITIONS INTO THE AMERICAN SECTOR IS FORBIDDEN! I walked up a wooden ramp and onto the narrow footway at one side of the bridge, reserved for pedestrian traffic, crossed over the breadth of the Landwehr canal and down a few steps at the other side of the bridge into the West. A lone West German policeman stood at the side of the roadway, armed only with a pistol buttoned into his holster.

I walked along the broad Wiener Strasse towards Spreewald Platz. It was a long street lined with trees and across the street from where I walked were high crumbling tenement buildings with shops beneath. Alongside the pavement on which I walked was a stark ten foot high red brick wall running along the full length of the street. It walled in the goods yard of the former Görlitzer station. It was a quiet street with almost no traffic, for it only led to the Wiener bridge and the sector frontier which was not open to vehicular traffic.

I reached Spreewald Platz and the front of the Görlitzer station, a massive yellow brick ruin with towers at either end, steps leading up to the entrance, and thick high walls with shattered windows leading out to the sky. The station had been built in late Prussian style with Saracenic columns built into the structure and Romanesque windows. It had once been the pride of Germany and symbolised Berlin as the heart of Europe and the connecting link with the Middle East, for it was from this station that the Berlin to Baghdad railway had originally been designed. Now it was nothing more than a gutted shell, its proud steps overgrown with grass and weeds, its doors sealed over with planks of wood crudely nailed across the entrance and its expanse of railway lines leading nowhere.

The spacious square in front of the station was a wide roadway encircling a small public park consisting of grass, some trees, flower beds, and a children's playground. I walked across the square to the buildings at the other side, most of which were seedy hotels and Pensions which in an earlier age had enjoyed prosperity. The facades were grimy and the grey rendering had crumbled away to reveal bare brickwork beneath. There was a ghostly emptiness, just a few small children shouting and chasing one another, as I passed along the pavement.

I found the pension, filled in the forms, and after passing along many passages and staircases, was shown to my room at the top of the building. I was handed an assortment of four heavy keys, and their uses were explained. The first was for entering the building and the second for entering the front door of the Pension. These keys were to be retained by me permanently during my stay. On entering the Pension I was to approach the duty reception clerk and ask for my room key. Two further keys would be handed me. I would then walk to the far end of a long passageway, open a door and leave the Pension by another exit where I would find myself by another staircase. I would climb to the sixth floor, open an annexe entrance to the Pension with the third key and then open my own room door with the fourth. On leaving the Pension, I would exit the annexe, go down the staircase till I reached the door where I had originally left the main part of the Pension, and ring a bell. (This is where I had been relieved the necessity for carrying a fifth key.) On entering the Pension I would surrender the two last keys and was then free to leave.

The room was small with a high ceiling and massive door. There was a small brass iron bedstead, a desk and chair, a wardrobe and a very old and cracked basin with running water. The room was decorated with a colourful William Morris style floral wallpaper, but despite this, it was depressingly dark and gloomy. The high narrow window was set into a deep wall and covered by a thick hanging of net curtains. But I could not complain, for the room was clean and cost a mere four marks a night – remarkably cheap for anywhere in Berlin.

I returned to the main part of the Pension, and glanced into the guests' sitting room. It had a comfortable clubby atmosphere, and about a dozen elderly ladies were seated in thickly upholstered armchairs with books and newspapers. They were clearly long-term residents, and the fine Pension of formers days which had possibly accommodated the well-to-do was now transformed into a home for geriatrics.

As I crossed the Wiener bridge into the East sector, I saw three Vopos crowded round a little old lady who had crossed the frontier some distance in front of me. One of the policemen was questioning her and all three had their hands in her little black shopping bag, and were taking out packets of groceries, glancing at them and returning them into the bag. A fourth Vopo was standing idly by, smoking at the side of the road. An example of police humour, I thought, as I passed by unnoticed.

On returning to the flat at No. 16, I took up my hold-all and went to Treptower Park station where I took the train to Ostkreuz and then changed for Warschauer Strasse, where I left the S-Bahn station and walked to the nearby Underground station of Warschauer Brücke where I took the train to the West sector. It was with a sense of relief that I reached the West together with my baggage without being intercepted. Fortunately, it was only during infrequent intervals when the Volkspolizei boarded trains at sector crossings checking passengers for suspicious packages – i.e. luggage suggesting a permanent migration from East to West. On arriving at the Görlitzer Underground station I realised that the long diversion had taken three quarters of an hour as contrasted with the direct walking distance of a mere eighteen minutes to reach my destination.

I unpacked my hold-all and washed in preparation for meeting Dagmar at her shop by closing time. The plumbing and water system connecting the taps of my basin gave cause for concern. First I turned the tap marked *Heiss* and nothing happened. I then turned the tap marked *Kalt*. I waited and still nothing. Both taps were turned full on. Suddenly there was a gurgling sound deep down in the bowels of the plumbing, followed by a vibrating and shrieking of the taps as if pandemonium were let loose. Frantically, I turned down the taps and there was a spluttering from the hot tap and dirty brown liquid splashed into the sink, and this was followed by a spluttering from the cold tap and dirty yellow liquid splashed into the other side of the sink. Then the noise subsided and the crisis of the water system abated as I let the taps run and the colour cleared to its desirable crystal clarity. Despite all the internal drama from the plumbing, however, the water from both taps remained cold.

I took the golden-foiled neck between thumb and fingers and turned the bottle in the ice bowl. Dagmar laughed, and despite an earlier reluctance, agreed that I should yet again fill her glass with the frothy bubbling Champagne. We were in high spirits and exchanging jokes, and Dagmar had been impersonating and telling amusing stories about eccentric customers she had served. Outside, crowds strolled leisurely along the wide pavement, and there was an environment of pleasure and affluence.

We were seated at a table within the enclosure of the pavement restaurant of the Roxy Hôtel – possibly at the same table we had occupied almost a year earlier. How much had happened during the intervening period! We had met in the little Art Shop in Stalin Allee; there had been the first outing in the Kurfürstendamm and the first expressions of affection between us; the strangely curious friendship during that time we had corresponded together; the quarrel and breaking of our friendship; our renewed correspondence some months later; and then my second visit to the great capital. So much had happened during the past year that time seemed to have been extended in allowing for so many events and experiences.

"But I'm afraid it'll make my head go round," said Dagmar waving her hand round the top of her head.

"Not after all we've eaten," I said consolingly.

"What did you do this afternoon. Go for another walk with Papa,?" asked Dagmar ironically.

I crossed my brows, and looking down I turned the stem of the Champagne glass between my fingers. I hadn't yet told Dagmar about the episode concerning Frau Hartmann and my moving to a Pension in the American sector.

"Or did you take Granny for a ride in her wheel chair,?" added Dagmar humorously.

"I went with your father to the police to try and get a Visitor's permit."

"What for,?" asked Dagmar alarmed.

"Because one of the neighbours told your mother Frau Hartmann had been gossiping about an Englishman in the flat."

"That could be dangerous," said Dagmar solemnly.

"I still don't understand what kind of a threat she's supposed to be," I said.

"She's an informer."

"But how? What's she exactly done?"

"People have gone missing and Frau Hartmann's believed to be responsible."

"Why – what proof?"

"She's the house Spitzel for the block"

"Has she shown you her credentials for that?"

"Of course not. But she's nosy and a gossip, and friendly to everyone. And she asks too many questions."

"That proves nothing."

"In the eyes of everyone she's a Stasi agent. The unanimity of feeling is proof enough. Besides, her son's in the State Security Service."

"But what has she to report on amongst all those decrepit old pensioners?"

"There are young people too in the block."

"And what have they got to betray themselves?"

"Usually small things like holding a membership card of an organisation in the West. Sometimes more serious things like persuading people to migrate – or black marketing; or attending political meetings in the West; or organising and participating in lotteries. Sometimes we all commit dishonest acts – just to survive - and so we're all at risk from Frau Hartmann."

"In that case I'm surprised life isn't made unpleasant for her by the other residents. After all, she does seem to be a minority of one against the rest."

"You don't understand. The authorities are ruthless. They have a hundred ways of keeping people in line. People are frightened here."

"Your mother seemed panic struck when she found out what happened this morning. I've never seen her like that before."

"That's because she's had a taste of what the authorities can do."

"Tell me about it."

"It's not nice. My mother wouldn't like me to tell. It was three years ago."

"Go on."

"I don't know if I can," said Dagmar spacing her words. "It was trouble with the Volkspolizei. It was humiliating for Mamma at the time. It was humiliating for us all."

Despite her reluctance Dagmar began to tell the story of her mother's traumatic experience. She spoke slowly and sometimes abruptly, hurrying over the more unpleasant aspects, but filling in every detail, and patiently answering those questions in response to the occasional interruption. She had not witnessed all the events, but her sister Gisela, had seen most of what passed, and then related them to Dagmar shortly afterwards. Then her mother, subsequently, in a mood of despondency and self-pity described her experiences in glaring detail to all who had had time to listen. But that was long ago, and since then,

Frau Renot had wanted to forget the episode and not be reminded of it again.

I sat forward resting my hands on the table, listening patiently as Dagmar related the story, and I was absorbed and at the same time aghast as the facts fell from her lips, and in satisfying my own curiosity, I often asked her to verify a point or describe the manner or mood in which an action had been carried out.

Chapter 28

The first event of this episode occurred on a street corner in Graetz Strasse. It was a Saturday morning and a fine Summer's day, and the pavements were crowded with shoppers. Frau Renot was amongst those shoppers, and had just left a grocery store with a basket of provisions for the weekend, when she began to make her way home.

After a few yards she came to a street corner – or almost so – where she intended crossing. On the same corner happened to be standing a People's policeman with machine gun over shoulder, but the good Frau never registered his presence – so common a sight was it to see People's policemen standing on street corners in that half of the city.

Neither did the good Frau notice (or at least so she claimed) when the Vopo called after her as she began to cross the street, and perhaps understandably so, since he merely shouted the word, "Comrade!" after her several times. It was not until after she had walked some yards into the middle of the road when a hand took hold of her shoulder that she realised something was amiss. She was brought back to the street corner, the policeman meanwhile holding his fingers onto the shoulder of her coat. The good Frau was alarmed at this unexpected occurrence, and as they stood at the kerb side, she asked nervously as to what was amiss.

"Did you hear me call after you,?" said the Vopo gruffly, glancing down at the little lady. He was a big thick-set chap, about nineteen years of age.

"I heard nothing," replied the good Frau.

"I shouted 'Comrade' after you three times. Didn't you hear that,?" said the Vopo. He spoke with an ugly Saxon dialect.

"I heard nothing," replied Frau Renot bewildered at the thought of having perhaps contravened the law.

"I spoke loud enough," said the Vopo encouraged by the timidity of the lady. "There were people who heard me on the other side of the street, because I saw them look up."

"I didn't hear."

"I take it you're not deaf, else you'd be wearing some kind of aid."

"I thought you were calling someone else."

"So you did hear me," exclaimed the Vopo proud at the success of his investigatory procedure. "Why didn't you return to the pavement when you heard me call?"

"I didn't know you were calling *me*," returned the good Frau.

"But you heard my voice call in your direction. Why didn't you turn to see what was the matter?"

"I said I didn't know you were calling me."

"Now my good Frau, you've already admitted you heard my voice," said the Vopo gesticulating.

"It could have been anybody's voice calling someone across the street."

"I called 'Comrade' three times – each time louder than before, and still you made no attempt to look up."

"Why address me as 'Comrade'? Do you address every citizen as 'Comrade'? What am I to understand by that,?" exclaimed the good Frau exasperated. "You can address your colleagues as 'Comrade,' but how do you expect any citizen to understand when you use that term?"

The Vopo began grinning, waving his hand up and down to calm the good lady.

"All right my good Frau, we understand you object to being addressed as 'Comrade,'" he said trying to quieten her.

"What do you want with me,?" exclaimed Frau Renot.

"Only to see your identity pass," explained the Vopo.

The good Frau laid down her shopping basket on the pavement, opened her coat, and put her hand into the pocket of her dress. Then she put her hands into her coat pockets, searching for the essential document. The Vopo stood by patiently.

"It must be in my bag," she said.

"She took her handbag out of the basket, opened it, and began searching through all the jumble of objects which were there, but it was nowhere to be found.

"I don't know where it is," said the good Frau helplessly.

"You mean you haven't got it," explained the Vopo.

"I always carry my pass – it's just that I can't find it," she replied.

"And let's hope you'll never be without it again," replied the policeman insolently. "You know it's an offence against the laws of the Democratic Republic to walk out without carrying an identity pass. I saw you come out of that shop there. Did you buy these things there?"

"Yes! They know me well."

"Let's see what's in that bag."

Frau Renot handed the shopping bag to the policeman who began to rummage through it.

"How did you buy these things without a pass,?" enquired the policeman glancing at one of the articles and then dropping it back into the bag again.

"I said – they know me well," answered the good Frau abruptly.

"It's a private shop – capitalist, yes?"

"What's that got to do with it?"

"It exploits labour for profit. Aren't there enough state run H.O. shops in the neighbourhood?"

"No! Besides, I shop where I choose," replied the good Frau indignantly.

The Vopo returned the shopping basket to Frau Renot.

"Are you carrying a library card, club identity card, or political or SED membership card,?" he asked.

"No, I'm non-political."

"No one's 'Non-political,'" said the Vopo significantly. "Give me your name and address," he added unbuttoning his top pocket and taking out a pad and pencil.

"Frau Maria Renot, sixteen Graetz Strasse," she returned.

"Sixteen," repeated the Vopo reflectively as he wrote down the address. "And you're returning home directly with this shopping?"

"Yes."

"Then, my good Frau, you're going in the wrong direction. Even numbers are on this side."

"I'm going to my mother's flat, that's at number" –

The Vopo threw up his head and laughed. Frau Renot stopped momentarily in her confusion.

"My mother's a pensioner. We live there, and cook, and eat there during the day. It's at number fifty-five."

The policeman waved his hand in disbelief.

"I think we misunderstand each other," he exclaimed smiling down at her.

"You could be anyone. This area's full of black marketers from across the border buying up our valued merchandise. You must come with me to headquarters."

"I'm guilty of nothing," exclaimed Frau Renot excitedly.

"Let me be fair, my good Frau," said the Vopo with a conciliatory gesture. "I'm not here to persecute honest citizens. But this morning I've been put on special alert. I've been asked to watch out for and apprehend non-passholding shoppers. If you're not the tenth you're the twentieth shopper I've questioned leaving this particular store. So put your mind to rest – you're not being picked-upon."

"Why pick on me? Why not somebody else,?" cried the good Frau. I'm well known in the district."

By this time a small crowd had gathered solemnly watching the proceedings.

"Then my good Frau you may bring a witness with you to the headquarters," said the Vopo consolingly. "Do any of you know this lady,?" he added addressing the crowd.

Several shook their heads, and wanting to avoid trouble, the crowd began to disperse.

"We'll go to the headquarters and find out just how well known you are," said the Vopo. "There's already too much here that doesn't add up."

As Frau Renot was escorted along Graetz Strasse she was bewildered, humiliated and indignant, and in no small way embarrassed, for the attention of the street was upon her, and how many of those passers-by might have known her by sight if not by name? What thoughts and suspicions might pass through their minds as they saw the good Frau being escorted down the street, a policeman's hand laid firmly on her shoulder? What felony had she committed – pilfered some article from a shop, or stolen a purse left on a counter, or quarrelled with and assaulted a peaceful citizen on the open street? How would she explain her predicament afterwards, and what mischief and what misapprehensions would result from her arrest on the highway and in view of the people who used that street?

On arrival at the headquarters, Frau Renot was taken to a small room and led up to a counter, behind which sat several Vopos at tables penning-in details on index cards. One of their number rose from his table warmly greeting the comrade who had just entered.

"Good morning, Theo, how goes it,?" he said stretching his hand across the counter.

"Fine, Erich," answered the other as the comrades shook hands. "I've brought in someone without a pass. No identity. Picked her up in Graetz Strasse."

"Let's have the name and address," said Erich casually, placing a pad of paper on the counter without glancing at Frau Renot.

"Says she lives in Graetz Strasse, but I suspect she's a currency swindler from the West," said Theo. "Came out with a lot of *quatsch* which didn't add up."

"I've said nothing untrue," exclaimed Frau Renot, but no notice was taken of her. "I want to bring witnesses to secure my release. This isn't justice."

"You've already committed an offence by not carrying a pass," exclaimed Erich, "so don't start playing the innocent."

"She admits buying all this from a private shop in Graetz Strasse," said Theo raising her shopping basket and placing it on the counter

"Those things are mine – you've no right to touch them," exclaimed Frau Renot as the policemen searched through her basket.

"Don't worry – they won't walk far. We're all honest here," said Erich with a chuckle.

"When am I free to go,?" enquired Frau Renot. "I have to prepare lunch for my family."

"That depends on the outcome of the investigation," replied Erich.

"When will that be,?" asked the good Frau.

"In about ten minutes, we hope."

"Who'll be seeing her,?" enquired Theo confidentially.

"Captain Kohn."

"Good! He'll put her through it."

"He's out now. I don't know exactly when he'll return," said Erich in an undertone, and he pressed a bell which lay atop the counter.

Again Frau Renot protested and the official across the counter waved his hand at her to remain silent. The door behind the two arrivals was opened and two Vopos entered.

"This lady's waiting for Captain Kohn," said the official behind the counter.

One of the Vopos nodded to the good Frau to follow them. She was taken to a large room stripped of furniture except for long benches fixed round the walls. There was a clock high up on one of the walls, and beneath it, a small speaking window leading into another office. The floor was bare and the walls painted a dark green. The minutes ticked by and still she sat there, patiently waiting to be called.

Twenty-five minutes ticked by, and Frau Renot became restless, and rising from the bench, she went over to the window and diffidently tapped it. She asked how much longer she would need to wait. The official waved his hand, saying it would only be a "few more minutes," and he slammed the window shut, and Frau Renot returned to the bench. More than an hour ticked by, and again Frau Renot returned to the window. She was in a fluster, explaining she had been kept waiting long enough, and that she had a sick daughter at home. She asked if she might send a message to her husband to let him know her whereabouts.

"It would take more than an hour to phone the West sector – the lines in Leipzig and Frankfurt are blocked at this time on a Saturday," replied the officer.*

---

* All telephone communications between East and West Berlin had to go via Leipzig in the East zone and Frankfurt am Main in West Germany, the main telephonic exchange centres of the two countries, since with the partition of Berlin, the telephone communications system between the two halves of the city had been cut.

"I'm an East German," exclaimed Frau Renot desperately.

"That's not what I've been told. – Besides it's forbidden to use the phone until the investigation's been wounded-up."

"I don't want to use the phone. We haven't got a phone. I want to send a message."

"Who send a message?"

"From the office," said the good Frau hesitantly.

"Sorry! Can't spare the staff."

"My husband will be anxious. He doesn't know where I am," pleaded the good Frau, but the window was slammed shut before she had finished the sentence.

She returned to the bench again and sat down. Another half hour ticked by. She rose from the bench, paced nervously across the room several times, trying to summon up courage, and then went over to the window, boldly tapping it. Then she tapped again, louder still. At last, the same face appeared.

"You must be patient," exclaimed the official. "The Captain won't be long."

"I want to go home," said the good Frau attempting to speak in a determined tone but somehow failing, and the window was again shut before she could finish her sentence.

Finally the door of the room was opened and a young Vopo stood at the entrance leading into the dark passage beyond. He indicated that she should follow him. Two hours ten minutes had elapsed since Frau Renot entered that room.

She was taken to another room and instructed to stand on a mat lying in front of an antique desk. On the floor at the side of the desk was Frau Renot's shopping basket. Captain Kohn sat behind the desk. On the wall behind him hung a portrait of Premier Walter Ulbricht and at the side of this was draped the East German flag. The Vopo Theo was also there. He stood a little to the left of Frau Renot. The Vopo who had escorted Frau Renot to the room stood just behind her, and so she felt hemmed in on all sides. There was a pause and no one spoke.

Captain Kohn broke the silence. He slowly pushed back the wooden armchair on which he sat, and the legs of the chair scraped on the floor. He stood up, rising to his full height and he clicked his heels and nodded his head in a little bow to Frau Renot, which might have been taken as a mocking gesture. Frau Renot remained standing to attention.

"Are you the lady claiming to be Frau Maria Renot of sixteen Graetz Strasse,?" said Captain Kohn politely, smiling just perceptibly.

"Yes I am, and that is my correct address," she replied nervously.

Captain Kohn took his seat again, and he pulled the chair comfortably beneath him so that its arms just touched the desk. He was a young man of about thirty with smooth brown hair.

"Volkspolizist Polanyi, what charges do you prefer against this woman,?" said the Captain calmly, but there was an insulting intonation in the tone as well as in the address, in which he pronounced the word "woman."

Polanyi clicked his heels in pulling himself to attention.

"I arrested the accused on the charge of her not carrying an identity pass," he replied. "But Captain, I would beg to reserve the charge until after the completion of this investigation."

"Yes,?" said the Captain.

"The accused was not carrying any kind of identity. I saw her leave the shop from which she admitted purchasing the articles you've already seen in this basket."

"Is this your basket,?" enquired Captain Kohn.

"Yes," replied Frau Renot.

"Did you buy these articles from the shop from which Volkspolizist Polanyi saw you leave?"

"Yes."

"I questioned the accused and suspected her of being a West sector resident," continued Polanyi. "For that reason I would beg to reserve my charge until the completion of this investigation, after her correct identity and address have been verified."

"Are you a citizen of the German Democratic Republic,?" asked Captain Kohn.

"Yes," replied Frau Renot.

"Volkspolizist Polanyi, the accused claims to be both a resident in Treptow and a citizen of the DDR," began the Captain in a measured tone. "It is understood she is not carrying any kind of identity, but can you substantiate your suspicions as to why this woman should be lying?"

"I can Captain. I can produce incriminating evidence," said Polanyi smartly.

"He can produce nothing," cried Frau Renot encouraged by the Captain's apparent scepticism.

"Silence,!" bawled Captain Kohn. "I want the facts which led up to this arrest, and then we shall carry out the investigation."

The young Vopo began his account of the episode. This was soon interrupted by Frau Renot who asked why she should have been "picked upon" in the first place. The Captain asked his subordinate to explain that.

There was a pause and Polanyi momentarily moved his weight from one leg to the other. It looked as if things were not to go his way.

"Haven't the People's Police got better things to do than ask law abiding citizens for identity documents,?" cried the good Frau encouraged.

"Captain," began Polanyi in reply, "Graetz Strasse is situated in that part of the Democratic sector on a corner of land jutting into the suburbs of Kreuzberg and Neukölln. These suburbs are situated in the American sector. The close proximity of Graetz Strasse to the West therefore makes it an easy temptation for illegal traffickers from across the frontier."

"I appreciate your conscientiousness," said Captain Kohn. "Continue your evidence."

"On seeing me, the accused walked to the kerb as if attempting to avoid my eye, and then proceeded to cross the street. My suspicions" –

"I never did that. I never attempted to avoid him. I never saw him in the first place," exclaimed Frau Renot.

"Don't interrupt," cried the Captain. "I want to hear the full account from the Volkspolizist. You may answer the charges later."

"My suspicions were aroused I called after the accused. I called loudly. I exclaimed the word 'Comrade' three times. Rather than responding to my call, she accelerated as if to make an escape."

"It's a lie – it's a lie,!" cried Frau Renot.

"Silence woman,!" bawled Captain Kohn banging his fist onto the desk. "If you interrupt again, I'll have you locked in a cell and the rest of this investigation will be deferred until Monday."

The young Vopo continued his account, dependent as it was upon circumstantial evidence filled with innuendo. At its conclusion, he clicked his heels, bowing to the Captain. There was a momentary pause as the Captain looked down thoughtfully in front of him fingering a paper knife.

"Is the information you've given us regarding your name and address correct,?" he said glancing up at last.

"Yes," replied Frau Renot.

"Then where were you taking this bag of provisions,?" asked Captain Kohn pointing with the paper knife towards the basket.

"To my mother's flat at number fifty-five. My mother's elderly and cannot leave her rooms. I do all the housework there, and my family live and eat there during the day to keep my mother company."

"Is the flat at number fifty-five in your mother's name?"

"Yes."

"Then technically you lied to the Volkspolizist when he questioned you. And if that was unintentional, it's no defence. And what is the name of your mother?"

"Frau Irmgard Brüning."

Captain Kohn wrote down the name and address on a memo pad. He tore off the top sheet.

"Check these names and addresses," he said nodding towards one of the Vopos.

The Vopo clicked his heels, approached the desk, and taking the slip of paper, left the room.

"Can I return home – as soon as the addresses have been verified,?" pleaded Frau Renot. "My husband and family must be fraught with worry."

"We haven't carried out the investigation," replied Captain Kohn.

"Why didn't you save time and check my name and address when I arrived here?"

"Only the investigating officer has authority to go to the files."

"It's all so stupid," said the good Frau under her breath. "I want to be released at once."

"Verifying the names and addresses with our records won't automatically secure your release," replied the Captain. "There are residents in this city with relatives in all parts of Berlin. We must have witnesses to identify you."

"When am I to be released then,?" exclaimed the good Frau in exasperation. "I've committed no crime, and I've already been here for more than two hours."

"The names and addresses are correct," announced the Vopo who had last left the room on his return.

"Then for the moment we'll assume you're Frau Maria Renot of the address you've given, and we'll accordingly carry out this investigation," said Captain Kohn slowly, and flattening some papers on his desk with outstretched fingers. "A charge will be preferred against you for failing to carry with you your identity pass whilst walking out on a public highway. You realise this is a serious office against the laws of the German Democratic Republic,?" said the Captain fixing the good Frau with his eyes.

Frau Renot nodded.

"You will therefore be charged according to the East German Criminal Code. Do you understand? Have you any answer to the charge?"

Frau Renot pleaded that her misdemeanour was unintentional, and when this line of defence was pushed aside, there followed a protracted argument on the petty details of the episode, which gave the appearance of a meaningless charade of cat and mouse pursued by a frustratingly under-employed bureaucracy. There seemed little attempt to support facts already agreed upon by both sides, but desperate attempts to inflate innuendo to impossible limits were pushed to antagonise or intimidate the defendant.

"This is getting us nowhere," exclaimed Captain Kohn in exasperation at last. "We'll let the court decide on the facts. – Let's find out what's on your police file," he added a moment later, picking up the phone to request the relevant papers.

Chapter 29

There was a tense silence of several minutes as the interrogator leaned forward; his elbows on the desk, resting his head in his hands. There was a knock on the door and a clerk entered and delivered the awaited documents.

Captain Kohn opened the folder, fingered through several sheets, and then glanced at the first page.

"Were you born in 1904 in the suburb of Treptow,?" asked the Captain without glancing up from the file.

"Yes, and in fifty-five Graetz Strasse," retorted Frau Renot.

"Is your maiden name Maria Annalise Brüning?"

"Yes."

"I see you married late in life," observed the Captain still without glancing up from the file.

Frau Renot shifted uneasily on her feet. What was that to do with him?

"Were you employed as a secretary in a trading company until your marriage in 1935?"

"Yes."

"Have you a brother living in the suburb of Britz – self-employed as an importer?"

"Yes."

"Did you give birth to a still child in 1936,?" said the Captain suddenly glancing up and fixing her with his eyes.

"Yes," replied Frau Renot after a pause.

The Captain turned over the top sheet of the file.

"Here's your photo," he exclaimed unclipping a passport image from the second sheet of the file and raising it in his hand for a closer look. "I think this helps establish your identity."

He replaced the photo and closed the folder, putting it to one side.

"Am I now free to leave,?" pleaded Frau Renot. "My family will be desparate."

"You'll remain in custody until the hearing on Monday."

"But why,?" exclaimed Frau Renot in utter astonishment.

"Because you have a relative in West Berlin. Experience has demonstrated too often in such situations that citizens flee the DDR. There can be no question of releasing you."

"I want to contact my husband – my family," sobbed Frau Renot.

"That doesn't fall within my remit. It belongs to another department. I'm only the investigating officer. This investigation has now been concluded," he said rising from his chair.

"But my relatives! When will they be told?"

"Ask the prison officer," said Captain Kohn, and he nodded to the Vopo standing behind her. "Take her to the cells."

Frau Renot was entered into the prison section of the police headquarters. She was placed in a cell below ground level in the detention block and a prison officer arranged to despatch a message to inform her family of the episode.

When the messenger arrived at fifty-five Graetz Strasse there was consternation within the flat.   Several neighbours had returned from searching nearby streets and shops, and telephone calls had been made to the emergency departments of hospitals, and Dagmar was in bed with influenza. As the assembled group stood around in the sitting room with expressions of concern Gisela poured out cups of tea. What was to be done?

"Why not go to the police,?" suggested Herr Schomberg, his eyes lighting up at the sudden inspiration.

"That's a good idea," agreed Papa Renot as the merit of the idea dawned on him.

"They might be able to help. They could make enquiries, and perhaps they could even send out a search party," continued Herr Schomberg.

It had never struck these good people that perhaps the police could assist them, so conditioned were they to identifying them as a militia rather than intended to serve every day public needs.

There were three loud knocks from outside. Gisela answered the door and after a moment she ran back to the sitting room.

"Papa, there's a policeman." She exclaimed.

Papa Renot left the sitting room and several inquisitive neighbours followed him down the passageway. The Vopo delivered his message briefly, explaining what had happened, and suggesting that Herr Renot should visit his wife and fetch the bag of shopping which had been left at the headquarters. There was gasps of shock and surprise, and as soon as the Vopo had left, it was decided that Papa Renot and Gisela should immediately leave for the Treptow Police presidium.

Frau Renot was brought up from her cell to speak with her husband through a wire grill as he sat in the visitors' room of the detention block. Gisela fetched the basket of shopping and returned home with it as Papa Renot had said it would be better if he saw "Mamma" alone. With self-pity and resentment, the good Frau gave an account of what had led up to her arrest and of the humiliation she had suffered during the investigation. Papa Renot consoled his wife, saying everything would turn out all right in the end; and on Monday she need only tell the truth, and after the hearing she would be released and all would soon be forgotten.

The identity pass was found later that afternoon. It was discovered on the good Frau's dressing table at number sixteen. It must have been put there the previous night or early that morning when she had changed into a different dress. Papa Renot took the pass to his wife when he visited her the following day.

Papa Renot, Gisela and several neighbours arrived at the Justice building in Litten Strasse, where the trial was to be held, well before the sitting of the courts on Monday morning, to enquire as to the procedure for the defence. The police were not helpful. Papa Renot and his small party were directed to a department and on arriving there, they knocked on the door, and pushed into the room as a group. They were seen by a legal adviser who told them bluntly that there *was* no real defence. The case was cut and dried – there was no question about guilt, and no facts to be disputed. Herr Renot said he would like to speak in defence of his wife. The official shook his head and doubted if that would be appropriate or even permitted. The old man had not been a witness to the events and so what could he say?

The accused would just have to defend herself as best she could. Herr Renot said he would like to present a character reference. Again the official shook his head, explaining that the case was not so complex to justify a character reference. In any event the husband of the defendant was not suitable for such a purpose. But was Frau Renot an active member of the SED or the Democratic Women's Association of Germany? No? That was a pity!

There was a stir behind the old man, and Herr Schomberg pushed forward, waving his fist in front of the adviser, saying the prosecution was a scandal and that Frau Renot was well-known and respected in Graetz Strasse. Besides that, everyone in the tenement block knew about the case and was discussing it, and so the authorities had better watch out. Old man Renot, encouraged by this outburst, banged his fist angrily on the desk at which the official sat, *demanding* an opportunity to defend his wife. The adviser relented nervously, taken aback by this protest – saying he promised to try and arrange for Herr Renot to be called into the witness box.

Herr Renot and his little group stood awkwardly at the back of the court with nervous apprehension, waiting for the session to begin.

"I wonder who the magistrate'll be,?" said one of the group.

"Let's only pray it's not Red Hilda," replied Papa Renot.[*]

"It won't be her – you can count on that – not in a small court like this," reassured Herr Schomberg.

The court was called to attention by the clerk, and the Comrade People's Judge and officials entered and took their places.　The magistrate was a lean man with thin greying hair, and a pallid complexion hidden behind thick-framed tortoiseshell spectacles.

"That's the man who condemned a worker to two years imprisonment last month, for stealing a handful of nails from a state owned factory," whispered Schomberg to Papa Renot.

The first case was called.

The little group waited nearly an hour in the courtroom as they witnessed the trials of felons of different degrees of culpability, and at last the little figure of Frau Renot emerged from below the courtroom, and stepped into the dock.

The judge had a dyspeptic finicky manner, a sharp high-pitched voice and a habit of pulling the sleeves of his black gown across him as they dropped beyond the arms of his chair, and that morning he had been erratic in the severity of his sentences.　At least he can't be too hard on her, thought Gisela, as her mother stepped into the dock.

The name and address of the accused was taken. Occupation? *Hausfrau*! Married? Yes! Husband's occupation? Proof-reader!

"Proof-reader for what – where employed,?" exclaiming the judge sharply, interrupting the clerk of the court.

"For the *Neue Zeit*," answered Frau Renot.

The magistrate took up his pencil and made a note.

The charge against the accused was read and she pleaded not guilty. Volkpolizist Polanyi was called into the witness box and he gave evidence reading from a typescript.　He seemed nervous and had little of the animation and self-confidence as when he had given evidence before Captain Kohn two days before.

"Mamma will win the case – look how hesitant the Vopo is," whispered Papa Renot to Herr Schomberg. "He can hardly stand upright."

"He's only a thug out for promotion," replied Schomberg.

Frau Renot was called upon to answer the charge.

Old man Renot turned round towards his group, momentarily flustered.

"I thought the Prosecutor would speak first," he exclaimed.

---

[*]　Hilda Benjamin, Minister for Justice in East Germany, notorious for the brutality of her sentences.

"I suppose he has a say later," replied Schomberg throwing up a hand to indicate his ignorance of the court's procedure.

Papa Renot left his group, pushing down towards the officers at the front of the court.

Holding tightly onto the rail of the dock, Frau Renot spoke boldly – hurriedly – in her staccato voice, saying that everything – everything Volkspolizist Polanyi had said was a tissue of lies. There was a titter from the officials in the court.

"Do you deny he arrested you,?" asked the judge.

"No."

"Do you deny you made no attempt to cross the street? Do you deny you were without your pass?"

"No."

"Then don't throw up a smokescreen by repudiating evidence you accept yourself."

Frau Renot denied she had seen the Volkspolizist in the first place; denied she had avoided him; denied she had heard him call after her; denied she had walked faster when he called her; and contended she was convinced she held the pass on leaving her house that morning.

Herr Renot alerted one of the officials at the front of the court who waved him to stand aside.

The Prosecutor, a man with eagle eyes and black bushy hair, took his stand.

"Is it necessary for the Prosecutor to address the court in this case,?" enquired the judge petulantly.

"The Prosecutor has certain facts he would he refer to from the investigation of the case," explained the clerk.

"The charge is clear and the evidence doubly incriminating. There is no defence in this case Comrade Volksrichter," began the Prosecutor addressing the judge in a crisp voice, hurrying over the words. He pointed his finger at the accused and shaking it, continued, "This woman is a blasphemous liar! How can she question the good name of the People's police who protect us daily from racketeers – not to mention fascist imperialist spies undermining our security. How dare she call Volkspolizist Polanyi a liar, and how dare she attempt to waste the time of this court with her defence!"

"It's lies your telling," shrieked Frau Renot.

The Prosecutor sniggered to himself.

"This woman has no defence and so she uses abuse and deceit," he continued. Let's glance at the facts brought up at the investigation."

Calling back Volkspolizist Polanyi to the witness stand, he made much of the defendant attempting a quick get-away from the Vopo using the pretence of deafness and feigning that it was not she who was being called by the authority of the law. He then listed the items in the shopping bag, citing the price of each, and underlined the significance of this and the loss to the Issuing Bank of the DDR had she been a black marketer from across the nearby border. The Vopo had been diligently carrying out his duty and the morale of the force must be upheld in the courts by ensuring convictions in cases of this kind. At the same time an example must be made of those failing to carry identity cards since this obstructed the duty of the police in apprehending criminals. It was not alleged that Frau Renot was a criminal, but in failing to carry her pass she had given rise to a great wastage of police time. There was legislation for punishing such persons, and an example must be made to warn others and the law must take its course.

There were interruptions from Frau Renot as the Prosecutor spoke and cross-examined the officer who initiated the case.

At last Herr Renot who had been standing near the front of the court, shifting on his feet with an appearance of increasing anger, suddenly banged his fist on a table exclaiming: "I demand to speak in the witness box!"

A nearby official began waving his hand at him to stand aside and then gesticulating with his finger to indicate that the old man should take a seat on a nearby bench.

Apart from this gesture of a single official, Herr Renot's short outburst had gone unnoticed, although there were whisperings amongst the small group which he had left near the back of the courtroom.

Chapter 30

The prosecutor said that Polanyi might leave the witness box which he did.

"Comrade Volksrichter, you can assess the hot-headed character of the accused for yourself," said the Prosecutor with a snigger before closing his evidence.

"Have you anything more to say before I pass sentence,?" said the judge afterwards when the Prosecutor had finished.

"I have nothing more to say, Comrade Volksrichter," said Frau Renot by now completely battered by the proceedings.

The Prosecutor smiled, glancing over to the judge with an expression of satisfaction before taking his seat.

"But I have," shouted Herr Renot rising from the bench and banging his fist on a lectern in front of him.

A paunchy Vopo sitting behind rose to his feet and tapped the old man on the shoulder, pouting his lips as he exclaimed, "Sh-h-h-h, Sh-h-h-h!"

The adviser whom Herr Renot and his small party had consulted earlier in the morning, rose nervously, explaining to the judge that the husband of the accused had "demanded" an opportunity to defend his wife in the witness box.

"I can't see what use such a witness would be," replied the judge. "We have all the facts and the husband of the accused was not a witness to the events described."

"I understand the witness wants to plead mitigating circumstances," replied the adviser bowing to the judge before taking his seat again.

"The witness may take his stand in the box if he refrains from taking up too much of the court's time," replied the judge testily, nodding towards Herr Renot.

There was a pause as the old man shuffled with his quick short footsteps towards the other side of the courtroom to the witness box.

The magistrate followed him with his eyes and the Prosecutor sniggered to several officials on either side waving his hand in the air as if to indicate that nothing the old man said could possibly have any bearing on the outcome.

Herr Renot hesitated by the witness box and an official directed him where to step in.

The judge glanced at the old man with an expression of petulance, leaning forward on his desk to see what was hindering his entering the box.

"Who is this man, anyway,?" exclaimed the judge irritably as Herr Renot stood in the box.

There was a momentary pause, and the old man looked awkward, not knowing exactly whether the judge had addressed a question to him or not, and if it were a question, as to how he was expected to answer it.

"Answer my question – what's your name?"

"Richard Rudolf Renot," answered the old man.

"What are you?" (Momentary pause.) "Occupation?"

"Proof-reader"

"Ah! Husband of the accused. Are you a member of a political association calling itself the Christian Democratic party?"

"I'm a member of a political association represented in the People's Assembly of the German Democratic Republic," replied the old man proudly.

"Hurry with your statement," said the judge contemptuously.

The old man spoke with self-assurance, appealing to the court's sense of justice. He complimented the court on its skill in the thorough presentation of the case, and he did not want it thought that he questioned the competence of the court, or that the law should be set aside. He did not doubt that his wife was "technically" guilty, but he pleaded that she was a simple and over-worked housewife, of good repute in the area where they lived, and that her only wish was to live a quiet and law-abiding existence.

At the end of the speech there was a thoughtful silence in the court.

"You've spoken with conviction but what you've said can have no bearing on the outcome," answered the judge with calm reflection. "The law must take its course. Pleading negligence, as you know, is no defence. You must know, Herr Renot, that the most serious crimes in a progressive Socialist state – especially political or economic crimes – are often caused through negligence. Your wife was charged with an offence which borders on an Economic Crime. It touches on the possibility of debasing the currency of the DDR had circumstances been otherwise. The time of this court has been wasted. Had the defendant pleaded guilty the sentence would be three days in prison. As the law stands the sentence is seven days."

Frau Renot began sobbing and dabbing her eyes with a handkerchief as she was taken from the dock, and the old man followed her to the well of the court, exclaiming consolingly: "Don't worry, Mamma, don't worry – it's not for long!"

Frau Renot never glanced up as she was taken down to the cells below. She was taken to the women's prison in Barnim Strasse, Friedrichshain, where there were felons of all kinds, and she was dressed in prison garments, and remained there for seven days.

The news of Frau Renot's arrest and imprisonment soon spread to Graetz Strasse. Some days later Gisela overheard a snippet of conversation between housewives on a street corner.

"There are too many Vopos lounging idly around this street," complained one woman resentfully.

"That's because it's too near the sector frontier," answered another.

"What are you complaining about? Aren't we living in a People's paradise,?" interjected another woman ironically passing by.

"Well, that's what they call it, don't they,?" added the second woman. "There isn't another country with a People's police like ours – a State police, yes, but never a People's police."

"And we're living in a democracy as well, of course," said the first woman. "There isn't a country in Western Europe calling itself a 'Democratic Republic' is there? *Ach mensch*,!" exclaimed the woman waving her hand in contempt, "a 'democratic republic,' indeed,!" and the party broke up on the pavement, and went their different ways.

By the time Dagmar finished telling me the story of her mother's unhappy experience at the hands of the Volkspolizei and the East German court of justice, we were strolling along Knesebeck Strasse between the Ku'damm and Savigny Platz.

We were silent awhile and I felt stunned and angry at what had happened, and I realised there was a hidden life of many in the East, which those affected were ashamed to admit or publicise, even though there was no true reason for their feelings of guilt. At that moment I wanted to expunge the memory from my mind.

"Let's think about something happier," I suggested after a while. "Tomorrow's your birthday."

"And the start of something better still," she replied joyfully, "my holiday!"

"We'll have all day to enjoy each other's company," I said.

"And we'll go on the Wannsee and visit Schloss Tegel."

"And swimming and lying on the warm sands by the lakeside," I said swinging her arm.

At Savigny Platz we took the S-Bahn home, and we were happy and high-spirited.

"Sh-h-h-h! Tip toe! Granny's asleep," whispered Dagmar.

"Quietly! Tread softly! Granny's in the land of nod," I responded, impersonating her manner.

"Last night Granny heard us – she knew you were here," said Dagmar glancing round and raising the key in her hand.

"We must be very quiet," I said raising my finger to my lips and nodding earnestly.

"Like fairies of the night," added Dagmar poetically.

The entrance hall of the tenement block was quite dark.

Dagmar pushed the key into the door and we entered, and I held onto her thighs so that she could lead the way in the dark, and I carefully closed the door behind us.

"No lights," said Dagmar, "not until the sitting room."

We tip-toed to the end of the hallway and into the sitting room. I closed the door, and Dagmar felt her way to the other end of the room and switched on the table lamp. Deftly, quietly, she lifted it from atop the radio to the little coffee table by the sofa.

"I have something to show you," said Dagmar with a provocative smile.

"I hope it's not a drawer full of mysterious objects," I replied.

"It's an English book," she said. "Will you give me an English lesson?"

"What, at this late hour,?" I exclaimed.

"What did we return for,?" said Dagmar smiling.

"I don't know," I said lamely.

"Then you can teach me a little English," said Dagmar pinching and kissing my chin. "Now just sit down and be a good boy."

She went over to the escritoire, opened a drawer, and took out a tattered book, and returned to the sofa, sitting down beside me. I read the cover of the book: " ' Learning English – Book Two.' – You're only a beginner, you want a First book," I said.

"My class read this book when I was at school."

"Did you learn English?"

"No, I learnt other things. Just some of our class had English."

"It's too late for English," I said throwing my arms round her shoulders and leaning back on the sofa.

"Now, we must be good," insisted Dagmar putting her finger to her lips. "Granny may be listening. Remember we're *ordentlich* people. It's very late. You've come home to give me an English lesson, and that's all."

"You begin to read and I'll correct your pronunciation," I said pulling Dagmar back onto the sofa so she was close beside me.

She opened the book at random and began to read: " 'Glimpses of England. – Four. – Mrs. Watts is a housewife in Newcastle.' I understand that; it's nearly like German," said Dagmar in delight.

I corrected her pronunciation of "Watts" and "Newcastle."

" 'Newcastle?' That's comic spelling for such a word," remarked Dagmar. She spelt the word as she thought it ought to be spelt. "English is difficult," she remarked.

"Not the grammar," I said.

" 'She lives in Redbrick Terrace,'" continued Dagmar. " 'Often the housewives in Redbrick Terrace seek her advice, because Mrs. Watts is a very important person. One morning last Spring the housewives in Redbrick Terrace were very angry. They organised themselves into a big group and marched down the street to where Mrs. Watts lived. They asked Mrs. Watts if she would help them.'"

"That's fine – you read beautifully," I said kissing her on the cheek.

"Sh-h-h-h! That kiss was too loud for so late at night," said Dagmar nodding towards the opposite wall. "It might have awoken Granny. – 'Mrs. Watts was the leader of the District Communist Party.' Ach! So political! – 'You remember, you met her husband in Lesson Two. He was the trades union leader who organised a strike of fifty-thousand coal miners. Mrs. Watts asked what was the matter. The housewives said the landlord had raised their rents from twenty-five to thirty shillings a week.'"

I stroked Dagmar's neck and kissed her forehead. Her head fell onto my shoulder.

"Read more softly," I told her.

" 'Mrs. Watts said she would help them. They would march through the streets and fight to the bitter end. If the housewives paid thirty shillings a week in rent they would face privation."

"How sweetly you read. – Read more softly," I said pulling her closer to me and kissing behind her ear.

" 'They would be unable to feed their husbands sufficiently or clothe their children properly. You remember that in Lesson Two the workers had been six weeks out on strike for twopence an hour more in their wage packets."

Dagmar let the book drop to the floor.

"I'm so tired," she said.

"What a pity," I replied smiling.

"I'm so tired and weak. I cannot even walk to the bedroom."

"Do you want me to carry you there and put you to bed?"

"No, Granny would discover you," she said quite shocked.

"Then you must sleep here," I returned.

"So uncomfortable!"

I took her into my arms, kissing her forehead, her nose and cheeks. She remained still and silent. I put my arms beneath her thighs and lifted her onto my lap. I brushed back her silky golden hair and kissed the shapely form of her neck.

"Oh, what a strange sort of English lesson this is," she said dreamily. "So un-pedagogic! We should be concentrating on the English book."

"Can you still concentrate?"

"I only want to sleep," she replied letting her head drop onto my chest.

I lifted her from the sofa and carried her to the couch which lay against the wall on the opposite side of the room. Gently, I laid her body onto the surface and knelt on the floor beside her and kissed her lips. She passed her fingers round my head and pressed me closely to her face. I stroked her thigh and caressed the smooth white skin of her shoulders. At last, our lips were parted and she brushed back my hair which had fallen across my forehead. She glanced at me searchingly.

"We must be good," she exclaimed significantly.

We lay relaxed on the couch, our love satisfied, and our minds were drowsed by the feeling of approaching sleep.

Dagmar was apparelled only in her pink silky undergarments, and as I held my arm beneath her head gently stroking the outside of her arm, she laid her warm head of hair against my shoulder, glancing dreamily towards the ceiling. I watched the slim and beauteous form of her figure with its smooth white skin, and I caressed her stomach, and as I kissed beneath her breasts, she breathed deeply and held my head firmly urging that I kiss again and again, and yet once more again.

"You have the most beautiful figure of any girl in the world," I said my fingers exploring her body.

"Do you really mean that,?" she replied turning towards me.

"With all my heart. Neither Michael Angelo nor Praxiteles could have sculptured a figure quite like yours."

"Oh, thank you,!" she cried in delight. "Many thanks!"

"What a funny answer to such a compliment," I laughed.

"Why? What should I say then,?" said Dagmar smiling.

"You don't have to thank me. I don't know what you 'should' say – no special phrase."

"What's wrong with saying 'thank you'?"

"There's nothing wrong with it," I returned.

"Isn't it the polite answer?"

"I suppose it is when you come to think about it," I mused. "But saying 'thank you' after a compliment like that is so typically Germanic."

"What would an English girl say?"

"That's difficult to answer. Perhaps she'd become a little confused, or laugh, or jokingly deny the compliment."

"But that's horrid," said Dagmar screwing up her nose. "It's so self-conscious and immature like a schoolgirl. If a girl can't accept compliments then there's no use in giving them, and what's love without compliments? Do English boys give many compliments?"

"Perhaps not so many as are given on the Continent. – Do you know the time,?" I said glancing at my watch. "I must return to the Pension," and I began to dress hurriedly.

"By law you still shouldn't be here," said Dagmar. "What will you say if the Volkpolizei stop and question you at the Wiener bridge?"

"I'll say I've been sleeping with the most beautiful girl in all Berlin," I replied.

"I won't say 'thank you,' – I'll be like an English girl," said Dagmar with mock seriousness. "Oh, James, I'm so terribly embarrassed and put-out, and I just don't know what to say.' – Is that how English girls talk?"

I laughed.

"Dagmar, Dagmar,!" came a voice from through the wall. "Come to bed at once."

I put my finger to my lips overcome with alarm. There was a momentary pause. Dagmar knelt upright on the couch. I felt painfully awkward, but not so Dagmar.

"It's after midnight, Grandmamma! I'm twenty-three today,!" she exclaimed joyously.

BOOK VII

Days of Joy and Sorrow

Love is a sour delight, a sugar'd grief,
A living death, an ever-dying life;
A breach of Reason's law, a secret thief,
A sea of tears, an everlasting strife;
A bait for fools, a scourge of noble wits,
A deadly wound, a shot which ever hits.

Thomas Watson, *The Passionate Centurie of Love*,
Sonnet xviii (1582).

Chapter 31

There was an atmosphere of lively activity, and a great exchange of confidential whisperings, as the flat at number sixteen was filled with a sense of happy anticipation. Almost as soon as I arrived there for breakfast, that morning, I was taken aside and quickly became involved in the general intrigue which lay ahead. As I passed the kitchen door on my way to the sitting room, I espied the pyjamed figure of Papa Renot sitting contentedly on a chair as he bathed his feet in a bowl of mustard water, and again, I saw his best clothes laid out nearby.

Even the good Frau had added some colour to her appearance, and instead of the drab brown dress she had usually worn previously, she now wore a colourful cotton blouse. Enormous red roses and yellow tulips were printed over the white fabric, and the design struck me as if it had been intended for furniture coverings rather than for adorning the human figure.

After breakfast, Frau Renot and I crossed the street to the flat at No. 55. She carried several small parcels under her arm and I carried a larger package. Today was a very important day! Dagmar was still dressing in Granny's bedroom on our arrival at the flat, but the good Frau said that that was "all right" as it gave us time to quickly make some little arrangements before Dagmar emerged.

I went into the sitting room, waiting idly by, and was touched by a suggestion of amusement at the inflated domestic drama which was planned for the day ahead, and with a feeling of mental relief my mind wandered back to the events of the previous night.

Frau Renot hurriedly entered the room with a glad expression, carrying a large cardboard box.

"This is for storing the presents for Dagmar," she said in a stage whisper that might have been heard through a wall twice the thickness as that dividing the sitting room from Granny's bedroom.

Dutifully, I dropped my package into the box on top of others.

"We'll put the box behind the escritoire by the window," said the good Frau carrying the box there, "so Dagmar won't see it. We must keep all the presents together. With your gift Dagmar will have had more presents than on any birthday before. – What have you given her,?" asked the good Frau in a confidential tone of intense curiosity.

"That's a secret," I replied. "What have you given her?"

"A set of toilet articles," replied the good Frau in delight. "Some perfume, three sticks of lipstick, powder and soap. She'll love them! And Papa has bought her a pair of white Summer gloves – so *petite*, and the best quality. He bought them yesterday in Woolworths, Neukölln. And Gisela has bought her some real nylon stockings – nylons suit Dagmar so well, don't you think?"

"Dagmar's birthday will be a great success."

"And there's Uncle Willy and Aunty Caroline's present still to come. I expect they'll bring theirs when they visit this evening. Dagmar mustn't open her presents until this evening when we'll all be there to see her."

There was a knock on the front door.

"I expect that'll be the post for Dagmar," said Frau Renot significantly, and she left the room, and in a few moments returned again, holding a wrapped bouquet.

"It was the florist," she exclaimed, and glancing at the label, "Why, it's from her colleagues in the art shop in Friedrich Strasse. How kind of them! Everyone likes Dagmar, you see," she said with emphasis.

Some minutes later Dagmar entered the room bearing the post. There was a birthday card from her friend Renata and from her former colleague, the plump girl, in the Art Shop in Stalin Allee.

"Isn't this card pretty, Mamma," she exclaimed holding up the latter for her mother to admire.

"Stand the cards on the centre table," replied her mother. Dagmar did so, and as she passed me, she kissed me on the cheek to the approval of her mother.

"Where did you go last night, Dagmar,?" enquired Frau Renot.

"We were in the Ku'damm, Mamma. We ate in the same restaurant where we were last year," replied Dagmar. "We had a thick mushroom and chicken soup – I've never had such a thick soup before – and then lamb chops and sauerkraut – and a vegetable I've never had before" –

"Corn off the cob," I reminded her.

"Oh yes, and potatoes and a fine sauce. And then we had two of the biggest ices I've ever seen, Mamma, with chocolate, nuts and many kinds of fruit."

"Wonderful,!" cried her mother clapping her hands.

"And to drink, we had Champagne. And do you know what the bill came to?"

"That's not important," I said nudging Dagmar, feeling a mixture of anger and embarrassment. "You weren't supposed to have seen the bill. Don't tell your mother."

"Thirty marks, Mamma!"

"Thirty West marks,!" exclaimed Frau Renot in delighted surprise. "Why, that would be a hundred and fifty marks in East German currency. Just think what you could buy with that!"

That morning Dagmar and I went to an art exhibition entitled the "Horse and Rider In Art," in the *Archivarion Gallery* in Cumberland House in the Ku'damm and saw an interesting collection of prints and paintings. On leaving the gallery we browsed through shops in the same street and spent an hour in an art book shop. It was past noon when we decided to spend the rest of the afternoon at the Pergamon museum in the East sector. We took the train to Friedrich Strasse intending to lunch in a large but inexpensive restaurant nearby, and it was here that we encountered one of those unique experiences only met with in Eastern Europe – in a country whose benefits are "organised" for the common good.

The H.O. restaurant was in a small street near the railway bridge crossing Friedrich Strasse. It was crowded but comfortable, with white table cloths, sets of silver cruets and upholstered leather chairs. We took our places and the waiter came to take our order, and I showed him my transit visa which he accepted as valid authority, and I placed the order and instructed him to bring a *dunkel* beer.

The *dunkel* beer arrived within five minutes and I began to refresh my thirst with the black sugary sweet liquid. The minutes passed but still no food arrived. Soon it was twenty minutes and then it was thirty minutes and still no service. We were impatient, and I called over the waiter. He was flustered and it was apparent that other patrons were in a similar situation. The waiter assured us we would be served "very soon." Thirty-five minutes passed and still nothing, and then we noticed a little plump man in white tie and tails (the head waiter) rushing hurriedly from table to table with a message which caused no little consternation. At last he reached our table, apologising for the delay. The restaurant's supply of potatoes had run out! A further supply had just been delivered, and we could be assured of service in another half hour.

"More like an hour and a half," I remarked to Dagmar when the little man had passed on. We left the restaurant and went straight to the Pergamon museum which was a five minute walk away.

The dining table was covered with tissue and colourful wrapping paper and a varied assortment of gifts, and there were cheerful shouts and a happy atmosphere in the room. Dagmar's slim fingers excitedly pulled off the string from around the present I had given her; then she tore away the wrapping paper.

Papa Renot, Franz, Gisela, the good Frau and I, were crowded round the table as with delight and anticipation we watched Dagmar open our gifts. Frau Brüning dressed in a long black evening gown, sat contentedly in her Bath chair against the wall. Papa Renot was in a bumptious mood, full of facetiousness as one witticism followed another, whilst his wife was overcome with a feeling of emotion (and perhaps even awe) at the auspicious occasion of her daughter's twenty-third birthday, and her eyes watered as she ran between Dagmar and me, frequently patting us on the shoulder and constantly repeating her daughter's name in a tone of emphatic significance. Gisela wore a new party frock of a fashionable if not attractive style, and her hair was tied up above her head and covered in spangles, whilst Franz was dressed in a light grey tweed suit with a yellow bow tie tucked beneath the flaps of his collar. Even by Western standards, he was dressed in the height of fashion.

"Oh, James, how beautiful,!" exclaimed Dagmar in delight as she pulled the wrappings away from my present. "*Knaur's Lexikon of Modern Art* – just the book I've wanted Mamma, for so long," she said holding up the gift, and she kissed me on the cheek.

"Isn't Herr Furner kind to you, Dagmar," answered her mother, tears of emotion filling her eyes, and then snatching the book from her daughter's hands and gently stroking the glossy cover with the tips of her fingers. "Yesterday the Ku'damm and today this beautiful book – he's the kindest of us all," she added reflectively, and at that moment, I could have sunk through the floor with embarrassment.

"Dagmar, open the next present," shouted Gisela excitedly.

Dagmar took up a small flat parcel from one of several gifts still lying unopened on the table.

"It's Granny's present," cried Frau Renot tense with excitement and clutching the art book to her breast. "Look Granny, now Dagmar's going to open your present," and the good Frau stood away from the table so that her mother could have a better view of Dagmar opening her next gift.

Papa Renot took up the art book which his wife had just placed on the table.

"Beautiful,!" he exclaimed running his thick thumb through the pages. Then he nudged me in the side with his elbow as he usually did if he had something confidential to say. "But it was a pity you didn't give her something smaller," he added in an undertone.

"Something smaller,?" I exclaimed momentarily perplexed.

"Yes, much smaller," replied the old man.

"Like what?"

"Round and gold. Something for her finger."

I blushed scarlet, and speechless, my mouth clammed up.

"Oh hankies! Delightful lace hankies,!" cried Dagmar. "Thank you, Grandmamma," and she kissed the old lady on the cheek.

"That's for when you're in bed with your next cold," said her grandmother.

"Oh, they're far too good for that, Granny," replied Dagamr. "I'll keep these to wear with my best party dresses."

"And to drop behind you, my dear, for attracting the attention of suitors," chuckled the old lady.

"I don't think Dagmar will need them for that," said Frau Renot with a suggestion of primness, emphasising her daughter's name. "We hope she's found her young man," she added in a significant undertone.

"Now open the next present," cried Gisela again.

Dagmar took up a small soft packet.

"Ach! That's mine," cried Gisela.

"Now Dagmar's opening Gisela's present," announced Frau Renot, throwing an arm around her younger daughter's waist. "I wonder what Gisela's brought you."

I picked up the bottle of scent out of the box of toilet articles which Frau Renot had presented to her daughter, and glanced at the label. At the base of the label printed in English were the words, *Made in the USSR.*

"How beautiful – real nylons," exclaimed Dagmar.

"I bought them in Neukölln," said Gisela.

"Beautiful nylons for beautiful legs,!" exclaimed Papa Renot, and he pointedly made the remark in my direction.

"Next time I shall give you a dress, Dagmar, perhaps like this one," said Gisela taking up a photographic magazine from a chair behind her and passing it across the table.

"Why, it's you Gisela," exclaimed Frau Renot in surprise. "You never told us before."

"It's a surprise Mamma. It only came out today."

"The photograph is beautiful," remarked Dagmar admiringly.

Papa Renot, who had taken up Gisela's magazine, and was thumbing through its pages, took me aside and nodded at a two-page spread of scantily dressed women.

"Beautiful girls,!" he exclaimed suggestively. "Just look at those breasts. *Wunderbar*,!" and he made a motion with his hands in front of his chest to indicate their size.

What's he behaving like this for, I asked myself? Does he think I'm under-sexed, or does he expect me to get his daughter pregnant?

Frau Renot re-entered the room gleefully carrying an enormous cream cake with twenty-three lit candles atop which she placed on the centre of the table.

"Oh, Mamma, I never expected this," exclaimed Dagmar.

"The ingredients came from the West sector," whispered Gisela into her sister's ear, and went to the sideboard to fetch plates which she laid on the table. In chocolate icing on the cake were written the words: *Für Dagmar's Geburtstag*!

As each family member placed a kiss on Dagmar's cheek as she stood over the cake, there came a knock on the front door.

"It'll be Uncle Willy and Aunty Caroline," exclaimed the good Frau.

There came shouts and a noisy exchange of greetings from the passageway, and a few moments later, a tall bald man with a red face, entered the room, accompanied by a little lady with a fixed smile dressed primly in a black costume.

Uncle Willy bowed to his mother in the wheelchair and took her hand as he kissed the side of her cheek. He was a heavily built man, neatly dressed in a light brown suit and colourful silk tie. He carried a square parcel and his presence seemed to dominate the company, not only on account of his size but because of his affluent appearance.

Chapter 32

Frau Renot patted her brother on the shoulder with a gesture suggesting admiration and sisterly affection, and began directing him towards me.

"I want you to meet Herr Furner, the young Englishman," said the good Frau with enthusiasm. "Of course you've heard of him many times before, Willy. He used to send those books to Dagmar, and now he's come to stay with us."

There was handshaking and bowing, and Uncle Willy approached Dagmar, handing over the gift which had been brought along.

"Such a tall man, isn't he,?" said the good Frau in a tone of admiration. "I don't expect you thought he'd be like that. And such a good businessman too – very rich,!" she added confidentially.

The latest present was unwrapped to reveal a box of chocolates, and Dagmar kissed her aunt and uncle for the cherished gift.

"We can't get chocolates here in the East," confided Gisela to me, "only bon-bons."

"Dagmar never eats them – she thinks of her figure," exclaimed Papa Renot facetiously.

"Oh *quatsch* Papa! I ate the box I had for Christmas in two days – with all of you to help of course," replied Dagmar, and she began handing them around.

"Now for something to drink," announced Papa Renot auspiciously, and he fetched a bottle of dark yellow liquid from the sideboard, whilst his wife laid out wine glasses on the table.

"Now you must blow out the candles," said the good Frau, and Dagmar leaned over the table and after seven puffs they were extinguished.

"Seven! A lucky number,!" exclaimed Papa Renot.

"To Dagmar on her birthday," said Frau Renot raising her glass.

We drank the sugary sweet wine which I noted had been bottled in Georgia.

"Let's hope that the next celebration will be for you both," announced the old man significantly glancing towards Dagmar and me.

Frau Renot nodded at me in agreement with her husband, but I averted my gaze, feigning not to have noticed the gesture. It seemed as if the pressure on Dagmar and me was being laid on pretty thick this evening!

As the cake was cut and slices served, there came another knock from the front door, and moments later, Renata came bounding into the room bearing a gift, and in her coy manner, began loudly greeting the other guests.

"Open the present," said Papa Renot who was curious about the latest package.

"Not here – open it later," said Renata awkwardly to her friend.

"I must open it now – to show the family," said Dagmar. "I've opened all my other presents in front of the family."

"Not that one – not in front of the men," said Renata trying to suppress a giggle.

"It must be interesting then," remarked Papa Renot who had no compunction about embarrassing anyone.

"What's wrong with the girl.?" I said aside to Franz.

"She's always like that," replied Franz indicating a sympathy with my own feelings.

"Why ever not open it here,?" asked Dagmar of her friend, holding up the packet which was already half torn open.

"It's private – not for the men to see," replied Renata with a giggle.

"Then I'll open it before I go to bed, and I'll thank you personally some other time," said Dagmar laying the packet on the table.

"No! Open it now, Dagmar," insisted Papa Renot showing all his teeth and grinning from ear to ear.

"Renata says it's private – not for the men," returned Dagmar.

"We're adults, not children," said the old man.

"I'm sure it can't be as private as all that," chimed in the good Frau.

"Oh, open it if you like," replied Renata throwing down her hand towards the gift, and averting her glance, she skipped away from the table.

The packet was torn open and Dagmar pulled out a chic little pair of pink panties with lace frills and matching bra. Everyone laughed.

"But how decorative," exclaimed Dagmar in quiet surprise, "They're charming."

"And now you must put them on, and be photographed for this magazine, like Gisela," suggested Papa Renot.

"Oh, how silly, Papa!"

"James, go and take the size of the garments now, so you can buy her the same another time – only in black," suggested Franz facetiously.

"Herr Furner's got better ways of taking her size than reading labels," exclaimed the old man with a wave of the hand.

"Oh really Papa, don't speak like that – it's so tasteless," chided Dagmar.

Frau Renot took me aside asking if it would be possible for me to extend my stay, as in little more than a week I would again have to leave Berlin. I expressed regret, explaining I had to return to Münster in time for the start of the new term.

"But couldn't you be transferred to Berlin University,?" she suggested.

"Not in the middle of a course and research project," I replied.

Uncle Willy announced he had brought something more potent than this Georgian wine, and he left the room returning a few moments later carrying a bottle of Doornkart high above his head. The earthenware bottle was uncorked and our spirits further enlivened by the potent schnapps, and then jellies and small pies were brought in to satisfy the appetites of the guests, as we settled to sit down at the table.

The party became louder and our glasses were charged again, and Uncle Willy told risqué jokes to Papa Renot and both men were thrown into fits of laughter, and Franz and I became involved in a political discussion, and the more he drank the more solemn he became. The good Frau, meanwhile, held her arm around Dagmar's shoulders waxing sentimental with reminiscences about her daughter's early childhood; whilst Gisela and Renata chatted on the joys and tribulations of a modelling career.

"Are you ready for your English lesson,?" I asked rising from the sofa as Dagmar tip-toed into the sitting room and closed the door behind her.

The party was over and the guests had left, and the sideboard was still covered with plates and empty wine glasses from which the Doornkart had been drunk.

"Yes," she replied. "And what new things are you going to teach me tonight,?" she added with a wicked smile.

"That depends on what you've remembered from last night," I said taking up the English book which lay on the coffee table. "If you've forgotten anything, then we'll have revision."

"I don't like revision," replied Dagmar screwing up her nose, "only new things."

"But tonight we must be very quiet, so as not to awaken Granny," I said.

"Don't worry, Granny won't wake up," replied Dagmar rising on her toes and kissing my forehead. "I've given her an extra strong dose of sleeping tablets."

"You wicked girl," I exclaimed. "Now for our next English lesson. First, reading," I announced placing the book in her lap.

"So difficult,!" she exclaimed.

"This lesson must be conducted according to the strict pedagogical rules of direct language teaching," I said with mock importance.

"I can see you intend being a stern schoolmaster tonight, carrying the big stick," replied Dagmar feigning a frown.

She opened the book at random and began to read: " 'Lesson Ten. – Jim MacKintie Speaks About His Holiday.' – MacKintie, what a comic name."

"That's Scottish," I explained.

" 'You first met the MacKinties in Lesson Five. Do you remember? They were the Scottish family who came from the Gorbals, and were evicted because they objected on principle to paying an increased rent demanded by the landlord. Now we shall meet the MacKinties again. They no longer live in the Gorbals because a slump deprived Jim

MacKintie of his job. Jim MacKintie, his wife and six children are now living in Liverpool, where they share a flat with four other families.'"

"Wonderful," I exclaimed. "Now read on."

" 'Jim MacKintie has just returned from a holiday. He has been to the Soviet Union, and today he feels a much wiser man. He was one of twelve happy delegates to be chosen by the Communist Party to visit the country where the daring dreams of humanity are being realised.' Ach! Political again, always political. – 'Jim MacKintie is in his flat surrounded by seven friends who are sitting in open-eyed wonder, hungry to hear about the glories of the Soviet Union..'"

"Your reading gets better all the time," I said stroking her neck.

" 'Jim MacKintie saw the May Day parade, and he reminds his friends that the Russian tanks and guns are weapons for peace. He tells his friends about the beautiful new workers' apartment houses where no more than two families share a three-bedroomed flat. His friends gasp in wonder when he tells them about the parks of Culture and Rest where Moscow workers in their leisure hours can admire beautiful statues and sit on benches in rose-scented gardens. Jim MacKintie says that the USSR is the envied paradise of the workers of the world.' I don't want to read any more," said Dagmar breaking off. "I can't follow the meaning of the text, but I do know when it gets political. I don't like politics."

"We're all 'political animals' as Aristotle once taught us. Politics affects all our lives," I said thoughtfully. "I wonder where we'll be this time next year."

"I'll still be here in East Berlin," she answered sadly.

"Come to the West, Dagmar," I pleaded with a sudden burst of enthusiasm.

"How could I possibly afford that,?" she replied.

"I'll pay for your fare from Tempelhof to Hanover."

"I'd like that, but you don't understand – there are things which bind me here in the East. – And where will you be this time next year,?" she said changing the topic and passing her fingers through my hair.

"I can't say. I'll have finished my studies though, and I suppose I'll be working somewhere."

"And where will Berlin be this time next year,?" she said sadly.

"The fate of Berlin will take no account of our lives," I replied.

"I suppose things will be much the same: the strange division of our city into two halves, the one rich, the other poor. We of the East will still look to the West for our entertainment and culture, and to learn about the outside world."

"I don't know about that. Things happen so quickly. So much has happened in Berlin during the past month," I said in a tone of concern. "Earlier this month was the five day closing of the sector frontier to West

Germans, and now we have the introduction of these visas to enter the East sector. What next – who knows?"

"You mean – you think things might become worse," said Dagmar hesitantly. "Like a permanent closure of the sector frontier?"

"There's no knowing. It's not impossible."

"That would be terrible! But I don't think it could really happen."

"Now you're the one who's being optimistic."

"In Berlin, anything is liable to happen any time," I remarked.

Chapter 33

I walked many times between my Pension in Spreewald Platz and Graetz Strasse, and soon became accustomed to the long bleak roadway of Wiener Strasse across the sector frontier. Despite the frequency of my crossing the frontier on only one occasion was I intercepted by the Vopos at the Wiener bridge. Perhaps they had come to recognise me.

In the early hours one morning as I approached the bridge a Vopo strode up to me and snatched away a newspaper tucked under my arm.

"What's this,?" he enquired holding the paper in his hand, in a tone suggesting he had discovered my carrying a contraband object.

"A newspaper," I replied casually, being the obvious answer.

He glanced at it curiously.

"West German,?" he enquired turning towards the light behind him.

"No – an English paper," I replied.

"Good,!" he exclaimed, and he returned the paper to me. "And where have you been at this late hour?"

"With a girl," I replied reluctantly, hurrying over the words.

He smiled and waved me on.

My trials and troubles with the water system in the little room of the Pension, were not yet at an end following that hectic afternoon when I first moved in. Tired of the discomforting inconvenience of washing in cold water I ventured to approach the landlady requesting if it might be possible to have a jug of hot water brought up to my room every morning. She looked at me with an expression of surprise and then replied, "But there *is* hot water in your room, Herr Furner. You must let the tap run awhile – but it'll come eventually." Accordingly, the following morning, I arose ten minutes earlier than usual, turned on the hot tap and returned to bed. Sure enough, after ten minutes there was hot water running into the basin. What extraordinary plumbing they must have in this city, I thought, as I let the water run over my hands.

The days passed and our relationship developed through the interaction of our experiences with one another, but as to the probable outcome of our friendship – as to whether it was progressing, or possibly even, regressing – I became ever more uncertain as each day drew to its close. This uncertainty did not arise from an increasing doubt as to our liking for one another, but rather from the sudden and unexpected mood changes marking our relationship, and the question as to whether such changes could sustain a friendship for the longer term. This uncertainty as to the direction of our friendship did not reflect a doubt as to our compatibility, but suggested rather, that external factors were acting as a divide between us. As each day drew to its close, I would be thrown into a quandary, sometimes with amusement and sometimes with anxiety at a failure to understand the strange wiles and ways of the fair Berlinerin, who seemed to be haunted by fears and difficulties she was loathed to express.

There were strange and inexplicable differences between us, followed by sulks and minor quarrels or short duration. These outbursts stemmed from the hypersensitive nature of the fair one, rather than from any intended offence on my part, and certainly not from grounds which would ordinarily ignite a quarrel between those of average sensibility. These differences, or rather, the petulance from which they arose, seemed therefore to originate from an internal battle the fair one was fighting within her own mind. I saw her moodiness as a symptom of nervous tension. It was true that as the days wore on an increased pressure was exerted by Mamma and Papa Renot to force the issue between us, and the "conspirator" Papa Renot (as I now nicknamed him in all certainty that the title was fitting) was particularly active during these days, often indulging in absurd or outrageous stratagems, but I felt convinced that Dagmar's uncertainty was not aroused by her parents' nagging solicitation, but by some secret she was harbouring in her mind. Her parents must surely have taken their daughter aside to assure themselves of her feelings before indulging in their questionable conspiratorial behaviour. I therefore became increasingly convinced there was a hidden mystery in Dagmar's life.

Albeit these factors, our days and nights remained pleasurable, unspoilt for the most part by quarrels of short duration, for as each quarrel ended it was soon forgotten, and so no accumulation of hard feelings was allowed to fester. We visited endless exhibitions, of which Dagmar never seemed to tire: *The Christian Art of Europe* at the Palace of Charlottenburg; *Berlin – The Place of Freedom For Art*, in the Orangery of the Palace; *The Art of Puerto Rico* in Reinickendorf townhall; The

Gallery of the Twentieth Century in Jebens Strasse; *The Young Generation* at the Hilton Hotel; the Bremer Gallery in Fasanen Strasse, as well as museums and other locations of interest.

Some of our most enjoyable hours were spent in strolling through the Grunewald, bathing in the Havel river and visiting old rustic buildings in the midst of the forest. Time was of little consequence as we became so enwrapped in one another's company as to forget the outside world. From breakfast, on my arrival at Graetz Strasse from the Pension in the West sector, till late at night, we were hardly for a moment parted. In the evenings, we attended a concert or film in the West, and on escorting her home to her grandmother's flat, I remained with her, an hour or so, before returning to Kreuzberg.

The flashpoint of our quarrels were explicable without explaining their deeper underlying origin. Inevitably, there were recurring themes in our conversation as for example my suggestions as to why she should leave the East at the earliest opportunity; discussions as to how this might be achieved, and not least, amongst the recurring themes of our conversation, concerned my frequent probes into all those little mysteries surrounding her. What was the real condition of her health? What had happened two years ago (or thereabouts) to upset her life, if indeed anything had happened, and she had hinted that it had? What explanation lay behind those strange souvenirs stored away in the drawer of little treasures? What was she doing with a packet of Russian cigarettes, and what explanation lay behind those new blank picture post cards from Friedrichshafen, and why had she refused to show me all the photos in the drawer? Was it any wonder that my curiosity was aroused?

Sometimes I would question her on these things, as we strolled in the depths of the forest or reclined by a lakeside. She would respond with a gesture of sulky ill-humour, turning her head with a moody expression.

"Why must you talk about Russian cigarettes,?" she once exclaimed in a tone of irritation as we lay on the banks of the Havel. "Can't we enjoy the beautiful nature all around and forget about life in the city?"

"I am enjoying the beautiful nature," I replied casually.

"Then why must you always let Russian cigarettes spoil your thoughts,?" she said sulkily, and I smiled.

"I thought it would be a good time to ask you," I replied after a pause. "Isn't it easier for us to talk together here in the countryside than in your home in Treptow?"

"Yes – in a way."

"Dagmar, why do you mistrust me,?" I asked pressing her hand.

"I don't mistrust you," she replied a little perplexed.

"Then why are you so secretive?"

"Do you resent that? Aren't there some things I can keep to myself?"

"The way you respond, anyone would think it was the most susceptible thing on your conscience."

"Sometimes curiosity can be mischievous," she replied irately.

"Dagmar, you know that if there's anything I could do for you I'd do it," I said.

"It's not a matter of that. It's a matter for my own judgement," she added quietly. "James, please don't question me any more on this. I don't like to think or speak about it."

"But you do think about it. You think about it sufficiently to consider worth keeping the box of cigarettes rather than throwing them away. Something is buried deep down in your heart, and you're filled with anxiety. Why can't you share your secret?"

"Because I choose not to," she replied sharply.

There was a pause of a few moments, and I picked up some pebbles, throwing them into the water, wondering what strange thought processes were passing through Dagmar's mind.

"What sort of person do you think I am,?" I said at last. "Someone who regards you as a true friend or someone you're not quite sure of? Tell me."

"I like you, James," replied Dagmar pressing her hand in mine.

"Why then don't you trust me?"

There was a pause, and I watched a serious thoughtful expression cross her face as she worked out her reply.

"It is because I like you very much," she said solemnly, "perhaps too much."

"Everything you say just piles one paradox on top of another," I replied throwing up a hand. "I cannot understand you."

Sometimes sharper words were exchanged between us. She would fend off my questioning, and then silence ensued. I would pass a humorously slighting remark which she would seize upon before retaliating with a bitter reply. I would attempt to fend off her bitter remarks with a half-apology, but she would accept no half measures, and so involuntarily, I found myself fending off a counter-attack. In this way, and because both of us tended unwisely to insist on the last word, we sometimes found ourselves in the midst of a heated quarrel. These exchanges often ended by our both speaking at once, so that neither was in a position to retaliate against the other, and then a sulking silence would follow.

Her health particularly aroused my concern. Every second day she visited a hospital for what she described as vitamin injections, and at least twice during my stay in Berlin she attended a physio-therapists' clinic for treatment she claimed was intended to aid her circulation and strengthen her nerves. On one occasion I suggested there was little wrong with her health which might not be improved by the enjoyment of our love rights, and that her nerves and circulation would certainly thereby be improved, but when despite these reassurances she continued to indulge in hypochondriacal outbursts, I was left to draw my own unsatisfactory conclusions. Was she tubercular or diabetic, or did she suffer from one of those incurable blood complaints under which she might linger for years before succumbing inevitably to a slow death? As to which of these complaints she might have been afflicted by, if any, I was uncertain, but the symptoms of her imperfect health all pointed to an ailment of some concern.

Once I tried to persuade her to visit a specialist in the West sector (most German doctors specialising in specific complaints) but she said it would be far too expensive. The shortage of doctors and trained medical personnel in East Germany was already critical, but despite this factor, I felt that Dagmar was being deprived of the best services available in her own country and might possibly have been better treated had she been affiliated to the SED. Quarrels arose from what she described as my attempts to "pry" into her health.

"Why do you make it so difficult,?" I said to her quietly one afternoon as we strolled through the Grunewald.

"How," she replied.

"Knowing you better."

"What don't you know about me?"

"That's what I'm trying to find out. Don't you understand why I ask you such questions,?" I said to her confidentially. "It's not out of idle curiosity."

"Your reasons for questioning never occur to me. I only think of the questions themselves."

"You know my feelings towards you, but these enigmas surrounding you are a barrier between us."

"Do you suspect our friendship is insincere?"

"Of course not."

"Or that our intimacy is not sufficiently close?"

"That couldn't be."

"Hasn't our friendship throughout the time we've known one another been spontaneous?"

"It has."

"Then why can't it remain so without your having to cross-examine me about other things?"

"Because I believe these other things are important to you. If our friendship continues merely on a 'spontaneous basis,' as you say, whilst ignoring these other things, perhaps one day we'll have to face them, and perhaps there might be difficulties for us both."

"In other words, you don't trust the basis on which our friendship is founded," she said.

"It's not quite that because I don't know what that basis is."

"You mistrust my character?"

"Not that, but merely the circumstances surrounding you. Love's not sufficient if a lasting relationship is intended. There must be no room for doubts. Can't you understand I ask these questions only because I love you?"

As the days passed by the quarrels and sulks became more frequent, and time was running out for us both. What would be the outcome of this affair? The quarrels increased in intensity even if they remained of short duration, like showers on an April day. Sometimes a quarrel might be settled after a tearful reconciliation, and sweet words followed bitter taunts, and she would cling tightly onto my arm, as we were enveloped in a beautiful rainbow atmosphere as after a violent storm. We felt our quarrel had inevitably subsided and that our love had been renewed. The sunshine always shone on us again!

However much the fair one might have enjoyed these conflictual situations and perhaps she found in them both a stimulation for her soul and "circulation," I eventually tired of her changing and unpredictable temperament. Her beauty lay in her pale features and in the delicate quality of her sensitive manner, but she was more than sensitive – she was hypersensitive; like a thermometer measuring the smallest degree of change. My every response needed to anticipate any sign of upset for the slightest lapse disturbed the delicate balance of her psyche.

Sometimes a quiet and apparently restful silence ensued between us as we leisurely strolled through the countryside, then unexpectedly I discovered the silence was far from restful – on her side. I would turn to her passing a remark, and she would reply gloomily with an air of irritation or depression. "What's the matter,?" I would say, and then the truth would be out. She had taken umbrage to a casual remark I made perhaps three hours earlier and the significance of it had meanwhile sunk deep into her brooding soul.

"That was tactless what you said," she would declare solemnly.

"Why didn't you tell me before, instead of burying it resentfully deep down in your heart,?" I would respond.

"You should have understood me," she would say solemnly.

"You never said I had offended you," I would reply. "It was only intended as innocent teasing."

"I suffer easily. I'm very sensitive," she would say with profound self-pity.

"I know you are," I would boldly reply. "It's a pity you haven't a little more humour and then you'd have seen it in another light."

I would feel her arm suddenly jog against the inside of my elbow as she thrust her hand into her coat pocket. The silence would be renewed between us as her morbid sensitivity (as I saw it, rightly or wrongly) brooded over a final comment.

Eventually I nicknamed her strange sulks as the Cold War from the East. "Is there another Cold War,?" I asked her sometimes, but she would see little humour in this, and made no reply. "Or perhaps you'd like another Hot War – a quarrel, to end the differences between us," I would add jokingly some moments later, "so we can make up our love again with tears and rainbow clouds and sunshine. Would you like that?" Still no reply.

As the days passed towards the end of my stay, and as I felt some kind of a decision or arrangement would need to be made before my departure from Berlin, and as the quarrels increased both in frequency and intensity, and as the parents became increasingly meddlesome and suggestive so that an engagement might materialise, I gradually began to feel the pressure of these persuasive and conflicting forces push me into a corner. I began to experience a nervous strain from the changing temperament and interminable moodiness and hypersensitivity of the fair one. Within the period of a single hour there might be a heated quarrel, followed by reconciliation, some intelligent discussion, some laughing and joking, some sulking, another quarrel, and again, reconciliation. Her temperament hardly remained stable for more than half an hour at a time, as it alternated between elation and bliss and darkness and despair.

"I just feel sad," she would moan when I enquired as to why she was so sullen. Sometimes, she even blamed inanimate objects for her changes of mood.

"What's wrong,?" I asked her once as we strolled through a gallery.

"It was that painting at the far end," she replied. "All that green and black and red paint is so disturbing. It frightens and depresses me."

We returned towards the painting and with a feeling of self-confidence I decided to re-interpret the picture for the sake of the fair one so that it projected a more optimistic image, perhaps even the joys of Spring. I felt myself obliged to do this for the sake of allaying yet another attack of doldrums with which she might be afflicted for an hour or more.

On reaching the painting again I was non-plussed.

"It's one of those Tacist paintings," I exclaimed in a tone which might have betrayed the philistine in me. "It doesn't mean anything. It's just one of those paintings where an artist chucks a lot of paint and

broken glass and crockery at a canvas from a six-metre distance. I can't
see what's so disturbing in it."

Suddenly, I checked myself. Now she's going to think I'm a
"moron," I thought.

"Look at that piece of glass in the centre of the painting," she said.
"It's like a knife thrust into a man's heart."

"I can't see any man," I replied in my ignorance.

"That brown paint is the man."

"Now I see. The splodge where the paint's hit the canvas is the
body, and those two lines where the paint's dribbled down are the legs."

"Exactly," she replied eagerly on discovering that I now shared her
enlightenment. "And the red above is the red flag of tyranny and those
jagged lines are the bonds of slavery and political imprisonment – don't
you see now?"

"And I suppose those two pieces of willow pattern crockery
represent the man's shoes," I added.

"Yes," she replied hesitantly.

"I shouldn't worry about it if I were you," I said consolingly.
"Remember it's not a conscious work of art. The artist never knew what
he was going to paint before he chucked all that stuff at the canvas. He
just looked at it afterwards and gave it a title; and then, hey-presto, a
great work of art was created! The picture was created through accident
not design."

"All the unpleasant things in life are created by accident," she
remarked sullenly.

"Now what do you mean by that,?" I said to her firmly. "Are you
referring to this painting as unpleasant, or to what it symbolises, or are
you just referring to things in life generally?"

"I mean the real things in life."

"Perhaps, but that's irrelevant to this painting, isn't it? Now let's
glance at the catalogue and see what it's really supposed to represent," I
said opening the glossy folder. "Number one hundred and sixty-two. Here
we are, *Sunset over Las Vegas*! Why, it's a happy picture. You've
nothing to worry about," I declared. "Don't you see the setting sun in the
centre of the picture – and those jagged lines are just people enjoying
themselves as the city comes to life."

"That's not what the artist conveys to me," she replied.

Dagmar remained unimpressed by my attempt at re-interpreting the
picture for her own peace of mind – at giving, even, an interpretation
which the painter himself had possibly intended.

Wire sculptures were her particular bugbear: she was forever
seeing in them symbols of bondage; political prisoners and a struggle for
survival. Whenever we came across these twisted pieces of wire or

contorted scraps of iron elevated on a pedestal, or when we were faced by an abstract painting, and I perceived that the fair one was yet again to be seized with an attack of the "black dog" by one of these monstrous pieces of art, I began to ridicule the object displayed, even though I risked the accusation of being thought "uncultured," but then I preferred such a label than having to endure her company when she lingered under these attacks of the "blues."

I accounted her attacks of depression and moodiness partly on the late nights and few hours of sleep, and partly on the unpleasant secret she possibly concealed within the recesses of her mind, and I hoped and believed that once I persuaded her to lay open her heart, that all the anxiety and quarrels between us would evaporate never to return.

It is said that every woman is a musical instrument, to be taken up by the man inclined to try her, and if he plays her well, he is successful and exposes her better qualities, but even a musical instrument may be imperfect, and to mix a metaphor, although it is the proverbial bad worker who blames his tools, the musician nonetheless demands a certain standard in the choosing of his instrument, for it is from the instrument itself that the art is created. The instrument known as Dagmar was as yet a delicate piece of equipment, strictly limited in pitch and mood: certain kinds of humour could not be played on it, the keys needed continual re-adjustment; the strings were constantly snapping and much time had to be employed in replacing them; and often, for some mysterious reason, no sound came from the instrument at all.

I loved the sweetness of her character; I loved her physically; we shared closely similar interests, and I saw no reason why our personalities should not be compatible. I hoped ardently our friendship would progress towards the culmination of a permanent union, when for eternity I should remain faithfully by her side, granting her everything which happiness required, but because of the critical political situation then existing in Berlin, I was reluctant to enter into an engagement – not to speak of marriage – until she had moved to the West.

This was because there remained the real possibility that the East sector might be permanently cut off from the West. What would happen if the East sector of the city were to be separated from its other half by an Iron Curtain, whilst our fingers still wore the rings symbolising the indissolubility of our vows and love for one another? Perhaps years of waiting, hoping and yearning, whilst we each tried to remain true to the other, as our lives wasted away.

Chapter 34

The conspiratorial behaviour of the parents and the awkwardness it aroused was something which had to be passed over tactfully as best it could without my seeming to convey unkindness or cruel embarrassment. Sometimes Papa Renot would nod to his daughter and take her aside for a *tête-à-tête*, and she too was perceptibly put-out, but I never enquired of her afterwards what happened during these clandestine Polonius-like interviews.

Often Papa and Mamma Renot were engaged in top-secret conspiratorial discussions as they stood in the middle of the kitchen or passageway, as Dagmar and I moved about the flat otherwise occupied. Then one of the parents would confidentially approach either Dagmar or me and ask a question or make a questioning statement, whilst the other parent stood some distance away observing the responses of the two persons so engaged. Then the parents would rejoin each other and another secret confab would ensue between them.

This behaviour bordering on the absurd, was a nuisance arousing my irritation. Only occasionally did I snatch pieces of such conversation between the parents, and usually when hanging up a coat in the passageway or walking towards the sitting room, as I overheard a whispered sentence or two through the half-opened door of the kitchen. "They're so much in love," I heard Mamma Renot exclaim one day in a tone overflowing with effusive sentimentality; "Be patient, Mamma – it's only English caution,!" confided Papa Renot to his wife on another occasion; "They're so happy to be young," said Mamma on another day; "I'll speak to her and find out," said Papa once; "Leave them alone, and it'll come late this evening – inevitable,!" exclaimed the old man in a confidential tone. I winced with mental pain on every occasion I overheard these altercations. Why were the parents so eagerly intent on fixing an engagement between us?

It was Papa Renot who conspiratorially arranged the details of the Pfaueninsel trip towards the end of my stay in Berlin. Dagmar and I were to leave very early one morning, taking a passenger barge from the Schiffahrt canal in Neukölln, which would carry us direct to the Wannsee. The old man had written down on paper the hour at which we were to meet for breakfast, the hour at which we were to leave the house and the time at which the barge left the quay at Wildenbruch Platz. The eve of the trip was full of suggestions as to how we should enjoy ourselves, whilst his wife prepared sandwiches to take with us for the day.

On the eve of the trip Dagmar and I had had a minor quarrel which was not entirely patched up before I left the flat on my return to

Kreuzberg, and on returning to Graetz Strasse for breakfast the following morning, I met her in the middle of the roadway.

"You're not late," she said in a tone of concern.

"What are you doing down this end of the street,?" I asked.

"I was coming to meet you. I didn't know if you'd come," she replied. "After that argument yesterday – I had no sleep last night."

"You shouldn't have been so concerned," I assured her gently.

"I was worrying, thinking about us, and trying to work out so many problems," she answered.

It was cloudy when the barge left the quay at Wildenbruch Platz but I nonetheless felt optimistic about the enjoyableness of the day ahead. As we sat in the barge we were both tired, for it was still early in the morning and we had retired late the night before. I carried the bag containing our provisions for the day and our towels and bathing suits.

It was to be a long boat trip. The barge stopped often to drop and pick up passengers, and we passed under many bridges and through continually changing scenery: alongside high tenement blocks which darkened the waterway beneath; through areas of rubble and new building development; by massive bleak walls in industrial areas; and then through the Hansa quarter and the Tiergarten. We passed through Charlottenburg and then into the River Spree, and through the suburb of Spandau where we caught a glimpse of the old keep of the Julius Fortress where were still imprisoned several of the surviving major War criminals.

As the barge entered the great Havel river, it began to rain heavily. Trust the old man's luck for choosing the wrong day, I thought to myself! But it was only a shower and the clouds cleared, and when the boat came to the quay at Wannsee there was bright sunshine. We strolled along the Pfaueninsel Chaussee, along the embankment of the Havel, and on finding a secluded spot, we jumped down to the shore and settled on a small patch of sand around which grew high reeds. We changed into our swimming suits and jumped into the river which was warm due to the shallowness of the water and the vegetation on the bed.

An hour later, after lunch, after resting awhile on the sand, as we strolled through the Stadt Forst (City Forest) behind the Pfaueninsel Chaussee, our attention was alerted to the sound of bells playing a tune of great beauty, and I asked Dagmar from whence unexpectedly came such music.

"Come and see," she replied in delight.

We passed through some trees and shrubbery, and there in a clearing stood an old Russian church complete with onion topped towers.

"It's the St. Peter and Paul Church," exclaimed Dagmar. "The bells are playing the Prussian soldiers' hymn. Isn't it beautiful? I used to know the words once, but I've forgotten them now. It's played every hour."

"Berlin is full of surprises," I said.

We walked a little further and it was then that we saw the Nikolskoe log cabin for the first time. It was then a restaurant, but had been built in 1819 in the style of a typical Russian farmhouse and given by Frederick William III to his daughter and her fiancé, Crown Prince Nicholas of Russia. We made our way to the river again and climbed into a small motor boat which took us away from the mainland to the island of Pfaueninsel. We climbed up the steep pathway to the high level of the island strolling through the woods.

As promised, Dagmar showed me the old farmhouse of the island and we went into the stables, and she stroked the noses of the small horses, and in the farmyard we nearly tripped over some piglets which ran into our path. How peaceful and rustic was the environment of the farm! Women with buckets walked casually by, and an old man with a couple of milk pales hanging from a yoke went into the brick and timber built cowshed with its thatched roof. This place was as idyllic in its rustic simplicity as a farm taken from a Moreland painting. We left the farm reaching some delightful old cottages in the midst of shrubbery and trees.

"See there – just look," exclaimed Dagmar.

I held her tightly as we glanced at one of the cottages.

"How would you like me to buy you such a cottage one day," I asked.

"Oh, that would be wonderful, James," she said gripping tightly onto my arm, "and we could live there always. Just think how restful it would be!"

We strolled to the aviary and then went to the Italian gothic mock ruin Schloss at the other side of the island, and on the lawn strutted peacocks which had given the island its name.

On returning by bus to the station of Wannsee, Dagmar was tired and sullen again.

"Berlin is so ugly," she exclaimed.

"You know the answer to that. I've told you many times before. Leave Berlin and come to the West," I replied.

"The houses are so old and dark and hideous," she continued. "They're too big and too crowded."

"Now you're talking about Treptow and the East sector, but when you leave the centre, then the surroundings of the city are enchanting."

"But always to be shut in by the zonal boundaries – it's terrible! Berlin is like a prison. I always feel I want to get out. I'd like to be free to travel through the countryside, and go on and on, in one straight line, in a fast car."

"So does every Berliner," I remarked.

"I'd like to live in a small house in the country – like one of those cottages we saw on Pfaueninsel. Graetz Strasse is so dirty and old."

"There are some very fine buildings in Treptow," I said. "On the Park Köpenicker Landstrasse are some well built blocks of flats. I'd say they were put up just before the War."

"It'd be impossible for our family to get an apartment in a luxury building like that," replied Dagmar. "They're all kept for Communist party bosses."

"Has your father ever tried to get a new apartment?"

"Yes, but we had a very bad experience," replied Dagmar. "We'd never try again."

She recounted how for many years her family had been on the waiting list for new housing. Her father's intention in applying for new housing did not arise from a feeling of dissatisfaction with the flats in Graetz Strasse, but rather from a wish to economise. The intention was to find a flat for the entire family including the ageing grandmother. As the family's need for housing was not as urgent as that of many thousands of East Berliners whose needs were desperate, the Renots were not placed high on the priority list. A further attraction in acquiring a new apartment in the East sector, was that rents were low for new housing constructed by and for the Communist state.

Two years previously Herr Renot had again visited the relevant office and enquired as to the likelihood of his receiving an apartment in the near future. He was told that the likelihood was remote, and reminded that in order to qualify for new housing that eight hours work from each member of the family would need to be undertaken in the service of the state organisation, the *Nationales Aufbau-Werk* (National Construction Work). He was told that there was a particular demand for volunteers for the NAW at that particular time, and that should his family agree to undertake to complete their service shortly, there might well be a chance of receiving priority housing in the near future. Work for the NAW was unpaid, consisting of cleaning bricks and removing rubble.

The family decided to volunteer their services to this excellent organisation. Arrangements were made and at last the great day arrived. The family rose early at five o'clock, and were optimistic and excited about the outcome of the work which lay ahead. They saw it as a refreshing break from drab routine, and Papa Renot put them all into good humour for the day with jokes and facetiousness. They had borrowed overalls and boots from neighbours, and laughed at one another as they stood in their ill-fitting garments. They must have looked an odd group. Dagmar's overalls had to be tied round her body with string to prevent them from falling off her shoulders, and the good Frau had to do some last minute darning on Papa Renot's overalls where he had split them down the side of one leg on climbing into the trousers. Papa Renot set the family into hoots of laughter by impersonating a broad Berlin dialect and using Berlin slang. At last the three left the flat, and were to work for an eight hour stretch spread over a two day period.

They reported to a building site near Stallin Allee. On arrival, they found they were amongst several hundreds of other volunteers, and after waiting an hour, they were divided into gangs of ten and put under the leadership of a foreman. The family was broken up: the good Frau and her daughters were put into a brick scraping gang, and Papa Renot was ordered to work in a rubble removing gang.

"*Viel spass*! (Have fun!) – till later," exclaimed Herr Renot cheerfully as he left the rest of his family and followed the other workers who had been picked out for the same gang.

"Hey! You there, old man, put some life into your feet and get a move on," shouted the foreman arrogantly at Papa Renot. "We haven't got all day to spare – we've got work to do and we're behind schedule."

The gang crossed a cleared area and passed a building site, from which came the crash of pile drivers and cement mixers, towards a vast pile of rubble and bomb sites beyond. The gang was a mixed bunch of men: several youngsters, laughing and joking amongst themselves as they ran ahead and kicked at pieces of rubble, whilst others were middle aged or elderly, and walked solemnly with bowed heads. Most looked awkward in their ill-fitting overalls or other kinds of makeshift working clothes, and one man even wore a housewive's apron over a business suit.

The foreman, a short man in his middle fifties with a square head and bull-like neck, was irritable, adopting the manner of a drill-sergeant who had just acquired a platoon of raw recruits.

"I want no idling," he exclaimed, "and no one wanders beyond sight. Have any of you done this kind of work before?"

Several put up their hands.

"As a trade,?" enquired the foreman gruffly of a tall thick-set man.

"No, as part time work," replied the man. "After the War."

"I mean as a trade," said the foreman.

The hands went down again.

"You're all clerks or business people sitting on your arses all day then," remarked the foreman

The small party continued to walk across the clearing, silently with bowed heads.

"You can be second in charge," said the foreman nudging the tall man in the side. "See that everyone keeps working. If anyone lays down his shovel I give you my authority to put your boot in his backside. You can all hand me the cards you've brought with you," continued the foreman turning to the rest of the party.

All handed their cards to the foreman. The cards bore the names, addresses and occupations of each volunteer, and required the signature of the foreman to certify that the required service for the NAW had been completed to satisfaction.

"So you're one of the Christian Democrats still remaining," sneered the foreman glancing with contempt from Herr Renot's card to the old man himself. "I thought you lot had been cleared out of the DDR years ago."

The old man said nothing.

"If that happened the DDR wouldn't be democratic any more," joked another, and there was caustic laughter from other members of the gang.

"I don't want any sarcasm," said the foreman gruffly. "I've got your cards, so now we can move onto the site."

The party continued walking towards the huge pile of rubble where there were queues of trucks waiting to be loaded, and dozens of men breaking up blocks of concrete with pneumatic drills, and others with sledge hammers and picks.

"What work are we doing – breaking concrete,?" enquired one man of the foreman.

"No, this is a loading gang," replied the foreman. "You lift the stone and concrete onto the trucks."

"Won't we have a chance to use the pneumatic drills,?" enquired one of the younger members.

"No," replied the foreman.

Herr Renot approached the foreman diffidently. Hitherto he had been lagging behind, and it had been as much as his strength required to keep up with the party.

"I want to do brick scraping," he said discreetly.

"You do, do you?   Well, that's women's work," returned the foreman.

"It's my stomach. I'm not strong enough for lifting," said the old man after a pause.

"You can lift a shovel, can't you?"

"Not like that. Not swinging rubble into the truck," replied the old man.

"What's wrong with your stomach? Indigestion? The work'll do you good," said the foreman with sarcasm. "You're thick set. You should be stronger than me. That's why I picked you out for my gang. I only choose strong men to work for me."

"I want to do brick scraping."

"It's too late to change. The gang's already made up, and we're late starting. Besides, transfers from one gang to another is not allowed – else everyone would be doing it."

"I've trouble with my stomach."

"You should have thought of that before."

"I must be careful of my health."

"So must we all. If you're not fit for working on a building site, you shouldn't have come along. If you want to do brick scraping, you can go home and come along tomorrow."

"I'll just be careful," mumbled the old man.

"But you'll work as hard as any other man here. I'll have no slackers. I'll see to that," said the foreman. "And put some life into your feet and keep up with the rest."

On arriving at the rubble there was a deafening din from pneumatic drills. The foreman put his men to work: six were given shovels and ordered to fill up the next truck which moved into position, whilst the other four were ordered to throw larger pieces of rubble into the truck with bare hands, and as a team, to cooperate in lifting the larger concrete blocks together. The old man was given a shovel and ordered to use that.

As soon as the first truck drew alongside, the foreman let down the back flap and jumped onto the back, and ordered the loading to begin.

"And any man who hits me with a piece of that stuff will get this shovel down his throat."

Work began and the foreman shovelled the rubble to the cabin end, but after a short while, several laid down their shovels and began coughing and spitting.

"What's the matter,?" cried the foreman.

"Dust," replied one of the men.

"Ignore it – it doesn't do you any harm. Lay down those shovels again and you'll be in trouble."

The old man, who was putting all his effort into the work, was not loading his shovel as effectively as the others.

"That's not the way to use a shovel," cried the foreman. "Fill it high. Where's my second in charge," he continued glancing round him. "Show that man how to use a shovel."

The "Second in charge" went hesitantly up to Herr Renot and taking the shovel demonstrated how it should be used correctly.

"Now give him back his shovel," said the foreman with contempt in his voice.

The old man made a greater effort in loading the shovel but half the load fell off before reaching the truck. The foreman glanced threateningly, and soon Papa Renot became the object of his particular dislike, and when the latter laid down his tool during a fit of coughing, he was subjected to a torrent of abuse.

"The dust – it's windy," returned the old man.

"I'll give you wind," sneered the foreman.

The old man persevered, but with painful difficulty, until the foreman ordered him to change places with one of the stronger men lifting heavy slabs.

The tall thick set man appointed as "Second in charge" was continually urged to help, watch over and reprimand the others, receiving occasional approbation from the foreman, but he was nonetheless, a reluctant overseer. Herr Renot had begun joking to those beside him, and most of the men were swearing under their breath over the "bastard" of a foreman.

"I dare you tell him to lick your arse," said one man to another.

Despite the suppressed resentment and anger, none dared answer the foreman back. Perhaps they were consoled with the realisation that it was only an eight hour stint, divided into two shifts, and then they'd never need see him again. After all any lip on their part could be prejudicial to receiving new housing priority. Such was their attitude, and so they remained silent, tolerating the intimidation with the traditional wit and cynical humour of the Berliner in lightening the environment if not the physical toil.

At last the foreman jumped down from the truck ordering the second in charge to take his place. The foreman showered abuse in all directions, insisting the gang must hurry to fill the truck. This was one of the laziest gangs he had ever had! He pointed towards another pile of rubble some distance away, saying that two loaded trucks had passed by whilst this truck was hardly more than three quarters filled.

"What are you laughing at now, funny man,?" cried the foreman at the old man who was sharing a joke with another whom he had nudged in the side. "This is work time, not laugh time!"

On another occasion the old man and another of the group were attempting to lift a huge slab of concrete. The second man, purple in the face and with beads of sweat on his temples, had lifted his end some centimetres off the ground. The old man had his fingers beneath the other end of the slab but apparently was having little success in lifting the heavy masonry.

"Grip the stone – grip with your fingers and then lift," cried the foreman. "Lift, lift – try harder." The old man tried with all his might but the slab never shifted. "Where are your muscles? What's that on your arms – fat and bone? Where's your strength?"

"I'm not as young as I was," replied the old man glancing up.

"Flabby and spineless you are! Of no more use to the People's Democracy than this stone," shouted the foreman kicking the piece of concrete. "Try again."

The old man tried again, his face becoming purple, beads of sweat rolling down his forehead. The slab was lifted some centimetres from the ground, but then he dropped it.

"I can't," he exclaimed breathlessly.

"All right, leave the stone, and I'll get someone stronger. You, take this man's place," said the foreman to another who had just swung a shovelful of rubble onto the truck. "But when you've got this rock onto the back, get back to the shovel again – this man can't be trusted with a tool – he's too idle. All right, get a move on!"

"Yes," replied the man thrusting his shovel into the pile and advancing to where the old man stood.

"Look, I've got something to show you," said the foreman to the old man, thrusting his hand with an impetuous movement into his pocket. "Something that'll show you the value of service to the State."

The foreman struggled in his pocket and the three men nearby crowded round with curious apprehension. The foreman pulled out his closed fist and stretched his arm across the slab of concrete. Slowly, he opened his fingers, and there in his grubby palm lay three dirty brass and silver medals with crumpled ribbons."

"What do you think these are,?" he exclaimed. "Medals! Medals in the service of war? No, these aren't war medals. I don't like war – war is for imperialists. I've never fought in any war. I've always believed in peace and I've lived for peace." Several of the men nearby winked at one another and touched their heads. "These are medals awarded for working with my hands, for working for the reconstruction of a world ruined by war," he exclaimed passionately. "This is the honour I've reaped for labour to the State. I wouldn't give you ten pfennigs for your war medals. Who of you can show me your medals for labour? None, because you've never worked with your hands. Now I've won these medals by working hard and making other men work, and I'm not going to lose them by having any idle man in my gang. Now I'm going to the engineer's shed over there, and if I catch any of you leaning on shovels when I get back, you'll get my boot up your backside."

"He's so good, they ought to put him on a postage stamp," said one of the men after the foreman had left, and they laughed at the joke.

The foreman was not absent for more than half an hour, and when he returned, he was no less irascible than before.

"How about a ten minute break,?" suggested one.

"You'll get your break in an hour's time," replied the foreman. "Don't you watch the other gangs – what they do is their business, not mine and not yours. When you work for me, you don't work for yourselves, you work for my reputation and for the State's reputation."

Soon the old man again became the victim of the foreman's spleen. He was accused of taking up pieces which were too small – pieces that should be left for the shovels.

"Take that piece," said the foreman knocking the side of a boulder with his foot.

The old man began struggling with the rock.

"Bend down to the job," commanded the foreman. "Get your fingers beneath the stone. Now lift, lift, you sapling!"

The efforts of the old man were in vain. Suddenly the foreman thrust his foot onto the boulder whilst the old man had his fingers beneath, and the latter quickly removed them stepping back. The foreman rolled up a trouser leg to the knee. Several put down their shovels and watched from a distance, bemused and curious as to what might follow.

"Do you see that,?" cried the foreman pointing to the inside of his leg. "It's a scar. A deep one. Eighteen centimetres long. That was in 1932 – a street fight in Neukölln. I fought under Ernst Thälmann, the Communist leader of Germany. It was a tough fight. One of our boys lost his life – got the spearhead of a banner thrust through his eye – but we killed two of the Nazis. I got this scar from a sabre wound. In those days it was Hitler or Thälmann. And what were you Christian Democrats doing then? Were you out in the streets? Were you out to fight the Nazis? Not likely! You were worrying how best to save your own skins. And where were you during the War? Helping to fight the capitalist cause like all the rest, I suppose. I can tell you where I was: five years in a concentration camp!"

The work continued, and the trucks were loaded and driven away, as the next drew alongside the pile of rubble, and the pile became smaller as the men strained and sweated to lift the heavy boulders as they shovelled the dusty rubble over the side of the trucks. The foreman swore and never for a moment did he rest, and the men coughed and spat and joked to one another, as they only could, and they cursed beneath their breath.

Sometime later that morning, the shrill siren of an ambulance was heard, as it drove at speed down Stalin Allee and turned down a narrow side street. It drove passed a building site and over some bumpy ground of cleared rubble, and the siren stopped as the vehicle braked by a crowd of men standing around something on the ground which was the object of their attention. The back of the ambulance was opened and a stretcher brought out, and the bearers pushed to the centre of the small crowd.

Some moments later the stretcher was carried into the ambulance bearing a corpulent figure wrapped in a red blanket.

Herr Renot remained in hospital for three months following a rupture and complications. His three hours of service to the *Nationale Aufbau-Werk* necessary for qualifying for new housing was invalidated for the reason of his incapacity and inability to complete the stipulated period of eight hours.

BOOK VIII

Towards A Dark Secret

I hold it true, whate'er befall;
    I feel it, when I sorrow most;
'Tis better to have loved and lost
Then never to have loved at all.

Tennyson, *In Memorium*, Pt. xxvii, St. 4.

Chapter 35

Dagmar and I were quietly walking down the narrow pathway of Bismarck Strasse. We had left the bus at Wannsee station, and I wanted to visit the grave of the great Prussian writer and playwright, Heinrich von Kleist, before returning to Treptow. Kleist's grave was only a five minute walk from Wannsee station.

We were quite silent as we went down the pathway towards the lakeside and Dagmar was introspective and depressed. No doubt she was pondering over the insults and humiliation her father had received at the hands of the Communist foreman.

At last we stood above the shore of the Kleiner Wannsee. At our feet, in the shade of a tree, lay a simple stone with a short inscription. My thoughts went back to the life of Heinrich von Kleist, and at that moment the tragedy of his life and death seemed especially poignant, for it threw a significant light on the national character.

Kleist had been one of the greatest Prussian patriots. It was whilst deeply aroused by Napoleon's subjugation of Germany that he wrote his play, *Die Hermannschlacht*. In this play he used the parallel of the battle of the Teutoberger Wald of AD 9 to dramatise the humiliation of defeat and to inflame his countrymen with hatred of the French invader. The play was suppressed by the authorities. The same purpose of patriotism inspired his projected weekly, *Germania*, and other writings of the period. For political reasons, the weekly proved impossible to launch.

After a mental breakdown resulting from the frustration of failure and other crises which harassed his life, Kleist wrote his last and finest play, *Prinz Friedrich von Homberg*. This proved to be the greatest manifesto of Prussian patriotism, and was besides a work of supreme dramatic excellence and psychological insight. This too was suppressed for political reasons. Kleist then founded the *Berliner Abendblätter*,

Berlin's first daily newspaper, which was successful at first but again was later throttled by government censorship.

Despairing of his country's plight and vexed with anger at the docility and pacification of the Prussian government which appeased the French conqueror, Kleist faced yet another breakdown. He was bitterly disappointed by failure and at the ineffectiveness of the political message he wished to transmit. Of all his plays only three were produced in his lifetime, and his greatest writings were suppressed by the authorities for fear of offending the French, and endangering a neutrality borne and maintained by fear. Eventually, he was disowned by his family and reduced to penury.

It was on the 21st November 1811 that Heinrich von Kleist together with Henriette Vogel came to the banks of the Wannsee where we now stood. Henriette Vogel was shot in the heart before Kleist turned the pistol into his own mouth, ending his life at the age of thirty-four.

Dagmar and I bent over the gravestone. It bore only the simple inscription: *He Sought Death and Found Eternity*.

"He knew the best way out of life's troubles," remarked Dagmar gloomily.

"Don't say that. Life's not quite so bad," I replied.

"He died for his true love," remarked Dagmar.

"He killed himself in despair," I returned firmly, " – in despair at the stupidity of his countrymen. He was the one man who had the courage to stand up against the foolish authority of the State."

"I admire him, anyway."

"All Germans admire him today, but they were a bit late in doing it. It took them fifty years to recognise his literary merits, and I don't know if the political significance of his life is even yet appreciated."

"How do you mean,?" asked Dagmar.

"He wanted to stand up against the French who were occupying his country, and he tried to flout the censorship of the press in expressing opinions he believed in. I'd like to ask if there are any von Kleists in East Germany today, not men who'd stand up against the Russians, but men and women with courage enough to stand up against the German State which claims its own autonomy from the occupying power."

"Perhaps there are."

"I think not."

"You've no right to say that," said Dagmar in unexpected anger. "You don't know everything that happens in the East."

"I've seen and heard a lot, and can draw my own conclusions," I replied.

"You've not seen or heard enough to suggest there are *no* men who'd not stand up against oppression."

"Then I'll wait till you assure me to the contrary," I replied smiling.

"I may even do that," said Dagmar significantly.

On arriving in Graetz Strasse early that evening, we saw at some distance in front of us on the pavement, a plump figure slowly moving along towards our direction bearing a white paper package. From behind the package came some grey wisps of smoke, clearly from a cigar.

"Why, it's your Papa," I exclaimed discreetly, "and he's carrying flowers."

"Yes," replied Dagmar leaning her head towards me and speaking in a confidential tone. "It's Saturday night. Papa always buys Mamma flowers on a Saturday night."

"How very sweet," I remarked.

Shortly after entering the flat I was met by a not inconsiderable embarrassment.

The good Frau, as usual, came out of the kitchen to greet us as soon as we arrived, and after patting me on the shoulder, she then led me by the wrist into the kitchen and in little more than a whisper, enquired gleefully, "Has Dagmar a ring?" I was so put-out I feigned not to understand, only shaking my head to indicate incomprehension. The good Frau was not in the least put out by my embarrassment, and she rushed out of the room and took her daughter aside.

As had happened before, when Dagmar and I remained at home for the evening, Granny was put to bed early, and at about nine o'clock the good Frau came into the sitting room and smiling gleefully, bid us, "Good night and sleep well!"

Dagmar and I were sitting innocently on the sofa, close together but stiffly upright with a book between our laps.

"Look, I'm learning English Mamma," exclaimed Dagmar in delight, holding up the volume.

The good Frau glanced at each of us in turn with an expression of benign appreciation, and then left the room, firmly closing the door behind her before leaving the flat.

The following morning I was awoken at the ungodly hour – that is, an ungodly hour for anyone enjoying the leisurely pace of life allowed by a vacation – of seven o'clock. This was not the first time this had occurred. In fact, to be exact, it was the fourth day running. The cause of my early awakening was not due to the deafening noises emanating from a building site (noises usually heard from every part of central Berlin) and neither was it due to the crashing of dustbin lids (to which I had become so accustomed in Graetz Strasse) for I had the good fortune to occupy a room in the front part of the Pension, facing the sleepy square of Spreewald Platz.

The cause of my early awakening was due to something at much closer quarters. In fact, it depended on the habits of the occupants in the adjoining rooms beyond the walls of my little apartment. I had already become accustomed to these same noises late at night or in the early hours of the morning, but since I returned invariably to the Pension quite late, I didn't consider them of special nuisance. This was not to suggest that the other occupants of the Pension were rowdy, raucously drunk or otherwise disorderly; quite the contrary, in fact, for I never heard the whisper of a voice from either side of the walls during the course of my stay there. This was an *ordentlich* (respectable) Pension. The noises caused by these other guests were something for which human blame could not be properly attributed. Blame lay only in the plumbing of the water supply.

As soon as taps were turned on on the other side of either wall, all hell seemed to be let loose. There was an impetuous gurgling and spluttering followed by a convulsion of the pipes of a violence which seemed to threaten the very fabric of the building. Many a time I had tucked myself well into bed pulling the duvet firmly over my head, in fear that the wall would collapse. After all, anything may happen in these old buildings following the bombing this city's been through, I thought, and one cannot be too cautious. No doubt, when attending to my own ablutions, I in my turn proved an equal threat to the feeling of security of the neighbouring occupants on the other side of the walls.

On this particular day, however, I did not consider my early awakening as something which was a gross disturbance of the peace, for I arose some minutes after seven. I breakfasted in the Pension for the first time during my stay there, eating butter and marmalade with *Schrippen* rolls and pumpernickel, and drinking coffee from delicate chinaware, in the company of the elderly ladies who permanently resided in the Pension.

That morning I paid a courtesy call on Frau Schultz, in Friedenau, presenting her with a small bouquet. My journey to Friedenau will remain memorable in one particular respect. On a map, the suburbs of Kreuzberg and Friedenau stand in close proximity. This was pleasing for I considered time of importance in executing my little mission before returning to Graetz Strasse later that morning. Friedenau was on the S-Bahn but there were no S-Bahn stations within two kilometres of my Pension in Spreewald Platz, but I was pleased to observe that a number 88 tram ran from Wiener Strasse (one minute's walk from the Pension) to that part of Friedenau where the Schultzes lived. This indeed seemed convenient!

I boarded the tram, a dusty noisy vehicle constructed perhaps fifty years ago, and the journey began. The tram moved steadily in one straight line, on and on, along Wiener Strasse and along Oranien Strasse, wide streets with vast grimy blocks and huge tenement structures which were gutted ruins, and then bomb sites, and more office blocks again, their plaster facades crumbling to the ground. The streets were so long that I began to wonder if they came to any end at all. The tram seemed to move neither left nor right, but to continue in a single direction as if determined to define the shortest distance between two points. Surely we must be nearly there now, I kept telling myself. The route seemed direct enough.

The tram moved at a speed of hardly more than fifteen miles an hour, and stopped every few hundred metres along the roadway to pick up or drop an elderly woman or two. There were never many people aboard the vehicle but several times during the journey, it was emptied and refilled again with a different set of passengers.

"Are we nearly there yet,?" I asked the conductor.

"A long way yet," he replied.

A long way yet! Always the same answer! I swore beneath my breath. The further we moved, the more perplexed and angry I became, as my feelings of desperation increased. The scene was unchanging – or almost so – the same dull grimy street and the same seven storey tenement and office blocks with their filthy unpainted fronts and crumbling facades. Surely we must be moving somewhere – moving towards some specific destination! Eventually, I began to doubt even that.

Again, I asked if we were nearly there. The conductor never deigned even to reply, but merely waved his hand at me to remain patient. Again, I swore beneath my breath. The journey was becoming ridiculous! I took out my map and glanced at it again. Yes, the suburb of Friedenau was practically adjacent to Kreuzberg, and maps can't lie, and yet judging by the time this journey was taking, anyone would have thought I had taken a street car to the moon! I glanced at my watch and began to work out a little scientific calculation. During the time I had sat in this filthy noisy clanking tram, a satellite had already orbited half way round the globe whilst I had not travelled between two districts of Berlin which were practically adjacent.

The tram was undoubtedly destined for Friedenau – I had assured myself of that several times from the conductor. But then, perhaps the transport authorities of Berlin were merely maintaining this line as a sort of practical joke on unwary travellers. Perhaps the tram would suddenly arrive at its terminal in Frohnau or Heiligensee. Was this yet another manifestation of Berliner humour? If so, it was in poor taste! And then again, perhaps the tram would finally arrive in Friedenau after a complete circuit of the city.

At last the vehicle crashed and clanked making a deafening row as it turned a sharp corner into another street. My sense of hopeful anticipation was suddenly aroused. Now perhaps we shall be arriving somewhere, I thought. But alas, the tram almost immediately turned another sharp corner and we seemed to resume the same direction as before. A few minutes later we passed nearby the Anhalter station. This is nowhere near Friedenau, I suddenly realised with concern. The tram made a few more turns, and then turned a sharp corner into Potsdamer Strasse. We now seemed to be travelling in the exact direction from which we had come. The tram had reversed its direction according to the points of the compass! It moved on and on, not once deviating from its straight course. The conductor waved his hand at me to remain seated. I considered the course of making a leap for freedom, irrespective of what the conductor might do – at jumping off at the sight of the next S-Bahn or Underground station, so completing the journey by another form of transport. At last my sense of desperation reached a state of total despair. I became apathetic, and for all I cared, the tram could go where it would and carry me with it.

"Only about another fifteen minutes," said the conductor passing down towards the other end of the vehicle (and there was a trace of sarcasm in his voice) as we left Kaiser Wilhelm Platz.

Finally, I was told we had arrived in Friedenau. It took my mind some seconds to register the reality of this fact, so unexpected was the announcement.

"Thanks for the lovely trip," I shouted at the conductor, perhaps with a trace of bitterness.

As I left the vehicle I swore to myself never again to board another tram in the city of Berlin and then I recollected the advice – alas too late remembered – which Martin had once given me: *never* to use a tram in his city!*

I stood in the middle of Haupt Strasse and realised I had in fact arrived in Friedenau, and I recognised the surrounding buildings from a year ago. The journey from Kreuzberg to Friedenau had taken sixty-five minutes.

I sat with Frau Schultz in Martin's room, and we drank tea and talked for an hour or so. We discussed the recent political situation in Berlin and about my stay in the East sector, on which she seemed reluctant to comment. Perhaps she thought my courting a girl from the East a foolish escapade.

---

* Trams were finally withdrawn from service in West Berlin in 1967.

"Today, it's a strain to live in Berlin," she exclaimed. "You don't know what may happen from one day to the next."

She explained that the stress of this anxiety had brought about a nervous complaint for which her doctor had prescribed medication. The allies had been slow to react during the brief crisis the previous month, when the East German authorities interfered with the city's communications, and she thought the wording of the protest to Moscow had been too mild. She had been particularly angered by the Western and especially the British press reactions to the refugee rallies, saying that the Western press had been "callous and most cruel," and I was made to feel uncomfortable by the bitterness of her accusations.

"All West Berlin was very angry during those days," she said. The indecision of the allies was what most exasperated the people of West Berlin.

"The Communists are *never* hesitant," said Frau Schultz with emphasis. "In that lies their strength. They have one will, and that is Moscow, but the decisions of the West require a compromise between the conflicting wills of three powers. How can decisions arising from the confusion of three heads possibly be expected to compete against the clear-cut clarity of one? The West has no clear policy to handle any eventuality that may arise."

"Only a federal government of a united Europe could solve that problem," I suggested in attempting to alleviate her resentment.

"That may be, but when shall we see that as a reality? And perhaps by then it may be too late. Sometimes I ask myself if we shall wake up one morning to see Russian tanks in the streets."

My visit to Frau Schutz was enlightening. It was clear the people of West Berlin were intensely worried by the unexpected turn of events, and there was here a greater concern and political consciousness than in the East. The ordinary people of the East had become passive through despair. Politically, they were no longer alive – no longer significant in any active sense. The people of the West sectors, by contrast, still retained their spirit and were fighting for their freedom, however pessimistic their hopes for the future might be.

I returned to Kreuzberg via the S-Bahn and Underground railways, completing the journey in less than half an hour. The morning's absence from Dagmar gave me an interval for thought away from the constant presence of her company. I had had time to reflect and to look at our relationship in a clearer perspective, but then suddenly I was seized with concern. I realised that in less than twenty-four hours some decision would need to be made between us as to the future of our friendship. Time, which for so long had been of little account, seemed suddenly to take on an aspect of urgency. It was now a Sunday morning and early on

Tuesday I would be returning to Münster. How could any decision be reached between us by then?

During the past week or more, our friendship had been marked by neither progress nor regression. Emotionally we had seemed inseparably bound, whilst the quarrels between us remained nonetheless a barrier towards the furtherance of our relationship. It seemed as if a mysterious force frustrated our psychic will, and this force seemed to lie behind the mystery surrounding the fair one. What decision would be made, and what would be the outcome of this affair? The answer to this question was more imponderable than the first. I decided to tackle her in a forthright manner that evening, by ignoring entirely the mysterious veil which shrouded her, and to dismiss the so-called "destiny" of her remaining in the East, as so much fog and confusion, and instead, to discuss the immediate practical problem of transporting her from Berlin to the Federal Republic, and the arrangements for her finding work and a dwelling place.

On returning to my Pension, I was told by the reception clerk that someone had called for me during my absence.

"When,?" I enquired.

"At about ten o'clock," replied the clerk.

"What sort of person?"

"An old man – *dick*! (fat!)," replied the clerk smiling just perceptibly and stretching out her hands to indicate the "thickness" of the caller.

"Did he leave a message?"

"No, no message."

"It was the same person as called yesterday then," I said.

Clearly, it had been Papa Renot again. Several times during the past week he had called on me early in the morning, and we had walked together down Wiener Strasse towards the flat in the East sector. I frequently asked myself (with a twinge of discomfort) what the hotel staff might have thought or supposed when this mysterious unprepossessing man (forever brushing his lapels of invisible specks of dust) called on me at the Pension. We must have seemed the most incongruous looking pair that ever stood together!

Even if the thoughts of the staff had been free of perverse suspicion, they must have regarded our relationship with nothing less than amusement. Who could have guessed that I was courting one of the most beautiful girls in Berlin who was the daughter of this very man? I resented the embarrassment caused by the old man calling at the Pension – but of course I could not prevent his calling – and when he stood in the hallway, he always looked so awkward and out of place. We would leave the Pension together and return towards Graetz Strasse.

During each of these walks, as we passed along the pavement beneath the high red brick wall which shut in the derelict goods yard of the Görlitzer station, he reminded me of a three week holiday he had had in Vienna with his wife and children, long ago, during the War years. Each day he recounted the same story, almost word for word, as if it had been quite new to me, and each day I politely condescended to receive the story as if he was telling it for the first time, expressing surprise and wonderment, and asking the same questions as I had on the day before.

"Once a great station,!" the old man exclaimed. "Today, it's nothing – everything *kaput*! Earlier trains left for Prague, for Vienna, for Budapest, for the Balkan states – thousands of kilometres away," he said throwing out his hands in front of him to indicate great distance. "Wonderful countries! Bulgaria and Turkey, where the sun always shines, and white mosques and high minarets – and harems with beautiful girls dancing in transparent silk." He grinned facetiously and looked thoughtful a moment. "Ach! That is the life, *Schön, nicht?*"

"Yes, that's the life," I assented.

The old man would nudge me in the side.

"During the War I took my wife and Gisela, and Dagmar when she was that small," he said lowering his hand to within a few feet of the pavement, "to Vienna. We were three weeks there. I didn't tell you about that did I?"

"No," I would reply, for I did not want to deprive him of telling a good story.

"The most beautiful city in the world! It has everything! We left from the Görlitzer station," he said stretching his hand towards the red wall. "But what a journey – never to be forgotten," he added cheerfully, "– boom, boom, boom! – all the way – every kilometre between Berlin and Vienna – British and American bombers, non-stop, all night long."

The old man laughed cheerfully.

On arriving at the flat at No. 55, Dagmar answered the door, and good-humouredly rebuked me for being late, saying that lunch had been kept waiting. I told her the story of my journey to Friedenau and she laughed. We talked for a while in the sitting room, and as the weather was dull, we decided to take a stroll in Treptower Park that afternoon and then return home for the rest of the day. This little programme, however, was not to materialise, for other persons in the house entertained alternative ideas as to our recreation that afternoon.

After lunch, as the plates were being cleared away, the good Herr and Frau Renot were engaged in an apparently conspiratorial discussion, and moments later the latter came gleefully into the sitting room, announcing to Dagmar and me that Papa would be taking us both to the races that afternoon.

I betrayed no response to the announcement, only turned towards Dagmar and waited for her comment. She responded coolly, accepting the decision as a *fait accompli*. We would go with Papa to the horse racing at Karlshorst! I felt apprehensive, and intuitively, knew that more lay behind this than merely "horses." There was a conspiracy at work! I had several times been taken out by the old man alone, but Dagmar and I had never before been taken out together. Perhaps the old man intended asking us point blank to enter into a formal engagement, and my forebodings led me to dread what lay ahead. Besides I felt Dagmar and I were being deprived of valuable time during which differences might be resolved, and possibly, a mutual arrangement agreed between us, and I felt nothing could be achieved during the time we were obliged to remain with Papa Renot.

The three of us went to Karlshorst by S-Bahn, and during the journey, hardly a word was exchanged between us. Dagmar and I stood silently side by side, she holding her arm in mine, whilst Papa Renot stood glancing up at us with an expressionless stare which was most unsettling. He probably wanted to say something and was thinking deeply how best to express it. The old man brushed his lapels and took out a cigar, which he lit, and the smoke came in our direction and into Dagmar's eyes.

"Oh really Papa, it's so dirty smoking in a crowded train," she exclaimed screwing up her nose.

The old man said nothing.

On arriving at Karlshorst we left the train as did most of the passengers, and on reaching the racing grounds we queued at the turnstiles behind a crowd of workers, and Papa Renot insisted on paying for our entry and a programme for the afternoon.

The horse racing, it transpired, was really trotting with little chariots, and for different reasons was the dullest race meeting I had ever attended. The track was spacious, and there were large covered stands where the punters might sit and be out of the rain. There was thick grey cloud and a chilly wind which pierced through our light Summer coats and made us shiver.

The three of us went into the large central stand and climbed the steps and sat on a seat high above the ground and well beneath the roof, commanding a bird's-eye view of the course. We sat huddled together in a place we hoped was protected from the wind. I sat between Dagmar and the thick figure of the old man who was on my left, but cold gusts blew against our clothing, and my fingers were numbed as I held the programme.

The stand was sparsely occupied. Few sat on our level, and none above, and groups of workers in scruffy attire sat silently in front of the stand, their eyes fixed on the course. Spectators stood crowded round the white fence barrier of the track, solemnly watching the proceedings, and others stood behind them, stamping their feet on the ground and throwing their arms around their bodies for warmth. A group of Russian soldiers stood together studying the odds, and every few minutes, several would leave the group going beneath the central stand to lay a bet.

Occasionally, a voice droned from the tannoy speakers announcing the details and odds for the next race, and a number of punters made their leisurely way to the betting kiosks in the long hallway below. Gloom pervaded the proceedings and how solemn were the spectators as with grim countenances they studied the odds. There was little of the excitement or thrilled anticipation as the horses came up to the finishing line as at a racing ground in the West, and there were no bookies calling or gesticulating to one another from different directions. This was a race meeting in a "People's" State and the proceedings were hemmed in by government restrictions of a kind which limited the excitement and removed the glamour found typically beyond the confines of the East bloc.

Dagmar complained of the cold, and so we moved to a higher seat but still we were unprotected from the bitter wind. We decided to warm our chilled bodies with coffee and something to eat, and went into the crowded restaurant, and I purchased refreshments, whilst Dagmar and her father reserved places at a table.

Later, Dagmar and I wandered aimlessly round the sides of the track whilst Papa Renot stood close to the barrier studiously studying the form, and occasionally pointing out the qualities and defects of various animals. There was an endless wait between one race and the next, for the clinker and dirt track had to be raked and levelled between each event. Suddenly, the old man brightened, announcing he would lay a two-mark bet, and he went off towards the booking area. It was the only bet he made during the afternoon, and he lost the two marks.

Again Dagmar complained, saying how boring everything was and that "both of us" were "frozen through" and some minutes later, we left the ground, Dagmar and I walking ahead, and she occasionally chiding her father with the words, "It's so cold, Papa, we must reach the station quickly."

As we stood on the platform of Karlshorst station, the old man exhausted and perspiring, took out an enormous handkerchief from his breast pocket and wiped it over his face.

"Oh really, Papa, do you have to do that,?" exclaimed Dagmar in an undertone. "You look just like a worker – it's terrible!"

The afternoon between the three of us was not yet over, and the old man had not given up all hope that it had been a wasted outing. Whilst standing close together in the crowded train he suddenly plucked up courage, and slapping one hand over the other, as if to catch a fly, he exclaimed, "*Heute Abend, der Ring*! (This evening, the ring!)" I never twitched a muscle nor blushed, and momentarily, it seemed as if the blood had stopped in my veins.

Dagmar only exclaimed, "Oh *quatsch*, Papa!"

There were a few moments of silence between us as the train sped along the rails, and then the old man exclaimed with a bright gesture: "This evening you'll be alone."

"And thank God,!" added Dagmar who had not yet recovered from her feeling of awkwardness at the old man's previous remark.

There was another pause, and then the old man exclaimed: "*Heute Abend, es kommt automatisch*! (This evening, it'll come automatically!)"

Chapter 36

Now Dagmar, I shan't listen to any more of your excuses," I exclaimed good-naturedly, firmly taking her shoulders.

"Such as what excuses,?" she replied.

"Such as those excuses where destiny is blamed," I answered, "and when you speak about the inevitability of fate."

We were standing in the sitting room and it was late in the evening, and the rest of the family had retired from the flat, except for Frau Brüning who had already been asleep in the adjacent room for several hours. We had had a stressful evening in the family circle, and a small party had been held which Renata and Franz and Gisela had attended, and throughout the evening Dagmar's parents had constantly dropped allusions for the furtherance of our relationship. These tiresome and blatant hints had embarrassed all the younger persons present and fending off these remarks in as good-humoured a way as possible, had eventually frayed the nerves of the couple to whom they were addressed.

"I don't know yet what I should makes excuses for," said Dagmar smiling, "since we haven't yet had a discussion on anything of consequence."

"I'm just telling you, before we have a discussion, not to mention directly or indirectly anything concerning your past life touching your future," I said firmly but in good humour.

"That depends on what you're going to ask," said Dagmar.

"I just want you to forget the past – if only for this evening."

"I think that's a tall order."

"Just think about the future – about the hopes and joys of a new life. But for this evening, don't look back – not for a second. Don't reflect – don't doubt – just think about what you want most in life. Be positive!"

There was a momentary pause. Dagmar looked into my eyes as I held her shoulders. She had been spellbound by my little speech.

"What are we to talk about,?" she asked.

"About practical things. Sit down and I'll explain," I said taking her hands and leading her to the sofa. "We'll discuss as to how you are to leave Berlin."

"If that could ever be a possibility," she sighed smiling.

"Don't think about impossibilities. This evening we'll only think about possibilities. Will you promise me that?"

"I'll try."

I took Dagmar's hands in mine.

"Now firstly, I understand it would be impossible for you or your parents to pay for your flight from West Berlin to the Federal Republic."

"Yes, that's the first impossibility," said Dagmar smiling.

"Secondly, I wouldn't like to see you stay in the refugee camp in Marienfelde – not even for a day. And so the first question would be money – just enough to pay for your fare from Tempelhof to West Germany."

"And how would it be paid for?"

"I'll pay the fare and transfer the money into a bank in the West sector. All you'd then do is book your ticket with an airline and fly from Tempelhof."

"It sounds fine, but it's not so simple," said Dagmar.

"Tomorrow we can talk about putting these and other things into practice. And now we can discuss about your reception in Western Germany. I could find you a room in Münster, and work also. As soon as I've secured these, you could fly to West Germany, and then your problems would be over."

"You said I'd only need money for the fare," said Dagmar. "Then how would I live for the first month in West Germany?"

"No problem! I'd lend you enough for basic living expenses. Anyway, if your employers are reasonable, they'll give you an advance."

"But I wouldn't have a job at that stage."

"There's plenty of work in West Germany. You'd soon get something – maybe not exactly what you want at first."

"It's still impossible."

"Why?"

"There are so many imponderables."

"Such as?"

"I'd be going to a new country. I'd want some kind of assurance – some kind of security beforehand," she said hesitantly in confusion.

"I'll give you any assurance you ask."

"I'd want some kind of guarantee."

"Just tell me the guarantee and I'll give it."

"It's difficult – I can't explain," she replied.

"Just tell me directly."

"You should know what guarantee I need," she exclaimed resentfully.

"I'll promise you that guarantee when all arrangements have been made."

"Why afterwards? Why ask me to leave all my friends and family, and expect me to commit my entire future whilst you risk nothing?"

"Don't be flustered. I'll promise you this guarantee beforehand. Can we now settle everything?"

"There are other things to consider."

"Then name them."

"They are more important than those things we've discussed this evening."

"Then it's important we consider them."

"They concern those things you've asked me to remain silent about."

"Are those things so important,?" I said slowly my voice trembling with a suggestion of anger. "Must they always intrude on what effects your future?"

"I can't run away from them – even if I wished to."

"Then we must discuss them."

"I will not," she said shaking her head stubbornly.

"You will not?"

"Because I cannot."

"Tell me about this great anxiety," I said taking her hands in mine. "Tell me the dark secret which has brought about this fatalism – your resignation in life?"

"My resignation in life?"

"Yes, from the day I first saw you in the little Art Shop in Stalin Allee, I asked myself, What lies in the secret of your resignation in life? Even then I felt that the memory of some great sad event was burdening your mind."

"I can say nothing."

"You're stubborn. I only see in your obstinacy an unfriendly gesture."

"It's for my own safety that I'm so."

"You can confide in me. Don't you, by this time, trust me as a friend?"

"Yes – it's not that."

"Then what is it?"

"I wish I could explain. It's so difficult for me," exclaimed Dagmar almost tearfully. "I wish I could make you understand, but I cannot."

"Tell me everything and put aside your inhibitions for this one evening."

"I won't tell you for this one reason: because I know it will upset our relationship," exclaimed Dagmar emotionally.

"You *know* it will upset our relationship? I can't believe you've committed some terrible wrong. Then some other person is involved?"

"Yes."

"Tell me about this person. Who is this person?"

"No! I shan't tell you anything."

"Then through involuntary circumstances, you're somehow involved with another person. That must be it. We'll free you from your relationship with this person."

"I'll tell you nothing. I don't wish to think or speak about this any longer. Don't question me any more. I refuse to argue with you any longer."

"I give up. Your attitude is incomprehensible. How do you expect me to understand? There's silliness in everything you say. It all makes such nonsense."

"Because you have no sympathy for my feelings. Why speak about things you know will hurt me?"

"Don't speak to me about your precious feelings, and my sympathy for them. I'm bored with them."

"Then perhaps you're bored with me too," said Dagmar with tearful self-pity.

"Who's this other person? Some person with whom you're emotionally involved? Perhaps it's your good friend Renata."

"Don't speak like that. Don't be so nasty," she returned angrily. "Is that all you can do – be insulting – just because I decide not to answer your stupid personal questions?"

"Dagmar, I'm sorry. I'm not jealous, just curious. Let's be calm for a moment. Let's try to be reasonable. You know I didn't come to Berlin because of a casual friendship. I came to take you away from Berlin. That's the only reason I came here."

"I'm from the East. I'm not from the free world."

"I know."

"You can take a girl from any city in the world, but not from East Berlin. Here we cannot act even of our own free will."

"But the frontiers to the West are still open for those choosing to flee from oppression. Dagmar, come with me to the West – tomorrow – next week – any time. You're free to come to the West – you know that – but for how long that freedom will be possible, we cannot say. Perhaps sometime in the future, the frontiers may be closed between the two halves of the city. Dagmar, come with me to the West before it's too late."

"I won't even consider coming to the West until our relationship is more secure," said Dagmar lowering her eyes.

"I'll do anything to further our relationship."

"I know Papa and Mamma have been very bad and very tactless today," began Dagmar awkwardly, "and I've felt very angry with them. They've made it difficult for us both, especially for you, James. It's not nice to be told what to do, but they want to see the furtherance of our relationship."

"And I want to see the furtherance of our relationship most of all. But there are many things to consider."

"So you, too, have things to 'consider,'" said Dagmar smiling. "And what things are those?"

"For me, too, an explanation is difficult," I began awkwardly. "I want to know about those things which are most important to your life, such as your health" –

"Which remember I wrote to you about in a letter some time ago," said Dagmar petulantly.

"And most of all, about the secret you're concealing from me in the deepest recesses of your heart."

Dagmar became pale with anger, stiffening her posture.

"Is that the condition on which our relationship will be furthered,?" she asked, her voice trembling.

"It is the condition," I replied. "It's not much to ask."

"And if I refuse?"

"I cannot see any good reason as to why you should."

"But if I should?"

"I don't know – our relationship may come to nothing."

At once I realised the indiscretion of the remark and the effect it might have on the fair one.

"Have I ever refused you anything,?" she exclaimed resentfully. "Have I ever extended to you an unfriendly gesture, or suggested to you that our friendship was insincere? Have you had any reason to suspect that?"

She was angry, but I could only talk with her on my own terms. The confusion between us was becoming irreconcilable.

"The subject we're discussing is of pre-eminent importance. A life relationship can't be entered into unless both partners are open and honest. I haven't concealed anything from you. You can ask me what you will. But you're hiding something from me, and for that, you must have an ulterior motive."

"First you ask me to leave Berlin – to leave my family and all my friends,whilst you promise nothing and I risk everything, and now you threaten that unless I divulge the secrets of my life, our relationship will come to nothing."

"Listen and be reasonable, Dagmar. I am prepared to tell you everything about myself – to conceal nothing. But you are not prepared to be open with me in the same way."

"But you are asking more. I don't understand that. You are free to do what you want, but what you ask of me involves the sacrifice of all I possess."

"We must know each other completely."

"Isn't our relationship as intimate as it could be?"

"Physically, yes, but that's not enough. More is needed for a life relationship. You know that," I said.

"Isn't our relationship mutual?   Haven't we expressed our innermost feelings to one another? Isn't that enough? If not, then on what grounds should the basis of such a relationship be made?"

"Feelings alone are not enough. That's where our opinions differ. We must consider rational factors – practical things bearing on our relationship."

"What shall we consider?"

"Tell me Dagmar, what's the secret around this other person?"

"For the last time, I won't tell you, and for reasons I'm convinced are sound."

"You're impossible! I can't argue with you because you're so unreasonable," I said rising from the couch.

"Then go – leave me if you will," exclaimed Dagmar tearfully.

"Your attitude is such stupid evasion."

"Then go!"

"I shall," I replied in anger, and suddenly it seemed as if our friendship was crumbling within minutes. I regretted the sharp retort but it was too late to backtrack or make amends.

"You've been cruel and unthoughtful," sobbed Dagmar.

"It was you who asked me to go," I replied as I made my way to the door.

It was too late to go back for I had reached the point of no return. A sharp pang of disillusion passed through me, and I was overcome with profound depression. In a flash, the events surrounding our friendship –

of our love and struggle – from our first meeting in the Art Shop to this present moment, rushed through my mind. But it was too late to go back – that would be weakness – a cowardly surrender to another's will. I knew our relationship was evaporating – but why? – I could not say.

I felt a pang of remorse at having allowed our argument to have run wild in this way – to have got out of hand – to poison our souls and ruin our friendship. But how had it happened? What dark force had crept into our souls and taken hold of our baser nature? Had it been my fault? She had sought only to fend off my questioning with reasons of her own – and perhaps they had been sound. We had both been stubborn, but the fault seemed to lie not so much within ourselves but externally. The blame lay in the secret burden which oppressed Dagmar and so frustrated the furtherance of our friendship.

"Come back,!" exclaimed Dagmar, and I turned towards her and she looked embarrassed as if she had uttered an involuntary cry.

"I'm sorry about what's happened, Dagmar," I exclaimed, my voice trembling, "but there's no coming back. I've asked nothing from you that's unreasonable. There must be no secrets which divide us."

"Wait, let me explain," she said, but her voice trembled with hesitancy.

"I'll call on you early tomorrow, and see you then, and say farewell to your parents."

"You cannot do this to me," exclaimed Dagmar tearfully.

"I'll call at nine tomorrow, so as to take the morning train from Berlin in the West sector."

"Don't go - wait!"

I opened the door and walked down the narrow passageway of the flat.

"Come back,!" I heard Dagmar cry from inside the room and her voice was choked.

I neither went back nor glanced back. I felt more profoundly depressed than I had ever done before as I walked down the little passageway I had come to know so well, and I wondered whether I should ever walk down it again. What memories it brought to mind! I saw Dagmar's blue coat hanging on the hallstand reflected by the light from the opened door of the sitting room. There came not a sound. Dagmar didn't intend then to see me off at the front door as she had always done before. I hesitated, wondering for a moment whether to return and seek a reconciliation. No, that would be weakness! I opened the front door. I felt a swelling in my throat, and it seemed as if all hopes were being dashed to the ground. I was overcome with a feeling of anguish and bitterness.

I stepped through the doorway of the flat and into the dark entrance hall of the tenement block, when suddenly I heard a sound behind me. Dagmar came running frantically down the passageway of the flat.

"Come back,!" she cried. "Don't leave Berlin tomorrow."

She reached the doorway of the flat.

"Don't leave Berlin. I'll tell you everything," she cried frantically.

"Quiet,!" I retorted sharply in a loud whisper. "You'll wake everyone in the block."

Her voice had resounded from the stone walls of the hallway.

"I promise to tell you everything," she exclaimed tearfully.

"Why need you? What would be the use,?" I returned cynically.

"James, promise you'll not leave Berlin tomorrow," she said pitifully, taking hold of my lapels.

"Why?"

"Because I must tell you everything. Now I realise the moment has arrived when you must know all."

"Will you tell me now?"

"No, not now. We're both too tired and upset. Tomorrow! Promise you'll come to me tomorrow. I'll explain everything. Come to me here, directly – not across the road – at ten o'clock."

"Why is it so necessary? Why must you suddenly tell all?"

"James, please – you must try to understand – this once," she cried, and again, her voice reverberated off the walls. "I'm engaged – engaged to be married!"

Momentarily I was transfixed and speechless with astonishment. Had I really heard aright?

"I'll come tomorrow," I replied at last.

My mind was numbed by the excitement, conflicting emotions and confusion, of the past few minutes.

"And try to be nice when you come tomorrow," sobbed Dagmar tightening her fingers round my lapels. "Try not to let Mamma and Papa know about our quarrel."

I took hold of her wrists and pulled them away from my jacket. I extended no parting gesture, and I walked towards the large doorway of the hall. She was still standing there, by the door of the flat, silent and motionless, watching me intently as I closed the heavy door behind me.

Briskly, I walked down Graetz Strasse towards my Pension in Kreuzberg and there was a mist in the night air. My mind was numbed by the confusion of events of the past few minutes. What feelings passed through my mind – anger, exasperation, resentment – I could not say. All was confusion. What had happened? I couldn't even answer that. It had happened so quickly – the sweetness of our love and friendship for one another, had crumbled within moments. Was this really the end of our friendship? Was that possible? What evil had dared to poison the sweetness of our friendship? How had it happened?

Perhaps we were just tired, I thought. Perhaps the strain and excitement of the day had brought on the quarrel. Perhaps tomorrow we would make up our friendship again, as we had done many a time before, but then a cloud of dejection crossed my mind. This quarrel was different from the others. I knew that. Why was it different? It seemed not so much a culmination of our quarrels, as the creation of a new synthesis of everything which had occurred. What was it which had made our quarrel so different? Suddenly, the answer hit me with the force of a hammer, and the realisation numbed my mind after a momentary pang of anger and perplexity. Had she really said that? Had she meant it? Was it true? Was she engaged – engaged to be married?

I came up to the Wiener bridge and the frontier police were lounging at the sides of the roadway, throwing their arms around their bodies to keep warm in the cool night air. Their figures made a black outline in the night, and they breathed cold air from their lungs and the butts of their machine guns rose from behind their shoulders. It was a reminder that Autumn was upon us and then the threat of Winter.

If Dagmar was engaged, then what strange mystery lay behind the secret of her engagement? Of what significance was my relationship to her now? How complex was the muddle in which she had involved herself? I felt angry rather than exasperated. It seemed as if she might possibly have regarded our friendship without sincerity. This was very possibly so! My anger became more intense. Then I thought of her implicit plea for the furtherance of our relationship. She had meant that with sincerity. I thought of all the love we had given each other, and of the joys we had shared together. How stood the emotional basis of our friendship? Everything stood in such confusion, that an attempt to guess, even, seemed futile.

Chapter 37

I arose late the following morning. I had overslept. I had lain awake many hours the previous night trying to unravel the confusion which had dashed our friendship. Sleepless, I tossed and turned, as I thought back over the course of our relationship. All the strange enigmas and inexplicable things surrounding Dagmar suddenly came to the fore.

I thought of her resignation in life, as I had described her countenance on first seeing her that day in the little Art Shop in Stalin Allee; of Martin's suggestion on the evening of the same day, that perhaps she was burdened by a great sorrow or had experienced great suffering, or was oppressed by fear or lived under a mysterious threat. I thought of the strange fatalistic conviction she had expressed, during our first evening together in the Kurfürstendamm, that she could not leave the East sector and settle in the West; and of the ambiguity of her letters, her reserve, her reproaches, and of her expressed indebtedness to me for my kindness to a girl who lived so far away and of whom I knew "so little." I thought of the renewal of our friendship and of the unpleasant dreams I had experienced prior to my second visit to Berlin; of the incident concerning the mirror, early one morning as she sat at her dressing table; of her sudden exclamation one night in the Tiergarten, pleading that I would never say she was a "bad girl;" of her hatred for Frau Hartmann; and of the mysterious objects she had hidden away in her drawer of personal belongings.

All these things had come to mind, and nagged at my heart with a piercing intensity. I lay awake and thought long over these things, thinking over the emotional basis of our relationship, weighing every alternative in turn, but try as I did, I could find no guiding clue as to the future of our friendship. Finally, I consoled myself, optimistically, that after the relaxation of a few hours sleep, I might awake the next day to find an answer to these questions, and perhaps even, see our relationship in a better light. Perhaps even the restful and peace-inducing effects of sleep might serve to cure all, and after the night had run its course and the bright sun shone on yet another day, the friendship between us would be renewed again, amidst expressions of mutual passion and tearful reconciliation.. With these thoughts, I consoled myself, and fell asleep.

I awoke to find the sun shining through the curtains of the room. I jumped out of bed and began to wash, not waiting for the interminable seven or ten minutes for the hot water to run from the tap. It was almost ten o'clock. I had slept well during the intervening hours. I was relaxed and rested. I threw cold water over my head and shoulders and the events of the previous night returned to mind. I felt comfortable and at ease, and I was resigned to the fact that in all probability my friendship with Dagmar was drawing to its close. The balm of sleep had done nothing to change or console my mind in that respect. I ate a quick breakfast in the Pension, and then speedily made my way to Graetz Strasse.

Frau Renot opened the door to me at the flat at No. 55, and I felt both surpised and awkward on finding her on that side of the street so early in the morning. Perhaps Dagmar won't be able to tell me her story after all, I thought, or perhaps she's just changed her mind again and has decided to tell me nothing.

"Good morning, Frau Renot," I said brightly.

"You're so late and Dagmar was expecting you earlier," she responded without smiling, leading me into the passageway of the flat.

I felt apprehensive. She knows everything, I thought.

"We've been so worried. Have you eaten,?" she asked.

"Yes," I replied.

"Are you sure? Have you had enough? I'll bring you some tea and something else to eat, if you'll first go and speak with Dagmar," said Frau Renot in excited concern. "It's nearly eleven o'clock. Dagmar expected you much earlier."

"Is there something wrong,?" I said awkwardly.

"Dagmar's told me about the quarrel," said the good Frau confidentially. "She's very upset about it. Please go and speak to her, and make it up. I'm sure she's sorry for anything she might have said last night."

I made no answer. I wondered what exactly had ensued between Frau Renot and her daughter since my departure last night. I walked down the passageway into the sitting room.

Dagmar was sitting on the sofa, and on the coffee table in front of her were breakfast things, open sandwiches and a cup of milk, for she rarely took tea or coffee, for her health's sake.

"I thought you were never coming. I thought you had left Berlin," she cried excitedly rising from the sofa.

She advanced towards me, throwing her arms tightly around my back, burying her face between my neck and shoulders. I was surprised by this sudden gesture, and in my present reflective mood was unprepared to receive this greeting. I placed my hands around her shoulders and gently patted her thick grey cardigan worn loosely round her body. Today, she was not wearing her blue dress with its handsome white belt – the dress she had worn for the first time for the outing we had had at the ballet in the West sector. Today she wore a dark green woollen spun skirt, a white blouse beneath her cardigan, and a pair of grey felt slippers which reduced her height some inches. She looked soft, in a cuddly kind of way, and homely. Then I realised she was dressed in those same clothes as when I had seen her a year ago in the Art Shop in Stalin Allee. I held her closer to me and she remained quite still.

"I thought you had gone. I thought you had left me forever," she murmured.

"Well, now I'm here and we can talk things over quietly," I said to her gently, and I firmly took her shoulders and pushed her away from me.

"I was so upset," she sobbed.

"Now sit down quietly and tell me everything – calmly from the beginning," I said leading her to the sofa.

"I'll tell you everything as best I can," she replied.

We sat down.

"Tell me, Dagmar, how much have you spoken about this to your mother,?" I asked.

"I told her everything about last night."

"Was it necessary?"

"I had to."

"You've only upset her. You know how susceptible your mother is regarding our relationship."

"I had to tell her. I was so worried about our quarrel last night; I had hardly any sleep. I was up early this morning, and I went across the road to tell Mamma what happened."

"And what did she say?"

"She was worried, but said we mustn't allow the quarrel to spoil our friendship – not on any account. We must make everything up again," said Dagmar fixing her eyes on mine.

"Anyway, we must both be reasonable with one another," I replied consolingly, and trying without success to avoid her glance.

"And now Mamma agrees also, that I must tell you about this other thing – this thing which has brought me such suffering and unhappiness," she said awkwardly, and her sentence became an undertone.

"Agrees 'also,'?" I said enquiringly.

"Yes, Mamma was always against my telling you about this other thing. I was against it too, of course, but Mamma and Papa were especially against it."

"But why,?" I exclaimed, and not knowing exactly why I had put the question.

"They said – that is – I don't know why Mamma and Papa thought that," said Dagmar confused and interrupting herself. "But Mamma says you'd be understanding and considerate if I told you the story, and that it wouldn't make any difference to our friendship. You are understanding and considerate, aren't you,?" she added earnestly, fixing me with her eyes.

"Yes, I think so," I replied unable to forebear a smile. "By now you should know me for what I am."

"James, I'm asking you to show more understanding than you've ever done before," she said taking my fingers into her hands.

"I've told you I'm understanding, but I don't know what exactly you're trying to ask of me," I replied smiling.

"Just listen patiently and don't be prejudiced. Wait until I've finished my story before deciding what you want."

"I'll listen patiently. And I won't draw any conclusions until you've explained everything."

"I'm asking nothing more than that, James."

"But don't try to extract any promises from me in advance."

"I won't. I ask only for your understanding."

"I promise you that."

"You've always been kind to me, and I think there's a mutual trust between us as to our feelings for one another."

I said nothing. I became more perplexed and curious with everything she said, and several unspeakable suspicions flashed through my mind. I decided to change the subject.

"And does your father know about our quarrel of last night,?" I asked.

"Mamma told him after I left the flat across the road, just before ten o'clock this morning."

"And what does he say about it?"

"Mamma hasn't told me."

There was a pause between us.

As to what the old man might have said, I had no idea, but I could make a pretty rough guess as to the probable trend of his thinking. He was possibly depressed and worried, frantically racking his brains in working out yet another silly stratagem. I regretted he had been told about our quarrel, especially in view of his obsessive concern over the course of our relationship. Perhaps in his own mind he even took credit for nurturing our friendship and the success of its outcome in view of the pressures he had already brought bear.

Frau Renot came into the room bearing a tray of cakes and biscuits and a pot of tea, glancing at us smiling, with a sad benign expression, as if urging that we make up our differences. The tray was laid on the coffee table, and Frau Renot left the room and not a word was exchanged between any of us. Dagmar and I were sitting quietly, on either end of the sofa, thoughtfully glancing at one another.

"Dagmar, I think you can begin to tell me now what's on your mind," I said at last.

"The door – I don't even want Mamma or Papa to overhear what we're saying," she said.

I rose from the sofa and went across the room, and as I took the handle of the door I saw Herr Renot just entering the flat and the good Frau rushing out of the kitchen to meet him, and I closed the door in time to avoid his glance and the need to exchange greetings. I returned to the sofa.

"Now you can begin," I said to Dagmar reassuringly.

"It's important you won't mention any of these things I tell you to any person or friend, however well you know them. You must promise to repeat nothing, either by spoken word or in writing."

There was a pause. I made no reply. I was mesmerised by the intense curiosity she aroused.

"Do you promise,?" she said.

"Why do you ask for such a promise,?" I asked.

"I only ask it for my own safety – for the security of my life and freedom," she said with resolution but in an undertone, lowering her eyes.

I passed no comment, and felt no inclination to question her further. I was overcome with a strange apprehension as if about to be led into the knowledge of forbidden secrets which were none of my concern and to which I had no right of access. I felt the weight of significance in the things she was about to reveal, and I felt bound by a responsibility to listen quietly to her story without comment or interruption.

Dagmar was tense, and she trembled nervously as her expression changed from that of concern to deep reflection tinged with pain, as if memories and conflicting emotions were all at once flooding her mind. I caught the feeling of her tension.

"All these things commenced long ago, but I remember them clearly – as if they happened yesterday," she began in agitation, as if trying to overcome the pain which those recollections aroused. There was a momentary pause. "There are some things in life we can never forget," she continued, "especially those happy things, and joys we experience for the first time in life. You see, James, I must tell you about those things which occurred during the happiest period of my life."

"Please go on," I said.

"And then I must tell you about those unhappy things," she said lowering her eyes. "They happened so suddenly and all at once, that at the time, I thought life was over. My years of happiness were shattered in a moment. Perhaps the tragedy of it all only helps to make those years seem all the happier in retrospect."

She bit her lip as an expression of pain and anger crossed her countenance.

"Go on," I said.

"I was younger then, and perhaps I didn't understand all the things happening in our city – or because I ignored them. And so I felt the tragedy with greater pain than I might otherwise have done. I enjoyed the pleasures of a girl just starting out in life, and I had little interest in the world beyond. In many ways, things were bad for us all in the everyday world, but what could we do to change the course of events? – only try to forget the big world of public events, and that's what I did. But fate is cruel. Here in Berlin, fate picks its victims at random. There's little consolation for an inner life. There's no freedom for the spirit within this unfree world.

"As I look back, it seems long ago when these events began. Since then – since the tragedy which occurred later, I've led a different life. I know you'll disagree with me – that you'll be cynical," said Dagmar hesitantly, fixing me with her eyes, "but I believe I've been enlightened by the fact of the inevitability of fate – that we have no control over our lives – that our will is nothing."

I made no comment, only nodded affirmatively. Now her obsession with abstraction or generalities is coming to the fore, I only thought.

"But as I look back to that first day,some years ago – before I was ever to begin that changed life I now lead – it seems as if it was one of the happiest occasions of my life; for it was a day which was to mark the beginning of new experiences. It was one of those days which at the time seemed so insignificant in itself and yet was to lead to so much. …."

Dagmar spoke slowly with deep conviction conveying the sincerity of her feelings; and I sat quietly, listening with increasing interest, as she warmed with intensity to the theme of her story.

BOOK IX

Dagmar's Story

Love seeketh not itself to please,
Nor for itself hath any care,
But for another gives its ease,
And builds a Heaven in Hell's despair.

William Blake, "The Clod & The Pebble,"
Songs of Experience.

1957 – 1958

Chapter 38

It was a warm sunny afternoon towards early evening, when the two girls had been attracted to the shore of the Langer See situated in that part of Köpenick not far distant from Treptow. It was at that happiest time of the year – most joyous to young people – a time of hopeful anticipation – not Midsummer, but late Spring, when leaves and blossom have just sprung into fullest bloom.

Not a breath of wind brushed through the treetops to disturb the silence of the forest nor the stillness of the day, and only the voice of a bird gave its song to the peace of the surrounding scene. The blue water of the lake lapped lazily along the length of the beach as small waves broke gently onto the sand. No one was to be seen along the length of the shore, and the sand was powdery and pale yellow, and high up on the beach by some tufts of long grass, lay a towel and two small piles of clothing, and nearby, a blue bag.

From the lake, suddenly came the sound of splashing and laughing, and two girls, hand-in-hand, each wearing bikinis, came running back to the shore, raising their knees high as their feet splashed through the water.

"That was wonderful," exclaimed Renata laughing.

"But too cold," replied Dagmar shaking her shoulders. "It's too early in the year, for swimming. I prefer to lie in the sun."

"But you need the water else your skin will be frizzled up," said Renata. "You've been sunbathing for a fortnight."

"But not for much longer," sighed Dagmar. "On Monday it's back to work," and she screwed up her nose in disapproval at the idea.

"You've had fourteen days of bliss without care," replied Renata, "whilst for most of my time I've been stuck in a dark room having to study and listen to a lot of dull lectures," and she sat down on the ground, landing on the sand with a bump.

"You can't complain about lack of free time, Renata," returned Dagmar sharply, "when next month you'll have a break of two or three months."

"I expect I'll have to find some kind of work," sighed Renata.

"One day you'll be a teacher, and then every year, for the rest of your life, you'll have more free time than most of us."

"If I pass my exams," exclaimed Renata. "I hate studying!"

They stretched out on the sand to absorb the last warm rays of sunshine, holding their hands across their brows.

"It won't be this quiet tomorrow if the weather's fine," mused Dagmar after a while. "There'll be the weekend crowds."

There came male shouts and laughter from the forest behind, and a moment later, a football was kicked onto the shore, and a youth in jeans and short-sleeved shirt jumped over a clump of grass onto the beach, some metres away from where the girls reclined in the sun. The young man, who carried a bundle beneath his arm, did not see the girls, but leapt down to the water's edge, the sand flying from the soles of his sandals, and began to dribble with the ball.

"You've spoken too soon about the 'quiet,'" said Renata glancing irritably at the newcomer. "Look what's followed in the wake of your words."

The young man began calling to companions who remained in the woods. Alarmed, the two girls sat up on the sand.

"Noisy youths," said Dagmar in the same spirit as her friend.

"Hooligans would be a better word," returned Renata.

The youth called to another, saying he had found a fine spot for their sports, and moments later, four of them were playing with the ball.

"We'll swim here," said one.

"We have ladies for company," said another but without glancing at the girls.

"We must undress in the woods then," said a third.

As the young men kicked around the ball, they edged closer to the girls, possibly with the idea of making an impression on the attractive bikini-clad couple. Renata and Dagmar observed the youths attentively, but they were rather concerned with the chance of being struck by the flying object, than the opportunity of striking up an acquaintanceship, and so no words were exchanged.

One of the youths, a tall boy with pale blue eyes and light hair, who had advanced nearest the girls, began to observe Dagmar with a curious look from the corner of his eye. Relaxing his attention on the game, he dawdled momentarily by the girls, and smiled at the object of his attraction, and Dagmar encouragingly returned the gesture.

"*Guten Tag*,!" exclaimed the fair youth, bowing his head towards the two girls as he stepped backwards with a modest gesture, as if hoping his greeting would not be taken as too precocious.

"Good afternoon,!" replied Dagmar brightly.

"You needn't encourage them," whispered Renata scalding, and the fair youth was called back to his companions.

"I wasn't encouraging them," parried Dagmar in reply. "I was only being polite."

"They take that sort of politeness for something else," said Renata.

"I don't mind if they're friendly."

"How can you speak so,?" scoffed Renata. "They're strangers. We know nothing about them."

"I liked that one who came closest to us. He was sweet."

"I don't care what they do, providing they're quiet," said Renata turning on her towel.

"If they get too rough with the ball, we'll ask them to be more careful where they kick it."

"If they become a nuisance, we'll move along the beach," said Renata sharply.

The young men who had disappeared into the woods some minutes earlier reappeared in trunks with towels across their shoulders, and the fair youth came boldly up to the two prostrate girls.

"How's the water,?" he enquired.

"Cold,!" replied Dagmar shaking her shoulder provocatively.

"Why don't you try it and see for yourself,?" responded Renata.

The fair youth looked askance at Renata, lost for a reply.

"Dieter's talking to the beautiful girls," chuckled one of the others as he ran to the water's edge.

The fair youth was called away, and joking, his companion exclaimed, "Did you ask for her phone number,?" and the four men dived into the lake.

"You needn't have spoken so sharply," said Dagmar to her friend.

"He shouldn't have asked such a stupid question," replied Renata. "The way you acted, anyone would think you'd fallen for him."

"*Schönes* warm ,yes,?" exclaimed one of the youths splashing in the water.

"Warm? *Scheiss, Mensch*! It's the Arctic!," exclaimed another.

"Mind your language, we have ladies listening," said another, feigning a feminine voice and a gesture of prudery.

"Aren't they presumptuous," said Renata scowling. "Just putting on airs to get our attention. It's typical of boys!"

When the young men emerged from the water, they rubbed themselves down, and again began playing with the ball, but this time provocatively and to show off, as they edged ever closer to the two girls. At last the game had its intended effect, for with a great thump, the ball landed on the towel between Dagmar and Renata.

"You're dangerous with that thing – can't you play elsewhere,?" exclaimed Renata irately.

"Please excuse – we didn't mean …," began one of the young men bowing to the girls, reclaiming the ball.

"Sour puss,!" exclaimed another of the youths laughing.

"Don't be so rough – and be careful with that ball," said Renata.

"And remember what the young lady says," exclaimed another of the youths ironically to the guilty party.

"We must play gently, like fine ladies – throwing the ball like this," said another impersonating a ballerina, to the laughter of his friends.

"Why aren't you at work,?" cried Renata in a bossy tone.

"Because we're on strike," replied one of their number.

"I thought strikes were forbidden in the German Democratic Republic," said Renata.

"They are," said another, "but that doesn't prevent us from striking."

"You're the first workers I've heard of who strike," said Renata.

"We're not workers," explained one of the youths laughing, "we're students."

"Then why aren't you studying,?" cried Renata.

"We've told you: we're on strike," said one.

"I've never heard of students striking," cried Renata waving her hand at them in contempt.

"None of us are studying," said another. "No one in the faculty."

"What sort of university is it where the students refuse to study,?" cried Renata.

"The Friedrich Wilhelm University," replied one.

"*Ach mensch*! Don't mention those words. It's a forbidden name! These girls are probably from the Stasi and will have us arrested for abusing the good name of the People's University," said one of the students to his companions.

"Have you heard of it,?" asked another of the students of the girls.

"That's still not the proper name," answered Renata.

"It's the place in the Unter den Linden re-named the Humboldt University," said another.

"And why are you on strike? To get degrees without taking your exams,?" cried Renata.

"We're demonstrating against the Soviet authorities," said one.

"And against the terror tactics of the secret police," said another.

"The whole faculty is out – a hundred and twenty of us," said another.

"What faculty is that,?" asked Renata.

"The Veterinary School," replied one.

"Why Renata, they're the students the West Berlin radio's been talking about over the past few days," exclaimed Dagmar to her friend.

"*Schlechte Menschen*! (Bad people!) What do you want to listen to the West Berlin radio for? You know it's forbidden," exclaimed one of the students ironically.

"We'll report you to the secret police," said another.

"You wouldn't dare," answered Renata.

"What's happened in the University,?" enquired Dagmar.

One of the students tucked the ball under his arm and the four gathered around the girls.

"The Dean of our faculty, Günther Schutzler, has been ousted from the University," said the youth turning to the girls. "He's received threats from the authorities, and has had to flee to the West for safety."

"And that's why we're on strike," said another.

"Several students have been arrested, and several have had to flee to the West," said the fair haired youth.

"And so now you can understand we have good reason to boycott lectures in the University," said another. "The students have no freedom to organise their clubs as they wish, and the secret police interfere and frustrate all our activities," he said throwing up his hands sadly with a despairing gesture.

"Of course we all know that – it's the same in every educational institute," said Renata, "but what can you do about it?"

"We can demonstrate," replied one of the students.

"Do you think you can influence the authorities by striking,?" said Renata.

"We can but try," said another.

"You're brave boys, but I think it's useless," said Renata smiling gently and turning her head from side to side.

"The fact is, we're not prepared to tolerate existing conditions," replied one of the students boldly.

"Conditions have been worsening for a long time now," said another, "and we're not going to be trodden on any longer."

"How long do you intend staying on strike,?" enquired Dagmar.

"We don't know yet," replied one.

"The authorities will force you to their way of behaving in the end – they always do. You can strike, but it'll make no difference to them," said Renata pointing her thumb downwards.

"We don't expect to win everything just by one strike," said one of the students.

"Think if you clashed with the authorities in a big way, all they need do is bring a few tanks into the city. They'd stop at nothing," said Renata. "Remember what happened three years ago – the Uprising!"

"But the authorities can't destroy the universities – they must go on. The authorities are dependent on them for drawing on the skills and brainpower for the future."

"That doesn't mean students can influence the authorities controlling the universities," replied Renata.

"It's a pity not all the students in East Germany come out on strike at once," said one of the students boldly. "Why is it always left to the Veterinary and Medical Schools to demonstrate for the freedom of the universities? We want sympathy and support, not criticism or 'Wise' advice."

"Only by throwing all doubt to the wind and putting trust in courage can we hope to win freedom," added another.

"Let's change the topic, and try not to get involved in a political argument with the young ladies," exclaimed one of the others in good humour, slapping his arm around the shoulders of his two companions who had last spoken. "May we introduce ourselves? This is Peter Wüstenhagen; this is Gustaf Maazel, and that is Dietrich Liebermann. And I am Wolf Spier."

The girls laughed shyly.

"I am Renata Manicker, and my friend here, is Dagmar Renot."

"May we sit on the ground,?" requested Dietrich, the fair youth, addressing his remark to Dagmar.

The girls nodded affirmatively, and the four boys sat down to join them, and there was some banter and small talk.

"You work in the city centre,?" asked Gustaf, who was also showing apparent interest in Dagmar.

"No, in Treptow."

"In an office,?" enquired Dietrich leaning in front of his companion who might take on the aspect of a rival for the attentions of the fair Berlinerin.

"In an art shop, but I earn so little money that I'm applying for another position - in the city centre. I've got an interview one afternoon next week."

"Where do you work in Treptow,?" asked Dietrich. "I'll come to your shop and buy a painting from you," he announced gallantly, to the laughter of his companions.

"Don't tell him where you work, Dagmar," said Renata smiling as she winked at Dietrich, "else he'll be a nuisance. You'll never get rid of him."

"It's a small shop in a tiny back street," replied Dagmar laughing. "You'd never find it."

"I'll come to your shop next week and buy a painting from you – and I'll ask you to choose it for me," said Dietrich moving closer towards Dagmar. "What's your address?"

Dagmar laughed, turning shyly to her friend.

"Don't give him your address," chuckled Renata.

"The only art he's interested in are photos of pretty girls," laughed Peter.

"My friends, I have an idea," announced Wolf brightly, slapping his hands onto the shoulders of the companions on either side. "We're all on holiday, - sort of. We're all free this evening, yes? How about taking the girls out to a film this evening in the West sector? Agreed?"

"*Schön*,!" exclaimed Dagmar, her face lighting up.

"How take the girls,?" said Gustaf.

"Dieter can drive us to the city centre, and from there we take the train into the West sector," suggested Wolf.

"Impossible,!" returned Dietrich laughing, "with six, the car would be *kaput*."

"Anyway, we have to be home by seven to meet friends," said Renata sharply.

Dagmar turned to her friend, frowning her disapproval.

"It's fixed then, yes? Tonight we go out together," exclaimed Wolf disregarding Renata's abrupt refusal. He rose to his feet. "We'll go and dress, and when we return, we'll have your assent, and then we'll discuss when and where to meet."

"That would be *Schön*,!" exclaimed Dagmar.

The three other students rose to their feet, following Wolf along the shore, before running, laughing and shouting, into the woods.

"That would be a nice arrangement, yes, Renata,?" said Dagmar to her friend.

"It would be impossible," returned Renata sharply. "We know nothing about them – and anyway, they could be in trouble with the authorities."

"Why did you give them that silly excuse about having to meet friends at home,?" said Dagmar annoyed.

"Because such an arrangement would be improper," returned Renata. "One can't go out with strangers. It's not respectable."

"We know they're veterinary students at the Humbldt University," pleaded Dagmar.

"And we know they could be getting themselves into deep trouble," replied Renata, "and if we play around with them, we could compromise ourselves."

"They seem decent intelligent boys. I'm sure we can trust their judgement."

"Today we can trust no one and nothing. Not in this country. Anything may be dangerous. The Stasi are everywhere."

"You're being paranoid, Renata. We must take an easy attitude sometimes, else life would be impossible."

"I know about these things because I'm a student myself. Informers are watching all the time. You don't know about such things because you work in a private shop. That's not the real world. It's not where people disappear."

"You've got a cheek, Renata. I've heard stories too, but I don't let them take over my life."

"I still think you're being impossible," insisted Renata. "It's a good thing we're mostly together, and I can watch over you, to keep you at trouble's length."

"I don't think that's funny," returned Dagmar irately. "I can see you'll be a good school ma'am one day – you're too fond of being bossy."

"Anyway, I'm not going out with them. I don't like them. Besides, I think they're only after one thing."

"That's unfair to say that."

"I think you've had a touch of the sun. – You go out with them yourself."

"I can't do that – not alone," said Dagmar almost tearfully.

Several of the students ran from the woods onto the shore, some distance from the girls, but on seeing them engaged in an argument, they hesitated momentarily to approach.

"What's the matter,?" called one.

"We're not coming," responded Renata.

"We've quarrelled," exclaimed Dagmar.

"We have to be home by seven," said Renata.

"A pity,!" exclaimed Wolf sadly. "Perhaps another day then."

"Perhaps,!" returned Renata ironically, and she ran into the woods to change.

Dagmar picked up her towel and clothing and began to follow her friend, and as she reached the trees, she glanced momentarily behind her. Dietrich had run forward some few metres in front of his friends. He stopped on meeting her glance.

"A moment, please,!" he called, but it was only a hesitant awkward exclamation.

"It makes no difference – leave them,!" cried Wolf with resignation.

Dietrich turned towards his companions and Dagmar followed her friend into the woods, disappearing behind the trees.

"They're little more than schoolgirls, anyway," Dagmar heard one of the students exclaim.

The two girls began to dress behind some bushes.

"I think you've been very mean," said Dagmar in anguish.

"Don't be a silly goose. They weren't worth getting to know."

"You had no right to behave like that."

"Just because you got a crush on that tall one!   How silly! Tomorrow it'll all be forgotten."

"The smaller one was a darling," came a voice through the bushes from the direction of the shore.

"Then ask her out, Dieter," came the voice of Gustaf.

"It's too late," replied Dietrich resigned. "Besides, I don't want to speak to her in front of that other girl."

"You could see the tall one was jealous – like a wallflower sharing the light of her prettier friend," laughed Peter.

"It's always like that when you meet a pretty girl," said Wolf reflectively. "You find a plain one tugging onto her arm saying 'No' to everything."

"Forget them," said Peter.

"Now you know what the boys think of you," whispered Dagmar spitefully.

"We'll walk back along the promenade to Grünau, so the boys can't follow us into the forest," Renata only replied.

Chapter 39

The sun shone down onto the vast desolate square of Alexander Platz, and the view of flattened rubble and ruins in all directions made the great junction seem larger, gloomier and greyer than it otherwise was. Vehicles, mostly lorries, rushed round the broad ring roadway at speed, and an ancient tram cut across the square clattering inevitably along the rails into Lenin Allee. The wide pavements were crowded with pedestrians, hurriedly moving in all directions, for it was at that time in the evening when work in the city was drawing to a close.

Dagmar was walking quickly along the pavement towards the S-Bahn station, and she was on that side of the square opposite from where the tall grey steel and concrete structure of the Warenhaus rose from the rubble lying around.

"Fräulein, *bitte entschuldigen* (please excuse me)," came a voice from behind.

Dagmar glanced round and a young man caught up with her.

"You remember me,?" he exclaimed brightly, pointing to himself and bowing just perceptibly.

"I don't know you," replied Dagmar in a curious tone.

"But surely,!" exclaimed the young man.

"Have we been introduced,?" said Dagmar feigning ignorance.

"Certainly," said the young man smiling in amusement. "Last week at the Langer See. The four students – remember?"

"You're dressed so differently."

"You also, but I knew I'd always recognise you again," said the young man boldly.

"It was a very casual acquaintanceship. I really can't be expected to remember everyone I meet," replied Dagmar good-naturedly.

"For me, it's a great pleasure we meet again."

"What is it that you want,?" said Dagmar as they continued along the street.

"It was just – I thought – I should like to thank you for the pleasure of your company during that afternoon last week," he exclaimed awkwardly.

"I don't think you enjoyed much of our company," replied Dagmar sympathetically. "After all, we parted almost as soon as we'd been introduced."

"I meant that sincerely as a compliment," said Dietrich.

"Then I thank you for the compliment, and now I must be hurrying home," said Dagmar increasing her pace.

"Please, a moment," said Dietrich excitedly as he moved in front of Dagmar.

"I'm late and my mother has food waiting for me," she said.

"I thought we might sit for a few minutes in a restaurant," said Dietrich.

"I said, I haven't the time."

"We have time for a coffee."

"You should know it's improper to accost girls on the street," said Dagmar in a mock chiding tone.

"Then I promise I shan't do it again when once we've been out together."

"Isn't that asking rather too much of someone you don't know? Do you usually stop girls in the street like this?"

"No! And never again – I promise. But for such a girl as you," began Dietrich boldly.

"It doesn't speak well for your character that you accost me in this way."

"I insist you come with me," said Dietrich with determination.

"Then only for a few minutes."

"*Wunderschön,*!" exclaimed Dietrich and he happily threw his arm around Dagmar's shoulder as they crossed the broad roadway towards the station.

"Where do we go,?" asked Dagmar.

"To a pavement café in Friedrich Strasse," replied Dietrich. "It's fine weather – too good to be inside. We'll take the S-Bahn – it's only two stops."

Dietrich pulled the chair from under the table and gallantly clicked his heels as Dagmar sat down and was joined by her escort. Few patrons sat in the open air restaurant but crowds hurriedly passed along the pavement beyond the low wicker barrier. At the table beside them sat sad looking Asians glumly looking out at the world passing by.

"Didn't your friends last week say you had a car,?" asked Dagmar.

"Yes, I have a Wartburg," replied Dietrich modestly.

"A Wartburg! You must be rich. And where is it now?"

"Well, you see, I don't have use of it every day. It's my father's. He has a greater need for it than I. He has to travel to the centre most days and his work takes him about the city quite a lot."

"Where do you live in Berlin?"

"I don't live in Berlin."

"Then where,?" exclaimed Dagmar surprised.

"I live in Werlsee – it's little more than a village."

"Where's Werlsee?"

"Not far from Berlin – just across the zonal frontier. You go to Friedrichshagen in Köpenick and then you drive down the Fürstenwalder Damm, through Rahnsdorf and through the zonal frontier by the Dämeritz See, and then it's about three kilometres beyond Erkner. It's about thirty kilometres from the city centre."

"It must be quiet and beautiful living there, so far from the city," remarked Dagmar.

"It's very peaceful, and we live in a large house which is all our own. There is forest all around and it's not too distant from a small lake."

"I should love to live in such a place," said Dagmar reflectively, glancing dreamily into Dieter's eyes as she rested her chin on her hands.

"But tell me, where were you coming from when I met you in Alexander Platz,?" said Dietrich taking Dagmar's fingers into his hands. "I thought you said you worked in Treptow."

"I do, but I'd just come from an interview for a new job."

"Did you get it?"

"Yes."

"Congratulations,!" exclaimed Dietrich, his eyes lighting up with pleasure. "Are you pleased?"

"I'm very happy. It's an art shop in Strausberger Platz, Stalin Allee. It's only a small shop and privately owned – but I think I'll like it there very much. They sell delightful oriental art works, and tapestries and oils, and many many prints."

"That's wonderful!"

"And the proprietor's very nice, and I'll get a much better salary than at my present job. But I expect it'll be very busy there, because it's Stalin Allee. People kept coming and leaving the shop all the time I was there when the proprietor was showing me where everything was kept."

"I expect you'll meet some interesting people when you work there."

"I hope so. The proprietor said all kinds of people come into the shop: doctors, scientists, engineers, teachers."

"I'll come and visit you as soon as you start work."

"But you must buy something," said Dagmar in a tone of concern.

"Of course, and I'll give a wonderful testimonial to the proprietor, saying you're the politest, the most charming, and the best little shop assistant in the world."

Dagmar laughed.

"But I won't be starting work there for two months. I'll start at the beginning of August. Meanwhile, I'll have to give notice to my present employer. I don't know how I'll do that, because he's become very attached to me and shown me every kindness. He's a very old man, and I've come to do nearly everything in the shop, but it's such a small business and I earn so little money. I don't know what he'll say when I tell him I'll be leaving."

"I expect he'll be upset. I would be. But then, that's the world," said Dietrich sadly.

"Perhaps the business will fold-up, although it's been going for eighty years."

"It's difficult for any private business to exist today."

"We live in a world of such strife and trouble," said Dagmar reflectively. "Which reminds me, how are your troubles – the strike?"

Dietrich shook his head with a melancholy gesture.

"Things have gone very badly," he replied.

"Have you returned to the University?"

"Yes."

"Just as my friend, Renata, said you would."

"The authorities have tightened the screw even further on the students of the University," said Dietrich in a deeply serious tone, biting his lips as he glanced down towards the table as if to suppress an outburst of emotion. "Some of my closest friends have been arrested by the Stasi on charges of having participated in the organisation of the strike. Others have had to flee to the West."

"I'm sorry about what's happened – especially for you personally," replied Dagmar, "but of course these things have happened before, and I suppose they'll happen again."

"Also, we've lost some of our finest lecturers as a result of the demonstration," continued Dietrich. "Professor Günther Bergman was one of the best teachers in the Veterinary School of the University. He has had to flee to the West."

"What happened?"

"He was charged by officials with sympathising with the striking students. His son had already escaped to the West with several fellow students, and that's what cast suspicion on him. The police don't need proof to act; all they need is suspicion and that stands for proof of guilt."

"Then my friend was right. Your little demonstration has come to nought, and now, you're again right under the yoke of the authorities – and perhaps it's even worse than before. It's just as she said."

Dietrich glanced thoughtfully at Dagmar, and was about to speak when he stopped himself.

"Do you know your friend well,?" he said at last.

"We've known each other ever since we were so high," replied Dagmar holding her hand about two feet from the pavement.

"Are you relatives,?" asked Dietrich.

"No, just best friends," laughed Dagmar.

Dietrich glanced thoughtfully at the table as if working out a little puzzle.

"You know, somehow, I don't think your friend liked us," said Dietrich hesitantly.

"I'm sure it wasn't that, but she's a very quiet girl," replied Dagmar.

"You're very kind to her when you say that."

"She has some old-fashioned ideas. You have to know and understand her first, and then she's a really nice girl and a good friend. You see, Renata's very introverted. She takes a long time to get to know people. They say inward looking people always make the best friends, don't they? And she's very sincere."

"But it was because of her that you both ran away that day, remember.?" Said Dietrich thoughtfully.

"Renata's frightened of strangers," replied Dagmar.

Dietrich chuckled in amusement.

"It was a pity for us all then, that afternoon," he said ironically, "but your friend had some pretty hard words for my companions and me. She wasn't frightened then."

"She didn't mean it," replied Dagmar.

"As you left us you said you had quarrelled," said Dietrich.

"Yes, it was a stupid quarrel, but now it's all over and forgotten. But you should have seen us when we made up. It was so funny, really," said Dagmar changing to a lively tone. "It was only three days ago, and I'd just got back from work, and Mamma said that Renata was waiting for me in the sitting room. I didn't know what to think because Renata and I had had such a bad quarrel that day at the lakeside. Mamma said Renata seemed awkward and embarrassed, and kept blushing, and she was carrying a bunch of flowers which she tried to hide behind her back, but Mamma saw the flowers, and she thought her behaviour very odd. Mamma said Renata kept trying to smile but she seemed upset, as if there was a lump in her throat, and her eyes were watery. Renata kept saying she wanted to speak to me alone, and when Mamma told her I wasn't home yet, Renata couldn't make up her mind whether to wait or call back, and she kept moving backwards and forwards between the door and the passageway. Mamma was very curious, but as Renata seemed so strange, she thought it better not to probe. Mamma asked me if I had quarrelled with Renata, but of course I didn't want to let on what happened at the Langer See that day.

"It was so funny when I went into the sitting room. Renata was sitting on the sofa, all stiff and awkward looking, with her knees pressed tightly together, and at first, she just didn't know what to say. Then she picked up the bunch of flowers she had hidden behind the sofa, and she said they were for me. I hardly knew what was happening – everything seemed to be in a daze – but I took the flowers, and thanked her. Then she began to apologise and say how sorry she was about what had happened last week. You should have seen her – she was so awkward, it was pititful – and I went up to her and took her hand, and said everything was all right. Then tears came to her eyes, and we had to embrace each other because we suddenly felt so weak and overcome with emotion, and we both cried in each others arms.

"You should have seen us, because it seems so funny now when I think of it afterwards. So you see, Renata and I really are best friends. It would be impossible for us to part really, because we've known each other since we were little schoolgirls."

Dietrich moved uneasily on his seat, glancing momentarily at passers-by in the street, as if disconcerted and wishing to change the topic of conversation.

"I'm glad then for your sake the friendship has been made up – if that's what you really wish," remarked Dietrich.

"Naturally I'm happy our quarrel is over and forgotten," said Dagmar.

"Do you mind if I ask how old you are,?" said Dietrich hesitantly.

"I'm nineteen," replied Dagmar. "And how old are you?"

"Twenty-two."

"Do you like being a veterinary student? You like animals?"

"Yes, naturally I like animals – and it's an interesting subject to study," said Dietrich thoughtfully, "but it's not really what I wanted to do. At first I didn't want to study science – not medical science. You see, my father's in medical science – he's a doctor and research worker. I think it reflects a kind of weakness – a lack of independence when a son follows in the footsteps of his father."

"You're very independent then,?" said Dagmar.

"It's in my nature. I've always been independent. I could never bend the knee to authority."

"You must find it difficult then, living in the DDR."

"I've worked out my own unique way of living with the authorities."

"Tell me."

"That's my secret," said Dietrich smiling.

"If you tell me, perhaps you'll be doing a favour for someone else."

"It's just my own joke with the authorities – inimitable in its own way."

"You make me curious," replied Dagmar.

A waiter came and laid a pot of coffee, some cups and cakes on the table, and Dietrich began to pour.

"What would you really like to study if you weren't doing medical science,?" enquired Dagmar.

"My prime interest is politics," replied Dietrich.

"But medical science is far more useful to society," said Dagmar.

"That depends on circumstances."

"I mean, every doctor and vet can claim to achieve some small good for society every day, but that couldn't be said of a politician. You can hardly measure that *real* good achieved by a politician, but the achievements of a doctor are always real and concrete."

"That's true. Of course it would be impossible for me to become a politician here in the DDR, and if I were to study politics or economic science in the University here, it would be a waste of time. Take economic theory, for example, such rubbish is taught here in our Humboldt University, that if a student attempted to outline the theories anywhere in the West, he'd be laughed at. No intelligent person can accept the fictions of Marxism-Leninism, or the labour theory of value, etc., etc."

"You must be careful what you say – especially in a public place like this," said Dagmar glancing around. "You're being very outspoken. You're not afraid of what you say."

"It's a luxury I'll not deny myself – come what may."

"It could be dangerous. I mean, we hardly know one another. How do you know you can trust me? I could be from the Stasi."

"You I would always trust – even my life," said Dietrich taking Dagmar's hand in his. "But seriously, I can always tell a Communist when I see one."

"Then what does a Communist look like?"

"He's a man who never wears a tie with his best suit."

Dagmar laughed.

"But what does a girl Communist look like,?" she asked.

"She's tight-lipped, has a shifty manner, and is dressed in dark ugly attire."

"Really, what a description,!" exclaimed Dagmar. "I think you must hate Communists."

"Who of us in the DDR doesn't,?" replied Dietrich. "We're all hypocrites forced to live under a regime which harms all our interests. How many ideologically convinced Communists are there in our country? Perhaps not more than a few thousand."

"And so because of all that, you turned to science."

"I had to. It's the only thing left in the University curriculum one can pursue safely without fear of Marxist-Leninist doctrines being stuffed down our throats –   although they even try that.   Even mathematics has been twisted to adhere to Marxist ideology – or doctrine as we're supposed to say – but you can't very easily introduce political doctrines into the study of medical science – although it has been done in the USSR."

"And yet you medical students have been more recalcitrant than the students of any other faculty. Why?"

"It's obvious. Firstly, there are students who like me, only study medicine because it's one of the few subjects on the curriculum relatively free of political bias. Secondly, a great proportion of students at the University have only been selected according to class criteria with the aim of turning out doctrinal Communists. And thirdly, medical students tend to be brighter and more free-thinking than those of some other faculties. You can turn anyone into a doctor of economic science – it's all imagination and theory – but not into a doctor of medicine. In selecting medical students the authorities – however reluctantly – are forced to make brainpower a priority over political reliability. After all, even the most convinced ideological Communist would prefer to be operated on by a surgeon *par excellence* than a surgeon qualified according to his political convictions."

Dagmar laughed.

"But you're still obliged to study Russian and Marxism-Leninism," said Dagmar.

"True, and that's why there's so much discontent."

"I would have thought anyone interested in politics the way you are, must be fond of people, and I'm surprised you wouldn't rather have been a people's doctor than an animal's doctor."

Dietrich laughed.

"In the DDR today it's hardly worth attempting to serve the people under any guise, whether it be politics, commerce, entertainment or even medicine," he replied.

"That's very cynical," laughed Dagmar.

"Everywhere there are restrictions and hindrances."

"And so you turned to animals."

"They're the only living things in the DDR for which it's worthwhile holding out any hope. Humans may be starved, beaten, and oppressed in the cause of expanding productivity, but we Germans are so sentimental, we'd never allow animals to suffer. And so the vet is still free to work in his own small world, but not so the doctor."

"Is that really true?"

"Today, a doctor cannot even stand by his professional code – the Hippocratic oath. He must sacrifice his integrity to political expediency. Remember what happened at Leipzig a few years ago? A doctor who purchased vital drugs (unobtainable in the East zone) from the West sector of Berlin, was charged by the authorities under the law for the Protection of Internal Trade. He had helped many people – the court admitted that – and yet, what happened to him? He was condemned to five and a half years hard labour in a concentration camp."

"I remember that – it was in all the papers," said Dagmar.

"As long as the SED remains in power, there can be no hope for humans in this so-called German Democratic Republic of ours."

"What other interests do you have,?" asked Dagmar dreamily gazing into Dieter's eyes.

"I'm interested in philosophy."

"So am I," responded Dagmar eagerly.

"What philosophy do you like,?" asked Dietrich.

Dagmar was hesitant, and began searching for the names of philosophers she knew.

"I like the essays of Schopenhauer – if you call that philosophy – and of course, Plato and a little bit of Aristotle," she answered.

Dietrich smiled sympathetically.

"I'm interested at the moment in the philosophy of the French Enlightenment – in Montesquieu, Helvetius, Holbach and Condorcet."

"They must be difficult – I've never heard of any of them," said Dagmar overcome with admiration.

"Not as difficult as our German philosophers," replied Dietrich.

"I think it's wonderful to read books like that."

"They're thinkers who have something relevant to tell us."

"Where do you get these books from?"

"From the American Memorial Library. It's one of the biggest in Berlin. They have more than two hundred and twenty-six thousand volumes."

"You'd get into trouble if the University authorities found out you belonged there," said Dagmar.

"They'd hardly be likely to find out. Hundreds of East Berliners belong there."

"Do you read English and French?"

"Naturally."

"It wouldn't be any use my joining then – I only understand German."

"There are thousands of German language books there. I could take you to the Library next week."

"That would be lovely."

"It's probably not too far from where you live. It's by the Hallesches Tor in Kreuzberg. – Do you like dancing, to do sixty-forty,?" added Dietrich smiling.[*]

"Not really – I don't dance," replied Dagmar screwing up her nose, "but I love concerts."

"Then come with me tomorrow night – to a concert at the Titania-Palast, in the West sector?"

"I will!"

---

[*] Dance orchestras in East Germany were required by law to play not less that sixty per cent Eastern dance music at any one session.

BOOK X

Rebel With A Cause

Love and desire are the spirits' wings to great deeds.
(Lust und Liebe sind die Fittige zu grossen Thaten.)

Goethe, *Iphigenia auf Tauris*, Act II, Sc. 1.

Chapter 40

That evening, when Dagmar arrived home she was in an exultant mood, and eagerly told the story to her parents of her chance meeting with the student Dietrich. As they sat at their evening meal, the good Frau listened patiently with a joyful countenance, and then Papa Renot rose from the table and made some facetious remark about his daughter having found her "young man." So began the eventful friendship between Dietrich and Dagmar.

The following day, they met in the city centre, and together went to the West sector, attending the concert at the Titania-Palast. Afterwards, they sat and talked vociferously for several hours in a café discussing their interests and aspirations in life, before he escorted her back to her home in Graetz Strasse. It was in the great hallway of the tenement block at No. 55 that he first attempted to steal a kiss from her delicate lips, but she resisted, and as she hurriedly disappeared into the doorway of her grandmother's flat, she promised "another time."

Dagmar was elated by and soon experienced a sense of bliss through her newly acquired friendship. A new emotional element had entered into her life. Almost from the start, the relationship was marked by mutual feelings, as the two were instinctively drawn to one another, and there was no battle of emotions or the casting of doubt to spoil the smooth progress of their friendship. But this is not to suggest Dagmar surrendered to her new friend as soon as she was sure of their mutual affection, for the contrary was the case.

Although Dietrich fondled her shoulder and was permitted to kiss the beauteous form of her forehead from that first evening when they went to the concert, it was not until after two weeks – after they had dated on seven occasions, that she finally allowed him to bring his lips to her own. On that occasion they were strolling in the Treptower Park near the banks of the Spree, on a warm Summer evening, when their lips met for the first time. They were walking along a quiet pathway, and the evening was so peaceful, and the scent of the flowers and newly mown grass so overpowering, and the water and river bank so refreshing, that she experienced a feeling of joy and surrender, as if all the goodness and beauty of nature had combined in creating the effect, and suddenly – spontaneously – she leaned her head against his shoulder and offered her lips to his.

For her, the occasion remained a warm and unique remembrance. Frequently, he had kissed her forehead, and sometimes he had stolen a kiss from her cheeks, and she had often snatched a quick kiss from his chin, but this event in Treptower Park was the occasion which she counted as the first real lovers' kiss. Immediately afterwards she was overcome with a feeling of awe and benediction at what had so suddenly occurred, as if she would somehow lock up the kiss and keep it for all time in a silver casket. She was overcome with a feeling of inviolability for every physical gesture of love expressed between them, and thereby, her sense of caution was resolved. It was not until six weeks later that the young lovers dispensed with the *Sie* term addressing each other as *du* for the first time.

Dagmar loved Dietrich for the modesty and gentleness of his manner, and the suave yet crisp movements of the gesture when he presented her his compliments. How perfect, how natural was every movement of his body! When they met, she was overwhelmed by his civility, and a strange enraptured feeling suddenly passed through her body as if she had succumbed to his will, as he clicked his heels bowing before her. The movement was such a spontaneous gesture of respect, so flattering in itself as to be seductive. No boy had ever complimented her in quite such a fashion.

In Dietrich she began to form in her mind the idealisation of perfect manhood, and then Dietrich himself became the Perfect Man, and finally, he became the Only Man – or the only man who mattered. She admired him for his knowledge and the breadth of his cultural interests, and she became mesmerised by his conversational ability and the vitality of his mind. She would listen to him speak, sometimes for hours on end, as he poured forth his ideas on politics, music, literature or any topic suggested to the two young lovers. Sometimes she interrupted him with a lively comment, or put a question, but always she accepted the opinions he expressed. As their friendship progressed, he was eventually to become the arbiter for all her ideas. He became not only her lover but her inspired teacher on everything touching the arts.

She loved the strength and protection he seemed to offer, and in her eyes, strength was the basis of his being. He was tall and well-proportioned, and there was strength in his body, and she loved to stroke his fine muscular arms with her delicate fingers, and his skin was covered with long blond hairs. She felt a feeling of tranquil bliss as she rested her head on his broad chest, and wished that time might stop forever as she experienced this joy. There was strength in his bearing and in every word he spoke, and his self-assurance was never in doubt.

His gentleness and boldness were contrasting characteristics in perfect harmony. Occasionally, they went out with a party of student friends, to a restaurant or concert, or other place of public entertainment. Dagmar became the object of his gentlest affection and every consideration. He would sit and talk and argue with friends, and invariably, he dominated the conversation, becoming the centre of the little group surrounding him. In emphasising a point and strengthening an argument, he would thump his fist onto the table, and with a sharp movement, brush his strong arm over the tops of the beer glasses, until his friends were brought round to his way of reasoning. Despite the concentration and heat of the argument which sometimes surrounded the subject under discussion, Dagmar was never far from Dieter's thoughts, and every ten minutes or so, when there came a lull in the conversation, he would gently turn to her and caress her shoulder and pass a compliment, before again returning to the heat of the debate.

Dagmar loved these little compliments and gestures which he then extended, and became doubly-reasssured she was never far from his thoughts. During these discussions she became ever more possessed with a feeling of surrender and belonging to his being. She began to lose her identity in his personality, so that her feeling of awe was enhanced, and she felt a sense of gratitude whenever she was near his person. As for participating in these discussions, that she would never dare. To think, even, of interrupting him with a remark intended to express assent would be bathos – absurd even – like holding up a candle to the sun. No, he was never to be interrupted – but Dagmar remained an attentive and intelligent listener to all he said.

Sometimes, a discussion ended in deadlock, when two strong minds of equal force came into collision, but despite this, no ill-feeling or unpleasantness was allowed to enter into these evenings of *gemütlich* entertainment – and entertainment – a pleasurable stimulation of the mind through searching out the truth, was all that was intended by these evenings of discussion. Never a rude nor an unkind nor a personal remark was ever exchanged – or hardly ever. When a heated discussion ended in deadlock, always the chief participants shook hands and bowed, before parting on an amicable basis.

Dagmar was enchanted, not only by Dieter's gentleness to herself, but by the civility he extended to all his friends on meeting them at a gathering, or in the street, or elsewhere. On meeting friends, his manner was always considerate and modest, and he extended his compliments with a spontaneous flattering gesture, often expressing the warmth of his feelings with a friendly pat on the shoulder, before asking after their health and situation.

It was shortly after the commencement of their friendship whilst strolling through the Lustgarten on a Summer's evening, that Dietrich met a professor of his faculty, a short fat man with dark thinning hair. As the three of them stopped on the pathway, the professor extended his hand to the student, and Dietrich, with a spontaneous gesture, expressing the warmth of friendship as well as the deepest respect, clicked his heels bowing low to his teacher as he firmly took hold of the out-stretched hand. Dagmar was overwhelmed by that same enraptured emotion as when he extended the same gesture to her, and the realisation dawned that her feelings were based not purely on the flattering and seductive gestures which he merely extended to her personally, but by something far deeper in the essence of his nature.

Although Dagmar admired and loved Dietrich for his boldness, she frequently warned him against the excesses of his outspokenness. It seemed to her as if one great hatred obsessed his mind, and that was the tyranny of the "system," and he saw this tyranny and the concept of tyranny in its most general terms, summed up in the tenets of Marxism-Leninism as interpreted specifically by the East German state. Dieter's explicit attacks on the theory and system of Communism were naturally reserved for those occasions when he was speaking alone with Dagmar, or when strolling through the woods or by a lakeside with a group of trusted friends.

How would the Berliner with his big mouth and instinctive pre-born inducement to speak his mind have ever fared in the East sector without the seclusion and privacy of the forests, where he might freely express his views – blow his top even – if he chose, with minimal risk of being overheard and apprehended as an "enemy" of the regime? Such caution was natural for no East Berliner in his proper mind would have freely discussed his political convictions in a public place, but despite such care, Dagmar nonetheless felt that Dietrich was often over-bold and outspoken. Once a discussion was well under way, and the participants had become heated to the topic, there was no effective way of controlling, curbing or censoring the direction of the debate. New and provocative ideas were all the while being thrown up and they had to be answered. There was no escaping them. No one could guarantee what he or anyone else might say in response to an intellectually provocative statement. Everyone spoke his mind, and reason is potent in the breadth of its imagination and the unpredictabililty of its outcome.

When persons are arguing hotly with each other on an intellectual plain, each tends, in a small way, to be influencing and instructing the minds of the others; and since all are amongst friends without the intention of confronting one another with insuperable truths, however hot-headed they may appear, and as each tends to push the subject under discussion towards an individual direction, any notion is liable to be floated, questioned or thrown away – even those "sacred" tenets of pseudo-science touching on Marxism-Leninism. Since the dialectical theories of Marxism-Leninism cover every aspect of life, social as well as political, and since Dietrich and his friends were living in a country where those tenets were enforced, it was not only natural but inevitable, that these theories should occasionally be brought up and discussed.

When this in fact occurred, one of the party would raise a finger to his lips exclaiming, "Sh-h-h-h,!" and they would bend their heads over the table, so continuing the discussion in a quieter tone. It sometimes occurred that Dagmar, who seldom participated or interrupted the discussions, was the first to smilingly raise a finger in this way, exclaiming, "Sh-h-h-h,!" as the others had been so hotly engaged in their argument as momentarily to have forgotten the need for caution.

When the couple were alone, and Dagmar affectionately pulled on the arm of her friend, chiding him for his defiance, she would ask, "Aren't you afraid of being so outspoken? Don't you fear the Stasi,?" and on one occasion, when she was so reproaching him, as they lay on the banks of the Müggel See, he replied by moving his hand aside with a nonchalant gesture, exclaiming only, "What is fear? I've never been touched by the feeling of fear." As to whether these words were merely intended as a boast or did in fact contain a seed of truth, Dagmar never really knew. She concluded he had intended such words as an ironic rebuff to her chiding him for his foolhardiness, and she therefore resolved not to reproach him again for his outspokenness.

After their friendship had progressed some weeks, Dagmar's thoughts became obsessed totally by the student Dietrich. As the rain poured down from the roof-tops into the dark narrow alley way outside her shop, and as she heard the water gush down the gulleys of the street, he was with her, closely beside her, in her workplace; as she tied up a parcel for a customer in the dismal back-room, with its peeling plaster and damp walls, he was there too, closely beside her; as she sat with her parents and Gisela, at No. 55, as they ate their evening meal, he was there too, sitting closely beside her; as she walked daily to her work, so he too walked with her; and as she lay in bed, thinking, hoping, and imagining for the future, so he too lay there – not where Granny lay, but on the other side of the bed, where she could grasp the duvet and press it to her breasts, as if it was he who was pressing his body so closely upon her.

Not only was he everywhere in terms of time and space, but his spirit pervaded everything, so that everything became a mirror reflecting his image. The door of the shop existed so that Dietrich could walk through it; a print which attracted the eye could only pose the question, What would Dietrich think of it;? every article of clothing had to be worn as Dietrich would have it worn; every piece of household furniture in the flat came gradually to be seen and assessed as Dietrich might view it – this chair became *kitsch* (and she would screw up her nose with an expression of disdain every time she saw it); and that table was only just to be tolerated; and as she climbed into the bed at night, she would even pose the question to herself, Would the springs bear the weight of Dietrich?

Her thoughts were always with him, and his thoughts influenced her thoughts, and his actions influenced her actions. He existed so that he might command and she obey, and in return, she might love him. He was her teacher and guide through life, and she would find maturity through him and he could do and say no wrong. Through his strength, knowledge and wisdom, culminating in the infallibility of his goodness and being, she found a sense of sublime contentment and happiness through which could be found a solution to all life's ills.

He became the only man who conceivably could form a part of her life – he was unique – irreplaceable. He was the inspirer of her imagination and the only subject of her day dreams, and her visions became magnificent ideals of happiness, and they were magnifications of real life where the mundane and ordinary found no place. She saw herself as the wife of the man who had become the heir to the house in Werlsee. She had not yet visited Dieter's parents in Werlsee, but in her mind the house had taken on a reality of its own. Now she was seated in the garden by the lily pond, watching her first born as he toddled unsteadily on the lawn in his blue smock, and now she had taken him into her arms and was kissing him affectionately, for he was Dieter's child, conceived in her womb. Now she was cutting flowers from the rose plants so they might adorn the evening dinner table and delight Dietrich on his return from the city, and now she was sewing on a button which had worked loose on his coat – and it was she who had first seen the drooping button which might otherwise have been lost; and now she was handing him his slippers, and now they were standing hand-in-hand over the cradle of their child as he thrust out his little limbs gurgling in his sleep. The house in the depths of the forest was her house, and she was mistress of the house in Werlsee, and every day she worked there, joyously, happily, so it might be clean, and the evening meal be ready, when Dietrich returned from the city.

Dagmar re-lived these dreams all day every day so they sunk so deeply into her mind as to become the basis of her emotional life. These were her elated and most ideal visions, but often she imagined things closer to her immediate existence. When the elderly proprietor was away upstairs in his little flat, Dietrich would visit her, and together, they would glance through some prints and discuss them, and sometimes they would discuss any other topic which entered their heads, and so Dagmar was never alone in the shop for very long. When a customer entered or when the proprietor returned from upstairs, then Dietrich would bow to her and politely take his leave. As she lay in bed at night, Dietrich would be with her, and they would lie quite naked together, kissing and embracing each other, but never more than this, for Dagmar would insist that the consummation of their love must wait until their wedding night.

The friendship between the young lovers progressed, and after they had known each other for two months, there was still no talk of introducing either to the home of the other – in Germany, an occasion of some significance – although the good Frau Renot once suggested at the dinner table that it might be nice if Dagmar could introduce her young man into the family circle. Papa Renot muttered something in reply about it being more usual for the girl to be introduced into the home of the boy's parents first. Naturally, there had been no talk – or even thought yet – between the lovers of an engagement.

Sometimes whilst strolling through the forest or lying half hidden between sand dunes by the shore of the Müggel See, as they kissed and embraced, expressing their deepest affection, Dietrich placed his hand on her thigh or gently stroked the smooth white skin of her naked back, and sometimes, he threw his body onto hers, kissing her passionately, and she felt the outline of his figure. On those occasions, she felt suddenly a thrilled sensation pass through her body. She lay there, quietly, restfully, her mind benumbed after receiving and giving tokens of affection to her loved one, but suddenly it seemed as if something had taken her unawares. She felt a weakness, as if an advantage had been taken of her. A shocked sensation flashed into her mind, and she would stiffen suddenly, or sit upright on the sand, resisting the advances of her loved one.

Dietrich would reply in a slow casual tone, "What's the matter?" Dagmar would momentarily be breathless. "I'm not that sort of girl," she would answer. Usually, Dietrich would say no more, but feign a casualness as the situation had been some minutes earlier, but occasionally he argued with her in a slow thoughtful tone, adopting a manner of indifference, fixing his eye on some inanimate object nearby.

"Our feelings for each other are mutual, *nicht*? We understand and trust each other, *nicht*? What is wrong? Why resist what is natural? It's only nature, *nicht*? I can't see that nature can commit any offence. Why not let our feelings take their course,?" he had once said in a tone of self-justification, almost of self-pity, as if answering to the charge of some misdemeanour for which he felt he was blameless.

After Dietrich had spoken in this way, there would be a pause, and Dagmar would reply with an equally lame argument as to why she should defend her innocence. As often with disagreements over questions the solution of which cannot be found through the pursuit of reason, for their basis is emotional rather than rational, the lovers would sit and argue feebly until their passion had subsided, with the consequence that no physical contact would ensue.

On two or three occasions, however, heated words were exchanged, as when Dagmar had suddenly lost patience with her lover and retorted with sharp words, accusing him of attempting to make her "cheap." Dietrich defended himself as best he could, speaking in a tone of self-pity, and taking her hand and trying to soothe and reassure her. In answer to this, she went into a sulk, whilst Dietrich kissed and clung onto her hand, and pleaded for foregiveness. When this occurred a new feeling and an enlightened realisation began to take shape in Dagmar's mind. The realisation was a new facet to be found and developed in their relationship. On one occasion, Dagmar extracted a promise from her lover that he would not attempt "those kind of advances" again. Dietrich solemnly promised.

Less than a week later whilst they were lying in their swimsuits on the sands of the Grosse Müggel See, and she was stroking her fingers through his hair and kissing his chin, he suddenly rolled over onto her body, firmly taking hold of her shoulders and showered a dozen kisses over her face. She laughed and pinched his cheeks, and then they fell into a passionate embrace. He began to caress her shoulders and back, and as he lay across her thigh, she began to feel a strangely increasing pressure from his body. Suddenly she protested, saying she wished to sit upright on the sand, but Dietrich would not allow this as he continued to gently kiss her neck and behind her ear. She began to struggle.

Still Dietrich ignored her pleading as he held her firmly. She began to beat her fists against the sides of his ribs, and then her hands took hold of his face as she averted her head to repulse his kisses. She protested pleadingly, but still Dietrich would not relax his grasp nor budge from her body. He had never before persevered with such tenacity when she had resisted his advances. He had always finally relented, and patiently listened to her as she lectured him on her "principles." Now Dagmar began to protest angrily, and in a louder tone of voice.

At last, Dietrich reacted, but he never moved from her body. He exclaimed, "Sh-h-h-h,!" and good-humouredly reminded her that if she was to speak as loudly as that, she might attract other persons nearby on the beach. Dagmar at that moment was in no mood for good humour.

Dietrich began to argue, in his customary slow, thoughtful, defensive tone, but Dagmar was in no mood for arguing either – at least, not whilst he was still lying across her body. Dietrich persisted in his attempts to make her see "reason" – but she would have none of it. She was not prepared to negotiate nor even talk, whilst imprisoned in his grasp. At last she made plain the real nature of her anger, poured out some spiteful words, and threatened to shout and draw attention to others on the beach if he did not immediately relent and free her from her prostrate position.

Dietrich calmly rolled over onto the sand, and nonchalantly asked her, What was the matter? He wanted to forget the episode, but her anger culminated in such an outburst that he felt obliged to make amends. In lieu of apology he wanted to convey astonishment at her indignation, as if to indicate there was no good reason for her attitude. He anticipated and hoped Dagmar would either lie silent awhile in a harmless sulk, or else exhaust her irritation in a few sharp words which would soon be forgotten.

On this occasion neither of these eventualities occurred. Instead, Dagmar continued to express her resentment, and not content with that, she began to accuse and to conjecture as to what might be the basis of their friendship from *his* viewpoint. She was unsparing in unleashing her anger, and she intended to be spiteful and succeeded. Dietrich had no option but to sit quietly, listening respectfully.

"All your feelings for me are insincere – hypocritical – you think of only one thing," she cried, "and that I shall *never* give you."

At the conclusion of her outburst, there was a pause. Dietrich made no attempt to reply; he only glanced down blankly at the sand in front of him, pouting his lips into an expression as if to convey ignorance of any wrongdoing.

Dagmar began speaking again, hesitantly, slowly, as she sat stiffly on the sand, in a slightly pompous pose.

"I've been thinking about our friendship during the past two weeks," she began, "and it's occurred to me that new factors have had to be considered. During the past two weeks you've attempted things which earlier had never come into our friendship. On more than one occasion I've explained to you what sort of girl I am, but you've chosen to ignore this. Last week I extracted a promise from you, but it seems you've chosen to ignore it. I don't think a boy who attempts to break such a solemn promise can have real respect for a girl – neither for her feelings nor her person. As I say, I've thought seriously about these things for two weeks now, and I've come to a conclusion."

There was a brief pause, and she glanced at Dietrich. He sat tensely, apprehensively, waiting for her to go on, as he looked into her face. Dagmar continued, speaking more hesitantly than before, stammering over several words, and apparently, there was emotion in her voice.

"I've decided therefore, and I am resolved, that this shall be the last occasion of our meeting."

Whether it was through inexperience, or merely because he was so suddenly overcome with uncontrollable remorse, it cannot be surmised; but certain it is, that Dietrich fell for one of the most common wiles of womankind.

He leapt over to her side, took her hand, which he kissed passionately, and pleaded for forgiveness. Now it was his turn to make a little speech. He protested his love for her, saying he would serve her always, honourably, faithfully – that she was the only girl who mattered in his life, and that nothing – nothing in the world could divide them. As he held her hand closely to his lips, he even muttered he would be broken hearted should she in reality think of leaving him.

In answer to this, Dagmar snatched away her hand from his lips, grabbed her towel and bag, rose to her feet, and began walking away along the length of the beach, moving with short firm footsteps. Dietrich sat still and watched after her. He waited for her to glance round. She continued to walk on, and she never glanced back. Was she really intending to leave him forever? Could such a thing be possible? He jumped to his feet and quickly ran after her. He caught her up, and again protested his love, asking her to be reasonable. He pleaded and argued, but she continued to look straight ahead, walking forward, and she made no reply.

He said she couldn't desert him like this – not in the middle of a Summer afternoon whilst they had been lying together on a public beach – it was unprecedented – girls didn't do that sort of thing! He told her she must dress first so he could see her home to her door as etiquette required, and that then she could desert him if she wished. Dagmar stopped in her track. She replied that they would return to their bathing place and lie down on the sand again, and that her final decision concerning the end of their friendship would be reserved until the evening when he would be judged according to his subsequent behaviour that afternoon.

They returned to their bathing spot, walking side by side but avoiding physical contact, and no words were exchanged. They lay down on the sand. Dagmar lay on her back going into an apparent sulk, whilst Dietrich lay on his side observing her closely with an expression of concern. No physical contact was made throughout the rest of that afternoon and when they dressed and left the shore of the Müggel See to return to the city, she shook off his arm when he laid it across her shoulder and put her arm through his, remarking that that was the proper way for young people to walk together. They went to the cinema that evening, and when he had escorted her back to the hallway of the tenement block at No. 55, he humbly asked her permission if he might be permitted to kiss her. Permission was granted.

Chapter 41

That Summer's day by the Müggel See proved to be of significance to the subsequent development of their relationship in more ways than one. For Dagmar, it was a day of victory; she had conspired and executed a stratagem succeeding to perfection. She had conquered, and the strong Dietrich – the bold and infallible Dietrich – had for one day been brought to his knees, begging and pleading for forgiveness.

The little trick had been planned with care and with the chance of almost certain success. The previous occasions on which Dagmar had rebuffed his advances had proven the likelihood of the plan's success. She knew that Dietrich loved her – she had never doubted that – but there was no harm in testing his love by putting it to a practical test – in fact, it could be amusing watching the outcome of the psychological experiment as anticipated. And this is just what had happened.

For Dagmar, it was the day when she first proved to herself the omnipotent power that woman might hold over man by withholding favours and the enjoyment of her body. On the night of that significant day by the Müggel See, as she undressed for bed, she felt both flattered and excited by what had occurred. She was thrilled by the idea that she could – and had made a plaything of Dietrich. On that occasion she had humiliated him, but she was never to humiliate him in quite that way again – anyway, not so grossly, with such obvious guile, since firstly, they were not to quarrel over such an issue, and for several months he never attempted to press his advances too far; and secondly, it was to be unnecessary, for when they came into conflict, she was to cultivate new and subtler methods of exerting her will.

Dagmar was developing her maturity. She no longer remained a passive being, idolising and worshipping her lover. She had begun to take a more positive role in their relationship. She chided him more frequently, but with all the charm of her affection, pinching her fingers on the inside of his arm as she held his elbow and softly laying her beautiful head of silken hair against his shoulder. She became more interested in expressing her preferences, and felt more free in forming her judgements. As they passed through an art gallery they would often dispute with one another, in low gentle tones as to the merit of a particular painting or piece of sculpture, as they held their arms around each other's waists. There was frequently, therefore, a battle of wills between them, but this was hardly ever allowed to become overtly intense or to break out into a quarrel. Their differences were sublimated into a form of good-humoured controversy, as she might tug on his arm and he caress her shoulder and even offer a kiss or two.

This battle of wills resulted in influencing the lovers in two ways. Firstly, their love for one another was thereby strengthened – made deeper and more real. He was no longer the absolute master and overlord and she was no longer a passive and adoring doll, to be merely looked upon and appreciated from a respectful distance. Their friendship was no longer predominantly based on mutual admiration for qualities which each saw in the other. Their relationship became emotionally intertwined. There was a process of adaptation, and so consequently, there were times when each felt uncertain of the feelings of the other, and because of this, they began to feel dependent on each other. In these circumstances a sense of mutual trust grew between them, and both felt the need for reassuring their love for one another.

The fever of love began to take it course. They had to meet regularly, and every meeting was anticipated with a feeling of impatience and excitement, and every parting was marked by a tinge of pain. After each tryst both lovers were left with sensations to ponder over after the evening's pleasure, and sometimes there were doubts, and sometimes they would lie long awake before sleep caught up with their fatigue. They met regularly throughout the Summer except for two weeks when Dietrich explained he was away on "holiday" in the East zone. They met three times weekly, every Wednesday, Saturday and Sunday – and three times was not enough, but Dietrich was studying, having to stay at home the other nights, reading and compiling notes for exams at the beginning of the Autumn term, until the early hours. Most painful was their parting on Sunday nights, for three whole long days had to elapse before their next meeting.

"Never mind, my sweet, think that but tomorrow only forty-eight hours must pass," consoled Dietrich, "and forty-eight hours surely cannot be too long."

The parting on Wednesday nights was not so painful. It was already passed the middle of the week, and on Saturday they might meet earlier in the day, and the weekend brought two days of freedom and leisure to be looked forward to.

The second way in which this battle of wills influenced the lovers, touched Dietrich alone. The individualistic and independent Dietrich, who resented authority in any guise, valuing his freedom above all else, was to respond in a particular way to their relationship. He rarely came into open collision with Dagmar as concerned the reconciling of differences between them, and because of her charm and feminine guile, perhaps he never realised the extent of the influence she exerted. Certain it is that consciously he never resented her magic power, although after some months of friendship, that influence attained considerable power.

This truth most clearly manifested itself in the pursuit of their interests together. The lively discussion evenings in a beer house or park restaurant, and the group outings to theatres and other places of public entertainment, became less frequent, as increasingly they spent their hours alone together. The pursuit of their interests together more often followed her interests than his. Visits to athletic and sporting events, as motor-cycle racing (of which Dietrch was fond) gave way to quieter afternoons in art galleries, museums and exhibitions of contemporary design.

Dagmar hated motor cycling, with its noise, dirt, danger and wild excitement, and she became "bored" by athletics which she thought "vain" and pointless. "What do all those men with big muscles want to pick up weights for, anyway,?" she once exclaimed in a tone of mild contempt, "haven't they got anything better to do with their strength? It all seems such a waste of time. I mean, they're not proving anything useful by it." Dietrich tried to explain weight lifting to her as something which was of value and significance in itself, but she was unable to accept this abstruse philosophical interpretation. Since Dietrich had a wider range of interests than Dagmar, perhaps it was only natural he should give way to his friend when it came to a choice of leisure pursuits, although he was never to become as keen as her on endlessly trailing around galleries, losing himself in the contemplation of the garish colours and abstractions of esoteric art.

If Dieter's character was tinged with egotism, this was certainly not reflected in his relationship with Dagmar, as their friendship stood after a process of three months adaptation, and by this time the basis of their friendship had reached a stage of stability. Although occasionally there were little squabbles between the two lovers Dietrich was always kind, considerate and generous to his beloved. Occasionally, he was unsparing in his generosity as when Dagmar pointed her finger at an attractive article in a shop window, and a few days later he would present it to her as a surprise gift. Before the Summer was out, he had already bought her a dress from the West sector (a costly article), a pair of shoes, and a set of Chinese prints. Then towards Autumn, for her birthday, he bought her a calf bound edition of Lessing's works.

Perhaps Dieter's friendship with Dagmar brought out in him a generosity which had hitherto remained but latent in his character, and perhaps he experienced a new joy in life which springs from feelings of spontaneous generosity and the desire to delight. There was, however, another facet of Dieter's character which was exposed as an outcome of his friendship with Dagmar and the hidden battle of wills between them. This facet was of a less likeable kind. It seemed as if the assertiveness of his character was being transformed into an arrogance towards those to whom he took an instinctive dislike, towards those with whom he lost patience, and occasionally, towards those in an inferior position.

Furthermore, his hatred and contempt for the "system" and everything resembling it became increasingly manifest, as made evident by his outspokenness and an increasing lack of discretion in public places. Concerning this latter tendency, Dagmar rarely attempted to chide him, since he had made that strange boast about not knowing what "fear" was. When he indulged in such plain speaking, she now adopted the stance of smiling at him, turning her eyes from side to side, suggesting that they might be overheard, but she never used a more explicit gesture in reminding him of the need for discretion. Perhaps her attitude – the delightful appearance of her smile, the seductive expression of her eyes as they narrowed and moved from side to sde, and the humorously shocked expression – served only to encourage his candid behaviour, so that he might arouse her attention to himself and see her smile in this seductive fashion.

It can be asserted as a fair probability that subconsciously at least, Dietrich found the weight of his friendship with Dagmar was limiting his sense of independence to which he had always been accustomed. He was an only child, intensely individualistic in his intellectual outook, in his interests, and in his relationship with others, and he resented interference or pressure of any kind. His friendship with Dagmar was an intense relationship – a new experience – so demanding a readjustment to fit his personality. That day when they had quarrelled on the beach at the Müggel See – that day which was to prove so significant to the future of their relationship – especially on Dagmar's part – was perhaps also significant in a different way when seen from Dieter's viewpoint.

For Dagmar it had been a day of triumph – for the cool and pleasant realisation of a new truth. For Dietrich it was a purely psychic event. Through inexperience or because he had been unable to comprehend the situation in time, he had been put-out and humiliated. His will had been bent so that Dagmar might use him as a plaything. Perhaps the humiliation of this experience had pierced his pride, hurting the most susceptible part of his soul, sinking into the recesses of his mind. The experience was never repeated but it was ever to be remembered, and from that day onward, his independence was to be eroded as a sacrifice to his friendship with Dagmar, and it might be argued that his increasing arrogance compensated for the independence he had relinquished in return for that friendship.

On several occasions he became irate with Vopos who pulled him up in his car for ignoring minor traffic regulations. He responded with short sharp words, and in the light of their apparent youth, he had insolently enquired as to whether they had yet graduated from "Kindergarten," before waving his hand contemptuously, and speeding off. "I don't mind admitting a wrong when I'm pulled up for committing a minor offence," he had explained to Dagmar as they drove forward, "but I'm damned if I'm going to bow down to those school kids playing 'Cops and Robbers.'"

Dietrich also became impatient with waiters, in locations where supposedly he was well known, on being badgered to show his pass. "Have you lost your memory tonight,?" or, "What's the matter – am I wearing a beard this evening,?" were responses which burst from his lips.

"I'm sorry, but we're watched by the police, and as a formality, we're obliged to glance at the passes of all patrons," explained a waiter apologetically one evening. "Last week, a colleague was sacked for failing to ask for the pass of a regular patron."

One incident which particularly stood out in Dagmar's mind occurred in the building of the Humboldt University. It was at the beginning of the Autumn term and Dagmar expressed a wish to see the inside of the old university building, and since the general public were not allowed inside, he took her there himself one evening. On reaching the barrier inside the entrance, he showed his university pass, but was told that it would be forbidden to bring in Dagmar. Dietrich politely explained to the uniformed official that he only wanted to show Dagmar round the building for a few minutes, to show her the lecture halls, some portraits hanging in the corridors, the library and the students' café.

The official shook his head. Orders were orders. No one was allowed into the building without showing an appropriate *Ausweis*. Dietrich told him he had shown him his *Ausweis* and that surely that was enough. Dagmar was his girl friend, his guest, and would remain his responsibility whilst in the building. The official still shook his head, saying it was "*Strengtens Verboten,*!" and that she must remain outside whilst he went in to complete his own business, and he waved his hand at Dagmar indicating she should stand aside. Dietrich said he hadn't come for any "business;" he had only come to show Dagmar the inside of the building. The official replied that in that case they must both go away. Dietrich said the official was trying to misuse the spirit of the regulations - he was being dictatorial. The official said the regulations didn't have any "spirit" only "plain instructions." There was a philosophical argument at the end of which Dieter exclaimed, "*Quatsch*!" The conscientious official responded: "How are we to know she's not an agent from the West? We have imperialist provocateurs trying to get into this place every day."

Dietrich took this as an insult to his friend and was infuriated. Dagmar bit her lips in anger. She opened her bag and was just about to produce her East German identity pass, when the next moment, her gesture was made unnecessary, for Dietrich had taken told of the official's neck, and was shaking him violently backwards and forwards. The poor afflicted creature gasped for breath becoming purple in the face. Dietrich banged him against the wall, lifted him off the floor and dropped him. He fell like a bundle where he remained doubled-up on his haunches between the wall and the ground making no attempt to move.

Dietrich pushed Dagmar through the barrier, and together, they ran up the steps beneath the long banner bearing a quotation from Marx, which hung from the wall above, and they passed quickly into the corridor beyond. Although there were students all the while hurriedly coming and going in the entrance hall, when the assault took place, none had taken note of the incident, nor bothered even in their rush to glance up.

"You shouldn't have done that," exclaimed Dagmar in a tone of concern as they came into the corridor.

"You can't say he didn't provoke it," replied Dietrich abruptly. "He behaved like a pig. I've never seen such petty officialdom carried to such limits."

"He was only acting under orders."

"Orders,!" exclaimed Dietrich ironically. "It seemed to me as if he was only trying to act like a tinpot dictator."

"But if he calls the police,?" exclaimed Dagmar in alarm.

"Let him call the police. I don't mind. He was insolent and provocative. I'd soon have him put in his place again. What did I do to him anyway? Only knock him to the floor, and he was lucky to get away with that. Someone else might have given him a black eye as well to keep as a souvenir for his bad manners."

"It's best we don't stay in here too long – something might happen," exclaimed Dagmar apprehensively.

"Don't worry – nothing will. He wouldn't dare call the police," replied Dietrich.

They passed along the corridor and Dietrich was fuming with anger.

"I'm fed up with the entire environment of this place – and I hold the University in contempt," he exclaimed loudly waving his hand aside.

"Don't speak so loudly – everyone can hear you," pleaded Dagmar.

"Let them," replied Dietrich. "This is no longer a place of learning; it's a factory for Communist *apparatchiks*."

In his burning anger it seemed as if he was intent on being overheard. He was in a fighting mood.

"And this is our first exhibit," he announced sarcastically as if acting the role of an appointed guide.

The couple stopped beneath a red cloth banner proclaiming, SUPPORT OUR NATIONAL PEOPLE'S ARMY! Beneath the banner hung some pictures depicting army life and training and guns and tanks and the latest weapons used by the publicised force.

"As you see, the students of our University are privileged to be well supplied with military propaganda," continued Dietrich in a loud voice. "In exchange for our education, the students are expected to volunteer and joyfully offer themselves to the glories of military science and warfare. Just look at these pictures and at all those happy faces! How wonderful it must feel to stand in the turret of a tank, or drive in a bren gun carrier, or sit behind a loaded machine gun with two thousand rounds of live ammunition at your side!"

"Don't talk so loudly," exclaimed Dagmar. "You're attracting attention – and it looks foolish."

"That's our solution to world peace – and who shall we be expected to attack and kill,?" continued Dietrich as if Dagmar had not spoken. "Why, of course our blood brethren in West Germany – our countrymen whom we're now being called upon to hate. Ach, People's Army! Of course, by international law, as laid down by the four power allies, it's illegal to organise an armed force of German citizens in the Free City of Berlin, but of course, here in the Demcratic Sector, the word 'law' means nothing. Here, only the illegal is legal!"

"Please don't speak so loudly," interjected Dagmar.

"This place is like an army recruiting centre," exclaimed Dietrich as they continued to pass down the corridor. "No one is free to say anything without risk of his being picked up by the Stasi – not even the leading ideologists themselves."

"Then be careful what you say," said Dagmar.

"Why, only last Winter one of the chief professors of Marxist philosophy was arrested by the SSD, accused of organising a group hostile to the Communist party. That was Professor Wolfgang Harich. If the Party's own leaders can't escape the long hand of the Stasi, then who can? But the authorities won't get me to bend down to the State."

They toured through the University building, as Dietrich vented his rage by denouncing anything which smelt of propaganda or party influence. As they left the building, the same official who had stopped them on entering, was still there. He expressed his resentment for the rough treatment he had received by turning his back on the couple as they came down the steps and left the building.

Those activities they enjoyed together initiated by Dietrich were usually concerned with visits to the West sector. He introduced her to the American Memorial Library in Blücher Strasse, and together, they often went to exchange their books there, and he was not tardy in presenting a reading list of "essential titles" for the fair one. He also had student friends in the West sector whom he had come to know through a cousin residing in Wilmersdorf and studying at the new Free University.

Sometimes Dietrich and Dagmar were invited to a party in the West sector, and on those occasions they usually found themselves the sole guests from the East. In these circumstances they must have encountered minor embarrassments, and sometimes, set-backs of a humiliating kind. They came from a different world, and in that situation there was no disguising the fact. When the conversation turned to holidays, trips to Federal Germany, or tours to foreign lands far away, where the seas were always blue and the sun shone down onto scorching beaches, then their part in the conversation could only be as passive listeners. These were talks of lands they would never have the means to visit, and even if they had – if they were rich beyond their dreams – then it was unlikely they would be granted exit visas to travel independently.

When the conversation turned to politics, there was often a feeling of awkwardness and uncertainty. Their sympathies were anti-Communist and pro-Western, but the fact remained they were citizens of the DDR. What stand could they take? To sympathise unconditionally with Western friends could place them at risk if an informer might by chance be listening in their midst, or if repeated to the wrong person. To take the stand of a West Berliner and to discuss problems as he would see them, might be an embarrassment for all, for even treason towards a much hated and illegally constituted regime might arouse scepticism in the minds of a listening group of West German students. Political discussion amongst a group of West Berliners with two East Berliners present was bound to evoke suspicion within the circle and caution into the proceedings. After all, who was to be quite certain of these East Berliners, and anyway, why were they there?

In fact, when the conversation turned to politics, Dietrich would start by announcing that he and Dagmar were from the East, so that no doubt could subsequently arise as to their identity and as to how they might see an issue from their particular angle. This apart, Dietrich was as forthright in expressing his views as ever, but he was sufficiently circumspect to discuss a problem as an East German might see it, and he liked to speak from personal experience and that of his friends and student colleagues in the East, for in this way he could more easily maintain the integrity of his convictions. For this reason he became an interesting speaker, invariably broaching a topic from a fresh viewpoint, and so adopting a bias not uncomfortable to others present. On finding himself amongst a party of trusted friends in the West sector, on the other hand, he then felt sufficiently free to speak in any way he chose.

When the conversation turned to the buying and selling of cars, or to the rising or falling prices on the bourse, or to some new luxury which had hit the market, then also, the lovers from the East would need to sit silently as passive listeners. After a time they found a way of partly alleviating the disadvantaged status felt inevitably by an East Berliner visiting the Western half of the city. The idea or joke was Dagmar's invention. One evening after Dietrich had taken her to *Die Stachelschweine* (the cabaret show, famous for its political skits, situated in Ranke Strasse off the Ku'damm) where they had met another young couple, Dagmar suggested to her friend, "Why don't we pretend to be West Berliners." Both lovers were in a high-spirited mood, and Dietrich endorsed the suggestion saying it was a "fine idea."

"After all, it'd be harmless, and we'd avoid that horrible awkwardness when people look at you with a pitying expression, reminding you that the price of potatoes in the East zone have gone up another few pfennigs per pound; and how terrible it all is, and so forth; and when they start asking the same old questions about living conditions again – it's such a bore," exclaimed Dagmar.

From that day onward, the joke grew until the fiction took on a feigned reality. An address was invented in Zehlendorf, Dietrich ran a Porsche, and Dagmar had wealthy relatives in Hamburg; this year they had travelled to Spain for a holiday and next year they were going to Italy – and so the great invention developed to cover every aspect of their lives. It became a huge joke kept strictly between the lovers. Whenever they made a casual acquaintance in a concert hall, theatre, or whilst strolling round a gallery, and sometimes, even, when meeting guests at a party, then the great fiction began to play its part. If, however, whilst they were at a function and a political discussion arose, then the idea of the joke would have to be suppressed for fear of consequent complications, and the possibility of the truth being somehow revealed and the joke backfiring. This was because political debate was a serious issue, and under no circumstances must practical jokes of such a kind be allowed to mix with politics!

The huge joke was immensely successful. It never seemed to occasion embarrassment to the lovers, and they were always accepted as credible.

"Didn't you notice how Johann seemed to envy us when we told him about the new Mercedes we're buying next week," said Dagmar one evening.

"Yes, it almost seemed to be hurting him," replied Dietrich.

"I almost feel sorry for him."

"Feel sorry for him,?" exclaimed Dietrich with a start. "He comes from one of the richest families in Berlin."

"You know, I think it would be so much funnier if we were West Berliners pretending to have come from the East," said Dietrich another day, "for then we could fawn on the pity of the West Berliners. Just think of all the sympathy we could arouse in their hearts for our sorrowful lot!"

"But the entire purpose of our joke is so they don't think we're East Berliners," replied Dagmar. "Don't you remember how it all began?"

"I was just assuming for the moment that if in reality we came from the West. If that were so, then we'd see everything so differently."

"I've an idea – and it'd be so simple to enact. Why don't we just pretend to be West Berliners pretending to be East Berliners,?" began Dagmar brightly. "No – somehow, I don't think it would quite work out," she added dolefully, a moment later.

When the evenings which had been marked by these hilarious practical jokes came to a close, the lovers would discuss at length what had been said to their different "victims," and they would compare the authenticity of their spoken accounts as it adhered to the truth of the story they had invented so far. In this way the great fiction was enlarged to ever more fantastic proportions.

"He asked me if we'd seen the paintings of the prehistoric caves in Altimara when we were in Spain earlier this year, and so I said we had," said Dagmar on one occasion. "I thought it was something we really should have seen – especially as I work in an art shop."

"And I told her we drove to Hamburg where we spent a long weekend at the beginning of last month," replied Dietreich.

"Scandalous,!" remarked Dagmar. "Oh, so much more to remember!"

They laughed over the reactions of their unsuspecting acquaintances, especially over their wonderment and envy. Despite all this, there was something pitiful, almost tragic, which gave rise to the huge joke. It was an easy way of making light of the grim circumstances of their own lives, but the bitter fact remained that it was they who became ultimately the victims of their own joke. It was a process by which they were ever bringing themselves into closer contact with the West without sharing in its reality.

On returning by train to the East sector, Dietrich often bitterly complained about the conditions and fate of that part of the world in which they lived, and he became morose and virulently critical of the "system" as they compared the two halves of the city. The couple became hypersensitively critical over the smallest differences: over the taste of coffee, over the manners of waiters, and over the shoddy condition of articles in shops in East Berlin. The purpose of their joke, which was a double-edged weapon, had begun to recoil. Their laughter was momentary and the humour short-lived, as it wore off to leave a bitter taste.

Whether it was because of these frequent visits to the West or for other reasons, of which Dagmar was not quite sure, Dieter's assertiveness manifested itself in a rising contempt and impatience with the regime, which to Dagmar bordered almost on the pathological. Added to this, Dietrich began defacing political posters with pencil marks, so that portraits of leading personalities became bearded or cross-eyed; to draw savage cartoons of the leaders of the East German state and to pin these in prominent places; to shout abuse and ironical remarks at selected demonstrators, who for one cause or another had been instructed to march through the streets, and on one occasion, whilst the two lovers were walking through Charlotten Strasse, he had even kicked to the ground a propaganda placard standing outside the ruined baroque shell of the French Cathedral.

On occasions, Dagmar was terrified by the thought of the immediate and possible outcome of these wild antics. In the apparent senselessness of this stupidity he was asking for trouble, and sometimes Dagmar reacted as if to disown him. If he was apprehended by the SSD, whilst indulging in these antics, he could have been arrested and detained for as long as the authorities pleased. Dagmar wondered why he did these things. By now she was certain it was not out of a vain desire to attract her favourable attention, and neither was it out of a desire to "prove" anything to anyone in particular, for at least he made sure of quickly slipping down a back street or into a crowded shop if he felt his behaviour exceeded even his lax standards of caution. His wild unpredictable antics went beyond the stage when they might have been excused as empty vanity or misplaced humour. His loathing of the regime was becoming surely symptomatic of a medical condition. There had to be an explanation which as yet was hidden from the fair one.

Chapter 42

One afternoon as the two lovers were quietly strolling through the Plänter Wald, less than a week after the incident when Dietrich kicked down the propaganda placard standing outside the French Cathedral, Dagmar decided to probe the reason for his increasingly unpredictable beahaviour with a view to eliciting some hidden anxiety which he might have been concealing from her. Since both lovers were in a relaxed mood, their minds absorbed by the melancholy beauty of the Autumn afternoon, it seemed to Dagmar an ideal opportunity for engaging Dieter's confidence in a discussion of this kind.

As a result of the conversation which followed and of Dagmar's discreet probing; she was to be surprised on learning a factor about Dieter's life which had hitherto remained unknown. It was a factor she would never have guessed,although had she been more insistent,during that first occasion they had met alone, she might have even then – at that early stage of their friendship – have cajoled the truth out of him. She received the revelation of this factor at first as if it were not to be credited and then as if it were absurd, before finally comprehending the full horror of its compromising significance.

"Dieter, why do you have to behave so recklessly – drawing cartoons and pinning them in the streets, and shouting at demonstrators,?" asked Dagmar confidentially.

"Because – as I've so often said – I hate the regime," replied Dieter evasively.

"You haven't always behaved like that – only since the last weeks."

"Perhaps it's because of the new term, when we students are brought closer to the authorities again."

"But it's dangerous – dangerous to yourself. You could be arrested any time."

"I'm cautious enough."

"You aren't. You don't know who might be standing beside you. The SSD could be watching and following your every move. You know how sensitive the police are to students."

"There was no one in the street when I pulled down that placard last week."

"But someone could have turned the next corner. It was in the city centre and every few minutes the police patrol those streets."

"You don't understand how resentful we students are at the oppression of the University authorities."

"Can't you find some less dangerous way of expressing your resentment?"

"It's difficult in this society to express any kind of resentment."

"Dieter, I've been thinking during the past few days, and it seems to me, as if it's not merely because of resentment and anger you've been doing these stupid reckless things. Tell me, Dieter, is it because of some hidden anxiety?"

There was a pause as they glanced down thoughtfully in front of them, as their slow even footsteps trod the ground beneath.

"Perhaps it's because of a bad canscience," replied Dieter.

"A bad conscience,?" said Dagmar alarmed.

"It's something I've not told you before. I don't know why – perhaps because I didn't think it important, or because I just didn't know how to tell you."

"Please explain."

"It's something that'll surprise you – and yet all my friends know – it's no secret from them – it seems silly you haven't heard before. I thought the fact would come up during one of our beer house discussion evenings, but it never did. It seems funny really that no one had cause to mention it – perhaps because it was of the sensitivity of my friends – they didn't want to let the cat out of the bag – although why they should think I'd be put out by your knowing, I just don't know."

"I still don't understand," exclaimed Dagmar with a suggestion of impatience.

"Let's sit down and I'll explain," replied Dieter, as the couple came to a park bench and took their seats. "You see, Dagmar, I'm a member of the Communist party," said Dieter.

Dagmar burst out laughing.

"A member of the Communist party? Oh, my sweet darling, what a wonderful joke," exclaimed Dagmar tugging on Dieter's arm and kissing his cheek. "How beautifully unbelievable!"

"I wish it was. But it's true – it really is true," insisted Dieter.

"And that's why you hate Communism," said Dagmar still laughing. "And how did all this come about?"

"That is, I'm not strictly a member of the Communist party, but I'm a member of the FDJ, the Free German Youth," continued Dieter as if Dagmar had not spoken. "But my parents are full members of the Communist party, that is, the SED, and when I'm thirty, I too will be expected to join the Socialist Unity Party."

By this time Dagmar had grasped onto the significance of what Dieter had said. She remained seriously thoughtful awhile.

"And so your parents are Communists – ideological believers in the party – and that's why you have that fine car," exclaimed Dagmar as if suddenly enlightened by an unpleasant discovery.

"No, not that – only beetroot Communists – red on the outside," explained Dieter hurriedly so as to avoid a false impression.

"But I still don't understand. Why have you been behaving in this reckless way? If you're a member of the party, you have all the more reason to be cautious and sensible. If a party member is arrested for a political offence, it's certain the punishment would be terrible."

"To me the reasons are clear – not necessarily for my 'recklessness' as you call it – but at least for my fervent criticism of the 'system' and everything it means."

"I count your recklessness, as tearing down placards in streets, as something quite separate and different from criticising the 'system' in beer house discussions with friends."

"Then let me at least explain the latter. I'm a member of the FDJ, yes? All the world knows it; all the world must know it; it can be kept as a secret from no one. There are certain duties and functions I'm obliged to carry out in the University in connection with the movement, such as canvassing, handing out notices, and all the usual things, etc. I'm known to every student there. You begin to understand, yes?"

"Go on."

"Everywhere my face is known. I'm known by my voice, and I'm known personally to every student in the faculty – and yet I loathe Communism in its every aspect. It's humiliating, isn't it? You remember when I was away from Berlin for two weeks in the Summer? I said I was on holiday, but I wasn't. I was on an FDJ cadre course near Rostock – drilling, rifle training, and learning how to throw grenades. It was a secret camp – all of us picked for the course were sworn to secrecy before we arrived at the base."

"Did you have to go?"

"Yes. We were chosen without right of option. Can you begin to understand my position now? Because I'm a member of the FDJ and because of my hatred for the regime and the ideology, I wish to escape from the horns of the dilemma which fate has forced upon me."

"What dilemma?"

"The dilemma which on the one side obliges my family and me to be members of the party, and on the other, the membership of the party itself."

"But your foolishness will give you away. Wouldn't it be better to renounce your membership and free yourself from this burden – this responsibility?"

"There'd be infinite – almost insuperable difficulties to face in renouncing party membership. Besides, I couldn't – for the sake of my parents. But I've discovered the next best thing. I've found a way of living with the authorities."

"You mean, by living a double life – a public life when you work for the party, and a private life when you work against it in your own small way?"

"That's it."

"Now I begin to understand. And is that what you meant by your unique and inimitable joke with the authorities? Do you remember what you told me that evening when we first met long ago, when we sat in that pavement restaurant in Friedrich Strasse?"

"Yes, that's what I meant by my joke with the authorities – it's part of the joke anyway."

"And is that what you meant by maintaining your independence? Is that what you call living your freedom in our totalitarian state?"

"Yes – just that."

"Dietrich, please give up this whole stupid play acting – and that's all it is, and you know it. Free yourself from membership of the party before it's too late and you find yourself in trouble."

"Dagmar, I cannot."

"Then become a bad indifferent party member, so they'll want to throw you out. Pretend to be crazy, or something."

"I cannot – my involvement with the party has gone beyond that."

"How? How deeply are you involved?"

"In a way I'm a sort of favoured – almost a privileged member of the FDJ. My name is known to some of the top party bosses in the country. You see, I've somehow won for myself the reputation of being a kind of brain-child of the party, to be lovingly nurtured and cared for until my talents can be fully made use of."

"I'm still perplexed," exclaimed Dagmar laughing.

"It all happened as an accident, and quite suddenly, and to me it came as a greater surprise than to anyone else. At the time, I had my tongue in the cheek. I was joking to myself. I could never have guessed it would go any further than that. What finally happened is that I found myself playing a practical joke on the authorities. At the time it seemed hilariously funny, but since then, things have gone wrong. I've become strangely inexplicably compromised by the outcome of my own joke."

"Please tell me," said Dagmar.

"It began some years ago during my last term at school. You know I've always been interested in politics, and at school I took an active part in debates, and was always a prominent pupil during the lessons on Marxism-Leninism. By a prominent pupil, I'm not saying a pliable, obedient pupil, learning and accepting the tenets of Marxism by heart and repeating them parrot fashion – because I wasn't. Quite the contrary, in fact. I provoked discussion, criticising everything we were taught – ridiculing every doctrine. Often I had the class in fits of laughter. I even ended up by teaching the master, surreptitiously, through the Socratic method. I'd ask him a string of questions needing only 'Yes' or 'No' answers, and finally, he'd find himself contradicting what he'd just told us five minutes beforehand. He was a graduate in Marxist philosophy, but every time we came into conflict, I'd have him floored. He found me quite a handful and was always reporting me to the headmaster, but of course, they couldn't do anything about it really, except call me into the study and reprimand me for simply putting the teacher's nose out of joint. I took all that as a joke.

"It was just after the East German Uprising in 1953 that this thing happened which was eventually to bring me some distinction. As you remember, the East German authorities were in a panic at the time, arbitrarily arresting hundreds of people, and everywhere asking for assurances of loyalty. Well, our class was called upon to write an essay or story illustrating the dangers of Western provocateurs in the Democratic Republic. Some of us were so upset at the time by what had just happened in Germany, that we refused to write anything, and I was amongst that number, but suddenly I had an idea. I asked myself, why not write such an essay as to ridicule the regime, and that's just what I set out to do."

"That was dangerous," remarked Dagmar.

"Listen! I wrote the essay – it was a long one – almost fourteen thousand words. I wrote it with care, and after much thought, and I used Marxist-Leninist writings as a source base. I analysed the psychology of 'reactionary elements' in a land newly 'liberated' by Soviet Socialism, and how such elements could lend themselves to be so easily seduced by 'fascist imperialist provocateurs' from Western Germany. I wrote about the enemies who may still be lurking in our midst and about the 'glorious Soviet Army' which had saved us from a terrible fate. I described the Bonn government as the most evil organisation of fascism – that it was intent on plunging the world into war, and I described the Soviet Army as the greatest and most sacred institution for world peace – that it had liberated and brought happiness to millions, that its tanks and bombs and guns were a joy to right-thinking democratic people the world over.

"The essay used the terminology and stale rationale of Marxism-Leninism whilst at the same time expressing the most rampant nonsense. No sane – no reasonable person could have accepted anything I'd written. It was a parody of what Marxism was supposed to be.

"We had two weeks in which to prepare the essay, and there was one day when they all had to be handed in. Only four pupils in our class wrote an essay, and when I handed mine in to the teacher he never glanced up at me, and even if he had, I could never have looked him in the eye and kept a straight face. When I gave him the essay, I had to bite the inside of my lip, and already I was immensely enjoying the joke I had invented only to satisfy my own satirical sense of humour.

"The essay wasn't to be corrected in the school, but sent to some central department – although I've no doubt our teacher took the opportunity of glancing through my contribution, even if only for his own 'education'. He never liked me much – you can understand that – and for a long time I was afraid he might destroy it, so it would never reach the great professors of Marxist philosophy sitting in some imposing building in the centre of Berlin. Then I began to have doubts. I thought perhaps I'd gone too far in my essay – that my irony had been too pointed – that it would be interpreted as grossly exaggerated, even a blasphemous interpretation of Marxist-Leninist philosophy – which of course was really intended.

"Those doubts were cleared away a month later. One morning we were suddenly called into the school hall. The entire school was assembled there, and we knew it must be something important because the lessons had been interrupted, and the school band of the Young Pioneers, and the Pioneer leaders were at the front of the hall. The headmaster came in and began making a speech. He spoke quickly and seemed very pleased and excited. He told us about the essay competition which had been set six weeks beforehand, and he said the pupils in the top grades in every school in Germany had been asked to write this essay, so the youth of Germany might prove its 'known loyalty' to the regime, and be vindicated from the suspicion of having fallen by the wayside to reactionary fascist influences, which some quarters had suggested.

"He said that all the essays had now been read and examined, not only by representatives of the leading educational authorities in the universities of the DDR but by members of the Marx-Engels-Lenin-Stalin Institute of the SED, and by representatives of the Ministry of Culture. Our headmaster said that this school in particular had proved its loyalty to the regime, and that one pupil had especially won distinction. He announced that an official from the Central Committee of the SED had come to the school to present a prize to one of the selected school pupils in Germany who had contributed the best essays pledging their loyalty to the regime. Our headmaster called for Dietrich Liebermann to take his stand on the platform."

"And how did you feel,?" asked Dagmar.

"I was so astonished, I couldn't believe it. Here was the headmaster of our school – a man who had many times called me into his study and reprimanded me for indiscipline and attempting to corrupt the minds of other pupils – who had called me a reactionary provocateur, and in his rage had called me worse things than that – here was this same man today announcing I'd won distinction as a loyal citizen of the DDR, inviting me to take a stand on the platform for a prize. What could I feel? It was unbelievable! I was known throughout the school for lampooning Marxist-Leninist philosophy. A loud murmur went up in the school again, and I think I even heard a few sniggers. Then someone nudged me, and I saw the headmaster smiling and beckoning me to go up onto the platform."

"What did you do?"

"What could I do? There were hundreds of people in the hall. I went up to the platform to fetch the prize. I felt confused. Still I couldn't believe what was happening. I was filled with misgiving, momentarily thinking they were playing some huge joke in return for my sarcasm, and I thought they would expose me to the school as a Western provocateur and then arrest me in a blare of publicity as an example to others. I felt that especially when I saw the headmaster smile at me – he seemed to be laughing inside himself.

"Then I saw the SED party official turning towards me, smiling, and holding the package in his hand, and I realised the truth. They were really trying to make a hero out of me. I felt embarrassed and angry. They had never consulted nor given me any warning beforehand. If they had, I'd refused the prize, or any other distinction they might have offered. After all, I wasn't really a suitable candidate for such a prize – that was clear. It was like giving a bishop membership to a society for promoting atheism. But what could I do? There were hundreds of people watching. I could only smile nicely, bow, shake hands and take the prize gratefully. There was a loud murmur in the hall until I reached the platform and the headmaster had to raise his hands for quiet, and as I took the package there was a dead silence, and then the murmur rose again.

"Then the headmaster asked the school to extend its congratulations to a very distinguished pupil. I turned towards the front of the platform and there was thunderous applause. Everyone was clapping and stamping as loudly as he and she could, and there were shouts and whistles, but the applause was clearly ironic – you could see that by the laughter on their faces. I felt furious inside – as if being exposed to ridicule, and that's exactly what it was. As I left the platform I saw my history teacher – the graduate in Marxist philosophy – and he too smiled at me, but it was a nasty sort of smile – derisive, insulting."

"But how did this thing come about,?" asked Dagmar.

"To this day I don't completely understand what happened. My guess is that the official from the Central Committee of the SED suddenly called on the school without warning, bringing the prize with him, and that the headmaster and school authorities were forced to make a snap decision amongst themselves. I suppose they thought it best to play up to the visiting representative of the SED, and let him know what a fine chap I was, and to cross their fingers and hope things would work out to plan. And that's just what happened. I suppose the headmaster backed on the conviction I wouldn't risk making a fool of myself in front of the school by refusing the prize."

"He was sly," remarked Dagmar.

"He had the choice of making me foolish or the SED official – and of course, himself as well. He decided to sacrifice my feelings. It would have looked strange if the headmaster had attempted to turn down the prize – he would have lowered the school's esteem as well as his own."

"And he would have made the government authorities look ridiculous," added Dagmar.

"I wish he had done that by advising them against presenting me with the prize. I'd love to have seen the headmaster repeat to the SED official what he'd often said to me, 'Provocateur,' 'Petty bourgeois,' 'Reactionary intellectual,' 'Capitalist thug,' 'Hireling of the West' – and all the other stale epithets from the tired terminology of Marxism-Leninism.   Can you imagine the face of the SED official if the headmaster had said those things?"

Dagmar laughed.

"And what would he have reported to his poor bosses and colleagues on returning to the Ministry later that day,?" exclaimed Dagmar. "The poor things would have been non-plussed."

"There would have been chaos and confusion in some government department for about twenty-four hours until they had chosen someone else to present the prize to," said Dieter.

"But really, the government authorities must have slipped up badly when they presented the prize to you. I mean, surely some kind of security check is kept on 'nuisances' like you who spend their time trying to wreck the credibility of Marxist-Leninist theories during school debates."

"They slipped up badly, yes. Somewhere in that school they must have kept a thick file on my activities during school breaks, and reports on what I'd said during discussion hours. I suppose after I won the prize, the file was just shredded and new forms filled in and countersigned again."

"But such reports must have gone further up than the school – a copy of the file must have been sent to the Ministry of the Interior. Isn't that what generally happens?"

"I don't know. The fact is the authorities slipped up by failing to check on my political reliability. Clearly, they were so excited and overcome on discovering a new propaganda brain-child in their midst who had succeeded so brilliantly in defending the regime, they decided to waive the usual routine security precautions, and go ahead in presenting the prize."

"And what was the prize?"

"A gilt edged red calf bound edition of *Das Kapital*."

Dagmar laughed.

"So that you might become an even more enlightened and patriotic citizen of our Democratic Republic," exclaimed Dagmar. "But what happened after you were presented with the prize? How did you become involved with the Party?"

"When I left the platform and joined my classmates again, and the applause died down, the SED official made a speech. It was terrible! He went on and on – for half an hour – repeating all the old shibboleths, exhorting us to be on our guard against traitors and 'provocateurs' in our midst. Little did he realise he had just presented a prize to the person in the hall who could be most aptly described as a 'provocateur.' When he'd finished, the meeting broke up and it was time for home-going and lunch. Then the jokes began. My friends began crowding round me and laughing, eager to take my hand, congratulating me on my success. I told them I didn't want to be congratulated, saying my joke had misfired – that I couldn't have anticipated anything like this would happen. They laughed all the more – they thought it uproariously funny – and eventually, I too took the attitude that the whole thing was a joke. It was the easiest – perhaps the only attitude I could take. It was futile remaining resentfully perplexed over the failure of a joke, or somebody else's intellectual shortsightedness, or lack of humour – call it what you will."

"The following day, I began impersonating the SED official, and had everyone in fits of laughter. There were several masters round about when this happened, but they pretended not to see, and they left with their tails between their legs. That morning our class had another debating session. Before it began, the teacher discreetly took me aside, asking me to behave myself, but I didn't take any notice of that, and I attacked and ridiculed the Party line. We discussed the recent dismissals of Wilhelm Zaisser and Rudolf Herrnstadt from the Central Committee of the SED, on charges of having formed a 'hostile and defeatist faction setting itself against the unity of the Party.' Zaisser had been Minister for State

Security and Herrnstadt had been the editor of *Neues Deutschland*, and it was during one of Ulbricht's get-tough purges."

"I remember. We were all frightened at the time by what might happen as a result of the ministerial changes," said Dagmar.

"Our Marxist-Leninist toady of a teacher – he was always cringing before the official Party line like an animal expecting to be whipped – said that Zaisser and Herrnstadt were weaklings who had betrayed the people; that they had conspired to turn the country into a bourgeois state. That really got me annoyed. I stood up and replied that these men had done nothing towards altering the official Party line as it had been a few weeks beforehand, and I argued that the dismissals had only been carried out because the Party was in the process of radically changing its own line of policy. I said it was deceitful and hypocritical to argue otherwise, and that the SED, because of its unpopularity, was being forced to revert to an oppressive get-tough policy.

"I was cheered by the entire class. Our teacher was furious. He went purple in the face, and I could see it was difficult for him to keep his self-control, because I'd implied he was a hypocrite. He tried to argue calmly but firmly with me, but he was so angry he lost control of his reasoning faculties, and kept repeating and contradicting himself, until he was so confused he didn't know what he was saying. I had him floored all through the lesson. He just couldn't think straight. At the end of the lesson I asked him, 'Why do you bother to argue with me? How can a man expect to win an argument when one day he swears blind that white is black when the next day he'll swear the opposite – and that's what you Communists are doing all the time?' He didn't answer that; he just walked out of the room, slamming the door behind him. The others in the class cheered and laughed.

"The next day I was called into the headmaster's study again. He didn't mention about what happened at the debating session the day before – although I've no doubt he was told about it. He spoke slowly, but was very firm and direct. I'd never seen him quite like that before. He told me I'd won distinction for myself and for the school through my essay, and that I'd have to live up to the reputation which I alone had created for myself. He said that perhaps I'd intended my essay as an ironic piece of writing, to which I replied, 'Yes.' He said I'd failed in my intention. I'd written a minor masterpiece giving a brilliant interpretation of Marxist-Leninist philosophy. My talent had been recognised and rewarded. He said under no circumstrances would he allow the risk of the school being ridiculed or its loss of reputation through the perpetuation of what he described as my senseless 'antics.' He said my behaviour was risking the reputation of too many party members.

"He said immediate measures would be taken to guarantee the school's reputation in the face of my capricious behaviour. He ordered me to join a number of societies affiliated to the SED, and to take a more active part in the FDJ,of which I was already – albeit a reluctant member. He said I should find no scruples about joining these societies, since my parents were already members of the Communist Party, and that very likely their membership was one of convenience rather than conviction. (I thought that insolent, but I said nothing.) I was about to protest against this peremptory order, when he asked me to stay silent until he'd said one last thing. He said that if I failed to join these societies, he personally would report me to the Ministry of State Security on the basis of my past behaviour, with the result I'd be arrested and interned."

"And so you joined these societies,?" exclaimed Dagar.

"I had no option. I filled in the forms and paid my dues, and that was all. After I left school, I never renewed my membership of these societies – but it was my involvement with the FDJ which really committed me to the Party. I was given a number of duties – they took up a lot of time when I should have been studying for final exams – and all these duties had to be fulfilled, and I was obliged to accept compulsory promotion because of the essay I'd written. What had started out as a practical joke was becoming a nightmare!"

"What happened to the essay? Was it published in a magazine,?" asked Dagmar.

"No, not in a magazine. A hundred thousand copies were printed as a pamphlet and circulated as free hand-outs throughout Germany."

"And so you weren't paid anything?"

"Only in spiritual kind – to feed my ideological fervour – with *Das Kapital*."

"Was your name on the pamphlet?"

"No, it was anonymous. All that was written were the words, 'By a schoolchild and young patriot of the FDJ,' and across the top was written the slogan, 'The youth of the DDR pledges its loyalty to the Central Committee of the Socialist Unity Party!'"

Dagmar laughed sardonically.

"I felt I wanted to vomit as I read it," continued Dieter. "Suddenly I became disgusted with everything I'd done – although the outcome was merely an accident. Worse than that, I kept being invited to receptions which I had to attend. I met top Party officials. I was even introduced to the President, Wilhelm Pieck. On one occasion I was introduced to an all Party delegation of British MPs. A crowd of grinning apes – sympathetic supporters of the Ulbricht regime – you know how hypocritical the British are with their eternal grimace. You never know what they're really thinking. They said I was a 'lucky fellow' to be living in the DDR.

I became nauseated by this vile form of political hospitality, and fortunately, the invitations stopped after a few weeks."

"And how was your school life after you'd won this reputation for yourself,?" asked Dagmar.

"The same as before. I continued to criticise every aspect of the Party line and ideology. During the school debates I was even more critical than at any time earlier. I wanted everyone to know I hated the 'system.' I was determined to let everyone know that, so no suspicions or doubts would arise as to the true place of my sympathies."

"Weren't you reported on by the school authorities?"

"No, not to my knowledge – nothing ever happened. I wasn't even called into the headmaster's study to be lectured and reprimanded. Firstly, I think he just gave up hope of influencing my behaviour, and secondly, I think he wanted to avoid the scandal of my being charged by the police as a provocateur whilst still attending the school. I had only a few more weeks there, anyway. I think he just decided to turn a blind eye to my behaviour, hoping that that would be the best way out of a dilemma."

"Still, it was dangerous to continue behaving as you did," said Dagmar.

"You can't imagine how I felt after all this," continued Dieter. "In writing the essay I became astonished and at the same time shocked by all the repercussions – horrified even, at what had happened. In carrying out what I'd intended as a joke, I'd created a monster – and I abhorred it. I re-read the essay and realised that in fact, by the standards of the Communist Party, I had unintentionally written a minor masterpiece. From the viewpoint of ordinary commonsense, the essay consisted of rampant nonsense – no reasonable person could have doubted that – but I'd used Marxist-Leninist dialectics as the framework for my essay. I had a total understanding of dialectical materialism, and I intended to use it ironically – as I still claim I did, by the standards of ordinary reasoning.

"However, the Marxist philosophers were not to see that. They only saw in my essay the perfect application of that pseudo-scientific method known as dialectical materialism. What shocked me most at the time was not the realisation of the publicity and embarrassment to which I'd be exposed, but the realisation that such lies and nonsense could be introduced into any method of 'scientific' thought, and be accepted as valid truths. It was that factor which hurt most. I'd never realised before that dialectics could be stretched to such limits. It became clear to me that dialectics, by any criteria of truth, was little more than a clever instrument for creating and perpetuating falsehood – merely a useful instrument of dictators of the ilk of Stalin to maintain power through the changing vicissitude of political fortune.

"I even began to lose my faith in reason itself. I began to re-read Hegel. I had been converted to Hegelianism by the, *Philosopphy of History*, and the theory of the development of the higher consciousness, and the progress of freedom which humankind attains through ever higher forms of civilisation. At that time I saw in Hegel a light for the future peace and freedom of the world. For the second time that year I read the, *Phenomenology of Mind*, and the, *Philosophy of Right*, and for the first time, I struggled through the three volumes of the, *Science of Logic*. For many weeks I sat and walked alone, battling out innumerable philosophical problems. I began to become disillusioned with Hegelianism and then I re-examined the theory of dialectical materialism as developed by Marx and Engels. It was then I realised Hegel had been turned upside down – appropriated – plundered - insulted – overthrown. Hegel was not to blame! And yet somehow, Hegel had been given – falsely – official recognition by the ideologists in their pantheon of great thinkers. When I returned to Hegel, as a thinker pure and undefiled, my faith in his philosophy was restored, and again, I could see the world in its proper perspective. Once more I could fall on my knees before the man who held the key to the eternal verities of existence."

"And now all that was some years ago – it's far behind you. How do you think about these things today,?" enquired Dagmar.

"The outcome of my essay, the publicity, my present role in the FDJ,?" exclaimed Dieter laughing. "Today my attitude is changed. I regard my membership of the FDJ as inevitable, and in a way, desirable. I've learnt how to lead a double life, and in that lies my joke against the authorities."

"It's a dangerous joke."

"Certain Party officials kept worrying me to write further pamphlets defending the regime. I refused. I even told them bluntly I wasn't in sympathy with the regime, and do you know, they were so thick-skinned, they wouldn't accept that as a final 'No.' They kept coming back. Then they offered me money, and jokingly, I began to bargain with them over a price, and I asked for a fantastic sum. Then they came back again in a few days. They came with a cheque in their hands, asking me to write the first pamphlet. They had paid me five hundred marks."

"And did you write the pamphlets?"

"What else could I have done? But it was on one condition. I didn't want my name publicised. They gave me a pseudonym."

"Was it a wise thing to do – to write the pamphlet?"

"I saw no harm in it at the time. Firstly, I'd just begun life as a student, and money was welcome, and secondly, no one in the DDR takes any notice of propaganda, anyway. It was on the latter count I justified the project to my own conscience. What was wrong in taking money from the hated department for propaganda which was anyway doomed to failure? If they weren't paying *me* for the propaganda, then the same money would have gone to someone else – most probably to a convinced ideologist. It seemed preferable that an anti-Communist rather than a pro-Communist should reap the monetary benefits of propaganda which all but a few regarded with contempt. What harm could come of that?"

"I don't know exactly," replied Dagmar, "but since you're so critical of the regime, I'd have thought any involvement with the authorities would be undesirable."

"The pamphlet was published, and then they came and asked me to write another, and they brought along another cheque for the same amount. That's how it began. Since then I've written about ten pamphlets – the last published two months ago. I've made a lot of money. Today, I feel quite indifferent about the whole thing. I regard it all as a sardonic joke on the authorities. I don't feel any scruples over it – I don't think so anyway – not as I did four years ago, when I received the prize for that essay."

Chapter 43

Y ou said earlier you had a bad conscience," said Dagmar.
"I suppose that comes from leading a double life. It's a schizophrenic existence. But of course I try to live up to my real beliefs – to show the world what I am – so no shadow can be cast on my integrity. Can you understand now, Dagmar, why I've behaved as I have?"

"No I can't – it does cast doubt on your integrity. It's a stupid way to behave. In the end, you'll betray yourself, your freedom, and your life. Can't you be discreet – conceal your thoughts and feelings entirely?"

"I cannot! I cannot go so far as to live that kind of lie. I must live freely and let people know what I am," replied Dieter emphatically.

"Why must you always prove yourself to others?   Is that important? For whom are you putting on this act?"

"I don't know – for the students of the University – for everyone who'll listen, I suppose," replied Dieter excitedly.

"Is it for me you're putting on this act, because you're hurt by a bad conscience,?" cried Dagmar.

"What is conscience? I don't exactly understand the reality of its existence," said Dieter evasively.

"Why didn't you tell me any of this before? Why have you only left it all till now?"

"I cannot say. It's just that it never came up in conversation before. But I'm glad you know now. Tell me, Dagmar, what are your thoughts about this episode in my life?"

"Why ask for my thoughts – of what use would they be? I think you were weak in accepting money for that first pamphlet. You shouldn't have done that. You've involved yourself deeply with the authorities. And I think you're wrong to see it as a joke. It's not a joke, and you must know that inside yourself. Politics can never become so trivial as to be a joke. I think you've been foolish, and must bear the burden of guilt. Now do you feel any better that I've acted as your conscience bearer?"

"Thank you anyway."

"And what, may I ask, do your friends think about this 'joke,' as you call it?"

"They share my attitude."

"Then they're either foolish as well, or else they're hiding their real feelings so as not to offend you. And if that's so, then they're not your real friends," said Dagmar.

"It's not that. They're just cynical like me. All of us who live in the DDR are cynical. We've no other choice. We're all unwilling victims of the system."

"And what do your parents think?"

"They take a calm reasonable attitude. They accept the fact that for the next decade or two Communism will be an everyday part of our lives, and that we must learn to live with it as best we can. They think my writing these pamphlets will help in overcoming hindrances – such as class bias – and eventually, it might even help my career."

"The political vet,!" laughed Dagmar.

"You see, our family is a very bourgeois one, and the authorities take an instinctive dislike to us. We must do everything to appease them, to prove our loyalty to the regime."

"How long have your parents been members of the SED,?" enquired Dagmar.

"Since 1948," replied Dietrch. "It was necessary – very necessary for my father's career, so he could continue to receive the financial resources vital for carrying on his scientific research. If he hadn't joined the Party he wouldn't have been able to continue his work independently. He has his own department, and he's supplied by the State with all the facilities he asks for. As far as my father's work's concerned, things couldn't be better. That's why our family hasn't left the DDR."

"Did you join the Young Pioneers at the time when your parents became members of the SED,?" enquired Dagmar.

"No, when my parents joined the SED in 1948, they confided to me it was only as a gesture of expediency. They saw no reason why I should become involved in the political aberrations of the time. I was pleased, for I'd been brought up during the previous three years to loathe everything that Communism meant. In that way, it was a shock when my parents said they were joining the SED, and I could see it was painful to them having to tell me, and I understood and accepted the decision as inevitable, and then they swore me to secrecy never to tell about their real political convictions. I was very young at the time and I kept the promise well. To this day I've spoken to very few people about the political convictions of my parents, and then only to closest friends.

"Perhaps the growth of my loathing for the system stems from the shock and realisation of my parents having to pledge themselves to a political faction they despised, so they could maintain their prestige and source of livelihood. It was a form of political prostitution forced on them, which disgusted me at the time. I was resolved *never* to involve myself in the organisation or activities of any movement remotely connected with the Communist cause."

"How did you first become involved with the Pioneers then,?" enquired Dagmar.

"The school began putting pressure on me to join the Pioneers – as indeed it puts pressure on all pupils – but I refused, and many others refused. Many could claim their parents were critical of them joining the Pioneers, since their parents were members of other incompatible political groups, but I couldn't claim that kind of exemption because my parents were already members of the SED. The teachers especially pressurised me, and frequently they were sarcastic and insulting, because they knew my parents were Communists, but I stubbornly resisted attempts at persuasion. Even at that time I was learning to stand up against the teachers – boldly, arrogantly – to resist their bullying.

"Eventually, they visited my parents, and calmly asked them why I was reluctant to join the Young Pioneers. They said they thought my behaviour strange, illogical – was I ill, or unhappy in my home life, or did I have a maladjusted personality? My parents told them they'd speak to me alone, and the teachers left. My parents asked me to join the Young Pioneers. I refused – I still stubbornly refused, with greater determination than before. I'd seen and felt something of the humiliation my parents had had to endure in being obliged to support the SED, and I told myself that that same thing would never happen to me. I'd fight for my right to freedom and independence at any cost. My parents argued with me but I withstood them, and eventually they gave up trying to persuade me.

"At school the coercion became even greater, but nothing moved me. Then the teachers resorted to ridicule: they made me stand up in the class, and asked awkward questions about my parents and about my political convictions. I replied I was a member of the Evangelical Youth Movement (which I was at the time) and that membership of the Young Pioneers would be incompatible with this. Then they asked me if I was trying to teach my parents to suck eggs by urging them against membership of the SED. Was I a threat to the political beliefs of my parents – would I perhaps bring them round to joining the CDU for example? Of course, the class laughed, although at heart their sympathies were with me rather than with the teachers.

"During these hours when they picked on different pupils trying to persuade them to join the Young Pioneers, there were usually two teachers in the classroom, so they could all the while confer together and quickly work out a line of strategy. They were always trying to catch you off your guard and you had to think fast before giving an answer. They were full of trick questions. I think that's how I first learnt to argue and hold my own when I came up against people who held different opinions from mine. On one occasion they even exposed me to ridicule in front of the entire school – together with other pre-selected pupils.

"Then the teachers visited my parents again, only this time they were more insistent. My parents tried to force me into the Young Pioneers, and we argued and quarrelled. I said membership of the Pioneers was incompatible with the Evangelical Youth Movement. My parents had to accept that explanation, but since that time, the relationship between us has remained difficult."

"Why – how do your mean,?" enquired Dagmar.

"Our way of thinking and attitude towards the authorities is different," replied Dietrich. "My parents are more inclined to remain by the letter if not by the spirit of the law – more discreet perhaps. I, on the other hand, am rebellious by nature. I cannot conceal my thoughts and convictions for very long. Perhaps the tension between us only reflects the contrast between youth and age. My parents are elderly – they're quiet retiring people. Naturally, I still express the exuberance of youth."

"But your exuberance might have endangered the status of your parents," suggested Dagmar.

"I don't know – perhaps in a small way," replied Dieter thoughtfully, "but I was determined against my parents persuading me to do something which inside themselves I knew they disliked my doing. At one time they had told me that my political involvement with the State would be unnecessary, and now they were playing a different tune – just because of a visit by a couple of school teachers. That's what I resented! However, after that second visit I might even have been persuaded to join the Young Pioneers had it not been for my active membership in the Evangelical Youth Movement."

"How did you come eventually to join the Pioneers then,?" asked Dagmar.

"It came as a result of two incidents. One day in 1952, ten pupils in our class were suddenly called to the headmaster's study. We weren't told what it was about, but as we left the classroom, we guessed it was in connection with our refusal to join the Pioneers, because it seemed as if all of us were non-members. Then suddenly we thought it couldn't be that, because when we glanced round, we found that in fact two of our number already belonged to the Pioneers. We felt anxious, naturally, because it was in the middle of the morning and one of the other teachers had come into the classroom to interrupt the lesson to pass on the message. He had seemed very grim, and we knew the interruption boded no good.

"On arriving at the headmaster's study, our surprise was even greater. On the table in the middle of the room lay a number of blank forms – they were laid all round the table, and there was a chair in front of each – and standing by the headmaster's desk was a green uniformed official. He looked very serious. Clearly something was up. For a moment I thought we were all to be arrested as provocateurs or for some other offence we'd committed. Then the headmaster spoke. He reminded us we were all members of the Evangelical Youth Movement. He said we were being called upon to renounce our membership of the Youth Movement, and that we must accordingly sign the statement laid out on the table confirming this as a promise. He said the police official would sign beneath each of our names as a witness to the statements. We were so astonished, we were stunned into silence, although we knew the relationship between the Church and State had been tense for quite some time.

"Then came the more astonishing part – the threat. The headmaster said if we refused to sign the statements and accept their conditions, then we should be expelled forthwith. We should be permitted to say farewell to our peers, and should then have to sign over all our text books to the chief monitor, and then leave the premises with an injunction laid against our returning to the buildings at any time in the future. Our education would be finished, and we'd be obliged to find whatever employment our present qualifications permitted. We were astonished – we couldn't believe it. The headmaster had spoken so calmly – almost benignly – as if congratulating us on something we'd done – that we were stunned into silence. But what could we do? Only throw up our hands despairingly and sign the statement. It was towards the end of our schooling, and we were studying for important exams to enter university. If we refused to sign the statements on grounds of principle, then our prospects for the future would be in ruins. That morning, pupils from the other top classes in the school were similarly ordered into the headmaster's study to sign the same statement. Eleven pupils in the school (eight of them girls) refused to sign – although we tried to persuade them to think again – and therefore, they were expelled that afternoon."

"Fourteen pupils were expelled from our school for refusing to sign the statement," said Dagmar.

"At that time, over two thousand pupils were expelled from schools in every part of the Democratic Republic," added Dieter.

"Did you join the Pioneers then?"

"No, I still refused to do that. But as you must remember, things began to get more and more difficult for young people in the DDR. The FDJ began an intensive campaign to win over the youth of Germany, and when it failed, they turned to terror tactics, beating up youths wearing the silver buttonhole of the German Evangelical Church, and wrecking church services by acts of hooliganism. Then the State began a process of direct persecution of the Church, seizing church property and arresting pastors and prominent laymen in every part of the country. At that time I began to give up hope for everything in the DDR. It seemed as if freedom of thought and speech would be banished forever. The country was undergoing a process of intensive Sovietisation. Also, I felt a bad conscience about having signed the statement, although I fully realised it was an action I could not have avoided. At that time I had reached the lowest ebb of depression.

"Then in April 1953, my conscience was set at rest somewhat, and my hopes for the future of Germany revived. Our bishop of Berlin and Brandenburg, Dr. Dibelius, published a letter addressed to the youth of the DDR. Even today I still remember some of the words of that letter. He said, 'The work of the Youth Groups goes on. I greet those who have remained firm in difficult times. To those from whom signatures have been extorted, I say this: God's forgiveness is greater than human failings. Extorted signatures have no validity in his eyes. God knows your consciences have every reason to be clear.'

"Those words set my mind at rest – I felt free. Then they set me towards a new way of thinking. How far would my guilt extend if I adhered to the letter but not to the spirit of the authorities? The question disturbed me for a few weeks, until I worked out my own answer. It seemed to me, that in a State where the rule of law had become non-existent – where the illegal was legal – surely justified no call on the allegiance of the individual. The fact that the illegal had become legal, surely rendered all oaths – and obligations even – to the State invalid, since government was no longer operating with the consent of the people. That was my reasoning, anyway."

"That was a new and striking way of viewing our difficulties in the DDR," said Dagmar. "Did that come from reading too much philosophy?"

"No, that was long before I began to read philosophy," replied Dieter abruptly. "Meanwhile, the school authorities were still trying to persuade me to join the Pioneers, and their pressure became more intense than ever. At last, I relented, and that was at the end of Spring 1953. As soon as I was in the Movement the leaders began to ensure that my membership would be active. I had to go on hikes, take part in forest games, participate in drill exercises and undergo semi-military training at a shooting range just beyond the zone frontier. I think the leaders were gloating over the fact of having at last got me into the Movement despite my earlier scruples. A few weeks beforehand I would have felt very angry about that, and would have resented being forced to participate in all their nonsense, and childish activities and the military training; but by now I didn't care what I did – I felt my will was no longer my own.

"Then came that day in June – the day that for many of us must have been the happiest and the unhappiest – and yet most memorable in our lives."

"The day of the Seventeenth,!" exclaimed Dagmar.

"The morning before I had been in the city centre. I had passed through Alexander Platz, and when I saw thousands of marching workers chanting in chorus, 'Berliners join our ranks; we don't want to be slaves,!' the sight was unbelievable. Somebody beside me asked, 'On whose instructions is this demonstration being held,?' and then somebody answered, 'This isn't a demonstration on instructions from the government, but a demonstration *against* the government.' It was almost too good to be true. And then the demonstrators' loudspeaker van, which they seized from the police, drove into the square announcing a general strike for tomorrow, and a mass meeting in Strausberger Platz, Stalin Allee."

"I remember when the news reached our school late that morning," said Dagmar eagerly. "We all made a bonfire of our Pioneer membership cards in the playground, and were so excited, we refused to attend lessons."

"At home-time we held a sing-song in the school hall," said Dieter, "and refused to go away. The masters tried to silence us and clear us out of the hall. We sang all the louder and refused to move. We were so happy! Then our history master – the graduate in Marxist philosophy – that despicable little man – climbed onto a table and began making a speech about the importance of loyalty to the great Communist cause, and the danger of spoiling the relationship with our beloved Soviet brothers, for whom we had to thank for our enlightenment and liberation. Do you know what happened then?"

"No."

"Four boys from our class moved over to the table, lifted him by the legs and arms, and carried him to the end of the hall. He started yelling but no one came to his rescue. We all laughed. Then he was thrown through a closed first floor window, and we set up a thunderous applause, stamping our feet on the floor, clapping and shouting."

"It must have been like that incident which set off the Thirty Years War," laughed Dagmar. "And what happened to him?"

"He was lucky. He escaped with a superficial cut across the back of his neck, and a broken ankle and fractured arm."

"A close shave," exclaimed Dagmar.

"And when I arrived home that night I received more news about the strike from my parents. The radio in the American sector had published a news bulletin and commentary on the day's events. The programme was heard throughout the entire Soviet zone. That evening we drank wine and I lay awake all night. I was up at four the following morning, and by six-thirty I was in Strausberger Platz – and even then it was crowded."

"The Art Shop where I work is in Strausberger Platz," interrupted Dagmar excitedly.

"The day was dull and it began to rain, but nothing could subdue our spirits," continued Dieter. "There were thousands of us there, and we began to sing. Nothing could suppress our exultation. It seemed as if the day of revolution had arrived. Our liberation from tyranny was guaranteed! Everywhere, the general strike was on!"

"It was our greatest day," exclaimed Dagmar. "It was the only time in my life when I've ever seen Papa drunk. Not even mamma had ever known Papa drunk before – not in all the years of their marriage."

"Did you go to the city centre?"

"No, we remained in Treptow, but Papa, Gisela and I watched the march of the nine thousand workers from the Stalin Electric Motor Factory, as they passed through Treptow on their way to the centre. Each of us carried flowers, which Papa had bought the night before in Graetz Strasse, and we threw them at the workers. That was very early in the morning. Mamma and Papa hadn't gone to bed at all the night before. They were listening to the West Berlin radio."

"Then we formed up in Strausberger Platz and began our march to the House of Ministries in Leipziger Strasse to present our petition to the government. On arriving there, a crowd of khaki-clad Barrack police swarmed out of the building and cordoned off the entrance. They had been waiting for us. A few seconds later, a half-dozen police trucks swept round another corner and came to a halt. Several hundred blue-uniformed civil police jumped out and formed a line across the street. The march continued, and moments later, truncheons were drawn and fighting began.   Some of our number were captured and carried away in handcuffs, and many more fell wounded to the ground.

"I was not in front of the marching column, and had been out of the fighting. A number of us moved round to the back of the building to try and force an entrance there, but it was too heavily guarded. Then we heard a great roar of engines, and armoured cars followed by truck loads of steel helmeted infantry appeared from all directions. The Red Army had arrived! Driving slowly they began to break up the crowd. Our chances of demonstrating in front of the House of Ministries had to be abandoned. We were broken up into small groups. We had to be united – to feel our strength in numbers.

"Then the word went round we were to re-assemble in Marx-Engels Platz.   Thousands of us left Leipziger Strasse. On arriving in Marx-Engels Platz, I was in the crowd amongst the first few thousand. But soon the square was filled. There came ten thousand men from Henningsdorf who had first assembled in the Walter Ulbricht Stadium in Chaussee Strasse, and then came another procession from Stalin Allee – twenty thousand men and women, their leaders carrying black, red and gold flags adorned with flowers. It was a wonderful sight! All of us were inspired! By midday there were fifty thousand of us in the square, and we felt our solidarity, although it was difficult for us to hear the hoarse voices of the successive speakers from the tribune.

"Then, suddenly from a side street we heard a deafening row of engines and vibrating steel. We were startled, and taken unawares. A movement of terror and confusion passed through the crowd. More armoured cars and steel helmeted divisions of infantry were not enough to repel a crowd of unarmed workers. It had to be tanks! The next moment, the worst had happened.   Wild panic seized the fifty thousand. Everywhere, there were yells of pain and screams of terror. For a moment I saw nothing – only wild confusion – and legs and arms moving frantically in all directions, and an expression which seemed to be imprinted on the faces of the crowd of a perpetual scream – like something from a Munch lithograph. There were bodies laid helplessly on the ground – bodies which would never rise again – and there were hundreds climbing, jumping and running over the shoulders of others. We all had only one thought in our minds: Escape; and only one instinct rushed through our minds, the instinct for self-preservation. During those few seconds, nothing else had meaning.

"Six Red Army tanks, lined up abreast, were charging us at full speed. There was no mercy in their endeavour to crush our bodies beneath their tracks, and there was no escape for the slow-footed or for those who had already fallen. All was finished! We fled in all directions, and in a few seconds the Marx-Engels Platz was cleared. Then the tanks changed direction, tearing up the paving stones beneath their tracks as they did so, and pursued a great section of the crowd down the Unter den Linden.

"At the corner of the Unter den Linden and the Marx-Engels Platz I saw a crowd standing over something in the middle of the roadway. I pushed my way through the crowd to the centre – as one does when confronted by a startling event. There was a long flattened piece of red cloth on the roadway, and a stink which was foul, and a pair of shoes which had been flattened like paper. At first I couldn't recognise what it was. Then I saw the face of a man. The face was thick with congealed blood – the eyes had come out of their sockets and the mouth had been distorted into an expression of agony. The back of the skull had been crushed and a grey mass lay on the road. A single severed arm lay nearby the flattened cloth. The fingers were tense and outstretched as if grasping for life. Nothing else remained – nothing! It was hideous – the mangled remains of a dead man – an image I'll never erase as long as I live.

"My body quivered with anger; a feelding of fury filled body and soul. We were all seized with a great rage. Our hearts cried out for the justice we'd been denied for so long. A section of the crowd took up stones and broken rubble left in the wake of the turning tanks, and running down the Unter den Linden, they attacked the tanks in their fury. Several jumped onto the turrets of the tanks and tried to tear off the radio masts. Several workers fixed together two pieces of wood and laid a cross over the dead man.

"I went down the Unter den Linden towards the Brandenburg Gate. I vowed a resolution I'd never break. I'd never surrender to the tyrants destroying our people. I'd live the life of a rebel as long as I was obliged to remain in the DDR. I felt I owed that oath as an obligation to those others who were to lay down their lives in the defence of freedom during the East German Uprising. They had laid down their lives for us and their offspring, that we might live in freedom. Was it right we should betray them by surrendering finally to the hated regime they had sought to destroy?

"I reached the end of the Unter den Linden. A great crowd was standing beneath the Brandenburg Gate, glancing upwards, anxiously – tensely. Three school kids were climbing the Gate. They were brave youngsters. They reached the top of the Gate. Suddenly, someone cried, 'Come down, they've got a machine gun trained on you from the Hotel Adlon!' The kids lay flat on their stomachs, and took out their pocket knives and began hacking at the tough cord, which held the Red Flag onto the mast on the centre of the Gate. The cord snapped, and they took the flag, and they stood upright on the Gate. Someone cried, 'Lie down, they'll shoot you,!" but the kids laughed and turned towards the government buildings, and waved the flag insultingly, as if waving a last farewell to the tyranny of the regime. They were brave youngsters, they were young heroes, and they knew it. They dropped the flag to the crowd below, and began to descend from the Gate. The crowd cheered; and tore the flag to shreds in a glorious tug-of-war.

"Another crowd of demonstrators marched up to the Gate and someone sent up the cry to march through the city. The column began to march down the Chaussee Allee – now renamed the Street of the 17th June. Several cars followed behind the column. The rumour spread that the cars carried Russian and East German agents, and the workers angrily crowded round the vehicles and threatened to turn them over, but suddenly, they saw a small Union Jack on the windscreen of one, and the demonstrators set up a thunderous applause. The cars were carrying Western journalists covering the story of the workers' struggle for freedom. I marched a little way with the workers, and then decided to return to the House of Ministries to see if the workers had re-assembled around the building.

"I walked down Ebert Strasse and on reaching Potsdamer Platz, there was a great crowd, and a propaganda booth was in flames, but across the square was a bigger fire. Thick black smoke was pouring from the windows of the vast Warenhaus building which had stood empty since Western purchases were banned there.

"I reached Leipziger Strasse. The strikers had strengthened their numbers, and forced the police cordon round the House of Ministries to withdraw several metres, but by this time the armoured cars were re-enforced by tanks. The tanks drove through Leipziger Strasse, and then turned in their tracks, forming up into a great panzer division, standing close together as an invincible phalanx which could never be pierced. All round was a deafening din, the ear-drum breaking roar of the tanks, and the shouts of thousands of workers crying for government leaders to address the people. 'Where is Ulbricht, Where is Pieck, Where is Grotewohl,?' they were crying. 'Why are they locking themselves behind closed doors? Why don't they make their appearance before the people?'

"Then a Russian officer stood up in the turret of his tank and ordered the police to advance. They were met by a hail of stones and were stopped short. Then a worker, stepped in front of the tanks, his hand raised in a gesture of supplication. Other men stepped forward also. 'We are unarmed and helpless,' they cried. 'We ask only for justice.' – 'We ask only for a free and secret election,' cried the first man. The Russian officers just smiled at one another in incomprehension. This was the funniest joke that they had heard! What were free elections? A moment later, there was a shriek of machine gun fire. Dozens of bodies were sprawled over the roadway, and yells of agony from the wounded and dying, as their limbs kicked and struggled in final death throes, pierced all other sounds. Their bodies sprawled and slipped in pools of blood, which gushed from frightful wounds and their mouths bit frantically at the dust and rubble in the roadway. The sight was terrible!

"I saw whiffs of smoke from the guns of the tanks, and the air was filled with the smell of powder. Thousands fled for their lives amidst the ruins all around. The tanks began to advance. There was no mercy for the helplessly wounded. I thought I saw several women throw up their hands in a gesture of surrender, and throw themselves beneath the tracks of the tanks. Smiling, the Russian officers still stood bravely in the turrets of their advancing tanks. I didn't stop or glance round to see any more. I fled to the rubble and ruins, away from the street.

"But the battle was not over! The fever pitch of our anger had yet to reach its apex. Someone gave the order to rally, and we advanced again. We grasped whatever we could from the heaps of rubble: stones, scrap iron, pieces of wood – anything we could find. Moments later, thousands of us descended into Leipziger Strasse. Some linked arms and advanced in line in front of the tanks, many jumped onto the tanks themselves, and the 'brave' Russian officers were terror stricken, and disappeared beneath the turrets, securing the safety hatches above them. Some thrust chunks of wood into the tanks' gun barrels, others tried to jam the tanks' tracks mechanism with pieces of scrap iron, whilst others tried to break off the radio aerials. We fought bravely, but it was a losing battle. The shells continued to boom from the tanks, and the scream of machine gun fire came from all directions. But we had won our courage. Bullets whizzed passed our ears and ricocheted off the stonework around. A half-dozen fires flared up from the ruins, where the shells of the tanks had exploded. Finally, we were driven back. We could do nothing more to resist, only choose to die bravely before the guns.

"I left Leipziger Strasse and went to see what was happening in other parts of the city. I arrived in Alexander Platz. The square was filled with thousands of demonstrators. Four police trucks had been overturned and were blazing. Someone said the Police Presidium had been stormed, and that armed sentries with fixed bayonets had been disarmed and their weapons smashed on the kerbside. The police had counter-attacked with fire hoses, but they'd been driven back. At that moment, many army trucks came into view at one end of the square. Hundreds of Red Army infantrymen jumped down from the trucks and began to take up positions. They were received with a hail of stones. The troops formed up into a line, and slowly marching forward and firing their rifles at the crowd, they began to clear the square. Within seconds the square was deserted, except for the dying and wounded, as we fled to the shelter of the surrounding ruins.

"Then a feeling of great anger and despair set in. By now it was mid-afternoon, and I wandered round Berlin, and everywhere the streets and squares were deserted, and everywhere tanks and troop units had taken up positions. The Red Army had won the day! That was the day of the 17th June. That was the day which will go down as the most courageous and most glorious in the annals of unarmed people power resistance. That was the day when the armed forces of the Soviet Union combined - infantry, armoured car divisions and tank units – into a mighty force to crush mercilessly eighteen million unarmed Germans pleading for basic civil rights."

"It was a terrible defeat," murmured Dagmar.

"Now you can understand the true meaning of my hatred for the system," said Dieter. "I've lived through and seen the worst. With my own eyes I've seen innocent unarmed men shot down in the streets. I've seen the dead and dying who've laid down their lives for the freedom of our country. Will the fate of history decide that the struggle of these men and women was in vain? Is their memory to perish with their bones? Are we to dishonour their memory and the cause for which they died by surrendering our struggle against oppression? Never! One day we'll re-fight the day of the 17th, and the names of these men and women shall be on our lips, and their memory shall live forever, and serve as a beacon of freedom to peoples everywhere."

"I hope that one day we'll be free of Russian oppression," said Dagmar. "It's terrible when one thinks of the crimes against humanity they've inflicted on us and other peoples."

"It's the doctrine of the system which is to blame," said Dieter. "It's easy to hate the Russians as a people, but that's wrong and I think we must avoid it. We must hate only the 'system' and blame that for all the evils. It's the false intellectual creed which has brought about these ills. Rarely has such a political doctrine brought such devastation to humanity – and most of all to the Russian peoples themselves."

"And to think we're supposed to be living in the 'Model' society. That's what they keep telling us. The German Democratic Republic – the 'Model' for the future."

"It's a model for the future as the Communists see it. According to the pseudo-scientific theories of Marxist-Leninist dialectics, we *are* living in the seminally perfect society. The Communist isn't concerned with empirical reality, he's only concerned with matching up hope with his own particular system of myth-making. So now, Dagmar, you can understand why I am as I am."

"I can understand your mind and the shock at the things you've been through, and I admire your courage," replied Dagmar. "But despite that, I still think you've been reckless and foolish during recent weeks."

"Perhaps I've been fighting an internal battle with my own conscience," said Dieter thoughtfully.

"I can understand you must have suffered," said Dagmar. "So many conflicting things have been put in your path. Things that have been forced upon you."

"Here in the DDR things that we loathe are forced upon us all."

"Dieter, I want you to know that I hold nothing against you because of what may have happened in your past," said Dagmar softly, placing her hand on his. "I want you to feel free inside yourself. I want to help you through difficulties which may worry or hurt you. In return, I ask only one thing of you: that you will be more discreet and sensible in your behaviour than you have been during the past weeks."

BOOK XI

The Lovers' Plan

Love is not love
Which alters when it alteration finds,
Or bends with the remover to remove:
O, no! it is an ever-fixéd mark
That looks on tempests and is never shaken;
It is the star to every wandering bark,
Whose worth's unknown, although his height
be taken.

Shakespeare, *Sonnet*, No. cxvi.

Chapter 44

On the following Wednesday when Dieter met Dagmar in the city centre, he was in a cheerful optimistic mood, and after they had eaten, he took her hands into his and announced that his parents had invited her to their home in Werlsee. He would meet her next Saturday afternoon after she had finished work in Stalin Allee, and then drive her to his parents' home. Dagmar expressed her joy on receiving this welcome invitation, saying that visiting Werlsee would be "*Schön!*"

The good Frau Renot received the news of the invitation with even more pleasure than her daughter, and certainly expressed greater concern as to the preparations necessary for the visit. There was an argument between mother and daughter as to what dress should be worn. The good Frau wanted her to wear a green party frock, but Dagmar said that she wanted to wear a dress she could also wear in the shop. Her mother said that Dagmar didn't possess a dress suitable for both occasions. Dagmar suggested she wear a new tartan skirt she had – it was very colourful and neat – and a white blouse with her grey cardigan, and she would look very smart and homely in that. Her mother insisted she must wear something more colourful and elegant, as this was such a special occasion – and she was in all probability visting a very elegant home.

"Remember, they'll be seeing you for the first time," said the good Frau, "and first impressions always count most."

"But I don't want to change in the shop Mamma," replied Dagmar screwing up her nose. "It's so small at the back, and perhaps the proprietor wouldn't like it, and I've only been there for three months."

"Nonsense, Dagmar, of course the proprietor wouldn't mind," said her mother. "Just tell him you're going to a party. Every girl's invited to a party sometime on a Saturday, and I'm sure the proprietor would be delighted to see you in your party frock."

Eventually, Dagmar was persuaded into wearing the party frock which she would have to change into at her work place.

No doubt the good Frau regarded the invitation as a significant prognostication of her daughter's future. She now felt even more insistent that Dieter should come and visit the family in Graetz Strasse. He could come on Saturday week. For five months Dagmar had been going out regularly with the boy Dietrich. Papa Renot, meanwhile, was accepting everything calmly, rarely commenting on his daughter's friendship with Dieter.

As the car sped down Fürstenwalder Allee towards the zone frontier, that Saturday afternoon, Dietrich began to tell Dagmar something more about his parents. It was a cold Autumn day and there was grey low-hanging cloud, and a mist in the air which made the atmosphere damp and depressing. It was one of those sad strangely haunting days in late Autumn which often casts the mind into a reflective mood, and the beauty of nature is not entirely bereft of its finery, and russet colours still bedeck the trees. The car sped through the village of Rahnsdorf and into the forest again, and the mist concealed the view of the long straight roadway beyond a distance of a hundred metres or so.

"You must understand my parents are quite elderly," said Dieter apologetically.

"Elderly,?" repeated Dagmar, wondering to herself as to what Dieter meant.

"My father is in his mid-seventies and my mother's just on sixty," he explained. "I suppose my father is old enough to be my grandparent."

"Why do you tell me this,?" asked Dagmar.

"You'll probably find them a little old fashioned," continued Dieter as if Dagmar had not spoken.

"I think it's rather nice to be old fashioned," said Dagmar reassuringly. "Old fashioned people are rather charming."

"They've seen better days. They live very much apart from the rest of the world."

"So do my parents – and so do many people in the DDR," answered Dagmar.

"My mother hardly ever leaves the grounds of the house even," said Dieter. "You see, she's partly crippled. She had polio about twenty years ago, and she's paralysed in one leg. She finds it difficult to move around."

"I'm sorry to hear that," replied Dagmar.

"A good neighbour comes in to do most of the shopping for us and help clean the house. The house is quite large to manage."

"Does your family live there alone?"

"Yes."

"You're lucky then," said Dagmar, "to have so much space for yourselves, when there are still so many people in Berlin living in such terrible conditions."

"We're very lucky – and highly privileged. For more than ten years after the War we had Russian officers billeted in the house – usually junior staff officers who were sent on special missions to Berlin, who only stayed in the city for two or three months. Officially, part of the house is still supposed to be kept ready for visting missions of the Russian Army, but we haven't had anyone in for more than a year now."

"Isn't that inconvenient for your parents to have troops billeted in the house?"

"We were confined to a small part of the house, but they brought their own kitchen staff and other servants with them – usually local people hired from the village – and so the house was kept clean and in good order. We're fortunate to have the house still in our possession. Many people who owned similar houses had their property requisitioned and were turned out and obliged to find other accommodation."

"I look forward to seeing the house."

"We have a large collection of antiques to show you also – most were acquired by my grandfather many years ago."

As the car sped towards the East, four uniformed figures with machine guns slung behind their shoulders and a barrier set across the way, emerged out of the mist, at the end of the long straight roadway. The figures loomed larger, until the car drove up to the barrier and braked. A Vopo stepped forward asking for identity passes of the occupants of the car. Dieter and Dagmar had reached the zonal boundary of Berlin. The young Vopo was known to Dieter, and the latter saluted him with a friendly gesture as he opened the window of the car and handed out the documents. The police official mumbled something in reply but remained as stiff as a poker. He glanced only superficially at Dieter's pass, but he bent down and looked inside the car when comparing Dagmar's photo with her original self. At last, he handed back the passes, instructed a colleague to raise the barrier, and waved the car on.

The car left the city of Berlin passing through a built up area.

"This is Erkner," said Dieter.

They passed down the Berliner Strasse, turned right and drove down the main street of the town, turning left at the Grosse Hauptmann Strasse.

"It's beautiful," exclaimed Dagmar.

The car left the town, drove for two kilometres through the forest again, crossed an autobahn, and then turned down a narrow unpaved lane which Dieter drove along at crawling pace, bumping over stones and potholes, for several hundred metres. Eventually, the trees gave way and the car passed by a wicker fence and a low hedge, and the vehicle braked alongside a pair of impressive gate posts.

"We're here," announced Dieter.

"How romantic," exclaimed Dagmar, craning forward her neck, her eyes lighting up with pleasure as she glanced through the gate posts and over the wicker fence to the garden and house beyond.

"As you can see, today nothing is very well kept outside," said Dieter. "Grass and weeds have overgrown everywhere, and the house has lost some of its former glory."

"But it's so wild and romantic – and right in the middle of the forest," said Dagmar.

A sandy gravel drive led from the gateway to the front entrance, where it divided left and right, passing along the front of the house and turning towards the back of the building. On either side of the drive was a lawn thickly overgrown with grass, and some small flower beds, and bushes which had been planted at random on the lawn.

The house was a long two-storied structure, not very high, built in typical early 19th century Prussian style. It was devoid of decoration, and the windows were simple square formations cut into the walls of the building, and the door was plain wood, with two low steps leading up to it and supported on either side by stone square pillars built into the wall. There was a black slate roof and two simple grey stone chimneys. On the left of the building was a small gothic tower with Romanesque arched windows. The walls of the house had an ochre tinted rendering, which in parts had crumbled away to reveal yellow brickwork beneath. In its simplicity, and surrounded as it was by high trees and wild vegetation, the house was homely in appearance.

The most impressive part of the property were perhaps the two gate posts leading into the garden. They were tall square posts covered with ornamental baroque plasterwork, surmounted by two savage looking eagles with wings outstretched, the claws of their feet gripping onto stone orbs which bore their weight, and their fangs were bared as they turned towards one another. The eagles had been cut from grey stone and painted black, and looked as if they might any moment take flight and engage each other in combat, although this was not to conceal the fact that both were damaged. Two small wooden gates connected the posts.

Dagmar expressed regret that the eagles were damaged.

"That happened about eight years ago," explained Dieter sadly. "One New Year's Even, a party of Russian officers arrived back here in the early hours of the morning, blind drunk, and began throwing stones at the eagles. They made enough row to awaken the dead. My father climbed out of bed and came into the garden and tried to quieten them, but they were so full of alcohol as to be uncontrollable. As you can see, the left eagle lost one of its wings, and the eagle on the right had the plumage knocked off its breast."

"They should have flown away," joked Dagmar.

"But they couldn't; they were made of stone," answered Dieter humourlessly. "Naturally, my father was furious – but he couldn't do anything, but just stand there and shout – and there were two lieutenant-colonels amongst them."

Dieter left the car and opened the gates and as he returned to the vehicle, he said: "Before the War, we had fine wrought iron gates, and high railings surrounding the property, but they were taken away to help with the War effort. The wicker fence and these gates were only put up a few years ago. When the Russians were billeted here, we were confined to living in that tower over on the left."

The car drove to the end of the drive, turning right before moving towards the back of the building. It was driven into a garage at the side of the building which originally had been stables. The back wall of the house was strangely decorated by an ornamentation not uncommon in Brandenburg houses of that period: broken pieces of Grecian frieze, pottery and mosaic, etc., being fixed onto the wall, pressed into plaster, in an odd assortment without any attempt at producing a unified design.

Dieter and Dagmar walked to the front of the house, hand in hand, smiling and laughing happily, and entered by the heavy plain oak door with its black iron knocker and large lock. Inside, the hall was dark and the ceiling low. There came the sound of voices in conversation from an adjoining room on the left and the door from the hallway was left ajar. Dieter took Dagmar's coat and hung it on the hallstand. The walls of the hall had dark panelling; and swords, spears and old fashioned firing weapons were hung around the walls, as well as oil paintings and a tapestry.

"It's beautiful," whispered Dagmar.

Dieter led Dagmar through the door on the left into a spacious living room, lavishly decorated with antiques and bric-a-brac, and a log fire was burning at one end, around which four people were seated in comfortable armchairs. Dagmar was introduced to Frau and Dr. Liebermann and then to a Dr. Goltz and his wife.

Dagmar was stunningly attractive that afternoon in her green party frock and long silky golden hair, and after the compliments and curtseyings, the company sat down, and for some minutes, she became the centre of attention. Dr. Goltz was enlivened by the young company, and began to flatter Dagmar and congratulate Dieter on his taste for "girls," in terms which raised laughter and embarrassed Dagmar.

He was a short plump man in his fifties with thinning red hair, and a round shiny face with bright blue eyes. He spoke quickly, dominating the conversation, and when he laughed, he slapped his knees and displayed a mouthful of gold-crowned teeth. Soon the conversation turned from Dagmar to other matters: to the work in the hospital and to the outcome of some recent laboratory experiments, and Frau Liebermann meanwhile turned to Dagmar, speaking to her with a motherly consideration.

Dr. Liebermann was a tall thin man with grey hair and a quiet retiring manner, and occasionally, he glanced with a disapproving countenance at his son, and Dagmar thought to herself that perhaps a divergence of personalities had divided father from son. Then Frau Liebermann, in a confidential tone, leaned towards Dieter saying that his father was displeased with him.

"Why,?" asked Dieter surprised.

"I don't know exactly – something to do with the University, I think," replied his mother.

Dieter threw up his hands and pursed his lips in indicating his ignorance of what might be the matter.

At last Frau Liebermann rose from her chair with the aid of her stick, saying she would prepare tea, and with apologies, Dr. Goltz said that he and his wife would be leaving as they had only made a surprise visit, but Frau Liebermann insisted they remain for refreshments, and after a short altercation this was agreed. There was a lull in the conversation after Frau Liebermann had left the room, and then her husband rose from his chair and turning to his son said he wished to speak with him privately in the study.

"What's the matter, Papa,?" replied Dieter concerned.

"It's in connection with something one of your professors has drawn to my attention," said his father.

Dieter followed his father to a small door at the end of the room which led into the study, and the door was closed behind them.

Dagmar experienced a feeling of awkwardness, but this was relieved by Dr. Goltz who engaged her in polite conversation as a distraction from the anxiety arising from father and son. As Dagmar conversed with her new acquaintance, she could not avoid overhearing the voices from the adjoining room.

"What's the meaning of this cartoon,?" asked the father gruffly.

"This cartoon – how did you get it, Papa,?" exclaimed Dieter in astonishment.

"Never mind how I got it – what's the meaning of if,?" exclaimed the father more angrily still.

"What do you mean by 'What's the meaning of it?' It's a cartoon, that's all."

"That's not all,!" replied the father. "This cartoon was found pinned in a lecture hall in the University. There are witnesses who say you drew it during a lecture on anatomy, and that you pinned it up in the hall at the end of the session."

"Impossible Papa!"

"Not impossible!"

"No one saw me draw this cartoon except for a couple of friends sitting on either side, and certainly no one saw me pin it in the lecture hall because there was no one there at the time."

"There are witnesses who said you did, and that's enough."

"What witnesses? How did you come by this cartoon anyway Papa?"

"Professor Buchholz handed it to me this morning. It was given him by a student yesterday who said you had drawn and pinned up the cartoon. Professor Buchholz wouldn't tell me the name of the student, but only said he was a committed FDJ member. The student warned the professor to have you put firmly in your place, or else trouble would follow."

"Ach! It's *quatsch*, Papa."

"It's not *quatsch*, because the student threatened both the professor and you as implicated in libelling the State. So you're not alone in this."

"I can't think who the student might be," exclaimed Dieter.

"Of course you can't. You don't think informers make themselves known, do you?"

"I can't see it's anything to get excited about."

"Not to get excited about? People have been shot for lesser misdemeanours than this."

"Ach, *quatsch*, Papa! Don't start speaking about misdemeanours like a Communist confessor."

"It's obscene and scurrilous! This man is a leading personality in the DDR. To think you've been lampooning him in this disgusting manner! Walter Ulbricht, Secretary-General of the SED, is the *one* man who must remain untouchable in the DDR."

"So what! Who loves Ulbricht,?" exclaimed Dieter.

"That's not the point."

"It's straight criticism, that's all."

"That's not the way to criticise the regime, or anything else for that matter."

"There are very few ways in this country to express any kind of criticism."

"Why bother to criticise? We're all Communists in this household, and we've got to maintain that front, come what may."

"Please Papa, don't start one of those lectures again."

"In the world of today, we must learn to think one way and act another. My God, hasn't the history of the last twenty-five years taught us that lesson?"

"That's where we differ, Papa."

"So be it! But your life's as much committed to the regime as mine, and as long as you continue living under this roof, you keep up the front of being a 'Good Comrade,' if not for your sake, then at least for mine and your mother's. I've no intention of losing hard won privileges and special work concessions just because of the gross foolishness and student pranks of my son. Is that clearly understood?"

"Yes, Papa."

"My God, I hope so. We enjoy a life-style infinitely better than the majority, but it's only on the sufferance of those who rule over us. Let there be no recurrence of an incident like this. The cartoon, naturally, must be destroyed," and there came the sound of tearing paper.

The door of the study was flung open, and Dieter re-emerged into the sitting room, his face flushed. Dagmar turned away from Dr. Goltz, to whom she had been feigning to listen, although she had not registered a word he had said, and glanced up at Dieter. Dieter put on a cheerful countenance, passed some pleasant remarks to the company present, sat down, and engaged the four of them in a lively conversation as if intent on quickly ensuring that the episode which had passed in the study would be quickly forgotten.

Dr. Liebermann remained in the study, and when he re-emerged about five minutes later, his wife came into the room, wheeling a trolley and tea was served.

"Dieter – I forgot to give it to you before – but this letter came for you this morning after you left," said Frau Liebermann taking up an envelope on the trolley.

"Thank you, Mamma," replied Dieter taking the letter and there was a suggestion of concern in his voice, and momentarily, he made as if to conceal the envelope.

"It looks an official letter," replied his mother.

Changing his mind, Dieter tore open the envelope and read its contents. His face dropped.

"It's from the Ministry of Defence," he exclaimed as he scanned the letter. "'Through the authority of the Secretary of State for High School and College Education, Order 113, for Student Military

Education, Dietrich Liebermann is obliged to report on the date given below, to the undermentioned unit for territorial training in the National People's Army.' Such time-wasting rubbish,!" he cursed beneath his breath.

Dagmar and Frau Liebermann consoled him by pointing out the insignificance of having to serve in the Volksarmee, and that many other students like himself would also be in the same boat.

"But it's all illegal in international law – as laid down by the four occupying powers," said Dietrich. "It's forbidden to raise an armed force of Germans in the Free City of Berlin. There's no West German Army in the West sectors of the city – in the Federal Republic they won't even allow a West German soldier to cross by rail to Berlin."

"You needn't bother your mind about that," replied Dr. Liebermann. "It's not illegal for you to be in the Volksarmee. We live in the East zone, not in Berlin."

The conversation turned to more agreeable topics and after tea Dr. Liebermann asked Dagmar if she would like to be shown the antiquities and old masterpieces in the house. Dagmar, who had been glancing curiously round the room, responded with enthusiasm, and the two left for their conducted tour accompanied by Dieter.

It was apparent Dr. Liebermann soon took a liking to the fair Berlinerin, and as he described an exhibit or as to how it had come into his possession, he edged towards her, speaking intimately, in affectionate fatherly terms. Dagmar dutifully took an interest in every object shown, and when the three stopped by a painting, she craned her neck in examining it aesthetically. Dieter, meanwhile, stood aside watching Dagmar, allowing his father to talk freely in cultivating a closer acquaintance with the fair one. Dr. Liebermann spoke at length and pendantically, clearly enjoying his role as guide, and all the rooms they passed through were lavishly decorated, but were dark because of the small windows and black panelling.

After they had toured the hallway, the dining room and another sitting room on the ground floor, the three went upstairs to the hallway above. The hall on the first floor was particularly dark, and as the light was switched on, Dagmar gasped on seeing two shining suits of armour, standing in all their magnificence, with closed visors and ostrich plumes rising from the back of their helmets, and again, the walls were crowded with swords, bayonets, antique pistols and all kinds of weapons, as well as paintings.

"*Wie wunderschön,*!" she marvelled.

"They were made in Nürnberg in the 16th century," said Dr. Liebermann. "Look closely at the engraving on the breast plate. It represents the deification of Alexander the Great after his conquests in the East. The suit was made for a powerful German prince."

"It's beautiful,!" said Dagmar again.

"But it's so difficult to clean when it has to be taken to pieces every six months or so," interjected Dieter.

"That's when Dieter can make himself useful by doing a job of work once in a while," joked Dr. Liebermann.

Dagmar was next shown a blood-stained pistel (or at least, she accepted it as being blood-stained although the stain had turned black) from the body of a dead French officer after the battle of Leipzig, when Napoleon's armies were on the retreat from Germany.

"There are so many things here, one would almost think the house to be haunted," exclaimed Dagmar jokingly. "I think I'd be frightened of living amongst so many old things."

"Not when you're brought up with them," returned Dr. Liebermann drily, before impatiently passing onto the next exhibit.

"What's this,?" exclaimed Dagmar gently placing her fingers on another object. "Why's it got such a funny handle?"

"It's a sword-bayonet," replied Dr. Liebermann.

"What a big heavy weapon for a bayonet," exclaimed Dagmar. "The blade's nearly a metre long."

"It's French," interjected Dieter. "It was picked up in France in 1870."

"At Sedan. That was the year we began to give our answer to Napoleon," chuckled Dr. Liebermann.

"And what's this,?" enquired Dagmar pointing to another object.

"You'd never geuss what that is," laughed Dr. Liebermann.

"It's Oriental – I can see that. There's Chinese writing down the side," said Dagmar.

"It's an old Japanese clock," said Dr. Liebermann taking the object from the wall. "It's clockwork. See, you wind it up like this so that the pointer is at the top, and then the pointer comes down to the bottom of the instrument, marking off the various periods of the day."

"It can't be very precise," remarked Dagmar critically. "You can't tell the hours or the minutes of the day."

Dr. Liebermann laughed as he replaced the object, and he put his arm around Dagmar's shoulder, and the three passed onto the next exhibit.

The three were absent for almost an hour, and when they returned to the sitting room, Dr. Liebermann had his arm placed across Dagmar's shoulder, and she wore a beautifully placid expression, and Dieter followed close behind. Dr. and Frau Goltz were standing in their coats, in the centre of the room, ready to leave, and when the three re-entered, he joked about their having perhaps lost themselves in the house, facetiously remarking that Dagmar's head must be in a whirl after absorbing so much information.

"The house is a real museum," he concluded.

"But I expect Dagmar is used to seeing antiques and pictures," said Frau Liebermann in a confidential whisper leaning towards Dr. and Frau Goltz. "She works in an art shop, you know."

"Yes,?" exclaimed Dr. Goltz in a tone of surprise turning to Dagmar. "Then she must come to our house and see the collection we have."

"Dr. Goltz has a really magnificent collection of oil paintings," exclaimed Dieter enthusiastically, "including some masterpieces by the greatest painters of 19th century Germany."

"I should love to see them," replied Dagmar.

"You're welcome to visit our house any time," said Dr. Goltz generously.

"Why don't both of you – Dieter and Dagmar – go with Dr. Goltz now," suggested Frau Liebermann, "only be sure to be back in two hours for dinner."

"That's an excellent idea," returned Dr. Goltz.

Dieter fetched Dagmar's coat, and the four left the house together. It was dark by now, and the mist had cleared somewhat, but a cold breeze chilled the night air, and with their hands thrust into their pockets, they walked briskly down the gravel drive towards the impressive gate posts at the end. On leaving the garden they walked down the narrow lane which cut through the thick forest.

"It's not far to go – about half a kilometre," said Dr. Goltz.

"Dr. Goltz's house is larger even than ours," confided Dieter, "and his garden or woodland area is over three times larger than ours. Also, his land borders a lake, and so in Summer you can imagine how fine it is."

"In Summer, we like to swim in the lake every morning before breakfast," said the doctor.

The four turned into an even narrower lane, and after walking down this for some distance, they came to a footway which was a narrow cutting between trees, and followed that.

"How haunting the forest is – aren't you afraid of encountering elves at night,?" asked Dagmar facetiously.

"We don't always have to walk through here to reach the house," explained Frau Goltz. "When we take the car, then we continue along the path we just left."

At last the path came to an end, and the four stood by the bank of a small lake. On the other side were to be seen moving lights and there came the sound of passing vehicles.

"That's part of the great autobahn encircling Berlin," said Dieter.

"In Summer both of you must come and swim here," said Dr. Goltz addressing Dagmar, "and then afterwards, you can come and join us for tea."

"That would be lovely," said Dagmar.

The four walked alongside the lake to a pathway which they walked down until they came to a lawn and a large house beyond, built in mock gothic style.

Dr. Goltz showed Dieter and Dagmar round the house, and she was delighted by the magnificent collection of 19th century paintings hung round the walls. There was an especially fine collection of Scandinavian pictures including paintings by such renowned artists as Schjerfbeck, J.C. Dahl and Järnefelt, and Dagmar was overjoyed by the revelation of these newly discovered works.

"These Scandinavian paintings touch the nerve-ends of our Nordic soul in a way your French Impressionists could never begin to do," exclaimed Dr. Goltz in awe.

"How many pictures do you have,?" asked Dagmar.

"Nearly three hundred," replied Dr. Goltz.

"Who's this painting by,?" enquired Dagmar pointing to a colourful abstract work.

"It's by Strindberg, the great Swedish writer," replied Dr. Goltz, "one of the profoundest abstract painters the world has seen – and this picture was painted long before abstractionism was to reach France."

Dagmar craned forward her neck and examined the picture critically, and then she was shown several weird and nighmarish masterpieces by the great Swiss painter Arnold Böcklin.

Dr. Goltz said he had something very special to show Dagmar, and he took the young couple into a small ante-room, and there on the centre of a blank wall hung a small painting hardly more than fifteen square inches in a large ornately gilded frame. The picture illustrated Frederick the Great and Voltaire in conversation, seated at a table drinking chocolate in the palace of *Sans Souci* in Potsdam. Dr. Goltz explained the picture was by Adolphe von Menzel, one of the greatest painters of Prussia. He recounted how the painting had been presented as a gift to his father by Menzel himself, at the turn of the century. Dieter and Dagmar were filled with delight and surprise at the discovery, and the three of them excitedly crowded round the painting as Dr. Gotz continued to enumerate its merits.

Chapter 45

The visit to Werlsee was a great success, and Dagmar was told she was always welcome, and favourable impressions were created in the minds of all. When the young couple returned from Dr. Goltz's for dinner, Frau Liebermann became most indulgent towards Dagmar, expressing as much motherly consideration as the doctor had show fatherly affection earlier in the evening. The four sat down to a sumptuous dinner, drinking French wine and liqueur, and toasts were drunk to each of them and to the friendship, although there was not yet any talk of an engagement.

As Dieter drove Dagmar home along the Fürstenwalder Damm towards Friedrichshagen, and as the car sped through the forest along the straight highway, she was pleasantly relaxed and happy, and she thought about the events of that afternoon and evening. As was only natural, she had felt a little apprehensive in advance of the visit – especially after all the fussing of her mother and after Dieter's apologetic explanation about his parents being "old fashioned," as they had driven towards the zonal frontier that day – but everything had worked out happily in the end. Perhaps Dieter, too, had been nervous about the visit, and perhaps that's why he had felt obliged to "explain" his parents. But everything had passed off successfully and there were no doubts left in Dagmar's mind. Still, she was glad the visit was over. Beforehand she had anticipated it as an ordeal, but now her mind was satisfied that in retrospect it would remain a pleasant memory.

Suddenly, the car slowed down, and Dieter turned off the road into a narrow unpaved lane leading into the forest.

"Where are we going,?" enquired Dagmar in a tone of mild alarm.

"Would you like to see the Müggel See by night,?" returned Dieter.

"Why – yes, of course," replied Dagmar sceptically.

"It's beautiful by night," exclaimed Dieter in a tone of enthusiasm, " – that great expanse of glittering shimmering water exposed to the moonlit sky."

"But I don't think there's any moon tonight," said Dagmar, " – it's so cloudy!"

"The Müggel See's always beautiful – so fresh and close to nature – always with the sound of water lapping gently on the sand," said Dieter poetically, seemingly quite unperturbed by the everyday practicality of Dagmar's statement.

The lane was short, and soon the car was parked by the shore of the lake, on the north bank of the Müggel See. Outside, there was the sound of the wind as it passed through the trees, and everything was black except for the outline of a few nearby tree trunks, and the glistening water of the lake as it was reflected from the headlamps of the car. Dieter switched off the headlights.

"*Schön, nicht,?*" he exclaimed.

"I can't see anything," replied Dagmar.

As their eyes became accustomed to the dark, still there was nothing around them except darkness. They were surrounded by the black woods and the black expanse of water in front – and only the outline of their head and shoulders made them visible to one another, and the only light came from the dials on the dashboard.

Dieter leaned forward towards Dagmar taking her shoulders into his hands. She said nothing, only leaned forward her head in a passive gesture, whilst he pulled her body closely to his. A moment later they were enclasped in a passionate embrace.

"You, most beautiful creature of God's creation," murmured Dieter as he kissed between her shoulder blades.

He unbuttoned her coat and slipped it from her shoulders. He placed his hands beneath her legs and lifted her onto his lap, and as he did so, she knocked her head against the roof of the car and exclaimed, "Ouch!"

"It's so small in here," she exclaimed.

"It's too cold for outside," muttered Dieter as he kissed the nape of her neck.

"Naturally," returned Dagmar.

She bent forward her neck and suddenly showered his face with kisses as she held the sides of his head between her hands. A moment later, Dieter thrust his hand beneath her petticoats and she squealed slightly, and he began to caress the inside of the upper part of her leg.

"Don't touch me there – no higher," she said softly almost hesitantly.

Dieter made no reply. She had told him not to "touch" her there, and then she had compromised, saying "No higher." He decided the compromise called for no comment, but at the same time realised that there was an implication he need not remove his hand from the inside of her leg. He had been told that he might touch "there" but "no higher," and providing he remembered and stood by this condition, all should remain well.

Dagmar was overcome with a feeling of blissful surrender, and her body was filled with a thrilled sensation. It was dark. She could neither see herself nor be seen. She felt free: both free of guilt and inhibitions. Her body was hidden in the blackness of the night – concealed from the eyes of man. Why not then relax and enjoy the blissful tingling sensations of the body, which God had kindly bestowed upon humankind for the enjoyment of rapturous pleasure.

She thought of her own body. She thought of her slim white legs, and the beauty and smoothness of her skin, and she saw her legs as she stood before the dressing table in the morning as she put on her stockings, for it was then when she most often admired the beauty of her own limbs. She thought of her delicate white breasts and of their velvety texture, and often she had stood before the mirror in the wash room, lost in contemplation of their beauty, and often she had pinched them between her slim fingers and enjoyed the sensation of this – especially when she was sad or worried.

She thought of the nakedness of her body, as she had often stood before the long mirror in the public bathhouse, and she saw her golden hair as it fell over her shoulders, and she saw her shapely hips and the slim white nakedness of her figure. As she became lost in the contemplation of herself, it often seemed to her, as if her body was hungry and forlorn, and craved for the awakening stimulation of latent sensations, bringing new strength and purpose to her body for which she thought its use was really intended.

She remembered how other girls had often glanced at her body on passing by. She remembered their looks suggesting envy, wonder or prurient curiosity, and she resented this for she was a proud modest girl, and disliked the visits to the public bathhouse. It seemed to her as if none of the other girls had glanced at her body kindly. Only her friend, Renata, had remarked on her body appreciatively, and as the two girls stood naked, washing themselves beneath the showers, they had often glanced at one another, and spoken about each other's bodies in an innocent sort of way. Dagmar remembered the snippets of conversation she had overheard from the other girls and women in the bathhouse and their crude laughter and jokes, as they discussed the most intimate details of their relationships with their menfolk, and this had shocked and disturbed her. Often, they had lowered their voices or edged away when Dagmar approached, for they surmised she was a virgin, and she despised them even more for their dismissive attitude towards her.

But now it was Dagmar's turn! Soon she would be one of them, she thought. Wasn't she waiting for the moment when a man would awaken her body from the sleep of virginity, and arouse the carnal sensations of her flesh? Her legs, too, would be opened to receive the consummation of a mutual love, and her legs, too, would be thrust around the naked thighs of a man. One day, too, a man's teeth would bite into her breasts as his hands caressed the most sensitive part of her naked shoulders.

Suddenly, she felt Dieter's fingers thrust to her most intimate parts. She was thrilled and at the same time frightened, but she was so overcome with a feeling of surrender that she felt any attempt at resistance would be futile. The potency of the French wine and the Benedictine liqueur was doing what Dionysius had intended! She leaned back, half closing her eyes, and began laughing softly as if with pleasure and abandon. She wished to close her legs, but she couldn't. She wished that Dieter's fingers were ten times larger but they weren't. Surely this was paradise on earth!

He unzipped the back of her dress, pulling it down away from her shoulders. He took his other hand away from her legs, firmly grasping her thighs, kissing her back and shoulders. She took in her breath, and a thrilling sensation filled her body as his lips met the white velvety texture of her skin.

"You shouldn't – we're very bad,!" she exclaimed under her breath.

Still Dieter said nothing. He placed his hands between her shoulder blades, and in a moment, he had unclipped the strap of her bra and thrown it to the floor. Involuntarily, overcome with modesty, Dagmar slapped her hands over her naked breasts.

"No, nothing more," she uttered.

"We'll sit at the back," said Dieter. "It's more comfortable."

"It's too cold to get out," said Dagmar.

"Not out – over the back seat," said Dieter, and he lifted his body and fell with a crash onto the floor of the back of the car whilst his feet hit the ceiling.

"What's the matter – are you hurt,?" exclaimed Dagmar in alarm.

"No, still alive, but I caught the back of my neck on the edge of the seat as I fell," said Dieter.

"Please be careful, my sweet," pleaded Dagmar.

"Now you come over," said Dieter. "Can you manage?"

"I think so," replied Dagmar as she turned and struggled in the car. "It's so small – so cramped in here. Ouch! My head's hit the ceiling. I don't think I can get over. It seems I'm too big."

"Where are you,?" said Dieter.

"Here," cried Dagmar.

"It's so dark at the back, you can see nothing," said Dieter, and he stretched out his hands and felt the top of Dagmar's shoulders. "Come over the other way – twist round your torso," he added.

Again, Dagmar turned and struggled with a great effort, and then there was a bump as her body landed on the back seat of the car, and she kicked her legs in the air.

"You've still got your shoes on," exclaimed Dieter. "Be careful you don't break the windows or tear the lining of the roof."

He leaned forward, snatched her shoes from her feet and threw them down onto the floor of the car. He took her legs and placed them across his lap.

"Now we're together again," he exclaimed embracing her.

Dagmar could see nothing, but she felt Dieter lift her thighs from his lap, as he pulled up her dress and petticoats. "My party frock will be creased and spoilt," she thought, but she was already resigned to her fate and so comfortable in body, as to be incapable of vociferating complaint. She felt his hands close to her thighs as he tugged at her little silk garment. A moment later, he pulled it away from her buttocks and thighs, and down her legs and then away from her feet. She felt momentarily frightened – more frightened than she had ever been – but there was no going back – she had reached the point of no return – she had surrendered to him the last vestige of her defence. She sat before him naked. Had she been rash – had she exceeded the limits of discretion? She did not know. She knew only she would surrender her entire self.

"Is it quite safe,?" she only exclaimed softly in a frightened tone.

"Quite safe," consoled Dieter as he took a little paper packet out of his breast pocket.

She heard him adjust his clothing, and he took hold of her thigh and drew her towards him. Her whole body quivered, but whether it was out of fear or a pleasurable sensation, she did not know. She felt him enter her body, and as his hands drew her buttocks towards him, as their stomachs were pressed together, he leaned over her and she grasped her arms tightly around his shoulders and panted and perspired in sheer excitement. She was thrilled with delight. So strangely intermingled are those feelings arising from the first experience of that greatest pleasure of all.

In this way Dagmar and Dieter consummated their love for one another after their friendship had happily progressed for a period of almost six months. This was not Dieter's first experience with a girl (as he later confided to the fair one) and doubtless he had found the six months waiting for the completion of this happy act both annoying and frustrating, but in view of Dagmar's virginity and the inevitable difficulties incurred in conquering a girl for the first time, he was prepared to accept this delay to the consummation of their love. His patience had been well rewarded, for their friendship had meanwhile grown into a profound love and respect for one another, and their subsequent physical relationship was to be fulfilled entirely.

For Dagmar, the act was of greater significance, for it was her first true sexual experience. As she was driven home that night in the car, she felt relaxed and happy. Any qualms she had previously felt about losing her virginity now melted away. Her conscience was clear and her innermost soul betrayed no doubts or misgivings. As the car sped through the suburb of Köpenick, she wondered why the first act of love was referred to as Loss of Virginity. She thought that perhaps the phrase was erroneous in meaning and emotional context. What had she lost? She felt and knew there was nothing she had lost – no positive thing or possession, or natural attribute, which she had nurtured or treasured within herself. She had lost her innocence, perhaps, but that was not to be wept over – for was that a loss of any consequence? Loss, was a wrong word surely. She had Shed her innocence – she had shed her virginity, as the snake sheds its skin, or as the young beast moults its first fur, or as the child loses its first teeth. She had shed her virginity and thereby gained maturity. The conception of lost virginity was a fictional bogey invented by religious ascetics, or so she concluded.

Now she felt equal to any other girl – she had had the experience – and there was no good reason why other women in the bathhouse should snub her by lowering their voices or edging away on her approach, as they discussed their menfolk. Doubtless they might continue to do this on seeing her slim unravished-looking body, but she wouldn't mind that any longer – she would continue to despise them anyway. She would despise them for the way they spoke about their menfolk in a public place, and for the way they so degraded their sex relationships by so doing. For Dagmar, the sex act would remain an intimate and cherished experience between herself and her lover, and she would never speak about Dieter in public – not like those women in the bathhouse – that disgusted her! If the details of her intimacies with Dieter were to be revealed to anyone, then it would only be to her closest friends, and then speaking quietly in a secluded place, where none might overhear.

When Dagmar arrived home, she was elated and blissfully contented as she thought back over the happy events of the day, and as she undressed in the little passageway so as not to turn on the light in the bedroom and awaken Granny, she thought about the details of her first love experience. As she pulled up her dress from her shoulders, she smiled to herself. She had been so frightened and worried at first, but there was nothing to it really. Some girls told her it hurt first time, and that sonetimes, you fainted even, but it had never hurt her and she had never fainted. It had been pleasurable from first to last – the experience had exceeded her highest expectations.

Then, one little incidental doubt re-entered her mind – something she had forgotten since she sat on the back seat of the car. Looking like a fairy in her pink underclothes and white petticoats, she tip-toed to the washroom toilet, switched on the light and stood before the long mirror. She lifted the front of her petticoats, and glanced down, closely examining the fabric. She took hold of her little silk garment and dragged it down beneath her thighs. She looked at it, and then touched and glanced closely at her most intimate parts. There was no blood! After her significant experience, she not only felt the same; she even looked the same!

On meeting the following day, Dagmar confirmed the invitation which her parents extended to Dieter to visit them next Saturday. Dieter said he would be pleased to visit Graetz Strasse. When they met the following Wednesday, Dieter asked Dagmar if they might meet every Tuesday on subsequent weeks. "Why,?" asked Dagmar. "Tuesday is not exactly the middle of the week, and it'll be a longer wait till Saturday." Dieter explained that on Tuesdays he might regularly borrow his father's car, whilst on Wednesdays the car was never free. Dagmar assented to the idea, but rather reluctantly. "After all, it's so nice to go for rides in the car – and it'll be something else to do after we've visited the theatre or a concert," remarked Dieter.

As the following Saturday drew near, Dagmar became increasingly concerned about the approaching event. She felt far more concerned about Dieter's visit to her parents' home than she had ever felt the previous week about her visit to his home. There was much bustling around the house, and secret whisperings between herself and Mamma. Dagmar became more apprehensive as the great day approached, and sometimes, she was irritable even. The secret whisperings were of a nagging kind, and it was Dagmar nagging her mother. Papa Renot remained oblivious to all of this, and continued to potter around the house, puffing contentedly at his cigars and occasionally passing a facetious remark or two.

Naturally, he knew about the approaching visit, and the good Frau frequently discussed her daughter's relationship with the boy Dietrich with her husband. During the past few weeks Papa Renot had even questioned Dagmar herself about the boy Dietrich, but he had never seemed to show a real interest (he was quite off-hand and casual about it all) and so Dagmar never had the inclination to open her heart to her father in describing the extent of her love for Dietrich, as she had sometimes opened her heart to her mother. Anyway, Papa Renot had a very matter-of-fact attitude to life, and so even if she had opened her heart to him, he would only have been embarrassed, or dismissed the affair with a flippant or irreverent remark.

It was well that Papa Renot's curiosity was not aroused by these secret whisperings, for they touched on matters which concerned him alone. In short, Dagmar was briefing her mother as to the essential preparations for the visit, and in Dagmar's mind, the most important preparations were connected with making Papa Renot presentable – or at least, passable. If he could not be improved upon by *additions*, then at least his worst and most unprepossessing faults could be erased by *subtractions*. It was not for Dagmar herself to advise, correct or otherwise nanny her father – she was not such a presumptuous girl – and anyway, she would not risk offending him, and so because of this, her mother had to act as an intermediary for her daughter.

"And please Mamma, tell Papa not to take that big handkerchief out of his pocket and wipe it over his face," said Dagmar in a confidential tone as she stood in the kitchen with her mother who was bent over the kitchen sink. "It looks awful when he does that. And Mamma, tell Papa to think what he's going to say before he says it. Sometimes he comes out with the most rude and stupid things without realising, and we're all so terribly embarrassed. And Mamma, tell him not to smoke at the table – and yes – tell him not to dig his elbow into people's sides when he has something important to say. Some people don't like that, and it's so impolite. And when the stove in the sitting room gets very hot, tell Papa not to remove his jacket – Papa looks really dreadful in braces. And what's Papa going to wear?"

"The blue suit with the white stripes," came the inevitable reply.

"But it's so stained and mouldy and old looking," said Dagmar screwing up her nose.

"It's Papa's best suit," said Frau Renot shaking her head sadly. "It was his proudest possession – his Sunday best – when he bought it in 1938."

"It's nearly twenty years old Mamma. And Mamma, tell Papa not to show too much hanky in his breast pocket, and tell him not to brush his lapels of invisible dust – it looks so silly, that habit."

And so it went on.

At last the great day arrived and Dieter met Dagmar in Stalin Allee after her work, and together they went to Treptow by bus and train. Now it was Dagmar's turn to tell Dieter something about her parents.

"As you know we live in a very modest flat," explained Dagmar, "and perhaps Mamma and Papa lead very simple lives. Our way of life is very modest, and you'll find our place quite different from your house in Werlsee."

Dieter was mildly put-out by Dagmar's explanation and he patted her shoulder and changed the subject.

As Frau Brüning was holding a small tea party for several of her old cronies at No. 55 that same afternoon, Dieter was taken to the flat at No. 16 and introduced to Dagmar's parents and Gisela. Tea and cakes were brought in by Dagmar and her mother, whilst the others talked and joked in the sitting room. Soon there was a lively and *gemütlich* atmosphere. All was going well! Papa Renot seemed to take a liking to Dieter after they had spoken together awhile, and he made some facetious remarks, and Dieter laughed at his witticisms.

Frau Renot was an indulgent hostess, and it was apparent that she too was prepared to welcome Dieter into the family circle with all her heart. As the evening progressed and the stove in the sitting room became hotter, Papa Renot (remaining true to his wife's entreaty) refrained from removing his jacket, although on one occasion, he did rise from his chair and flap the sides of his jacket up and down to cool himself. However, Dagmar decided to overlook this slight impropriety, but when he subsequently pulled out a handkerchief from his pocket and began dabbing it over his face, she frowned at him chidingly, although this breach of good behaviour on the part of the old man seemed to go entirely unnoticed by Dieter.

Later, it was decided that the party would move across the road to see how Granny and her cronies were enjoying themselves, and to afford Dieter the opportunity of being introduced to Frau Brüning. The party at No. 55 was a noisy event and as soon as the door of the flat was opened, there came the sound of loud voices and much laughter. Dieter was introduced to Frau Brüning, Herr Schomberg, Frau Klingberg and Frau Hartmann. All the company settled down into chairs in the sitting room, and more food and tea was brought in. Herr Schomberg was in an especially lively mood, and doubtless he was being flattered by the company of the three ladies entertaining him during the afternoon. Herr Renot and Herr Schomberg were completely in their element amongst so many ladies, and together they joked and laughed and generally buffooned in front of the rest of the company. This was a party for the older folk, and Dagmar and Dieter, who sat on the sofa hand-in-hand, looked quietly on the others.

Frau Hartmann turned to Dieter with a friendly gesture and began enquiring as to who and what he was. She spoke in a quiet confidential tone, and Dagmar leaned forward on the sofa trying to catch what was being said between them.

"So you're a veterinary student,!" exclaimed Frau Hartmann. "Some students from that faculty have been bad boys during the last year – a real worry to the authorities."

"Yes," laughed Dieter in reply – Frau Hartmann seemed such a facetious old lady, he thought.

"I'm glad you agree with me," said Frau Hartmann.

Dieter thought he had a sympathetic listener. He began confiding to her his innermost thoughts. The students of the DDR will remain the backbone for any opposition to the authorities. The state is dependent on the universities for the future of the country, and the universities cannot be deprived completely of the last vestige of their freedom. Always there will be a voice of dissent raised against the oppression of the authorities. One day the regime will be destroyed from within, and the students will lead the movement for its destruction. The regime is doomed to collapse by its very nature, for it is unpopular with all sections of the populace. Nobody believes in the regime.

"Many people believe in the regime," replied Frau Hartmann firmly, but still pleasant.

"Only the rotten," replied Dieter, and he continued to expound his ideas as he lambasted the system. He was oblivious to Dagmar's nudging for he was too absorbed in communicating his thoughts to the old woman.

He said he was an active member of the FDJ, that he had been sent on several cadres in the East zone, that he made propaganda in the University, and would soon be joining the Volksarmee.

"From that you'd conclude I was a keen ideological Communist, yes,?" he concluded.

"Most certainly I should," replied Frau Hartmann sharply.

"Well, I'm not. I loathe the system and everything it means," said Dieter.

"You're a reactionary bourgeois then,?" exclaimed Frau Hartmann sharply.

"Not in reality," returned Dieter laughing, "but the authorities would like to describe me as such should they know my convictions."

"How is it you hold such a fine position in the FDJ,?" enquired Frau Hartmann, the sympathetic listener.

Dieter told her the story of the prize winning essay which had won him such distinction, and the outcome of this. He explained how he was forced into serving the Party, but he justified his doing so on the grounds that no one in the DDR was stupid enough to be persuaded by Communist propaganda, however great the resources of the SED. He cited the case of the SPD in Berlin shortly after the end of the War. At that time the SED held all the propaganda resources; the officials enjoyed immense privileges, and the Russian authorities granted the Party every facility it required: buildings, vehicles and such technical aids as loudspeakers – and lastly but not least, an espionage system to hunt down and break up opposition elements. Dieter was referring to the first and last free election to be held of all the citizenry of post-War Berlin in October 1946, when the Berlin SPD (which a few months earlier had been contemptuously referred to as the "Zehlendorf Hospital Club," and later, as the "SPD Splinter") won 48.7 % of the votes as against the SED's 19.8%. He joked about it being preferable that a non-Communist rather than a Communist be paid for making pro-Communist propaganda. Dieter added, though, that it was unfortunate that anyone should be obliged to make Communist propaganda, but sadly, that that was a result of the strange situation in which the world now found itself.

"And so you're a traitor," exclaimed Frau Hartmann.

"Yes, maybe, a potential traitor, in a purely technical sense," replied Dieter cheerfully, "but then comes the question, how legal is the regime itself? It's not based on the authority of the people; it's something forced on us from above by the Soviets. Is there a moral right which justifies such a regime to call on the allegiance of the people? Does one commit treason in defying the authority of such a regime?"

"I don't think you understand me, young man," said Frau Hartmann slowly in a grimly serious tone; "when I said you were a traitor, I meant it in a derogatory and not a complimentary sense."

"I'm afraid, I don't quite understand you," said Dieter vaguely put-out.

"I was speaking in sincerity," said Frau Hartmann.

"She's a Communist," said Dagmar tugging on Dieter's sleeve.

"I should never have known it,!" said Dieter in astonishment to himself, and then turning to Frau Hartmann, he said, "Why didn't you tell me before?"

"Why should I,?" retorted Frau Hartmann sharply. "You never asked. Does one normally spell out one's party affiliations before starting a conversation? I think not! We were both talking at cross purposes. There was no intentional concealment on my part."

"I trust I haven't caused you offence," said Dieter apologetically.

"Me offence? You needn't worry about my feelings," retorted Frau Hartmann indignantly. "My worry is only for the security of the State. It's my son who wouldn't like what you have to say."

"Doubtless, your son is a very honourable man," said Dieter nodding politely.

"Every officer in the SSD is honourable," retorted Frau Hartmann sharply.

"In the SSD,!" exclaimed Dieter astonished.

Frau Hartman chose to ignore his exclamation of surprise, and began instead to upraid him for his disloyal feelings towards the regime.

"Recationary bourgeous of your kind are a threat to the democratic development of our country. Some day the authorities will catch up with you," she said irately.

"I can assure you, there's nothing reactionary in my ideas," responded Dieter.

"We're living on the edge of a new era," continued Frau Hartmann without having registered Dieter's response. "Of course, it's no good telling you that because you don't believe it, and you've got to have faith. It's all a matter of *faith* in the system – it's no good doubting – that way nothing is achieved."

"I can't accept 'faith' has a place in political life comparable with that which it clearly has in the realm of religion," remarked Dieter under his breath.

"Of course, us old ones will never live to see the great day," continued Frau Hartmann who by this time was listless to anything Dieter had to say, "but it's a fine future which lies ahead for the young people."

Frau Hartmann's little speech and her raised voice attracted the uncertain attention of others in the room. Out of civility, they feigned not to register the abrasive environment created, and this was all the more embarrassing to Dieter. By now he had been cowed into submission by the old woman, and he merely sat nodding his head in stupid affirmation to all she said. He wanted an end to the discussion. When, however, Frau Hartmann continued to chatter away on the need for maintaining loyalty to the regime, Dagmar at last interrupted her, saying: "Please, Frau Hartmann, let's end this discussion; you can see it's embarrassing my friend."

"Well, just remember what I've said young man," concluded Frau Hartmann, and she nodded with a significant gesture, before turning away and good-humouredly nudging Herr Schomberg who stood with his back to her.

Apart from Dieter's encounter with Frau Hartmann, the party progressed pleasantly enough and all were in high spirits, and fortunately, he was not brought into direct contact with her again that evening.

About an hour later, the three elderly guests of Frau Brüning began to take their leave. There was much handshaking and bowing and curtseying in all parts of the room. When Frau Hartmann reached Dieter, she asked for his name again. Dieter blushed, hesitating to offer a reply, but she saved him his embarrassment by exclaiming, "Liebermann, wasn't it? Dietrich Liebermann?"

"That'll do – Liebermann," answered Dieter awkwardly with a sickly smile.

"I'll remember that, and just take care of yourself, young man, else you'll find yourself in deeper water than you care to be," she said in a sinister tone, and curtseying with exaggerated formality, she passed on.

Dieter turned pale at these words, delivered with the solemnity of a prophetess, and he became meditative and seemingly dispirited for the duration of the party; but this went unnoticed by the others who remained in high spirits, but Dagmar once or twice edged closely beside Dieter, quietly whispering into his ear, telling him to forget the "beastly" Frau Hartmann, but Dieter said nothing in answer to this alleviating gesture.

When Dagmar walked with Dieter to Treptower Park station, they were in a quiet reflective mood as with even steps they trod on the paving stones of the street, and then he turned to her and enquired who and what exactly Frau Hartmann was.

"She's a friend of Granny," replied Dagmar.

"A close friend,?" enquired Dieter in a casual tone.

"No, not really – just one of her elderly companions living in the block."

"I don't like her politics," said Dieter earnestly.

"The old people don't usually discuss politics amongst themselves – or at least, politics doesn't seem to count in their relationships with one another."

"Still, she's a dangerous friend to have around – and her son, a member of the SSD! She must be a genuine Communist. Did you hear what she said about the SSD?"

"It was unfortunate you spoke to her so freely. We all make a point of *never* discussing politics when Frau Hartmann's around. She's suspected of being a *Spitzel*."

"A *Spitzel*! How can your grandmother entertain a *Spitzel* in her house?"

"You know Dieter, the old people really have only two things in common: their old age and their loneliness. They've seen so much storm and stress in their long lives that they've no more energy to worry about the *Stasi*. They just don't care any more. They're just happy with the opportunity of talking and laughing with one another, and occasionally, being dependent on each other's help."

"A woman who's suspected of being a *Spitzel* can never be trusted – especially when her son's in the SSD."

"Sometimes Frau Hartmann's very kind to Granny – especially last year, when Granny was confined to bed for six weeks with rheumatism. You see, it's difficult to keep home life separate from the possible complications of political life all the time."

"I can see that. It's all part of the totalitarian agenda," moaned Dieter.

"I shouldn't worry. I can't see she could do you any harm," consoled Dagmar.

Some days later, as Dagmar was returning from work to the flat at No. 55, she met Frau Hartmann in the hallway of the tenement block.

Frau Hartmann beckoned to her with her finger with a confiding gesture, and Dagmar walked over to the old woman with a feeling of curious apprehension.

"I don't think that young man is made for you, my dear," said Frau Hartmann benevolently.

Dagmar stood in front of the old woman and her eyes widened with astonishment.

"I mean, Dietrich Liebermann, my dear," explained Frau Hartmann. "He's not your kind at all. You've been going out with him quite a lot recently, haven't you? He's been escorting you back to your flat quite late at night. I couldn't help noticing you both from my window over the courtyard. I could recognise your footsteps anywhwere, my dear, and as for Herr Liebermann, he has such heavy hard-soled shoes that I wake with a start every time he comes into the courtyard – and three times a week it is."

"I think you're being very nosey and interfering, Frau Hartmann," exclaimed Dagmar in breathless anger.

"No offence, my dear. You know your grandmother's my best friend, and I wouldn't offend her granddaughter for all the world," assured Frau Hartmann. "I wouldn't say anything that wasn't intended as a piece of friendly advice."

"What advice,?" enquired Dagmar sharply.

"Herr Liebermann is a mischievous young man," said the old woman. "He's a threat to the well-being of our young country. He's not the type of young man for you to go out with. He doesn't deserve you, my dear."

"I don't think you know what you're talking about," returned Dagmar.

"Follow my advice and don't meet him again. Heed my words before it's too late. Find yourself a young man who's a credit to our new society."

"You're an insolent interfering old witch," cried Dagmar turning on her heel and stepping up to the door of her grandmother's flat.

"You've been warned, my dear, and I'd never wish you any harm," called Frau Hartmann after her, but Dagmar ignored the final threatening words, as she went into the flat and closed the door behind her.

She was frightened by Frau Hartmann's warning and by the tone in which it was uttered, but she never spoke about this encounter to Dieter or to anyone else, despite the marked impression it made on her mind and despite the remarkable insolence of the old woman. Perhaps she felt that an encounter boding such ill-will was best forgotten for there was no way that such a sinister threat could be countered by word or action.

Chapter 46

The weeks passed by and the Winter's cold settled over the city of Berlin, and the unpleasant encounters with Frau Hartmann were soon forgotten by Dieter and Dagmar. Tuesday remained the day kept as the mid-week tryst between the lovers, and on that day, the car was free for their use. After visiting a theatre or other place of entertainment, the lovers took a ride in the car around the city or to the outlying suburbs, instead of sitting in a crowded smokey café as previously. Dagmar disliked noisy cafés, far preferring a car ride. Sometimes she brought along a flask of tea or coffee and sandwiches, and these refreshments were enjoyed by the lovers as they sat together parked in some quiet place.

Every Tuesday, and often on Saturdays and Sundays also, they would sit on the back seat of the car expressing their love for one another. It was a cold Winter and there was no heater in the car, and as the lovers reclined on the back seat, their heads leaning against one of the back side windows, their legs propped up on the back of the front seat, as they lay in each other's arms in a state of partial undress, they must have felt the Winter chill, but after a time they found a way of partly overcoming this. Four lighted candles were placed on a small mat on the floor. Later, Dieter brought a rug, this proving more effective than the candles, and in this situation, they would often lie passively for an hour or so in each other's arms after expressing their closest intimacies.

Dagmar liked the candles because of their soft light, and after their physical relationship progressed for some weeks and a freer intimacy grew between them, she liked to see the gentle candlelight reflected against their white bodies and the black coverings of the car. She was no longer inhibited by the need for concealment as she enjoyed the delights of love. She liked to lie in his arms and to look at his naked body, at his strong fair-haired limbs and his smooth muscular chest, and she would lose herself in the contemplation of his body. On one occasion, after they had fulfilled their pleasure, she plucked one of the long shiny hairs from his body, and the hair curled round her slim finger as if it would never part company from her.

"I shall keep this forever," she promised solemnly.

She plucked a hair from her own body. It was much shorter than his and fairer and more silky, for those hairs from the most intimate part of her body had a silky softness of the rarest quality. She tied the two hairs together.

"This shall remain a symbol of our sacred indivisibility," she declared.

"And of our undying love for one another," added Dieter.

"I shall keep it in the back of my watch," she said.

Dagmar plucked two more hairs from their bodies, trying them together, and gave them to Dieter. He too promised to put them into the back of his watch.

The lovers were careful and discreet when engaged in the pursuit of their most intimate pleasures. They were ever conscientious in parking in a place where the likelihood of disturbance was remote: at the end of a ruined street, on a bomb site, in a woodland area, or some other place which humans were unlikely (be it hoped) to frequent. Nothing would have upset them more than the shock of being caught in the act with the risk of public shame. Their precautions, of course, were no guarantee that they might not at some time be discovered and caught, and on one occasion they did experience an unfortunate episode.

Early one afternoon in January when the ground was laden with snow, as the car drove at great speed along the autobahn in the East zone, south of Berlin, towards the direction of Potsdam, Dagmar hinted that it might be nice to "rest awhile" in the car during daylight. To "rest awhile" was a polite euphemism used between the lovers. Dieter replied it would leave them less time to spend in Potsdam, for they had arranged to visit the Palace and exhibition of *Sans Souci*.

"But we've never 'rested' in daylight," pleaded Dagmar, "and with all the beautiful snow, there's so much natural light in the atmosphere. Let's take advantage of the crisp, dry, ice-cold beautiful part of Winter. It would be so nice to enjoy the full benefits of the season."

Dieter remained silent a moment, continuing to look straight ahead as the car sped along the highway. In his own mind he must have thought she was tiring of candlelight.

"*Sans Souci* closes early in Winter," he said at last.

"It's so nice today. The first day of snow," said Dagmar reflectively. "This is how I think Winter should always be."

Dieter made no reply and neither did he turn towards her. He continued to look ahead, wearing a serious expression, his eyes intently fixed on the road in front. The car sped onwards, but suddenly, it braked and Dagmar was thrown forward on her seat.

"Where are we going,?" she enquired with mild surprise.

"To 'rest awhile,'" replied Dieter nonchalantly, and he turned off the autobahn, driving onto a smaller road pointing to a village called Genshagen.

Perhaps it was with reluctance he had decided to delay the visit to *Sans Souci* for the sake of the fair one, for he still wore a tired unsmiling expression.

The car drove through the village of Genshagen and on reaching a wooded area, Dieter slowed on seeing a pathway between the trees and he drove down this.

"Are you sure it's all right to go down here,?" asked Dagmar as the car bumped over the crevices in the narrow pathway.

"Yes – why not,?" replied Dieter casually throwing up a hand.

"I think I saw a notice at the end of the pathway saying this was a state owned timber forest," said Dagmar.

"There was no gateway at the end of the pathway," said Dieter.

"But if it's state owned property," said Dagmar in concern.

"Any vehicle can come down here if it wants," replied Dieter. "There was no notice forbidding traffic. In any case, forests are always open to anyone who wants to use them."

"I'm not sure about that," remarked Dagmar.

The car drove into a clearing and parked.

"Here it is safe," exclaimed Dieter.

"So near the road,?" replied Dagmar.

"It's Sunday. No one will be coming through here to disturb us."

"It's beautiful here," exclaimed Dagmar. "Everything's so white and peaceful."

"We're in the middle of a snow white forest, where the animals sleep through the Winter's cold," added Dieter poetically.

He opened the lid of the pocket in the dashboard taking out the candles and a little mat. He placed the mat on the floor and carefully stood the candles upright; then he took out a box of matches and lit each candle.

"It's like lighting up a birthday cake," remarked Dagmar as she watched this.

The couple got out of the car and settled into the back seats. Half an hour later they lay resting comfortably, naked in each other's arms.

"It's wonderful to 'rest awhile' in daylight, isn't it,?" remarked Dagmar dreamily.

Dieter mumbled a reply indicating assent.

"Our bodies look quite different in daylight, don't you think,?" continued Dagmar. "Somehow, they look more real. I mean, they look so white, and all the marks show up: the goose pimples, little spots, blue veins – and every line on our skin. Our bodies seem smaller and more in proportion with nature and the things of the world."

"How do you mean,?" asked Dieter.

"They lose something of their mystery and sensuality, and the idealised proportions they attain in candlelight. Still, it's wonderful to 'rest awhile' in daylight," she mused.

At that moment there came a tapping on the front window of the car. The lovers glanced up, and involuntarily tightened their arms around each others' bodies. An ugly red face with a large bulbous nose looked angrily through the window. Terror seized the lovers, and Dagmar gave a little scream, and Dieter held her closer to his body. Was it a hobgoblin or phantom of the woods which had so had rudely disturbed them whilst enjoying the rites of love? A moment later they were to learn it was something far more concrete.

The figure in the snow began tapping a grey hairy hand more threateningly on the window, and then ranting furiously, stamping his feet up and down on the ground.

"What shall we do,?" cried Dagmar frantically.

"Get out of the forest and back onto the autobahn," cried Dieter in reply as he disengaged himself from Dagmar and jumped over the front seat of the car, " – come quickly,!" he added.

Legs first, Dagmar pushed herself over the front seat, and her naked body landed with a plonk into the seat of the car. Exclaiming "Ouch,!" she gave a little cry of pain. She had knocked over the candles and scorched her feet on the hot wax. Meanwhile, Dieter started the engine and began reversing. The old man who had disturbed them, a forester in a dirty green hat and leather boots, stepped back, waving a club-like stick in the air, ranting with indignation. Such behaviour was "unheard of" on state-owned property! They were not being "*Ordentlich*." Such acts were "*Verboten*" in the forest. It was unprecedented! Cars were not designed for such activities. There was no law or custom to justify such behaviour – and so the accusations went on. The lovers remained in a state of terror, their eyes wide open with fear, for not a stitch of clothing covered their nakedness.

The car swerved round, before driving down the narrow pathway. The old man gave chase. The pathway was crooked and the surface potholed, and the bumps difficult to anticipate because of the snow. Dieter drove as fast as circumstances permitted, without risk of damaging the car or slipping the front wheels into the furrows at either side of the pathway and so stranding the vehicle in an underlay of mud. Still, the old man followed them, running on his bandy legs, lifting his knees high, shaking his stick threateningly in the air, and shouting furiously. The car bumped sharply over every crevice swerving uncomfortably round every corner, but it could not accelerate for more than a few metres at a stretch, and always as it came to a corner, the running figure of the old man could be seen appearing round the last bend the vehicle had taken.

"We've nearly reached the main roadway," exclaimed Dieter. "Get some of our clothes from the back."

Dagmar twisted round on the seat, springing her legs beneath her body, and knelt over the back seat. She stretched her hand down to the floor at the rear of the car where the clothes lay.

"I can't reach them," she exclaimed desperately.

Dieter said nothing for a moment. He bit his lip, an expression of tense anxiety crossing his face. He glanced into the mirror above him. Still the old man was giving chase.

"If we're seen, we're lost! Try to reach the clothes again," exclaimed Dieter.

Again Dagmar stretched out her hand.

"I've told you, I can't reach them," she cried.

"That's impossible,!" cried Dieter in a spasm of anger. "What are people going to think if they see us like this? It'll be scandalous! Respectable people don't drive around naked in cars."

"If you stop, then I could climb over the seat and retrieve our clothes."

"*Mensch*, don't be stupid! How can I stop with that lunatic on our trail?"

"Don't call me stupid," replied Dagmar angrily.

"If that maniac catches us, he'll murder us both – and worse still, knock every bit of enamel off the car. What would Papa say then?"

"It's the car and not us you're worried about," said Dagmar with a suggestion of contempt.

"*Quatsch*,!" exclaimed Dieter.

"If you wanted to, you could get out and fight him."

"What, with nothing on?"

"What can we do then,?" cried Dagmar frantically.

"Firstly, let's keep cool. We're both over-excited."

"But we must stop to dress."

"We can't stop now. We're too near the roadway, and if that madman were to raise a hue and cry, we'd never get away."

"When can we dress then?"

"We must drive away and find another quiet spot to readjust ourselves."

The car drove onto the main roadway. The old man stood at the end of the pathway, still shouting, and banging his stick on a red and white hoarding fixed to a tree by the entrance to the woods. As to whether the old man's fury had really been aroused by the state of disarray in which he found the lovers, or by their trespassing on state owned property, they never stopped to discover, but certain it is, that he caused a memorable commotion.

The car began speeding along the main road.

"Fasten your safety belt," ordered Dieter. "We're driving back to the autobahn, and naturally we've got to pass through the village of Genshagen again. We must attract as little attention as we can. If possible, I'll get the speed up to a hundred kilos an hour."

Dagmar obediently secured her belt and Dieter requested her to fasten his. He pressed his foot down onto the accelerator, and the car shot forward like a rocket, the air beating against the sides of the vehicle. Soon the village of Genshagen came into view. There was no attempt at deceleration and continuous hooting was the only warning Dieter gave of his approach. The car rushed through Genshagen, and several elderly villagers waved their fists irately as they stood on the doorsteps of their cottages, sweeping away snow with shovels and brushes, and beyond Genshagen were fields and then the autobahn.

"When do we dress,?" enquired Dagmar anxiously.

"As soon as we see a quiet clearing," replied Dieter. "Meanwhile, hope to God we cross no other traffic."

They reached the autobahn, speeding forward, and the young couple were lucky. They encountered no vehicles in either direction except for a timber truck which they overtook, and it was not for another two kilometres before they finally reached a small clearing in woodland, and by that time they were frozen to the marrow, shivering convulsively, their bodies covered in goose pimples. They dressed hurriedly, and then left the car to jump up and down on the ground and slap their arms around their bodies for warmth, before returning to the vehicle and continuing the journey to Potsdam.

That memorable day in January was the first and last occasion when the young couple "rested awhile" in daylight. It had taught them a lesson, and never again were they to be caught in such a compromising situation.

The physical relationship between the lovers furthered their bonds of friendship through facilitating an adaptation to one another's differing or individual temperaments, and they recognised an indivisible relationship was theirs for life. It also became apparent to Dagmar that Dieter's approach to life became more equable – almost matter-of-fact. This was especially reflected in his political feelings for he was no longer so vehement in the expression of opinions; he maintained a greater discretion; and there was no repetition of any incident comparable to that when he kicked down the propaganda placard outside the French Cathedral.

One Tuesday early in February when the two lovers met in the city centre, Dieter was in a state of elated excitement, and bowing before the fair one, and taking her hands into his, he confided that he had some good news.

"What,?" exclaimed Dagmar in a state of anticipation.

"I'll tell you as oon as we're alone," replied Dieter, and he took her round the corner to where the car was parked, and they drove towards a restaurant in Friedrich Strasse.

"What's the good news,?" enquired Dagmar as the car sped round Alexander Platz.

"I'll tell you as soon as we're settled in the restaurant," replied Dieter brightly.

"Why not now,?" said Dagmar. "We're alone together."

"Well, you see, I want to prepare you for the news – so you can take it in the right way," said Dieter evasively but still in a bright tone.

"What do you mean, 'prepare me,?'" exclaimed Dagmar with suspicion in her voice. "Do you mean there's something unpleasant in it?"

"No, I assure you it's entirely pleasant."

"Do you want to persuade me to do something which you think might be against my wishes, or perhaps, against my better judgement?"

"I promise, it'll be nothing against your better judgement."

"Then it might be against my wishes?"

"I don't know – no I don't think so – not against your wishes exactly."

"I'm quite confused! What is it you've got to tell or ask me?"

"You'll see," replied Dieter significantly.

The couple went to a restaurant in Friedrich Strasse and they sat down at a table for two in a far corner. The restaurant was empty except for a group of Vopo officers dining handsomely on boar's head and champagne at the opposite end of the room.

"Now tell me," exclaimed Dagmar impatiently in a loud whisper.

"Sh-h-h-h! We mustn't be overheard," replied Dieter smiling, nodding towards the Vopos. "It's all very secret."

"Then it must be exciting," said Dagmar.

"How would you like to go to Friedrichshafen,?" exclaimed Dieter brightly.

"Where's Friedrichshafen?"

"You don't know,?" exclaimed Dieter in good-humoured surprise.

"Is that the place on the North Sea in West Germany?"

"No, that's Wilhelmshaven. Friedrichshafen's on lake Konstanz – right in the south of Germany. It's a hundred kilometres from Austria and only fifteen kilometres across the water from Switzerland."

"It must be beautiful there."

"It is! It's situated in the most beautiful part of Europe. Not far, are forests, mountains, vineyards – and there are hot Summers and snow-laden Winters."

"But what do you mean by 'go to Friedrichshafen?' We can't do that; we live in the DDR," replied Dagmar laughing. "It would be too expensive – and anyway, we'd never get a visa."

"Not for a holiday – to live!"

"But why to Friedrichshafen?"

"I'll tell you. I've an uncle in Friedrichshafen who's a veterinary surgeon. He has a prosperous practice; he travels to many farms and villages in the neighbourhood, and he runs a large kennel where he employs assistants. Until 1948 he had a large practice in Fürstenwede, east of Berlin, and then he and his family went to West Germany as refugees. Since that time, he's founded and built up the practice in Friedrichshafen. Now he's becoming elderly; he's over-worked, and none of his children (who are already married and settled) will take over the business. Last month, my uncle sent a letter to my father suggesting the idea of my taking over the practice. Naturally, my uncle prefers the practice should remain in the family, if it's possible, rather than selling out to a stranger. I've discussed it at length with my father, and we've written to my uncle and already received a reply. The letter came yesterday. My uncle has consulted his lawyers, and they've drawn up proposals for an agreement as to my taking over the business."

"It sounds wonderful,!" replied Dagmar clapping her hands, "but where would the money come from to buy the practice?"

"For the first two years I'd work as a partner with my uncle. That would form part of the agreement. During that time, I'd work on a good salary and have time to settle comfortably into the neighbourhood. Then, the practice would be passed entirely over to me, and my uncle would go into retirement."

"For what sum would your uncle sell you the practice?"

"For about fifty thousand marks."

"But if we went to the West, we'd have practically no money. Could you buy the practice from the salary of your first two years in Friedrichshafen?"

"No, that would be impossible. There'd be so many other things we'd have to spend money on, in building up a home."

"Would we loan the money from a bank?"

"No. We'd pay over an agreed amount annually to my uncle in monthly instalments – and on his decease (if he died before the purchase completion) to his heirs via their lawyers acting as trustees."

"It would be wonderful,!" exclaimed Dagmar, her eyes lighting up with joy and happiness. "I should love to live in South Germany."

"I'm glad, then, we both feel the same about it," said Dieter taking her hands into his. "At first I was worried what your reaction might be about leaving your relatives here in Berlin. I think we'd be very happy in Friedrichshafen."

"When would we be able to go,?" asked Dagmar as a waiter served the couple with soup and rolls.

"Naturally, I must complete my studies here in Berlin first," replied Dieter. "Next year I'll finish my studies and leave the University. Next year, we'll go to Friedrichshafen."

"I'm so happy, I can hardly wait for the day to arrive. To go to West Germany – it'll be wonderful!"

"To think, and say, and do as we like – to live in freedom!"

"We'd be free to travel where we liked – everything would be so much cheaper, and life would be so luxurious! Just think, it would be wonderful,!" exclaimed Dagmar suddenly raising her voice in an outburst of joy.

"Sh-h-h-h-h! Quiet,!" whispered Dieter raising a finger to his lips. "Everything must remain a secret. We don't want our Vopo friends to overhear us."

"They're too busy stuffing themselves," said Dagmar smiling and glancing across the room to where the Vopos sat. "Just look at them!"

"They're certainly enjoying themselves," replied Dieter with a smile, "but if they're going to eat all of that head, they've got a lot to get through."

"How shall we travel to West Germany,?" said Dagmar returning to the topic, laying her fingers on Dieter's hand.

"By air, of course, from Tempelhof."

"Will your father give us the money for that?"

"No, that would be dangerous – for my father. Our going to the West must be made to seem like a sudden impetuous action – as if the whole thing had been unplanned. If my father were suspected of aiding or abetting our flight from the DDR, he could lose everything. Even if he were suspected of *knowing* of our escape in advance, he might be punished."

But how can we escape from the DDR without the authorities suspecting your father knew about it?"

"Listen! My father and I have thought up a plan," said Dieter leaning over the table speaking in a whisper. "We can make our flight to the West seem like a romantic elopement. My father can feign disapproval of our attachment – to have done everything in his power to prevent our marriage."

"But on what grounds?"

"On the grounds that neither you nor any of your family are members of the SED."

"Would the authorities really believe that?"

"If they don't believe the excuse itself, then I still think they can be made to believe my father's disapproved of our friendship on other grounds, and did everything in his power to end it." Dieter hesitated momentarily, and made an airy gesture with his hand as if to overcome a slight awkwardness as to the wording of his sentence. "My father might refer with contempt to yourself and your family, when questioned by the authorities. He could refer contemptuously to the CDU and especially to your father. If the authorities disbelieved him, which is possible, they'd still be led to believe my father disapproved of our friendship on the grounds of social differences between our families."

"That's clever – really clever,!" exclaimed Dagmar, her eyes lighting up. "Who'd need to doubt that? Your father is elderly and might still have old-fashioned ideas about class, despite his membership of the Communist Party. And he'd overcome the embarrassment of openly suggesting such class-based bias by personal and contemptuous remarks aimed at my family in view of their CDU involvement."

"Exactly! And meanwhile, we'd have eloped to the West without our families having received any indications beforehand."

"Neither of our families?"

"Yes – why not? And then we'd send letters to our parents in Berlin from Friedrichshafen, explaining convincingly the motives for our flight to the West."

"That's wonderful! What an alibi for our parents if they're confronted by the authorities! But still you haven't explained the financial side – our flight from Tempelhof."

"I've relatives in the West sector, remember. We'll borrow enough money for our flight from Berlin to Hanover, and for our fare from there to Friedrichshafen from my uncle. That'll be the first of our debts to be paid back."

"It sounds so wonderful,!" exclaimed Dagmar. "But can it ever be true?"

"Of course! Next year we go to West Germany, to live in freedom,!" replied Dieter, his face radiating joy and enthusiasm.

BOOK XII

Hope Looks Westward

Love is above the laws, above the opinion of men; it is
the truth, the flame, the pure element, the primary idea
of the moral world.

Germaine de Staël, *Zulma and Other Tales.*

Chapter 47

The idea and prospect of fleeing from East Germany and settling in the little Swabian town of Friedrichshafen, soon began to obsess the minds of the young lovers. Their excitement and joy increased as each practical detail was considered, decided and acted upon. There were so many things which had to be thought out, so many difficulties to be overcome, and so many preparations to be made, that there was always something new for the lovers to discuss on every occasion they met, despite the fact that more than a year lay ahead of them before they would leave for the West.

The details of their registration as refugees and their subsequent registration as citizens of West Germany and the issue of new passports had to be considered, and then there were all the details concerning the agreement transferring the veterinary pratice over to Dieter, and then there were a hundred things to read up in books about their new life and the people of Württemburg.

For security reasons the letters between Dieter's family and the uncle in Friedrichshafen were transmitted via relatives in West Berlin, as a sensible precaution against the correspondence being intercepted by the East German authorities. The correspondence between Dieter and his uncle soon became a busy all-absorbing affair, and as letters were regularly exchanged between them every two weeks, Dieter soon accumulated enough letters from his uncle to become a thick packet tied firmly together by string and kept locked in a small box. Evenings would be set aside for writing the letters, and sometimes, the two lovers would settle down and write a letter together. All the letters received from Friedrichshafen, and most of those sent by Dieter, were read by Dagmar, and often, he asked for her advice on a point before completing a paragraph or sealing down the envelope.

Dieter's letters to his uncle usually took a questioning form: asking for advice on legal or business matters as things presently stood within the Federal *Land* of Baden-Württemburg, requesting clarification or enlargement on some point raised in an earlier letter, and questions about the life and people of the locality. Whatever pains were taken by Dieter in composing the letters, the results of his correspondence were rewarding in one respect. His uncle was a keen letter writer, and they arrived in thick envelopes, often twenty or more pages at a time, and even if they were packed full of unsought-for advice on peripheral matters (and offering advice is an irrepressible German characteristic) and even if they were verbose, at least they were also full of intimate and often amusing details descriptive of the local scene. Sometimes he enclosed pictures and post cards of Friedrichshafen, and these Dieter gave to Dagmar.

Eventually, an agreement was drawn up in Friedrichshafen as to Dieter taking over his uncle's practice, and a copy sent to Berlin. This necessitated that Dieter and his father consult a lawyer in the West sector, and several amendments were suggested, and several more weeks of correspondence ensued, before the agreement was finalised to the satisfaction of all parties. All practical details were being brought up, examined and settled long before the lovers were to make their flight, and every day, the move to Friedrichshafen seemed to become a closer reality, and in view of their detailed preparations there seemed no reason as to why they should believe otherwise.

Their dreams, their hopes, their life aspirations were centred on the prospects of their future in West Germany. There they would find freedom, happiness and prosperity, as well as an immediate relief from the material deprivation enforced on the people of the East. No more food shortages; no more hunger; no more need for enduring the Winter's cold in unheated buildings; no more extortionate expenses for clothing in the West sectors just to look presentable, and no more living in fear of being watched or overheard by the People's police! Also, the lovers were exceptionally fortunate in being able to go directly from East Berlin to Friedrichshafen to find both a home and work awaiting their arrival.

True, they would leave behind nearly all their worldly chattels, apart from what could be stuffed into a small suitcase each, which they might carry with them in the S-Bahn train, and if necessary, push under a seat and disown, should the Vopos board the train before the sector boundary, but unlike several millions of others who preceded them, they would avoid the gruelling experience of life in a refugee camp with all its discomforts. Indeed, Dieter and Dagmar had good reason to think themselves exceptionally fortunate. There were no major problems or crises which faced them in the West. They even had the perfect alibi for ensuring the safety of relatives left behind. A new world lay before them!

It was not surprising that hardly a week passed when Dagmar did not dream about the life which lay before her. She dreamt about the sunshine and warmth of Summer in the south of Germany, about villages and pretty cottages overgrown and permeated with the scent of honeysuckle, about baroque white-walled churches with onion topped towers, and blue lakes and high white capped mountains, and forests and fields of corn, and meadows and the sound of cowbells. It would all be so different from the drab greyness of East Berlin! Her mind became haunted by the beauty of South Germany. Her dreams were vivid pictures of the life there as she imagined it, and her dreams aroused her conscious imagination and her impatience to leave the East, and often, she would experience the same dream on consecutive nights, and sometimes a dream would recur at intervals over a period of many weeks or months.

In one recurring dream, she found herself strolling along a narrow cobbled roadway in a quiet part of the town, and on one side was a wall overgrown with creeper, and on the other, old houses and rose gardens, and the roadway led down to a sandy beach and the blue lake. In another dream, she visualised the house in which Dieter and she might live. It was a small grey stone cottage with quaint windows and a slate roof, and in the garden was a lilley pond and goldfish, and there were baroque statues and an aviary with many-coloured birds.

Her parents expressed their approval of their daughter's prospective flight to the West, despite the sorrow they occasionally expressed of her leaving them. – "I expect you'll feel homesick at first," confided her mother on one occasion. (Dagmar had never for a single night been away from the home of her parents.) - "I expect I shall be at first," replied Dagmar sadly. The good Frau Renot felt particularly upset at the prospect of her daughter leaving, and although she tried to conceal this fact from her daughter, it soon became clear to Dagmar how her mother felt. Sometimes when the good Frau spoke to Papa Renot about the arrangements for her daughter's flight to the West, she even clutched a handkerchief in her hand, to hold back tears which by chance might flood her eyes.

"What will it be like Papa, when there's no Dagmar around to care for, and to keep us company,?" bemoaned the good Frau. "We'll feel so alone in the evenings when there's an empty place for her at the table, and when the sound of her feet and her voice will never be heard in our house again."

Papa Renot consoled his wife when she became depressed in this way, speaking of the good life that lay ahead for their daughter. Whenever the parents spoke to Dagmar herself about her flight to the West, they were sure to speak in a bright optimistic tone and to encourage her aspirations for the life which lay ahead. They knew that her flight and settlement in the West was in her own best interests, and they tried to conceal their personal feelings of sorrow on her future departure. After all, they knew that the eventual aspirations of every young German in the East – of every German with initiative who held out hope for his or her own future – was to fly to the West – to the land of freedom!

Naturally, the arrangements for the young couple's flight was kept in the strictest secrecy. This was of prime importance. Dagmar's parents did not whisper a word about it to a soul outside the immediate family circle, and Dagmar confided the matter only to her friend Renata. Any discovery by the authorities of the planned flight might have resulted in prison sentences for the persons knowing about the matter in advance.

It was now very frequent that Dieter and Dagmar visited the West sectors in connection with arrangements for their future. Not only did they visit the West with a view to fixing the immediate practical arrangements, but they visited the libraries and read all the books they could lay their hands on, descriptive of the life and people of South Germany. Their journey from East to West, from a world of oppression to the world of freedom, would not be the only significant change entailed in moving to their new habitat.

They soon realised that the people and temperament of South Germany was a far cry from that of the North. Some of the older South Germans might in their own minds (for historical and cultural – as well as religious reasons) wish to dissociate themselves from the North. Sometimes, Dagmar wanted to laugh at and regard with amusement the people of the South, whilst also liking them from a distance for their quaint habits and customs and a strange fascination they might arouse. She wanted to regard them as a tourist might look on the natives of another country.

The Prussian (this including the Berliner) is a very subjective animal, finding it difficult to identify with others, although others may not find it difficult to identify with him or her. In view of this, Dieter realised that the move to the South would necessitate a process of cultural assimilation, although Dagmar seemed to remain oblivious to this factor. She still wanted to regard the Swabians (people of Württemburg) with their outlandish dialect as somehow quaint or even comic.

"They speak a terrible German there – just like a lot of old farmers," exclaimed Dagmar on one occasion. "Do you think we'll be able to understand what they say? If we don't, then we'll just have to ask them to speak High German. I can even understand *Platt deutsch*, a little, but that Swabian – it's terrible!"

"You mustn't speak like that," replied Dieter in a mock chiding tone. "The President of West Germany is a Swabian and he speaks with a strong Swabian accent, and if he were to be told what you say about Swabians, he might withhold the issuing of our West German passports."

"Oh, *quatsch*,!" replied Dagmar sharply.

"Won't it be funny to see all those fat old men running around in leather pants and green forest caps," exclaimed Dagmar on another occasion.

"You shouldn't say that," replied Dieter. "Remember, they won't take to us either so easily. As soon as we settle in, the neighbours will say that two more 'bloody sow Prussians' have arrived again from the East. They regard us as barbarians. They still think we walk around in spiked helmets with swords clanking at our sides."

"What a silly notion ,!" exclaimed Dagmar screwing up her nose with an expression of disapproval.

"They say we Berliners have got a big mouth and a bitter tongue," continued Dieter. "They say we're rude and got rough manners. Remember what uncle said in his last letter? We mustn't give nicknames to everything, because they don't like cynicism, and they'll take it to heart as a piece of ill-humour."

"Then they haven't got any humour," said Dagmar.

"Their humour is different from ours. They have a different temperament."

"They don't understand us," said Dagmar.

"The history and traditions of the South are different from the North," explained Dieter. "They are Catholic, we are Evangelical. They are more fond of pleasure and expressing their feelings. We are more reflective and intellectual. A hundred years ago Germany was divided into many self-governing sovereign states. Since then much has happened to unite us, both politically and in spirit. Still, the world is changing, and in a hundred years, perhaps all Europe may be likewise united. Let's hope so!"

"The people of the South should regard us as a credit to Germany because of our role in uniting the country," said Dagmar proudly.

"Perhaps, but you mustn't tell them that," replied Dieter. "Some of the very old people still hate Prussians – they resented our power. Of course, most of that is disappearing now, but they still have some distorted ideas about us. They even blame us for two world wars – which is cheek – because all the leading Nazis were South Germans, and it was Prussians who opposed Hitler all along from the start, and actually planned and carried out the assassination plot of July 20th in 1944."

"Still, it will be wonderful when we arrive there – in Friedrichshafen,!" exclaimed Dagmar clapping her hands.

Because of the secrecy of the young couple in planning their flight to the West, and to leave a plausible story behind them, so that if necessary their parents might extricate themselves from any charge by the authorities in the matter, it was wisely decided that they defer their official engagement until a much later date. As to the exact time of their future engagement, they were as yet undecided, but their flight to the West would be made to seem like a sudden and impetuous action of a young couple hopelessly in love, acting in conflict against their parents. It was thought best, by those involved in the conspiracy, that the official engagement should be announced several weeks, or two or three months, prior to the actual flight, and that then a pretence would be made by Dieter's parents expressing their displeasure at the match. It was all very Machiavellian, and everything seemed to be working out to plan.

It was a sunny although cold day, when Dagmar walked along Stalin Allee to Andreas Strasse to meet Dieter at the appointed time, and on arriving at the street corner, she certainly met someone she knew – expected even, but the sight confronting her was so different from that she had ever seen before, that her eyes lit up with astonishment and delight.

"You like it, yes,?" said Dieter beaming with pride at his appearance.

"It's beautiful,!" exclaimed Dagmar stretching forward her hand. "May I feel the material?"

"Of course," replied Dieter.

"Why didn't you tell me before you'd be dressed like this, then I'd have worn my best party frock,?" said Dagmar.

"I wanted to keep it as a big surprise for you," replied Dieter. "The material is really expensive – even in the West something like this would cost a fortune – and you see these gold tabs on the cuffs," he continued, raising his elbows to the chest, "they're made from real gold thread."

"It's beautiful,!" repeated Dagmar. "You look just like a field-marshall. I'll feel so proud to be with you. And the cap makes you seem even taller than you are. How high it is at the front!"

"And the boots are made of the softest leather," said Dieter glancing down at his feet. "They could almost be made of kid skin."

It was a Saturday afternoon at the beginning of Spring. Dieter had been in the National People's Army for more than two months. He had spoken little about his training, and for several weekends he had been away from Berlin on manoeuvres in the East zone, and two or three times he had even had to cancel his Tuesday meetings with Dagmar for reasons of training. Once before, Dagmar had seen him in uniform (when they had met on a Sunday night) but that was in a course grey uniform, which had had previous wearers and the fabric gave out an unpleasant smell, and he had worn thick shapeless looking boots and been shirtless without a tie. On that occasion Dagmar had also been surprised to see him in uniform, but he had been evasive and slightly awkward, apologising for not having had time to return home and change first. His occasional offhand references to the Volksarmee had always been marked by contempt – that it was time-wasting and a nuisance.

The couple went to the car which was parked nearby and drove to Werlsee, where Dagmar was a frequent visitor.

"It'll be a surprise for my parents also," said Dieter, "to see me dressed like this. They don't know I've been made an officer yet."

"You've kept it as a surprise for everyone then," said Dagmar.

"This time last week I didn't know I'd be an officer myself," said Dieter. "I only had the uniform fitted up this morning."

"How did it come about? How did you become commissioned so soon?"

"Earlier this week I was called into the Commandant's office – or rather, the assistant Commandant's office, and he said that last month enquiries had come down from higher quarters as to my military bearing and proficiency. Well, he sent back a good report, and then instructions reached my unit from the Central Staff headquarters that I'd be transferred to the Political Section of the Army."

"I suppose because of your political pamphlets," said Dagmar.

"That's it,!" replied Dieter. "The Commandant said I'd be commissioned and promoted to the rank of *Leutnant*, and then transferred to the Political Officers School of the Volksarmee in Treptow."

"In Treptow,!" exclaimed Dagmar.

"Yes, I'll be able to come and visit you more frequently in the evenings," said Dieter. "All the arrangements for my promotion have been made during the last two days. You can understand, I've been doing quite some rushing around, from one place to another, filling in forms and completing all the formalities."

"It's wonderful that you'll be in Treptow, and able to come and visit us in uniform."

"Of course, more of my time will be taken up by military duties now, which'll be unfortunate," continued Dieter brightly, "but eventually, I'll be made a Captain. The Commandant even said I might be called upon to take up a position in the School as a lecturer in Marxist-Leninist Military philosophy."

"Do they have such a department of philosophy?"

"Of course they do."

"The material of the uniform is so soft to the touch," exclaimed Dagmar feeling his cuffs again.

"Yes," replied Dieter, and then a thoughtful expression crossed his face. "The uniform's all right; it's the cause behind it that's all wrong," he added despondently.

On arriving at the house in Werlsee, the two lovers were in high spirits.

"We must put the car in the garage and then reach the front door of the house without my parents seeing us," said Dieter as he drove the car down the drive.

Two minutes later, the young couple were running quickly around the outside of the house, close to the walls, crouching down so that their heads were below sill level of the ground floor windows, towards the front door. Dieter held Dagmar's hand tightly in his begging her to crouch lower, and with his other hand, he held onto his cap so that it might not fall and be spoilt on the path.

"It's a pity we won't be able to bring your uniform to Friedrichshafen with us," joked Dagmar breathlessly, as they arrived at the front door of the house, "to keep as a memento of your old life in Berlin."

The door was opened quietly, and Dieter exclaimed, "Sh-h-h,!" and the couple entered on tip toe. Dagmar's coat was hung in the hallway, and then to announce their entry, he banged his fist loudly on the sitting room door, and they entered boldly, hand-in-hand. Frau Liebermann was darning socks and the doctor, who was also seated comfortably in an armchair, had his head buried behind a copy of *Neues Deutschland*.

"*Leutnant* Liebermann, reporting for duty,!" exclaimed Dieter clicking his heels with a smart military salute.

Frau Liebermann rose from her chair, and with outstretched arms, greeted Dagmar effusively. Dagmar left Dieter's side, approaching her hostess, and the two ladies kissed – so far advanced had their feelings of friendship, trust and familiarity progressed since that cold misty day the previous November.

Dr. Liebermann lowered his paper, and glanced up at his son who was beaming with pride, still holding his hand in a smart military salute. Dr. Liebermann was not amused. Dieter still stood there, beaming happily.

"What's all this nonsense,?" exclaimed Dr. Liebermann at last.

Dieter's face dropped.

"Nonsense? I'm an officer, Papa," he replied.

"Since when were you made an officer in the Volksarmee,?" said Dr. Liebermann irritably.

"Why, only last week, Papa. It all came quite suddenly," replied Dieter in an offended tone, surprised by his father's response.

"I should think it did come suddenly,!" exclaimed Dr. Liebermann.

"What's wrong, anyway, Papa?"

"What's wrong? That should be clearer to you than to me."

Frau Liebermann and Dagmar stood together, looking on with surprise at this interlocution between father and son.

"I don't understand, Papa," said Dieter throwing up his hands.

"When did you know you'd be commissioned,?" enquired Dr. Liebermann.

"On Monday."

"Why didn't you come back here and discuss it first? Why didn't you tell us beforehand?"

"Do I have to tell you everything I do beforehand? I'm not in Kindergarten any more."

"Anyone would think you still were by this stupidity."

"Stupidity? I thought you'd be pleased to see me in the uniform of an officer."

"Now we're all Communists in this house – good beetroot Communists – I know that," began Dr. Liebermann irately, "but this is going too far. We don't all have to gang up as officers in the Volksarmee – that's taking risks beyond a sensible limit."

"Now I begin to understand. You have to act both as my conscience bearer and the censor of my political activities," began Dieter angrily. "When I was a small child, you brought me up to hate and despise Communism and everything it meant. When you joined the SED, you still taught me to hate Communism. Then one day, two school teachers called here, and after they left, you spent years trying to persuade me to join the Young Pioneers, but by that time I was so mentally conditioned to loathing Communism that I refused to co-operate in any Communistic organisation. Then after I won the prize for that essay and began writing those pamphlets, you had to frown on that. Then I joined the FDJ and you said that that was the only good thing I'd done in years. Then I began drawing those cartoons, and you criticised me for that – for expressing my genuine political beliefs. And now I've become an officer in the Volksarmee, and you take an exception to that. What do you want me to do then?"

"Just not to go too far, that's all," replied Dr. Liebermann, "and taking a commission in the Volksarmee *is* going too far. I don't think you understand the implications of what you've done."

"What implications?"

"When were you commissioned?"

"On Wednesday, Papa."

"And can you repeat to me, word for word, the oath of loyalty taken by an officer in the Volksarmee,?" said Dr. Liebermann.

"Er – no, not exactly – everything was done so quickly, Papa – they're transferring me to the Political Officers School in Treptow, and for some administrative reasons, they had to commission me first."

"Political Officers School? That's worse still. Did you see the oath?"

"Everything was done in a hurry, Papa. Everyone was in a rush. I was given a lot of forms and papers to sign – and I signed them."

"That was gross stupidity," exclaimed Dr. Liebermann angrily, banging his arm onto the side of his chair.

"I couldn't have read everything I was given – there was so much. In any case, the instructions for my commission were sent down from above – on orders of the Central Staff headquarters – perhaps even sent from the office of Colonel-General Willi Stoph himself. I had to accept the commission whether I liked it or not. You see, persons with my kind of ability and background are short on the ground. They were desperate to use my expertise."

"Involving yourself that deeply with the Volksarmee is courting trouble. You must know the People's Army is one of the main organisations ensuring the security of the State in times of trouble. Therefore, its internal security is ruthless. No one under the slightest suspicion of holding subversive views would be allowed to run amok for long. With the things you've been up to, the security authorities must have tabs on you by this time – or they will do pretty shortly."

"Well, I don't know about that," said Dieter suddenly overcome with qualms of doubt, "but they must have had their own reasons for promoting me. My promotion came on orders from the top."

"Their reasons for promoting you are clear enough: they want to use you as a political officer," replied Dr. Liebermann.

"It was something I couldn't evade. Had I hesitated even, in accepting promotion, it would have struck the military authorities as pretty strange, and might have aroused the worst kind of suspicions. They must have received good reports on me, else I wouldn't be an officer today."

"You just be careful in everything you do and say in the future then," said Dr. Liebermann in a slow threatening tone.

"I shall," replied Dieter impressed by his father's manner.

"If the military authorities have any lingering doubts as to your reliability, they'll be watching you – you can be assured of that."

"I'll take care."

"Your entering the West sectors of Berlin would be enough to incriminate you on any number of charges. Your oath as an officer in the Volksarmee isn't something to be taken lightly – it's real and binding – not like being in the FDJ."

"I'll take care I'm neither watched nor followed, and I'll account for every movement I take – just in case I am questioned."

"You'll need to do that," said Dr. Liebermann. "With your plans for leaving the East, it's unfortunate you've had to become involved with the Volksarmee at this juncture."

The discussion came to an end, and during that afternoon, the subject of Dieter's service with the Volksarmee was not touched on again, and before he drove Dagmar back to Berlin, he went up to his room and changed back into civilian clothes.

His subsequent attitude towards service in the Volksarmee whilst attending the Political Officers School in Treptow was ambiguous. He was careful in everything he did and said, both in and outside the School and in the University, which might possibly cause suspicion or betray the conspiracy of his flight, and perhaps his very reticence might have aroused the suspicions of those who knew him as a characteristic which was out of keeping with his personality. On the other hand, he could not suppress an instinctive feeling of pride in the uniform itself, and in the evenings, he often visited Dagmar and her family in Graetz Strasse in his recently acquired field grey attire.

The good Frau, in her naïve way, was delighted to see him in such a "glorious looking" uniform – it reflected so flatteringly on Dagmar – but Papa Renot reacted with marked disinterest on seeing Dieter in what he described as a "tin soldier's costume," and he passed other flippantly irreverent remarks. After several calls, Dieter noticed this displeasure and it seemed as if the sight of the uniform was distasteful to the old man, for he was silent and even left the room on occasion, when Dieter was entertaining the family with his conversation and laughter. Because of this, Dieter began to change at the School into civilian clothes, before visiting the family in Graetz Strasse.

As a result of these evening calls at Graetz Strasse, Dagmar was able to entertain Dieter alone in the sitting room of the flat at No. 55, after her grandmother had been put to bed. These were clandestine meetings between the young lovers. When the family stayed up late in the evenings, they always sat and entertained themselves at No. 16, whilst Frau Brüning had meanwhile been put to bed to sleep in peace without fear of being awoken at the other side of the street. When the time came for Dieter to finally take his leave (and it was usually by then late in the evening) it was not unnatural, therefore, for Dagmar to excuse herself from the company, and the young couple left the flat together.

Once outside the flat, it then naturally became Dieter's duty to escort Dagmar to her door. Once the lovers had reached the door, and begun to exchange parting kisses and parting wishes for the night, it was not uneasy for Dieter to persuade the fair one to allow him to "sit" in the sitting room awhile and "rest," before returning on that "arduous" ten minute walk to Treptower Park station. Once they were seated on the sofa in the said sitting room, it was neither surpising nor unexpected that after a brief struggle, that the lovers would have discovered to one another to have yet again enacted the rites of love. "It's so much more comfortable here than in the car," Dagmar shrewdly observed.

During these occasions when they expressed their love for one another at No. 55, the utmost caution was observed by the lovers. The light was never switched on in the passageway in case Granny's door was ajar, with the result that she'd awaken; shoes were removed by the front door of the flat; tip-toeing had to be strictly adhered to, and the opening and closing of doors done with the greatest care; no speaking louder than a soft whisper was allowed, and the physical act had to be performed on the floor, as the sofa was not long enough, and the couch standing against the opposite wall could not be depended upon for the reason of noisy springs. On several occasions, when the couple returned to No. 55, they crossed Frau Hartmann in the main hallway, but they never took notice of her, and she only glanced at them with a suspiciously inquisitive look, although on one occasion on seeing Dieter in his uniform, she glanced after him with a shocked expression as if to say, "What scum to be serving as an officer in the honourable People's Army!"

Chapter 48

One evening when Dagmar met Dieter at the corner of Luisen Strasse and Karl Platz, which was very near the Veterinary School where he studied, before going to the Deutsches Theatre nearby, she noticed he was more introspective than usual. They made their way to the theatre, and at first she refrained from remarking on his quiet frame of mind. When, however, a few minutes later, they were seated in some comfortable chairs, opposite a low coffee table spread with light refreshments, and Dieter remained silent and meditative, Dagmar suspected that some new anxiety was gnawing at his mind.

Was it in connection with his studies, or with the arrangements for their flight – had some new and inexplicable difficulty arisen, or had a misfortune of some other kind occurred? They were seated in the crowded handsomely furnished foyer restaurant of the theatre. Dieter stirred his coffee, and crossed his brows, as he glanced down at the table with a serious expression. Dagmar asked him what was the matter.

At first Dieter was evasive, saying that nothing was really the matter, or at least nothing of consequence. Then he said that something strange had occurred at the University that day – nothing serious or important even – but which nonetheless had disturbed his peace of mind.

"What,?" enquired Dagmar.

"Perhaps it's silly – I shouldn't allow the incident to worry me. I'm sure there can't be anything in it – but I'll tell you what happened, all the same," said Dieter.

That afternoon Dieter had been confidentially approached and taken aside by one of his teachers, Professor Buchholz, and told to "Watch out for himself." The two were alone in that room in the University set aside for the Professor's own use. Dieter was surprised on receiving this warning which had been given in the most earnest tones. He responded with a feeling of resentment, for he saw this warning as a kind of implied threat on the Professor's part – although he knew not of what kind. On an earlier occasion the Professor had reported him to his father, and Dieter remembered him for that action which he considered "mean and malicious."

"I always watch out," replied Dieter defensively, not knowing what the Professor was driving at.

"You'll have to take greater care of yourself in the future, Liebermann – I'm warning you," said the Professor shaking his finger, his voice vibrating with emotion.

"Please explain,?" enquired Dieter arrogantly.

"I can't say anything more than that," replied the Professor. He was a tall elderly man.

"You can't say more? What are you asking of me? Why did you bring me to this room – just to deliver a baseless threat which you and I know to be nonsense? No, Herr Professor, what is it you really have to say to me? If you really know something, then please tell me."

"I have nothing more to say than what I've said."

"It seems as if you're fond of secrecy, Herr Professor. You make me curious."

"I can tell you nothing more."

"Why then did you have to worry my peace of mind by telling me anything then? Why bother? Why say, 'Watch out for yourself?' What am I supposed to do – stop at every street corner and look over my shoulder? Are you trying to make me paranoid?"

"You know what I mean," answered the Professor firmly. "I've brought you here for your own good. In warning you I'm risking my own security – so don't ask me more."

"I suppose you were risking your own security when you handed that cartoon to my father, a few months ago"

"That cartoon was handed to me by another person."

"What person?"

"Don't be absurd! How can you expect me to tell you? It suffices only to say by a person connected with the security authorities in this University."

"Security authorities! If you tell me who this person is, then perhaps you'll really be doing something for my good."

"That's enough of this conversation," replied the Professor irately. "I've told you enough – too much even. My warning alone (should it be discovered) would be enough to incriminate me. I intend holding down my position here, come what may, and I'm not going to risk my neck by revealing more. You should be grateful for my pains, not petulant."

"I'm sorry, Herr Professor. Perhaps I was impolite," said Dieter bowing, "but naturally you've disturbed my peace of mind by bringing me here. Naturally, I'd like to know more."

"I know nothing more myself. I've only been instructed to watch you closely, reporting everything you say which could be given a political interpretation."

"On 'everything I say,!'" exclaimed Dieter astonished. "If they have anything against me, then why don't they have me apprehended and cross-examined?"

"That's not the way they operate in this country – you should know that. Anyhow, I don't expect they have specific suspicions against you. I should think it's merely routine, because of your post in the Volksarmee," said the Professor consolingly.

"That's possibly so," replied Dieter.

"You haven't done anything wrong, have you,?" said the Professor in sudden concern. "You're not involved in clandestine activity of any kind?"

"No, nothing," reassured Dieter.

"Your behaviour in the University hasn't been too discreet in the past. Your position in the FDJ hasn't really been a cover. You've always been outspoken – remember those cartoons you drew and pinned up. They came to the knowledge of the security authorities. It might stem from that."

"But that was months ago. I've been discreet since then. Why should they want to start keeping a watch on me now?"

"A few months is nothing. Years, yes, but not months. These things don't blow over overnight."

"As you say, perhaps it's only a routine check because of my new post in the Volksarmee. The reliability of newly commissioned officers has to be ascertained through their past. – When did this person who approached you, tell you to keep an eye on me?"

"About a month ago."

"That would be it then," said Dieter, his mind at ease. "If they really held something against me, then they'd have arrested me or called me before a tribunal for a dose of criticism and self-criticism long ago."

"I should still take care and watch your step," said the Professor grimly.

"Thanks for your advice," replied Dieter.

"I don't want to lose a valued pupil," added the Professor as Dieter made towards the door.

As the young couple sat in the foyer of the Deutsches Theatre, Dagmar became no less concerned than Dieter over the episode earlier that day.

"Do you think anyone might have discovered the plans for our flight,?" enquired Dagmar.

Dieter replied that he thought this most unlikely, and he added that they might start imagining all kinds of things, after receiving certain knowledge that he was in fact being watched in the University.

"Do you think we should go to the West before completing your studies,?" suggested Dagmar.

Dieter replied that that would be most inadvisable and would create a whole packet of problems. He told her not to worry, saying everything would be all right. They had only to remain calm, and act as they had always done before, never breathing a word to anyone about the plans for their flight.

"Remember, only one more year in Berlin, and then we leave for Friedrichshafen," said Dieter encouragingly.

The couple acted with the utmost caution in everything they did and said. The Professor's warning had been a sobering experience. Anything which might possibly arouse the remotest suspicion was undertaken with the greatest circumspection.

"Providing the Stasi are only watching me in the University, we have nothing to worry about," said Dieter on one occasion. "As far as they're concerned I'm still a good member of the FDJ, obediently handing out leaflets and giving all the good old propaganda talk for the Party. Anything I might have done in the past can't arouse their suspicions now because I'm acting like a new man."

"I hope you're not acting too differently," said Dagmar.

"Just differently enough to convince them I've been converted ideologically to the Party line," replied Dieter.

"Well, I hope they really are convinced of that," said Dagmar anxiously.

"They should be," said Dieter. "I've lost several friends because of what I've done or not done, clever play-acting, and snubbing old acquaintances (in the University restaurant) known for their criticism of the regime."

"If the change has been too sudden though, you're bound to arouse the suspicion of the Stasi," said Dagmar.

"They can account my ideological conversion to the Party from the time of my commission in the Volksarmee. My mind was seduced by the uniform."

"Do they think you're that simple?"

"It's a reason that'll suffice. After all, it must have happened many times before."

"Let's hope that'll be so," said Dagmar.

"Providing we're careful in everything we do outside as well as inside the University, nothing can go wrong," said Dieter.

The young couple took the precaution of never discussing their plans within hearing range, and on passing along the street, they occasionally turned round to see that no one was following, and Dieter used the driving mirror to take a note of and write down the number of vehicles apparently tracking them.

On going to the West sectors they always used the S-Bahn or Underground, and usually in the evening when the trains were most crowded, so it was almost impossible for them to be followed; whilst both kept their eyes alert; intermingled with the crowds on the platform; and jumped onto trains just before the doors closed. Both travelled separately when going from East to West, and usually, they sat or stood at either end of the same carriage, and before the train left the penultimate station in the East sector, they would check that no frontier police had boarded the carriage, and if in fact this happened they would quickly hop off the train.

There was nothing to encumber Dagmar travelling between the East West sectors if she chose, but during the past few weeks, the authorities had begun enforcing travel restrictions on students going to the West – a periodical fact of life for the Eastern half of the city. Naturally, these restrictions were difficult to enforce but several students had in fact been caught by the frontier police and punished. Therefore, whenever the couple crossed the frontier from East to West Berlin, they began to experience the journey as an adventure of risk. Despite this, it was still the safest way of crossing from one half of the city to the other. The frontier Vopos only boarded trains infrequently to check passengers. Had the couple crossed on foot, the chances of being stopped by the police would have been very much greater.

On one occasion when the couple were together, Dieter opened the inside of his jacket, and smiling, pointed to where the lining met the arm of the coat.

"What's that,?" asked Dagmar.

"It's a secret pocket," confided Dieter. "On my suggestion, my mother sewed it into the jacket last night."

"What's it for?"

"For carrying letters and other secret documents from the West sectors to the East. It wouldn't do if I was caught carrying one of my uncle's letters, would it? The entire show would be given away! See, the pocket's quite well concealed."

"But if they made a close search, they'd soon find it."

"Yes, but how often do they do that?"

The obsessive care of the young couple in safeguarding the great secret of their flight arose from their fear after the Professor's warning. It was not unnatural that their caution and forethought arising from an inevitable feeling of apprehension should further promote all kinds of new suspicions in their minds. Despite this, they never at any time found evidence of being followed or overheard in conversation. On only one occasion did they encounter an experience which seemed strange at the time but was soon afterwards forgotten.

It occurred one day as the young couple were changing books in the American Memorial Library in Blücher Strasse. Dieter had just chosen several books and laid them on a table, and had returned to the shelves, to the reference section, a little distance away, and was consulting something in the *Grosse Brockhaus*, when Dagmar discreetly nudged him in the side.

"What's that man doing over there by your books,?" she asked him.

Dieter turned round, glancing towards the table where he had laid tha books. A young man with pencil and notebook in hand was looking furtively about him, opening the covers of the books as he busily took down some notes. He was dressed in grey trousers, a sports jacket and a white open necked shirt. He had dark hair and was heavily built.

"What do you think he wants,?" said Dagmar.

"I don't know," said Dieter without taking his eyes off the man, "but he's acting strangely."

The couple walked back to the table.

"What are you doing,?" enquired Dieter abruptly.

The stranger started.

"I'm sorry – are these books yours,?" he responded.

"Yes – I'm just taking them out of the library. I've just lain them there for a moment."

"You're taking them out, not returning them then,?" said the stranger awkwardly.

"Correct,!" replied Dieter abruptly.

"The fact is I only wanted to borrow one of them. I was just taking down the serial number to reserve it."

"Then there's no need to look at them all," replied Dieter.

"I noticed they all covered the same topic: Hayek, von Mises, and others, on the critique of Socialist theory – a subject close to my heart. I thought I might reserve them all," said the stranger grinning condescendingly.

Dieter looked the man up and down, taking an instant dislike to him for his apparent insolence.

"Well, you've got the information you wanted, and so now you can go," he said.

"Yes, thanking you for your understanding," said the stranger pocketing his pencil and notebook and bowing, before making a hasty exit.

"What do you think he wanted,?" asked Dagmar again.

"I don't know," said Dieter, "but his excuses were lame enough. Let's just forget it."

"Still, it was strange," remarked Dagmar in bewilderment, glancing towards the exit.

Towards the end of Spring the lovers held a small party at Werlsee to celebrate the first anniversary of their meeting. It was strictly a young people's party, and the friends were mostly Dieter's who brought girl friends, fiancées and wives. Renata and the plump girl who worked in the little Art Shop in Stalin Allee, were the sole friends invited by Dagmar. It was Renata's first meeting with Dieter since that day exactly a year previously when she had been so abrupt and unpleasant to him and his friends on the occasion of their first meeting.

Two other friends of Dieter's who had also been with him at the Langer See on that far-away day were also at the party. They (Wolf Spier and Gustaf Maazel) were perceptibly amused at meeting Renata again under such different circumstances. How much had happened since then! Who would have guessed at the time, that such a firm friendship could have blossomed between two of those persons who had by chance met at the Langer See? Certainly, Renata least of all. She was slightly awkward on meeting Wolf and Gustaf again, but whether it was due to any feelings of foolishness for her odd behaviour during that day at the Langer See, cannot with certainty be said, for Renata was often awkward in company, and then she was never at her best with strangers.

Soon all were in high spirits once the drink began to flow, and Wolf and another friend had brought guitars, and the young couple went into the garden and sang and danced until late in the evening. Gustaf (who had also been attracted to Dagmar during that day at the Langer

See) suddenly stood on a chair and delivered an impromptu speech, emotionally conveying his good wishes to the young couple and to a "much envied friend" who had won the heart of the most beautiful girl in Berlin.

"We now only await the engagement day when we can extend to the happy pair the best wishes for their future," concluded Gustaf passionately.

There was loud applause, and when Gustaf descended from the chair, the two friends embraced warmly. Then Dieter stood on the same chair and gave a short speech of thanks. None of the friends at the party (apart from Renata and the plump girl, who worked at the Art Shop) yet knew of the plans for the couple's flight to the West.

"What a pity they won't be able to attend our wedding in Friedrichshafen," confided Dagmar to Dieter when they were left momentarily alone.

Soon it was Summer again, and it was that year when all Europe was gorgeously bathed in sun. Dagmar visited Werlsee most weekends, both Saturday and Sunday, often staying at the house over Saturday night. Many flowers grew in the garden surrounding the house, and often the family ate outside. For Dagmar, they were blissful days of relaxation and peace.

The young couple were often visitors at Dr. Goltz's house nearby. They swam in the small lake, and lay on the warm soft yellow sand, and sunbathed until they were tanned. Dr. Goltz said they might come to the lake and swim and lie on the sands (which bordered his grounds) whenever they chose, and then he insisted they visit the house afterwards. Since the weather was constantly fine, the couple chose to swim in the lake most weekends, and since Dr. Goltz and his wife were so informal in their hospitality, and liked to keep open house, they felt free to avail themselves of their kindness whenever they went to the lake.

Both Dr. and Frau Goltz welcomed the young couple warmly (perhaps because they were childless) and they would sit in the garden for many hours and sip tea, or drink beer or wine, and talk about art and literature. Perhaps a significant reason why the young couple spent so much time with the Goltzes was to be found in the fact that Dieter found a friend and fellow spirit in Dr. Goltz which he did not find in the coldness and critical attitude of his own father. Dr. Goltz and Dieter engaged in long arguments on aesthetics and the function of art, whilst Dagmar sat quietly listening, ever more impressed by the conversational ability of her beloved. Dr. Goltz was always good-humoured, and when the evenings drew in, and the small party entered the house, settling into comfortable chairs, the glasses were refilled with wine, cigars lit, and then he began to retell jokes taken from his store of wit.

When the conversation between the men became too abstract or obscure, Dagmar would wander around the house alone, losing herself in the beauty of the paintings. The naturalistic Scandinavian pictures were of particular interest to her, and there was one picture she particularly liked: a painting by Schjerfbeck of a little girl sitting in a field by a lakeside on a bright Summer's day. Dagmar would stand before this picture, which hung in the main hall on the first floor for minutes at a time, losing herself in the beauty of its imagery. Letting her mind wander, she would imagine a future time, and that little girl was her child, and that place was Friedrichshafen.

Chapter 49

Towards the end of August, Dagmar was due for a two week holiday from the little Art Shop where she worked in Stalin Allee. By that time she would have been there for just over a year. It was natural that the young couple should wish to holiday together, and much thought and discussion took place between them as to where they might go.

"Would you like to go to the Baltic, or to the island of Rügen,?" said Dieter. "Today I've been to the State Travel agency and collected some brochures showing the nicest seaside resorts."

"As this'll be our last Summer in the DDR, I thought it would be nice to go on some kind of tour," replied Dagmar.

"That would be fine," said Dieter. "Perhaps I could even persuade Papa to lend us the car for two weeks, and then we could go around the countryside."

"That would be wonderful,!" responded Dagmar. "Where would we go?"

"How about touring Mecklenburg and visiting some of the seaside resorts,?" suggested Dieter.

"Why don't we go to the heart of Germany – to Thüring – there it would be most beautiful," said Dagmar. "Mecklenburg is so impoverished by comparison with the south – all lakes and marshy ground."

"That's an excellent idea," replied Dieter with enthusiasm.

"We could go to Naumburg and Weimar, and then to the very south, where are mountains and beautifully forested hills."

"And perhaps we could go east to Saxony, and visit Dresden, the most beautiful city in all Germany," suggested Dieter.

"Not to Dresden, it's so ruined," said Dagmar sadly. "Renata's mother comes from Dresden, and she went back there last year to visit for the first time since the War, and she cried and cried, because all the beautiful streets and palaces lay in ruins."

"Then we'll go to Thüring," agreed Dieter.

Dieter persuaded his father to lend him the car for the last two weeks of August, and then the young couple planned out in detail the route for their holiday. It was also decided (and with the consent of both parents) that they should become secretly engaged at the end of the holiday. Their sense of anticipation rose as each day brought them closer to the date of their holiday, and they read up all the guide books on Thüring, making extensive notes on places to be visited.

At last, the great day arrived, and when the sun rose, there was a mist in the air, predicting yet again many hours of heat and sunshine. Dagmar arose very early that morning, and moving quietly around the flat, she prepared some sandwiches for the journey, finished her packing, bid her grandmother farewell, and left the flat. She went across the road, kissed her parents goodbye, and walked along the quiet streets to Treptower Park station. She took the S-Bahn train to Ostkreuz and then to Erkner, where Dieter met her at the station in his car. They drove back to his home, where they breakfasted, prepared some more food for the journey, and at nine o'clock in the morning, to a great send-off from Dieter's parents, the couple drove down the drive, leaving on their long car journey south to Thüring.

The mist cleared, and there was blue sky and the bright sun shone above them. The destination for their first night's stay was Wittenberg, and after a three hour drive, they reached the beautiful old city. As Dieter drove the car down the winding streets towards the Pension where they were to stay, Dagmar's face lit up with excitement as she turned her head in several directions. A host of historical associations with the city rushed through her mind, and all at once, she turned to Dieter impatiently asking where this or that place was.

"Wait – we'll book into the Pension first, and then we'll find our way round the town," replied Dieter good humouredly trying to quieten her excitement.

This was the city of Martin Luther. From the little city of Wittenberg was to spread the fire of revolt against the oppression and tyranny of a corrupt church – a revolt which was to spread to the four corners of Europe, and the name of Wittenberg was to be imprinted on the lips of free men everywhere. From Wittenberg was born the Reformation, and from Wittenberg was born the autonomous man – freed from the shackles of superstition and ignorance which had burdened his forefathers for centuries. Wittenberg the city of iconoclasts! Wittenberg, the city which sired the modern era!

It was a little Pension in an old timber built house, at one side of the town, where the young couple took up their abode. They occupied a room with windows overlooking a little garden at the back of the house. When they had unpacked and washed, they left the house, carrying a guide and notebook between them and a small bag containing refreshments, and began to wander about the town.

"This is where Shakespeare's Hamlet went to college," remarked Dieter. "It was because of Hamlet's education in this city that he searched so ruthlessly for the truth which gave him the courage to avenge his father's death on his recall to Denmark. Shakespeare understood the greatness and freedom cherished in our German city of Wittenberg," added Dieter proudly.

They visited the Augustinian monastery where Luther dwelt, first as a monk and later as the owner with his wife and family. The monastery had been restored and fitted up as a museum. Then they visited the old 15th century Schlosskirche to the door of which Luther nailed his famous Ninety-Five Theses on that historic day in 1517. The old wooden doors had long since disappeared and been replaced by bronze doors bearing the Latin text of Luther's theses. The couple went into the quiet refreshingly cool interior of the church. It was pleasant to escape for a few minutes from the heat of the sun! They saw the tombs of Martin Luther and of the more moderate Protestant, Melanchton, standing peacefully on the cold stone floor of the church like monuments to eternity. They visited the parish church where Luther had preached, although it had been much altered since it was built in the 15th century. Inside, they saw the magnificent painting by Lucas Cranach the Elder, representing the Lord's Supper, Baptism and Confession, and a beautiful and ancient font designed by Herman Vischer.

On leaving the church, they strolled to the Elbe, and sat down on the banks of the river, eating their refreshments. They rested in each others arms and watched the boats pass by, then they returned to the city centre and sat in a café and took beer and cake. How relaxed were their minds, and how beautiful was the city and surroundings in which they immersed themselves! By now they had left all cares behind and Berlin was far away. In the evening they attended a chamber concert in an old hall in the town, and that night, for the first time during their friendship, they slept together until dawn the following day.

They arose at nine o'clock, and after breakfasting in the Pension, they drove to their next destination. After a two hour drive they reached the great city of Halle. They booked into their Pension and drove to the city centre. They saw the medieval town hall at the side of the market square, and the 16th century Marienkirche, and in the centre of the square, they saw the fine bronze statue of Georg Friedrich Händel, for this city was the birthplace of the great composer. They lunched in an old beer house, before visiting the 12th century St. Moritzkirche with its fine collection of wood carvings and sculptures.

The following day they continued their journey south-west, through the province of Sachsen-Anhalt towards Thüring. They arose early that morning as they had slept long the night before, and then, they particularly wished to arrive early at their next destination to afford time to study the art treasures of the city. After an hour's drive they arrived at the ancient cathedral city of Naumberg, and after settling into their Pension in the city centre (and they occupied a room beneath the high roof of an old house, and the windows overlooked a narrow cobbled street) they made their way to the cathedral.

It was a magnificent 13th century Romanesque building with a pair of towers at both East and West ends of the cathedral with a gothic choir at either side. After strolling arm in arm around the outside of the immensely long cathedral, and glancing up at the high towers, seemingly so strong and permanent, and at the buttresses surmounted by gargoyles glaring down at the ground far below, the young couple went into the building through the West door. How well proportioned and majestic seemed the interior and how disciplined and finely wrought was every decorative feature! The church was quite silent except for the footsteps of the young lovers as they trod the stone floor, and an occasional cough from other visitors admiring the art works.

Dagmar pointed up at the delicate tracery above the columns in the north aisle, and then at the beautiful leaf sculptured capitals in the West end of the church. Most beautiful were the sets of stone figures representing scenes from Christ's life. How real and sensitive and full of expression were the small statues! Surely they reflected the genius of the medieval craftsman at his best. There was the scene representing the Holy Communion, and then, the Payment of Judas; the Capture of Christ; Peter's Disownment; the Guards; Handwashing; Flogging, and finally, the Carrying of the Cross. For a long time Dagmar stood before the statues, and she moved her head aesthetically as she admired them. Then she looked at the life-size crucifixion scene in the doorway leading to the choir and altar at the West end. The wooden figure of Christ was fixed to a cross dividing the doorway into two parts. On either side of the doorway stood the stone figures of Mary and John in lamentation.

They left the cathedral with the intention of returning later, and they dined in an old beer hose, and then strolled towards the outskirts of the town walking alongside the banks of the river Saale. It was a swelteringly hot day and the sight of the flowing water refreshed them, and with liveliness they discussed the art treasures they had seen that morning. Later in the afternoon, they returned to the cathedral, seeing the other life size stone figures which stood in the West choir.

"Look, there's you Dietrich, armed with your sword and shield," remarked Dagmar humorously, pointing up to the statue of the medieval Knight, Dietrich von Brehne.

Dieter laughed quietly as he held the fair one closer to his side.

The statues represented the donors of the cathredral, the great Knights and their ladies who had lived and died in that part of Germany. Most famous were the statues of Ekkehard and Uta, and the Uta figure was famed throughout the world as being amongst the greatest of medieval statues. Dagmar said she liked best the statue of Timo von Kistritz.

"But he looks so solemn and serious – almost as if he were trying to put on a false front," replied Dieter.

"But he has such strength and determination," said Dagmar. "I think no one can move his will. And which figure to you prefer?"

"I like Reglindis, the wife of Hermann," replied Dieter. "She looks so happy and full of gaiety and fun."

Dagmar frowned disapprovingly.

"But she looks as if she might be a naughty girl. I don't think she can be trusted with men," answered Dagmar.

On the following morning the lovers continued their journey southwards. They were in high spirits, and the weather continued to favour them. They left Sachsen-Anhalt behind as they entered Thüring. Within an hour of having left Naumberg, they reached the city of Weimar, and they drove down the narrow winding streets to their Pension which was not far from the market place. They occupied a small room with wooden beams across the ceiling and whitewashed walls, an uneven and partly sunken floor, and furniture which was rustic and ancient. The small windows of the room (and you had to bend low to look out of them) faced the back of the building and small garden below.

"It's furnished just as it might have been three hundred years ago," exclaimed Dieter.

"You have some white on your sleeve – you must be careful not to touch the walls," said Dagmar.

Dieter brushed the whitewash from his sleeve.

"It's beautiful, but everything's so old here," continued Dagmar brightly. "I wonder if the electricity works."

"Our bedroom is far away from the street; we'll be able to sleep until late in the morning," said Dieter.

The couple left the Pension, making their way to the most prominent building in the city – the Palace of Weimar. They passed through the quaint old market place surrounded by houses with high pitched gables and roofs, and after a short walk, they reached the Palace. This building had been erected under the superintendence of Goethe at the end of the 18th and beginning of the 19th centuries on the site of an earlier palace burnt down in 1774. They saw a remnant of the older palace with a surviving tower, rising high above the buildings around – a landmark of the city. How quiet and peaceful were the surroundings of the Palace, with its spacious parkland and woodland beyond – a thick forest of oak trees to fend it from the environs of the city. Dieter and Dagmar went into the Palace and saw the collection. In one of the wings they saw a fascinating series of rooms dedicated to the poets, Goethe, Schiller, Herder and Wieland.

At last they returned to the city to eat.

"We must remain here for more than one day," said Dagmar over luncheon, "there's so much to see."

"We must stay here for three or four days," answered Dieter.

That afternoon they drove to the Belvedere Palace, and walked in the enchanting park with its abundant variety of trees and plants, and the open air theatre, before strolling around the great palace itself, around the Cavalier house and the Orangerie, and then into the interior. In the evening, they attended a concert.

The young couple arose late the following morning, and after breakfasting, they went to the Stadtkirche, a gothic church dating from the beginning of the 15th century – although much altered later under classical influence. Dagmar was especially impressed by the altarpiece in the form of a triptych. The centrepiece depicted the Crucifixion, and beside the Cross was represented the figure of Luther with Bible in hand, as the blood-pierced side of the Saviour dripped down onto his head. On leaving the church they went to the ancient Jakobs Hofkirche.

After lunching, the couple drove to the Palace of Tiefurt. They strolled through the park, keeping to the sides of the long narrow pathways so they might be shaded from the heat. They saw the Temple of the Muses, the impressive Roman style Cenotaph for Prince Konstantin with an elegant inscription composed by Goethe engraved on the side, and the Herder memorial stone; but Dagmar was most delighted by the little seated stone figure of Cupid as the feeder of the nightingales.

"How sweet he is,!" exclaimed Dagmar tugging on Dieter's arm.

After inspecting the Palace, the couple returned to the city, visiting the old ducal dowerhouse (Wittumspalais) and then the museum.

That evening, the lovers strolled in the city park, perhaps the most beautiful monument of Goethe's genius in Weimar. On the instructions of the ruling prince of Weimar, Goethe alone had landscaped and supervised the planning of the great "English park." The young lovers saw the Sphinx statue, the Triton relief, the weirdly fascinating Snake stone set in a mock gothic grotto, and then the monuments to Liszt and Shakespeare, and after the Soviet occupation, the Russians had even initiated raising a monument to their cultural heritage, by erecting in the park a bust of the poet Pushkin. Then the young couple saw the Pan statue, the Knights' Templars house, a ruined wall (which looked more real than a real ruin) and a Roman house, which looked as ancient and as genuine as any real Roman house might have looked. When they saw the lion fighter's Portal, and the tablet with its Latin inscription set into the wall beneath the house, Dagmar turned to Dieter asking if the Romans had really come so far, and Dieter laughed, replying that these things in the park had been built to take mens' minds away from the present era and back to what was imagined to be greater or more romantic ages in the distant past.

"Why? Weren't these princes contented with their own era,?" enquired Dagmar. "Surely they had everything to be thankful for."

"These monuments were erected at a time when Europe was racked by fear and suspicion of what the future held for humanity," replied Dieter. "Europe was in ferment at that time. It was during the French Revolution."

Before the lovers returned to the city centre, they strolled leisurely along the banks of the river Ilm, bordering one side of the park. The river was little wider than a stream, and the scent of the trees and the undergrowth and the refreshing sensation of the water and surroundings of the park were strangely enchanting as the sun set on that hot August day.

The next day the lovers visited the Schiller Haus in Schiller Strasse, seeing the humble rooms in which the great poet and dramatist had lived and died. Dagmar was moved to pity on seeing the small room and bare furniture which had served as the poet's home.

"How different this is from those stately palaces we've seen of all those princes and dukes who lived around the city of Weimar," exclaimed Dagmar. "How contrasted was the humble abode of this poet compared to the luxury that must have surrounded them!"

"In those days, I think the courtiers and servants who lived and worked in those palaces must have represented half the population of the little city of Weimar," replied Dieter, "although some of those palaces were only used as Summer residences."

On leaving the Schiller Haus, they visited yet another palace and its extensive grounds and park, that of Ettersburg. It was here, that for a few weeks in 1800, Schiller had worked on his play, *Mary Stuart*. After lunch, they walked from the city centre towards the Park, stopping briefly to inspect the house of Frau von Stein (which also had the proportions and magnificence of a palace) before passing through the Park, and over the river Ilm across the quaint rustic Nature bridge, towards Goethe's Summer house.

"Look, there's the house," exclaimed Dagmar suddenly in delight, pointing her finger out in front of her.

Behind some trees in the near distance emerged the high pitched roof and then the timber and white plaster walls of a little cottage, and one wall was attractively overgrown with creeper.

"How beautiful it is," exclaimed Dagmar as they came nearer. "I should love to live in such a sweet little house."

"It's just like a doll's house," replied Dieter.

They entered the garden through old handsomely designed wooden gates, paid their entrance fee to the elderly curator sitting behind the table at the door, and inspected the rooms. Dagmar was enchanted by the simplicity and classical forms of the furnishings and hangings in the house, and after leaving, they strolled round the garden. They sat awhile on the old wooden seat where Goethe and Frau von Stein had often sat together, and they kissed in front of the memorial of "Good Fortune." That evening they attended an excellent (albeit amateur) production of a play by Schiller, acted by the citizens of that cultured city.

The next day the young couple visited the house where Goethe lived from 1762 until his death in 1832. It was a complete example of a German nobleman's house at the beginning of the 19th century. The couple remained there for three hours inspecting the house and the exhibition within. On leaving, they lunched, and visited the city cemetery. In the grand ducal family vault, they saw the tombs of the two great poets, Goethe and Schiller, lying side by side. That evening – the eve of their departure from Weimar – the lovers once again strolled through the Park to take in something more of the great beauty of that monument of Goethe's genius.

"A pity we must leave Weimar so soon," exclaimed Dagmar dreamily, leaning her warm head against Dieter's shoulder. "I shall be so sad to leave this city. I have begun to love Weimar."

"We've been here for four days," replied Dieter softly. "Tomorrow we must continue our journey southward, through the hills and forests of Thüring."

And so ended the stay of the young lovers in Weimar, and such were their impressions of the old ducal city. Not once during their sojourn had the reminder occurred that this was the city where the constitution and government had been drawn up for a new Germany – of the Weimar Republic in 1918. Indeed, they saw nothing to remind them of that historic fact, but then, Germans everywhere had long since turned their backs on the memory even of the Weimar Republic as something belonging to the forgotten past of a well-deserved oblivion. The chaos, shame and disgrace which had been the outcome of its tragedy and failure served only to embarrass the living. Weimar would always and only be remembered as the city of Goethe and the cultured literary elite which surrounded the great poet and thinker during those many years he had flourished there.

The following morning, the couple were driving through the beautiful countryside of Thüring, speeding over hills and through forests, continuing their journey south west, towards their next destination. In just over two hours they reached the little town of Meiningen.

"Do you know, Dagmar," said Dieter as they drove passed the old town church with its twin towers, "we're only ten kilometres from the frontier with West Germany?"

"Really,?" exclaimed Dagmar in delighted surprise. "Then we must drive to the frontier and take a look at our future homeland."

"Across the frontier is the Federal *Land* of Bavaria," said Dieter.

They went to a small Pension in the town centre, and after lunch, they visited the Elisabethenburg, the old late 17th century ducal palace, containing some interesting collections, being the focal point of the town.

"It's so quiet and peaceful here," said Dagmar as the two lovers strolled by the banks of the river Werra later that afternoon. "Let's stay and rest here for several days."

Accordingly, the young couple remained in Meiningen for several days, taking it easy, walking over the rolling hills overlooking the small town, swimming, and sunbathing on the banks of the river. They had become tired after the extensive sightseeing in Weimar, and wanted to relax so that the impressions they had experienced in that city might begin to mellow in their memory. The weather remained fine and the sun scorched the earth, and they strolled through the yellow fields, watching the farmers and their families bringing in the crops for the year.

The menfolk, stripped to the waist, their tanned and perspiring skin reflecting the sunlight, advanced through the fields in rows, skilfully swinging their scythes from side to side. The women and children followed, with their long wooden rakes, gathering the corn together and tying the bundles into sheaves.

"How idyllic it is,!" exclaimed Dagmar as the couple watched the scene from the side of the field.

The lovers walked onwards, arm in arm, until they came to an old farmstead. There they heard much noise and the sounds of merrymaking, and they hurried forward in anticipation, and behind the barn were gathered a number of people in a threshing area. Some were seated at a table drinking from Steins, where a giant barrel had been set up on a trestle, whilst the rest were busily working in bringing in the harvest or threshing. A large wagon drawn by two horses and loaded with sheaves had just been brought into the area, and a number of the men were unloading the wagon, whilst others were carrying away and untying sheaves. There came the neighing of horses, and another wagon which had been unloaded, was driven out of the area, as the farmer stood up on the board at the front of the vehicle, raising the reins high and shouting at the great beasts. In the centre of the area, a dozen or more people were threshing corn, raising long flails and beating the grain in separating it from the chaff.

The young couple from the great capital were delighted and envigorated by the rustic scene. Dieter began speaking with one of the drinkers, although at first he had difficulty in understanding the old peasant. He suggested he would like to try his hand at threshing, and a few minutes later, he was wielding a flail up and down in his hands, and Dagmar laughed at what she saw as a most incongruous sight.

"Careful there – keep your distance from the others," cried the old peasant who had been instructing him in the use of the implement.

"It's good exercise," cried Dieter pointing to the muscles on his arms.

After a while, Dieter was rewarded with a Stein of beer, and the couple from Berlin were invited to attend a dance that evening held in the barn of the farmstead. Dieter said they would gladly accept the invitation (although Dagmar felt reluctant as she was not a good dancer) and that evening they attended the rustic dance, which was a noisy event, enjoyed by young and old alike, lasting until the early hours of the following morning.

Another day, they visited the 11th century church of Meiningen which had been built by the Holy Roman Emperor, Henry II, and then they inspected the collection of antiquities in the Henneberger Haus. One day as they walked towards the old farmstead where they had attended the dance, they saw the same field being ploughed where a few days earlier they had seen the farm workers reaping crops. Dieter was struck by the apparent speed with which the field was being turned to fallow.

"You're fast workers here," cried Dieter to the ploughman as he passed by.

"Fast workers? Ach, nothing,!" replied the ploughman waving his hands dismissively, before pulling on the reins of the horses. It was apparent the ploughman was in an ill-natured mood, although willing to stop work and grouse to another. "We farmers have no say any more as to what goes on around here. We can't even be responsible for our own failures because they've taken from us the right to use our own heads. All orders come from above, nowadays," said the old farmer pointing to the sky.

Dieter was surprised at meeting the old man in such a disgruntled frame of mind after seeing him in the high spirits of a few days earlier.

"They know nothing about farming, and it's no good arguing with them either. There's no educating them," continued the old ploughman, "because they're too ignorant to listen to us farmers. You know who I'm talking about: the Communist overseers, sitting in their offices and controlling the collectives. They're all theory and no practice."

"That's Communism through and through," remarked Dieter. "Theory and Plan is everything, and the realistic and experimental is discounted."

"They're as crazy as raving dogs," continued the old man pointing to his head. "The orders coming through from that office could be made nonsense of by a six year old - and every other day they contradict themselves. When you put two and two together they try to tell you it doesn't make four. They're not farmers who give us our orders, they're ideologists. The State sends them on a tour of the Ukraine, and they come back thinking they've found a cure for all our ills. My God, in Russia they've seen famine enough over the past thirty years, you'd have thought that'd teach them the failure of collective farming."

"Once they've accepted the ideology, their heads are too thick to take in anything else," remarked Dieter.

"Once all this land was mine," said the old farmer stretching out his hand towards the field, "but because the farm was over two hundred and forty-seven acres in extent, my land was expropriated without compensation. Everything I owned has been collectivised into an Angricultural Production Co-operative. I receive the same pay as any of my farmhands, and I've been deprived of all real authority. This farm's never begun to produce anything like the overall total of pre-War days, and I don't expect it ever will so long as it's controlled by the LPG – and that's what they call 'Land Reform,' these theorists sitting in their closed offices!"

"Why don't you leave the DDR.?" asked Dieter.

"I'm too old to hope for a new life in the West. I only pray and hope for another day like the Seventeenth of June," said the farmer.

"We all pray for such a day," said Dieter.

"And those crops, they should never have been taken so soon from the fields," said the farmer, "but we had orders to begin ploughing by today, and ploughing's always a slow job. We have no plough but this."

"You need a plough with two blades," suggested Dieter.

"Not on this land – it's too hilly – we wouldn't get the even furrows," said the farmer.

"Then you need a tractor to speed up the work."

"That's our tractor over there, against the wall of the silo," said the farmer pointing his finger across the field to where a rusted vehicle stood against the grey stone wall of a tower. "The Russians took away the engine for War reparations – although I don't know what use a tractor engine is without a tractor."

Chapter 50

On the day preceding the lovers departure from Meiningen, they arose and breakfasted early, and drove to the south west frontier of the German Democratic Republic. It had been raining heavily the night before, but by dawn there was clear sky, and when the sun rose and its rays brought heat to the land, it took up the moisture from the ground, so that an orange mist rose from above the fields and hills.

After a twenty minute drive over hills and through valleys, past forests and farms, they left the narrow winding roadway into a lane climbing the side of a steep hill.

"How beautiful is the morning nature,!" exclaimed Dagmar glancing out of the window down at the countryside from where they had come. At last the car drove into a siding and braked.

"From here we can walk," said Dieter.

They left the car, and continued up the lane, past a cottage, through a meadow, and through a gate to woodland beyond. Up and up they climbed, and a little footpath between the undergrowth led them towards the top of the hill. The red disk of the sun rose higher and the day became warmer. How beautiful was the wooded hill at that early hour! They passed through a forest of pines, their tall slim copper red trunks reflecting the sunlight, and through the tops of their ever-green finery, from the blue sky above, shone down a long yellow sunbeam onto the ground below. The undergrowth was thick with shrubbery, a green mantle of grass, and everywhere, plants in bloom with purple and yellow flowers. Dieter took Dagmar's hand, and with long firm strides, he led the way, as the lovers joyously climbed towards the summit.

"How much further,?" enquired Dagmar.

"I cannot say," replied Dieter as he passed his fingers through the stalk of a curled dock weed and brushed away its red brown segments, "but let's stop awhile."

The lovers turned round, glancing down at the route from which they had come.

"How beautiful is the land,!" exclaimed Dagmar enchanted by the scene confronting them.

"So beautiful is Germany,!" replied Dieter in a quiet tone, over-awed by the landscape.

In the near distance before them, rose a vapour of mist from the undergrowth towards the sky, and the gentle forms of green ferns topped their stalks above the rest of the greenery, and their light green leaves were reflected in the sunlight. Through a clearing on their left, not far below from that part of the steep hillside from where they stood, shone down the rays of the sun, and from the ground had sprung a cluster of rosebay willowherbs, their stalks rising proudly above the greenery around, their mass of pink flowers bringing colour to the forest. At their feet grew a cluster of violet headed thistles, and from the patch of deep green grass and beneath the tall trunks of the red pines were scattered the butterfly orchid with its white fragrant flower, and from every part of the undergrowth rose the yellow head of the dandelion. In the far distance, and beyond the light vapour rising from the greenery, and far below where the two lovers stood, were the rolling hills and forests of Thüring.

"Come, we must climb to the top," exclaimed Dieter at last, and he threw his arm around Dagmar's waist, pulling her body closely to his, and together, the lovers continued their climb. "I think we have not so far to go," he added, "there's the top of the hill."

"How peaceful is everything here, so far from town and village,!" exclaimed Dagmar.

"Here nature lies pure and uncorrupted at the hands of man," said Dieter. "Here every plant and blade of grass has the freedom to exert its will."

The forest was full of woodland sounds. From the high branch of a tree came the trilling song of a warbler, and from a cluster of bushes came the loud melodious call of the wren. A red squirrel ran across the path of the lovers, and stretching forward her slim fingers, Dagmar bent down and called to it sweetly. The little furry animal jumped round and faced the couple, glancing at them curiously, as it threw up its bushy tail blinking in the sunlight. It sniffed the air holding its paw before its chest with an anticipatory gesture. It jumped several feet closer towards Dagmar, and when she bent down the little animal turned, and ran up a tree. Dieter laughed in delight, and taking Dagmar's hand, the couple continued their upward climb. He snatched a long green blade from a clump of grass and began chewing the stalk.

Dagmar stopped by a cluster of flowers and broke off the stalk of a purple clustered bellflower with its yellow stamen.

"This is for your buttonhole," said Dagmar fixing the stalk of the flower to Dieter's jacket as he stood quietly to attention, and then she kissed him on the chin.

"*Danke schön*,!" he replied bowing with a smile.

"And this is for me," said Dagmar breaking off another stalk of the flower and fixing it to her dress.

Onward they climbed. Suddenly Dieter stopped by the path pointing to a flapping movement in some low-lying undergrowth.

"See there, a nest in a deserted rabbit hole," he exclaimed, "and some young."

A small bird was fluttering near the ground.

"She's feeding them," added Dagmar in delight. "See, the bird is carrying an insect – a spider I think."

"The bird is a wheatear," said Dieter. "Do you see its white rump?"

"But how near the footpath it's nesting! It shows this path is rarely frequented," said Dagmar.

The lovers continued towards the summit, and after several minutes, they reached the top, and they walked along the ridge towards the downward incline at the other side. The trees gave way; the bright sun shone down, and a vast expanse of blue sky and small white clouds opened to their view.

They stood at the summit of the hill at the other side, and glancing down saw miles of rolling hills and forests stretching to the distant horizon, where a light mist met the blue sky. How vast and magnificent was the scene! The meandering course of a river could be seen in the distance, its water glistening brightly in the sunlight. Yellow fields were there, some farm buildings, a hamlet and a village or two. A light breeze blew through the tree-tops, and as they bowed their heads, it seemed to the two lovers as if the trees were almost extending a gesture of welcome. Dieter clasped his arms firmly around Dagmar's shoulder, and she held her hand around his waist, as they stood silently surveying the glory of the landscape which met their view, and a gentle breeze from the south west refreshed them, cooling the warmth of their bodies. Their hearts were overwhelmed by the significance of the scene, and a thousand cherished hopes and aspirations suddenly overwhelmed their souls. Their eyes filled with emotion. Before them lay the bastion of the free world – their free world – the Federal Republic of Germany!

"How beautiful is everything,!" cried Dieter joyously, throwing up his hand and striding forward.

"Our first glimpse of Western Germany – our future homeland,!" exclaimed Dagmar.

"And so this is Bavaria,!" cried Dieter. "So beautiful is the South of Germany."

"*Alles ist schön*,!" cried Dagmar joyously.

Dieter threw his hands onto his hips, and glancing round him, strode boldly forward, his heart filled with exultation, his face expressing joy.

"How glorious the gleam
 To me the Nature!
 How glistens the Sun!
 How laughs the Field!"

Dieter had begun to recite, his voice filled with emotion, gesticulating with great gestures towards the trees and forests, the sky, and other objects of nature round about, both near and far.

"There breaks forth the Blossom
 Out of every Branch
 And a thousand Voices
 From the Shrubbery around.

"And joy and bliss
 Out of every Breast.
 Oh earth, Oh Sun!
 Oh happiness, Delight!"

"Do you know those lines,?" cried Dieter glancing up at Dagmar.

"Naturally,!" replied Dagmar, her face breaking into a smile, and she continued to recite them:-

"Oh most agreeable!
 So golden, beautiful,
 How the morning Clouds
 Are scorned!

"You sail gloriously
 The fresh Field
 To the blossom Scent
 The world to fill."

"After our visit to Weimar I think all the poems we ever learnt of Goethe are suddenly recollected," exclaimed Dieter laughing.

"During those four days, we lived close to the remembrance of everything that was Goethe," replied Dagmar.

"Then let me make love to you as Goethe would make love," exclaimed Dieter, and he strode up to Dagmar with his hand laid across his heart, and with an airy gesture, he briskly threw out his arm as he bowed his head low and gallantly prostrated himself on one knee. "Madamoiselle, your humble and obedient servant, Johann Wolfgang Goethe." Dieter took the hem of Dagmar's dress into his hand and kissed it.

Dagmar laughed softly, extending her hand towards him.

"Madamoiselle says that you may kiss her hand," she said.

Dieter took Dagmar's hand into both of his, and kissed it passionately.

"What more beautiful or more slender hand is there than this in all Germany," he exclaimed gallantly.

"How sweet you are,!" exclaimed Dagmar chuckling, and she bent forward and kissed him on the forehead as he knelt on the ground.

Dieter stretched forward his arm on either side of Dagmar and continued to recite:-

> "Oh Maiden, Maiden,
>   How I love you!
>   How glance your Eyes!
>   How you love me!

> "So loves the Lark
>   Song and Air,
>   And morning flowers
>   That scent the Sky."

Dieter rose to his feet and clasped Dagmar in his arms, and the lovers embraced and kissed, and then he continued:-

> "How I love you
>   With warm Blood,
>   You gave me Youth
>   And Joy and Courage,"

and Dagmar joined him in the recitation of the final verse:-

> "To sing and dance
>   anew,
>   Eternally Happy
>   How you love me!"[*]

The lovers laughed joyously, kissed, embraced, and again faced the happy and expansive scene which lay before them.

"*So schön*,!" exclaimed Dagmar again. "Wouldn't it be wonderful if we could walk to the bottom of the hill, and cross to the other side, and just lay our hands on the soil! Then we could return to Berlin and say that with our own hands we had touched the free soul of West Germany."

"Or to break off a twig from a tree on the other side, and return with that to Berlin," added Dieter. "That would be fine indeed!"

"Or to pluck some wild flowers from the land on the other side, and bring them to Berlin," suggested Dagmar.

"What a souvenir,!" exclaimed Dieter impressed by the idea.

But these things were not possible for the two lovers. Far below them to the right, but high up on the hillside stood a wooden tower on tall spindly legs. Out of the openings of the cabin at the summit of the tower protruded the barrels of several machine guns. In the far distance, at the

---

[*] Goethe's *Mailied* an Friederike Brion, Strasbourg, 1771. Author's translation.

bottom of the hillside was a barbed-wire fence running along the length of the frontier. Beyond the fence was a narrow strip of ploughed land, and then another similar barbed fence. The grey figures of two soldiers of the People's Army could just be distinguished as they strolled together alongside the inner fence, machine guns slung over their shoulders. At some distance away, two more soldiers were strolling together in the opposite direction. The entire area was alive with soldiers and police, and the watchtower had a dominating view of the landscape.

"And so there lies our future homeland," exclaimed Dagmar dreamily.

"And now we must say farewell to the sight of our future homeland until next year," replied Dieter.

"Until our feet shall touch the land which will be really ours," added Dagmar.

There came a rustling noise from some bushes nearby where the lovers stood, and then a trampling sound of heavy footsteps on the undergrowth. The footsteps approached nearer, and in sudden alarm, Dagmar broke away from Dieter's side and advanced towards the direction of the disturbance. Dieter remained still, calmly nonchalant, as he stood atop the hillside with hands on hips, continuing to observe the scene.

Suddenly, Dagmar let out a shrill cry. A green-uniformed figure emerged from behind the bushes, holding a rifle with bayonet at the ready, pointing the weapon towards the fair one. With a sharp movement and a metallic click, the figure drew back the bolt and cocked the rifle.

"Halt! Who goes there? Put up your hands,!" shrieked the Vopo as he strode into the clearing.

Startled, the young couple instantly raised their hands to shoulder level, and faced the Vopo to show they were not only unarmed but carried nothing with them.

"What are you doing here,?" demanded the Vopo gruffly.

"We're tourists," replied Dieter. "We're walking in the country."

"This is a forbidden area. Get out your passes," ordered the Vopo.

The couple lowered their hands.

"Put that gun down, we're frightened," cried Dieter.

The couple took out their identity passes and handed them to the policeman. The latter glanced from the passes to the young couple, scrutinising them closely.

"You've no right to be here," he exclaimed at last.

"We saw nothing to indicate this was forbidden territory," replied Dieter indignantly.

"Didn't you? The entire area's wired off," said the Vopo.

"I can assure you, we didn't cross any fences or force an entry," said Dieter.

"How did you get in?"

"We came up the hill from the other side. We passed a cottage, walked through a meadow, and came through a gate to the woodland."

"Wasn't the gate locked?"

"We never saw any lock"

"Thanks for the information. Now we know who's to blame. He won't escape lightly."

"May we now have our passes back,?" requested Dieter stretching out his hand.

The Vopo glanced at each of them suspiciously.

"Where are you staying,?" he enquired.

"In Meiningen," replied Dieter.

"All right. Now get out of here, and at double speed," exclaimed the Vopo handing back the passes. "We have orders to shoot on sight in this area. I should really be taking you in for questioning."

"Thank you," replied Dieter pocketing his pass.

"Now get out of here to save your necks," cried the policeman impatiently.

The couple walked off rapidly without another word.

"I'm glad we came, anyway," exclaimed Dagmar as the couple ran down the footpath hand in hand at the other side of the hill.

"It was a lucky escape," replied Dieter. "He could have taken us in."

"It was decent of him to let us go."

"Still, it was dangerous to have gone there. We might have been shot – and no questions asked. Had he been in a worse frame of mind, there's no knowing what might have happened. There'd be an award for bagging a couple of prospective escapees."

Early the next morning the lovers left Meiningen, driving north west towards their next destination, and within an hour they reached the city of Eisenach, birthplace of Sebastian Bach. They booked into a hotel on the outskirts of the town and unpacked their luggage.

"Look we have a radio," exclaimed Dagmar pointing to the bedside table.

"What luxury," replied Dieter in happy surprise. "Does it really work?"

"It should do," said Dagmar, "else it wouldn't be here."

Dieter sat down on the bed switching on the set.

"It's very old," he said.

"Just think, we'll be able to lie in bed in the morning and listen to music and the news," said Dagmar.

Some crackling came from the set, followed by the stirring tones of patriotic Russian music, and then a rhetorical voice in Russian shouting a speech into the microphone.

"That's Moscow," said Dieter, and he began turning the knobs on the set. There was crackling and the sound of a German voice speaking in a quiet intimate tone addressing listeners in the familiar *du* term. "That's *Deutschland Sende*, you can tell by the tone of voice alone," said Dieter and he immediately switched away from the wavelength, and then came the tune of the Star Spangled Banner followed by an American voice announcing, "This is AFN Frankfurt!"

"This radio's fine," exclaimed Dieter. "We can switch to any programme we want."

A few minutes later the young couple were driving along a roadway just outside the city, for the main attraction which had brought them to Eisenach was something which lay beyond the environs of the town. They drove along a quiet country road, with hills and forests in all directions.

"Look, there it is," cried Dieter at last, pointing towards a mountainous summit. "Do you see, on top there?"

Dagmar craned forward her neck towards the offside direction.

"Yes – it's wonderful,!" she cried excitedly.

"An invincible fortress dominating the land,!" exclaimed Dieter.

The car drove into a siding at the foot of the hill and braked. The young couple climbed out and stood and surveyed the impressive scene. High up on the thickly forested hill above precipitous cliffs stood a vast fortress, the towers of which soared to the sky, seeming almost to touch the white clouds high above the land where the lovers stood. Atop the great precipitous cliffs stood the Wartburg, famed in history and legend alike.

"What a sight,!" exclaimed Dieter. "No wonder it inspired the great musical genius of Wagner to write an opera. Already I can hear the sounds of *Tannhäuser* ringing in my ears, like music sent down from the heavens."

"The seductive themes of the Venusburg and the Pilgrims' chorus,"cried Dagmar joyously. "*Schönes* music!"

"Perhaps on this very rock the young shepherd boy had sat whilst piping his ode to Spring," cried Dieter placing his foot on a block of stone. "And perhaps Tannhäuser had stood on this very spot whilst the pilgrims passed by on the roadside."

The lovers climbed the steep roadway leading to the North East gateway into the fortress. It was a long climb, and the higher they ascended, the finer the view of the landscape. At last they reached the summit, arriving at the drawbridge entrance into the castle.

"How silent and still is everything," said Dieter. "There's not a soul to be seen and there's hardly a breath of wind. Just think, seven hundred years ago the Wartburg was the home of a boisterous court and riotous living.   The court was famed throughout the land, and the minstrels and wandering folk of all kinds streamed here to seek the patronage and hospitality of the great Landgrave Hermann I.   It's recorded by the chroniclers of that time that the Wartburg was the scene of constant revelry, and that from this same gateway, crowds of people constantly rushed in and out, both during night and day."

"I don't think I'd have liked that," replied Dagmar. "I don't like noise and rowdiness."

The couple crossed the drawbridge and walked through the little doorway cut as a pedestrian entrance through a pair of massive wooden gates. They passed through a tunnel beneath the Gate house, their feet resounding on the cobble stones, and into the courtyard of the fort. They paid their entrance fee and began to inspect the ancient buildings.

The fortress had been built by Louis the Springer, Landgrave of Thüring, at the beginning of the 12th century, and from that time until the middle of the 15th century, the Wartburg remained the seat of the Landgraves of Thüring. The couple began inspecting the Knights' and Harsdörferschen houses with their stone and timber built walls and white plaster. Then they passed to the most impressive part of the Wartburg, to the great stone palace, a firm and erect structure, that in strength seemed as eternal as the precipice on which it stood. It was one of the few well preserved Romanesque palaces anywhere to be found.

They entered the Landgraves' room with its fine timber ceiling, and high up around the walls were the beautiful frescoes of the great Pre-Raphaelite style painter, Moritz von Schwind, illustrating the legends of the Wartburg. They saw the banquet hall with its wildly ornate almost oriental decoration, and then they went into Elisabeth's room with its fine vaulted ceiling and brilliant mosaics. They saw the Chapel and then the Singing Hall, where in 1207 took place the great Minnesingers' song contest.   Dagmar went over to the large fresco painted by Moritz von Schwind of the *Sängerkrieg*, and arching her neck, she examined it aesthetically, whilst Dieter strode excitedly up and down the hall, exclaiming that this was the room where Tannhäuser had so scandalised the court of the Wartburg and shocked the ladies by singing to the glory of Venus. The couple glanced out of the Romanesque windows and down at the rolling hills and forests far below stretching to the distant horizon.

They saw the harp of the Wartburg, Cranach's portraits of the Emperor Charles V, of Luther and his wife, and of noblemen connected with the fort. Then they went into Elisabeth's gallery where Dagmar became lost in the contemplation of a beautiful painting by Moritz von Schwind illustrating the sad parting between Elisabeth and the Landgrave Ludwig IV. They went into Luther's room, a modest chamber with bare walls and simple furniture. They saw his silver and gold plated travelling spoon, which he carried everywhere with him, with its ornate handle and engraved crucifix in the bowl. It was on 4th June 1521 that the great reformer had been brought to the Wartburg for his own safety, at the instigation of Frederick the Wise, Elector of Saxony. Luther remained in the Wartburg for ten months, completing his translation of the New Testament. In another room they saw an attractive pencil drawing by Goethe of the bulwark of the fortress. The great thinker had visited the Wartburg in 1777, and nearby the drawing hung a framed copy of a letter to his intimate friend, Frau von Stein in Weimar, expressing his sense of joy and happiness at having been received in the great fortress, describing with passion the surrounding scenary.

It was late in the afternoon when the lovers returned to Eisenach, and they were tired and hungry, for in their absorption in the antiquities of the Wartburg, they had forgotten lunch. They ate well, and Dieter drank several glasses of beer, and they said they felt drowsy and fatigued, and decided to retire early.

"Still, we can rest for several more days and do just as we choose," said Dagmar encouragingly as Dieter leaned back on his chair stretching his arms.

"And then back to Berlin – worse luck,!" he replied. "If only we could stay here in Thüring for a week longer."

"But now we have next year to look forward to," said Dagmar significantly.

BOOK XIII

Forewarned Is Forearmed

Love is too young to know what conscience is;
Yet who knows not conscience is born of love?

Shakespeare, *Sonnet*, No. cli.

Chapter 51

The young couple remained in bed until late the following morning. Dieter switched on the radio as a "wakener," but the couple remained lying in bed, close together, half way between consciousness and sleep. It was true the programme was not of a kind conducive to arousing one from sleep. There was no music. A quiet voice spoke steadily in a measured confidential tone, whispering *du* with every phrase into the listeners' ear. From the tone of voice it was as if the speaker was careful not to offend his audience whilst presenting an argument which he felt might well arouse mistrust.

"Can't we switch to another programme,?" requested Dagmar drowsily. "I hate listening to all this propaganda. These *Deutschland Sende* programmes are horrid."

"I think this programme is designed for people on the other side of the frontier," said Dieter. "He's telling the people of West Germany all about the people's paradise of the German Democratic Republic."

"What *quatsch*! Did you hear that? He said East German workers have the highest living standard of any in Europe. He says the West German workers are brutally oppressed by Adenauer and the American imperialists and that there's a critical food shortage in the Ruhrgebiet. And that there's growing unrest amongst the working people in West Germany."

"I can't understand how anyone can be persuaded by such programmes," said Dieter.

"I suppose they only do it to frighten ignorant people in the DDR," replied Dagmar.

"Can anyone really be as ignorant as that,?" asked Dieter.

"Thank God in a year we'll be in freedom, and all this'll be behind us," remarked Dagmar.

The talk on the radio came to a close, and after a pause there came the rhetorical declaration: "Long live our beloved Saviour Lenin; long live the glorious Soviet Union; long live the People's German Democratic Republic!" This was followed by the playing of the Red Flag.

"Let's switch to RIAS," suggested Dieter.

"Then we must have it very quiet," replied Dagmar putting her finger to her lips, "because it's forbidden to tune into that wavelength. We're in a hotel and we don't know who could be on the other side of the wall."

Dieter played around with the knobs, finding the programme they wanted.

"Listen! It's the news," he said.

The young couple lay quietly, as a voice on the radio continued: "Yesterday, Professor Josef Hamel, former Rector of the Friedrich Schiller University in Jena, held a press conference in West Berlin. Professor Hamel, a dermatologist, who had fled from East Germany on August 20th , said he had found 'unbearable' the Communist demands to 'convert East German universities into political institutions.' The Professor had fled from the East on the occasion of the four hundredth Anniversary of Jena University."

"Now Rectors of universities are fleeing to the West! Where will it all end,?" exclaimed Dieter.

"And from Jena – here in Thüring," added Dagmar.

"Do you remember when we were driving from Weimar to Meiningen, and we saw that convoy of lorries, full of cheering students and schoolchildren, festooned with flowers and streamers?"

"Yes, and we wondered what it was for."

"They must have been going to Jena for the Anniversary celebrations."

The report on the radio continued: "He said that the Communist regime in the East zone was increasing its efforts to turn the universities into bastions of Marxism. Statements by Party leaders about a 'softer' course had little significance, he said. It was true the Party leaders allowed recalcitrant professors a certain latitude, but this in no way modified their main aim of bringing up Central German[*] students as true Communists. Professor Hamel reported that although large numbers of the faculty and students were only pretending to be Commuists, they were 'fighting a long losing battle to retain intellectual freedom.' He said that the 'Socialisation of the student body is already far advanced.' Professor Hamel declared it had not been easy for him to leave the University with his patients and hospital with a hundred and eighty beds. He said, 'I had battled with the idea of flight for months. Had I been a historian, for

---

[*] In the Federal Republic, for many years in the post-War period, a clear distinction was always made between three Germanies:- West Germany, the BRD; Central Germanhy, the DDR; and, East Germany, the territories lost to Poland and the USSR, e.g. Silesia and East Prussia, following the 1945 defeat.

example, I would have turned my back on the regime long ago.' He now only had one wish: to carry on his scientific work in freedom.

"He said that the flight of doctors from the East zone was already endangering the medical care of the population. Professor Hamel declared that the chief reason for this flight of doctors who fared well materially, was the ban on foreign travel to West Germany and anxiety about the education of their children who were being increasingly exposed to Marxist influences. The children of the bourgeoisie were being more and more shut out of studying at the universities. The sons of professors and prominent people could not naturally be refused, but the sons of artisans, merchants, tradesmen and lawyers, suffered the worst discrimination. – That was the news and now ..."

Dieter switched off the set.

"Our plans to flee the DDR are none too early. The situation is worsening by the hour," he remarked.

It was a fine day when the lovers arose that morning, and after breakfast, they visited the old ducal palace inspecting the exhibition, and they visisted the Lutherhaus where Luther stayed with the Cotta family in 1498. They remained in Eisenach for several days – leisurely sunshine days – losing themselves in the beauty and antiquities of the city and its surroundings, and forgetting the outside world to which they still belonged.

Their only reminder of the real everyday world in which they lived was the morning news from the little bedside radio in the hotel. They had read no newspapers since leaving Berlin, as there was a tacit agreement between them to ignore the everyday news for the duration of their holiday, so they might fully enjoy the peace and beauty of the country in which they immersed themselves. The presence of the radio in their hotel room, was however, too great a temptation, but after two days they even tired of that.

The young couple returned more than once to the Wartburg during their stay in Eisenach, and then they visited the mid-12th century Nikolaikirche, and the Klemda, a small 13th century castle; the late gothic St. Georgenkirche; the birthplace of Sebastian Bach, and the Richard Wagner Musuem. They strolled in the forest behind the town, swam in the confluence of the rivers Nessa and Härsel, and sunbathed and rested on the peaceful banks of the rivers. The weather remained kind, and without a care in the world, the lovers continued to immerse themselves in the unreal illusions of the past as an escape from the harshness of the present.

On the eve of their departure from the city, the young couple wandered around the town, browsed in the shops, and bought souvenirs for relatives in Berlin. Dieter bought an antique Meissen milk jug for his parents, whilst Dagmar bought a box of cigars for Papa Renot, an ebony Chinese casket for the good Frau, an Indian silk scarf for her grandmother and sweets for Gisela.

"You know, Dieter, we must buy something for the Goltzes – they've been so good to us," said Dagmar.

"And we must get them something special," added Dieter.

After searching around the shops a second time, the young couple bought the Goltzes a small but charming pair of Dresden figurines, and before arriving back at the hotel, they had already decided where they might ideally be placed in the Goltzes sitting room.

The little alarm clock on the bedside table had gone off and the young couple lay drowsily in bed. It was still early in the morning but they were to arise punctually that day for the long drive back to Berlin.

Dieter turned towards Dagmar suggesting they might switch on the radio for the news. After all, their holiday was coming to a close, and it might be as well to acclimatise themselves to the real world before their return.

"Today, we must leave Luther and Bach and Goethe behind us," said Dieter. "Today we must return from the world of contemplation to the world of struggle."

"But not too loud – the people in the other rooms,!" warned Dagmar.

There was some music, and then a pause, and a voice spoke: "This is the Radio In The American Sector, calling from Berlin. Good morning everybody! The time is six o'clock. Here is the news for Monday, the first of September 1958. Today is the start of a new term for several million schoolchildren in the East zone of Germany, but for all those between the ages of thirteen and seventeen, it will be a new term with a difference. A new curriculum has been added to the school syllabus. Today a new scheme comes into force described by the Soviet Zone authorities as 'Polytechnical Education.' This will oblige every child between thirteen and seventeen to engage in manual labour for one full working day of each week in factories throughout the East Zone of Germany.

"The ostensible motive of the East German government for introducing this scheme of enforced child labour (so politely and deceptively term 'Polytechnical Education') is to bring children into closer contact with production work, and to teach them to love labour and the working class. Other sources are led to believe that the scheme has been introduced to overcome the permanent and now critical labour shortage felt throughout the East Zone of Germany.

"The increasing discontent of the general population in the East Zone, has been reflected in Berlin during recent weeks by a sudden rise in the number of people admitted to refugee camps in the West sectors. In the week ending August 29th, the total of refugees rose sharply to six thousand and seventy-nine compared with five thousand and seventy in the preceding week. The refugees have come from every strata of the community, including eight hundred and thirteen doctors during the first eight months of this year, and they've brought with them their tales of deprivation and threats, and persecution and brutality they had suffered at the hands of the East Zone authorities.

"Many said they had been living for months in constant fear of their lives and in fear of incarceration at the hands of the People's Police, before finally making the decision to come to the West. A number of farmers and peasants whose land had recently been collectivised under the government's policy to hasten the collectivisation of all land throughout the Soviet Zone, said they had 'just found it impossible' to make ends meet.

"Herr Lemmer, Federal Minister for All German Questions, sent an appeal to the Kremlin to put an end to what he described as the 'gruesome play' now taking place in Central Germany,"

"Thank God we'll be out of all this by this time next year,!" exclaimed Dieter.

"Let's turn the radio off – we don't want to hear any more," said Dagmar screwing up her nose with an expression of disapproval. Dieter switched off the set. "All news is bad news, and so why should we bother to listen to it,?" added Dagmar defensively. "I mean, none of it can affect us, can it?"

Chapter 52

It was a long journey back to Berlin that day, but Dieter drove at a leisurely speed, and the young couple stopped at Wittenberg again, making a second visit to the old parish church where Dagmar wanted to take another look at the magnificent painting of the Lord's Supper, Baptism and Confession by Lucas Cranach the Elder. Then they stopped by the roadside to pick wild flowers at the edge of a field, and they gathered enough for three bunches for their parents and the Goltzes.

Before they had approached within fifty kilometres of Berlin and were still in the heart of the countryside, Dieter suddenly drove the car into a siding by the quiet roadway, and braked by the side of a meadow and nearby lake.

"Why have we stopped,?" enquired Dagmar.

"I wish to ask you a very important question," replied Dieter in mock solemnity.

"What kind of a question,?" said Dagmar curiously.

"In a way it bears on the significance of our holiday – as the climax and summit of all our pleasures and everything we've done," said Dieter in a formal tone, betraying difficulty in directly expressing his meaning.

"I think you're being rather obscure," said Dagmar frowning at him.

"In short, I have a formal proposal to make: will you marry me?"

"Yes, I will," replied Dagmar, her face breaking into a smile, and then she kissed Dieter on the chin and put her arm through his. "Now we are really engaged," she added.

"All except for the rings," said Dieter, "and for those we must wait until we reach the West."

"I'm so happy,!" exclaimed Dagmar in a sudden burst of ecstasy, and she threw her arms around Dieter's neck, and for some moments, the lovers were enclasped in a firm embrace, kissing passionately.

As they continued their journey to Berlin Dagmar thought back over the entire course of her friendship with Dieter, and she felt as if she had never been happier. It seemed as if her friendship culminating in her engagement with Dieter marked the desire and consummation of all she had wished for in life. She had suffered in the past. As a child she had suffered immense deprivation and borne great discomfort through the effects of War and its aftermath. For years, she had experienced cold and hunger, and seen the far worse sufferings of others – especially after a night of saturation bombing – and perhaps because of the deprivation she had experienced, her desires and hopes for the future were more intense. In the past she had dreamt great dreams for the future, and now at last it seemed as if they were materialising. The prospects for her life and marriage with Dieter, and their journey to the West offered the greatest happiness. What was there which could possibly mar their plans already so far advanced?

Suddenly, Dieter distracted Dagmar from her daydreams.

"Next Saturday your parents can come and visit us at Werlsee," announced Dieter joyously. "It's all arranged as far as my parents are concerned – we've discussed the date and the details of entertaining them."

"That's fine," replied Dagmar, but after a moment's reflection, a frown passed over her brow. Again, she was reminded of the problem of having to make Papa presentable. How could this be done? How would the Liebermanns take to the Renots?

"You know, I'm worried about Papa," said Dagmar at last.

"Why? What's wrong with him,?" replied Dieter in a curious yet nonchalant tone.

"He doesn't always look so good," said Dagmar for want of better words.

"Look so good? What's wrong with his looks?"

"You know what I mean, Dieter," replied Dagmar. "His clothes are so terrible, and he hasn't so much money to spend on clothes as your family."

"Dagmar, please don't think about anything like that," replied Dieter consolingly, laying his hand on hers. "Everything will be all right, I promise you. I've spoken all about your parents at home, and they'll be very welcome at our house and receive the best hospitality, I can assure you. All will go well!"

Dagmar was reassured by the consoling words of her lover, and Dieter turned the conversation to other matters, and soon their mood was changed and they were laughing and lively again.

In high spirits, they arrived at Werlsee by early evening, and drove down the narrow lane leading to the Liebermanns' house. It was a warm evening, and when the car drove off the lane and down the drive of the house, Dieter was surprised to see the front door wide open. It had not been customary to leave open the door of the house – not even on hot Summer afternoons when the family frequently spent its time in the garden. Dieter was more surprised a few moments later to see two elderly ladies supporting one another emerge from the doorway of the house and make towards the lane. They were certainly not friends of the family, and indeed, did not have the appearance of ordinary visitors – for there was no one in the doorway to bid them farewell.

"Who are those people,?" asked Dagmar.

"I don't know," replied Dieter, his voice betraying anxiety. "I've never seen them before."

"Have your parents begun to take in lodgers?"

"That's most unlikely."

The car drove to the back of the house and into the garage. As the couple were about to return to the front of the building, Dieter caught sight of something through one of the back windows – the heads and shoulders of several persons who must have been seated inside. The young couple went close to the window and glancing in noted a crowd of waiting and mostly elderly people, perusing newspapers and old magazines, or sitting idly by.

"They must be patients," said Dagmar.

"I can't understand it," responded Dieter in bewilderment. "My father doesn't take patients. He devotes his time to experimental research at the laboratory – and to hospital work."

"They can't be there for any other reason," said Dagmar as the couple hurried round to the front of the house.

Dieter carried a suitcase and two bunches of flowers whilst Dagmar carried the wrapped gifts, and when they reached the front door, they stood aside to allow an elderly man to leave the building.

"Your father must be busy," whispered Dagmar as they entered the hallway.

They went into the sitting room where Frau Liebermann was seated by the light of the side window busily occupied with a sewing machine, and she rose from her work, greeting them warmly.

"We're engaged, Mamma,!" announced Dieter proudly.

After congratulations, Frau Liebermann kissed them both, asking after their holiday; and the young lovers, speaking in loud excitement and interrupting one another, replied they had never before so enjoyed themselves.

"We've brought you these flowers, Mamma," said Dieter.

"And here is a present for you both," added Dagmar.

"You can open it when Papa's here, and we're all together at dinner tonight," said Dieter.

"And have you driven all the way from Eisenach today,?" enquired Frau Liebermann as she took the gifts.

"Yes, we arose very early this morning," replied Dieter.

"Then you must be tired. I'll prepare tea, and then you can tell me more about what you did and saw," said Frau Liebermann as she made towards the doorway.

"Mamma, what are all those people doing in the house, and why is the front door being left open,?" enquired Dieter.

Frau Liebermann turned towards the engaged couple, and remained stationary a moment, as if in shock or lost for words.

"Yes – it's terrible! – It's been like this for a week now – and your father's been dreadfully overworked," she exclaimed, waving her hand aside with a despairing gesture.

"But why? What do you mean,?" cried Dieter in exasperation.

"Your father's been leaving here at seven-thirty every morning for his work at the hospital."

"Which is his usual time," said Dieter.

"And on arriving back here in the evenings, he has dozens of patients waiting. He's been working until past ten o'clock every night."

"That's madness – for a man his age."

"Sometimes till eleven. It's too much for him. He's getting old – and when his work's finished, he's just irritable and unpleasant, and doesn't feel like dinner."

"But why this new routine? What's happened,?" said Dieter.

At that moment, Dr. Liebermann entered the sitting room from the hallway, a stethoscope round his neck, and wearing the long white coat buttoned up to the neck which doctors in Germany always wear when attending patients. He stopped suddenly on seeing the young couple, glanced at them firmly, but never smiled.

"Hullo Papa, I hear you've been overworking yourself," said Dieter brightly after a momentary pause. "We've brought you a present back from Thüring."

"Aren't you going to welcome them back from their holiday,?" exclaimed Frau Liebermann good-humouredly to her husband.

The doctor came forward and shook the hands of the young couple, but he never smiled.

"I hope you both enjoyed yourselves," he said dryly.

"You can be sure we did, Papa," replied Dieter, beaming with a broad smile. "And now we're engaged."

"Congratulations! And now I must leave you – I'm very busy nowadays. I only came to fetch something from the study," said the doctor gruffly making towards the other side of the room.

"Won't you open the present we've brought you, now you're here,?" said Dieter.

"I expect your father's too busy to stop now," said Frau Liebermann. "That'll have to wait until we're seated at dinner."

"And God only knows when that will be," added Dr. Liebermann.

"And we've brought something for the Goltzes," said Dieter.

"As they've been so kind to us," added Dagmar.

On reaching the study door, Dr. Liebermann turned on his heel and faced the couple again.

"You can forget the Goltzes," he exclaimed.

"Will someone tell me what's going on here? Nothing makes sense," cried Dieter in exasperation.

"They've gone," said Frau Liebermann.

The doctor unbuttoned the top of his coat and took out an envelope from inside his jacket.

"We received this letter from them," he said presenting the article to his son. "It arrived last week."

After a momentary hesitation, Dieter took the letter and feverishly opened it.

"It's a long letter," he exclaimed. "From Hanover!"

"They fled to West Germany ten days ago," replied Dr. Liebermann.

"And so that explains all the patients. You've inherited Dr. Goltz's work."

"Some 'inheritance!' That's not the word. I was the only doctor in the neighbourhood who could take them on."

"But I can't understand why they fled," exclaimed Dieter. "They had everything they wanted. There was nothing they missed. And they had no children whose future to worry about."

"It was unexpected to us all. They told no one," said the doctor.

"I'd have thought they'd be amongst the last to leave the DDR," said Dieter. "They seemed so happy and contented in their house and grounds. They lived in a world of their own."

"We all thought that," said Frau Liebermann. "There was nothing to suspect otherwise. They had no relatives to go to in the West and none to worry about here in the East."

"Then why did they leave,?" asked Dieter.

"They had their own reasons. Read on," said Dr. Liebermann.

Dieter moved his head from side to side as he continued to read the long letter, and he was filled with intense interest and apprehension.

" 'I could no longer go on practising in the DDR as I found the conditions of work intolerable,'" said Dieter reading from the letter. " 'Doctors practising in the East Zone of Germany are deprived from carrying out those basic obligations of their profession recognised throughout the civilised world.' – 'You will ask for the reasons of my flight from the East Zone. I fled on the grounds of humanity. I fled from the DDR so I might practice my profession in freedom and honour, and fulfil those obligations essential to the profession, and help all those sick in mind or body, irrespective of ideology or religious conviction or status in life.' – 'to serve young and old alike, and to reserve the right entirely, to prescribe treatment for my patients according to need, without the intervention of having to succumb to economic sanctions according to known political loyalty.

" 'I had long been opposed in principle to the policy of the Communist Party touching the care of the population of the East Zone; I had long been opposed to administrative interference in hospitals by Communist Party officials having neither knowledge nor expertise in the medical profession. I had been opposed to the privileges extended to Communist Party members, whilst non-Communists were deprived of certain treatments and costly drugs necessary to their recovery. I had been opposed to the gross inhumanity of the Communist regime as it touched the medical care of the people of the East Zone, and I had been shocked by the reports of cruelty, and the denial of proper medical aid to the thousands in concentration camps throughout the East Zone, which reports had reached me through reliable first hand accounts from colleagues in the medical profession.

" 'Only selfishness had delayed my earlier flight from the East – the concern for the house and property at Werlsee, which had been in the possession of my family for over a hundred years. It was a selfishness of which I felt increasingly ashamed, and am now proud to have turned my back on. Now my conscience is free! The final decision between my wife and I to leave the East Zone was made in October of last year.

" 'At that time I received in the casualty department of my clinic in the city centre five sixteen year old youths suffering from indescribable injuries. The youths who were unconscious at the time of admittance, were taken to the surgical ward, and their clothing (which was caked in blood) removed with difficulty by my assistants. The youths were examined. I refused to operate until I had first been informed of the circumstances in which these injuries had been inflicted. That State Security official, who with the help of a group of young Vopos had brought the youths to the clinic, declared that the youths would have to be taken to another medical centre. I replied that the youths would remain here in my clinic until I had been fully satisfied as to the cause of the inflicted injuries. I insisted that someone would have to answer for these atrocities.

" 'The SSD officer broke down blubbering. He said the atrocities had not been committed by Germans – but as we were to discover later, that was not entirely true. Western literature had been found in the youths desks at school, and this had led to their arrest and interrogation by the SSD. The youths were cross-examined in the HQ in Lichtenberg. Orders came down from the Ministry of State Security instructing that the youths should be charged with complicity in an American imperialist fascist conspiracy to incite incendiarism and sedition throughout the Soviet Zone. No charge (not even of a spurious nature) could be made against the youths, and no confession following an interrogation could be extracted by the State Security officers. Someone in the SS Ministry was exasperated, explaining that demotions would follow such incompetence.

" 'The following day, the youths were taken to Karlshorst and handed over to the KGB.' – The Russian security service,!" exclaimed Dieter in surprise.

" 'It's horrible,!" interrupted Dagmar.

"There's nothing surprising in that. The Russians control the Ministry of State Security," said Dr. Liebermann. "Even junior members of the KGB work alongside and watch over their German counterparts in the SSD."

" 'The youths were ordered to reveal factual information they did not possess. They were heavily fettered, thrown into small dark dirty cells, and kept in captivity for fourteen days, during which time they were subjected to the conventional tortures recognised by the legal code of the

USSR, for the purpose of extracting information from persons suspected of working against, or intending to work against, the Socialist State. No coherent information could be extracted from the youths. The KGB began to despair of their abilities. Then one night, after a long drinking session, a group of hardened KGB interrogators, came to the cells where the youths were imprisoned, bringing with them less conventional instruments of torture, and it was then that the atrocities took place. At that point they were joined by two SSD officers. The yells of the youths were so loud that German SSD officers in a neighbouring building, were awoken from their sleep, and came to the dungeons.

" 'They found the worst atrocities had already been committed, but all the youths were conscious and smelling-salts had been used to ensure this. The Russians were very drunk, and an argument took place between them and the Germans, but after further altercation, they relented, and allowed the Germans to take the youths from the prison to a clinic for treatment.

" 'In these circumstances I received the five youths. None survived to see the morning. There was nothing I could do with the limited resources at my disposal.'"

"It's terrible, terrible,!" cried Dagmar.

"Was any court of enquiry held to apprehend the criminals responsible for these atrocities,?" asked Dieter of his father.

"Yes," replied Dr. Liebermann. "Read on."

Dieter continued to read: " 'I was called upon by the Soviet authorities to make out death certificates for the five youths, and I was then required to attend an inquest to be held in camera. I certified the cause of death, adding that the youths had been murdered through injuries to vital organs and the loss of blood. My statement was challenged by a group of Soviet medical practitioners who appeared in court. It was argued that the KGB had not intended to inflict permanent injuries on the five, but that they had died as a result of *accidental misfortune*, primarily because no medical officer had been present at the torture scene as customary in such circumstances. My evidence was dismissed as an attempt to slander the reputation of the Soviet Security Service.

" 'A lengthy technical discussion followed concerning the autopsy carried out on the youths. The Soviet medical officer and I were in agreement that the youths might have died as a result of torture but definitive proof was lacking. Evidence suggested they had rather died of complications arising from bayonet wounds received two days previous to their death. These wounds, it was contended, were not inflicted through interrogation methds, but by the prison guards in the course of preventing an organised escape. The youths had not received proper medical attention after the inflication of these wounds.

" 'I argued they had lost consciousness through shock – or the loss of blood. This was accepted by the court. But then to my astonishment and horror, the tables were turned and I alone was blamed as being ultimately responsible for their deaths. The charge was incompetence for failing to fix up a blood transfusion on their immediately being admitted. My plea that at that early hour in the morning I had not had the facilities available in my small clinic was rejected. They had been brought to my clinic for the reason of secrecy. The magistrate declared I had been guilty of manslaughter, but that thanks to the leniency of the administrative system, no action would be taken against me.' "

Dieter glanced up from the letter.

"It's terrible,!" exclaimed Dagmar again.

"But nothing's surprising in this letter," said Dieter. "We've heard such similar stories so many times before."

"What was the court's decision on the youths' direct cause of death,?" asked Dagmar.

Dieter continued to read: " 'The immediate cause of the youths' death remained in doubt for the results of the autopsy were inconclusive, but it was agreed by the court that the most dangerous injuries were the bayonet wounds. Since the interrogators had not been responsible for the infliction of these wounds the KGB were exonerated from any suspicion of guilt.' "

Dieter glanced up from the letter.

"What happened to the youths' bodies? Were they handed back to their families for a Christian burial,?" asked Dagmar.

Dieter continued to read: " 'The law took its inevitable course. As the interrogators had failed to clear the youths of the charges, they were adjudged guilty of treason in attempting to provoke sedition as instigated by the American imperialists.' "

"Tortured to death to prove their innocence! Is that justice when there's no evidence of guilt in the first place,?" exclaimed Frau Liebermann.

"Why didn't Dr. Goltz tell anyone about these terrible things before,?" exclaimed Dagmar.

"I should think that's clear," replied Dieter. "He had his life to think of."

"But how could he hide such horrible things in his mind for so long, without revealing them to anyone,?" insisted Dagmar. "How could he keep such a secret as that?"

"Doctors are good at keeping secrets," said Dieter with an ironic smile and winking at his father. "They do it all the time. It's part of their work."

"And I don't expect that that's a secret any man would like to let out easily," added Dr. Liebermann. "And it remains a secret between us in this room, and goes no further. Dr. Goltz's flight to the West will make no difference to the revelation of secrets of this kind. There are Soviet agents everywhere, and they could handle him as they pleased in their own way at any time, if they thought it necessary."

Dieter continued to read the letter silently.

"He says he sent a letter to the Soviet Commandant complaining there was already a critical shortage of doctors in the East zone to handle those suffering from ordinary accidents without having to attend to those intentionally injured by the Soviet security forces," said Dieter. "That must have been a fine smack in the face for the Commandant!"

"He didn't receive a reply to the letter," added Dr. Liebermann as his son continued to peruse the letter.

"But he was called to an office in Karlshorst a few days later and received an oral threat to keep silent," said Dieter glancing up from the letter again.

"That was usual procedure after all he had witnessed," remarked Dr. Liebermann.

"He wishes to bind us under a promise to whisper nothing of what he's written," exclaimed Dieter without glancing up.

"Only the four of us here in this room will know anything of this matter. That's the wish of Dr. Goltz, and that's how it'll stay," said the doctor.

" 'I am glad to share the burden of this secret with several of my old friends to whose hospitality and good companionship I have long been grateful, and whom I know can honour the keeping of this secret,'" read Dieter in a slow solemn tone.

"That's the most significant part of the letter as far as we in this room are concerned," said Dr. Liebermann. "You can leave the rest for now and read it later. It's full of little requests and business matters."

"But I can't understand why the Goltzes never told us anything about this before. I mean, about their intention and plans for leaving the DDR," said Dieter folding the letter and handing it back to his father.

"I can't understand it either," replied the doctor shaking his head sadly. "Fleeing like that without telling us a word, and after the number of times we've entertained them here. It's that which hurts me most."

"You know, I don't think the Goltzes ever really trusted us – not after we joined the SED in 1948," said Frau Liebermann.

"Surely they must have known we were only beetroot Communists," said Dieter.

"Even beetroot Communists are prepared to betray their 'friends' in certain circumstances or under pressure, else they wouldn't have joined in the first place," remarked Frau Liebermann. "Aren't there times when all of us in the East zone suspect our closest neighbours? How many people can we count on our hands whom we really trust? Not many!"

"It's a terrible world we live in if Germans can no longer trust their closest friends," said the doctor shaking his head despondently.

"But that's how it is today," replied his wife.

"And to think of what that man's left behind here,!" exclaimed the doctor throwing out his arm with an eloquent gesture. "The fabulous art treasures lying in that house! Of course the State will take the lot."

"Did the Goltzes succeed in taking anything with them,?" asked Dieter.

"He says in his letter that since last October he's been taking out various amounts of cash from his bank and storing the notes, in readiness for his flight to the West," said Dr. Liebermann.

"That must have set off alarm bells at the bank," replied Dieter.

"Well, it wasn't exactly all one way. He was depositing cash as well at regular intervals, but in smaller amounts," said his father. "On the day he left for the West, he tried to take out five thousand marks. The bank wouldn't give him a pfennig. He took fright quickly. He left the building with his wife, went to the nearest Underground station checking that no one was following, and a few minutes later, they were in West Berlin – and they've never returned since."

"And so they blocked his bank balance as quickly as that," exclaimed Dieter.

"Not entirely. When I received his letter, it enclosed three cheques: two thousand marks for your mother and me; and one thousand marks each for you and Dagmar. I've cashed our cheque and yours Dieter, at the bank, and I've heard that the payments have gone through."

"That was an unnecessary kindness. It'll always be remembered," said Dieter.

"As for Dagmar," said the doctor turning towards her, "I went to several banks in Berlin trying to ascertain whether or not you held an account."

"I haven't got a bank account," replied Dagmar.

"Even if you opened one now, I don't think the cheque would go through at this late stage," said the doctor. "They must have blocked his account for certain. Anyway, I'll give you the cheque to keep as a memento of your friendship with Dr. and Frau Goltz. You can frame it, and if you meet them in the West at some future date, you can return their hospitality."

"I don't see what's the use of a dud cheque," remarked Dieter.

"The flight of the Goltzes has been so sudden and unexpected," exclaimed Frau Liebermann. "It's been a great shock to us all. Nowadays in this country we don't know what to expect from one day to the next."

Chapter 53

After she had returned home to Treptow that night, Dagmar passed on the invitation to her parents to visit Werlsee the following Saturday. Dieter would fetch the three of them in the car and drive to their hosts. For the rest of the week, Dagmar's mind was preoccupied with the imminent party, and again, she was engaged in a whispering conspiracy with her mother. For the second time that year there came the problem of making Papa Renot presentable, only this time the problem seemed to take on greater proportions than before.

How would Dieter's parents take to the old man,? was a question which worried Dagmar throughout the week. The first meeting between Dieter and Papa Renot had gone off well, but then introducing the latter to Dieter's parents might be quite a different proposition. After much discussion, the problem of making Papa Renot presentable was very simply solved. It was solved through the acquisition of two small purchases: a new tie from Woolworths in Neukölln (the good Frau's gift) and a box of fine handkerchiefs (also from the West sector) which was Dagmar's gift. One of the handkerchiefs was to be placed in the old man's pocket.

"And don't show too much hanky, Papa," advised Dagmar as the old man opened the box, after she had explained the reason for the purchase. "And remember, it's only for show – for your pocket – not for face-wiping," Dagmar made so bold to add.

On the Tuesday of that week, Dagmar and Dieter went out together as always on that day, and they attended a concert in the West sector. On Thursday evening, after her return from work, Papa Renot said he wished to speak with her seriously.

"What is it Papa? Do you have to be so grim,?" replied Dagmar, taken aback by the gravity of her father's manner.

"It's about your visits to the West sector," said the old man.

"What about them?"

"Have you read the papers?"

"I don't read them like you do," replied Dagmar.

"The Volkspolizei have been stepping up their interference with DDR citizens going into the West sectors of the city," said her father.

"Well,?"

"Yesterday, according to the radio, the three Western Commandants sent identical letters of protest to the Soviet Cammandant, Major-General Zakharov, against what they described as the 'harassment of border crossers.' Apparently, detentions, threats, deprivations of identity documents and economic pressure have been used against our citizens."

"But I expect that's only against people carrying luggage – refugees, Papa," replied Dagmar.

"Still, I'd be careful. It's wise not to cross too often. You never know what they might do next."

"Of course, Papa," replied Dagmar solemnly.

"And remember, one day you'll be a refugee yourself."

"We're always careful, Papa, when we cross to the West sectors – although I always fear for Dieter."

"You should drop a hint to him not to cross to the West sectors so often," advised the old man. "I can't be responsible for him – and it's not my business."

That Saturday Dieter fetched the three of them from Treptow and drove to Werlsee. The subsequent party was a great success. They ate a fine tea shortly after arrival, and afterwards, wine was brought out and served, and the old man remained discreet and modest for the duration of the afternoon and evening to his daughter's complete satisfaction. He neither wiped his face with the handkerchief nor dug his elbow into anyone's side, although he did on several occasions brush some invisible spots of dust away from his lapels. Shortly after tea he was engaged in a long discussion with Dr. Liebermann about the present state of the CDU in the DDR, as both men leaned over a table with fine cigars. Frau Renot was enchanted by the house and hinted she might like to be shown all the pictures and antiquities, and so Frau Liebermann was drawn in as her guide.

That evening they ate an excellent dinner, and joked and laughed over glasses of wine and liqueur. Then the four parents played cards in the sitting room, whilst Dieter and Dagmar went off to his room to be alone awhile. It was almost midnight when the party ended, and the Renots were given a great send-off by their hosts and told they would be welcome many times again, and Dr. Liebermann said he looked forward to hearing some more of those side-splitting jokes Papa Renot had related about Walter Ulbricht.

"But I shouldn't let the jokes get too scurrilous," advised the doctor with a wink as the old man climbed into the car, "or else the First Secretary might come to hear of them himself one day, and try finding out who invented them."

Papa Renot laughed as the doctor slammed the door of the car, and as Dieter drove the Renots back to Treptow, the parents were talking and laughing all the while as they sat in the back seat.

Dagmar told Dieter about her father's warning against too often crossing the East-West borders of the city. Dieter shared her apprehension, and after some thought and planning he obtained a library card to the Free University and cards to various societies attached to the same institution in West Berlin. He obtained these membership cards through the help of his cousin in the West, for the purpose of flashing them in front of the East German border guards (should he be stopped any time) so leading them to believe he was an East German attending the West Berlin University.

The new term began again at the Humboldt University, and soon, new orders, warnings, threats and reiterations of older threats came down through the authorities, and the students were especially warned against visiting West Berlin. New spies were appointed to watch over the activities of the students, and the authorities made this clear through a high-focused arrogance and close supervision of the student body. Their education was free, and for that reason, they had to serve absolutely and without question the State which was giving them this education, and this lesson was hammered home by the authorities again and again.

Soon there were rumours of arrests of students and tales of tenement blocks which the SSD had visited in the early hours of the morning, before removing students and other youths. Sometimes a professor disappeared or was mysteriously replaced under unusual circumstances. There were those who witnessed various events and happenings, and rumours spread, but nothing certain was confirmed as to what had occurred. Everywhere there was suspicion and fear and everywhere there were things which went unexplained. Discontent amongst the student body in the Humboldt University ran high and Dieter felt something of this anger, but he suppressed his natural instinct of resentment.

Sometimes as he sat listening to one of the compulsory propaganda lectures, or whilst attending a compulsory Russian lesson, when the students were being exhorted to cherish the memory of Comrade Stalin, he would clinch his fists with anger as indeed did other students.

One evening when outside the University, a couple of old friends ran up to him on an urgent matter.

"Dieter,!" one of them cried, "you must help us."

"What's up,?" returned Dieter.

"You remember about the professor in the medical faculty who was displaced last week?"

"Yes."

"Well, it's been confirmed. He's been arrested on ideological grounds."

"So what,?" returned Dieter.

"Dieter, listen,!" said one of the others, as the three youths continued briskly along the pavement. "We're organising a strike."

"But the medical faculty isn't our faculty," said Dieter. "We're veterinary students."

"I know, but this time we're trying to organise a strike throughout the entire University," replied the other.

"Then count me out," said Dieter.

"A universal strike may even undermine the foundations of the State,"

"I'm sorry, Karl, I can't help you," said Dieter.

"But why? At one time you were one of our best agitators – behind the scenes," replied Karl. "Do you remember the demonstrations of May last year, when our entire faculty came out on strike?"

"And the publicity the West German press gave us,?" added his companion.

"I remember its collapse and the aftermath," said Dieter. "The situation, Hans, has become far too hot for a repetition of that."

"But this strike is *really* important," said Hans. "The new professor's useless. They say he can't even distinguish the difference between the anatomy of a human and and a chimpanzee – that's how bad it is! The students learn nothing from him. He's just a political stooge."

"He's only interested in giving a Marxist-Leninist interpretation to every appendectomy he performs," said Karl.

"It's unfortunate for the students, but I can't help," replied Dieter.

"We need concerted action from the entire University," continued Karl unabated. "Only in that way can we hope for some relief from tyranny."

"Conditions are already unbearable without this latest episode," put in Hans.

"How much longer can we put up with these conditions,?" said Karl.

"I understand everything, but I can do nothing," said Dieter.

"Why not,?" exclaimed both students at once.

"For one thing, you know my position in the FDJ, and for another, I'm an officer in the Volksarmee," replied Dieter. "If I was accused by the authorities of complicity against them, the penalty would be merciless. It's not as if I was an ordinary student."

With this explanation, the two students took their leave of Dieter after expressing regret. Dieter meanwhile felt a pang of self-reproach at his inability to help his companions in the University where he had studied so long. Deep inside he felt he owed it to them to help in their struggle, but he also recognised that his future life lay beyond the frontiers of East Germany, and all his hopes and aspirations now only looked forward to the day when he and Dagmar would fly to the West, to their new life in Friedrichshafen.

In October, a new order came down from the authorities. All students (including schoolchildren) were ordered to pledge themselves at the disposal of the government for a period of three years after leaving school or university. The wording of the pledge began: "My education is made possible by our workers' and peasants' State. I, therefore, assume the obligation to support the policy of the German Democratic government at all times, and to pursue the studies of dialectical materialism which at the end of my studies will be used for further Socialist construction."

In that same month, the fear and caution of the young couple when crossing between the East-West sectors of the city, was well justified by public events. In that month a number of students were arrested, tried and condemned to a period of fifteen years imprisonment for "clandestinely" entering and leaving West Berlin, on a charge of trying to promote German unification.

Discontent ran higher in the University, bursting into minor demonstrations, shouts of defiance and the boycotting of lectures. There was conspiracy against the authorities, and more common, talk of plots, but as yet all seemed in vain and all gestures against oppression impotent. Everywhere was suspicion and acts interpreted as espionage, followed by more arrests, but always the iron fist of the authorities was unremitting. Still the students refused to give up the struggle. Still they risked arrest, internment and the suffering and humiliation of incarceration in concentration camps throughout the Soviet zone, rather than surrender the last hope of freedom to the oppression of the system. They chose not to surrender because they knew that that led to everlasting despair.

For the second time that term, Dieter was approached by student companions to help in the struggle against authority. He was asked to petition and help demonstrate for the release of students who had been condemned to the brutal sentence of fifteen years imprisonment for crossing into the Western half of their own city.

"If I signed that thing they'd string me up by the neck," replied Dieter.

"But if we can collect hundreds, or maybe, thousands of signatures," argued one of his companions, "perhaps we can secure some leniency even if not the release of our imprisoned colleagues."

"I think it'd be useless," replied Dieter. "Do you think this petition would ever reach the eyes of any member of the Central Committee of the SED?"

"We can but try," said one.

"Any such petition would go straight to the Ministry of State Security," said Dieter. "It's madness!"

"That may be. We understand the risks."

"It would lead to more arrests," persisted Dieter. "You'll probably get yourselves arrested before you have a hundred signatures."

"Nonetheless, we're prepared to carry on the struggle," replied the other student defiantly.

"That's just what two other students told me less than a month ago," responded Dieter. "You remember Karl and Hans? Well, they've disappeared and no one's heard of their whereabouts since."

Because of increasing arrests and renewed tension felt in East Berlin, Dagmar begged Dieter that they should evacuate the city earlier than the time already projected for their final departure.

"I cannot. I must complete my studies first," replied Dieter.

"I feel so afraid. From day to day things have been worsening here in the East. Horrible things are happening all the time," said Dagmar holding her arm tightly around her lover and burying her head in his chest.

"Soon I'll have completed the course, then we can leave," consoled Dieter. "There's not much longer to wait."

"I hope and pray nothing will happen before then," exclaimed Dagmar.

"Why should it,?" asked Dieter.

"Sometimes I have terrible premonitions – although I try not to believe them," she replied.

The young couple cut down drastically on their visits to the West sectors.

The struggle of the students continued, despite the hopelessness of attaining their ends and despite the brutality of the authorities. Although the widespread use of informers was employed throughout every level of the community and despite the use of varying intimidation tactics, still the smouldering embers of discontent could not be smothered. The struggle only succeeded in convincing the authorities they faced a problem of insuperable proportions requiring yet more oppressive measures, and it was with this in mind that towards the end of October, a conference of East German educators was held for the purpose of planning a new drive to stamp out student unrest and crack down on anyone dissenting from the party line. Over 900 students – FDJ enthusiasts – and professors were summoned to Berlin for the conference. It was devoted to the problems of colleges and technical schools enrolling some 100,000 East German young people annually.

The conference was conducted according to Marxist-Leninist thinking, rarely rising above the level of the credulously inane whilst sometimes sinking to the depths of Alice In Wonderland absurdity. Practicality was laid aside so that the dogmas of Marxism-Leninism could be pursued to their logical conclusion. Professor Robert Neumann, deputy director of the Institute of Social Sciences at the Humboldt University, told the conference that the "bourgeois" idea still persists that students should be admitted on the basis of talent and mental aptitude. A candidate for the medical faculty, for example, should not be admitted to the University on the potentiality of his or her being a competent doctor, but rather on the potentiality of his being a good Marxist in the workers' and peasants' State.

The same professor also reported to the conference the "highly regrettable fact" that students still resisted having to learn Russian, and that some professors still have "peculiar" ideas, as for example that "capitalist pride of property in production was not gained by means of robbery." From the conference came three recommendations: firstly, that all teachers should study Marxism-Leninism; secondly, that action should be taken against professors who had fled to the West by the withdrawal of academic degrees; and thirdly, that Party members should be recruited from amongst the students. The urgency of holding such a conference devoted to the problems of university discontent was underlined by the fact that between the years 1953 and 1957 inclusive, more than 24,000 students had fled from the DDR.

On one occasion when Dagmar tried to persuade Dieter on the advisability of their leaving the East earlier than planned, he took her aside solemnly requesting she no longer speak to him about the daily events occurring around them, and he even extracted a promise from her to this effect.

"Remember, in a few months, we'll no longer be living in Berlin," he urged. "What happens around us is no longer any concern of ours. Please remember that. You're only apprehensive because the time for our flight is drawing ever nearer. Can't you see that? Your premonitions have no more substance than that. They're in your own mind – not out there in the real world."

Dagmar kept her promise, and on no future occasion did she mention to him anything about the day to day events occurring in East Berlin. Indeed, she closed her mind entirely to what was reported in the news. Dieter studied hard in preparation for his final exams, and took part in as few University and FDJ activities as was possible, although he was still obliged to attend the Political Officers training School of the Volksarmee in Treptow twice weekly.

In this way the young lovers became gradually more oblivious to the political environment in which they lived. What happened in East Berlin or in the East zone of Germany was no longer of interest to them. They now only looked forward with keen anticipation to their flight to the West and to their new life in Friedrichshafen, and they were not going to risk losing such a life opportunity for any inducement which perchance might come their way.

BOOK XIV

The Uninvited Guest

Love is the mind's strong physic, and the pill
That leaves the heart sick and o'erturns the will.

Thomas Middleton, *Blurt, Master Constable*, Act III, Sc. 1.

Chapter 54

It was in the middle of November and under the most unexpected circumstances that the fate and future of the two lovers was sealed. For almost a year Dieter had maintained the utmost discretion in expressing his true political convictions. In view of the rosy prospects facing him and his fiancée in West Germany he had good reason to remain cautious, but considering his natural loquacity and the "big mouth" of the Berliner, he must often have found this reticence both difficult and unnatural. It sometimes happens that transgressions committed at an earlier period, and long since thought to be absolved and forgotten, must unexpectedly be paid for in an unknown future. It sometimes happens that such transgressions are paid for under extraordinary and the least expected circumstances, and this was so as concerned the fate of Dietrich Liebermann.

Dieter's cousin, Irmgard, who lived in West Berlin, attending the Free University, had recently become engaged to another student of the University, Max Möller. Both Dieter and Dagmar already knew Max, for he had been a close friend of Irmgard for more than a year prior to the engagement, and the couple from the East had often visited Irmgard's home and attended parties at Max's apartment.

Irmgard Liebermann was an attractive girl with a large bone structure, attractive limbs, a well bronzed skin, platinum blonde hair and deeply set pale blue eyes. She was lively, with broad cultural interests, gregarious and passionately keen on the study of comparative politics. As with Max, she belonged to the faculty of Social Sciences, and it was the ideal of a unified Europe which had first brought the young couple together, sealing a spiritual relationship between them.

Max Möller lived in a large five-bedroomed flat, shared with four other foreign students, in a fine apartment house just off Onkel Tom Strasse in the prosperous suburb of Zehlendorf. The five students who were close friends, were also members of the Social Science faculty, and often, they held bottle parties, which they called *Soirées*, in the apartment on Saturday nights.   The four foreign students, well liked for their extroverted good nature and wit, were already known to Dieter and Dagmar.   There was Alexis Cremidis, a Greek; Luigi Romariz, a Portuguese; Lars Grunqvist, a Swede, and Carl Schauwecher, a Swiss.

Alexis Cremidis was a tall muscular youth who looked older than his years, not only on account of his large figure, but because of a deep bass voice, a pointed black beard and dark tanned complexion. He was well liked for the warmth and civility of his manner, and his other student companions had first nicknamed him the Ancient Greek as he loved to recite the *Choruses* from several of the major Greek plays. Then one day, in a book of Greek legends, Max found an 18th century engraving of the hero Achilles, the beard and face of which resembled that of Alexis Cremidis, and from that day on Alex was jokingly re-named Achilles. Alex had long been a devotee of the Greek drama and in his native land he had taken part in open air amateur productions. In the flat in Berlin, he was often seen to be pacing up and down the sitting room eloquently reciting from Aeschylus (usually from the *Oresteia*) or from one of the other Greek dramatists, to refresh his memory on what he had learnt by heart. A small stool was used as an altar before which he would pray or beseech the gods.

"Alex, I can't understand what you're saying, but whatever it is, I can see it's most impressive," said Max on one occasion glancing up from the book he sat reading. "You act with pathos, and somehow, you arouse in me deep feelings of pity and intense emotion."

Alexis Cremidis reacted with uncertainty to this response, not knowing what was meant by these remarks.

"I really mean it sincerely," continued Max. "To listen and watch you recite from the ancient Greeks is quite an electrifying experience. You must recite at our next party."

From that day, Alexis recited at every party held in the flat, and he was applauded by his friends and captivated them by his acting, although none understood the meaning of his words, until the five students clubbed together buying copies of the German translation of the plays so they could follow the sense of the recitations at subsequent events. One day, Alex boasted that if anyone quoted any ten lines from any of the fifty or so complete plays still extant of the four great Greek dramatists, he could name which play it had come from and exactly place the lines. As none of those present understood Greek, he could not be challenged, but one day, a Spanidard, Manuel Ruiz, joined their lively set, and he challenged Alex.

Manuel Ruiz was a student of philology, who was fluent in Greek and Latin in addition to a smattering of six modern foreign languages. Dieter and Dagmar witnessed the challenge when it was made. It was very late on a Saturday night and most of the guests were full of drink. Manuel said he would take twenty-five quotations from the Greek dramas and would pay Alex two marks for each quotation correctly placed. Alex responded by defiantly rejecting the terms of the challenge, saying he would pay Manuel a straight sum of fifty marks if he failed to place any one of the twenty-five quotations. The challenge was accepted and hands shaken, and Max announced that a party would be held in the apartment next Saturday, to which all present were invited, and that the quiz would then take place. For a week, Alex was nervous, re-reading the plays, wondering whether he had been too bold in making such a challenge. Dieter and Dagmar attended the party that Saturday. With perfect ease, Alex was able to place each of the twenty-five quotations, and he won the fifty marks. From that day onward, Alex and Manuel were the best of friends.

Luigi Romariz, the Portuguese, was older than the other students in the apartment, for he had begun his university education later in life. For seven years he had served in the French Foreign Legion, had been wounded five times, winning medals of distinction. After leaving the force, he had wandered over Europe, thinking deeply and formulating his ideas from the experiences of his travels before arriving in Berlin. Through his extensive travels, he had come to believe that the future of Europe lay only in her unification under a Federal government. As with many who had gained that practical experience of life which comes after a period in the armed services, he had a broad-minded, generous and humane outlook on life.

Lars Grunqvist, the Swede, was a tall ginger haired boy, and as with Max, he was a student of philosophy in the faculty of Social Sciences. He was deep thinking and intelligent (even if deficient in a sense of humour) and for many hours, until late into the night, he and Max were often engaged in conversation as they discussed Schopenhauer, Hegelian idealism or different aspects of Kantian metaphysics. Lars was a heavy drinker although his friends had never seen him drunk.

During a party on one occasion, an Englishman, George Watson, also a member of the circle, asked Lars why he never seemed tipsy. It was the kind of insolent question which could only have been put through that curious bent of inquisitiveness unique to the English mind. Lars nonchalantly replied that he happened to be built in such a way that alcohol just never went to his head (which was partly but not entirely true) on the condition he took the precaution of engaging in physical or mental exertion after drinking. He explained that will-power had something to do with it, and that providing he never lay down or otherwise remained inactive the effects of alcohol never effected him adversely.

At that moment, the Englishman and Swede were rudely startled from behind by the loud exclamation, "Boy, that's impossible!" These words came from Milton Malone, one of many Americans on exchange schemes spending a year at the Free University, and he jumped in front of the couple, and shaking a finger in the Swede's face, challenged to drink him under the table. It was already late in the evening and Milton Malone had by that time drunk more than was good for him. Lars, maintaining his usual sang-froid in face of this challenge from an unexpected quarter, coolly accepted the contest.

"Name the weapons – your tipple," said the Swede with complete indifference as he sat, as he always did, stiffly upright on the low sofa.

"Whiskey,!" retorted Milton Malone without a moment's hesitation.

"Accepted,!" replied Lars. "Name the time and place."

"In this apartment next Saturday night at nine o'clock," said Milton. "And fifty marks to win or lose."

"Agreed,!" said the Swede.

It was that same night when Alexis Cremidis had earlier picked up his fifty marks from Manuel Ruiz, and had it not been for the heroic outcome of that event and the temptation of the financial winnings, as a precious bundle of crisp new green five mark notes was passed from one pair of hands to another, then Milton Malone would never have been inspired to make so bold a challenge. All present at the party were again invited to attend another evening at the apartment the following Saturday.

At last, the anticipated day arrived, and at nine o'clock precisely in the presence of the assembled company, a table was placed in the centre of the sitting room, and the Swede and Irish-American were seated back-to-back cross legged on the table, and two bottles of Whiskey had been purchased and brought by the umpires for the contest, and handed to the competitors for their consumption. The Swede and the American quickly stripped off the wrappings around the necks of the bottles.

With perfect ease, and as if quenching his thirst with water on a Summer's day, Lars drank down the bottle to the last drop within sixty seconds. The assembled company watched him pour the "water of life" into his mouth, as if emptying it into a drain, and they saw the movement of his neck muscles as the liquid gurgled down his throat. The girls gasped in amazement, and then Lars leapt off the table and bowed to the company, receiving a thunderous applause. Apparently, he suffered no ill effects, remaining in full control of his faculties, although he did belch on laying the empty bottle onto the table. It was true that Lars had prepared himself for the competition that afternoon, by filling his stomach with buttermilk, raw eggs and cheese; but despite that, it remained a remarkable achievement.

Milton Malone, soon discovered that by making the challenge he had "gulped" down more than he could "swallow." He became a pitiful figure, sitting alone on the table, belching loudly and bravely gulping down great mouthfuls of Scotch at ten-second intervals. The company were reluctant to let him go until he had emptied the container, and anyway, Milton would never have pocketed his pride and jumped down from the table until he had accomplished what the Swede achieved. Eventually, Milton threw down the empty bottle onto the floor, and received the applause which was his due. Immediately afterwards, however, and before he had taken a bow from the company, he was seized with convulsions, writhing and vomiting. Consternation broke out amongst the company. Max, Alex and Luigi called for calm, and in their presence of mind, they were led to carry the American into the bathroom, and Dieter, being the only medic present, was called upon to diagnose the patient.

A probable attack of acute pacreatitis was diagnosed, and the patient was urged to eat nothing for thirty-six hours. That evening, after Milton had been put to bed in the flat, Dagmar and other girls took turns to sit by and nurse the patient throughout the night, and he remained bedridden in the flat for the following five days.

Lars was fascinated by the pointed well-pruned beard of Alexis Cremidis, deciding to make a similar attempt himself. He succeeded. Max looked at his face one day with a critical eye exclaiming, "We can't call *you* an ancient Greek, you look too much like a Viking." After some discussion amongst the students, they decided to name Lars, Rurik, after the legendary Swede who had led the Scandinavian tribe of Rus across the Eastern plains of Europe, so giving the name to the Continent's largest country.

Carl Schauwecher, the Swiss, was younger than the others who shared Max's apartment in Zehlendorf and he had joined them later. He was a student of political economy, with a practical business outlook on life, and rather quieter than the others, but despite his reticence and puritanical outlook on life, he was well-liked by his companions. He had a passion for fencing and athletics, attending a nearby gymnastics hall several nights a week. Sometimes at the parties held in the flat, he arranged fencing matches between himself and friends. On one occasion he brought a Dutchman back to the flat named Hendrik Everts, whom he had met at the gym, and after the Swiss and the Dutchman had fenced for an hour, they sat down for coffee with the other students in the flat, and it was soon discovered that Hendrik Everts shared political views similar to the other students.

These then, were the friends of Irmgard and Max Möller. The parties or *Soirées* held in Max's apartment usually took place on alternate

Saturdays. To broaden the objectivity of his outlook and rid himself of a lingering subjectivity which tended to limit the Prussian mind, he had decided that none but foreigners share his apartment, and preferably those from diverse parts of the Continent. He therefore considered a Greek, a Portuguese, a Swede and a Swiss to be a suitable combination of nationalities with whom to share his company. The parties held in the apartment were therefore always international, attended by as many as twenty to thirty persons who in so large a flat could be easily accommodated. The boys brought their drink and usually their womenfolk, and Irmgard always invited a number of her female friends to ensure that numbers were even. The guests began arriving at seven and all were usually there by eight.

Irmgard and several of the girls attended to the serving of drinks and food, and the proceedings often began with Alexis Cremidis delivering one of his dramatic recitations, and then an old school friend of Max, Manfred Herfurth, sang some *Lieder*, to his fiancée's accompaniment, for there was a fine grand piano; Hendrik and Carl Schauwecher might have a few rounds of fencing; someone else delivered another recitation or impersonated a well-known personality; others told jokes, and then Leon Deveaux, a Belgian music student, played the violin, and finally, the political discussions began.

During these discussions, the girls often preferred to play a passive role, sitting quietly by their menfolk serving them with drinks and refreshments and listening to the conversation. Even Irmgard, who was usually a voluble speaker, said little during these evenings, for as a hostess she was often busily engaged in the kitchen attending to the comforts of her guests. The political discussions continued until the early hours, when the men would escort their womenfolk home, or sleep with them in the apartment, but occasionally, discussions continued without a break until midday Sunday.

Shortly after the engagement was announced between Irmgard and Max Möller, a special engagement party was arranged in Max's apartment in Zehlendorf. The young couple from the East were naturally invited, and it had been many weeks since they had last attended a party at Max's, because of their reluctance in too often crossing the East-West sectors of the city. At first Dieter shook his head with a gesture of dismay exclaiming, "I don't think I can go. It's on the eve of the national elections in the DDR, and I'm supposed to be canvassing with the FDJ for Communist votes."

"Just don't turn up," replied Dagmar, "and if they ask afterwards, say you had a sore throat and stayed at home. I don't expect the Communists will lose the election just because you won't go canvassing for them for one night."

"They couldn't lose the election anyway," replied Dieter. "There's only one list of candidates."

The couple decided to attend the party in the West sector. They bought a gift for the newly engaged couple, a set of records of Brahm's *Deutches Requiem*, a cheap bottle of Caucasian wine, and a fine bouquet of flowers. Dieter decided that if they were stopped and questioned by the border police, to reply they were going to lay flowers on his grandmother's grave in the Heer Strasse Cemetery in the suburb of Westend.

They reached Max's at eighty thirty and Luigi Romariz opened the door to the young couple warmly welcoming them into the flat. Loud voices and laughter came from within, and in the background, the strains from a Bruckner symphony.

"I hope we're not the last here," exclaimed Dieter full of anticipation, quickly pulling off his coat, which Luigi took from the new arrivals.

"The party's hardly begun yet," replied Luigi beaming with liveliness and good cheer. "You'd better take those things into the kitchen to the hostess," he added pointing to the packages.

The young couple went towards the kitchen, and as they passed the doorway leading to the sitting room, they heard someone clapping his hands and calling for silence, and as they glanced into the crowded smoke-filled room, they saw Max in the centre standing beside the tall black bearded figure of Alexis Cremidis. The couple from the East went into the kitchen and were greeted by Irmgard, who kissed them both, taking their gifts and thanking them profusely.

"We wish you every happiness for the future," exclaimed Dieter and Dagmar both at once.

"We haven't seen you for so long," cried Irmgard excitedly, laying down the gifts on the kitchen table which was already piled high with presents.

"Such terrible thngs have been happening in the East during the past few weeks, that we're afraid of being apprehended and arrested every time we cross the sector frontier," replied Dagmar.

"And you've brought us flowers too," exclaimed Irmgard. "Hilda, put these in the washing mug in Max's room," added Irmgard to one of two girls who were pouring out trays of drinks and preparing open sandwiches.

"You have many guests tonight,?" exclaimed Dieter.

"More than ever before," replied Irmgard.

"And gifts from so many," said Dieter winking. "You'll have a lot of letter writing to do."

"It was funny earlier this evening," said Irmgard moving closer to her cousin and speaking confidentially. "You know George Watson, the Englishman. He arrived here at seven-thirty with Waltraute dressed in a loose pullover, carryng a bottle beneath his arm. Already some of the guests had arrived, and when he saw everyone in dark lounge suits and white or silver ties and flowers and presents everywhere, he suddenly looked awkward, and said he had left something behind and would go and return later. Poor George! He didn't understand this was a special party."

"These poor English don't understand our Continental customs," laughed Dieter. "And what happened?"

"Well, he lives quite near, and he returned half an hour later wearing a dark suit and silver tie, and carrying a present and bouquet.

"I always knew George was a well-meaning chap," replied Dieter.

From the direction of the sitting room came a reverberating rendition in a foreign tongue, and Alexis Cremidis had begun his dramatic recitation.

"Tonight it's Orestes," exclaimed Irmgard with a smile.

Max hurried into the kitchen greeting the new arrivals, and there was more handshaking, bowing, curtseying and laughing.

"Not too loud – Alexis is reciting," urged Max.

"Hi! How do folks? Sorry I'm late," came a voice from behind Dieter and Dagmar, and a short stocky fellow in a light blue suit and a green hat pushed onto the back of his head, came bouncing self-confidently into the room. He wore a large carnation buttonhole, and carried a package and bouquet.

"This is for the prettiest bride-to-be in Berlin," exclaimed the newcomer speaking quickly, stretching out his arms and holding up the gift and flowers at chest level.

"Thank you, Milton," cried Irmgard taking the gifts.

"Welcome,!" exclaimed Max.

"Hi! Here's another happy couple," exclaimed Milton shaking hands with the couple from the East. "Seems everyone's getting married around here nowadays. – Say, I haven't seen you two around lately."

"We don't like crossing the East-West sectors too often," replied Dieter.

"You mean, 'cause of Ulbricht and his Vopos,?" exclaimed Milton.

"That's about it," replied Dieter.

"You ought to sort those guys out sometime. Haven't you got an election coming up tomorrow?"

"That doesn't mean much to us," said Dieter with a smile.

"I pity you guys,!" replied Milton adopting a patronising pose.

"See you inside," said Dieter impatient to get away.

"Do you see this flower,?" exclaimed Milton holding out the lapel of his buttonhole towards Max. "It's real, isn't it?"

"Seems so, and the scent is delicious," replied Max bending forward.

A stream of water squirted Max in the eye, and Milton burst into laughter, and the others too, as Max wiped his face with a handkerchief.

"Really, Milton, not another of your practical jokes," chided Irmgard good-humouredly.

"You like it? Great, isn't it,?" exclaimed Milton. "It's the latest craze in Berlin. No guy would have expected that. See, you can fix it into any ordinary buttonhole," he added showing the mechanism. "That's what you need at a party like this!"

"You're always up to new tricks," exclaimed Irmgard shaking an admonishing finger in Milton's face.

"Say, Sir, Max, can I make a very special request,?" said Milton.

"You can but ask."

"May I kiss the bride-to-be of the luckiest man in town?"

"I can't very well refuse, can I,?" chuckled Max.

"Thank you, Sir," said Milton, and he quickly threw his arms round Irmgard, kissing her on the lips to the laughter of the company.

"Max, that was a kiss I'll cherish all my life," exclaimed Milton wiping his lips free of colour with a handkerchief. "Max, I'm telling you, with this dame, you've sure got the best oomph value in Berlin. Now I want to rush off and hear that Greek. Somehow, he can really get the feelings worked up inside me. That Greek can sure act!"

"Aren't you going to take your hat off first,?" exclaimed Irmgard as Milton turned to leave the kitchen.

"Gee, I'm going crazy tonight," replied Milton shaking his head and snatching off his hat to reveal a crew-cut of russet coloured hair. "It's all the excitement and happiness around. I've been hurrying so, I don't know what I'm doing from one moment to the next. – Say, anyway, what's this guy acting tonight?"

"The *Oresteia*," replied Irmgard.

"Which *Oresteia*?"

"From the *Choephoroe*."

"Aeschylus! The greatest,!" exclaimed Milton and he trotted out of the kitchen to the living room.

"And take care of yourself tonight," cried Irmgard after him.

"We'll join the others, and leave you two to open the presents together," said Dieter throwing his arm around Dagmar's waist as the couple left the kitchen.

On reaching the entrance to the sitting room, they saw Alexis Cremidis kneeling in the centre of the floor before the Biedermeier piano stool, shaking his enclasped hands before him, as his bass voice boomed throughout the room with his passionate declamation, his fiery eyes staring out of their deep sockets and dark complexion, like shafts of lightening, and the end of his beard shaking with every movement of the jaw. His audience sat motionless, huddled close together on sofas, chairs, cushions and on the bare floor, as they listened, captivated and entranced by the performance. There was a pungent smell of cigars, cognac and beer.

One of the girls whom they had just seen in the kitchen, pushed passed them, with a tray of drinks, and as the young couple entered, Carl Schauwecher, who was standing by the doorway, thrust a small booklet into their hands.

"The tomb of Agamemnon – page one, and then page sixteen, beginning, 'Great Loxias word shall never play me false,'" he hurriedly whispered into their ear.

Dieter nodded affirmatively, and the couple tip-toed into the room and sat down on the floor, nearby the tomb of Agamemnon (the piano stool) and just in front of Milton Malone, who was sitting stiffly upright on a cushion with wide-open eyes suggesting mystical wonder, as if enjoying an apocalyptic experience.

Several lengths of cut string lay above the piano stool. Alexis Cremidis rose from his knees, and his voice thundered even louder, as he gesticulated with hands and arms and every movement of his body, his eyes glistening as they watered with emotion.

"He's just placed two locks of his hair on the tomb of his dead father," whispered Leon Deveaux after Dieter had nudged him in the side. "Now it's to page sixteen."

"That's where the guy resolves to kill his mother," whispered Milton Malone from behind.

Chapter 55

Dagmar glanced round the room to pick out those friends of Max and Irmgard whom she knew, and many of the guests were already known to the young couple from the East. They were crowded against the walls of the room, so that Alexis Cremidis had sufficient floor space for his performance, and the girls sat close to their menfolk, sometimes on their laps, or with their legs tucked beneath their thighs, as they followed the German text of the recitation from the little booklets they had been given, or fixed their eyes intently on the actor who strutted, gestured and soliloquised in the centre of the room. Most the guests wore dark suits and silvery silk ties, and the girls wore colourful party frocks.

Hendrik Everts was there and Manuel Ruiz, the philologist, and Lovell McGraw, a Californian of Princeton University, a tall fair-haired boy and history student spending a year in Berlin. Then behind him and his girl, sat the tall muscular figure of Sigismund Parnitski, a Pole. Apart from Luigi Romariz, Sigismund Parnitski was perhaps the oldest student present at the party that night, for he was already in his mid-thirties. His life had been interesting and eventful.

Living in the city of Görlitz on the eastern side of the river Neisse, he had witnessed the demonstrations of the East German Uprising of 17th June 1953, from across the water. Like many of his countrymen in that city, he had watched the demonstrations from a distance with keen anticipation, hoping and praying that they might mark the opening of a new era in East European history. Sigismund was one of a small party of Poles who actually swam across the river in the face of Polish border guards, to help the German rebels on the other bank. He and his friends were warmly received and given food, drink and cigarettes by their German hosts. That day he marched in the streets in the ranks of the German workers, threw Vopos from the windows of the barracks, and hurled stones at Russian tanks. He considered that day as marking a turning point in German-Polish relations, and he hoped that a genuine reconciliation and settlement might grow between the two peoples in their common struggle against foreign domination.

On the defeat of the East German Uprising, at the end of that long day, he tearfully parted from his new friends, and he and his companions swam across the river again to their own land. Inevitably he fell under the suspicion of the authorities for the story of his hopeless adventure across the Neisse spread to all and sundry. Sigismund Parnitski, the student and a well known swimmer and athlete in his own country, was denounced by the Secretary of the local Communist party. Warned by a friend in the Komsomel that he was to be arrested, he packed a briefcase and fled overnight to the north.

Having hitched a lift on a lorry he arrived in Gdansk, early the following morning, where he smuggled himself aboard a cargo boat, and within twenty-four hours, he had left his native land, and was voyaging on the open sea, he knew not where, or in what direction. He fed himself on a diet of wheat grain and flour mixed with Polish vodka which the boat was carrying in bulk, but before the day had darkened on the first night at sea, he was found by the crew and dragged before the Captain who ordered him to be locked in a cell. The following day he was allowed to wander freely about the decks, and at midday he sighted land at both sides of the ship.

He decided to make a leap for freedom, but still had no idea as to the whereabouts of the boat. Glancing around to see that none of the crew were above decks, he dived into the water from the stern, and began swimming to the nearest point of land which lay to the portside of the ship. He had dived into what he subsequently learnt was the Öresund. He soon found himself in difficulties, for there was a strong current and the water was colder than he had anticipated, but he struggled bravely against the sea, and six hours later, exhausted and on the verge of collapse, he dragged himself ashore before the little town of Rungsted, some forty kilometres along the coast to the north of Copenhagen.

He found work in a factory just outside the great capital, and as he already spoke German, he managed to learn Danish fluently within the next three months. In the evenings he worked in a restaurant, and then, until late into the night he studied in preparation for entrance to a university. Saving every öre he earned, he prepared himself for entrance to the Free University of West Berlin, for he felt contemporary Berlin at that time to be an especially significant city in central Europe. After four years, he finally achieved his goal, and after moving to the old German capital, he worked part-time in a restaurant to supplement his resources to cover the expenses of his university course in economic science.

Also at the party and already known to the young couple from the East, was André Peyron, a Frenchman, Manfred Herfurth, and George Watson, the Englishman.

The latter was a curious personality, and although reticent and withdrawn, he had a lively sense of humour. He was almost seven feet tall, with a long pale complexion, thin lips, and smooth dark-brown hair parted in the English fashion. He had blue dreamy eyes, a high forehead furrowed with lines, and a countenance suggestive of permanent absorption in deep thought.

Dagmar was glancing towards George, who sat on the floor, with an introspective expression, resting his head in one of his large hands with their long pale delicate fingers. What was he thinking? Perhaps he was working out some difficult economic problem in his cool practical mind, thought Dagmar. He wore a black suit with a silver tie - the latter probably borrowed from the German friend with whom he shared an apartment, for it was an article of clothing which had never been in fashion in his own country.

Clinging tightly onto his free arm was a small plump girl with black hair and large dark eyes. Waltraute and George had been friends for almost six months, and it was apparent she adored the Englishman. She was an old school friend of Irmgard's and had first met George at a party of Max's, and Irmgard confided to Dagmar that she hoped the affair between Waltraute and George might ultimately lead to an engagement between the couple. During the parties at Max's, Waltraute rarely left George's side for more than a moment, and she liked to gaze into his face for minutes at a time and be constantly reassured that she was the true object of his affection. During the long political discussions George would reassure her by pressing her hand in his, and occasionally, he would offer a smile, but apart from these innocent gestures, he maintained a cool reserve, and Waltraute accepted such reserve as "natural" since he was, "after all, an Englishman."

Dagmar was suddenly awakened from her wandering thoughts by the noise of clapping, stamping on the floor and shouts of "bravo!" The tall bearded figure of Alexis was bowing to his audience.

"Bo-oy or bo-oy,!" came the voice of Milton Malone from behind the young couple from the East.

Dieter and Dagmar glanced behind them. Milton sat stiffly upright on his cushion, visibly impressed by the dramatic recitation, his eyes watering with emotion.

"That guy Aeschylus sure knew how to work up the pathos," exclaimed Milton over-awed by the performance.

Meanwhile, a newly-arrived guest was being introduced to others in the room – a short dark-haired heavily built young man.

"Dagmar, do you know that man from somewhere,?" exclaimed Dieter with suspicion in his voice. "I'm sure I've seen him before."

"I can't recognise him," replied Dagmar. "Where might you have seen him?"

"I can't recollect," said Dieter, "but at the back of my mind, the association is not a pleasant one."

"I expect you've seen him at one of Max's parties."

"No, I've never seen him here. Of that I'm sure," said Dieter. "Somehow, I feel I've seen him in the East sector."

"That'd be impossible," replied Dagmar. "Max and Irmgard would never entertain anyone from the East unless they were relatives. – You must ask him who he is."

"I shall," said Dieter. "I'm most curious."

By this time there was again the noise of loud voices and laughter in the room, and several girls were passing round trays of drinks, and someone had put Strauss's tone poem, *Ein Heldenleben*, on the radiogram. Dieter took a glass of light beer and a cognac, pouring the latter into the former, and Dagmar took a glass of lemonade.

The new guest was at last introduced to the young couple as Wolfgang Fortner.

"I believe we've met before," exclaimed Dieter bowing politely and shaking hands with the newcomer.

"Yes,?" replied Fortner. "Where?"

"Do you occasionally eat in the restaurant of the Humboldt University,?" enquired Dieter.

"I've never in my life been inside the building, if by that you mean the Friedrich Wilhelm University," replied Fortner.

"I do mean that," said Dieter.

"Of course he hasn't,!" chided Irmgard at Dieter.

"Then perhaps we've met here before," said Dieter.

"No! This is the first time I've enjoyed the privilege of being entertained in the apartment of Max Möller," replied Fortner suavely, bowing his head again.

"Then have I met you at the local headquarters of the FDJ?"

"I've never belonged to that movement," replied Fortner.

"Really Dieter, don't say such stupid things," Irmgard scolded. "As if we would entertain a Communist from across the frontier. It's most laughable!"

"Do you swim,?" enquired Dieter.

"I occasionally enjoy bathing," replied Fortner.

"Then perhaps we've seen each other on the shore of the Müggel See at some time in the past."

"That would hardly have been possible. Firstly, I neither swim nor live in the East sector, and secondly, I don't recollect having ever seen you before," said Fortner ending his sentence in a tone of irritation.

"Then at least you know the Müggel See's in the East sector."

"Geography was never my weak point," responded the newcomer.

"He's a student at the Technical University," explained Irmgard, cross at her cousin's rudeness. "And so now you can bury your suspicions."

"I'm sorry then," replied Dieter again bowing to Fortner.

Without another word being exchanged, Wolfgang Fortner was taken away from the young couple and introduced to other guests standing nearby.

"Man, do you now what they used to give a guy for writing stuff like that," exclaimed a loud voice nearby. "A lot of fig leaves to put round his head."

"Laurel leaves," corrected Lars in a blasé tone as he sat bolt upright on the edge of the sofa in that peculiarly uncomfortable way of sitting on sofas only known to Scandinavians.

"Now if that ain't an exploitation of great talent, what is? If a guy like that was living today, he'd be earning millions of dollars back home in Broadway."

"But he'd be a Greek citizen," Lars nonchalantly replied as he sat poker-faced listening to Milton Malone.

"It'd make no difference where he came from. We'd pay him the rights and ship him over to the States. I'd like to shake the hand of a guy like that. Tennessee Williams ain't got nothing on him. Greek drama had every headline sensation: matricide, infanticide, perversion, wild illicit love and raw sex! Why, they were the first to exploit the Oedipus complex. Boy, they knew it all – and three thousand years before our time. They had everything – even science fiction."

"Science fiction,?" repeated Lars glancing up at Milton with an indifferent expression on his long face.

"Sure! Take that piece of Aeschylus, the *Eumenides*. If a lot of half naked women running around with snakes in their hair ain't science fiction, I don't know what is."

The two were engaged in a discussion (as yet monologous) on Greek culture. Milton Malone stood holding a glass of beer, whilst with his free hand he gesticulated with sudden sharp movements. Lars Grunqvist sat in his favourite place at the end of the sofa, which he usually monopolised for the duration of the evening during these parties at Max's. It was the most confortable sofa in the room, and should he vacate it, he risked losing his seat – perhaps even, for the rest of the evening. In his hand, he held a full size souvenir *Hofbräu Haus* stein. Whilst Milton Malone had been speaking to Lars, Dagmar had watched the latter uncork a bottle of Burgundy and empty its contents into the tankard.

Dagmar did not witness this scene with particular surprise for she already knew about the drinking habits of the Swede. Irmgard had confided to Dagmar about the struggle which Max had had with Lars in trying to teach him to drink wine out of a wine glass. So far, all attempts had failed and Max was beginning to give up hope of changing the Swede. Dagmar watched Lars raise the stein to his lips and take down several draughts of the red wine. Then, with a genteel, effeminate gesture, he took out the neatly folded handkerchief from the breast pocket of his dark suit, gently dabbed his lips, before carefully replacing it. Poker-faced, he sat primly on the edge of the sofa listening to Milton Malone – his old rival – expounding his idiosyncratic views.

Chapter 56

Dieter again brought back Dagmar's attention to the newcomer who had arrived as a guest at Max's.

"He looks so much alone and separate from the rest of the company," remarked Dagmar thoughtfully.

"A solitary individual in a crowd! He's out of place and that's suspicious. He seems different in an unsocial sort of way," said Dieter.

"He doesn't seem to know anyone here, and he doesn't seem very much interested in getting to know anyone," said Dagmar.

"Are you sure you've never seen him,?" enquired Dieter.

"Now that I've been looking at him, I'm not so sure I haven't seen him," replied Dagmar. "But I can't make any connection. But somehow, in the back of my mind too, he evokes an unpleasant association."

"Exactly,!" exclaimed Dieter with emphasis. "We've both seen him before. I know we have."

"But what difference does it make if we have,?" said Dagmar. "After all, we could have seen him in a thousand places."

"The significant fact to my mind is that the association for both of us is unpleasant. That's the significant connecting link," replied Dieter.

"Look how strangely he's behaving now," said Dagmar. "He's just standing listening to the conversation of those two over there. You can see his ear's cocked to one side."

"He's clearly a creep," said Dieter.

"It looks as if he's come here to spy," added Dagmar.

"Now he's moved round and is standing behind André and Rita, listening to what they're saying," said Dieter. "It looks as if he's fastidious in his drinking habits too. That's often a bad sign in a man. He's drinking beer. Did you notice when Hilda offered him cognac, a moment ago, he refused it?"

"Perhaps he has a weak stomach," suggested Dagmar.

"More likely to keep his mouth shut," said Dieter scornfully. "See his wary look. He's intent on keeping his wits about him. Self-possession carried to that degree is just unnatural."

"He is behaving like a *Spitzel*," said Dagmar, "but what can we do?"

"It was his behaviour when introduced to us which really arouses my suspicion," said Dieter. "He was affectedly suave, and when I suggested we had met before, he wasn't all that surprised."

"He reacted as if he wanted to avoid your recognising him," said Dagmar. "In a normal situation he would only have joked about your remark."

"That could explain his strange manner," said Dieter.

"He wasn't even offended or amused at your insisting you'd seen him in the East sector," continued Dagmar. "It was only when you insisted that he became irate."

"Where have I seen him then,?" exclaimed Dieter. "Can't you remember where it might have been?"

"You know Dieter, we shouldn't really be talking about Max and Irmgard's guests in this way. Even if we dislike the man, he's still a guest and he must have got himself invited somehow."

"But how?"

"Why don't you ask Max and Irmgard who and what he is,?" urged Dagmar.

"I shall. Come, we can ask Max now – for a moment he's free," said Dieter as he put his arm around Dagmar's shoulder and led her towards Max who was standing at the other side of the room. Max stood by the radiogram, and had just been speaking with Leon Deveaux who was standing beside him holding his bow and violin. Discreetly, Dieter made his enquiry.

"Wolfgang Fortner? I don't know the name," replied Max in bemused surprise.

"See, that fellow there," said Dieter indicating the newcomer.

"I've never seen him before," replied Max. "Why, what do you want to know about him?"

"I'm sure I've seen him somewhere – I think, in the East sector – but I can't exactly remember. In fact, we've both seen him before and he arouses an unpleasant association."

"Why don't you ask him yourselves,?" suggested Max.

"He denies having met us," replied Dieter.

"Perhaps he only looks like someone you've seen before."

"But we wouldn't both feel that way," said Dagmar.

"If you insist on finding out who he is, you'd better ask Irmgard. He must be an old flame of hers."

"We'll do that," said Dieter.

"But not now. Now we have something special," said Max.

Max removed the record from the radiogram, and raised his hands in calling for silence. He announced that their old friend, Leon Deveaux, would again be playing for them another piece from his extensive repertoire. He asked everyone to be seated, and there was a movement towards the chairs and cushions laid out on the floor. Lars, who had just taken a glass of cognac from a tray of drinks, poured it into his stein to give piquancy to the Burgundy, and raising his brows with a blasé expression he glanced up at Leon Deveaux who strolled into the centre of the room.

Leon announced a piece by Debussy which he hoped the company would enjoy. After tuning his instrument whilst Irmgard struck up several keys on the piano, he began playing his piece with verve and sensitivity, mastering the instrument with lightness and perfect control. His audience sat silently,watching and listening with a critical ear. After ten minutes, he bowed to the company, receiving their warm applause.

"Sure, the man's great – he's got the knack of handling that thing," came the voice of Milton Malone from across the room. "Hey man, could you take a request for Rogers and Hammerstein,?" he added as Leon passed by where he sat, but the request was not acknowledged.

"Now we can ask Irmgard about Fortner," exclaimed Dieter rising from the cushion on which he sat, and pulling Dagmar after him.

They went over to Irmgard who was bent over a small table partly hidden in the corner of the room by the grand piano and a music cabinet, and they were surprised to find her adjusting the knobs and pushing the buttons on a piece of electrical equipment.

"What are you doing,?" exclaimed Dieter.

"Sh-h-h-h-h,!" responded Irmgard putting a finger to her lips. "We're going to have some fun, and we don't want the others to find out yet. This is a tape recorder and later we'll play it back to the party."

"Where's it from,?" said Dieter in surprise.

"It belongs to Manfred – and I've hidden the microphone under the piano. It's the best place for it."

"Irmgard, who is this Wolfgang Fortner,?" said Dieter coming to the point at last.

"Dieter, I'm very annoyed with you," said Irmgard in a mock chiding tone, shaking her finger in his face. "I thought you were very rude to him."

"Who is he, anyway?"

"I don't know," replied Irmgard evasively after she had begun attending to the Grundig recorder again.

"What do you mean, you don't know? Is he your secret lover,?" exclaimed Dieter.

"His secret lover,?" exclaimed Irmgard bursting out laughing. "With a man like that? Of course not."

"Who is he then?"

"I've never seen him before tonight."

"Then what's he doing here? Max says he's never seen him either. Either one of you is lying, or hiding a dark secret, or else he's a great mystery man who's bluffed his way into gatecrashing into the party."

"He's a friend of Klaus Gebhart," replied Irmgard.

"Who's Klaus Gebhart?"

"A friend of Max's."

"Is he here tonight?"

"Klaus sent Wolfgang Fortner along in his place tonight. The story is – and it'll lay all your suspicions to rest – Klaus caught a cold and is confined to bed, and he suggested that his friend take his place instead, so that the numbers between boys and girls would remain even. So there couldn't be anything more straightforward than that, could there? Klaus was only doing Max and me a favour."

"Still, it wasn't really the right thing of Klaus to do without phoning himself, was it,?" said Dieter in some relief at this explanation.

"I suppose not. I think he should have phoned to apologise for his absence. Anyway, why are you so curious about this Fortner?"

"Somewhere, we're both convinced we've seen him before, and it's not a pleasant memory – but we just can't place him."

"I must say, I didn't take to him myself," said Irmgard thoughtfully. "He doesn't seem to fit in, but I can't make out why."

"That's what we thought," said Dagmar.

"But he's here, and we can't very well turn him away," said Irmgard. "If I get a chance later, I'll speak with him, or try to get him hooked to one of the girls."

"That should put a stop to his eavesdropping," said Dieter.

"I still find it difficult to believe he's a friend of Klaus Gebhart. Klaus is such an out-going personality."

"Irmgard, I must tell you, we are anxious," said Dieter. "You know we have to be careful – especially because of my commitments over the other side – and in view of all the strange things happening around us in Berlin nowadays. No one and nothing can be trusted which has a whiff of the unusual."

"I understand that, Dieter, but what can we do,?" said Irmgard sympathetically.

"I have an idea. Is this chap Klaus Gebhart on the phone?"

"I don't know, but I expect so. I'll have to ask Max."

"Just to play safe, why not ask Max to phone him, just to check everything's bona fide? Max could use the excuse of good-humouredly admonishing Klaus for not letting him know beforehand about this arrangement."

"We'll do that now," said Irmgard.

There came the sounds of clapping, and again, Max called for silence, asking all to be seated.

"We'll have to ask him later," whispered Irmgard.

The three crossed the room and sat down on a sofa. Again, they found themselves seated in front of Milton Malone, who was standing behind the sofa leaning on his arms against its back.

Max announced that Waltraute would sing four Schubert songs. Waltraute was already standing by the piano, whilst Manfred's fiancée sat at the piano, strumming a few notes whilst Waltraute trimmed her voice to the keys on the scale. She sang the four songs in her fine soprano, giving expression to the meaning of the words as well as a melodious rendition of the music, and when she made her curtsey, she was received with enthusiastic applause. Before she had finished curtseying, she had begun beckoning to George, indicating he should rise from the floor and stand beside her, but he responded by smiling coyly and shaking his head sideways.

When at last the applause had died down, she ran over to him, and seizing his hand, tried to drag him onto the floor. George, laughed awkwardly, resisting, continuing to shake his head negatively. Then, shouting to Max at the other end of the room, she cried, "Now it's George's turn!"

When Max hesitated, she cried, "I only did it on a promise from George. He said he'd get up after me and perform." Then turning to her friend, she exclaimed, "We had an agreement, George. You shouldn't break a promise."

Still George refused to budge, laughing and blushing, and perceptibly embarrassed.

"Perhaps George doesn't want to," cried Max.

"He's only pretending to be shy," replied Waltraute. "He wants to recite – you do want to recite, don't you George? It's only his false modesty. Come everybody, clap, and then he'll get up and recite."

In response to a slow handclap from all parts of the room, George smiled down at the floor, shook his head with a sharp self-effacing gesture, and then slowly rose to his feet and strolled modestly towards the piano, head lowered.

"I knew he would,!" shrieked Waltraute in delight, wildly clapping her hands, and the slow clapping broke into a spontaneous applause.

George Watson appreciated the early Romantic poets and this naturally complemented his more mundane interest in the "dismal science," and this was not the first time he had been called upon to recite at Max's.

"I bet that guy's going to give another recitation from *Lalla Rookh*," exclaimed Milton breathing down Dieter's neck.

George stepped forward from the piano towards the centre of the room, and his great height seemed to command silence and the attention of all. Clasping his hands before him and lifting his gaze from the floor to the ceiling, and fixing his dreamy blue eyes on the far wall, as he spoke in a slow measured tone, he announced he would recite from a poet whom he had not hitherto introduced at these *Soirées* – from Wordsworth.

Milton Malone poked his finger into the top of Dieter's shoulder.

"Ain't that the guy who wrote up the English lake country,?" he exclaimed.

"I believe so, but I'm not too well up on the poets," replied Dieter brusquely, annoyed at having been poked in the shoulder.

"You haven't heard of Wordsworth? How ignorant,!" exclaimed a tall blonde girl scornfully, glancing behind her at Milton Malone.

"Sure, I've heard of Wordsworth," replied Milton defensively. "We know him coast to boast back home. He's the guy the British put on their travel posters to sell the North country."

Pausing, George glanced severely towards Milton Malone, waiting for him to cease prattling. He then gave a short introduction to the poem – it was from the later period – and the recitation began. The poem was abstruse, and soon guests began glancing at one another with looks of bewilderment. At first George was oblivious to this, for he was looking above the guests, gesticulating with slow languid movements of his long slim fingers, lost in the rhythm and beauty of the verses. When, however, he was alerted to the perplexed look and the uncomfortable and impatient shifting of the guests on their cushions and chairs, he wisely brought the recitation to an early close.

The applause was markedly lukewarm, interspersed with slow handclapping, and he bowed stiffly, blushing with a feeling of discomfort at the thought of having failed to satisfy his audience.

"We couldn't understand you George," shouted several girls in unison.

"I couldn't get what the guy was trying to put over in that poem," said Milton to himself.

"George, recite one of your comic poems to us," shouted Waltraute. "It's not George's fault we couldn't understand him," she added defensively.

At last, George drew himself up to his full height and lifting his hands for silence, he announced he would recite a poem he hoped they would all enjoy, by England's great comic poet, Thomas Hood. Reciting slowly and pausing after every pun, he gave them, "Ben Battle was a Soldier Bold," which was received with laughter and great applause.

"A poet who appeals to our cynical sense of humour," exclaimed Max with satisfaction. "Someone we can all understand."

"And quite in the tradition of our Wilhelm Busch," remarked Manfred.

"I guess that guy Wordworth's not for export," muttered Milton. "Say there, how about some Robert Frost? That's a poet of living America," but by that time it was too late, for George was already returning to Waltraute's side.

A general bustle broke out in the room, as the guests rose and formed groups again, and several girls re-entered with refreshments and trays of drinks, and Irmgard put a Mahler symphony on the radiogram.

"Look, do you notice Fortner across the room there,?" exclaimed Dieter clutching Dagmar's hand. "He's been watching us for quite some time now."

"I've noticed it myself," replied Dagmar.

"And now he's removing his tie and unbuttoning his shirt," said Dieter.

"Now he fits your definition of a Communist," laughed Dagmar. "A man who doesn't wear a tie with his best suit."

"He's staring at us. I'm convinced he's up to no good," said Dieter. "We'll ask Irmgard and Max to phone this Klaus right away."

The couple went over to their hosts who stood talking by the piano, and after an altercation on the awkward problem of how best to handle the uninvited guest, Max exclaimed: "But we can't very well turn him away."

"I know, but we've got to understand Dieter's and Dagmar's concern about their own safety," replied Irmgard. "Do you have Klaus's phone number?"

"Yes, why?"

"Then be a sweet and phone him – just for Dieter's sake. We must take precautions. You know Dieter's an officer in the Volksarmee, and being in this part of the city could get him into trouble."

"He doesn't look like a spy to me – just a quiet, retiring short of chap," said Max.

"Well, really, what is a spy supposed to look like,?" responded Irmgard with mounting impatience.

"Then if you insist, I'll phone Klaus. We'll take the phone into my room where it's quiet," said Max.

The four went into the hall, unplugged the phone, and took it into Max's bedroom, away from the noise of the party. After having gone through his pocket book, Max dialled the number and they stood silently by with a feeling of anticipation.

"I hope he's fit enough to answer the phone," said Max glancing up.

"I rather hope his landlady will be able to answer for him," said Irmgard. "If Klaus's alone in the house, I expect he'll just stay in bed and hope the call is for someone else, if he's feeling bed."

"Hullo! Good evening! I'd like to speak to Herr Gebhart if that's possible," said Max into the phone. "I hope you don't mind having to get him out of bed, but it's important. This is Max Möller. – What? – At what time? – Are you sure?"

"What does she say,?" whispered Irmgard leaning over the bed towards Max.

"Sh-h-h,!" replied Max waving his hand in the face of his fiancée. "Could you tell me when he'll be back? I see. No – no message. Thank you. *Auf wiederhören!*" Max slowly replaced the receiver. "That's strange," he muttered.

"What happened,?" said Irmgard.

"Klaus left the house at seven o'clock this evening with his girl friend, saying they were going to the cinema. His landlady didn't say anything about his having a cold. She doesn't know when he'll be back."

"I can't understand it," exclaimed Irmgard. "Why should Klaus want to do a silly thing like that? If he didn't want to come to our party, then why didn't he just excuse himself?"

"Perhaps he changed his mind at the last moment," suggested Dagmar.

"There's something strange in all this," mused Max. "There must be something afoot."

"It seems our suspicions were justified," said Dieter.

"I don't think it can be put down to Klaus Gebhert simply being a bloody liar. This entire episode is so out of character," said Max. "We must try phoning him again after eleven."

"And we must keep an eye on Fortner," said Irmgard. "I'm sure he's behind all this mystery."

Chapter 57

When the four returned to the sitting room, they found the guests seated, listening intently to several of their number in heated discussion.

"They can't expect sensational gains over previous targets," exclaimed Lovell McGraw. "I guess they've almost ninety-nine per cent of the vote. Say, Manfred, you're well up on these facts. Do you know what the figure was last time?"

"In 1954 the Communists got 99.46% of the vote," replied Manfred.

"That's what I thought. It's well over 99%," said Lovell McGraw. "You can't do much better than that. If they shoot the figures up much higher, I guess people'll start thinking there's political skulduggery in some place."

"But in 1950, they had a higher percentage," said Manfred. "Then it was 99.61%."

"Boy, that's a good sign! The Commies are on the downward path," exclaimed another American facetiously, who was unknown to the young couple from the East.

"Man, just think, if the opposition keep up an increase on those figures, why in nine thousand nine hundred and ninety-nine years from today, the Commies may even lose an election in East Germany," quipped Milton Malone to laughter throughout the room.

"That's if they had an opposition which they haven't got," added Lovell McGraw.

"It was a drop of only point fifteen per cent," said Manfred, "but apparently, even that has got the Communists worried. My guess is that the results of tomorrow's election will put the vote even higher than it was in 1950."

"You know, I can't understand why they bother with elections," said the American who was unknown to the young couple. "They have only one list of candidates, and both the electorate and the authorities know beforehand that not only can there be *no* change of government, but that the pro-Communist vote will never be less that 99%. It beats me why they bother with a sham democracy which everyone sees through."

"Maybe, it's only because they hope to bluff some people in the Western world that they really have democracy," said George Watson.

"After all, they're obliged to keep up an outer appearance of democracy, even to satisfy their own people," said André Peyron.

"But does it satisfy them, when nearly three million people have voted with their feet to leave the country?," said Hendrik Everts.

"But what beats me, is that if the majority in the Soviet Zone are opposed to the regime (as indeed, we're led to believe) then why do the people go to the polls in the first place,?" said the American who had spoken before. "If the people stuck together and boycotted the polls, then even if they couldn't bring down the Communist government, they could at least destroy its credibility in the eyes of the world as to any pretensions of democracy."

"And that in itself would be a victory," said Leon Deveaux.

"It would be a moral victory of a kind – for the cause of democracy," continued the same American. "It would destroy the swindle which is making a mockery of democracy. If people in the East zone are opposed to the regime, then why don't they abstain from voting instead of acting like a lot of zombies under some kind of hypnotic trance?"

"Well Raymond, I guess you ought to ask that question from this guy over here," said Lovell McGraw. "This is Dietrich Liebermann, and he's from the East."

"It's a pleasure meeting someone from the East," exclaimed Raymond, his eyes lighting up with interest. "This is the last place I'd've expected to meet someone from across the other side. I've been making a study of Communist societies of East Europe, and I've been waiting to meet some guys like you to get first hand impressions."

"I think your best bet would be to go to the East sector, and then you could speak with as many people as you chose," said Dieter. "What you need are first hand impressions of a good cross section of the community."

"You won't get me crossing to the other side," replied Raymond smiling.

"Why not,?" asked Dieter with surprise. "This is still a Free City. You can go where you want."

"Not me. I've heard too many stories. I'd be afraid of those Vopos."

"You needn't worry about them. They wouldn't touch you. You're a foreigner – and being one of the occupying powers, you're in a privileged position."

"Well, I've heard some pretty unpleasant stories from the landlady of the apartment where I'm staying."

"You'll hear lots of unpleasant stories from landladies here in Berlin," replied Dieter, "but those stories are about West Berliners – and possibly West Germans, not foreigners. A few years ago there were kidnappings all over West Berlin, but there's not so much of that today. But for foreigners in the East sector, the authorities like to lay down the red carpet."

"Then maybe I'll spend a half-day in the East sector some day – but I'd feel wary about going there. I haven't met many people in Berlin who go there too often, and I've already had plenty of advice to stay out."

"I shouldn't take that advice too seriously," said Dieter.

"But I've already had a clear visual impression of East Berlin from a distance. I live in a high apartment block in Wedding, right on the Sector frontier, and my window looks out onto the East. I guess it's the most depressing view I've ever seen from any window – just miles of grey ruins and rubble stretching into the distance. The War might have ended yesterday. Sometimes, I ask myself, how can those guys go on living in a place like that?"

"It's tough, but we have to survive as best we can," replied Dieter.

"Getting back to the topic, why is it then that you guys go to the polls in East Germany if you're so opposed to the regime,?" asked Raymond.

"Many of us are foced to. If we didn't, the police authorities would take action. Everything is done to ensure the majority cast their vote."

"Sort of democracy at the bayonet point," remarked Raymond.

"Except that real democracy offers options which we don't have," replied Dieter.

"I can't understand a people who tolerate such oppression on a day-to-day basis," exclaimed André Peyron. "I mean, why don't you revolt – go on strike, or just march in the streets."

"East Germans have already done that," said Dieter. "Haven't you heard of the Uprising of the 17th June?   Many lives were lost. It's hard fighting against tanks."

"Many lives lost,?" exclaimed George Watson incredulously.

"Yes, many! The Western press outside Germany didn't give us too much publicity, but we fought bravely and laid down our lives. I think the Western press didn't want to raise the Cold War temperature too much. Berlin has seen many uprisings in her history, but the day of 17th June 1953 was a spontaneous uprising of all East Germany. That day marked a new turning point in the soul of the German people: it marked the birth of the German revolutionary spirit."

"The idea persists still in the minds of people, that the Germans are unquestioning in their acceptance of the iron hand of the law," said Leon Deveaux.

"That's no longer true," said Dieter. "We Germans have suffered and lived through so much. The charge of parochialism can no longer be made against us. Today we're outward looking and sceptical. And 17th June put that to the test."

"Then why did the Uprising fail,?" enquired George.

"There were twenty-two divisions of Soviet troops against seventeen million unarmed Germans," replied Dieter.

"I don't remember it in the news," said George.

"The British press were there – I remember them at the Brandenburg Gate on that day," said Dieter.

"It's the editors who don't print the facts," said George.

"Don't you remember the Uprising of 17th June, George,?" exclaimed Lovell McGraw. "Back in the States it hit the headlines of every paper in the country. It sticks in my mind as clear as D-day."

"I remember the Uprising of June 17th – I was there. I helped fight the Russians," said Sigismund Parnitski excitedly. "I swam across the Neisse and marched with the railway workers from the Christoph-Lüderstrasse Works. I helped beat up the Communist Party district Secretary, Comrade Weichold, and I helped storm the SSD headquarters and burn their precious card index files recording the political reliability of the citizens of Görlitz, and I helped storm the two prisons in the city, and to free the prisoners. In the men's prison, we set free more than a hundred farmers and tradesmen who'd been incarcerated without trial. The farmers had been arrested as criminals for being in arrears with deliveries, and the tradesmen had been those unable to pay taxes. We stormed the women's prison in the Postplatz, defying the fire hoses and machine gun bullets of the guards within, and we freed the four hundred women prisoners, and they came out into the square in their prison clothing. It was just like out of that scene in Beethoven's *Fidelio*. Amongst them was an old lady, white haired and thin – and do you know what her offence had been? She had bought a packet of coffee in the West sector of Berlin!"

"And that's how it is in the 'Paradise' of the German Democratic Republic," said Dieter. "Take the truth from a foreigner."

"I threw Vopos from the windows of their offices. Then, that afternoon, the Red Army closed in on the city. Tanks and armoured cars thundered through the streets. Everywhere came the burst of gunfire, and everywhere was the smell of cordite and powder. It was 1945 all over again. I helped stone the tanks and to attack the Red Army. I was there! But soon we were defeated. We were unarmed. We could do nothing more than make a great gesture for freedom."

"Now Sigismund has told you why our Uprising of the 17th June failed to succeed," said Dieter. "It was put down by bloodshed."

"It's terrible, terrible,!" exclaimed George. "We heard almost nothing of these things in Britain."

"Killing women and children is a recurring occupation of the Russian army," said Sigismund. "They did it before the Winter Palace in 1905, they did it on the steps of Odessa in the same year – they've done it a hundred times in Poland over the past century and a half – and they did it in Germany in 1953."

"We must cherish in our hearts forever the men and women who fought and laid down their lives for freedom on that historic day – not only the people of Berlin and Görlitz, but those of Brandenburg, Jena, Halle, Bitterfeld, Leuna, Magdeburg, Chemnitz, Dresden, and a hundred other cities and villages throughout the Soviet Zone of Germany," said Manfred.

He took a glass of Schnapps, which was offered him on a tray, and swallowed it.

"Why don't you strike at the University,?" suggested André.

"We've done that time and again," replied Dieter downing a glass of Schnapps and then taking a cognac. "The Humboldt University is just one great ferment of discontent and clandestine conspiracy. Our strikes have got us nowhere, and the ringleaders are usually arrested before anything of consequence has materialised. Everywhere there are informers, and everywhere there is mistrust and suspicion. The man or woman whom you thought was your best friend may betray your life. That's the degree of uncertainty. There is nothing left for us but despair."

"My friends, Berlin is a city alone in the world," began Manfred. "Our fate lies not in our hands – not in the hands of Berliners – but in the rule of the four occupiers. Our status still remains that of an occupied city. In the East, the occupiers are enemies of peace and freedom – they encircle our city with a massive force threatening our existence. Militarily, Berlin is the most vulnerable fortress in history. If we were attacked, our position would be untenable – no matter how large an army we had within the city boundary. Krushchev has boasted that within an hour, his tanks could be thundering down the main streets of West Berlin.

"We know the occupiers in the West sectors are allies and friends, but how far would they be prepared to go in protecting our city if the chips were down? That, we cannot know. In the past, our friendly occupiers have been slow and hesitatent in responding to the machinations of the Soviets. On technical grounds we cannot blame them for that. The three occupying Commandants in the West sectors can only act on the orders of their respective governments, and those governments are divided amongst themselves. They can never think and act alike. The West is divided against itself. Not so the East. We cannot know what one day may bring after the next. For these reasons Berlin is alone in the world."

"Berlin is not quite alone. The position of Berlin in the world is not entirely unique," began Hendrik Everts. "One of your great Christain Democrats, Jakob Kaiser, one of the last men who tried to prevent the final dismemberment of Germany, once declared in this city: 'Berlin is Germany in miniature and Berlin is Europe in miniature. We want a free Germany and a free Europe.' There is much truth in that contention. It gives us food for thought. All Europe has suffered the ravages of war, just as has Berlin. Europe is no more master of its fate than is Berlin. If war was brought upon us (which God forbid) the conduct of that war would be directed from foreign non-European capitals, even though Europe alone might be the battleground."

"And because of that – because of our vulnerable situation, we want a united – a Federal Euopre," exclaimed Luigi Romariz. "We want a Europe united into one people and into one State. Only then will Europe be strong enough to pursue her own interests and concurrently, under the same banner, as a neutral power bloc, those of world peace."

Applause throughout the room greeted this passionate address.

Chapter 58

The disputants were interrupted at this moment by the sound of voices from a microphone in the direction of the piano. Irmgard was playing back the tape she had made of her guests, and this was met with laughter.

"Now you have the opportunity to admire your own voices," joked Irmgard. "Your words of wisdom have been preserved for posterity!"

Several of the boys seated near the piano, including Fortner, rose curiously from their chairs for a closer look at the machine. Questions were raised, and Max, Manfred and Irmgard explained how they had spent the afternoon experimenting with the apparatus for achieving best results.

"The sound is very clear," remarked Fortner to Manfred with interest. "Can you show me how you use this machine?"

Manfred obliged, explaining in detail the switches and buttons, and how the tapes were changed and removed, until Max at last intervened by saying they would resume recording the conversation of the guests in taking up the thread of the discussion.

"Max, you ought to publish full reports on the debates we have in your apartment - a sort of Hansard," joked George as he puffed out a cloud of smoke from his pipe.

"If you'll cover the cost," responded Max facetiously.

George laughed, and the party returned to their political discussion which became increasingly heated as the evening progressed. As Dagmar was becoming visibly fatigued due to the noise, smoke and trend of the discussion, she was joined by Irmgard, who sat between her and her cousin, engaging the two of them in lighter conversation.

"That Wolfgang Fortner is really strange," remarked Irmgard. "I don't like him at all. I was speaking with him a little while back. He gives me the creeps."

"What did he say about himself,?" asked Dagmar.

"Almost nothing personal. He says he's a student of bio-chemistry. I can't understand how he and Klaus could have met."

"I noticed he was curious about the tape recorder," said Dagmar.

"It was the first time he really spoke," said Irmgard, "and fancy asking about the tape recorder! Of what interest can that be," she added laughing."

"Perhaps that was his way of making a pass at you," chuckled Dagmar.

"Oh don't,!" said Irmgard laughing.

"And there's another problem to the creation of a Federal Europe, which seems to make the reality so remote," said Manuel. "All European countries are so different in culture – not to mention conflicting economic aspirations. And again, how can we hope for a united Europe in a world where even so homogeneous a people as the Germans are betraying one another as we see in the East zone."

A cry of protest met these remarks.

"People don't betray their own kind without good reason," said Luigi. "If what you say is true, it's either because half the people believe in the system, or out of fear, or for the basest form of personal gain."

"Then maybe it's out of fear and threats," said Dieter. "It's a vicious circle of fear, for in the East, everyone goes in fear."

"Do you go in fear,?" asked Fortner suddenly, as he walked in front of Dieter taking down a draught from his glass.

The gesture was so unexpected and sudden that there was a momentary pause – a stunned silence – for Fortner seemed suddenly to appear from nowhere, so reserved and reticent had he been until that moment. He had been unseen – standing at the back of the room – and his presence had been forgotten during the absorbing discussion. Dieter looked him up and down with an expression of unashamed suspicion. A feeling of apprehension passed through the room.

"That's a curious question to put," replied Dieter at last.

"It's a valid question," said Fortner with unconcealed insolence.

"Since, then, you ask the question, yes, I do live in fear," replied Dieter with candour.

"But why must you live in fear,?" asked Fortner. "Is it that you've done something wrong? Do you have a heavy conscience? This fear cannot be inexplicable. It cannot come from nothing."

"You're putting a very strange question," said Dieter. "I cannot imagine anyone else in this room asking it. I mean, the answer to your question is to be found merely in feelings and commonsense. We all know there's fear in the East."

"But let's keep away from abstract generalities," said Fortner. "I didn't ask you why there's fear in the East. I asked why *you* as an individual feel fear. As an individual you must be able to give some specific explanation. It's the answer to that question which would be interesting."

"It's a curious question."

"It's still a valid question."

"I don't think I accept the context in which you put it."

"Please don't think me rude," said Fortner raising his palm defensively. "I'm not trying to pry. The fact is, I have an interest in the psychology of the motivation of fear – especially as it relates to the political conditions of society."

"That seems a legitimate interest," responded Dieter. "In the East we live in fear because of injustice, and because we can be punished for a thousand things we do or fail to do – things which would be unpunishable in the West."

"You're being abstract again," said Fortner. "Those generalities are not of interest. We can learn nothing from them. What is it that you fear on a close personal basis? Where is the hand which will be placed on your shoulder and for what reason?"

Dieter swallowed the rest of his cognac, and took up another which was offered from a tray.

"I'm a member of the FDJ and I'm an officer in the Volksarmee. I'm attached to the political section," said Dieter fixing Fortner with his eyes as he came out with this confession.

"That must be a responsible post in their eyes," said Fortner.

"It is," said Dieter. "It's my duty to make propaganda, yet I loathe and despise the regime."

"Do you really expect everyone in this room to believe that,?" responded Fortner. "Do you believe that the East German authorities are so incompetent as to place someone allegedly so opposed to the regime in such a responsible position? I don't. Either you're lying to us, or you're lying to yourself, or you're not what you say you are. I don't know which. But I don't want to be offensive, I'm just sceptical – and I want to be convinced."

"I'm telling the truth," said Dieter. "People know me here and they trust me – or I like to think they do. In any event I wouldn't speak like this if that wasn't so."

"Are you saying everyone in this room knows you're an officer in the Volksarmee?"

"Not quite that. But my cousin here, Irmgard, and Max, and several others."

"Now that's very different. Just a handful of friends out of this great assembly. To the rest, it's new."

"But I'm not ashamed of admitting the truth to the world. I've nothing to hide. I've no wish to hide anything."

"But now that these others – these others you don't know so well – know you're an officer in the Volksarmee, do you think they'll trust you in the future? Do you think it was wise to have admitted such a thing? They'll have many questions they'll want to ask – at least in their own minds. Who's to know you're not a spy for the East? Now that's my first thought."

"You've forced me, by your questioning, to openly proclaim my position in the Volksarmee."

"And aren't you embarrassed – in front of these people from the West – many of them strangers – to proclaim that?"

"Momentarily, yes, maybe," said Dieter.

"And nothing will clear away those lingering suspicions by what you say. Only deeds are convincing," continued Fortner.

"I think I can set your mind at rest on that score," said Dieter. "Next year, with my fiancée here, we'll be going to West Germany, leaving behind forever our sordid past in the East."

"So you can use the word 'sordid' for your own actions. At least that's a confession of faith."

"I meant by that, escaping from a world of deceit and oppression – nothing more," said Dieter. "As I've said, I've nothing on my conscience."

"That's something you can't answer yourself," said Fortner. "I think you have a bad conscience about these things – deep down. Time will tell. After what you've done – after the commitments you've taken on, you must have a conflict with yourself."

"I take that as insulting," cried Dieter.

"No offence intended," replied Fortner, raising a hand again. "And you'll desert the Army? Turn your back on the State which nurtured you? Commit treason even?"

"What questions are these? – Yes, all those things. The DDR can have the allegiance of no one. On the day I cross over to the West, I'll throw my uniform into the Spree. All the world shall know how I feel."

"With your candour, all the world already knows it. And do you think treason can be justified on any grounds?"

"It wouldn't be treason in the strict sense," replied Dieter. "Ulbricht and his henchmen have committed treason against Germany. They're the traitors. The DDR is not an autonomous state. Power lies elsewhere. Under no definition is it democratically constitutional."

"Democracy, freedom and the social order! Shades of Hayek and von Mises," exclaimed Fortner under his breath. "Of course, I remember, you follow the teachings of some esoteric thinkers."

"What do you mean by that,?" asked Dieter with anger.

"Forget it,!" replied Fortner waving his hand aside. "As we were saying, you would still commit technical treason against the DDR if it would help fulfil your own ideals?"

"I suppose so – but then so would most," said Dieter.

"We are approaching a new age when we must learn to put European loyalties above national loyalties," said André. "Surely all of us in Europe have learnt that by now."

"You'll find that such ideas are unacceptable to the powers that be," said Fortner, and he walked away to the back of the room, not waiting for an answer.

"Yes, we must learn to think in European terms," said Dieter. "We must live as Europeans, re-formulating a new set of values."

"Dieter, you are right," cried André slapping his arm across Dieter's shoulders.

Hendrik began to expostulate on the nature of the new Europe which would emerge out of the polyglot collection of smaller countries in forming a neutral world power bloc.

After some minutes, whilst Hendrik was still speaking, Dieter suddenly nudged Dagmar.

"I remember where we've seen Fortner before," he whispered.

"Where,?" asked Dagmar.

"It was when he referred to Hayek and von Mises that gave me the clue."

"Where have we seen him,?" asked Dagmar again.

"Do you remember that day we visited the American Memorial Library together, and we caught that man copying down serial numbers of the books I'd taken out?"

"Yes, now I remember," exclaimed Dagmar excitedly.

"Let's go and speak to Max now."

"What can he do?"

"We now know for sure that Fortner's a *Spitzel*," said Dieter. "Max and I can force him into another room and grill him."

"If Max'll agree."

"He'll have to now," said Dieter, and he rose from the floor, pulling up Dagmar after him.

The couple strode across to Max who was seated on an upright chair, listening meditatively to Hendrik.

"We need a word with you in private," whispered Dieter.

Without a word, Max rose and the three moved to the far side of the room, away from the discussion group.

"We know where we've seen Fortner," whispered Dieter. "It wasn't in the East sector. It was here in the West. We caught him spying on the books I'd just taken out of the American Library. That was last Spring – more than six months ago. I can tell you he was acting very suspiciously indeed, and he had no alibi."

"That's true, Max," confirmed Dagmar.

"Then we'll take him into my room and ask him some questions," said Max. "Just the two of us. We don't want anyone else involved. Let's keep this discreet."

"Just what I was going to suggest," said Dieter.

"Where's Fortner now,?" said Max glancing around.

"He was sitting near the piano a moment ago," said Dagmar.

"Max! Why have you removed the tape,?" exclaimed Irmgard in dismay from across the room.

"I've done no such thing," responded Max.

"The tape's missing. It's gone,!" said Irmgard throwing up her hands.

"I haven't touched it. I haven't been near the Grundig all the evening," said Max.

"Have you removed the tape, Manfred,?" enquired Irmgard.

"Not me," answered Manfred.

"Then someone must be playing a practical joke," exclaimed Irmgrad glancing around at the guests.

"Don't say our brilliant discussion has been lost to posterity," chuckled George, puffing out a cloud of tobacco smoke.

"Indeed, I hope not,!" added André smiling.

"Come on – own up – who's ever taken it," exclaimed Irmgard.

"None of us here," responded Alexis. "We've been too busy talking."

"Someone must have taken it," said Irmgard.

"I saw that dark quiet man leaving the room a few minutes ago, carryng a flat round tin," said a small blonde girl sitting near the piano.

"It's Fortner,!" exclaimed Dieter. "He's taken the tape."

"Irmgard, go and see if he's in the kitchen or toilet," said Max. "If he's not, then he's left the flat."

Irmgard rushed from the room.

"Why didn't you tell us before he'd taken the tape,?" asked Dieter angrily of the small blonde.

"I thought nothing of it," she replied defensively. "It just didn't connect. I'm not to blame. But it was only a moment ago – he couldn't have gone far."

"He's not in any of the rooms," shouted Irmgard breathlessly as she stood in the doorway. "He's left the flat."

"We must catch him before he escapes," cried Dieter rhetorically. "He works for the *Stasi*, and he's carrying incriminating material."

All in the room rose to their feet, some turning to one another not knowing what exactly was expected of them.

"I could see he was an informer as soon as he arrived at the party," exclaimed Leon. "He had a shifty look."

"It was clear he'd been sent here to spy on someone," added Manuel. "He never said a word all evening until he picked on Dieter."

"He was even chary about accepting food and drink," said Hilda. "Anyone could see he was no ordinary guest."

"It's a pity no one said anything before, if you were all so convinced," cried Dieter.

"What could we do? He was still a guest," cried several.

Max ran to the large windows, pulled back the curtain, and opened the double frames. A breath of cold air and grey night mist entered the room, as the curtains were blown back by a momentary breeze. Max glanced down into the street below, and Dieter and Dagmar rushed to join him, as did others.

"See, the window is directly above the house entrance," said Max. "We'll see him come out, and we'll call him back, and raise a hue and cry if he doesn't – even if we awaken the street. – Manfred, Luigi! Get down the staircase into the street quickly,!" cried Max into the room. "And bring him back – by force if necessary."

"We'll need some help," cried Luigi.

"We'll all be helping," responded Max.

"He mustn't be allowed to escape – not at any cost," cried Dieter, as Manfred and Luigi rushed from the room.

"Here's something to drop on his head when he comes out," said Manuel handing some beer bottles to those by the window.

"And here's my Burgundy bottle," added Lars. "That should knock him into tomorrow!"

"Please, no violence," pleaded Max. "We must try to lure him back. Only then – if he runs – do we raise a hue and cry."

"Do you think he'll take notice of that,?" said Dagmar.

"We can but try," said Max. "The street isn't empty and if he tried to escape, we'd soon catch him."

"If those in the street don't think we're a bunch of hoodlums," said Alexis.

"I don't think shouting from the window is going to be much help," said Dieter. "He's quite unprincipled."

"But we must avoid street fighting," reiterated Max. "If we were picked up in the street, we'd all be in trouble – and worse still, we could be thrown out of the flat for causing a public nuisance."

"That's a minor consideration," said Irmgard, "when we know what's at stake."

"And that's our life and freedom – Dagmar's and mine," said Dieter.

"Don't worry. Fortner will be caught," consoled Leon from behind the young couple.

"Once we've got him back in the apartment, we'll cross-examine him, and hold our own trial, before handing him over to the police," said Max. "We can't do more than that."

"That's the idea," cried Carl.

"And boy, that guy won't escape alive," exclaimed Milton Malone.

"We've got a fine bombing range here," cried Lovell McGraw holding a beer bottle over the sill. "A three storey drop!"

"Don't throw anything," cried Max. "It's forbidden! Besides, it might damage the cars on the pavement."

Dagmar glanced down onto the pavement directly below the window. A figure emerged from the front of the house.

"It's Fortner,!" cried Dieter.

"Fortner! Come back! We want to speak with you," cried Max.

"You're stealing our tape," cried Irmgard.

"He's taking no notice," said Manuel. "He's crossing the road. Now he's running!"

"There's a policeman, just up the street across the road," said Dagmar. "Call him!"

"Police, police,!" cried Max at the top of his voice. "Catch that man!"

The policeman began running along the street towards Fortner. Fortner stopped in the middle of the roadway. He glanced up at the window high above.

"Keep quiet you bunch of rowdies! What kind of practical joke is this,?" he cried.

"It's no joke," returned Max.

"He calls us rowdies, does he? I'll teach him," cried Lovell Mcgraw, and he hurled his beer bottle out of the window, which smashed into fragments on the roadway near Fortner.

Lars took hold of Manuel's shoulder, pulling him back, before hurling his Burgundy bottle into the street where it smashed into smitherines at Fortner's feet.

"Nice shot,!" cried Lovell. "That'll shake him."

"Idiot,!" cried Max at Lars. "They'll think we're a crowd of drunks. We'll all be arrested, whilst Fortner'll escape in the confusion."

Manfred and Luigi appeared in the street below.

"Arrest them, not me – you can see they're crazy," cried Fortner at the policeman.

The policeman stopped in his path, bewildered. Manfred and Luigi ran towards Fortner. Fortner ran to the pavement on the other side of the street, taking cover behind a car.

"Police! Catch him,!" cried Max hysterically. "He's a *Spitzel* from the East."

"He has a car – he'll escape," cried Dagmar as she saw Fortner struggle to open the driving door of an Opel.

The policeman blew his whistle and again ran at Fortner. Fortner glanced round him, running to the other side of the car where he came up against the policeman. There was a scuffle and a thud, as the policeman was sent sprawling to the ground. Then came the sound of two shots, their sound reverberating throughout the street. Dagmar raised her hand to her mouth and gave a little cry.

"Luigi's been hit," she cried.

"André, Carl, George, Hendrik! Go down into the street and help them," cried Max, and several of the boys rushed from the room.

"Stand back or I fire again," cried Fortner from the street below. "Next time it'll be to kill."

He was standing behind the bonnet of the Opel, revolver in hand, covering the two youths who had followed him. Manfred and Luigi stood in the middle of the roadway, their arms raised above their heads. On Luigi's hand, from the lamplight in the street, was reflected a stream of blood. Slowly, the two boys edged forward.

"Get back, or I fire again," cried Fortner. "This gun has a longer range than you think. It'll be to your own best interests to let me get out of here."

"You won't escape with this, Fortner," cried Lovell McGraw.

"Drop your gun now and surrender," cried Sigismund.

"You must be mad," shouted back Fortner. "You're all drunk. Play safe and get back into the house. Only one of you's involved in this mess and that's Dietrich Liebermann. I advise you: let him fight his own battles. Don't get involved. You'll regret it."

"Just hand back the tape and you'll be free to go," cried Dieter.

"Never,!" cried Fortner triumphantly. "This evidence will destroy you."

By this time, the curtains had been drawn back from many windows in the street, and alarmed, curious and angry faces were peering into the street.

"*Was ist los,*?" cried an elderly man from across the street.

"There's enough noise to awaken the dead," cried another.

"It's the middle of the night," cried a woman in curlers.

"That man's a *Spitzel* from the East," cried Max in return. "He was spying in our apartment, and he's stolen an incriminating tape."

"Then call the police," cried a pyjamed figure.

The policeman who had lain sprawled on the pavement, gained consciousness and slowly struggled to his feet. A moment later, he was wrestling with Fortner. Max and his companions standing by the window set up a cheer, but it was a premature gesture, for Fortner was not to be so easily overcome. Manfred edged forward slowly on the roadway towards Fortner and the policeman.

"Stop! Don't go closer," advised Luigi. "He still has the gun."

The two students stopped in their path. André, Carl, George and Hendrik emerged from the front of the building, running onto the pavement.

Fortner freed an arm, and with the butt of the revolver, dealt the policeman a heavy blow on the crown of the head through the soft cap which he wore. He fell a dead mass to the pavement.

The four students who had just emerged from the building spread out along the roadway around Fortner.

"Stand back,!" cried Fortner again as he held the revolver over the bonnet of the car. "I'll shoot to kill. Now get back onto the pavement and into the building – all of you."

Slowly, the six students edged back towards the pavement.

"George! Be careful – don't let him shoot you – he's wicked,!" shrieked Waltraute from the window.

Fortner unlocked the driving door and opened it.

"Quick! All into the street below before he makes a getaway," cried Max leaving the window.

"He must not escape," cried Dieter.

Those remaining in the room excitedly left the flat, charging down the staircase to the street.

"How can we catch him if he drives off in the car,?" cried Dagmar desperately.

"We've got three cars to give chase, if need be," replied Max.

"And boy, it looks as if we'll need them all with this guy," remarked Milton Malone.

"It's sixteen unarmed men against one armed thug," added Lovell McGraw, "and we need everything we've got. This guy's desperate!"

In the hallway of the flat Max came up against Irmgard.

"What are we doing,?" she asked.

"Giving chase," replied Max.

"Is the party over?"

"No! We'll return as soon as we've caught Fortner."

"If we do catch him," exclaimed Dagmar.

"Don't worry Miss, we'll catch him dead or alive," replied Milton Malone.

"Keep all the girls in the flat," said Max. "Only the men will be going on this chase."

"Can't I go with George,?" pleaded Waltraute.

"No! This ain't any game for women," responded Milton Malone. "There's going to be fighting and shooting."

"No place for a lady," put in Lovell Mcgraw.

"Come, we'll get down to the street," cried Max beckoning to the others to follow.

"Sure, you're the boss this evening, Max," replied Milton.

"You come into the street as well, Irmgard," added Max.

All those in the hallway, left the flat for the landing of the staircase of the apartment house. At the top of the staircase, Max came up against an old man standing in his slippers and nightdress.

"What's all this row,?" he enquired disgruntled.

"We're sorry Herr Becke, we haven't time to explain now," replied Max brushing passed him, leaping down the staircase.

"Max! See George doesn't get shot," shrieked Waltraute from the top of the staircase, as she leaned over the banisters.

"I guess that dame's crazy on George," remarked Milton as he ran down the staircase with Max.

"We caught a *Spitzel* from the East spying in the apartment, and we're giving chase," explained Irmgard to the old man.

"Then I wish you'd find your *Spitzels* in the daytime not at night," replied the man. "It seems you've woken the street."

"We'll explain everything later, Herr Becke," said Irmgard. "Please go up into the flat, and we'll give you something to eat and drink in a moment."

Irmgard and the others ran downstairs whilst the old man went over towards the still opened door of the flat.

"Who was that guy,?" said Lovell McGraw.

"The housekeeper," replied Irmgard. "We have to keep in with him."

"What cars have we got for the chase,?" enquired Dieter of Max as they leapt down the stairs together.

"Lovell has a Buick; Manfred a VW, and Manual a Morris Minor."

"We should be able to catch him with those," answered Dieter.

On arriving in the street, they found Fortner already safely in his car but without having escaped far from his pursuers. The car had moved into the middle of the roadway, but was still opposite the apartment house where the students lived. The engine was being revved as the car stood stationary, and brakes were off, and the vehicle rolled backwards and forwards in readiness to shoot forward.

Four of the boys stood with linked arms, in the middle of the roadway, some metres in front of the car, so blocking its path. Three others stood with outstretched arms behind the car, so blocking its recverse path.

"Give up Fortner – you're trapped,!" screamed Hendrik, as with his companions, he blocked the way in front.

"Get out of the way or I run you all down," responded Fortner leaning out of the window.

"We dare you,!" screamed André defiantly.

Several of the girls attended the policeman on the far pavement. As he gained consciousness, they lifted him to his feet, and helped hm across the street to the apartment house.

Luigi stood by the entrance to the house, tying a handkerchief around his hand. His face was contorted in pain as blood still poured from his wound. On seeing him Dagmar gasped with horror.

"Is it bad,?" she asked.

"It's nothing," said Luigi. "He just took a bit of flesh off the side of my hand."

"We must rush you to hospital," said Max.

"One of the girls has already called an ambulance," replied Luigi.

By this time, silent groups of horrified onlookers stood by the entrances of their apartment blocks, most in night attire.

"Get out of the car and surrender to the police," cried Max as he advanced into the roadway. "They'll be coming here to pick you up in a few minutes anyway."

"You can't escape now, Fortner," cried André.

"Max! Watch out – he's still armed,!" screamed Alexis.

Another shot rang out in the street, and as Max involuntarily ducked, a bullet hit the kerb of the pavement, ricocheting into the road.

"The guy's crazy," remarked Milton.

"Keep away from him," screamed Carl.

Max jumped back onto the pavement. Again the engine of the car was revved.

"All right, let him drive off and we'll give chase," cried Max. "We can't risk anyone else being hurt by staying here."

Hooting the horn, the car shot forward, as the four boys in front jumped quickly to either side as the vehicle drove through them, and they yelled at the tops of their voices, thrusting their fists into the sides of the Opel as it passed by.

"Lovell, how many can you take in the Buick,?" cried Max.

"Up to ten, if need be!"

"Okay! Leon, Dieter, Lars, Milton, Carl and Hendrik, get into the Buick and start off after him," cried Max, and his instructions were followed. "Sigismund, Raymond, André, you go with Manfred."

Manfred was already in the VW beetle starting the engine, and his passengers jumped in. The Buick shot away from the pavement, giving chase after the Opel, which had reached the end of the street and was driving into Onkel Tom Strasse.

"George, Alexis, get into the Morris," cried Max, and Manuel was joined by his passengers as he drove from the pavement.

"Irmgard! Take the policeman into the apartment, and give him coffee and something to eat, before the ambulance arrives," cried Max, and he jumped into the Morris, slamming the door behind him, as the third car shot down the roadway giving chase.

BOOK XV

A Spitzel On The Run

Love is the emblem of eternity: it confounds all notion
of time: effaces all memory of a beginning, all fear of
an end.

Madame de Staël, *Corinne*, Bk. viii, Ch. 2.

Chapter 59

As the Morris turned the corner into Onkel Tom Strasse, an ambulance, its siren screaming, rushed passed in the opposite direction.

The Opel sped down the straight wide roadway of Onkel Tom Strasse towards north Berlin, and the Buick followed in hot pursuit some fifty metres behind, and the two cars in the rear were similarly spaced.

To the north of Onkel Tom Strasse, there were few roads leading onto the major highway, and those tended to be narrow lanes with little traffic. Fortner pressed his foot down on the accelerator, as the speedometer moved steadily up to three digits. The three pursuing cars accelerated in response. The chase became desperate as the four cars exceeded the hundred kilometre limit. They left the suburb of Zehlendorf, passed Onkel-Toms-Hutte; and then the toboggan run; raced over the bridge crossing the Riemeister and Langes Fenn, before speeding into the Grunewald forest. It was a dark night with a thin mist in the air, and when the car had left the built-up area, they switched on their headlights.

"How can the guy get up a speed like that in an Opel,?" exclaimed Milton as he sat in the back of the Buick.

"Judging by the acceleration, that guy hasn't got the motor of an Opel – he's got the engine of a police car," replied Lovell as he clutched at the driving wheel keeping his eyes tensely on the roadway.

"He must be making for the city centre and then for the Brandenburg Gate," exclaimed Carl as he sat in the front of the car with Hendrik, a large map spread over their knees.

"We must stop him before he reaches the Brandenburg Gate," cried Dieter excitedly as he sat in a corner seat at the rear of the vehicle.

"Don't worry – we've got a good fifteen kilometres to go before we reach the Brandenburg Gate," replied Lovell.

"Clearly we must catch him before the Brandenburg Gate," said Lars as he sat stiffly upright in the back of the car. "We can't follow him into the East sector."

"Man, we follow him any place, until we've caught him," exclaimed Milton arrogantly as he sat in the corner seat beside the Swede.

"We don't seem to be gaining on him," exclaimed Dieter.

"And he's not gaining on us either," replied Lovell.

"Can't we go faster,?" cried Dieter.

"No," replied Lovell.

"Can't we chase him down into the side of the road,?" suggested Dieter.

"We don't want to be shot at," replied Lovell.

"We're in the open country. This is the best opportunity to run him down," cried Dieter.

"All right! You pay for damage to the car and we'll do that," replied Lovell irately.

"It wouldn't be a good idea, anyway," said Carl. "He'd just stop, jump into the forest, and be lost forever."

"We're on a straight road without traffic barring our path," said Dieter.

"As soon as we reach the city, we'll run him down," said Lovell. "Then he'll think twice about firing a shot at us."

"We could lose him in the traffic," said Dieter.

"We won't," said replied Lovell. "We'll keep close to his tail."

"There shouldn't be all that much traffic at this time," said Carl, "and he's unlikely to go anywhere near the Ku'damm or streets where there could be a traffic hold up."

"Look at the map,!" cried Hendrik as he took Carl by the arm. "He may be attempting to reach the Avus Autobahn, if he turns to the left at Pückler Strasse."

"He must never be allowed to reach the autobahn – not at any cost,!" screamed Dieter frantically.

"That would be his easiest escape route," cried Hendrik, "and the quickest. He'd have a straight eight kilometre run to the Dreilinden control point."

"That would mean his escaping into Potsdam and the East zone," cried Dieter. "We couldn't follow him there. Better chase him into the East sector – and follow them there – than that."

"But he'd still have to go through the Western control point if he made for the East zone," said Carl. "That would give us time to catch up."

"How about overtaking him, and blocking his way down Pückler Strasse to the autobahn,?" suggested Hendrik to Lovell. "Of course, he could dodge us by driving down the Alte Post Strasse, but we'd have to take that risk."

"It's best to overtake him after he's passed the Alte Post Strasse," suggested Carl glancing closely at the map. "If he went down the Post Strasse he could still drive down the narrow Teltower Weg, and that would be a short cut to the autobahn."

"Right! Let's overtake him at the next crossing, and then speed on ahead and block Pückler Strasse," exclaimed Hendrik.

"That would be our only chance of keeping him off the autobahn," cried Dieter leaning over the front seat of the car as he glanced at the map.

"Okay everyone, hold tight,!" exclaimed Lovell as he pressed his foot down on the accelerator. "We'll drive right up to his tail."

"And the Alte Post Strasse is only fifty metres ahead," cried Carl.

"And duck down everyone as we pass," cried Lovell. "He may fire."

The car sped forward, gaining rapidly on the Opel, until it came up within a few feet of its tail.

"We've left the others miles behind," exclaimed Leon glancing out of the back window.

"Now we've crossed the Alte Post Strasse," cried Hendrik.

"And only half a kilometre to Pückler Strasse," said Carl.

"We're going to let him gain on us a few yards," said Lovell braking. "Then we can overtake him on the wide semi-circle at the other side of the road. Okay everyone, duck down in case he fires. Here goes!"

The six passengers ducked beneath window level and the Buick shot forward, overtaking the Opel on the far left side of the road. No shot was fired, but Fortner pressed his foot down on the accelerator in trying to race his pursuer. The Buick overtook with ease and sped forward towards Pückler Strasse.

"How far is he behind,?" enquired Lovell.

"About fifty metres," said Leon.

The Buick reached the junction with Pückler Strasse, turned sharp left, and braked in the middle of the roadway, ready (if necessary) to jam the Opel should it attempt to drive down the right side of the street. Seconds later, the Opel rushed passed, continuing along the roadway up Koenigs Allee.

"Right! Now we can tail him for another two kilometres to the end of the Grunewald, and then we chase him down into the suburb of Wilmersdorf," cried Lovell, his finger on the map.

The car moved forward, but before it could cross the junction to Koenigs Allee, a convoy of three huge trucks with trailers, moved slowly across the junction from the city end of Pückler Strasse making towards the direction of the autobahn. The pathway of the Buick was blocked.

"Damn,!" cried Lovell, and in his anger, he pressed his thumb down on the horn of the car.

"They're food trucks going to West Germany to fetch supplies for the city," said Lars.

"Why the hell do they have to choose this one moment to block the junction,?" cried Lovell angrily. "Fortner'll get to the end of the roadway before we've made a start."

The VW and the Morris, with the other passengers, braked behind the Buick. As the third truck drove by, its driver waved an angry fist at Lovell who was still impatiently blasting his horn. At last, the three pursuing cars moved off again, speeding up Koenigs Allee.

"He's got a good start on us," cried Hendrik. "There he is – in the distance."

The Buick moved at top speed, as its passengers sat tightly in their seats staring tensely out of the front window at the car in front; but still the pursuers had not reached within fifty metres distance of the Opel – not even by the time they had left the Grunewald forest.

"We must gain on him now," cried Dieter frantically, "else he'll be lost in the traffic, or we'll be held up, or something."

Lovell said nothing. He steadily pressed his foot down on the accelerator, and gradually – just perceptibly, he gained within fifty metres distance of the Opel.

The chase was now in a heavily built-up area. The Opel sped across the junction of Hagen Platz. Making a wide semi-circle, turning violently in several directions as it dodged oncoming vehicles from Hagen Strasse, the brakes screeching, the Buick shot across Hagen Platz in pursuit of the other car. A policeman standing on the pavement of Koenigs Allee, blew his whistle, waving his truncheon at the Buick, indicating it to stop.

The cars raced by the Diana and König lakes as they sped towards the end of Koenigs Allee, and the VW and Morris followed not far behind. Lovell clutched frantically at the steering wheel, his eyes fixed tensely on the roadway as he glanced from side to side, dodging other vehicles, and drops of sweat began to form on his brow.

"We're gaining on him – we're not thirty yards behind," cried Milton.

"Now the chase is going to be difficult," said Hendrik. "We're reaching the city centre and Westkreuz, and there's a chaos of junctions, bridges, over- and underpasses and one way streets ahead."

"Then let's get right up to his tail," cried Dieter.

"We're doing our best," said Lovell. "We have to be careful in overtaking here. We don't want to be run down by the police."

"There's not too much traffic to worry about," remarked Leon.

"My bet is that he'll cross Rathenau Platz and go down the Ku'damm, making for the East sector," said Carl.

"Then we'll run him down at the far end of the Ku'damm," replied Lovell. "The street will still be crowded with pedestrians at this time of night and I don't think he'll risk firing a shot at us then."

"And he'll give us a nice long wide run to get behind his tail," exclaimed Hendrik.

"And the Ku'damm's his quickest escape route to the Brandenburg Gate," added Carl.

"Okay Fortner, just make for the Ku'damm and we'll have you licked," remarked Milton to himself.

The cars raced up Koenigs Allee, passing nearby the Halen lake, and Lovell pressed his foot down firmly on the accelerator, and within a few seconds, he came within five metres of the Opel.

"Boy, we're right on his tail,!" exclaimed Milton.

Seconds later, the cars reached Rathenau Platz.

"I'm going to run him down now," cried Lovell. "Duck beneath the windows."

The Buick moved out to the left, driving into the centre of the roadway, and then shot forward to move alongside the Opel, so as to force it to a halt in the middle of the circular junction. Suddenly, Lovell jammed down the brakes, and all were violently thrown forward.

"The maniac,!" he shrieked. "What's he up to?"

Without warning, Fortner turned sharply to the left, coming within inches of the Buick, driving against the oncoming traffic of the circular junction.

"Is he trying to crash and kill us all,?" cried Carl.

"He's avoiding the Ku'damm. He's making for Halensee Strasse," cried Dieter.

"What do we do," said Lars.

"Same as he. Take the short cut; break the rules of the road and follow him," replied Lovell.

The engine stalled. Lovell cursed beneath his breath as he started it again, and amidst hooting from vehicles in all directions, he reversed and shot forward against the oncoming traffic.

The Opel had had a good start, having already reached the right hand side of Halensee Strasse, which had an island running down the centre dividing the two-way traffic. The Buick sped forward in pursuit, but was again forced to halt as a lone vehicle drove out of Halensee Strasse into Rathenau Platz.

"Damn it,!" cried Lovell banging his palms down onto the steering wheel. "If Fortner thinks he can break the rules of the road in throwing us off his tracks, perhaps we can go one better in showing him who's master here."

The Buick turned in direction, and speeding forward, raced down the left hand side of Halensee Strasse, to the accompaniment of angry hooting from oncoming vehicles.

"My guess is that he'll try to throw us off his tracks in some of the smaller streets in north Berlin," cried Carl.

"There he is – just a few metres in front," cried Dieter.

At that moment, from behind the car, came the shrill of a siren.

"It's the police,!" cried Leon. "They're right behind us!"

"If they stop us, the chase is over," cried Lovell.

"We can't give up the chase. We must catch Fortner at any price," screamed Dieter.

"I'm in a foreign country. I'm not risking breaking the law here," replied Lovell. "I could lose my residence permit, and they could throw me out tomorrow."

"Where are the other cars,?" enquired Hendrik.

"They're miles behind us," replied Milton.

"I can't see them," said Leon. "They're probably right off our tracks."

"I've told you, if we're stopped by the police, the chase is over," repeated Lovell.

"And I'll be finished as well,!" remarked Dieter to himself.

The police car drew alongside the Buick, and an officer dressed in a green leather great coat and peaked cap, rested his elbow on the opened window leaning out his head. Lovell lowered his window, and Dieter who was seated immediately behind, lowered his too; as the vehicles raced along the highway at equal speed.

"Hey Yankee! Is that the way you drive an Auto back in New Jersey,?" cried the officer in English.

"No! We're chasing some guy from the East," replied Lovell.

"You're on the wrong side of the road," cried the police officer.

"We're sorry," cried Lovell. "We don't mean any harm."

"We're after a *Spitzel* we caught spying in our apartment," cried Dieter leaning out of the window. "It's that Opel there. We must catch him!"

"If you want to play cops and robbers, you do it on the right side of the road," said the officer. "In Germany you must respect our laws and read our road signs."

"We'll do that next time," replied Lovell casually as he raised his hand in a salute.

"If you're involved in an accident we'll throw the book at you," said the officer, and he disappeared from the window, and the police car dropped behind.

"That was a near one," exclaimed Lovell sighing with relief.

"It was decent of the guy to let us go," exclaimed Milton.

"It was possibly the foreign number plates which saved us," remarked Leon. "I couldn't see them doing that with one of their own people."

The island dividing the two-way traffic came to an end, and Lovell drove the car onto the right side of the road. The Opel was some way ahead.

"Now we must drive alongside him," cried Hendrik. "The start of the Avus autobahn is less than one kilometre ahead, on the left hand side."

"We must run him into the right side of the road," said Carl.

"Okay everyone! Hold on tight. We're going faster now than before," said Lovell, and he pressed his foot down onto the accelerator as far as it would go, and the car shot forward like a rocket, overtaking other vehicles which seemed almost stationary by comparison.

The wheels of the Buick sped with lightening speed, the body of the car seeming almost to leave the road surface. The passengers clung tightly onto the seats and side straps as the car rushed beneath the main line railway bridge, moving into the centre of the roadway.

"We're right on his tail – just five metres behind," cried Milton.

"And this time he isn't going to play another trick – no sharp left hand turns,!" cried Lovell.

The Buick reached the back offside corner of the Opel, and the race was desperate. The Opel moved out some inches towards the centre of the roadway.

"The autobahn's a few metres ahead," cried Carl.

"Keep well down in case he fires," said Lovell. "We'll be moving within inches of him."

The Buick drew alongside the Opel – but not levelling with its bonnet – for the two cars began driving in towards one another in a battle of wills to dominate the highway. The Buick tried to ram the Opel to a halt by the kerb, and the Opel tried to make for the centre. The two cars sped along the street, threatening one another as each edged towards the other.

"Why don't we come level with him,?" cried Dieter. "He's still ahead of us. Why must we give him the lead?"

"I'm not driving closer than this and I'm not retreating either," replied Lovell. "I don't know how desperate he is. If I level with his bonnet, he may panic, drive into our front wheels, and knock us off the roadway. I'm not getting us all killed!"

"We're crossing the autobahn over on the left now," cried Carl.

"Say then, how come we ram him down if we're not levelling up,?" asked Milton.

"We'll just wait until he's forced to slow down some place," replied Lovell. "I'm not risking a smash-up at this speed."

The two cars continued along the highway, speeding up the Messe Damm.

"He's not going to use that gun," said Leon.

"We're driving too fast for him," replied Lovell. "He needs all his concentration to keep out of our way."

They raced alongside the great exhibition grounds, and a few moments later, reached the junction with Neue Kant Strasse. The Buick braked suddenly, and again its occupants were thrown forward. A car speeding down from Masuren Allee had suddenly crossed their path.

"Damn! He's gained on us again," cried Lovell.

The Opel turned sharply to the left, racing up Masuren Allee.

"Look who's behind us," cried Leon joyously. "The others have caught up."

In the distance behind, speeding up the Messe Damm, were the VW and Morris. Several of their occupants were waving their hands in greeting the vanguard pursuers.

The Buick turned sharply to the left, shooting up Masuren Allee in pursuit of the Opel. Again, the intensity of the chase became desperate as the cars raced passed the St. Hildegard Hospital and then into the spacious Reichskanzler Platz, in the centre of which burned the great gas flame in a bronze bowl erected on a high concrete plinth – a flame which would burn until the day of German unification – and a memorial to those who had laid down their lives for freedom on the 17th June.

The Opel sped round the great square and the Buick chased frantically, and there was skidding and a great screeching of brakes. The VW rushed into the square, driving to the left in an attempt to block the path of the oncoming Opel.

"They're going to crash – a head on collision,!" cried Carl.

"Manfred, you idiot – get out of the way – you don't know how desperate he is," shrieked Lovell.

Fortner bit his lip, pulling round at the steering wheel, and the cars were no longer in the control of their drivers as they swerved and skidded. A great crashing filled the square. The VW was knocked out of its path, and a piece of metal went flying across the roadway. The Morris rushed into the square, driving alongside the pursued car. A shot rang out and a side window of the Morris was splintered.

The Buick braked before the VW.

"Are you all right,?" cried Lovell.

"Yes," replied Manfred who had got out of the vehicle and was inspecting the damage. "It's nothing – just a dent in the mudguard and we've lost the front bumper. Let's get after him.!"

Manfred jumped back into the car and both vehicles sped off again.

"The Morris was already well in pursuit of the Opel as it reached down the wide roadway of Kaiser Damm.

"He's making direct for the Brandemburg Gate," said Dieter.

"It's a straight seven kilometre run all the way," cried Carl.

"Now we must drive him down at any cost," cried Dieter.

"Don't worry – we've got more than seven kilometres to do it in," replied Lovell.

"I guess we'll have to run him down at top speed, too," remarked Milton. "There won't be much chance of his being forced to slow down on this highway at this time of night."

"We'll just await our chance," replied Lovell.

"Wait! If we wait for anything we'll lose him," cried Dieter irately.

"He's quite a way ahead of us," said Hendrik.

"And it looks as if he's keeping well to the centre of the roadway," said Milton. "He's not going to risk being run down into the kerb again."

"He's determined then to wriggle out of any position," remarked Leon.

"That means we'll have to run up to the front of his bonnet if we're going to force him to stop at all," exclaimed Dieter, "no matter how fast a speed he keeps up."

"Just sit back and keep cool everyone," said Lovell.

"How do you intend stopping him,?" asked Dieter.

"We don't know yet. We'll just have to see when we get close," replied Lovell.

"We must think out a tactic to force him to stop, or he'll slip us again," cried Dieter.

"These things aren't a matter for thinking – they're a matter for split-second timing," replied Lovell.

"Why not try to jam him between two of the cars," suggested Leon. "That way, we could force down his speed, and then run in front of his bonnet and force him to halt."

"That would be a sure way of damaging all three cars," replied Lovell.

"Ah-h-h! What damage is that,?" exclaimed Milton. "Nothing more serious than a few dents. We'll all muck in together, and pay out of our pockets, to have your mudguards straightened out."

"It would depend if the speed of the Morris in front could keep up," said Lovell.

"Let's try it," insisted Dieter. "It's a good plan."

"That little Morris has got a powerful engine. It's been in front for quite some distance now," said Carl.

"Okay then, we'll drive forward and speak with Manuel," replied Lovell.

The Buick sped forward, reaching the Morris, and the windows of both cars were wound down.

"Were you much damaged by that shot you got back in Reichskanzler Platz," cried Lovell to George who leaned his head out of the front window of the Morris.

"It was nothing," replied George. "It splintered the window and the bullet ricocheted off into the roadway."

"We thought you had lost track of us at the end of Koenigs Allee," said Dieter to Alexis.

"We just caught sight of you after you braked in Rathenau Platz. If we hadn't seen you then, we would have gone chasing down the Ku'damm," replied Alexis. "Our guess was that Fortner would take that route to the Brandenburg Gate."

"We thought the same," said Dieter.

"We have the idea of trapping him between the two cars," said Lovell. "It'd be the only way of slowing him down and forcing a halt. Can you ask Manuel if he can go much faster?"

George's head momentarily left the window.

"He says he'll try, but he hasn't much hope of beating the Opel," replied George.

"Fine! We'll jam him from the outside of the road," said Lovell and he raised his thumb as he wound up the window.

George raised his thumb in return and disappeared from view. The Buick shot ahead down the roadway, and now the cars were chasing along Bismarck Strasse. Again, the Buick reached the tail of the Opel.

"We can't drive on the outside of him – he's right in the middle of the roadway – and if we tried, the police would run us in for speeding on the wrong side of the street," exclaimed Lovell.

"It wouldn't be any use, anyway, the Morris is now miles behind," said Leon.

"Just our luck,!" exclaimed Lovell cursing beneath his breath. "Then the entire chase is up to us."

The cars raced passed the Schiller Theatre and the Technical University, and over the Charlottenburg bridge and the Landwehr canal, and a moment later, they were driving passed the Tiergarten on their right. They raced beneath a railway bridge, and then the Tiergarten was spread out on both sides of the wide roadway, and in the distance, in front, rose the Victory column, its floodlit golden winged figure surmounted on a high column, magnificently dominating the surrounding scene.

"How are we to stop him,?" cried Dieter. "It's no good just tailing him like that."

"How about ramming the car into his back wheel and knocking him off course,?" suggested Milton.

"Don't be stupid,!" replied Lovell.

"All we can do then is run alongside him on the inside of the road," said Hendrik.

"Okay! Now get below the windows in case he fires again," said Lovell.

The Buick drove to the inside of the road moving alongside the Opel, so that not more than two feet divided the two vehicles.

"All right, you can sit upright now. He's got his windows closed, so he can't shoot out," said Lovell.

Dieter pulled down the window.

"Fortner, you can't escape! Stop the car and give yourself up now," cried Dieter.

Fortner wound down the window of his car.

"We'll see who'll win in the end," he replied. "Here I've got a tin full of treason. "Clearer evidence could never be hoped for."

"He's got the tape in his hand," cried Leon.

The cars reached the Victory monument and the junction with other major streets, and the vehicles began to swerve round the roundabout.

"Jam him into the side of this truck," cried Milton.

The Buick shot forward – to the front of the Opel, forcing the latter close to the side of a large truck.

"Now we have him trapped," cried Leon.

There was a crashing metallic sound, and the Opel shot forward, tearing away part of the bumper of the truck whilst several men in the cabin of the vehicle shouted furiously waving their fists.

"That's the second smash-up,!" remarked Milton.

"Rather they than us," replied Lovell.

"We should have had him trapped. Why did we let him slip,?" cried Dieter in desperation.

"We were as close as could be bar risking a crash," replied Lovell.

The Opel sped down the Street of the 17th of June, the Buick speeding closely behind. In the far distance at the far end of the street was the floodlit Brandenburg Gate.

"Now we *must* ram him down somehow," cried Dieter.

"We'll do it if we can," replied Lovell calmly.

"Don't worry Diet – we'll get the bastard," cried Milton.

"If only we could get him off the centre of the road," exclaimed Lovell.

The Buick drove ahead, again sidling up beside the Opel, moving threateningly close to the pursued car.

"Just try to ram him onto the wrong side of the road," cried Milton.

"What does it matter now if we're all picked up by the police for dangerous driving,?" cried Leon.

"There's no traffic coming up from the other side of the road, so we've got the whole highway to play on," said Carl.

"We'll do our best," replied Lovell.

The two cars sped along the street, each battling desperately for the centre of the roadway. Each in turn neared and dodged away from the other, but dared not come into contact. As every moment passed, the grey floodlit form of the massive Brandenburg Gate loomed nearer and larger.

"Why don't we ram him down now,?" cried Dieter.

"It would be impossible at this speed," replied Lovell.

"Then he'll reach the Brandenburg Gate before us," said Leon.

"What happens then,?" cried Lars.

"What then? We follow him, man. What else,?" replied Milton.

"Through the Brandenburg Gate? Into the East sector? We can't do that,!" cried Lars in outrage.

"We're going to see this through – see,?" said Milton threateningly.

"They'll arrest us all. We'll end up in Siberia," cried Lars.

"We've got our buddy to think about," said Milton. "We're going to get that tape back and destroy it."

"I think I'm getting out now," said Lars leaning over towards the door. "I'll meet you back at the apartment when you return."

"No man's getting out of here," said Milton barring his way. "You'll stay, and if necessary, fight with the rest of us."

"It's suicide! We're all lost – we can do nothing,!" cried Lars. "It's madness!"

"Just forget yourself for once and think of others," said Milton. "See how the rest of us are behaving. Muck in! And don't try jumping from the car 'cause we've got you trapped on both sides, and won't let you go."

"I'm surrounded by maniacs,!" screamed Lars. "I'm the only sane man in sight."

"Keep that guy cool in the back," said Lovell, "else the Vopos'll think we're a bunch of loonies when we reach the Gate."

"They won't let us through at this time of night," cried Lars. "We should turn back now."

"We'll get through somehow. If they try to stop us, we'll shoot down the Under den Linden in top gear," said Milton.

"They'll shoot after us," cried Lars.

"We'll do nothing of the sort," said Lovell.

Lovell lifted his foot from the accelerator allowing the Opel to go on ahead, before driving the Buick directly behind the tail of the pursued car.

"Our following Fortner into the East sector will depend on one thing," said Lovell calmly. "We'll brake at the Gate directly behind him. If he merely shows his passport to the police and then drives on without speaking, we'll follow. If he begins talking with the police or if there is any kind of delay, then we stay this side of the Gate, and we have to call the chase to a finish. There's no sense in falling into any kind of trap. That's all I'm saying, and that's the beginning and end of the matter."

"That's sensible enough," remarked Leon.

"What do we do after tracking him down,?" asked Lars.

"That'll depend on circumstances," replied Lovell.

"Do we risk a fight,?" asked Lars.

"We don't know what we'll risk yet," replied Lovell.

The Opel braked in front of the Brandenburg Gate and the Buick pulled up behind it. Lovell and the other occupants in the car, sat silently, watching and waiting tensely to see what would happen in front. A Vopo went up to the Opel and Fortner handed out his pass. The Vopo glanced at it, handed it back again and waved on the car. The Morris and VW braked behind the Buick. The Buick drew alongside the policeman, and Lovell handed out his pass and those of the other occupants.

"Who are these people,?" asked the Vopo.

"Friends," replied Lovell ambiguously.

"Anyone resident in the East sector,?" asked the policeman addressing the passengers.

"No," replied Lovell firmly.

"Good," said the Vopo and he returned the passes, waving on the car.

"That was a near one," said Hendrik as the car moved off. "It was lucky he couldn't count – didn't know the difference between six and seven."

This was said as Dieter had been the exception since his identity document had not been shown. The Buick chased the Opel down the Unter den Linden at top speed, passed the Russian embassy, passed the headquarters of the Young Pioneers, passed the State Library and the Opera House, and passed the Humboldt University. Suddenly, the brakes of the Opel screeched as the car turned right, down the narrow street of

Oberwall Strasse. Frantically, the Buick chased it, the Morris and VW not far behind.

Lovell kept his eyes intently on the roadway in front, as the car swerved sharply around a number of corners into a confusion of narrow back streets. The occupants of the car said nothing, only clutched onto the seats and dashboard in front, so as not to be thrown forward as the car lurched violently this way and that. They kept their eyes intently on the tail of the Opel which was never more than several metres in front. Lovell switched on the headlights, for the narrow back streets in the city in the oldest part of Berlin were quite dark, only lit by dim gas lamps at infrequent intervals. They met with no other vehicles in the deserted streets and no pedestrians except for occasional Vopos with machine guns slung over their shoulders, lounging at street corners.

They crossed a narrow bridge over a tributary of the river Spree, and raced down another street, swerving round yet another corner.

"He thinks he can throw us off his tracks in this part of the city," remarked Milton.

"We're making it difficult for him," replied Lovell.

"I wonder where he can be making for,?" mused Carl.

"Let's only hope it's not to the KGB headquarters," responded Hendrik.

At a street corner, where the Opel made a sharp turn to the left, moving on the wrong side of the road, a green Zil raced out of the street at top speed, crossing the junction, continuing up the other side of the street. The Opel, meanwhile, served and skidded, and the Buick followed quickly behind. There was a deafening crash followed by the dull thud of an explosion, and all at once, the street was lit up by a great blaze. The Buick braked in the middle of the roadway, its occupants glaring in wide-eyed horror at the sight confronting them. The Opel had crashed into the brick wall of a bombed ruin in a narrow street. The car was in flames.

Chapter 60

It's all over,!" cried Hendrik, but he spoke too soon, for the door of the Opel was opened, and Fortner jumped out of the vehicle, still with the tape in his hand.

"He's unhurt," cried Dieter.

Fortner ran through the front doorway of the bombed house and began climbing the pile of rubble at the other side.

"Get after him quick – all of you – and bring back the tape," cried Lovell. "I'll drive the car round to the next corner on the left and wait there."

The doors flew open and the six passengers leaped out and ran through the doorway of the remaining façade in quick pursuit.

The Morris braked alongside the Buick.

"Drive round to the parallel street at the back of this block, and catch him there before he can slip out of the area," cried Lovell to Manuel who was leaning out of the window. Manuel shot off and the VW stopped where the Morris had been.

"What's happened,?" cried Manfred leaning out.

"He crashed into the wall before escaping with the tape onto the bomb site," replied Lovell. "Drive round to the back of the block and trap him there."

Manfred drove on ahead, and as Lovell started the car to follow, there came the sound of a shot and then a cry of pain from the direction of the bomb site.

"Lars, Milton, don't go after him – he may fire again," cried Dieter; but heedlessly, the Swede and the Irish-American disappeared from view over the pile of rubble as they continued in pursuit of Fortner.

Dieter who had climbed half way up the pile, ran down again to join Hendrik and Leon who were standing around Carl. Leon was holding Carl's jacket, whilst Hendrik was rolling up the former's shirt sleeve. Carl winced in pain but he never let out a groan.

"How is it,?" cried Dieter anxiously.

"It's nothing," cried Hendrik glancing at the wound on Carl's shoulder. "You've had worse than that from a sabre before now."

"It's damned painful," muttered Carl.

"Here, take this – it's quite clean," said Dieter taking out his pocket handkerchief and splitting it into two as he handed it to Hendrik.

"It's bound to be painful – the bullet's gone through the flesh," said Hendrik, "but still, he's hit you on the outside of the arm, and the wound won't be dangerous."

The blood ran freely down Carl's arm.

"Use this as a wad," said Leon taking his pocket handerchief, folding it once and handing it to Hendrik.

Hendrik bound up Carl's arm, then the latter pulled down his shirt sleeve.

"Get back to the car," cried Dieter. "We'll return in a minute or two when we've got Fortner, then we'll rush you to a hospital on our way back."

Carl took his jacket from Leon, folding it over his arm, and placing his hand on his painfully wounded shoulder, he made towards the exit leading into the street, whilst the others began nimbly climbing the pile of rubble in pursuit of Fortner. They had already taken a half dozen steps when they heard a terrified cry behind them – uttered like a stage whisper – *Volkspolizei*! Startled, they stopped, glancing behind them.

A Vopo, his machine gun held out in front, was standing in the doorway of the building, barring the exit to the street. Carl remained quite still, standing in front of him.

"*Was ist los*,?" cried the Vopo.

"We run,!" whispered Leon into Dieter's ear.

"We make a break," cried Hendrik.

"Stop,!" cried Dieter as he stood between his two companions, and he grabbed their arms so they could not run forward. "I have a plan."

"What's the matter,?" repeated the Vopo.

"We've been attacked by a maniac," replied Dieter advancing towards the young policeman who looked at them suspiciously. "See, our friend here has been shot."

"You're all under arrest," cried the Vopo. "Stand back, else I fire," he added addressing Hendrik who had stepped forward towards him threateningly.

"You can't arrest us for nothing," cried Hendrik excitedly.

"This is a mistake," cried Leon.

"I know my business," replied the Vopo irately. "If it's a mistake, then the office will see to that. You're under arrest for causing a public disturbance."

"I think you're arresting the wrong people," said Dieter in an authoritative tone. "I think also, you're not aware of your duties. It's your duty to protect people and safeguard the interests of the State. We've just chased down an armed and desperate criminal to this spot, and it's our duty to see he doesn't escape."

"Who are you,?" enquired the Vopo impressed by Dieter's authoritative manner.

Dieter handed the policeman an identity pass, and the latter examined it in the light of the burning vehicle which shone through the doorway from the street. Suddenly, the Vopo clicked his heels, and making a smart military salute, he returned the pass.

"Apologies, Leutnant,!" he exclaimed making a stiff little military bow from the waist. "Who is this criminal,?" he asked.

"An imperialist agent from the West who's stolen important taped documents, which it is my duty to return immediately to the appropriate authorities," replied Dieter crisply.

"Ach! I understand," replied the Vopo seemingly enlightened. "Secrets bearing on the political section of the Army!"

"Exactly,!" returned Dieter. "As you see from my pass, I'm a political officer."

"And who are these men,?" enquired the Vopo.

"They're counter-espionage agents working for the SSD in the West sectors of the city," replied Dieter. "They're under my command."

"Where was this criminal first apprehended,?" asked the Vopo.

"He was followed by my agents and I came across the sector frontier," replied Dieter. "Then his car crashed into this street."

"The case seems unusual," said the Vopo perplexed.

"We'd request that you come with us to shoot down the criminal – unless he's prepared to surrender of course," said Dieter. "I must warn you, he's desperate and would shoot his way through us to escape. Because of the nature of our work in the West sectors of the city, we were forbidden to carry arms. That's why we need your help now."

"I'd prefer to act on orders from my immedieate superior," said the Vopo hesitantly.

"But this is a special situation," said Dieter. I make it an order you accompany us – covering us with your firearm. Naturally, I take full responsibility for everything you do. – Carl, go back to the car."

Carl left the bomb site, disappearing into the street. The Vopo hesitated, as if doubt still lingered, and then lifting his machine gun and saluting lazily, he exclaimed a reluctant, "*Jawohl,!*" and followed Dieter and the others up the pile of rubble. Dieter and Hendrik slapped the Vopo on the shoulders and the latter seemed gratified by the comradely gesture.

They had not gone far, when again, the small group was stopped by a voice from behind.

"What's up,?" cried an excited voice.

Dieter and his friends glanced round. An officer of the Volkspolizei stood in the doorway to the street, his hand held over a pistol.

"A Western agent is on the loose," replied the subordinate Vopo intent on justifying his action in being with the other youths.

"How was this car set alight,?" cried the officer running up the pile of rubble to join the group.

"A Western agent was chased here and crashed into the wall," replied the subordinate. "He's armed and is attempting to make his escape through the bomb site."

"Have you notified the police and the fire brigade of the accident,?" asked the officer.

"No," replied the subordinate. "I heard a shot and voices in this direction and came to investigate."

"The fire service must be called."

"Yes," replied the subordinate saluting.

"What's this about a Western agent?"

"He's armed and desperate and has already shot one of these men."

"That man who had just come into the street had been shot?"

"Yes."

"And who are these men?"

"They're working under my authority for the SSD," replied Dieter handing the officer his military pass.

"I see," replied the officer glancing at the pass and then saluting Dieter.

"It's vital this agent must be apprehended at once – and if necessary shot," said Dieter. "He's carrying important taped documents which it is my duty to return to the appropriate authorities. We're unarmed and beg you to assist in his capture."

"We'll do that," replied the officer, but in a reluctrant tone and glancing at Dieter suspiciously as he placed his hand over his revolver. "But afterwards, you must all be escorted back to police headquarters for an investigation."

"That goes without saying," said Dieter bowing politely.

"You take that area over on the right, and I'll advance from the left," said the officer to his junior, and both Vopos began nimbly climbing the rubble as they ran in different directions.

"What happens now,?" said Hendrik in a whisper.

"You, Hendrik, cover the officer, and you, Leon, cover his subordinate," answered Dieter in a whisper. "If you happen to come up against Fortner, get them to shoot him, and then overpower the Vopos, knock them out, grab their firearms, take the tape from Fortner, then run for it."

"What if we don't come up against Fortner,?" asked Leon.

"I'll be running across to the other side to assist the others," replied Dieter. "If and when we happen to catch Fortner from the other side of the bomb site, then we'll shout the word, *Ende*! That'll be the signal to overpower the Vopos and make a run for it."

"Hey there – come on,!" cried the police officer from the mist in the distance.

The three youths ran off in different directions, Dieter running into the street again, and round the block to join and alert his other companions to the developing stratagem.

Meanwhile, the Morris followed by the VW, turned sharply and raced down the street on the left, and the Buick was not far behind. It was a long street, and the area on the left was walled in by a high wooden fence crowned with barbed wire, and behind this, rose massive grey ruins crumbling to the ground. Towards the end of the street, the fence gave way, and only rubble lay beyond the pavement.

Again, the cars skidded, their brakes screeching as they swerved round the next corner to the left, and there they braked behind each other. Along the length of the street on the left was only rubble and large boulders of masonry.

"Manfred, Manuel, stay in the cars and be prepared to drive off at a moment's notice," cried Max. "We'll try not to be more than a moment. – Raymond, André, Sigismund, spread out and advance from the left side of the street. George, Alexis and I will advance from the right. If any of you see him, just shout his name and we'll close in. We'll attack him with stones – but don't get too close."

The youths ran quickly onto the rubble, spreading out along the length of the street. Manfred and Manuel returned to their cars, slamming the doors behind them.

Max and his companions sprang nimbly over the blocks of masonry, jumping across the crevices and trenches in the ground, and running over mounds of dirt overgrown with weeds and grass. The mist was thicker in this part of the city than in the West sectors, possibly because of the close proximity of the river.

They had not gone far from the roadway when André caught sight of a black figure darting quickly behind a block of masonry. He picked up a rock and hurled it towards the black figure, before running in a semicircle around the block. A shot was fired, and a bullet whizzed passed André's arrm and ricocheted off a boulder behind him. As the black figure of Fortner darted away in front, the tails of his coat flying behind him, André picked up another rock and hurled it. There came the sound of voices from several directions. André ran frantically after the disappearing figure, picking up another stone and hurling that too. It struck Fortner's shoulder. Fortner stopped suddenly to face his pursuers, and bending down to take up a rock himself, he was hit in the face by another stone. Momentarily stunned, he dropped the pistol and tin which he held in each hand, and groaning, he staggered back, leaning against a high wall behind. He raised his hand to his face and a stream of blood came from between his fingers.

André uttered a stifled shout of exultation and throwing himself onto Fortner like a tiger, began beating him with his fists, until the latter collapsed onto the ground.

"I've caught Fortner,!" cried André and his voice echoed around the masonry.

From the distance came the cry of "Vopos!" Raymond had seen half a dozen Vopos armed with machine guns, run onto the bomb site, and he shouted a warning.

"We'll fight them,!" came the voice of Milton Malone from another direction.

"They're armed,!" cried George from another direction.

"*Nur Halbstärker*!" (only teddy boys), came the voice of a Vopo.

"Now Lars, prove your mettle," cried Milton encouragingly as the two ran across a flat piece of ground.

From the distance came the sound of several shots. Through the mist loomed the figure of a Vopo standing atop a high wall, his back turned to the advancing students.

"We'll creep up on him quietly, then take him by surprise," exclaimed Milton in a whisper. "You knock him off the rock first and I'll take his gun."

Stealthily, treading only on tufts of grass and soft earth, the youths advanced nimbly up to the policeman. Standing beneath and flat against the wall, Lars grabbed the Vopo by his ankles, pulling his feet from under him. With a short cry, the victim fell flat on his face and Lars lifted himself onto the wall, placing his foot firmly on the Vopo's back so that he was unable to rise. The Swede snatched away the machine gun, throwing it down to Milton who hurled it far away into the mist. A moment later, Lars and the Vopo were engaged in a desperate struggle but after several seconds, the latter was thrown over the other side of the wall into a muddy pool of water some fifteen feet below.

"Hands up,!" came a cry.

Shocked, exclaiming beneath his breath, Milton raised his hands. Another Vopo had emerged from the other end of the wall, gun at the ready.

"You too, get off the wall, and stand alongside your companion – else I shoot him," he cried to Lars.

"Spare us,!" exclaimed Milton in horror, and his plea was answered, for a large figure loomed up behind the Vopo, who was unceremoniously seized by the scruff of his neck and the seat of his trousers, lifted into the air, and thrown headlong into a pool of dirty water more than a metre deep. Sigismund was standing above the wall.

"He can wait there with his comrade until the fire brigade pull them out," said Sigismund as he jumped down from the wall.

There came the sounds of heavy footsteps running towards them. The black outline of another Vopo loomed through the mist.

"Quick! We make a dash for it," cried Milton tugging on the sleeves of his companions, but before another word could be said, a bullet whizzed passed them ricocheting off the wall behind.

"Hands up! You're all under arrest," came the cry of the approaching policeman.

The three students raised their hands.

"Now walk on ahead of me, back to the street, and join your other companions," cried the Vopo. "They're all under arrest."

The three students began walking back towards the street, the machine gun of the Vopo pointing into their backs.

"To think it would all come to this,!" muttered Milton.

After Raymond had shouted his warning cry of "Vopos,!" he was arrested at bayonet point, ordered to raise his hands, and led back to the street. At the same moment, several other Vopos ran onto the bomb site along the entire length of the street, searching for the rest of the gang. Max and Alexis, who were crouching down in a trench, some distance in front of Raymond, saw the arrest and the police moving onto the area.

"We're in danger of being surrounded," exclaimed Max glancing around him. "Alexis, run forward and tell Dieter that Raymond's been arrested, and that we need all the help we can get – and tell him that Fortner's been caught."

Alexis jumped out of the trench, quickly running into the mist, and several bullets whizzed passed him, before escaping from the visibility of his pursuers. Max heard heavy footsteps running up from behind, and crouching down in the trench as he ran along its length, he tried to make a getaway, but moments later, he heard the word, "Halt,!" and looking up, he saw a bayoneted rifle pointed at his head.

"Out of the trench," ordered the Vopo. "You're under arrest."

Max put up his hands before being led back to the street at bayonet point.

André was still standing by Fortner, when a hand was placed firmly onto his shoulder and a voice behind exclaimed, "All right, *Halbstärke*, come with us."

André glanced behind to see two Vopos covering him with machine guns. Without a word, he raised his hands, and was led towards the street.

On approaching the end of the bomb site, he saw Raymond, Max and George huddled together in a little group nearby a police officer who held his hands on his hips, and the students were covered by the guns of three other Vopos. From another direction, out of the mist, came Lars, Milton and Sigismund, escorted by yet another Vopo.

"Say nothng – nothing that can compromise us in any way," exclaimed Max excitedly to his companions in English.

"No foreign talk," responded one of the guards.

"What were you doing on this site,?" asked the police officer firmly.

"We had our private business," replied Max firmly but politely.

"Private! We'll see how private a business it is causing a breach of the peace on a bomb site in the middle of the night,!" exclaimed the officer angrily. "Do you all live in the neighbourhood?"

"No," replied Max.

"Show me your passes."

"We're not carrying them," replied Max.

"Why not?"

"We had a special reason for that."

"You'll all be taken to police headquarters for questioning."

"I can assure you none of us can be held responsible for any wrongdoing."

"We'll find that out for ourselves."

"This man is a *Halbstarke* – he was caught beating up another youth," said one of the Vopos as he brought André to the rest of the group.

"Which of you is armed – we heard a shot from a small automatic,?" said the officer.

"None of us is armed," replied Max.

"I didn't ask you to act as spokesman for the group. Let the others speak for themselves," said the officer abruptly. "You – who's the gang leader here,?" he added addressing Raymond.

"I guess there isn't a gang leader. We're all equal here," replied Raymond.

"Are you foreign,?" asked the officer.

"Sort of," replied Raymond trying to be evasive.

"Where do you come from?"

"I'd prefer not to say right now, but I could give you some pretty good guesses when I tell you I'm of mixed descent."

The officer glanced suspiciously at Raymond as if not quite understanding what he meant.

"I guess we'll be catching the next slow train to Siberia," exclaimed Milton nonchalantly in English as he was led with his two companions into the group of other students standing on the pavement.

"Sh-h-h-h,!" cried George nudging Milton in the side. "Max's doing all the talking."

"I said no foreign language talk," repeated the same guard again.

"You're all from the West sectors,?" exclaimed the officer. "This'll be interesting. Are you American,?" he added addressing Milton.

"What am I supposed to say to this guy,?" said Milton turning to the others.

"I asked the question, not them," said the officer.

"No, I'm not American – I'm Irish," replied Milton.

"One of the fighting Irish, as they say," chortled the officer. "It seems we've got all nationalities here."

"God only knows what Ike'll say when he comes to hear of this,!" exclaimed Milton beneath his breath in English. "We've sure got ourselves into a real pickle this time!"

"Are those cars down in the street there yours,?" asked the officer.

"No,!" replied Max sharply.

"Well, it doesn't make any difference – they've got foreign number plates and they'll be impounded anyway," said the officer. "Braun, hold these men whilst I contact the police headquarters for re-enforcements and a van," added the officer addressing one of the Vopos who looked about sixteen years of age.

"*Jawohl*,!" replied Braun clicking his heels, saluting smartly.

"There may be other youths on the bomb site, and I'll instruct headquarters to send down a contingent to surround and comb the area," said the officer.

"We already saw one youth run over to the other side, and we fired but he escaped into the mist," said one of the Vopos.

"Two of our comrades are still covering the area, and they'll capture him," said Braun reassuringly.

"That's what they think," muttered Milton.

"We should send for an ambulance, Captain," said another of the Vopos. "One of the youths is unconscious – seriously wounded."

"I'll see to that," replied the officer curtly nodding his head, and he briskly walked across the street, disappearing down a narrow alley way opposite.

When Alexis ran off into the mist away from his pursuers, he crossed the bomb site as fast as his legs would go. It was vital that Dieter should be immediately told about the crisis which had marked the turn of events. It was all up as far as Raymond was concerned, and perhaps several others would be arrested too. Dieter and his companions who were still with him at that side of the bomb site would need to escape as best they could through the back streets of the city to the nearest Underground station and get back to the West sector. They could not risk waiting for the cars to pick them up – the vehicles, conspicuous with their foreign number plates might have already been seized by the police.

Alexis thought it of primary importance that Dieter should make his own escape before the others, so dissociating himself from the group. In this way, the youths from the West would have to invent their own story for causing a public affray on a bomb site in the middle of the night. What story they told would be up to them – it could be a party game car chase, a treasure hunt, anything – but it was vital that as far as possible they should be dissociated from having had any connection with anyone from the East. If Fortner involved the group of youths in trouble (and certainly that seemed probable) it would make things bad, and if Dieter was arrested, that might make things far worse for them all. After all, Fortner had clearly attended the party to spy on Dieter, not on the others. If Dieter was arrested with the group, a trumped-up charge of conspiracy against the security of the DDR might be held against them all, and perhaps even, a major political incident could be the outcome.

Alexis jumped across a deep crevice, ran round a boulder and then over a small pile of rubble, and across an area of cleared land. He came to a high wall, and pulled himself up with the strength of his hands, putting the tips of his shoes between the brickwork. On the other side of the wall was a deep drop of some twenty feet and a pool of black water. He ran along the wall towards the left, until reaching a vast block of ruined buildings which were fenced in and lined the roadway. He jumped down from the wall and ran frantically through a doorway into the back of the building. It was quite dark and he could see nothing. He bumped into a wall and then tripped over a piece of cast iron lying on the floor in an inner room. There was a foul smell of refuse, and he heard something scuttle quickly away.

He saw a light and ran towards it, and as he left the building he heard a crash behind, as a piece of masonry fell through the building to the ground – the delayed consequence of a bomb which had been dropped on the building on some historic night many years previously. His nostrils were filled with the dust of cement and plaster. He saw a small hole in the fence in front of him where a board had broken away, and he heard footsteps frantically running down the pavement towards him from the other side. Intuition told him that this was Dieter or one of his companions from the other side of the bomb site.

He ran up to the fence breaking away two more planks, kicking them into the street, and climbed through the barrier.

"Dieter, Raymond has been arrested and the others are surrounded by the police," cried Alexis as Dieter almost crashed into his arms. "We must flee instantly!"

"Raymond arrested! Have the police taken them away,?" cried Dieter in return.

"I don't know. Anything could have happened during the last two minutes," replied Alexis.

"Then we must rescue them."

"We can do nothing," cried Alexis. "We must flee. You mustn't be arrested with them at any cost. It would be worse for us all."

"They mustn't fall into the hands of the authorities. I'll bluff the police."

"You can't do that," cried Alexis excitedly, holding onto Dieter's arms to prevent his running off.

"Has Fortner been seen?"

"Yes – and captured," replied Alexis.

"Then go up to the other end of the bomb site and shout the code word *Ende*," said Dieter. "That'll call Leon and Hendrik off the hunt. They're with a couple of Vopos, so if they have any trouble, you can help them."

"Vopos,?" exclaimed Alexis.

"Yes – they're being bluffed," replied Dieter. "There's no time for explaining. Now go along and find them both."

Both youths ran in opposite directions down the pavement of the street.

Two minutes later Dieter had already turned the corner of the next street, and was fast approaching his friends standing huddled together on the pavement under the close guard of the People's Police.

As he ran up to the group recognising the figures of his friends from a distance, a sensation of horror ran down his spine. Had they all been arrested? So quickly? Had none of them escaped? Was it possible they had all been captured when only five minutes before they had been free men chasing through the streets of the city in their own cars? He saw only one consolation as he ran up closer towards the group. Fortner was not amongst them! Perhaps he'd been knocked unconscious, or had run off in another direction to escape his pursuers without knowing what had subsequently occurred.

Chapter 61

As a question of honour, Dieter felt it was his responsibility at any cost to ensure the release of his friends. He could only attempt this through bluff and grandiloquent play-acting – something not foreign to his nature. Perhaps his friends had already admitted too much – entangling themselves beyond hope of rescue – he did not know – he could only try to deliver them from a horrible fate. Perhaps in so attempting, he was merely surrendering himself into the hands of the authorities, so condemning himself to certain death.

He knew the risk he was taking, but instinctively, he felt the rescue of his friends was an imperative of honour, exceeding any other consideration. They had pursued Fortner from Zehlendorf merely as a gesture of friendship towards him, and likewise, he felt morally obliged to return that gesture of friendship by attempting to rescue them.

"Halt! Who goes there,?" cried one of the Vopos pointing his bayoneted rifle at Dieter as he ran up to the group.

"Put down that rifle! I demand the release of these men," commanded Dieter. He prayed that he might be able to sustain the courage of his cheek, but he felt that the vehemence of his outburst helped embolden him – and then cheek was a natural attribute of the Berliner.

"Who do you think you are,?" cried another of the Vopos in an insolent tone throwing his hands onto his hips.

"These men are working under my command," cried Dieter shouting defiantly, and eloquently throwing up an arm.

"Ha! Who are you bluffing,?" cried another of the Vopos angrily.

How much do they know,? thought Dieter. Perhaps they'll think my outburst is merely a mark of insanity. Never mind – I must carry on with the act against all odds, until I'm either arrested or my friends are released.

"These men are in the employment of the State Security Service. They're acting under the direct orders of Colonel-General Mielke," screamed Dieter at the top of his voice.

"Under the orders of Colonel-General Mielke,!" exclaimed one of the Vopos astonished.

"We didn't know that," exclaimed another.

"They were found causing a disturbance on this bomb site," said a third.

"One was armed with a small automatic," exclaimed a fourth.

"That's what brought us onto the scene," said another. "We were alarmed by shots and shouting."

"They were hunting down a dangerous political criminal whom we chased into the city centre from the West sectors," cried Dieter.

"This guy's a genius," muttered Milton in English to Lars as he nudged him in the side.

"He's the one who's armed," cried Dieter.

"That's what we said," exclaimed Max.

"He's over there – we knocked him out on the bomb site," replied André pointing.

"What does this mean,?" exclaimed one of the Vopos confused.

"These men are foreigners," said another. "What are they doing in the service of the SSD?"

"They're members of the KGB seconded to the SSD," cried Dieter.

"Members of the KGB,!" exclaimed several of the Vopos at once.

"They're a counter espionage unit from West Berlin," continued Dieter.

"We cannot risk upsetting the Soviet authorities," said one of the Vopos to another. "Then we'd all end up in the soup!"

"Why wasn't this explained before,?" demanded another in resentful anger.

"How was that possible when for obvious reasons they're carrying no kind of identity,?" replied Dieter angrily.

"But they never attempted to identify themselves."

"They were ordered not to. They're under orders of secrecy."

"Then we can't be blamed for that."

"Why were they arrested?"

"For causing a disturbance."

"They must be released at once."

"Impossible! We've orders to hold them here until they've been picked up by a police van."

"Who's in charge here?"

"I," replied Braun clicking his heels.

"Release these men immediately," ordered Dieter. "This dangerous criminal must be caught at any cost. He's carrying vital top secret taped documents stolen from the SSD headquarters in Lichtenburg. I can assure you, that if you prevent us from carrying out our duty, the consequences will be serious, not only for the country but for yourselves. You're committing a grave mistake by holding these men. If you don't immediately release these men, I personally, shall see you're demoted."

"Can you show us papers to prove your identification,?" said Braun impressed by Dieter's speech with its mounting anger.

"Naturally,!" replied Dieter thrusting his pass into Braun's hand.

Braun clicked his heels and saluted smartly.

"Apologies, Herr *Leutnant*,!" he said returning the pass. "I'm sure everything's in order. He's a political officer attached to the School in Treptow," he added addressing his comrades.

"Now you can appreciate the importance of immediately releasing my men," said Dieter.

"With due respect, Herr *Leutnant*, we've had instructions to hold the men here until the return of our superior officer," replied Braun bowing politely.

"Who is your superior officer?"

"Captain Eggerath."

"Ach! A personal friend of mine," replied Dieter. "I'm sure he'd appreciate the exceptional circumstances of my countermanding his orders."

"In view of the circumstances, then, we can overrule the instructions of the superior officer – the Captain,?" said Braun.

"You can,!" replied Dieter firmly.

"We can all hunt for the political criminal, then return in the police van to the headquarters when it arrives, just the same,?" said Braun.

"Naturally – I wouldn't intend otherwise," replied Dieter bowing politely. "I wasn't suggesting Captain Eggerath's orders should be overruled entirely."

"Then I suggest we spread out along the length of the street, advancing across the bomb site to the other side in a straight line," said Braun.

"Excellent,!" exclaimed Dieter. "That way he should never slip between our ranks. I suggest you take your men and cover the right half of the street from the centre, whilst my men cover the left half of the street."

"Agreed *Leutnant*! We're under your orders. – Schmidt! You take the contigent onto the bomb site. I must wait here for the return of the Captain and the police van."

"Yes, Corporal,!" replied Schmidt, and he and the other Vopos excepting only for Braun ran onto the bomb site and spread out.

"And hurry now,!" cried Braun after them, " – before the criminal escapes to the other side."

"We go this way," cried Dieter and he and his companions ran onto the bomb site in a bunch, as fast as their legs could carry them, away from the Vopos.

They had not run far when they stopped behind a boulder.

"Now listen," cried Dieter breathlessly. "Our escape still depends on split second timing and luck. The police van will arrive any moment. – Who knows what's happened to Fortner? Alexis said he was caught."

"I beat him up," said André. "He's lying unconscious."

"Then André, George and Max, recover the tape and take his revolver," said Dieter. "The rest of you, run round the bomb site in a semicircle, keeping just beyond the view of the roadway, so the Corporal on the pavement can't see you. His suspicions mustn't be aroused. Reach the cars at the end of the roadway as soon as you can, and André, George and Max, follow on immediately afterwards and under no circumstances allow for delay."

"Right,!" replied several at once.

Breathlessly, they had been listening to Dieter with wide-open eyes, filled with nervous excitement. None had attempted to interrupt him since he had so cleverly secured their release, and none dared congratulate themselves for fear of speaking too soon, and then their sudden release from capture was as great a shock as their sudden arrest. As soon as Dieter had finished speaking they all ran off to the left.

Fortner, his face badly cut and bruised, slowly reached out for the round tin and the pistol, as he lay on the ground, besmirched with mud.

Painfully, he dragged himself to his feet, supporting himself with an upstretched arm against the boulder behind which he had lain.   He stumbled forward several steps, shook his head clear, then clenched the pistol threateningly in front of him.   He stepped forward again, his eyes glistening with anger, and drew back his bleeding lips which were badly cut. He heard footsteps running up behind him, and he lurched round, aiming the pistol, to see who would emerge out of the mist.

Corporal Braun stood on the pavement alone, waiting for the imminent return of his superior officer. His machine gun was slung across his shoulder, and he slouched lazily against the doorway as he lit up a cigarette and glanced across the street at the corner of the alley opposite. He heard heavy footsteps quickly approaching, and a moment later, the police officer reappeared running across the street.

"Where are the others,?" he exclaimed in horror as he crossed the street.

"Their arrest was all a mistake Captain," replied Braun with devastating complacency.

"A mistake,?" returned the Captain glancing at his subordinate as the latter lazily took a draw on his cigarette. "Who told you that?"

"They're SSD agents," said Braun, "seconded from the KGB. They're working under the direct orders of Colonel-General Mielke."

"What nonsense is this,?" exclaimed the Captain. "And stand properly when I address you – the wall can stand up without you supporting it."

Braun clicked his heels and saluted.

"They were hunting a dangerous political criminal from the West sector, who was carrying top secret documents stolen from the SSD headquarters in Lichtenburg."

"Where did you get this information from,?" exclaimed the Captain with mounting anger."

"A close friend of yours, Captain," replied Braun grinning, and not at all disconcerted by the officer's rising anger.

"Friend?"

"Yes, Captain!   *Leutnant* Liebermann," replied Braun complacently as if making a happy revelation to his superior officer.

"Liebermann? I've never heard the name."

"From the Political Officers School of the Volksarmee. Remember,?" said Braun attempting to knock the amnesia out of his superior's head.

"What idiocy is this,?" screamed the officer shaking his fist in the air. "I don't know anyone from the Political Officers School."

"He showed his pass, Captain."

"And take that cigarette out of your mouth when you're talking to me. And where are those men who were arrested five minutes ago?"

"They're searching for the armed political criminal on the bomb site," replied Braun.

"And where are your comrades?"

"They're also searching."

"And so the arrested men have been released?"

"Yes Captain, but …"

"Who gave authority for that,?" yelled the officer.

"But they're coming back with us voluntarily to the headquarters just the same," replied Braun. "It was mutally agreed."

"Mutually? What's that mean? When you let a fish off the line, is that mutual? What nonsense is that? Agreed between whom?"

"Why, between *Leutnant* Liebermann and myself, Captain."

"I don't believe that any such officer exists as *Leutnant* Liebermann. Who gave authority for the release of these men?"

"*Leutnant* Liebermann, Captain."

"Over my authority,?" yelled the officer pointing to his tabs. "Is that bird shit on my shoulders?"

"Under the exceptional circumstances it was decided …"

"*Quatsch*! I'll not listen to you any more. I'll have you shot for this Corporal,!" yelled the officer, his face red with rage. "You're a blithering idiot! You'll be stripped as soon as we return to headquarters."

"His papers seemed quite in order," muttered Braun quivering in front of his superior.

"You've been duped,!" yelled the Captain waving his arms with rage and advancing from the pavement onto the bomb site.

"He spoke so authoritatively," pleaded Braun.

"Authoritatively – my foot! It was mere play acting. These men must be re-arrested at once. They must be shot down. The entire area must be sprayed with machine gun fire. Not one must be allowed to escape."

The officer drew his pistoil, firing into the air. Both Vopos began shouting for the recall of their men, crying that the men who had been taken from the bomb site must be re-arrested instantly or shot down. The Captain and the Corporal ran forward onto the bomb site in different directions, rounding up their men, shouting, and excitedly giving orders.

Within moments there was pandemonium. By this time Braun's subordinates had spread out over a large area of the bomb site, and several were beyond hearing range of their superiors, and some only heard the distant shouts indistinctly and were undecided. What had happened? What were they supposed to do? Some continued across the bomb site searching for the "dangerous political criminal," whilst others, on hearing that the "foreigners" were to be re-arrested and that the area was to be sprayed with gunfire, began advancing towards the left, shooting wildly.

André, George and Max continued running through the mist until a black figure loomed in front of them.

"He's recovered," cried André.

"Don't go near him – he's armed,!" cried Max.

There came the sound of more shots and then shouting from the distance.

"Surround him and stone him down," suggested André.

Fortner fired a shot at the three youths, and then retreated quickly, disappearing into the mist. The students picked up some rocks and hurled them in the direction of Fortner.

"Now surround him," cried Goerge, and the three students ran in different directions.

Suddenly, Dieter's voice pierced through the night air from the distance. He shouted that the three students must instantly return to the street as the police were again covering the area and that the cars could not afford to wait. Heedless of danger, the students continued to hurl several more rocks after the retreating figure. Again, the *Spitzel* fired at his pursuers.

The youths heard footsteps running towards them from the near distance.

"We cannot delay longer," cried Max. "We must fly!"

There was a burst of machine gun fire, and bullets ricocheted off stonework around the youths. The three of them ran as fast as they could back towards the street where the cars, hopefully, were still parked. They heard shouting not far behind. They had run a fair way of the distance when suddenly George tripped over a protruding girder and fell flat onto his face. He cried out in pain and struggling to his feet, limped several steps forward. He cried out for help, pleading he could not reach the car alone. André and Max ran back, lifted him onto their shoulders, and quickly ran forward again.

When Alexis reached the other end of the bomb site, where the crashed Opel was still burning against the wall, several persons and a Vopo were standing around the vehicle. To avoid attracting their attention or arousing suspicion, Alexis ceased running as soon as he turned the corner into the street, and crept along light-footedly at normal walking pace.

"The driver must have gone off to fetch the fire brigade himself," he heard one man say who was standing by.

"He clearly escaped in good time from the wreck," said another. "There's no sign of a body inside."

"He must have been pretty drunk to crash the car in a back street like that," said a woman.

Alexis went onto the bomb site without drawing attention to himself, running towards the left. He decided not to shout the code word *Ende* for fear of bringing the people in the street onto the bomb site, and then he wanted to find Hendrik and Leon separately, so that he might in turn help them to overpower the two Vopos.

He climbed the pile of rubble and ran down the other side, crossing over an area of cleared ground. He had not gone far, when he saw two figures in the distance way over on the left. He ran quickly towards them, soon recognising Hendrik and a police officer carrying a pistol several metres to the left. Hendrik and the officer turned on hearing Alexis approach.

"What's happened,?" cried Hendrik as Alexis came up to him.

"*Ende*,!" exclaimed Alexis in a loud whisper.

Without another word, both youths moved towards the Vopo, and Alexis made to run to the other side of him.

"Have a cigarette," said Hendrik holding out a packet to the Vopo.

"Thanks," replied the Vopo stretching forward a hand, and at the same moment, Hendrik dealt him a heavy right-hander beneath the jaw, throwing the policeman flat onto his back. Hendrik grabbed the pistol and threw it into the mist. The Vopo groaned semi-consciously.

"Let him come to in his own good time," said Alexis. "We must find Leon and get back to the cars," and the two youths ran off in their search.

Leon and the Vopo moved slowly across an area of flat rubble, their eyes searching through the mist for any sign of a human figure.

"I heard something," cried the Vopo.

"Where,?" cried Leon.

"Straight ahead – from the left."

"What?"

"A stumbling."

From the distance behind them came the sound of the word *Ende*,! a ghostly whisper piercing the mist.

"What's that," exclaimed the Vopo.

"I don't know," replied Leon.

"It was a voice from behind us."

"Wasn't that what you heard just before?"

"No! There's someone approaching us from the front."

"Are you sure?"

"Yes," replied the Vopo and he ran forward a few steps.

Glancing furtively at the policeman before him Leon picked up a heavy rock.

"Look! A figure approaching us," cried the Vopo excitedly.

Leon dropped the rock, running to the side of the Vopo. There was a stumbling sound, and then a black thick-set figure with dishevelled hair carrying a revolver, emerged from the mist. The figure stumbled aimlessly towards the two men as if half-conscious or on the verge of collapse, and as if oblivious to what was ahead.

"It's him,!" cried Leon. "Fortner! We have you now. Give yourself up."

From behind the two mend came the word *Ende,*! exclaimed louder than before and from a closer quarter.

"Fortner, drop your gun," cried Leon.

Fortner shook his head, stopped in his path, drawing himself up to his full height. A shot was fired, and a bullet ricocheted off the ground between Leon and the Vopo.

"Get on the ground – he's firing at us," cried the Vopo.

Both men threw themselves onto their stomachs, and the Vopo adjusted his machine gun for burst firing and aimed in front.

"We have you now, Fortner," cried Leon.

Fortner began stumbling forward again – almost running towards the two men.

"No, no – not that – there's a mistake – wait, wait – I work for the KGB,!" he cried frantically, and he threw down his revolver, running forward quickly, holding out his bared hand and in his other was held the tin containing the tape.

"Is that a pistol in his other hand,?" cried the Vopo confused.

"Seems so," replied Leon.

The air was pierced by the deafening scream of machine gunfire, as the Vopo clung firmly onto the automatic as it vibrated beneath him, his fingers clutching round the form of the weapon. Fortner was thrown into the air by the force of the gunfire, landing a dead mass on the stony rubble.

The Vopo grinned at his accomplice and slapping him on the shoulder, offered his hand. As Leon returned the handshake, he stretched out his other arm along the ground, blindly feeling for a suitable object.

"We made it then," exclaimed the Vopo, before he was struck on the skull by a rock which was forced down onto his soft green cap, and he was left senseless on the ground.

There came the sound of running footsteps from the direction of where Fornter had emerged from the mist. Leon leaped to his feet and was about to retrieve the tape, when he was stopped by the sound of voices in front, and the figures of three running Vopos came into view.

"Look, a body,!" exclaimed one.

Leon's heart sank when he realised that any chance for the recovery of the tape was gone and that hence the mission – costing so much effort – had failed. He turned and ran as fast as his feet would carry him.

"Halt there,!" cried another of the Vopos.

Leon hid behind a boulder and then ran again, and he never slackened his pace until reaching the street. Several bursts of machine gunfire came from behind, but he escaped into the mist, beyond the visibility of his pursuers. On reaching the street, he almost creashed into Hendrik and Alexis.

"What's happened,?" cried Hendrik as they quickly followed after Leon.

"Fortner's been killed," replied Leon, "but it was impossible to recover the tape."

"We thought Fortner had been captured at the other end of the bomb site," cried Alexis. "We were looking for you to call off the chase."

"Then it was lucky you didn't find me too soon," replied Leon.

Further up the street, they heard their names shouted. Dieter was waiting by the Buick.

"Hurry! Get into the car," he cried. "We're being chased by the police."

As the four youths ran along the pavement, the Buick began to slowly move off. Frantically, they ran at the car, jumping into the back. Dieter, the last to jump into the vehicle, slammed the door behind him, whilst Lovell pressed his foot down onto the accelerator, and the car sped forward.

"The others have gone on ahead," exclaimed Dieter.

The Buick swerved round a corner, racing down another street.

"It seems as if you guys have been getting yourselves into difficulties," cried Lovell.

"We had a lot of bad luck," replied Alexis. "Everything seemed to go wrong."

"Then if we get out of the East sector unscathed, you can count us darned lucky," said Lovell as he drove the car across a bridge over the river Spree.

"How's your shoulder, Carl,?" enquired Hendrik.

"Painful," replied Carl.

"We'll rush you into hospital as soon as we get into the West sector," said Lovell.

"We can drop him at the St. Gertrauden Hospital – it's on the direct route back to Zehlendorf," said Hendrik pointing at the map.

Speeding along the narrow back streets of the city, the car took the quickest route back to the Unter den Linden.

"There are the others just in front of us," cried Milton.

"Listen, this is how we've planned to get out of the sector in case of trouble," said Lovell, " – as arranged between the three of us drivers. We'll drive up to the Brandenburg Gate and brake closely behind one another. If the police try to block the roadway before our approach, we'll drive straight through the Gate at top speed, so you'll have to duck down beneath the windows in case of gunfire."

"What if we're held up after we're stopped at the Gate,?" enquired Leon.

"The cars will park in such a way as to be able to drive out from behind one another, rush forward and knock aside anyone holding up the first car, so escaping into the West," replied Lovell.

"Sounds great," said Milton. "Not much else we can do anyway."

The Buick shot forward, overtook the other two cars, but remained only a short distance in front of them.

"Now we slow down, so as not to arouse their suspicion at the Gate," said Lovell lifting his foot from the accelerator. "We want to avoid trouble if we can."

The Gate came ever closer, and no one rushed out from the guard house into the middle of the roadway, although a couple of Vopos paced lazily up and down the just in front of the Gate.

The cars reached the Gate and braked behind one another. One of the Vopos went up to Lovell and took his pass, glancing at it superficially.

"Where have you been,?" he asked.

"For a drive round the city," replied Lovell.

"You should have been out of here before this time," said the Vopo returning the pass and waving the car on.

The passengers drew a sigh of relief as Lovell started the car and drove through the Gate. They had returned to the free world! As they passed the Soviet memorial in the Street of the 17th June, they glanced behind them and saw the Morris and VW following behind. Milton cracked a joke and the others laughed, and they began to talk excitedly and describe the adventures they had experienced. They were free – they had luckily escaped the imminent danger of arrest and internment at the hands of the Commuist police. They had escaped by the skin of their teeth. They laughed, congratulating one another on their pluck and presence of mind. All were in high spirits – all except for Dieter who sat quietly with a thoughtful expression, in the back corner seat of the car. He knew that the mission had failed.

BOOK XVI

The Day of Reckoning

Love is a flame to burn out human wills,
Love is a flame to set the will on fire,
Love is a flame to cheat men into mire. …
Love puts such bitter poison on fate's arrow.

John Masefield, *The Widow in the Bye Street*, Pt. II.

Chapter 62

There was the sound of laughter, talking and singing in the flat. The party had reached the height of merriment. Manfred, Lovell, Ray and André were standing around the piano singing some beer hall songs to the accompaniment of Leon's violin, and Manfred's fiancée played the piano, whilst behind them, stood Alexis beating a saucepan with a wooden spoon.

More than an hour had passed since they had raced through the Brandenburg Gate in their three cars. Carl had been taken to the hospital where he was being treated for a minor operation to remove the bullet from his shoulder, and to complete a routine police enquiry into the circumstances of the accident, and Luigi had been taken to the Red Cross hospital in Charlottenburg where his hand had been stitched and bound up, and from where he had just returned.

Laughing, as he joked with Milton, he downed a glass of beer with his free hand as the other was held in a sling.

"I guess Sigismund made a pretty showy job of chucking that Vopo over the wall," exclaimed Milton as Sigismund stood by beaming with pride. "A guy has to have muscles to do a thing like that."

Lars emptied a bottle of Hock into his Stein as he watched Milton speak. Again, the Swede was seated in his favourite place at the end of the sofa.

"And even Lars proved to us he's got fighting courage," added Milton nodding to his friend.

Herr Becke, the housekeeper, and his wife, sat in their dressing gowns on another sofa, and were royally served with food and drink by several of the girls. They sat close together, silent but contented, grinning with pleasure, overcome by the hospitality of their hosts. They were receiving ample compensation for the interruption to their night's sleep.

From another part of the room, George let out a little yell of pain.

"It's as it should be, George," cried Waltraute insistently. "Now put your foot right in."

George was sitting on an upright chair with one trouser leg rolled up to the knee, whilst Waltraute knelt at his feet with a bowl of hot mustard water, coaxing him to put his swollen foot into the emollient. Waltraute had already sent one of her friends out to a nearby chemist to buy a poultice.

Dieter and Dagmar sat quietly together in another part of the room. The fair one held a glass of lemonade whilst Dieter stared thoughtfully into his glass of cognac.

"Don't worry, Dieter – we'll think of a way," said Dagmar softly as she laid her hand on his.

"Think of a way for what,?" said Dieter as if startled.

"For escaping the danger in which you now find yourself," replied Dagmar.

"I'm in no danger," said Dieter with a shrug and a strange kind of smile.

"What do you mean by that,?" asked Dagmar intently, looking straight into his eyes.

"I mean – I've no intention of escaping from anything," said Dieter.

"But you're in terrible danger – perhaps both of us are," said Dagmar. "You know what you've done. You cannot return to the East."

"Dagmar, don't speak like that," said Dieter firmly but gently as he took her hands into his, after she had laid down her glass on a table. "I must return to the East – my studies – everything – everything I possess is still in the East."

"They'll arrest you," said Dagmar.

"I'll find a way of evading them – if that becomes necessary," said Dieter in a strange tone.

"How?"

Max, beaming happily, came up to the young couple.

"I think we might phone Klaus Gebhart now," he said brightly. "It's rather late, and I don't suppose his landlady will like it, but I think this call is important and can't wait till morning."

"You're right," replied Dieter rising from his chair.

"We'll take the phone in my room again," said Max.

The three went to Max's room, and whilst Dieter and Dagmar sat down in basket chairs, Max sat on the bed and dialled the number. In tense anticipation, the three waited as the phone rang at the other end.

"Hullo, Klaus, I'm sorry to phone so late," said Max at last, "but it's an urgent matter. It couldn't wait until tomorrow. Irmgard and I didn't know what had happened to you tonight. We heard you were ill earlier, and tried to phone but you were out. The fact is, we've had a long episode of trouble tonight and all because of a friend of yours called Fortner. Not a friend? ... He introduced himself as a friend. Only an acquaintance, I see. The truth is, he nearly succeeded in killing several of us with a revolver. Who is this Fortner? ... A student at the Technical University! How well do you know him? ... How is it he came to the party tonight – and why weren't you there? ... Ha! That seems to explain a lot. Fifty marks? Sounds like a well-planned conspiracy. Now I begin to understand everything. ... I haven't time now to explain everything. ... Yes, Klaus, it was that bad. We're not blaming you – you couldn't have known what was to transpire. Good night Klaus," and Max replaced the receiver.

"What happened,?" cried Dieter.

"He was duped," replied Max, "but cleverly duped. Apparently, this Wolfgang Fortner had been a casual acquaintance of Klaus for some time. Klaus never really liked him because he was a creep, but he did once visit a room he had in Steglitz."

"And so Fortner actually had an address in the West sector," exclaimed Dieter.

"Apparently," said Max. "And tomorrow we can contact the police, and they can send their own agents along to search the apartment."

"But how did Fortner get to the party?"

"Fortner told Klaus he'd heard about the party, and that he wanted to meet a girl there whom he'd had his eye on for some time. He offered Klaus fifty marks to feign illness so allowing him to attend in his stead. Naturally, Klaus fell for the profitable offer - who wouldn't? – and he saw nothing compromising in it."

"It was still mean to sell himself like that," said Dieter.

"It was clearly part of a much larger conspiracy to track you down and put you on a trumped-up charge of treason," said Max.

"That's just what I've been telling Dieter," said Dagmar.

"The authorities were diligent," said Dieter thoughtfully.

"They were more than that," said Max. "They must have been determined to nail you down to have gone that far. They must have shadowed your friends and acquaintances to have set up this evening's little episode."

"And now it's over and done with. It's no good discussing it further," said Dieter dismissively.

"Over and done with,?" exclaimed Max in astonishment. "Dieter, your troubles have only just begun. You're living on a knife-edge. Even if you moved to West Berlin, they'd still catch you. You're a marked man now. The *Stasi* are everywhere."

"It's ironic to think this could have happened to us," interrupted Dagmar. "For more than a year, we've done everything to avoid suspicion. We've taken every precaution, and Dieter has even lost friends at the University through refusing to associate with critics of the regime."

"That's probably the very reason why they've gone to such lengths to set up this trap," said Max. "Their doubts about your reliabililty must go further back than you think. – Now we must discuss your immediate future."

"My future? What is there to discuss,?" exclaimed Dieter feigning an attitude of surprise.

"For a start, you can't remain in Berlin," said Max.

"I've no intention of playing cat and mouse," said Dieter.

"You won't have a chance, my friend," answered Max. "If you don't go into immediate hiding, the *Stasi* will have you within hours."

"No one will have me on the run," said Dieter emphatically.

"Look how you've been compromised. Don't you realise that? What about the fracas in East Berlin tonight? They know your name and your rank, and the lies you told the Volkspolizei."

"But Fortner's dead, and the dead can't speak. What happened in the East sector will just blow over. The Volkspolitzei were double-crossed, but they won't make fools of themselves by publicising the episode. They'll write it off. I'd rather consider the matter forgotten and done with."

"Don't be stupid,!" cried Max. "They'll check with the Political Officers School."

"If they haven't forgotten my name in the meantime," said Dieter.

"Why should they?"

"Because they're stupid. They made such a bungled job of what happened tonight, they'll want to suppress all evidence of the matter. They'd only get themselves into further trouble."

"I'm not so sure," insisted Max. "After all, they've got a body on their hands. There'll have to be some kind of investigation."

"I know these people," said Dieter laughing. "You'd not credit their cowardice in the face of incompetence."

"You're merely indulging in hopeful speculation," said Max.

"If I'm held for questioning concerning the pass, I'll simply deny all knowledge of it."

"What stupidity! They have witnesses. – And what about the tape? They may be listening to it as we're talking now."

"I've every intention of returning to the East," said Dieter firmly and rising from the chair.

"You're mad! It's suicidal," cried Max throwing up his hands.

"I'll somehow talk my way out of the problem," said Dieter nonchalantly. "I've always succeeded in the past and I see why not now."

"But how?"

"It'll depend on circumstances," replied Dieter impatiently waving a hand.

"You should at least go to the West German police and make a statement, and take their advice," said Max.

"That's the last thing I'd do," said Dieter. "Do you think they'd trust an officer of the Volksarmee – and attached to the Political section to boot? Never!"

"You have friends here, who'll stand security for you."

"I don't want that kind of involvement."

"But why not,?" cried Max.

"I've no wish to confide the whole of my private life and thoughts to the West Berlin police or to any other police."

"But it'll be necessary if you're to flee Berlin. You'll need their help, and the assistance of the refugee organisations in getting you out of the city unscathed."

"I know that, but I don't want to call on those channels for help."

"And why?"

"Because I don't want to. – Too many inconvenient explanations would be necessary."

"Then how are you to get out of this mess,?" cried Max exasperated.

"I'll use my own methods. I've talked myself out of trouble before, and I'll do it again. But standing as a supplicant before the West German authorities is one thing I'll not do."

"I still don't understand why you can't be helped by the West German police. That's what they're there for."

"Because Max," said Dieter faltering, "as you yourself know, I'm already deeply involved with the East German authorities. I'd be no ordinary refugee. I'd be under constant suspicion. I'm a political officer in the Volksarmee and an active member of the FDJ, and through a set of unintentional and ironic circumstances, I've become a well-known propagandist in the SED."

"So it's your sense of pride which prevents you from going to the West German police – you're afraid of losing face – of being ridiculed," said Max contemptuously, nodding his head as if to say, "and so that's it!"

"It's not quite that, Max," replied Dieter. "My public life's been such a mess over the past two years, that in explaining it, it would be impossible to create a credible impression. Who would believe me for a start? I would need to reveal my most inner thoughts – explain all the motives for the things I did – and who would accept it as truth? In some ways I'm hardly credible to myself, so how can I begin to be credible to others?"

"You'd just have to try your best," said Max.

"I've no inclination to embark on the attempt," said Dieter. "I haven't the will. Simply, I couldn't."

"Your attitude is suicidal. I'm even beginning to believe you're fraught with self-hate. What other explanation can there be? Have you no courage left?"

"Not courage of that kind. My courage is of a different sort."

"Of what sort? To throw away your life into the hands of the East German authorities?"

"Firstly, not to risk disgrace. Secondly, not to run away from danger, but to stand up and face it."

"*Quatsch*! That's not courage – that's foolhardiness. Nothing's achieved for yourself or anyone else by that kind of attitude. Do you think there's any credit in surrendering to the *Stasi*? Of course not! It's not even martyrdom."

"I'm not seeking martyrdom – nothing could be further from my thoughts," said Dieter. "I'm just prepared to face fate – the inevitable! I ask you, Max, how is it possible for a highly-successful propagandist to ever prove he's never believed in any of the things he's propagated for years on end? And I've not merely been cynical about the DDR – there are plenty of cynics around who've comfortably sold their beliefs for thirty pieces of silver – I've positively loathed the DDR and all it stands for. My mind has never been – and could never be at peace with anything I've done. That's something more than cynicism. It's a betrayal – a polarised reversal even of everything I've believed in and lived for. Now explain that."

"In the final analysis, Dieter, it doesn't matter a damn what other individuals or authorities make of anything you tell them," said Max. "What's important is that they accept your explanation at face value – and I see no reason why they shouldn't."

"But that's no answer to the difficulties in having to present my case," said Dieter.

"You'd not be the first man to have faced the West Berlin police in a similar situation," replied Max. "Perhaps hundreds have gone before you. I see the situation differently. As you've already won a curious distinction for yourself in the East zone, the Western security authorities must already have you on their files. What's happened tonight could be turned to your advantage. If you'd moved to Friedrichshafen without the occurrence of this episode, you'd still possibly be under the lingering suspicion of Western intelligence. Now that need never be. With one of the Soviet agents dead and the police duped – and all the witnesses to these events – your integrity need never now be suspected. Do you follow?"

"Max is right,!" cried Dagmar.

"I think not," said Dieter. "Intelligence matters are not so simple as that. Any involvement with the police is compromising."

"What are we to do then,?" cried Dagmar.

"What more can I say to him,?" cried Max in desperation. "I've exhausted every avenue looking for a way out. – If for no other reason then, take our advice for the sake of Dagmar – for the sake of your friends and those who love you."

"What do you want me to do,?" said Dieter dreamily.

"Why, stay in the West, of course."

"Take Max's advice," urged Dagmar.

"Sleep here for what remains of tonight, and maybe, when your head's clearer, later this morning, you'll see things differently," said Max.

"We cannot stay here tonight – I cannot anyway," protested Dieter. "Tomorrow are the elections, and I must be up early, to help bring people to the polls. FDJ orders!"

"What insanity! You're exhausted and don't know what you're saying"

"I must go," persisted Dieter. "I must return to the East. I had never contemplated having to leave the East under such circumstances – and I never shall. If I left now, everything would be in chaos."

"It already is. You can't escape that," said Max.

"I still have final exams, and other essential arrangements to be made for our departure from the East."

"You'll have to live with those inconveniences," said Max.

"As I've said, I think the risk in returning to the East sector is minimal," said Dieter. "And besides, if the East German intelligence were really out to get me, it wouldn't matter where I was. Under such circumstances I reckon Friedrichshafen's hardly safer than West Berlin."

"I doubt if they'd go that far," remarked Max.

"And so you see, Max, we have to return tonight," said Dieter.

"Well, I can't stop you, though God only knows I've done my best," muttered Max grimly beneath his breath.

The three left the bedroom returning to the noise of the party in the sitting room. Dieter and Dagmar remained for another half hour, and Irmgard in her turn, tried to induce her cousin to remain for the rest of the night in the West sector, but her persuasion fell on deaf ears. Dieter was obdurate, and he insisted that his practical duties during the election day were imperative. Max and Irmgard, therefore, had to leave Dieter to his own fate. They concluded between them that he intended regarding the evening's dramatic events as ephemeral and melaningless as a passing dream and not as an episode of consequential facts.

The young couple from the East caught the last train from Zehlendorf to Friedrich Strasse. It was a long slow journey in an almost empty train, picking up guards and other S-Bahn personnel at every station, and taking them towards their homes in the East sector, and the young couple remained silent and thoughtful for most of the way. On arriving at Friedrich Strasse, they found the station almost closed, and from there to Treptow, they needed to take a taxi.

As the taxi sped down the wide empty roadway of Stalin Allee, the grim colourless outline of its immense buildings lit up by the dim light of old fashioned candelabra style street lamps, Dagmar asked Dieter why he had refused to heed Max's advice to remain in the West sector.

"Everything we have is still in the East," replied Dieter.

"I feel so afraid for you," said Dagmar snuggling up against his chest.

"You mustn't be afraid," said Dieter. "You must forget everything that's happened tonight."

"How can we,?" said Dagmar startled. "Is that your only response? These events are now part of our lives."

"No good can come of remembering them," said Dieter.

"These things are real – not just a bad dream."

"There's no other way to regard them than as the fevered invention of our imagination," said Dieter.

"What will you do if you're apprehended?"

"Nothing!"

"Nothing? Then why have you risked your life – our lives, in returning to the East?"

"We can do nothing, absolutely nothing, in the event of repercussions," said Dieter. " That's why we must forget."

Dagmar said nothing more, but snuggled closer to Dieter's chest, an expression of anxiety crossing her face.

Dieter had parked his car in Graetz Strasse, and when they left the taxi in Puschkin Allee, he walked her home to number 55 where they parted on the doorstep, before he drove back to Werlsee. Whilst they both stood in the hallway of the tenement block enclasped in one anothers' arms, she pleaded with him that he return to her in Treptow as early as possible that Sunday.

"I'll be very busy later this morning," replied Dieter smiling and looking down into her soulful eyes.

"I feel so worried," she said tightening her arms around his back. "I'll not be able to sleep until I see you safe again."

"Don't speak like that," said Dieter comforting her.

"Then can you promise me a time when we meet later today?"

"At two in the afternoon. I'll promise to be here then. Now please don't worry about me," he said kissing her on the forehead. "I'll be safe - I promise you."

"But you mustn't be late," she excalaimed in anxiety.

"Just go inside and get some sleep," urged Dieter trying to console her. "You'll feel better tomorrow."

"Be careful Dieter – in everything," said Dagmar kissing his lips. "Not until I see you again will my mind be at rest."

Chapter 63

That morning brought a bright day and Dagmar was awoken by the sun shining through her window. For a long time, she lay in bed thinking and worrying, as she rested the back of her head on the palms of her hands staring out of the window at the rooftops of the buildings across the courtyard. Although she had awoken early (for a Sunday) she had slept deeply during the night after taking one of her grandmother's sleeping pills. But still her mind was unchanged from the previous night – she knew that her fiancé might be in the direst peril.

What occurred the previous evening had been far from a dream, and after a night's sleep, she was in no way consoled by the facts as she recollected them. She realised that this was something which could not be slept "over" or slept "away." It was a real episode – to be faced with consequences – something from which there was no escape – for it would lead inevitably to a chain of worsening events. Why had Dieter on the previous night chosen to regard it all as a dream? It seemed so unlike him to run away from reality – and that's what he had done. Why had Dieter done this? Suddenly, Dagmar's mind was overcast by a dark shadow. Was Dieter prepared to surrender himself to the authorities? He had said that if he was apprehended, all would be up. Had he given up, even, the idea of attempting to escape? If so, then why had he reached such a conclusion? It was true he had acted strangely the previous night.

Now Dagmar regretted she had not more forcefully argued with Max and Irmgard in persuading Dieter to remain overnight in the West sector – but then she had become unused to arguing with her fiancé when she felt his mind was made up. She should have insisted by herself in refusing under any circumstances to return to the East sector. That might have persuaded Dieter to remain in the West - he would anyway have been put on the spot. But they were tired and it was late, and it was so easy to rationalise after the event as to what might have been the wiser course. The resolution of the problem seemed easier in retrospect than it had been at the time. That was so often the case. She was struck by the horror of his being arrested and lost forever. She knew that if he was taken by the authorities, he would never return. Then, everything would be lost – her life would no longer be worth living. She would have been widowed before life had begun, for the thought of ever having another man was unthinkable. Perhaps he had already been arrested. She would feel no peace of mind until he called for her that afternoon.

Suddenly, she was rudely started out of her pondering state of mind by loud knocking on the front door. Momentarily, she clutched the sheets as a pang of fear ran through her body. Was this the proverbial knock on the door – the police who had come for Dieter? She took up her watch from the bedside table and glanced at it. It was not yet nine o'clock. Who would call so early on a Sunday? There was more banging. The caller was urgent for an answer.

"Go to the door," said her grandmother who was lying beside her.

Dagmar jumped out of bed, put on her slippers and blue coat, and went out into the passageway towards the front door. She resolved that if it were the police, to say nothing that could possibly cast suspicion on her beloved or betray his probable whereabouts, and her heart beat nervously. Just before she reached the latch, she decided to misdirect the police by telling them that Dieter had remained in the West, and then that morning she herself would go to Werlsee and warn her fiancé's parents that the police were already on his trail – if he had not already been arrested or had not made his escape.

When she opened the door, she found to her surprise, a little fat man with a grinning red complexion, dressed in his Sunday best with a white open-necked shirt, and a lapel covered with political association badges, standing on the step.

"Fräulein Renot and Frau Brüning,?" he exclaimed beaming brightly with a happy grin.

"Yes," said Dagmar, startled by the sight of the man confronting her.

"Today is a great day for the people of the German Democratic Republic! A day to prove your loyalty to our glorious Communist State, and to our beloved First Secretary, Comrade Walter Ulbricht. I have your names on the electoral roll and I'll know when you've voted," said the little man. "You should report to the polling station early to avoid queuing."

Whilst the little man had been speaking, Dagmar heard loud knocking on several of the front doors throughout the tenement block. The Communist Party enthusiasts had invaded the building *en masse*. She heard their voices calling on the occupants to vote, and she heard the slamming of doors, and occasionally, the shrill caustic replies which some of the canvassers received.

"It's very early – it's a Sunday morning – I don't like being woken at this hour," replied Dagmar annoyed at having been unnecessarily dragged out of bed. "I thought you were the police come to arrest someone."

"But today will make history. Today is a very special day," replied the fat man brightly. "Today everyone in the DDR is granted the privilege of pledging his loyalty to the regime."

"I don't regard it as such a privilege," said Dagmar flatly.

"Not a privilege to vote? But we must have democracy my dear Fräulein," responded the canvasser taken aback. "Tut-tut, where should we be without democracy?"

"Voting is not a privilege, it's a right," said Dagmar.

"Our rights are only guaranteed through the workings of our glorious Marxist-Leninist state. Therefore, we should regard all rights as privileges," replied the fat man happily.

"In other words, the people should serve the State rather than the State serve the people."

"Precisely, Fräulein! That's the correct way of seeing it – although the reverse is also true. You have an exact understanding of the Marxist-Leninist theory of the State. That way, we can go through life having all the right answers without the need of doubting."

"I'm still not attracted by the 'privilege' of going to the polls," said Dagmar. "I think there should be more than one list of candidates."

"Oh no, Fräulein, that wouldn't do at all," said the fat man shocked. "That way, an opposition party might come to power, and the natural logic of progress would be overturned. There's only one way ahead.!"

"Will you be voting for the Communist Party this morning – the SED,?" said a canvasser diffidently across the hallway, speaking to an old man in pyjamas.

"No, I'll be voting for General Eisenhower," said the old man disgruntled, slamming the door in the canvasser's face.

"I can't stand here arguing with you now," said Dagmar. "It's cold and I want to get inside."

"I'll be checking later Fräulein, to see that you and Frau Brüning go to the polls," said the little man, "and I'll be keeping a watch in the future on all bad citizens who fail to cast their votes," he added brightly as he began to leave the doorway.

"But my grandmother, Frau Brüning, is very old and cannot walk easily," called Dagmar after him.

"Never mind, a bus will come at noon to fetch the old people," said the little man as he walked up the hallway. "We in the Communist Party have consideration for everyone you know."

"How very kind,!" said Dagmar, and she slammed the door behind her as she returned inside the flat.

Later that morning she left the flat to cast her vote at the polling station. The streets were more crowded than usual on a Sunday morning, and everywhere there were Communist officials urging people to use their vote. Just outside No. 18, a loudspeaker van was ordering people to report to the polling station, appealing to their sense of patriotism and civic pride, and to cast their votes as a first duty to the State. As Dagmar reached the corner of Bouche Strasse, the voice from the speaker gave way to stirring Russian march music, which sounded painfully high-pitched and metallic as it came from the tinney tannoy.

As she advanced down Bouche Strasse, as the noise from the speaker van receded, this was replaced by an even louder sound from the other end of the street. In the Busch Park, by the corner of Am Treptower, a fifty piece brass band was playing German march music, and outside the entrance to every tenement block, Communist agitators were calling on all who left or entered the buildings to cast their vote before attending to any other outside activities. And most significantly, the people were reminded that a record was kept of those failing to perform their civic duty.

On arriving at the polling station, Dagmar encountered another brass band playing outside the building. They were forming into three ranks with a group of happy Communist Party enthusiasts carrying red flags, before marching through the streets of the suburb of Treptow.

Inside the polling station, Dagmar saw a streamer running across the entire length of the hall, with the words, VOTE FOR THE SOCIALIST UNITY PARTY! Dagmar was struck by the absurdity of the exhortation. There was no other party for which it was possible to vote. To make voting easier for the electorate, the SED and other parties belonging to the National Front had combined to produce a single list of candidates. Therefore, no candidate for election to the People's Assembly need worry about fighting for his seat – his seat was already guaranteed – and irrespective of whether he received the vote of all or none of the electorate, his place in the People's Assembly remained a foregone conclusion. Across the opposite wall of the hall was a streamer announcing, THE SED FOR PEACE AND FREEDOM!

Dagmar went up to one of the tables, giving the officials her name and address.

"Graetz Strasse! Table ten," came the reply.

She went up to table ten, and her name and address was checked with the list, and she was given a voting slip. She walked across the hall, dropping the paper unmarked and unfolded into the ballet box, for it was not necessary even to put a cross beside the name of the single candidate – so simplified had the system of voting been made for the electors. She was overcome with a feelling of disgust at the proceedings and at their meaninglessness.

Before she left the hall, she saw at the far end, and placed in a prominent position, a lone voting booth. This had been put there for the benefit of any exceptional or eccentric individual who might wish to vote for a non-Communist and unlisted candidate. In the privacy of the booth, he (or she) was entitled to cross out the name of the listed candidate, and write instead, the name of his best friend or any other person whom he should like to elect to the People's Assembly. This marked the furthest limits of practical democracy on the impractical level in the German Democratic Republic.

At each side of the voting booth were two Vopos, machine guns slung over their shoulders – hardly an encouraging presence to the unconventional voter. Dagmar didn't feel quite sure as to their purpose in standing there. Were they there to protect from the risk of assault or abuse anyone inclined to use the prerogative of the booth, or were they there to frighten away with grim looks anyone so bold as to think of using it?

Dagmar left the hall and returned towards home. The brass band and the contingent of Party enthusiasts were already marching up the street in close formation, kicking their heels into the roadway, slowly waving their red banners, and singing a Communist Party song with all the gusto they could muster. Others were glancing from the windows of their apartment blocks along the length of the street. Every attempt was being made to draw the people to the polls, so that the hoped-for results could be used as a propaganda ploy in the outside world, in demonstrating the solidarity of world Communism.

When the results of the election were published, it was reported that 98.89% of the electorate had participated, and that 99.87% of the votes were for the SED. Manfred's guess at Max's party the previous night that the Communist vote at this election would be higher than those in 1954 and 1950, was therefore proved correct. The 1958 elections succeeded in giving the Communists in the DDR a higher percentage of votes than they had ever had before! Surely this was sproof of their rising popularity!

For the rest of the morning and the earlier part of the afternoon Dagmar was tense with worry at what meanwhile might have happened to Dieter. She told nothing to her parents of what had occurred the previous night. She sat quietly in the sitting room at No. 55, reading a Tolstoy novel, trying to seem inconspicuous, and hoping the time would pass quickly until Dieter's expected arrival at two o'clock. She found the novel of little consolation to her present state of mind, for she was reading the final chapters of *Ressurection* where she was following the account describing the long trek of hundreds of political and other prisoners to camps in Siberia. She became more depressed as she read on, for the book only served to remind her of the real danger in which her fiancé was now in.

During lunch, Dagmar was especially quiet, and Papa Renot made some facetious remarks as to the probable reason for her reserve and apparently melancholic mood. Dagmar reacted awkwardly, exclaiming only, "*Quatsch*, Papa!" Her grandmother commented, saying that perhaps she was tired after going to bed so late the night before. When Dagmar left a lot of food at the side of her plate, her mother asked why she had lost her appetite, to which she could only answer that she didn't know.

The hour arrived, and Dagmar's heart beat violently, tense with anticipation, as she awaited the expected knock on the front door. Soon it was fifteen minutes passed the hour, and still he had not arrived. Her heart began to sink. Had something happened? Had he been arrested? Her anxiety became a torture without rest, and she busied herself around the house with minor household chores.

At ten to three there was a loud knock on the door. Dagmar dropped what she was doing, running out of the kitchen to answer. She opened the door, and there was Dieter standing before her, beaming happily, and in his hand he held a small bouquet. She jumped at him, throwing her arms around his neck, embracing him tightly, burying her head in his chest, as if they had not met for a year.

"So you're still safe," she muttered.

"Of course I am," he replied smiling, gently patting her shoulders.

"*Was für ein Liebespaar!*" (What a pair of lovers!), came a voice behind them.

The young couple immediately disengaged themselves, and saw Papa Renot standing in the passageway of the flat, grinning in amusement. The old man clapped his hands.

"Very romantic,!" he exclaimed. "A beautiful sight!"

Dieter exchanged greetings with the old man, but Dagmar felt momentarily awkward, annoyed at her father having caught her whilst the free outlet of her emotions had so taken advantage of her.

Dieter was welcomed into the flat, and the entire family sat, talked and joked awhile in the sitting room. As Dieter had not visited the family for more than three weeks, the good Frau was especially indulgent, patting him on the shoulder, and insisting that he take the most comfortable seat in the room. Tea and cakes were brought in, and later, Papa Renot offered the guest a cigar which was gratefully accepted.

After an hour or so, the young couple left the flat to take a stroll in Treptower Park. When they came into the courtyard of the tenement block, they met Frau Hartmann approaching them from the other side. She eyed them curiously.

"I bet she's going to ask if you've voted," said Dagmar whispering in Dieter's ear. "She's such a busybody – there's no need to tell her you have."

"Have you voted yet, young man,?" said Frau Hartmann as she came up to the couple.

"No, Frau Hartmann," replied Dieter facetiously, "but if you go to the polling station, you can tell them you have my permission to vote for me."

"That would be political corruption,!" she retorted in shocked anger.

The lovers laughed and passed on.

It was a beautiful day in late Autumn as they strolled in Treptower Park, and the sun shone down from a blue sky, and the air was chill, and Dagmar remarked that there were more shades of colour in the Park at this time of the year than at any other. The leaves had not yet fallen, and there were yellow and russet hues bedecking the branches with gentle shades, as well as the ground beneath. They strolled round the Karpfen pond and saw some children feeding the ducks and drakes, and then they looked at the permanent exhibition of sculpture. They strolled along the narrow sandy pathways, between the bushes and beneath the branches of high trees, and Dagmar thought back to a year ago. It was almost exactly a year since she had first visited the house at Werlsee on that misty November day and it was on that day that she had lost her virginity.

That evening, the family sat in the flat at No. 18 enjoying an evening's entertainment, talking, joking and listening to the radio. Papa Renot was in particularly high spirits, joking constantly, and as it became especially cold that night, the good Frau lit the stove in the sitting room for the first time that Autumn. The family usually spent their evenings in the sitting room at the other side of the road, but when guests were invited and Frau Brüning retired early, then parties were usually held at No. 18. Later, the family sat round the table and played a parlour game.

Dieter and Dagmar left the party and bid the others good night at eleven o'clock, when they returned to No. 55 and quietly entered the flat.

Nearly an hour had passed. They lay close together on the couch naked in one another's arms. They rested quietly, but Dagmar clung tightly onto Dieter's body as if afraid of losing him.

"All day I've been waiting only for this moment. I've been so afraid," exclaimed Dagmar softly.

"Why afraid,?" replied Dieter gently, caressing her shoulders.

"Because of last night. I felt sure something would – that something must happen. Still I feel sure, and still I'm afraid."

"Don't be afraid," said Dieter consoling her.

"It's so good to be near you – to feel the strength and warmth of your body. Now – during these moments, I feel safe," she said tightening her embrace.

Dieter kissed her on the forehead.

"What would happen if they arrested you,?" said Dagmar suddenly.

"I don't know. It's better we don't think about it."

"They would never free you again. – What would you do if the police arrested you?"

"I should stand up truthfully against them and answer their charges."

"Truthfully? Tell them what you think?"

"Yes, everything!"

"That wouldn't be wise. All their charges against you would stick. It would provoke them. They would evoke the extreme penalty – they would have to."

"If I was arrested, I'd never be freed anyway. It wouldn't matter what I said or did."

"But you must fight for our freedom – for yourself – for us."

"I shall, but I'll fight them with the truth."

"That would be self-destructive."

"I'm tired of lying. I've lied enough. The last few years of my life have been nothing but a great lie. All of us in the DDR have lied out of the cowardice of our hearts, and our lies are chains of bondage. Sometimes we must stand up to the truth and fight."

"Even if it means to face death?"

"Yes, even that. Look at my life. Have I not been guilty of lying? The pamphlets I've written, my service in the FDJ, and now the Volksarmee – suddenly it all fills me with disgust."

"But your motives have been those of expediency. In the society of fear and oppression in which we live, it's excusable. There are thousands of others in the same position as you. They've done the same. You're not alone in that."

"I know. We're all guilty. But if I'm arrested, I'll lie no more."

"We're both tired. Maybe tomorrow you'll see these things differently."

"I know, it's late," said Dieter glancing at his watch and stirring from the couch. "It's gone midnight. I must be returning."

"Don't go yet," cried Dagmar clinging onto his body. "Stay till half past the hour. Let me continue to feel the warmth of your body till then."

"All right," relented Dieter and he kissed her forehead again.

"You seem so brave," said Dagmar after a pause, glancing in his eyes.

"Brave? Why?," replied Dieter chuckling.

"Because you don't seem afraid – almost as if you didn't know the meaning of fear."

"I fear nothing – then why should you have reason to fear?"

"Why is it you don't feel fear? You remind me of when I first knew you. Do you remember that hot Summer's day when we were lying on the branks of the Müggel See, and I asked you if you ever feared the authorities? Still, I remember the answer you gave me that day – you said, 'What is fear? – I have never been touched by the feeling of fear.'"

"That was a long time ago," mused Dieter smiling.

"On that day when we first met together in Alexander Platz, and you took me to that café in Friedrich Strasse, I remember you said that free speech was a luxury you'd never deny yourself."

"I remember," replied Dieter thoughtfully, "but since that day, I've broken that promise to myself. I've denied myself free speech for more than a year now – not out of fear but out of caution for our safety and future."

"That's when fear can be useful."

"But not moral fear in the political context – not in the long term. It leads to cowardice. The sensation of fear is an evil no man should feel."

"What do you mean?"

"Men only experience moral fear out of the selfish interests for their own skins. Fear is cowardice. Fear has accomplished nothing in history except defeat. Fear is the basis of tyranny and totalitarianism, without which the latter could never thrive. If you destroy fear, then you destroy tyranny."

"I understand. That's true," said Dagmar.

"Fear is the millstone around the neck of the German people. It's their eternal curse – the one thing which keeps us all in bondage. That's why I refuse to fear – for fear in man is not an inherent instinctive thing, but something taught and cultivated in the mind. Hence man is the one animal on earth with the power within himself to destroy fear. That's why I don't feel fear: because I've conquered it."

"You are brave," said Dagmar softly kissing Dieter's chest.

The couple lay quiet awhile, lying restfully and glancing up at the ceiling above, until Dagmar thought she heard a knock outside.

"What was that,?" she said startled.

"I heard nothing," replied Dieter soothingly.

"There was a knock on the door."

"It was nothing. Just in your own mind."

Then came two knocks – a little louder than before.

"You heard that,?" cried Dagmar in alarm.

"It was someone at the door," said Dieter calmly. "Don't worry. You must go and answer it."

The couple quickly jumped off the couch and began to dress. There was more knocking – louder still.

"You must hurry," said Dieter.

"Who can it be,?" said Dagmar, " – and at this hour."

"A neighbour, I expect. No cause for alarm."

"It's like the knocking at the front door this morning, when I was so afraid."

"But now you are not afraid," said Dieter consoling her.

Having pulled up her stockings and slipped on her dress, which Dieter zipped up at the back; she put on her shoes; hid her undergarments beneath a cushion on the couch, and went out into the passageway to answer the door. Dieter remained sitting on the couch in his underwear, waiting.

Dagmar became deathly pale, shivering with fear, knowing that the knocking was no good omen, and time seemed suspended with the tension of the situation, as if a knife was suddenly dividing one part of her life from another. She knew it was the political police – that the worst had come – and that she could do nothing to avert the inevitable.

She opened the door, seeing two large men in front of her. One was tall and thin; the other was shorter, but thick set. Both wore felt hats and black leather greatcoats, and their hands were thrust into their pockets.

"We've come for Dietrich Liebermann," said the shorter man.

"He doesn't live here," replied Dagmar.

"We'll search the apartment," said the taller man.

Dagmar felt a pressure against her stomach. She looked down to see that a revolver had been pointed at her. She was too frightened even to let out a little cry of horror.

"We've had reliable information from an occupant in the tenement block that Liebermann's in this apartment now," said the shorter man. He spoke with a foreign accent.

"He was seen to enter the block more than an hour ago, and our source of information has assured us he hasn't left yet," said the taller.

They pushed passed her and walked down the passageway towards the sitting room. The light guided them towards their prospective captive. Dagmar closed the door behind her. They were grim strong men with immovable expressionless faces, and an iron will. They spoke quietly with calm self-assurance, and their word was law. They betrayed no feelings, not even the self-important attitude of officiousness, and their every gesture seemed inevitable in its finality.

Dagmar followed them down the passageway. She wanted to cry out to warn Dieter, but she was so terrified that she couldn't utter a sound, and anyway, she knew it would be useless. She wished with all her will that somehow Dieter would miraculously disappear from the apartment, or that he would take the initiative whilst she was out of the room, and leave the apartment by the window and so escape into the West sector where she could join him later. She wished this with all her will, and prayed it to God, that somehow he would have left the room by the time she re-entered it again.

She followed the two men into the room. Dieter was still there. Her heart which had been pounding violently, seemed to stop. Dieter was pulling on his trousers as he sat on the couch. He glanced up at the two men insolently, with an expression of indifference.

"I'm from the Komitet Gossudarstwennoi Besopassnosti," exclaimed the shorter man waving a pass in front of Dieter's face. "Are you Dietrich Liebermann?"

"*Da, da*,!" replied Dieter nodding at the man nonchalantly.

"I'm with my colleague here, from the German State Security Service," continued the man, taking out a packet and lighting a cigarette. He threw the packet onto the little table in front of Dieter, in offering him a cigarette. Dieter nodded in refusal.

"You must get dressed and come with us," said the taller man. "You're under arrest."

"What are the charges,?" said Dieter nonchalantly without glancing at the men as he tied his shoe laces.

"The charges are serious," said the shorter official taking a paper out from his breast pocket. "I can read them to you – they've already been listed in detail."

"I'd only deny them, so why bother,?" said Dieter insolently.

"Unfortunately, that would not help you," said the official. "Your judges already have the evidence they need, and care has been taken to prove your guilt irrefutably. The outcome is a foregone conclusion."

"That's the way it always is," said Dieter ironically.

"How did you know he was here – in this apartment,?" exclaimed Dagmar from behind the two men.

The shorter official half turned towards the girl at this minor annoyance, whilst the other turned quite towards her, replying, "We don't reveal our sources of intelligence, Fräulein, but every block has its own agents, and they keep us informed."

Dagmar collapsed into a chair.

"And our agents have had you under surveillance for a long time now, Liebermann," said the taller official. "You were finally caught in circumstances surprising to us all."

"Just for interest, what are the charges,?" said Dieter.

"Firstly, you're charged with complicity in the murder of Dmitri Semionovitch Korabylaev, alias Wolfgang Fortner, of the KGB," began the shorter official.

"So Fortner was a Russian,!" exclaimed Dieter. "I'd never have guessed it."

"Secondly, you're charged with plotting with Western imperialist agents, to overthrow the regime of the DDR," continued the official.

"I deny that charge and the first one," replied Dieter. "They're both nonsense."

"We have the tape in our possession recording your voice and the voices of others actively engaged in the imperialist conspiracy," said the official glancing up. "We'll have plenty of time to go through the tape together in detail, and discuss at length the entire conversation."

"Is the tape to be used in evidence against me?"

"As the motivational basis for evidence on all charges – including that of complicity to murder," answered the official. "The evidence of the tape is definitive and irrefutable. Thirdly, you're charged as a provocateur, with inciting others to overthrow the regime."

"I deny that."

"Fourthly, you're charged with attempting to sabotage the work of the SSD in your role as an officer in the Volksarmee."

"I deny that."

"Fifthly, with advocating sedition and mutiny against the authorities of the DDR."

"Yes, I gladly admit to that," said Dieter grinning. "At least you have the sense to formulate one charge correctly."

"Dieter, don't say that,!" cried Dagmar alarmed.

"Sixth, you're charged with betraying your oaths of loyalty to the FDJ and the Volksarmee."

"I proudly admit that."

"Please Dieter, don't make it worse for youself," cried Dagmar. "Think of our future."

"Your ready admittance is helpful and will save time in extracting an open confession. As for your pride in treating lightly the oaths of the

Communist Party, you'll soon learn a lesson from that," said the official glancing up. "Then I think you'll sing a different tune. – Seventh, you're charged with committing treason against the People's German Democratic Republic and betraying a Socialist State and the cause of Marxism-Leninism."

"If you prove that charge against me, it'll be my proudest boast," exclaimed Dieter.

"He doesn't know what he's saying," cried Dagmar to the officials. "His mind's confused. You must believe that. He's not himself."

"I've betrayed Germany, and worse still, I've betrayed Europe, through selling myself to the 'System,'" said Dieter as he slipped on his jacket, standing up, fully dressed. "That's the one crime of which I cannot now forgive myself.   All other alleged crimes against me are meaningless."

Dagmar could say no more in preventing her lover and fiancé from sacrificing their future. She sat, stunned, as she watched him speak.

"Eighth, you're charged with conspiracy to desert the Army, and Ninth, with conspiracy to leave the DDR," continued the official.

"Yes, to escape from slavery,!" cried Dieter.

"Now come with us," said the taller official.

"You can do what you want with me. I care no longer for anything you mean. I'm sick of you. I refuse to recognise your authority. You're no longer real. This is a dream existence."

"Leave your speeches for the judges," said the taller official taking Dieter by the arm.

Dieter turned towards Dagmar. She rose from the chair and stepped towards him. Her eyes were filled with tears but he said nothing.

"Have you nothing to say,?" she said tearfully.

"Remember me! Wait for me – you know, Dagmar, I'm yours forever," said Dieter dreamily. "We're promised to one another. I'll return – sometime!"

"Have you nothing more to say? Is there no message,?" said Dagmar.

"Just, that I love you always," replied Dieter. "Be true to me. It's now that I deserve your love."

"Now come with us," said the taller official.

"Where's he going – can I visit him,?" said Dagmar pitifully.

"Impossible! His place of interrogation and confinement is secret," replied the shorter official. "He's a political prisoner, and is besides, an officer in the Army. This is not a civil matter."

"So his trial will not be public even," exclaimed Dagmar.

"Military trials are never public – anywhere," said the same official. "He'll be brought before a court martial. All proceedings and the outcome will be secret. State security dictates that."

"Which means, Fräulein, that you mustn't breathe a word to anyone, either about your fiancé's arrest, or as to your knowledge of his disappearance," said the taller official.

"That means, you'll know nothing whatsoever about the circumstances of his disappearance," said his colleague. "As far as you're concerned, you'll presume he's deserted you – is that clear? If rumours start spreading as to his having been arrested by the SSD, we'll hear of them, and it'll make it worse for him – as well as for yourself."

"We have informers in this building and elsewhere, and we'll put you to the test by using them to extract information. So see that you say nothing to anyone," said the taller official.

"But if you do start blabbering, you'll be arrested and interned," said his colleague. "If you're questioned, just plead ignorance. Keep your mouth shut and you'll be safe."

"All right. Now come with us into the street," said the other official taking Dieter by the shoulder.

"Dieter – what'll happen,?" cried Dagmar desperately, suddenly running towards him as tears rolled down her cheeks.

She threw herself into his arms, and the lovers embraced.

"Dagmar, I ask only one thing of you," exclaimed Dieter kissing her forehead. "Do nothing foolish which would hinder my release. I'll fight for my release, and maybe, one day I'll be free."

"That's a distant hope," said the shorter official. "We've ten more charges against you. I could go on – causing an affray; inciting a riot against and causing bodily injury to members of the People's Police; slandering the State through pictorial misrepresentation, etc., etc."

"We'll remain true to each other for all time,"sobbed Dagmar. "I promise.!"

The two men parted the lovers, and Dieter was led from the room.

Dagmar followed them into the passageway. The front door was opened, and Dieter was led into the hallway of the tenement block. Dagmar ran to the door and stood there, watching Dieter being led between the two men to the end of the hallway. Just as they reached the door leading into the courtyard, he turned his head and glanced towards her.

"Remember me,!" he cried.

Dagmar said nothing in reply. She was too frightened and grief stricken to utter a sound. The men tightened their grip on Dieter's arms and roughly pushed him through the doorway. Dagmar remained motionless, and with an expression of horror and despair, she watched her lover disappear.

Then he was gone. Dagmar grasped her fingers round the framework of the door, lowered her head over her hands, and collapsed onto her knees on the doorstep of the apartment. She broke down sobbing, and as she held her hands over her face, her golden hair parted at the back of her neck and fell across her cheeks, and some large glistening tears dropped from between her delicate fingers onto the lap of her dress.

She knew the worst had transpired – that all was over. She knew he would never return, and yet somehow she held out the hope that one day he would miraculously come back to her.

That night whilst standing on the threshold of her grandmother's apartment was the last occasion when Dagmar set eyes on her fiancé Dietrich Liebermann.

BOOK XVII

Destiny Takes Its Course

For time makes all but true love old;
The burning thoughts that then were told
Run molten still in memory's mould.

Thomas Campbell, *Hallowed Ground*, 1, 19.

September 1960 – August 1961

Chapter 64

We were sitting quietly together on the sofa, and on our laps lay Dagmar's drawer of strange personal belongings she had taken from the cabinet by the window. For some moments we were silent. Carefully, I took the objects out of the drawer. I glanced at the sketches of faces and fashion designs and at the political cartoons – drawings pencilled by Dieter more than two years ago. I came to the envelope containing the bundle of photos, and I glanced at Dagmar with a questioning look for her permission to see them for myself, and she nodded affirmatively. I went through the photos and came to several pictures of Dietrich Leibermann. He was just as Dagmar had described: tall and slim with fine light blond hair smoothly brushed back. He was handsome, and in the pictures with Dagmar, he was fondling her with the tenderest affection. I replaced the photos.

I laid the objects, which I had rested on my arm, onto the coffee table in front of us, and then I removed the other things from the drawer. I came to the second envelope containing the packet of cigarettes. I took out the packet and glanced at it. It was a course cardboard packet, almost yellow with age. There was a crudely printed picture of two Soviet soldiers racing along on a motor bike with side-car. They were helmeted and in battle dress, and the soldier in the side-car held out a machine gun in front of him. The march to the West! Even on cigarette packets, there was the suggestion of glorifying Soviet warfare and aggressive militarism. On the background of the motorbike and side-car, was a large red star: the terrible symbol of the will to world dominion. In black letters in Cyrillic script were written the words, *Krasnaya Zvezda* – Red Star.

This packet was the only remaining material evidence of Dietrich Liebermann's arrest in the apartment at No. 55 that Dagmar still possessed. Dagmar remained quiet and thoughtful, with an anxious expression. I put everything into the drawer again, placing the drawer onto the table beside the coffee things.

"And what did you do after that night he was taken away,?" I said at last.

"I was so frightened and upset, I couldn't sleep, and I had to take some pills, and the following morning I overslept till very late," replied Dagmar. "Still I was frightened, and I daren't tell anyone anything. I thought that perhaps they might come and arrest me. After all, they must have known that I as well as Dieter was guilty of the ninth charge they had made against him, that is, conspiracy to leave the DDR."

"When did you tell your parents?"

"I had to tell them after three days – they knew that something was wrong – I'd entirely lost my appetite – I was so depressed."

"What happened?"

"Mamma was terribly upset, but Papa said not to worry, and that we'd go to the police together and try to find out what had happened. I tried to persuade Papa against that, explaining how the police had threatened me, but he thought nothing of that, saying the police wouldn't arrest me. He said it was only natural I should tell my parents about my fiancé's arrest – the police would allow for that – and that anyway, it was inevitable my parents would come to ask about him."

"And so what did you do?"

"Papa and I went to the police, and we made our enquiry. They said they'd try to find out, and told us to call back in a week. When we called back, they kept us waiting an hour, and then apologised, saying they'd been so overrun by work that they hadn't had time to find out about Dietrich Liebermann. They said, call back in another week. We did that, and they said an enquiry had gone through but no answer had come back. They said, call back in a month. When we called back, they reacted as if surprised at seeing us, and impatiently asked what we wanted. Papa reminded them of our enquiry about Dieter. They replied they know nothing about it, and that they weren't competent to find out either. Papa asked if we might see the officer whom we'd seen a month ago – the officer who said he'd put through an enquiry – but we were told he'd been transferred to another station. Then we asked what police department we should go to, but they were so uncooperative, they would tell us nothing. They just pleaded ignorance and knowing nothing.

"I was so upset, I broke down crying in the station. I was in despair. What could Papa and I do next? In East Berlin there are no telephone or address books, so it makes it difficult when you want to visit a government department or find a special department of the police.

"Eventually, a friend advised Papa that we should visit the Criminal Police Inspectorate, and he gave us the address which was in Dirken Strasse. We were politely received there and given the name of a particular officer whom we'd have to see. However, we were told he was very busy and that callers could only be seen through an appointment. Papa said we'd make an appointment. They fetched his appointment book, and it was very full, and we could only be seen between ten and four which meant I'd have to get time off from work. We made an appointment for three weeks ahead – it was the earliest time we could get – but before we left the Inspectorate, we had to fill in a long questionnaire – it was four foolscap pages. I had to fill in all the particulars about myself, and then about Dieter, and about the circumstances of his arrest, and as to the purpose of my making the enquiry. It was dreadful!

"And so another three weeks passed. When we arrived at the Inspectorate for the second time, we were put into a room and had to wait a long time. We were told that the officer was dealing with a very trying case taking up a lot of time, but at last we got in to see him. He was an elderly man in civilian clothes with thin hair and gold framed spectacles, and he received us very politely, and had a nice gentle reassuring manner. He sat in a large comfortably furnished room. He apologised for drinking coffee in our presence but said he'd had a trying day, and had had no time for lunch. He seemed very modest. We told him our story and he listened patiently without interruption.

"Afterwards, he shook his head and said it was all very sad and that he sympathised with us deeply. He regretted, however, that he'd be unable to help. It wasn't in his department. He explained that his job was only concerned with helping the relatives and families of Economic Criminals. He interviewed those who on grounds of exceptional hardship wished to secure the temporary release from prison of relatives awaiting trial; or those whom on humane grounds were seeking a mitigation on the sentence of relatives for such economic crimes as debt (mostly private trades or commercial people) or those who had failed to fulfil quotas (mostly tradesmen whose businesses had been incorporated into co-operative associations); or those who had been found guilty of more serious crimes, such as the purchasing of forbidden goods from the West sectors of the city.

"We asked him to what department we should go to put our case. He shook his head and said it was difficult – very difficult indeed. He said that purely political cases (and our case was compounded by the fact of its also being a court martial matter) were always difficult. Then after a pause, he advised us, saying that perhaps it would be better if we waited a bit until the police informed us, rather than we inform them. We reminded him we'd already waited over two months and had heard nothing of Dieter's whereabouts. He began hedging and mumbling to himself, and then he tried to console us, saying he thought the police would inform us sometime, but emphasised that they were never in a hurry with that kind of thing.

"He strongly urged us against unnecessarily worrying the police, explaining in a confidential tone that worrying them might irritate rather than soothe things, for the police were sensitive – very sensitive about political matters. We asked him what police department, anyway, we should consult. He seemed momentarily put out by the question, and hummed and ha-ed again, and then began to speak and stopped himself, and then he suddenly brightened, and announced that he thought he'd found the right solution for us. He'd make an enquiry for us through several police departments, and then write to us within four to five days. We thanked him for his kindness and consideration and left."

"And did you hear from him?"

"We waited a fortnight, but we heard nothing."

"What did you do then – go back to the Inspectorate and ask for another interview?"

"No. Another friend of Papa's advised us to go direct to the SSD headquarters in Lichtenburg – after all, it was the SSD who arrested Dieter. We went along there and told them our story, and were immediately shown into the office of a senior official. We told him everything. He said he hadn't heard about the case before, but that it was all very serious. He thought that the trial and outcome would all be carried out in the strictest secrecy as it seemed a matter where the security of the State was concerned. He said that *Leutnant* Liebermann had clearly held a responsible position, and that a case of that seriousness was rare. We asked what would be the probable penalty for the offence he'd committed. The officer hesitated, and then replied that it was impossible to say, but he thought it would be very severe indeed. We asked if arrangements could be made to see Dieter. He assured us we'd come to the right department for that, and that only his office was competent to arrange such a thing, but that he'd have to make enquiries first. He said we must say nothing about this case to anyone, and that if rumours got out, the security of our family would be put at risk. He told us to call back in a month."

"And what happened then?"

"Well, the following week, I received a letter asking me to report to the SSD headquarters. It seemed a pleasant surprise after having anticipated waiting a month. I went alone, as they'd only asked to see me, and I saw the same official as I'd seen before. He said he'd completed an enquiry into the matter, but that for reasons of security he could tell me nothing about the outcome of Dieter's trial or his present whereabouts. He said it would not be possible for me or any of his relatives or friends to see him. He then said he'd be obliged to put me under oath to say nothing about the circumstances of Dieter's arrest; to plead ignorance as to his whereabouts in answer to unauthorised enquiries, and to repeat nothing of what he (the police official) had told me. I was taken to a special room for the oath. It had already been made out in writing. There were two other police officials who acted as witnesses, and it was all carried out very solemnly.

"Then I was taken back to the office from where I had just come. I was told that a criminal charge could be made out against me on the grounds of conspiracy to leave the DDR and for failing to report on the misdemeanours and crimes of Dietrich Liebermann, but that the authorities had decided to take a lenient attitude, on the grounds that Dieter had seduced me into thinking unpatriotic thoughts. They warned me, however, that should I leave the DDR, there would then be no hope for Dieter. My remaining in the East sector of Berlin would continue to be dependent on Dieter's being exempt from the ultimate penalty. I felt puzzled by this threat. They said this condition had been made to ensure that I couldn't go to the West and attempt to work for Dieter's release from the other side of the city – perhaps through some refugee or underground organisation. Lastly, they said I would be kept under surveillance. I asked if Dieter would ever be released. They replied that that question could not be answered. They could only assure me that his welfare could only be safeguarded by my remaining in the East. He then said that that was all, and he rose from behind his desk and clicked his heels, and I left."

"Now I understand so much," I said meditatively. "Your fatalism and vague hopes and an underlying pessimism which seems to have been so great a part of your character. Now I understand the pessimism in your letters I received in London. Now I begin to understand everything. – And did you make any further attempts to contact Dieter after that day when you last visited the SSD headquarters in Lichtenburg?"

"Yes, I went to Werlsee and visited Dieter's parents," said Dagmar. "We'd already exchanged letters, but we'd been unable to inform each other much about Dieter's whereabouts or circumstances."

"And what did they know?"

"They knew nothing more than me, except that they'd been told he'd received a long term of imprisonment for political offences. They'd been told nothing about the exact nature of those offences or the circumstances of his arrest, and neither had they been told the exact term of his imprisonment. We must have been a very sorrowful looking group during that afternoon at Werlsee as we exchanged our little bits of information and hearsay about Dieter's circumstances and whereabouts. Like me, the Libermanns had been put under oath to say nothing about Dieter and they'd also been warned not to leave the DDR."

"How had they got their information about Dieter?"

"They did nothing until Monday night when they then became very worried. When he hadn't returned by Monday morning they thought he'd spent the night with me, and then gone straight to the University, but when he hadn't returned by the evening, they knew for sure that something was very wrong. They thought he'd had a motor accident because he'd taken the car, and that night the Liebermanns went to the local police headquarters. The police phoned the various hospitals and emergency clinics throughout East Berlin, but no one of Dieter's description had been admitted. Then one of the police officials who'd just come into the room, asked them the number of the missing car, and this was given. The police official told them to sit down, whilst he made a telephone enquiry in the next room. He returned in fifteen minutes and gave them a name and address in Lichtenburg where he said they could fetch the car.

"The police official said he could say nothing more, and naturally, the Liebermanns felt surprised and worried. On arriving at the address, they were even more surprised to find it was the headquarters of the SSD. They were immediately led in to see the official whose name they'd been given. They were told that Dieter had been arrested and charged with committing serious political crimes. No more details could then be given. They were told to say nothing to anyone, and to call back in a fortnight. They were given the car keys, and told they could pick up the vehicle which was parked in a nearby street.

"It was a terrible blow for the Liebermanns on hearing what had happened to their only son – especially to Frau Liebermann, but Dr. Liebermann had suspected for some time that something like that might happen. On the following night Irmgard met her uncle and aunt in East Berlin, and told them what had happened at the party the previous night. Irmgard said that every attempt had been made to dissuade Dieter from returning to the East sector, and that she and Max had exactly anticipated what might happen if he did return. The Liebermanns said that Dieter had told them nothing about the events of Saturday night on the following morning when he had been with them for the last time – that was at breakfast before rushing off to attend duties concerned with the election. The next day, the Liebermanns received their first letter from me. Two weeks later, they returned to the SSD headquarters, and were told that Dieter had been given a long prison term. They were then put under the oath of secrecy."

"So you knew Dieter had received a long prison term long before you went to the SSD headquarters yourself, whilst you were still chasing around for his whereabouts from a lot of other police authorities?"

"Yes. I learnt about Dieter's imprisonment some four weeks after his arrest. Naturally, Papa and I couldn't explicitly reveal our knowledge of that information to the police authorities without endangering the security of the Liebermanns. We couldn't break our trust to the Liebermanns. Our only purpose was to find out more for ourselves with a view to visiting Dieter, and then attempting to secure a mitigation of his sentence."

"But if you'd been communicating with the Liebermanns for so long, why didn't you visit the SSD headquarters sooner?"

"The Liebermanns and I only exchanged a few letters before I finally went over to Werlsee, when we told one another everything we knew. Those few letters were kept short and written with caution, against the high probability of their being intercepted by the police. Both the Liebermanns and I knew the chances of our being kept under surveillance. In those few letters we both said nothing about the sources of our information concerning Dieter. In my first letter to the Liebermanns, I only asked them if they knew where Dieter was, suggesting that I thought he was in some kind of trouble with the law. In their letter to me saying he'd received a long prison term they only said that they'd 'heard that.' Both of us were too frightened to write anything more."

"What happened meanwhile in West Berlin? Late that Saturday night during the party, Max said he was going to the police the following day."

"He did. Two weeks after Dieter's arrest, I visited Irmgard's home in the West sector. I told her my side of the story about Dieter's disappearance and she told me about how the Liebermanns had recovered their car and found out about Dieter's arrest."

"Why didn't you visit the Liebermanns at a much earlier date than you did?"

"Why not? Because we'd both been warned by the police not to say anything to anyone about the case, and we were possibly being trailed by the police. Had we visited one another earlier, we might have aroused the suspicions of the police."

"You might have aroused their suspicions had you visited one another at any time."

"Yes, but when I finally visited Werlsee, it was only after careful preparations. Herr Liebermann picked me up in his car in the Wulheide, near Köpenick, and when I entered and left the Zonal frontier, I was hidden under a blanket on the floor beneath the back seat of the car. Not a soul saw me arrive or leave the Liebermanns' house in Werlsee. Everything was done in the closest secrecy."

"I see. You were going to tell me about what happened when Max visited the West Berlin police."

"Yes. On the Sunday following the party, Max met Klaus and they went to the police and told them their story. Later, they all went to Fortner's, or rather Korabylaev's apartment, and were surprised to find it already cleared of all his possessions. The landlady explained that three men had come early that morning (at six o'clock) saying that Fortner had had a traffic accident during the night, and that at present he was in the German Red Cross hospital in Drontheimer Strasse. The men said they'd come for some of his belongings which he'd asked for. The landlady showed them his room, then returned to bed. She said she was annoyed at having been awoken so early. Later that morning, however, she found that the men had cleared everything of Fortner's out of the apartment. She phoned the hospital to find out how he was – and of course, to ascertain whether he'd permanently vacated the flat, for in that event she wanted a month's rent in lieu of notice. Of course the hospital knew nothing, and then she phoned several other hospitals without result, before becoming suspicious and then angry. She decided to contact the police to trace his whereabouts, so she could sue for non-payment of advance rent, and just then, Max and Klaus and the police arrived to investigate."

"Was anything else found out about Korabylaev?"

"No, nothing more to compromise him as an informer. It was concluded he'd been employed as a spy by the KGB, where he'd been masquerading in West Berlin as a West German student at the Technical University. They discovered he'd been carrying a complete set of forged documents to prove his citizenship and origins."

"A pretty clever set-up then."

"It's terrible to think that such dangerous people can exist in the West," said Dagmar.

"When the police arrested Dieter, they said they'd employ their informers in trying to extract information out of you about Dieter's disappearance. Did this in fact happen?"

"I don't know – I don't think so. I think they said it to frighten me. Of course one doesn't really know – unless Frau Hartmann was their informer. She came out with the odd remark from time to time."

"When they came to arrest Dieter, they said they'd had reliable information from an occupant in the tenement block, that he was in your apartment. Do you know who that occupant could have been?"

"Of course it was Frau Hartmann," replied Dagmar emphatically.

"What makes you so very sure of that,?" I asked.

"Just a casual remark she made lesss than a week after Dieter's arrest. I met her one evening in the courtyard after returning from work, and she curtsied to me with a '*Guten Abend*,' saying that someone had told her that Dieter was in trouble with the police."

"It seems to put suspicion on her."

"Suspicion? It's proof! How else could she have known that?"

"What did you say to Frau Hartmann when you met her then?"

"I could have killed her. I just walked on and said nothing. But from that moment, I had proof it was her who betrayed Dieter."

"How many people found out from you about the circumstances of Dieter's arrest?"

"Just the family and two friends of Papa's, and of course, my best friend, Renata."

"It's all terrible – terrible,!" I said. "To think that such things can really happen!"

We sat silently thoughtful awhile. I thought over the story that Dagmar had told me, and for a time, my mind was in a whirl of conflicting emotions. Why had she told me the story? I had forced it from her, or rather, our relationship had reached a point when she could no longer continue to hide the truth about herself. Why had her parents felt even more strongly about the necessity of her hiding the truth from me? Why had Dagmar delayed telling me the story for so long? Was it that after a period of almost two years she still feared the SSD in case the story might somehow come into the open? I thought it was not this. Before revealing the secrets hidden in her breast, what had she meant earlier that morning, when begging for a greater understanding and consideration than before? What had she meant when asking me not to form prejudices as to the likely outcome of our friendship until she had finished her story? She was clearly anticipating the possibility of my reassessing our relationship.

I thought over her friendship with Dieter, and of the great part he had played in her life. He had been her first love; she had found maturity through him; she had shed her virginity and became sexually experienced through him; she had been (and in all probability still was) his fiancée, and for many months, all her ideals and hopes for a future life in the free world had been planned with him. Then I thought, I should ask myself the question not what had been her relationship with him in the past, but rather, what were her likely feelings for him in the present and the future. Perhaps in fact, he had been shot or hanged by the authorities. There was no knowing, but this was very probably so, considering the extreme seriousness of the charges brought against him, but certainly it was not for me to suggest such a likelihood to Dagmar.

Even if he had been executed by the authorities and even if she came to know of this, I saw the prospect of this as no consolation in solving the emotional relationship between Dagmar and me. In her heart, she would always be his. Because of the bitterly unhappy circumstances in which her lover – her first love, had disappeared, the possibility remained (especially in view of her extreme sensitivity) that she'd forever be afflicted with a longing for his return. Inwardly, she might always pray for this – hanker for the past – for none could replace him. Her love for Dieter had become an eternal part of her being, and possibly the shattering experience of Dieter's disappearance had already unbalanced her personality. Our relationship from the beginning had never been smooth. There had always been enigmas in communication between us, suggesting a disturbed soul, and perhaps our relationship had even been doomed to failure from the beginning because of this.

Chapter 65

Then I pondered on the possibility of Dietrich Liebermann still being alive. It was a probability that could not be discounted, especially in view of the threat which had been held over the fair one. If he should return, he could still have a claim over her on moral grounds – even if the affair between Dagmar and I had materialised into marriage. There was the possibility that he might be released from a concentration camp and given his freedom within the next ten to fifteen years. If that indeed occurred, and he sought and found her, and if meanwhile the affair between Dagmar and I had progressed into marriage, I felt that the weight of moral obligation would necessitate my surrendering the fair one to him, and perhaps also, any children which had resulted from the union.

In the final resort, a spiritual union and unspoken promises between a first and ideal love must be given a higher moral priority over the material outcome of a later physical union with another partner. The mere legal bases of the latter, howsoever entrenched in religious decrees, when confronted by the demands of a first and greater love, must be swept aside in the name of a greater truth and humanity. Even the children of a recognised union become the issue of a usurpation when a woman is claimed by and accepts the reappearance of her first love from the mists of lost time.

The bonds of mere legal formalities cannot have a higher demand than those of real love and the truth of our own hearts – for those are eternal now and forever after – so having a greater moral priority than the more pedantic obligations of the earthly world. Furthermore, I felt that any obligation towards Dietrich Liebermann in the event of his unexpected return, stemmed not merely from the promise made between the two lovers, but because of the circumstances in which he had been arrested and taken away. I pitied him for the circumstances of his conviction, and for his courage during those moments of greatest stress, that is, during his arrest.

He was no mere ordinary felon. He had to be seen in the light of a political martyr who had sacrificed himself for the cause of freedom. He could have spared himself from martyrdom by heeding the persuasion of Max and his cousin Irmgard by remaining in West Berlin, but he had chosen to return to the East even though he must have known (despite his half-hearted suggestions to the contrary during that fateful Saturday night) that this would result in certain death or long imprisonment. During his arrest, he had admitted the charges and openly defied the great "cause." He had acted with bravado in such a way as to diminish the possibility of leniency at the hands of his accusers. Who in those circumstances, therefore, could claim to be worthy enough to take his place in claiming the hand of the fair one? Only he who could claim an equal measure of heroism and courage – and I did not think I could aspire to such exceptional qualities of nobility. Least of all was I prepared to diminish my sense of moral worth by playing the cuckoo, or being perceived as the scavenger of a wronged-man's rightful possession.

On being led away by the police, he had extracted a promise from Dagmar to await his return and to live only for that day. That promise must have sunk permanently into her heart, and somehow, I felt she still honoured that promise deep inside herself, even if she was to be self-condemned to an eternal "widowhood." Such a widowhood would have been her moral choice – the perseverance of an ideal – and only an evil suitor would have attempted to persuade her otherwise. If Dieter returned tomorrow, she would return to him without a murmur or twinge of doubt. She would be morally obliged to return to him, and I could not question her choice in so doing. I now felt that the emotional conflict and all the enigmas surrounding her behaviour were explained by this.

Dieter was her lover and fiancé now and forever. It was her duty to love him and serve him – even if it was only his memory. Dagmar was a Prussian – reputedly amongst the most self-denying and dutiful of peoples – and she had the virtues of a Prussian deeply ingrained within her soul: of loyalty, perseverance and modesty. Now that I knew the truth behind the secrets she had been hiding, I felt no compunction in refraining from attempting to move her indomitable will, or to change the true allegiance of her virtuous heart. I would only have betrayed her - as well as myself – in pursuing the courtship.

I was profoundly moved by her story, but I knew the direction that her life would have to take, and it would be a life of reluctant self-denial, and perhaps of suffering. Her life would be devoted to one cause: to the hope for Dieter's return. She would be doomed to wait, patiently, like Tennysons's *Marianne* of the moated grange, and perhaps she would wait a lifetime for his return, and perhaps he would never return, but still her loyalty and love would persevere in the single object of her heart's desire.

Perhaps, meanwhile, she might enjoy reluctantly contact with other men – perhaps even bear them children, but these other men would only have a secondary place in her heart as she still dreamed for Dieter's return. There is more truth and intensity in love unfulfilled than can ever be realised in its final consummation. The purest love lies in the heart alone, unsullied by the limitations of physical contact. True love can only really be experienced through the concept of the Platonic *Form* and never through the imperfections of its *Actuality*. This is because the reality of a thing in terms of *quality* can only be assessed through the original idea of its ideal *form*, to which all pale imitations of the real must somehow strive to conform, unspoilt by the corrupting or commonplace influence of everyday life. We all know this but few live by it, and yet in this was to be seen the potential for Dagmar's future. It was not for me to turn her from such a path.

Perhaps deep down in her subsconscious she wished to break off the friendship we had had. Perhaps my ending the affair would put an end to her internal conflict, and perhaps my ending it would be the kindest course. I loved her dearly, and I could not doubt that her affection for me had been anything less than *love apparent*, but I also realised that her love for Dieter was a profounder spiritual experience, whilst the depth of her love for me was masked by the bonds of mere physical attraction. I had not been the inspirer of all her ideas on art, literature and politics, and no amount of sex could hope to compensate for these spiritual and more substantial things she had received from Dieter. Doubtless a deeper spiritual relationship could grow between Dagmar and I, and our love had formed a basis for that, but through Dieter, she had found the maturity of her youth. Because of this, Dieter would forever be ineradicable from her mind.

Because of Dagmar's apparent state of mind, and because I felt a sense of obligation towards her fiancé, Dietrich Liebermann, irrespective of the fact of his being alive or dead, I decided, with a heavy heart, as we sat there quietly on the couch, to terminate the relationship. Perhaps it was because she had anticipated such a state of mind that she had been reluctant to tell me her story earlier. If this was so, then I secretly blamed her for the guile in motivating her course of action.

We had been sitting silently for some minutes, and many conflicting thoughts had passed through my mind before I finally reached this resolution. I returned to Dagmar, saying, "Perhaps one day he'll return to you," and as I spoke I realised a faltering in my voice which betrayed my thoughts, and a lame attempt to evade resolving the issue existing between us.

Dagmar looked at me with surprise.

"What do you mean,?" she replied.

"Exactly what I've said. Perhaps he'll return. What would happen then?"

"It's been nearly two years since he's gone."

"Two years isn't long in a life-span," I said. "He may return in five years – or in ten – but he may still return."

"What are you thinking then,?" said Dagmar trembling.

I felt momentarily awkward. She's reading all my thoughts, I reflected. My voice betrays everything.

"I don't know what I'm thinking," I replied unconvincingly, and Dagmar glanced at me accusingly.

"What do you think I should do,?" she said slowly, her voice trembling again.

Again, I was taken aback by the question. Again, my mind was racked by conflicting thoughts. Did she really love me after all – perhaps, with a passionate spiritual love? Had she perhaps told me the story so that I could make a heroic conquest of her and so tear her away from the past forever? Her tone of voice touched me with a pang of guilt.

"It's not for me to tell you what you should do," I answered. "I don't know what you should do. You must decide for yourself."

It was the logical answer to her question, and yet I was touched by guilt at my own logic, for it was such a conveniently evasive answer.

"How long should I be expected to wait,?" she asked.

"That's impossible to say – as long as you yourself want to wait," I said. She looked thoughtful, confused and upset. "How do you feel about this,?" I said at last to relieve her apparent quandary.

"I don't know," she replied.

"How do you feel towards Dieter today?"

"I don't know."

"Do you love him?"

"I don't know," she replied, her voice trembling, her face betraying perplexity and mental pain.

"Then how can I help you if you don't know your own mind,?" I said. "What can I say or do?"

"I suppose I've said too much about myself," she said in an undertone, her voice choking.

"Not at all. I admire you for your candour," I said.

Now it was my turn to read her thoughts. It seemed as if she had told me the story so that I could snatch her away forever from the past, so that she might move and live in a new world. She had made her confession so I should be free to conquer her whilst knowing the truth, so that a true spiritual love might freely grow and flourish between us, unhindered by the horrors of the past.

But despite this, I still somehow felt I couldn't go back on the impetuous resolution I had made. Why? I tried to answer this question some months later, when again my mind was thrust back to Dagmar by a major political event which shook the world, but I never found a final all-satisfying resolution to the issue. Perhaps it was due to the fact that the story which Dagmar had told me, combined with the strain and stress of our friendship during the preceding weeks, had put me on my guard against coming to any final arrangements with the fair one, or perhaps it was due to the fact I had become tired by the ups and downs of her temperamental nature.

"I'm glad you've told me the truth," I added.

"Is that all you can say,?" she said looking into my eyes.

"I should like to say more – but what can I say,?" I replied stupidly, trying to avoid her gaze.

"Do you truthfully think that Dieter will return?"

"I don't know," I said.

"What then, do you think I should do,?" she said hesitantly, her voice trembling.

"I think you should wait for Dieter," I replied suddenly. "He's your first love, and you love him still, and he loves you. There's no love like first love – and you're both promised to each other."

At once – too late – I felt the cruelty of my words – the cruelty of finality – a ruthless practical logic evading a deeper truth in overthrowing the sphere of feeling and affection. Then I added, as if to give some moral justification to what I had said: "What would happen if he returned, and found you had broken your promise to him? Wouldn't the affair between us both then come to an end? Wouldn't you feel obliged to return to him?"

Somehow, I felt relieved after expressing these deceitful sentiments.

"I suppose you're right," she said. Then she swallowed a lump in her throat, saying, "then I suppose it's not entirely over between Dieter and me."

"I suppose it's not," I said, "not until you receive definite confirmation as to whether he's alive or dead."

"I've tried to get confirmation during the past two years, but I can't."

"Then you must keep trying."

"Supposing they never let me know one way or the other?"

"It makes it very difficult. I can't say what you should do."

"Then suppose I find out he's alive?"

"Then you must wait for him."

"But perhaps they'll keep him in prison for life."

"If he's alive, the likelihood is that he'll be released sometime. Everyone gets their freedom in due course. Of course, it may be a long wait."

"Like twenty or twenty-five years."

"It could be,"

"Should I wait that long?"

"If you feel it's your duty, then you should. After all, it's not only your feelings – it's his as well."

"And what if I get confirmation he's dead?"

"Then you're free," I said, and then correcting myself, " – I mean, we're free."

"It's difficult for me, isn't it?"

"It is," I said.

"And in the meantime, what about us,?" she said, and she glanced up at me with that same significant expression as she had done a year ago, just as I was about to make a dignified departure from the Art Shop in Stalin Allee. Again I was struck by the significance of her glance, but this time I felt there was no going back.

For some moments I was unable to reply. Then I said: "We must leave things as they are."

I caught her glance and suddenly I was shocked. Her eyes were tear-filled.

"You promised you'd be reasonable if I told you the story," she said.

I could no longer bear the sight of seeing her so emotionally perturbed. I wanted to make an instant departure. I rose from the sofa.

"I'll write to you from the West," I said.

"Is it all over between us,?" she said.

"We'll write," I said evading a direct answer to her question. "If and when you find your obligations to Dieter no longer standing, then you can come to the West."

Immediately I had spoken, I was hurt by the callousness of my own words, but I had spoken without reflection.

"You know that's not possible," she said. "I mean, such an arrangement."

She began to rise from the sofa, but I took her shoulders and pushed her down onto the seat again. I could no longer take another gesture similar to that when she had welcomed me into the sitting room earlier that morning. I could no longer have her kiss or embrace me. My mind was made up, and I could no longer allow her women's wiles to alter my will.

"I'll write to you," I repeated. "Please don't try to stop me." Her head was buried in her hands. She said nothing. "I'm sorry about everything," I added.

I went over to the door, and as I opened it, I saw Papa Renot diffidently retreating from me down the passageway. I had clearly caught him spying, with his ear to the door. I felt suddenly alarmed and angry.

"What's happened,?" he said as if to relieve my sense of surprise.

"I'll be writing to you all, to thank you for everything, as soon as I'm back in Münster," I replied as I made towards the coat stand.

"Come into the kitchen a moment," he murmured awkwardly indicating with his hand.

I obeyed his instruction, and found the good Frau there, standing over the sink by some soap suds and washing. She glanced at me with an expression of concern, and Papa Renot made a significant nod to his wife, and closed the kitchen door behind him. He wore a thoughtful intensely worried expression. I felt hemmed in by the atmosphere of the room, and all exits of escape were barred. Even the window was closed. I wondered what ordeal I should now have to undergo. I wondered what new conspiracy was at hand.

"I heard most of what was said at the end," admitted the old man awkwardly and glancing at the floor.

"I thought you might have done," I replied just as awkwardly.

"Of course, he won't return," he said.

"I suppose he won't," I answered.

"He would have been shot within two weeks of his arrest – for a certainty. The charges were so serious. But you couldn't tell Dagmar that."

The good Frau shook the soap suds from her hands and sat down on a chair nearby.

"He was such a stupid young man, really," she said.

"He made his own fate himself. He could have saved himself, but he didn't," said the old man.

"And he should have acted differently," said Frau Renot. "He should have taken Max's advice and stayed in the West sector. He should have done that for Dagmar's sake, instead of making a martyr of himself. It was all so foolish and in vain!"

"These things are often difficult to think of at the time," I only replied.

"It was his own fault," said the old man.

"What'll happen now? Will you take Dagmar,?" said Frau Renot brightly, her eyes lighting up with an expression of hope.

I was taken aback by the good Frau's question. Instinctively, I was put on my guard. The parents had done so much in attempting to force the issue between Dagmar and me, that I had become constantly wary of everything they said or did. They had made me impervious to persuasion, and by now I felt they were powerless.

"I think these things depend on feeling," I replied.

"What do you mean,?" replied Frau Renot suspiciously. "Don't you want to take her?"

"Of course," I said. "But the matter concerns Dagmar, not me."

"I don't understand," said Frau Renot in a tone of mounting concern. "She's yours to take. You're the man – you can persuade her – you can force her will. She'll go with you."

I felt trapped. For reasons of courtesy I had begun by using evasion and I would have to continue along that path. It was no longer possible to speak the truth as man to man or man to woman. Had Herr Renot sensibly taken me aside and truthfully stated his anxiety concerning my state of mind, we might have got somewhere, but he never did this. Instead, he had chosen to take me into the kitchen and attempt to press-gang me with the aid of his wife.

"I don't think that's the crux of the matter," I replied to Frau Renot. "It rather depends on Dagmar's present attitude and feelings towards Dieter."

"But Dieter's dead,!" cried Frau Renot emphatically.

"There's no proof of that. Nothing's been confirmed."

"He'll never come back," said the old man shaking his head.

"But she's made a promise to him, and inside herself, I think she still feels the obligation of that promise," I replied.

"Please take her," said Frau Renot pleadingly.

"I cannot do what I believe might be contrary to her inclinations," I responded.

"As my wife said, she'll go with you if you ask her," said the old man.

"Perhaps, but perhaps also I'd be wrenching her away from the real obligations she feels within herself."

"But if you took her away, her feelings would soon be with you. Love accomplishes anything,!" exclaimed the old man.

"O course," I replied abruptly.

"Have you asked her the vital question,?" said the good Frau.

I hesitated.

"The ring,!" exclaimed the old man slapping his hand down onto his fist.

I felt intensely awkward and was momentarily thrown into a quandary by the question.

"No," I only replied.

"Why haven't you done that,?" exclaimed the good Frau resentfully.

I blushed – more with anger than embarrassment, for the bluntness of the question struck me as being of unparalleled insolence.

"I don't know," I said. "An engagement is a vastly complex matter."

"What do you mean,?" said the old man. "It's just a matter of love."

"And other things," I said. "It's not as simple as that. All kinds of criteria have to be satisfied in the complex society we live in – such as friends and relatives. For example, one has to have the agreement of one's own parents to avoid offence. And most of all, there's the question of money."

"Wouldn't you be in a position to borrow some,?" said the good Frau. "You come from the West. You must be very rich."

"I really don't think this discussion is getting us anywhere," I said trembling with anger. "I thank you for everything, and shall write to you as soon as I've returned to Münster."

"Oh! I'm sorry! What have I said,?" exclaimed the good Frau in sudden alarm and raising her hands to her cheeks.

I turned away from her. I felt too embarrassed to wait for her apologies.

"Cheer up Mamma – don't be so upset," exclaimed the old man consolingly, and he walked across the room and patted her on the shoulder, and the next moment, I noticed the good Frau was in tears. This was more than I could endure.

"Come, we'll all go into the sitting room and talk it over," said the old man.

A few moments earlier, I might have turned down such a suggestion and made my departure, but I felt so sorrowful at the emotional upsets for which I was plainly responsible, that I felt obliged to follow the good couple out of the kitchen, along the passageway, and into the sitting room at the end.

We found Dagmar still seated on the sofa, pale and depressed, as when I had left her.

"Dagmar, you want to go with Herr Furner, don't you,?" said the old man coming directly to the point.

Again, I felt acutely embarrassed, and began to anticipate the blunders which the old man in his reckless stupidity was about to make.

Dagmar glanced up at her father with an expression of surprise.

"You want Herr Furner to take you with him, don't you,?" he repeated.

I stood half behind the good Frau and tried to look inconspicuous. I didn't want it to appear to Dagmar as if I was in any way responsible for the plotting and carrying out of these absurd antics.

"Take me where,?" asked Dagmar in surprise.

I was struck by the pertinacity of her question. How would he answer that one now?

"To the West," said the old man.

"He's never asked me," replied Dagmar.

"But if he did ask you?"

"If he did ask me? What sort of supposition is that, Papa,?" exclaimed Dagmar in justified exasperation. "What if the man in the moon asked me to go with him?"

"But you don't know the man in the moon, whilst you do know Herr Furner," answered the good Frau as if impressed by her piece of sophistry.

Dagmar glanced at her parents resentfully.

"What do you want me to say,?" she said.

"It's for you to answer," replied her mother.

"Am I to dictate to Herr Furner what he should do,?" exclaimed Dagmar.

"Listen, listen,!" said the old man consolingly and going over to his daughter and patting her on the shoulder. "Herr Furner's suggested he thinks you're still in love with Dieter. That's the only reason he hasn't asked you."

"I've never said anything of the sort," I said angrily to the old man – angry at the presumption of his having pretended to read my thoughts, and then using them as a pretext to force the issue between Dagmar and me.

The old man ignored me. He continued to blunder – stubbornly maintaining the same line of argument.

"Now, Dagmar, tell us that Dieter's no longer in your thoughts – that he's forgotten – in the past," he said.

"I don't think Dagmar's in a position to say that," I said, shocked at the old man's attempt to bully his daughter in front of me.

"It's for the best. She'll answer, she'll answer," said the old man in an undertone, nodding towards me.

"I can't say – it's impossible,!" cried Dagmar. "Why are you both trying to force something between us like this?"

"We're not trying to force anything," replied her mother. "We're only concerned for your own future. We only want to know why Herr Furner's not asked you to marry him."

"Then you should ask *him*, not me."

"We have, and we know it's about Dieter, and we want to help you both," said the good Frau.

By now the conversation had become absurd, and I was filled with exasperation. I wanted only to make my excuses and take my leave.

"I think it's better if we just leave everything as it is," I said. "None of us wants to force the issue. Dagmar and I shall write to one another, and I'm sure everything'll work out all right in the end."

"Don't you want to take her,?" cried her mother resentfully at me.

Momentarily I said nothing.

"Don't speak like that Mamma," said the old man going over to his wife, consoling her again. "Herr Furner's right – they'll write to one another, and everything'll smooth out in the end. We mustn't force anything."

At last the old man was beginning to see the light and come to his senses.

"But they should come to some agreement now between one another," cried his wife.

"Not necessarily, Mamma, not necessarily," returned her husband consolingly.

"I really don't think there's anything more to be said," I interrupted at last. "I think it's time for me to take my leave. Dagmar's tired and depressed – it's been a great strain on her having to tell me everything about her past. I think she only wants to rest awhile."

"Won't you stay by her for the rest of the day,?" exclaimed her mother.

"I don't think any good would come of it. We'd only get on one another's nerves," I replied.

"You two get on one another's nerves? How would that be possible,?" exclaimed the good Frau in vexed surprise.

"Besides, I have several friends to call on in the West sectors of the city," I said.

"Won't you even stay with the family,?" exclaimed the good Frau quite upset.

"Don't stop him, Mamma – he knows best," said Papa Renot consoling his wife who was in tears again.

"I've got a lot of packing to do and other arrangements for my return to West Germany tomorrow morning," I said. "I haven't booked my train seat yet. Tomorrow morning, I'll call early, at eight o'clock, and say goodbye to you all then, if that'll be all right."

"You'll breakfast here, won't you,?" said the good Frau insistently but still upset. "You'll be here by seven thirty, yes?"

"Yes, I'll breakfast here, I promise you, Frau Renot," I replied. "You've all been so good to me. I don't quite know how to thank you – but I'll do it tomorrow," I said awkwardly glancing round at each of them in turn.

"And come and eat with us tonight if you can," said Frau Renot. "We'd all enjoy that so much if you could."

"I'll try," I said.

"And think about Dagmar – she's such a precious girl – and try to come to some arrangement with her when you call tomorrow morning," pleaded the good Frau.

"She won't be far from my thoughts," I replied. "Well, goodbye, and until tomorrow morning."

I shook hands with them all, and then the old man led me down the passageway to the front door at the end. I bowed my head towards the floor, treading lightly as I followed him, feeling awkward and a little guilty. Perhaps I'd been impolite – I'd certainly offended them, on so insistently making my departure, but I felt I couldn't bear to remain in the house a moment longer whilst being the constant victim of hints, persuasion, and a mild form of bullying.

I took down my coat from the stand, folding it over my arm, and as the old man opened the door, I shook his hand once more.

"Bring Dagmar something tomorrow," said the old man confidentially, slapping his hand down onto his wedding ring. "You'd be surprised how it could solve everything. All difficulties disappear,!" he added throwing his arms into the air.

"I'll turn it over in my mind," I replied to console him, and then I left the apartment.

Some seconds later, I was briskly walking down Graetz Strasse towards Kreuzberg and the West sector – a free man!

Chapter 66

The train moved slowly along the platform, beneath the high arched green and glass roof of the station, and into the open. I glanced at the two other lone occupants of the compartment, a man reading a Danish business magazine, who sat in the middle of the seat on my left, and another, who sat in the far corner, reading the latest issue of *Newsweek*. It seemed as if none of us felt any inclination to speak to another, and certainly, my mood was one of depressed pondering and cool reserve. The long train was almost empty as it left the Zoo station.

I turned from the two passengers, and glanced outside, resting my chin in the palm of my hand as I leaned forward, with my elbow on the little collapsible table in front of the window. Outside, the scene was dreary: grey roof-tops and an overclouded sky. I was making my final departure from Berlin, and at the time, my feelings were not those of regret.

The past twenty-four hours had been hectic. I had been rushing around West Berlin visiting old friends; I had offended those to whom I owed most, and through absentmindedness or just thoughtlessness or both, had bungled my final plans before leaving the city. There was no excuse for those things I had left undone, and I didn't attempt to make excuses, but the feeling of concern plus overmuch mental strain concerning these things, had been exhausting. I had passed through the stages of exasperation which in turn had given way to desperation which in turn had given way to ennui, which I was just now experiencing.

During the past twenty-four hours I had been handsomely entertained by my good West Berliner friends, but their hospitality, instead of contributing to my feeling of well-being, had finally ended by filling me with nausea, boredom and a sense of guilt. I had betrayed my good hosts the Renots. Finally, as I glanced out of the window of the train onto the gloomy scene outside, I was overcome with a feeling of physical fatigue and sleepiness. I had been drinking and dancing until the early hours, and had had only three and a half hours sleep.

On returning from Graetz Strasse to the West sector the previous morning, I went to the Pension and packed in readiness for the next day, gone to the Zoo station to confirm the train times, changed back my remaining East currency for West marks, and then phoned Fritz Krela. I learnt he was no longer living with his parents in their villa in Schlachtensee. He was married and had an apartment in Schmargendorf. His mother advised me to call at his office in Kant Strasse not far from the Zoo station.

I went there immediately, and met Fritz whom I had not seen for a year, since we had last parted in Breitenbach Platz outside the Eierschale night club. He was surprised at seeing me and greeted me warmly. I told him I'd been in Berlin for several weeks, and regretted my having been unable to call on him before, and that I'd be leaving the city early the next morning. He insisted on my visiting him and his wife in their new flat that evening for a little celebration. We'd eat and then go to a night club in the town centre to drink and dance, and meanwhile, he'd phone his wife to ask her to arrange a partner for me. He told me to be there by seven.

He picked up a bundle of papers on his desk and threw them down again, complaining of overwork, saying he was in the office for ten hours a day, eighty-thirty to six-thirty. I laughed, saying he was anyway working two hours less a day than last year, and that if he kept up that reduction of hours for the next few years, he might even find himself working a mere eight hour day. I thanked him again for the invitation and hurriedly left, as I could see he was pressed by a load of work.

It was already midday, and I decided to lunch in the Free University canteen in Dahlem, in the possibility of encountering any of Martin's friends or acquaintances whom I had known from the previous year. I went there and ate lunch and smoked awhile, and after I'd sat less than an hour, I espied someone whom I recognised. It was one of the students whom I had met at the dance in the Grunewald, on the eve of my first taking out Dagmar to the Kurfürstendamm. He was a student of political science who had buttonholed me and become so insistent on discussing the technicalities of British parliamentary government, and I rose from the table and made myself known to him.

He seemed overjoyed at seeing me, asking me to join him. He laid down his lunch tray at a free table and we sat together, and soon we were discussing the recent political situation of Berlin. "The security of Berlin, as of Europe and the free world, lies in the demonstration of strength of the allies," he said. I assented to what my friend said, but my thoughts were elsewhere. He said that after lunch, he was returning home, and invited me to spend the afternoon with him, and I replied I should be pleased to do so. We returned to his house, which was a large villa in Dahlem surrounded by a high red brick wall, within walking distance of the University. There was a large attractively laid out garden around the villa, and he showed me a small botanical exhibition of tropical plants kept in a heated conservatory, before we entered the villa. I learnt that his father was a businessman as well as a Senator in the Berlin government. On entering the house, he led me into the drawing room, richly furnished with tropical plants and cacti, and large French windows, overlooking the back of the garden.

He bad me sit down on a sofa, offering a cigar. The surroundings were affluent, and a pleasant contrast from those to which I had become accustomed during the past few weeks. I was relaxed and satisfied as I lit up the cigar and leaned back on the sofa. My friend asked if I liked Wagner, and he put a new record on the radiogram of Kirsten Flagstad singing the *Wesendonck* lieder. He sat down, and we continued our political discussion. Later, we were joined by his mother and small sister who called us into tea. I was embarrassed at not having brought flowers, but my friend explained how we had unexpectedly met at the University before he had brought me straight to the house.

We sat down to tea in the dining room. The tea was rich and appetizing: egg and shrimp open sandwiches, a variety of fish dishes and a choice of bread, cakes of several kinds, and a plum tart which had been baked by the Senator's wife. Such food was indeed a treat after the modest fare I had become used to during the past few weeks in Treptow. We talked about London and British politics, and the little girl all the while laughed, glancing across the table at the curious foreigner sitting at the other side, and she asked if I would speak some English since she was learning it at school. Afterwards, we returned to the sitting room, and I was offered another cigar and a glass of wine, and my friend and I continued our more serious discussion which had been interrupted by the entry of his mother. At six I regretted having to take my leave – regretfully since I deprived myself from the opportunity of meeting the Senator, who had not yet returned from the government offices in Schöneberg.

Before going to Fritz's, I bought a large box of fine cigars and an attractive potted plant, as gifts for the good Frau and Papa Renot – Dagmar having already received a birthday present.

On arriving at the address I had been given in Schmargendorf, I was welcomed by Fritz Krela and his charming wife, Anne, to whom I presented a small bouquet. I was shown into the newly furnished flat, and Fritz and I sat down over a glass of wine and talked and joked awhile, whilst his wife busied herself in the kitchen. By way of apologising for not having called on him earlier, I was obliged to tell him about my affair in the East sector. I would like to have discussed the relationship with him in greater depth and to have asked his advice, but I sensed he was listless to the story and dismissive of its significance. He joked and talked lightly about the affair, being clearly under the false impression that I regarded it merely as an "amusing flirtation." I was despondent at his attitude, but only grinned, and took down the rest of my wine – for there was no sense in expecting from him a sounder understanding of the total situation.

After all, I pondered, after some minutes had passed, I couldn't blame him for his attitude towards my affair with Dagmar. What was I, a man from the West, doing in the East sector, anyway? What serious interest was an Englishman with my background likely to have in an East German shop assistant? What sort of people lived in Treptow – were they anyway worth such serious attention as to justify a long-term relationship? Certainly they were a far cry from those who lived in such well-to-do suburbs as Dahlem or Grunewald.

Fritz, therefore, naturally thought there was nothing objectionable in his joking about my relationship with Dagmar, or in his congratulating me on "an easy conquest," and at the same time exploiting the hospitality and full board of the girl's parents into the bargain. He thought the latter especially funny, and laughing loudly, he punched me in the chest, calling me a "young devil!"

I tried to explain that Dagmar was an educated well-mannered girl, who socially, seemed different from her parents, but Fritz interrupted, knocking me in the chest again, saying that "those girls in the East" would accept any favours, if someone from the West made it worth their while. "They've got nothing to lose," he cried. "And what did you eat,?" he asked. "Potatoes, I bet. They've got so many potatoes in the East, they don't know how to get rid of them." After some more personal remarks on the physical side of our relationship, he thoughtfully puffed at his cigar and then burst into laughter.

"You English, you have no heart. You're so cold-blooded and calculating. You know which side your bread is buttered on. – Don't get me wrong," he hastened to add, holding out his hands, as if startled by my reaction, "I admire you for it. Your attitude to life is so commercial and serpentine in all your relationships. 'Perfidious Albion,' they call you. We Germans are so silly and sentimental – so soft and simple – all emotion. We're so easy to understand – we can be manipulated like automatons once you know our character. But you English are complex – unfathomable. One can never learn to read your thoughts. I should like to be like you English – without feelings and sentiment. Life becomes much simpler. You can face the world better."

He paused, puffing thoughtfully on his cigar, and I sat stunned by his candour. Did he really suspect such things about me? Did he really think I was so crafty and cynical? Did I seem so unfeeling – so hypocritical? Was that really his opinion of my character? Then he burst into laughter again. "But I still can't imagine you staying with those good simple people in Treptow, and you ravishing their daughter. You're a devil,!" he added knocking me in the chest again.

"It wasn't quite like that," I said swallowing a lump in my throat, and trying to force through a grin.

"Come off it – none of your English hypocrisy," he said with a sly wink. Then after a pause, he added, "I still can't understand how you could have got yourself into such a situation."

"Sometimes – at the beginning – I found it difficult to understand myself," I replied. "I suppose it was fate and mutual feelings."

"It's so incongruous," he cried. "Why, I bet you must have tricked her parents into thinking you wanted to marry the girl."

I could only smile sadly at what he said. How completely he had missed the truth about my relationship with Dagmar! But then Dagmar came from the East, I reflected, and those from the East were often seen as "pariahs" in the Western half of their own city. I recollected Martin's attitude of vague contempt towards those people from the East queuing up outside the grounds of the Industrial Exhibition last year, and I remembered the attitude of cool reserve and suspicion of many other West Berliners towards their compatriots from the other half of the city. Fritz's attitude towards my affair with Dagmar, was neither better nor worse than that of many of his fellow citizens towards their countrymen in the East.

Fritz was a West Berliner from a smart suburb in the Westernmost part of the city. He lived for his work and for his fun and enjoyment, and now he was married to an attractive affectionate wife, and lived in a new apartment which was elegantly furnished. What more did he need from life? What need had he to think or worry about those from the East? What concern were they of his? What could he do for them? Their situation was beyond help or hope. Perhaps Fritz had no time, even, to think about the people from the other half of his city – he worked for so many hours at his office desk, and I thought that perhaps only a major political crisis was likely to awaken Fritz's active sympathy for the people of the East.

Anne called us into dinner and Fritz and I rose from our chairs, and he showed me round the flat which was newly furnished in Scandinavian style – which was all the rage then – with solid utilitarian pieces in teak, upholstered in colourful textiles. The dining room and bedroom suites were Danish, and there was Finnish glass – glass ashtrays, glass vases and glass dishes – Fritz assuring me it was the finest glass in the world. I dutifully expressed my admiration, congratulating them on the care they had taken in planning their flat.

"It must have cost you a packet," I said making the appropriate remark which I knew would be appreciated.

"It did – many thousands of deutschmarks – but then I worked twelve to fourteen hours a day for over a year, so I could pay for everything cash down," replied Fritz proudly.

We went into the dining room and sat down beneath a wooden Swedish mobile. Anne had prepared a thick mushroom soup, followed by *Wienerschnitzel*, fresh vegetables and potatoes, and then a dessert of Black Forest cake and clotted cream.

Afterwards, whilst Anne was clearing away and washing up, Fritz and I remained at the table, smoking cigars and drinking Schnapps, and we discussed the new Volkswagen shares which had recently appeared on the market, for it was at that time in Germany when they were heavily marketed for the first time for popular purchase. The bell rang and Anne answered the door and another guest arrived, and I was introduced to an attractive blonde called Gudrun, whom I was to escort for the evening – an old school friend of Anne's. The flat was filled with the noise of laughter and greetings, and we all sat down for some minutes and enjoyed a glass of wine, before departing for a night club.

Fritz drove us to the centre, and already, we were a merry crowd, laughing and joking. At last we came to Kant Strasse, parked the car, and strolled along the pavement, Fritz leading the way, galloping on ahead, turning round and putting his hands to his head and making funny faces, and generally buffooning, which threw us into laughter. We turned into Joachimstaler Strasse, and went through a doorway. We had arrived! We handed in our coats, and my paper shopping bag, containing the cigars and potted plant, was put under the cloakroom attendant's counter, and we went into the club room. Around the walls were fishnets, lifebuoys, lobster baskets – even diving suits – and other paraphernalia suggesting the sea. We were in Remde's St. Pauli Am Zoo. We sat down at a table near the dance floor, and Fritz ordered the first round of drinks.

There was a *gemütlich* atmosphere as we drank cognac, and Fritz and I added ours to the beer, whilst the girls had coca-cola, and Fritz entertained us with his store of jokes, and we laughed and banged our hands onto the table. Gudrun was good company – friendly and warm-hearted. We danced on the packed floor – and I felt the shapely form of her body pressed against mine – and we ordered more drinks, and Fritz continued to entertain us with his lively wit. We were never for a moment silent as our voices crossed one another, but at last our attention was distracted by a voice on the microphone from the little stage at the end of the room. A compere announced that the cabaret was to begin. Fritz called over one of the waitresses for a confidential word in her ear, and a few moments later, Fritz and I were handed fishing rods, and I glanced at mine with an expression of puzzlement.

"What are we supposed to do with these,?" I called over the table to Fritz.

"Fish,!" he replied with the obvious answer. "What do you think?"

"Married men shouldn't be fishing here," said Anne to her husband with an expression of mock scorn.

"And married women shouldn't be here," retorted Fritz laughing. "All the men are married here, I bet – except for our friend here."

"He's free," said Anne.

"They're an elderly lot – they're beyond it, anyway," said Fritz with a naughty wink, "so I don't think it matters much if they are married."

"It's full of sugar-daddies this place," said Anne.

"Just right for the cabaret girls," returned Fritz. "It's full of rich pickings for them after the show."

There was a fanfare and a tall blonde strangely attired in a costume of loosely attached odds and ends of clothing, appeared from behind the curtains in the spotlight after the lights had dimmed. She danced erotically on the little stage, and then began the fun of the evening! All were thrown into fits of laughter and merriment, as seductively, the blonde walked amongst the guests, whilst fishing rods were stretched forward in snatching at her pieces of flimsily attached clothing. Cries of triumph filled the room as slowly but surely she was stripped of her garments.

As she passed by our table, Fritz pulled away a silk stole draped round her shoulders, whilst I, with a quick movement hooked my rod onto the strap of her bra, and with a sharp tug, snatched it away. A cheer of applause went up in the room, as laughing, I held up the rod with a victorious gesture, displaying the captured object dangling at the end. Fritz downed his cognac, rose from the table, and slapped me on the shoulders, and other guests at nearby tables nodded their approval.

"You know what you must do with that," said Fritz. "Wrap it into a parcel and present it as a new gift to your girl friend in the East."

"If it'll fit," said Anne smiling as I unhooked the bra.

"She has a smaller bust," I remarked.

"A pity," said Fritz. "A genuine product from the West! I bet she doesn't have a bra as sexy as that. A gift not to be sneezed at. Those girls from the East don't even know what silk is - not real silk."

"What's this, James, about having a girl from the East,?" exclaimed Gudrun tugging on my arm.

"You needn't tell her about that," exclaimed Fritz winking at me across the table.

"Come on, tell me James – I'm interested," insisted Gudrun. "It's nothing serious, I hope," she added with mock scorn.

"No, nothing serious – just a casual friendship," I replied evasively.

"I hope so," laughed Gudrun. "You must stay clear of those girls. They're only out to make a good match for themselves. Money is the only thing they think about."

"I'm sure James knows how to take care of himself," said Fritz. "He's got his head screwed on the right way. He just likes to have a good time."

We were distracted by a great applause which went up in the room, and I turned to look. An elderly roué, grotesquely fat with white hair, sitting at a table across the other side of the floor, held up a pair of black panties from the end of his rod. He guffawed loudly and his large pouch shook with triumphant laughter. His face was red, and drops of sweat formed on his brow. He had stripped the shapely blonde of her last item of defence.

She stood naked before him. She curtsied with a provocative gesture, and leaning over his chair, kissed him on his bald patch. He reciprocated with a sensuous guffaw, and seizing hold of her hips with his large hands, he drew her torso towards him and kissed her naval, and cries of "Bravo!" met this unexpected gesture of audacious gallantry. He tried to induce the stripper to sit on his lap, and there was laughter as she struggled away, curtsied to the company in all directions, and disappeared behind the curtains of the stage.

"A gorgeous girl – what,?" exclaimed Fritz clapping.

"She has a superb figure," I replied.

Another round of drinks was ordered, and we danced, and Fritz told more stories, and again we were thrown into fits of laughter, and so the evening progressed, but Fritz's reminder of Dagmar, the girl from East Berlin, in his tasteless joke over presenting her with the stripper's bra, had made me depressed. For an hour or two I had forgotten about Dagmar, as we had enjoyed ourselves in the club, and now I was reminded of her again, and I was filled with a feeling of sorrow and guilt. Frau Renot had asked me to go to Graetz Strasse and eat with the family, and although I had made no promise, I realised it was an obligation I should have rightly fulfilled whether I chose to or not.

It was whilst travelling by Underground from Kreuzberg to the Zoo station that morning, that I fully recognised the obligation of eating with the family that evening as a minimum gesture of civility, and it was then I decided to do just that. When, however, I eventually called on Fritz, I felt obliged to accept his invitation also, since he had reproached me for not having called on him earlier during my stay in Berlin. Had he been less busy at the time of my calling, I would have explained to him about my affair with Dagmar and the necessity of having to spend my last evening in Berlin with the Renots. As it was, Fritz made the invitation and rattled off the arrangements for my entertainment before I had had an opportunity to decline the proposal. He then picked up the pile of papers on his desk and threw them down again, which I took as my cue to depart. I realised there was no time to offer excuses for refusing the invitation, and that therefore, I should have to accept his hospitality in the evening. With these thoughts – with the inevitabililty of having to spend the evening with Fritz – I tried to console my conscience that that was a sufficient excuse for not spending my last night with the Renots, and yet, I was still afflicted with feelings of regret.

The Renots had been good to me during my stay, and given everything within their means to ensure my material comfort. For some days they had surrendered their sitting room as a bedroom, and had given me full board for the duration of my stay. I had spent my entire time with them, except for this last day, and surely I owed it to them to spend this final evening in Treptow. Deserting them on this last day, after their weeks of hospitality and kindness, seemed especially cruel, and callously ungrateful. They had given me so much, and I had given little in return. I recollected the exceptional circumstances of that morning which had persuaded me to part company with the Renots until the following day, but the elapse of time had diminished the significance of those circumstances, so they seemed to act as no mitigation for the course I had taken.

Then I realised this was my first occasion in a West Berlin night club since before that time when I had met Dagmar in the Art Shop in Stalin Allee almost a year ago. I had previously enjoyed myself in the company of Martin and his friends, and then I remembered the people of the East, and my curiosity in their way of life and thinking, and my pity for their unhappy plight. I remembered Martin's evasiveness and his tactics of procrastination in putting off our visit to the East sector of Berlin – to that part of the city where the "untouchables" lived – those beyond hope or help.

Then finally, unexpectedly, one sunshine Saturday morning, I had met Dagmar in the Art Shop in Stalin Allee. That seemed an historic event! So much had happened since then. Dagmar suddenly became the focal point securing my attachment to Berlin. My relationship with her marked a slowly changing perspective of the city, its significance and situation. I had come to see so many things in a different light, and as my understanding of the city broadened, so I learnt to perceive its problems with a greater objectivity. My sympathy had deepened for the people of the East and was substantiated by a wealth of information, and I saw the contrasts dividing the people between the two halves of the city in glaring detail.

For these reasons, my feelings of guilt for not having spent my last evening with the Renot family became all the more intense. It was so easy to accept and enjoy the hospitality of my friends from the West, with their high living standards and good food and drink, and luxuriously furnished houses. How different it was with the Renots and those who like them were forced to live under the oppressive Communist regime. As I sat in Remde's night club drinking cognac and beer and listening to the jokes and light conversation of my friends as I leaned back in a comfortable chair, I thought of the Renot family and asked myself what perhaps they were doing and thinking at that particular hour.

Perhaps they had laid a dinner place for me that evening in the hopeful expectation of my arrival, and perhaps they had sat down to eat in silence, still waiting half-expectantly for the knock on the door, when I would join them at that place by the table which had always been laid, and share in the modest fare they had prepared. I knew that in view of the good Frau's highly sensitive nature I must have offended her through my absence, and that probably, she was worrying and even reproaching herself for her involuntary piece of tactlessness that morning. I wondered what both parents were thinking together, and if their minds were tortured by reproachful thoughts, interspersed with outbursts of mutual consolation and stoical acceptance that the friendship between Dagmar and I was drawing inevitably to a close.

Then I thought of Dagmar. What was she thinking? This question, I could not answer – my relationship had become so complex and involved; but there was one thing I knew for certain: I still loved her. I thought of her beauty – her slim figure – and the figure of the striptease girl in Remde's from whom I had jokingly removed the black bra with a fishing rod, reminded me of Dagmar's figure. I thought of her golden silky hair, her comeliness, and the sweet gentleness of her nature, and the tranquil movements of her body and gestures, which seemed to express her strange spirit of resignation and peace and harmony with the world. I thought of her kindness towards all living things, and I remembered the gentleness and affection with which she had caressed the fawns in East Berlin's Tierpark.

As I sat in Remde's, I felt I missed her more than at any time before. I began to regret the sudden decision that morning which had led me to desert the Renot family, but I realised that the indiscretion of hasty acts are often not seen for what they are until long after the event – that time alone is the path to real knowing. I still loved Dagmar and yet I had deserted her, and here I was enjoying myself with other friends in a West Berlin night club. Gudrun was amusing and pleasant company, but she was not Dagmar. I was reproached with a sense of guilt at spending the evening with Gudrun, and after a time – after we had sat and enjoyed ourselves in the club for some hours, I was overcome with a feeling of profound depression, which was difficult to choke back.

I took down the cognac and laughed with the others, and I caressed Gudrun's shapely shoulder and felt her cheek against mine as we danced and sat together, but inside, my feelings were very different. Eventually, I became listless to the jokes and small talk, only laughing mechanically, as I was overcome with an oppressive melancholy.

Chapter 67

At last it was time to leave the club. Most of the guests had departed, and it was already the early hours of the morning. Despite my melancholy state of mind, and because I had become listless to the jokes and conversation of the past few hours, and because I had buried myself in my own thoughts, and perhaps also because of the strange illusion of timelessness induced by drink, the time had passed quickly. I was glad we were leaving.

Fritz laughingly reminded us he had to be up at five-thirty that morning – he seemed especially proud of the fact that he worked a ten hour day. Anne said she had to be up before that time, to prepare her husband's breakfast, although she did not have to arrive at her work until eight o'clock; Gudrun said she did not have to attend her first lecture at the University till ten; and I promptly added I had to be up early that morning to catch a train for West Germany and was looking forward to a good night's sleep.

We strolled into the cloakroom, picked up our coats, and went out into the street. It had begun to drizzle, and the street surface was wet, and several people passed quickly along the pavement with their coat collars buttoned tightly round their necks, or with raised umbrellas. For some moments, our group stood huddled together on the pavement as we discussed ways of reaching our different destinations. Gudrun lived in Lankwitz and I felt no inclination to see her back at that late hour, and so I said nothing in leaving the others to make the decisions. Anne reminded us that the Underground and S-Bahn had long since closed, and that the buses had ceased running, and that taxis would be "prohibitively" expensive at that late hour, and finally, Fritz offered to drive us all to our various abodes.

We went to the car and drove towards Kreuzberg, where I was the first to be dropped, outside my Pension in Spreewald Platz. I left the car, shook hands with my friends, thanking them effusively for "a most enjoyable evening," and we laughed, showing feelings proper at such a departure, and after more farewells and promises to write, I slammed the door and it slowly moved off. I watched it disappear behind the next street corner, and all the while, I waved until it was out of sight. Then I was alone in the quiet, wet and empty street.

Before I went up to the door of the Pension, I glanced behind me, looking through the mist and drizzle at the Wiener Strasse, which led down to the bridge crossing the Landwehr canal to the East sector of Berlin. It was early in the morning and the streets were depressing in their emptiness, and silent but for the falling rain. The city was asleep, and only a few hundred yards away, across the frontier, so too was the Renot family. Perhaps they had been asleep for many hours, and I wondered as to their sleeping thoughts and dreams on that particular night.

I opened the front door of the building, switched on the light in the hallway, and walked up the wide stone staircase, my shoes resounding on the concrete. I opened the door of the Pension and entered. It was quite dark except for a night light over the reception desk, and I went up to the desk and pushed an electric bell to fetch the night porter to ask for the keys of my room. All was silent as I waited. After some moments, the landlady appeared in her night dress and gown, her head in curlers, carrying the keys in her hand. She smiled, seeming not at all put-out by my awakening her at this late hour.

"There was a caller for you today," she exclaimed quietly.

My heart beat suddenly with anticipation, although I knew not why.

"Who,?" I enquired.

"The same as before – the fat man," replied the landlady smiling.

"Was there any message?"

"He said, only to expect you for dinner tonight in Graetz Strasse."

"When did he call?"

"Just after four this afternoon."

I thanked the landlady for the keys and the message and made the way up to my room on the sixth floor of the building. I was suddenly overcome with the deepest melancholy. So the old man had even troubled himself in going that far in calling at the Pension and begging for my presence at the dinner table of his family for that final evening. He had even stooped to do that!

Then it occurred that there was something unusual in the old man's request. Despite the feeling of obligation that I should have dined with them that evening, I remembered that on parting from the family the previous morning, it had been understood I should not see them again until the day of my departure. Why then had the old man therefore bothered to call on me to make this request?

I was standing by the bedside and had just hung my jacket over the back of the chair, when I was shocked by a dreadful realisation. As I climbed the stairs of the Pension I had carried nothing in my hand. Then I remembered as I got into the car in Kant Strasse that night, I had also carried nothing. The gifts I had brought for the Renots had been left in the cloakroom of Remde's club. I cursed beneath my breath, and pulled off my tie contemptuously, realising that only I was to blame. The paper shopping bag containing the gifts had been put under the cloakroom attendant's counter away from my coat. He could not have been expected to remember all the odds and ends the many patrons brought into the club. I was to blame, and my forgetfulness had badly cheated me.

I felt hot and excited, filled with self-resentment and anger at my stupidity. I had to recover the shopping bag – somehow, I told myself. I must return to the club immediately, by taxi – and then I thought of the cost that that would incur. Never mind, it had to be done, I thought, spurring myself with determination. I glanced at my watch. Three a.m. already! I realised the club would be closed and locked up by this time – Fritz and our party had been almost the last to leave. What was to be done – arise before dawn and return to Remde's and somehow try to arouse the housekeeper? I realised the hopelessness of the idea. The premises would be locked up and no one would be there until about ten or eleven in the morning with the arrival of the cleaners.

In desperation, I sat down on the edge of the bed. I had to do something. During the past day I'd already treated the Renots badly enough – with cruelty and ingratitude. My leaving Berlin without offering them a parting gift would be inconceivable, after the kindness and hospitality they'd given. It would be an affront even – interpreted as the most horrible snub, in response, perhaps, to their tactlessness of the previous morning. What could be done? I would have to bear the financial loss of the gifts I had purchased, and buy cigars and a potted plant on arising later that morning, before going to Graetz Strasse. As for the gifts which now lay in Remde's, I would write a humorous note to Fritz relating the entire tragic story, explaining the impossibility of sending the Renots there to fetch the gifts – the full treachery of my ingratitude would then have been laid bare to those "humble people" from the East! – and presenting the gifts, with all best wishes, to Fritz and Anne themselves.

Then I realised that even this plan would be unworkable. I was expected at Graetz Strasse for breakfast at seven-thirty that morning. No shops or stalls would be open by that time. I had reached the lowest point of despair. I thought of writing a letter to either Fritz, or my friend, the Senator's son. It would be a cringing begging letter; full of polite phrases and finely rounded sentences, half-humorously trying to excuse and explain my absentmindedness; apologising for the trouble of how the shopping bag came to be left in Remde's; humbly requesting that it with the contents be delivered to the proper recipients; explaining the immense importance of the delivery of the gifts, both as concerned the donees (and more important) my own peace of mind; again apologising for trouble caused; and finally, extending profuse anticipatory thanks for the request being carried out.

Then suddenly, the idea of writing such a letter filled me with nausea. Why should I write a humiliating letter, full of self-reproach and excuses for my forgetfulness and failing memory, perhaps suggesting even the first signs of premature dementia, to persons I hardly knew? What right, anyway, had I to worry them with such petty troubles? I thought that in writing such a letter, I should bring ridicule on myself in attempting to fawn on their good nature or pleading for their indulgence because of my own stupidity. I pondered over their curious speculations on delivering the shopping bag to the Renots in Treptow. Whatever was that "funny Englishman" doing in this unlikely part of the city, associating himself with such unprepossessing people?

It was then I realised I should have to send the Renots to Remde's club to fetch their own gifts. The idea filled me with dread but there was no alternative. Writing a quick note and sealing it into an envelope, and handing it to Papa Renot and sending him to the other side of the city as a messenger for his own gift was bad enough, but sending him to Remde's was even worse! The premises might be locked on his arrival, or perhaps there would only be a small group of disgruntled cleaners who would feel unauthorised to open the note, or be unable to offer information as to the opening times of the club. Or perhaps the shopping bag would have been taken from under the counter and locked away safely in the manager's office where it would necessarily remain until the evening with the arrival of the manager himself.

The conclusions which the old man might draw as to the voluptuous pleasures I might have enjoyed during my last night in Berlin, when I should have been accompanying his daughter, pained me, filling me with acute embarrassment. On arriving at the club he would be confronted by the erotic publicity photographs behind their locked display cases in the lobby. I was loathed to think he should surmise I had ever danced or caressed any girl other than his precious Dagmar, not to mention the fact I had helped to pull off the last garments of a striptease artiste with a fishing rod. He might well fall under the false impression that I had spent a small fortune in the club on drink and women – money saved during the past few weeks due to his kind hospitality and full board. His visit to Remde's would undoubtedly reveal my treachery in its blackest form.

No – the idea was impossible – I couldn't allow the Renots to go within a mile of Remde's club. Somehow, I'd have to prevent it – somehow find another alternative. My mind was in a whirl of perplexity and vexation. What could I do? I'd already decided against using third parties for delivering the shopping bag to Treptow – so I couldn't go back on that idea. I thought of consulting the post office on arising early that morning, and enquiring as to the possibility of hiring a special messenger, but didn't feel sure as to whether the post office offered such services.

Again, I was thrown back onto the stark reality of the fact that the Renots would *have* to fetch their own gifts from Remde's.

I thought of inventing a fictitious explanation for the shopping bag being there. As a citizen from the West, I was afraid the potted plant might arouse the suspicions of the People's Police as some kind of contraband, so I handed it for safe keeping to the cloakroom attendant at Remde's. The central heating in the room of my Pension was set at such a temperature that I was afraid the plant would become dehydrated, so I decided to leave it in the town centre, and I handed it for safe keeping to the cloakroom attendant at Remde's. I had just bought the cigars in Zoo station and I went to the flower shop next door and pointed to the potted plant of my choice, when the assistant explained it had been sold – but no worry, another would be delivered tomorrow, and if I wanted it urgently, I could pay for the order, and the plant would be left for safe keeping with the cloakroom attendant at Remde's. I shook my head with an expression of disbelief. No – none of those excuses would suffice – none were credible.

Again, my mind was thrown into a welter of confusion and indecision. It all seemed so problematical. I got up from the bed and continued undressing. Perhaps after a night's sleep – after a very few hours sleep – I should wake in the morning with an inspiration, and with these hopeful reflections, I retired to bed.

On rising later that morning, I felt no more consoled by the difficulties which had worried me the previous night, but I was resigned to one thing: there was no escaping the truth. Everything would have to make itself known in due course. There would be no excuses. My sense of resignation to reality was only hardened. I was impatient to dismiss the problems of the Renot family as quickly as possible, and these problems and my absentmindedness which had been their cause (which absentmindedness I had cursed so bitterly the night before) now only touched me with a feeling of ennui.

After dressing, I took out my writing pad, and sat down at the little desk. I sat still for some moments, impatiently fiddling with my pen before writing the following note:-

TO WHOM IT MAY CONCERN

Please hand bearer of note, paper shopping bag under counter containing 1 box of cigars and 1 potted plant. With thanks,

| Club patron, | Stuben-Gasse |
| James Furner | Münster |

I folded the note, putting it into an evelope which I sealed, and on the outside, I wrote in large capitals: "To the Manager or Cloakroom Attendant, Remde's St. Pauli Am Zoo."

I sighed. My duty is done, I thought with a feeling of relief and indifference. I finished packing, and left my room for the last time – the room which for so long had been mine. I left my hold-all in the reception hall of the Pension, and made my way to Graetz Strasse. It was no longer drizzling but the sky was dark and overcast.

As I walked quickly down Wiener Strasse alongside the high red brick wall of the Görlitzer goods yard station, I thought of how differently my affair with Dagmar might have progressed had I been residing in Berlin the previous year when first we met, instead of the brief encounter during the last two days of a holiday. Had the former been the case, her parents would hardly have had the opportunity to interfere so disastrously with our relationship. I would have met Dagmar in the West sectors and taken her to the Grunewald and Wannsee and those other places which she liked, and the friendship would have developed spontaneously at its own pace, without the need for third parties trying to push the issue either way, but I realised the hopelessness of wishing for what was already long past and done with.

I still loved Dagmar and everything she meant, but the stupidity of her parents had raised insuperable difficulties. I decided that on reaching Graetz Strasse, to take Dagmar aside, in a room away from her parents, and make one last attempt at persuading her to come to the West as a refugee and seek work in Münster. I would promise her an engagement within one month of arriving in Münster, and marriage within six months. I felt the chances of Dagmar accepting such a proposal better now than at any time previously, and I thought it unlikely that her parents would attempt to raise any objection to such an arrangement. The good prospects of her accepting me on these terms filled me with renewed hope and enthusiasm, and I quickened my pace as I crossed the Wiener bridge over the Landwehr canal. Now she would be mine – really mine – after so many months of hope, sorrow, tears and struggle!

I was uncertain as to whether I would be breakfasting at No. 18 or at No. 55, and I rather thought it would be at the parents' apartment at No. 18, given the early hour. This was encouraging – it would give me an opportunity to first call and speak with Dagmar alone on the other side of the road, before we then went together to her parents' flat, telling them of the happy arrangement. It would even be an occasion for Papa Renot to bring out a bottle of Georgian wine – even that early in the morning!

On arriving at No. 55 I was surprised and a little disconcerted on seeing the good Frau open the door to me. It looked as if my plan might be spoilt after all, and it seemed as if I would be breakfasting this side of the road.

"We were expecting you last night," she said in a tone of concern.

"I'm sorry, but I didn't arrive back and get your message until quite late," I replied.

I took off my coat, handing it to her, and she hung it up on a peg, before leading me down the passageway to the sitting room. She wore an anxious look, although she was as kindly and indulgent as ever, despite the fact that she had lost her bright gleeful manner.

In the sitting room, the table was already laid for breakfast, and I met Herr Renot and shook hands with him, and he too was solemn. I felt awkward at carrying no gifts, and explained in detail and as light-heartedly as I could, how they came to be left in Remde's club, but I feared my voice sounded heavy throughout the exposition. Even the little joke about my absentmindedness and the "first signs of dementia" fell flat, and certainly the Renots saw nothing humorous in the account. They asked no questions either – I wished that they had – any lead to have opened up a new line of conversation, to help transform the heavy atmosphere. Frau Renot only muttered that she was grateful for the present, and Herr Renot cleared his throat and thanked me also, and I modestly waved aside their gestures of gratitude, saying that the gifts were "nothing," before we hurriedly sat down at the table.

Little was said during breakfast, although both parents were indulgent, continuously asking if I would have some more, and kept filling my cup as soon as it was emptied, but I was surprised by the atmosphere of silence. It didn't appear as if the parents were necessarily displeased or peevish – it seemed as if their minds were somehow wandering – as if I was no longer the centre of their concern. They no longer glanced up at me with that questioning or expectant look as if trying to read my thoughts or persuade me to take some course of action through their hypnotic will. Still, they looked thoughtful, wearing an anxious expression, but it was not I who was the centre of their anxiety.

It was not until after I had been sitting at the table for some minutes, that I began to question in my mind as to the whereabouts of Dagmar. I had imagined that perhaps she was meanwhile dressing in her grandmother's room, but I heard no sounds from that direction. Then I noticed to my surprise that no place was laid for her at the table.

"Where's Dagmar,?" I asked Frau Renot.

She hesitated, glancing up at her husband who gave her a strange significant look.

"She's not here," replied Frau Renot.

"She left early this morning," replied the old man distinctly, showing all his teeth.

I took the determinedness of the reply to be a final answer to a matter which should not be questioned or gone into further, without risk of causing embarrassment. I concluded that Dagmar must have suddenly become so resentful at my action in leaving the family yesterday that she was resolved never to see me again.

"I'm sorry she's not here to see me off," I replied sadly.

I felt momentarily downcast. My last hopes for repairing our friendship at the eleventh hour had been dashed. The apartment seemed empty and oppressively gloomy without her presence.

It was not until some weeks after I arrived back in Münster that I learnt the real reason for Dagmar's absence from the house at that time.

After breakfast, farewells were exchanged, and I thanked them for everything and we shook hands and bowed and curtsied, and then the good Frau went into the kitchen and came out with a big bag of luncheon refreshments for the journey, and I thanked them again, and then I reminded Papa Renot to be at Remde's without fail by ten this morning, as the potted plant was wrapped in paper and might be urgently in need of water, and then I thanked them once again, and made my departure from the flat, and they even came out into the street to wave me off until I finally disappeared from view. My last sight of them both – that kind and hospitable couple – was just before I reached the Wiener bridge, when I finally saw them disappear into the tenement building.

When I crossed the Landwehr canal into the West sector, I felt a feeling of relief and freedom, but I realised that my affair with Dagmar was now a thing of the past.

I felt the jog of the train as it braked. Thinking over the discordant events of the past twenty-four hours, I had fallen asleep with my head in my arms as they rested on the little table before the window. I glanced up leaning back in the seat. The train had stopped in the little station of Griebnitz-See, the Zonal check point for entering the DDR. The train remained stationary for half an hour and the usual formalities were completed before moving off again.

I glanced out of the window as we passed through Potsdam, and then again, I was overcome with a feeling of heavy fatigue. I laid out my copy of yesterday's *Times* on the seat opposite, put up my feet and leaned back, and within minutes, was asleep.

I felt the pull of the train as it seemed to be moving in a great semicircle. The train was moving slower now and I felt the bump of the wheels over the joins of the rails. Stretching my limbs, I glanced at my watch. Several hours had passed since we left Berlin. The other two occupants in the compartment were asleep. I heard a loud clattering from the wheels, as the train passed over the girders of a steel bridge.

I looked out of the window. We were crossing a suspension bridge over a wide river – the Elbe. Far below, several coal carrying barges were passing up the river. The train came towards the end of the bridge, and I saw the high grey muddy banks of the river, and on the land beyond, were several large gasometers. We were approaching a city! I pulled down the window and leaned out. As I had thought, the train was moving in a great semicircle, white smoke puffing from the locomotive far in front.

In the distance beyond was laid out the great expanse of a city over the flat land. In the middle of the city, and dominating the buildings around, rose two tall towers – identical and Romanesque. We had reached the outskirts of Magdeburg! I remembered the first occasion I passed through the city of Magdeburg. Nearly a year had gone since then – and so much had happened. At that time I was merely a tourist, going to Berlin to see the sights and enjoy the pleasures of the city. Berlin had meant little to me then – it was a name – a tourist attraction. How much I had experienced! How little I anticipated the things I should see and feel in Berlin, on first passing through the city of Magdeburg! I remembered my fellow passengers in the compartment during that evening long ago, as the train entered that ancient city in the East zone with its desolate ruins.

I remembered the worker from the East, with his ill-fitting clothes and tubercular cough, and of how he seemed to sit apart from the other passengers. He came from a different world from the rest of us and yet for several hours, we had all sat together in the same compartment. Apart from the green uniformed officials, that man was the first I had seen who lived behind the Iron Curtain. How typically he had seemed to represent the wretchedness, misery and despair of the many millions who like him were forced to live behind that Iron Curtain re-enforced by minefields, barbed wire and alarmed fences, and armed sentries!

The train was approaching ever nearer the city centre and outside the window were factories and slag heaps, and bomb sites and crumbling grey tenement blocks. The twin towers came nearer to view as they rose high above the rest of the city. Still the train was moving round in a great semicircle, and it passed over a bridge, the wheels clattering loudly over the rails beneath, and far below was a wide roadway, and some grimy streets which led off from a junction.

There was little traffic below: a group of workers on bicycles rode beneath the bridge; three large trucks with trailers, belching diesel drove in the opposite direction; a car crossed the junction, and two motor bikes with side-cars were parked at the side of the roadway – but that was all. Several Vopos stood together on one of the street corners, machine guns slung over their shoulders. People on the pavements moved busily to and fro, and the buildings around were grey and desolate – their windows sometimes boarded over with wood. The streets were colourless and depressing: no bright advertisement hoardings – just a few political posters, each glaring in its crudity – and no sign anywhere of fresh paint. And this was Magdeburg, one of the great industrial centres of Germany, and the fifth largest city in the East zone!

As the train moved round towards the West front of the Cathedral, I glanced up at the high grey towers and noticed how damaged and pit-holed they were by bombing and strafing, and yet, still they rose proudly above the city dominating the buildings around. There was an aloof and eternal quality about the Romanesque towers, which their badly scarred stonework could not diminish.

As the train came parallel to the West front, I saw that the massive doors of the Cathedral were locked and boarded over with planks. It seemed as if the Communist authorities had taken more than effective measures to ensure that no one could enter this place of worship. No attempt had been made to repair the outside of the Cathedral or to clean its grimy stonework. It stood in the heart of the city, an ignored and forgotten monument, shut off from the streets around by railings and a wooden fence, whilst hundreds rushed to and fro like diminutive ants beneath its walls, oblivious to the existence of a mighty giant. But despite this rebuff and the War damage, and the cross which had been blasted from the right tower, which damage alone distinguished one tower from the other, the Cathedral maintained its dominance over the city; and the strength and simplicity of its Romanesque form gave it an expression of disdain over the surrounding buildings.

The Cathedral of Magdeburg stood undaunted over the city, a symbol of sorrow over the past and yet of hope for the future. And yet it had not been the first time it had experienced the sorrows of war, for it was the city which will always be remembered in the annals of history, which had been so cruelly destroyed and put to the sword by the atrocities of that Flemish mercenary, Tilly, during the horrors of the Thirty Years War.

Chapter 68

It was on August 13th that it happened. At twenty-eight minutes to two on Sunday morning, the silent night prevailing over East Berlin, was shattered by the scream of sirens and the thundering convoys of vehicles rushing through the grim streets of the city. Residents occupying tenement blocks and other buildings overlooking streets leading to the Western half of the city were startled out of their sleep by the deafening row, as in bewildered alarm, they glanced from their windows to the darkened streets below.

They saw the headlights of police cars, motorcycles, and truckloads of armed men and barbed wire speeding westwards. What was happening? Was there a general alert of the armed forces? Had a political crisis during the night precipitated a state of emergency being declared throughout the city?

All main streets leading to the West sectors of the city were alive with military transport carrying units of the People's Police and the Volksarmee to the boundary dividing the two halves of the city. Shortly after 1.25 a.m. thousands of armed men assembled along the length of streets; along pavements; across roadways; along the length of canals; across the middle of great squares and junctions; across graveyards and parks; across bomb sites; by gardens; along the backs and fronts of houses, factories, stores; across bridges; and along the length of the railway tracks of the S-Bahn – they assembled along every section of the forty or so kilometres of boundary running from north to south Berlin, dividing the two halves of the city.

Armed with rifles and machine guns, they took up positions on the Sector frontiers, from north to south, dividing the West and East suburbs of Reinickendorf from Pankow; Wedding from Prenzlauer Berg; Tiergarten from Mitte; Kreuzberg from Friedrichshain; and Neukölln from Treptow. They were under orders to block the Sector boundary of all traffic, vehicular or pedestrian, and to shoot to kill, in the event of persons attempting to escape to the Western half of the city. Tank formations and armoured cars moved into positions at many points.

Some minutes later, further convoys of trucks sped through the streets towards many points along the East-West frontier of the city. They carried thousands of Combat Groups from the People's Own Works, dressed in their floppy caps and loose fitting garments, armed with machine guns and in full battle order. Most belonged to companies brought into the city from as far away as Saxony and Thüring.

Behind the Combat Groups, came trucks carrying building workers with picks, drills, shovels and other tools, and behind them came trucks bearing rolls of barbed wire, steel and concrete posts, and other building implements.

Early that Sunday morning in August and still before dawn, many Berliners living on both sides of the border, were awoken by the deafening scream of pneumatic drills, the shouting of orders, the running of men to and fro, and the crashing of picks and hammers against concrete stonework. Ditches were dug, roads and pavements torn up, steel and concrete piles driven into the earth, and concrete blocks and other obstacles moved into position. Rolls of barbed wire were laid out along the entire length of the frontier.

A permanent blockade between the East and West Sectors of the city was being effectively constructed.

It was being carried out as a reprisal of the government against the people of the Soviet Zone of Germany – against those who lived in the People's German Democratic Republic. Between 1945 and August 13th 1961, 3,600,000 persons – a number corresponding to the entire population of the Federal *Land* of Rhineland-Palatinate – had voted with their feet to flee from the Communist State to the free West, rather than endure privation and oppression which had become intolerable.

The rulers of the Soviet Zone of Germany, however, had other pretexts prepared for the moves which were under way. During the first half of the month, there had been an atmosphere of increasing tension throughout the DDR. Ulbricht had declared in a speech to workers in a factory, "that the borders of the DDR must if necessary be defended militarily against the militarists in Bonn by the forces of the Soviet Zone as well as by the National People's Army." Without attempting to demonstrate the truth of the imputation against the West, Ulbricht continued, "that the strengthening of the DDR in all fields will show that the war hysteria ignited in West Germany is madness and completely without sense."

From the beginning of the month, there had been an intensified agitation in the East Zone press against what was described as the "slave trading" and "enticement to flee" of East Berliners working in the West Sectors. On 2nd August the Soviet Zone Supreme Court sentenced five persons to terms between two and fifteen years imprisonment on charges of "slave trading" and "spying," and on 4th, the city authorities of the Soviet Sector, ordered the compulsory registration of all East Berliners employed in the West. They were instructed that as from the start of the month, to pay rent, lease interest, electricity, gas, water, and fees for public services in West marks. Contraventions were to be punished with imprisonment or fines. Because of currency laws already standing affecting East Berliners employed in the West, whereby earnings had to be exchanged at the rate of one East mark for one West mark, they were faced by an awkward dilemma. Either they give up their employment and find work in the East Sector, or else, they give up their apartments and houses and go over to the West as refugees. Many chose the latter.

It was not until 11th that the first rumblings occurred to give any indication of what might happen on August 13th. On that day, Willi Stoph, Prime Minister of the DDR, announced in the People's Assembly that "new protective measures against slave traders, enticers to flee and saboteurs" would have to be taken, which might "bring certain discomforts to citizens." To prevent slave trading, he hinted that measures against travelling from the Soviet Zone to the Federal Republic and West Berlin would be taken. That same day, the People's Assembly instructed the Council of Ministers in general terms to prepare and execute appropriate measures.

The atmosphere throughout East Berlin and the East Zone of Germany was marked by rising fear and tension, and evidently as a consequence of Stoph's speech and the decision of the People's Assembly, the number of refugees received in camps in West Berlin increased dramatically. On the following day, the Warsaw Pact states published an instruction asking for effective measures to be taken in East Germany because of the "perfidious agitation campaign of the West," and "to introduce a state of order on the West Berlin boundary such as will guarantee a reliable watch and a genuine control." The Volkspolizei tightened their control on trains, particularly at the S-Bahn stations of Potsdam, Babelsberg and Griebnitz-See, and that night trains from Potsdam through West Berlin to Friedrich Strasse, had few passengers, for travellers intending to go from Potsdam to the Soviet Sector of Berlin, were forced off the trains, and told to use the outer ring of Berlin to reach their destination – a diversion of eighty kilometres! Then, two hours after midnight the blockade between the two halves of the city was put into effect.

Throughout the week leading up to August 13th there was a greater stream of refugees than at any time during the sixteen years following the end of the War, excepting only for in 1953, when the flight of thousands was brought about by the East German Uprising.

Whilst during the previous sixteen years, the history of West Germany had been marked by the re-building of a shattered economy through perseverance and hard work, and the creation of living standards higher than at any time before, the history of East Germany had only been marked by an increasing oppression over the people as the Communist noose was tightened. Whilst the West had seen the development of industry and commerce benefiting ordinary people, the East had experienced a relative worsening of all the conditions of social and economic life as the tenets of Marxism-Leninism were put into practice, bringing bankruptcy and economic chaos in their wake. The loathing of the people of the DDR for the regime, was the final proof – if that was needed – of the failure of the system.

I was staying with friends for the weekend on the South coast when I first heard the news. It was from the Sunday papers on the morning of 13th that I first heard what had happened in Berlin in the early hours. A friend rushed into the room, throwing the papers onto my bed whilst I was still enjoying a cup of early morning coffee. During breakfast that morning, as eight of us sat round the table, the situation in Berlin became the sole topic of conversation, just as it must have been in millions of other British homes, and many millions more throughout Continental Europe and the world. Overnight, the image of Berlin as the metaphor of threatened freedom in the eyes of the world was re-enforced, and the people of Berlin in their unhappy plight, won the sympathy of the world.

I refrained from telling my friends about the intimate relationship which had brought me into such close contact with the city, and after breakfast, I sat down with the papers studying the reports in detail. I was shattered by what had happened, and throughout the day feverishly listened to the latest bulletins as they came over the air.

Only eleven months had elapsed since I was last in Berlin, sharing and enjoying the life of the city with Dagmar. Much had happened since then. I had graduated, achieved a satisfactory post in London, and lived in an apartment in a salubrious area, enjoying comparative affluence. Many months had passed since I last heard from Dagmar and the Renot family. On returning to Münster, I wrote to Herr and Frau Renot, thanking them for their hospitality, and I wrote to Dagmar. Within a week I received a warm-hearted letter from Frau Renot thanking me for the potted plant and extending her husband's thanks for the cigars. She sent me greetings from Gisela, Franz and Frau Brüning, saying she would deliver the letter I had sent to Dagmar – which phrase I thought strange – and that I would receive a reply from her shortly. Finally, she expressed the hope I would be returning to Berlin in the not too distant future.

It was not until two weeks after receiving Frau Renot's letter, that I heard from Dagmar. I thought she had been so piqued by my behaviour before leaving Berlin that she had resolved not to write, and it was with a feeling of relief and mild surprise that I received her letter. But my surprise was greater on reading its contents on discovering it was written from the Charité University hospital in Schumann Strasse. The handwriting was untidy and smudged as if written by an invalid propped up in bed. I was shocked at receiving a letter from her under such circumstances, and hurriedly read it through. She regretted having been unable to see me off at Graetz Strasse, explaining she had been taken ill during the afternoon previous to my departure, necessitating immediate hospitalisation. She said she was surrounded by flowers, and that Papa Renot came to visit her daily, and Renata twice weekly. She gave no indication what her illness was, but from her letter, it was evident she enjoyed receiving friends and relatives at her bedside and that special sympathy and attention usually given to the sick.

I wondered why her parents had not told me about her illness before my departure from Berlin. When I thought back to that last morning in Graetz Strasse, I realised they must have lied intentionally –

or at least concealed the truth – in view of Papa Renot's explanation in answer to my enquiry that Dagmar had left "early that morning." By her own account, she had been taken to the hospital the previous afternoon, and then I recollected the message which the old man had left at the Pension on the day previous to my departure. He had called at the Pension at four o'clock in the afternoon. Perhaps he had called with the intention of telling me about Dagmar's illness with the idea of our visiting her together in hospital, and perhaps as a result of my not visiting them that evening, and because of the consequent impossibility through lack of time in exchanging last farewells, her parents had decided to conceal the news from me of their duaghter's illness.

I replied to Dagmar's letter a week after receiving hers. I enquired after her illness, sent my best wishes for a speedy recovery, and wired flowers. I received a second letter from her two weeks later. I was surprised by its tone. It was full of reproaches and self-pity. She accused me of being callous, of having failed to write to her earlier whilst she was meanwhile lying "seriously" ill in hospital, and of my being hypocritical in my concern for her health. I took this as a strange response and my feelings cooled. She made no mention of the flowers I sent or as to the nature of her illness, and the letter was more untidy and smudged than the previous communication. It seemed as if our relationship had gone full circle since a year previously, when I had begun to receive those strange temperamental letters.

I ignored the letter, concealing it away under a pile of papers. A week later, I received another letter, again full of self-pity but without the reproaches. The handwriting was more feeble and smudged than before, as if written by a very weak invalid. Again, it was addressed from the Charité hospital. I was surprised by the protracted nature of her illness and even more concerned as to its cause, for she had now been confined for well over six weeks. She thanked me for the flowers and apologised for the unfriendliness of her previous letter, explaining she was now very weak and nervous and undergoing complicated treatment, but still gave no indication of the nature of that illness. She begged me to write again soon, but I made no reply, and from that day until August 1961, neither of us had corresponded.

And now on August 13th and during the critical days which followed, my mind was suddenly thrown back to Dagmar and to the happy eventful days we had enjoyed together long ago in Berlin. Berlin remained an intimate memory, and as I read about events in the city – about incidents and barricades across streets and squares I had come to know so well, I thought inevitably of Dagmar the fair Berlinerin from the East. In the light of these events and the stress and tragedy which faced the people of Berlin, I began to reassess the course of our friendship.

On August 14th, tank units took up positions in many parts of East Berlin, especially in the Marx-Engels Platz and in the side streets of the Unter den Linden, to pre-empt a repetition of what had occurred on 17th June 1953. The Russian embassy (one of the most loathed buildings in East Berlin) was cordoned off by heavily armed units, and the government quarter and the House of Ministries were hermetically sealed with barbed wire, and later, with a high stone wall to protect them against the demonstrations of an angry mob. Hence even the government buildings of the DDR had to be turned into fortresses. The running of the Underground and S-Bahn trains between the two halves of the city had been stopped the day before, and subsequently, at the Sector and Zonal boundaries, lines were removed or blocked with iron sleepers and concrete slabs.

On Monday 14th, none of the fifty-three thousand East Berliners working in the Western half of the city, reached their places of employment, except for those few who were fortunate enough to escape to the West under cover of darkness through the barbed wire entanglements laid across the length of the Sector boundary. During the day, along many parts of the Sector border, East German workers were busy driving concrete posts into the ground in erecting wire fences. After work and throughout the evening, crowds of West Berliners demonstrated their anger against the East German authorities at various points along the border. At one point, smoke and tear gas bombs and water hoses were used by the East Germans to disperse a crowd of several hundred youths who had taunted police and armed factory brigades trying to explain the necessity for the measures, and meanwhile, two hundred police were brought up to the Brandenburg Gate in trucks, and the area was roped off to prevent a major clash.

Foreigners and West Berliners were still allowed to drive into the Eastern half of the city and visit friends and relatives, but within the next few days, the security check on West Berliners became ever more intense, and ruthless measures were taken against anyone attempting to break the letter of East German law. Before the end of the month, a young West Berliner was condemned to seven years imprisonment for attempting to smuggle his fiancée out of the East Sector with false identity papers.

As the lovely Summer day darkened on the evening of 14th, a crowd of four thousand West Berliners gathered before the rope barrier in front of the Brandenburg Gate, chanting, "Hang Ulbricht,!" and "Put down your guns," to the Vopos and Combat Groups stationed beneath the pillars of the Gate. From the other side, armoured cars and trucks had been brought up to the pillars of the Gate. Crowds of West Berliners threatened the two Russian sentries guarding the Memorial in the Street of the 17th June, and it was only with difficulty, that the West Berlin police pushed back the crowds before roping off the area. Several days later, the Memorial was cordoned off with barbed wire entanglements and put under the protection of British troops. During the night, searchlights were played along the Sector border, and the police stood on guard, machine guns at the ready, to shoot down escapees, but despite this, a number of East Berliners succeeded in reaching the West by jumping fences and swimming canals.

Within the next few days the mood in West Berlin was marked by rising anger and a sense of increasing exasperation which in view of the situation in the city could well be understood. The Berliners had good reason to be angry and to vent their rage in the city. For a time it seemed as if the West had no intention of introducing counter-measures. The politicians dithered, overcome with anxiety at this latest demonstration of strength by the might of Soviet Russia. The Berliners were only angered by the Soviet measures, having no time to consider the possibility of fear, for as the politicians debated in privacy, the Communists were all the while tightening their squeeze on the city.

On 15th, telephone and teleprinting communications were cut between the two Germanies; West Berliners vehicles' were refused entry into the East Sector after an announcement explaining that the freedom of movement of West Berliners in the East was being abused for espionage purposes; the rumour was confirmed that two Soviet divisions had encircled Berlin; and the Brandenburg Gate, the symbol of the city, and standing between its two greatest thoroughfares, was closed to traffic, because of what were described as "continual provocations." A few days later the Gate was boarded and finally walled-up to prevent any passage, although one escapee did succeed in crashing a car through the boarding in making his escape to the West. The 15th was also the day marking the start of the building of the Berlin Wall of brick and mortar.

West Berliners became ever more embittered at the failure of the allies to act against the Soviets, and five thousand workers marched to Schöneberg town hall, despite torrential rain, to demand action and to hear their Lord Mayor, Willy Brandt. Many of the crowd had marched straight from their factories, carrying banners bearing slogans reflecting their anger and exasperation, as, "You can't stop tanks with paper,!" and "Kennedy come to Berlin!" The crowd cheered Mayor Brandt's call for action, but whistled derisively at any mention of the ineffective protests which the three Commandants had sent to their opposite number in the East. As could be understood, Willy Brandt was critical of the allies in his speech, warning the crowd of the imminent danger of another Munich, for which he was loudly applauded.

That same day, a group of students in Bonn, had the same thought in mind when they sent the American President an umbrella, to which was attached the following note: "We are sorry to say, Mr. President, that because of your reserved reaction to the happenings in Berlin, you have at the moment become the most worthy possesser of this symbol of a fatal policy. Because your doubtlessly very determined words in this present crisis were not followed by equally determined actions, there arises a comfortless memory of an era of European history from which the world is still suffering."

Meanwhile, in East Berlin, a brick Wall was constructed during the night across the great Potsdamer Platz, and during the day, other extensions to the Wall were constructed and heightened and crowned with barbed wire. The FDJ suddenly called on its members to report for two years service with the armed forces, and still the West introduced no effective counter-measures.

As the Berlin crisis intensified, so increased my personal concern for Dagmar and the unfortunate people who had been imprisoned in a vast "concentration camp" on the other side of the Wall. The people of East Berlin were imprisoned by thousands of armed police and troops surrounding the entire Sector of the city. Some could escape to the East Zone, if they wished, to a much larger concentration camp, but many preferred to remain in Berlin and try their luck in escaping through the Sector boundary, which although consisting of a high concrete Wall topped with barbed wire and occasionally even watch towers, was a less impenetrable boundary than the Zonal frontier with its minefields, its broad strip of forbidden territory and trip wires, its searchlights, and its police dogs prowling along the border day and night.

Nonetheless, many were to lose their lives in attempting to escape through the Sector boundary, and frequently, they were to be shot and left dying – bleeding to death – deprived of medical aid – as they lay helpless on the ground. In this way – through bloodshed and atrocities – one of the most hated regimes in modern history was to prevent its own citizens from escaping from its frontiers. With the building of the Berlin Wall, the Soviets filled in the last hole in the Iron Curtain. For too long, West Berlin as the mirror of the free world, had been a source of irritation to the Soviets. August 13th must have been a day of victory and celebration in the Kremlin and sympathisers throughout Eastern Europe. It was the day from which fool-proof lies could be propagated in a closed environment in the hope that they might flourish with success in an unknown future.

As the situation in Berlin worsened from day to day, and the Wall rose higher and stronger, and the possibility of escape ever more difficult, so I was drawn to renew my contact with the city. Accordingly, I wrote off to Martin Schultz, expressing my deepest sympathy for the plight of his unhappy citizens, and asking for his first hand account of the latest events.

Then I contemplated writing to Dagmar, but hesitated, and for some days was uncertain as to the reason of this hesitancy. Would she regard my writing to her after so long a silence as an affront, or as a simple way of satisfying an uneasy conscience in the event of my having wronged her by so long a silence, or would she regard my asking after her as merely a piece of hypocrisy hidden behind the guise of compassion? If she were to suspect the sincerity of my feelings, I would prefer not to write, and yet my concern and interest in her fate was real and increasing with each passing day, until my desire to write became a heartfelt necessity. These were the questions tormenting my mind. Prior to the Berlin crisis of August 13th, I had never experienced these issues with intensity. Had I been in the wrong in failing to enter into an engagement with Dagmar in view of my sincere love? Had I been over-cautious – callous even – in declining to formalise our friendship? Pushing aside all doubt, I finally resolved attempting to renew contact, and I wrote a cautiously amiable letter, posting it to Berlin. I was anxious to receive her reply, but uncertain as to whether she would respond.

Meanwhile, more protests were delivered, and finally, measures taken to counter the Berlin situation. On 17th, the British government expressed the wish to indict the East German regime in the United Nations for suppressing human rights, and the West German government banned the export of certain vital goods to East Germany, and refused negotiations for a Soviet-West German cultural accord unless the agreement recognised West Berlin as part of the Federal Republic, but it was not until the following day that the first serious counter-measures were taken.

On 18th, the American government ordered the movement of fifteen hundred troops into the city to help bolster the morale of the Berliners, and on 19th, Vice President Johnson and Lucius D. Clay, the great American general who had done so much after the War in helping to rehabilitate the German people, flew from the States to the old German capital. They received a tumultuous welcome. On 20th, General Clay and the Ambassador Extraordinary, Charles Bohlen, made a tour of the East Sector, and on returning to the West, the General said, "My impressions were very bad. The city was like an army camp. I saw more soldiers there than in 1945."

On the same day, the American battle group consisting of fifteen hundred men arrived in the city to a tremendous welcome from Berliners who tossed flowers at the troops. Also, tanks arrived to re-enforce the British garrison, and France too, announced it would strengthen its garrison. The Vice President welcomed his countrymen into the city with the words, "Never before in the past have American troops carried a greater responsibility as guardians of peace than here in Berlin." He then toured the Western half of the city, and the greeting he received was so great that neither cordons nor protocol were heeded. The route had to be changed several times, and to the regret of Berliners, had to be curtailed because the enthusiasm of the crowds so delayed the procession. It was during the tour, that the Vice President delivered his historic pledge in the name of the American people, "To the survival and the creative future of this city we Americans have pledged, in effect, what our ancestors pledged in forming the United States, 'Our lives, our fortunes and our sacred honour.'"

When he left the city at 4.0 a.m. the following day, despite the early hour, hundreds of Berliners gathered at the airport to see him off and to throw flowers in his path. In his farewell message to the people of Berlin, the Vice President declared, "I have just seen the soul of a city and a people that will never submit to conquest. I am going home to tell the President and the people of the United States that the Western powers – the United States, France and Britain – have never had better nor braver allies than we have in the citizens of this city. … For many years this city, which has worn its tribulation like a crown of glory, has compelled our admiration. … I have seen the fruits of democracy in this city. … I salute with honour and gratitude the great-hearted people of West Berlin, the city of unconquerable freedom."

From that day, the Berliners won the friendship and respect of freedom loving peoples everywhere. The city of Berlin was finally recognised in the eyes of the world as the symbol of freedom and democracy in adversity.

With the arrival of American troops, thousands of grateful West Berliners began to invite the GIs into their homes for meals, and especially Sunday lunch, but internally, the situation in the city was no more improved – on the contrary, it continued to worsen. New restrictions were enforced by the East German authorities on West Berliners wishing to visit relatives in the other half of the city. West Berliners had to apply for a pass, and later, East Berliners had to apply for entry permits for West Berliner relatives, and finally, West Berliners were refused entry on any conditions to the other half of the city. Thus, they were permanently cut off from seeing friends and relatives. Meanwhile, on the East Zonal frontier of the city, restrictions were laid down for East Germans wishing to enter the capital of their own country.

Everywhere along the Sector border, the Chinese Wall was heightened and strengthened to prevent the increasing number of escapees crashing heavy trucks through sections of the Wall. The number of clandestine Sector crossings which before August 13th had been approximately eighty, were reduced to twelve, and then to seven. More officers of the Volkspolizei, Volksarmee, FDJ, and Workers' Combat Groups replaced non-commissioned sentries at the crossings and along the Sector frontier since desertions from members of these forces to the West averaged from between twelve to fourteen daily after August 13th. On August 13th, entrance to houses in the East Sector facing the West, were walled up, and before the end of the month, windows were also walled up. Then, forced evictions were carried out. Without previous warning, furniture vans and police drove up to the buildings, ordering their inhabitants to immediately pack up belongings and clear out. Their homes were no longer theirs. Their homes were to be turned into part of the massive Wall dividing the two halves of the city.

For the first few days after August 13th, friends and relatives were able to talk to one another or exchange packages over the wire fence or the brick Wall, if they kept beyond sight of the sentries, but on 23rd, the Minister of the Interior in the Soviet Zone called on the population "in the interest of their own safety to remain outside a distance of a hundred metres on either side of the boundary between the capital of the DDR and West Berlin." In the East Sector, this was strictly enforced as a regulation, but in the West, Mayor Brandt described this attempt at an infraction of the freedom of movement in West Berlin as "an unheard-of piece of effrontery," and the three Western Commandants at once protested against this new restriction in a statement accusing the East Berlin authorities of encroachment, and ordered a thousand troops and tanks to take up positions along the Sector boundary to ensure complete freedom of movement of West Berliners in their own city up to the Chinese Wall. Two days later, Gerhart Eisler, the East German propaganda chief instructed and encouraged youths everywhere, to climb rooftops and pull down the antennae of people receiving West Berlin television programmes.

Within two weeks of writing to Martin, I received his reply. The first half of his letter was full of personal news. He described the pleasure and usefulness of his six month sojourn in France. He had recently graduated and now held a well-paid post in Charlottenburg. The second half of his letter was devoted to the political crisis in Berlin. He said that the atmosphere was despondent and pessimistic, and that since the Sector frontier had been closed, East Germans were using the most desperate means of escaping into West Berlin through the heavily guarded Zonal frontier round the city, cutting their way through wire fences, running over dangerous marshland and mined strips, crawling on their stomachs through meadows overgrown with high grass and reeds, in the view of watchtowers and searchlights, and swimming across the wide Havel river. Along the Sector frontier, meanwhile, there were almost daily incidents:

stonings by angry West Berliners of the East German police, and retaliation with smoke bombs, tear gas and water hoses. West Berliners were even leaving the city and settling in Western Germany because the strain was becoming unbearable.

Martin expressed the view that the events of August 13th had only been made possible by the West European press attacks on Berlin and West Germany of almost exactly a year earlier. He said that this was a subjective view, and he reminded me of the events of August and September 1960 – but he need hardly have done so for the events were still fresh in my memory. It was at that time when I was in Münster and had written to Dagmar for the first time since the first breaking of our friendship. The East German authorities in protesting against what they absurdly described as a revanchist rally, had then initiated restrictions on those wishing to enter the Eastern half of the city.

I remembered how angered my student friends and I had been by the reactions of the Western press to this infraction on free movement within Berlin, and of how the East German papers had quoted widely from the Western press. I remembered Eberhard's outbursts of rage and how amused we were by them, but since then a year had passed, and he had been proven right in the theory he so doggedly propounded. The restrictions of the East German authorities preventing free movement in Berlin at the end of the August 1960 were merely a trial run – a dress rehearsal for the events of August 13th 1961. In August-September 1960, the West had given the green light to the Reds. The West – or at least, the Western press had callously betrayed the people of Berlin. Because of its attitude at that time, the blame had to some extent to be laid at the feet of the press for the events of August 13th. I could not but agree with Martin's bitter analysis.

As I folded the letter placing it in a drawer in my desk, I remembered the first occasion I met Martin at the Café Royal. It was long ago – that first meeting – but I remembered the urgency with which he had told me about the problems of his native city. Thanks to my chance meeting with Martin Schultz, I had seen and experienced much since that historic day three years previously.

Dagmar's reply never came, and finally, I accepted the sad truth that the bonds between us had been severed forever. What remained was the memory of the experience – so much joy and pain – and the scar which is left across the heart with all such broken friendships. But the outcome of our relationship had been pre-ordained. It could never have been otherwise. We had been ill-starred lovers from the moment of our first meeting in Stalin Allee. If I recollected with remorse that I had wronged her in thought and deed – by hasty actions and thoughtless omissions leading to the termination of our friendship – I recollected that nonetheless there remained an inextricable conflict between us.

In our parting, both of us were forced to carry our different crosses. I remembered the terrible secret she was bound to carry to the grave – the scar which marked her wounded soul. She was such a sensitive creature, strangely perplexed by confusing emotions, and her life was eternally bound with the fate of her native city. As her letter never arrived, I never found out what became of the girl from East Berlin.

Epilogue
Sixty Years On

"What is time? The shadow on the dial, the striking of the
clock, the running of the sand, day and night, summer and
winter, months, years, centuries – these are but arbitrary
and outward signs, the measure of Time, not Time itself.
Time is the life of the soul."

Longfellow, *Hyperion*, Bk. ii, ch. 6.

The aircraft was high above a blanket of cloud when it began its
descent on approaching Berlin, and I was apprehensive over the
days which would follow. It was some sixty years since I first
visited the city, and now I was using a very different mode of travel from
that of many years ago. The German railway system may still have been
amongst the finest in Europe, but who arrived today from a foreign
destination except by air? This was the age of bargain flights and tight
time schedules, and few in a hurry were tempted away by an alternative
form of transport.

I was visiting Berlin to search the whereabouts of half-forgotten
friends and discover their fate in the intervening years, and particularly
that of my past love, Dagmar Renot. Such a curiosity was only natural in
view of the deep impressions I had experienced in the city, and I was
apprehensive at the prospect of meeting the "fair one."

It was with some misgiving I had embarked on such a venture –
and with good reason. It was audacious and impossible to anticipate the
response I might arouse. The first steps towards planning such a trip had
been cautious and discreet, but after some initial enquiries, I had
unwittingly become entangled in the scheming of another, who for her
own motives of prurient curiosity, was impelled to arrange a meeting
between the two former lovers from the distant past – and irrespective of
what their feelings might now be towards one another. I had wanted to
step with care and negotiate with tact, but in this situation I felt no longer
in control in anticipating what was to be the outcome. Overcome with
trepidation and realising the risks, I was induced to ask the question:
under such circumstances, did I really after all want to meet with
Dagmar?

Why should I wish to meet her? And there was less reason for her
wishing to meet me. Our lives had diverged. I had moved in a direction
far removed from the life and events of Berlin, and had developed other
aspirations and interests which had brought me some success and
fulfilment in life. Dagmar had been consigned to the past – or so I

thought – and other women had gained my affection, and is not the past best forgotten in avoiding to upset the relationships of the present? The tragedy of our broken friendship had left an open wound on my heart for some six months or so after I departed Berlin in that Summer of 1960, and it was a wound re-opened in that dreadful August which shocked the world the following year.

But six decades had passed since that shameful event, and a busy life and the striving for personal achievement and the formation of new relationships and a domestic life (which irrespective of its fulfilment) was seen as average by friends and acquaintances beyond the family circle, had together with the passing of time created a distance from that love affair of limited duration of long ago. And yet, over the past few decades, inexplicably and out of nowhere, I had been haunted by a recurring dream which was unchanging in its imagery and relentless in the repetition in its course of action.

Conscious that many years had passed since our last meeting, and that I had meanwhile led a long and lonely bachelorhood, and after a brief correspondence with Dagmar, I found myself once again in the divided city. Walking along a broad empty street in the Western half of Berlin, with the grey Wall on my right, I made hurriedly for the Sector crossing point. The formalities at the crossing point were, surprisingly, almost waived aside, and I entered East Berlin, and was confronted by an open square with Moscow style apartment blocks and buildings with onion-domed roofs, and crowds of drably-dressed people moving quickly to and fro.

Immediately I was met by Papa Renot, and after a perfunctory exchange of greetings after which no more was spoken, we re-traced the direction I had come, but this time walking alongside the Wall in the Eastern half of the city, and dusk was closing in. Perhaps the silence of the old man was partly explained by his annoyance at the protracted period of my return. After a long distance we reached Dagmar's house, and the front door was opened by her mother, who simply exclaimed, "She's been waiting for you," and I was shown into Dagmar's bedroom where we were left alone.

It was a small dark room and she was seated nervously at the edge of the bed. At once I was relieved that she had hardly aged during the long intervening years and my heart was filled with hope and happiness. Nonetheless, we both remained momentarily silent, with serious downcast expressions, neither betraying feelings to the other.

"The years have hardly changed you," I said at last.

"That's because I was waiting for your return," she responded with a strange weariness.

"You look thirty-three rather than twenty-three, but that's given you an added lustre and beauty."

"And you, too, have not aged," she said.

"We must have been made for one another that we've retained our looks after all these years," I remarked with optimism. "What have you done since I left Berlin?"

"I knew you'd return. I've just been waiting."

I was astonished by her reply, and the patience of her heart which this reflected, and by her trust in such an eventual outcome.

"Then let us continue our friendship as if it was never broken," I said.

"Yes, we can do that," she replied, but in a tone which was strangely casual.

I was surprised by her reply, but reassured by her calm finality, and felt that the future was truly ours.

"We do share the same interests and I know we'll be happy together," I said.

"I think so, too," she answered.

Her calm resignation raised my optimism further.

"Too many wasted years have passed in our lives," I said. "We must make up for lost time, and re-capture the years of our lost youth."

"Yes, we must do that," she said simply. "Have you ever been married,?" she added raising her head and looking into my eyes.

"No, never," I answered. "I'm sorry I've been so long returning but I've been busy. Work commitments have kept me away."

"I'll be sorry to leave home," she said sadly.

"But we must," I said, " – and now. An opportunity has arisen. I know a crossing point where the security is lax. We'll tell them we're a married couple. I know they'll let us through. Take up your coat and let us leave now."

"Yes," she said, and she rose from the bed, taking up her blue light weight coat which was lying there.

"We'll cross the Sector and be married in West Berlin tomorrow," I said.

"Yes," she answered calmly, almost with indifference.

"Come, let us say goodbye to your parents," I said taking her arm.

At that point I awoke, and the realism of the dream had been so intense that for some seconds my happiness was sustained, until it dawned on my waking consciousness – which momentarily I tried to push back – that it was after all only a dream, and I realised that in actuality I had already been married for many years.

The aircraft was now approaching Schoenefeld, the airport to the south east of Berlin, at one time the main entry point for international flights ariving at the capital of the DDR, but now the main airport for budget carriers. Below was a huge expanse of deciduous forest broken by lakes, rivers and connecting canals, and on cleared areas of meadowland, for as far as the eye could see, were clusters of white generating windtowers in their dozens. Clearly the environmental cause of self-generating energy had captured the imagination of the Berlin authorities!

Over the previous few weeks I had researched the whereabouts and fate of the Renot family, at first through the web and then through a series of telephone calls, and to my relief at enquiries from a stranger out of the blue, I had been met invariably by a helpful response. Perhaps such an attitude was a legacy from the past, when following the upheaval of the post-War period, millions of displaced and possibly deceased persons, both civilian and military, had been sought by relatives and loved ones. In any event, I felt that such enquiries out of the unknown would not have been met by quite such friendliness by any other people.

Eventually I tracked down Dagmar to an address in Erkner, beyond the eastern limits of Berlin. My first thoughts were that she had possibly moved closer to Werlsee as a tribute to the memory of her first love and affianced, who lived there in the idyllic home of his parents. Or had he perchance even returned, possibly after a long term of imprisonment, and had she welcomed with open arms the return of a long-lost lover, and had all been resolved to the happiness of them both, and were they now living in wedded bliss? This move to Erkner and the close proximity to Werlsee seemed to suggest such a happy outcome. But alas, the evidence for such an outcome was soon contradicted. I had indeed elicited the fact she was married, but her name was not Lierbermann but Beck.

More curious was the fact that both sisters – both married, lived at the same address, or rather, shared the same house number. I concluded, therefore, that such an address must be that of a large apartment block, typical of the city. As Gisela's husband's first name was Franz, I hazarded she had married the friend I had known in Berlin. Close family ties must have brought all four of them together to an address in Erkner.

The provisional arrangements to meet the family had not been arranged through either Dagmar or her sister, but through the too-willing participation of the latter's married daughter, Angela Kohler. We had first communicated through email and then by phone. She was very curious about my enquiry, saying she knew nothing about her aunt having once formed a friendship with an Englishman. She humorously remarked she half-suspected her aunt had had "a past," since she was so reticent about her youth, whilst also indicating that in reality she believed she had lived a very ordinary and uneventful life as a shop assistant. I gathered from

Angela Kohler that I must have known very much more about Dagmar's "past" than her, but I drew this conclusion not on account of my own friendship, which was of short duration, but on account of her friendship with her first love, Dietrich Liebermann.

Angela promised to approach both her mother and her aunt on the matter, in setting up a meeting either in their home or in a restaurant in central Berlin.

"Please tread carefully," I pleaded. "I would not like any feelings to be upset unnecessarily."

"I know what you mean," said Angela. "I'll ask them for my sake. If they see it from my viewpoint there's a better chance of my aunt agreeing. Leave it to me. I'm curious to know more."

"I know I can rely on your discretion," I answered.

It was suggested I phone back in a week. On that occasion Angela intimated there was a "slight difficulty," but not to worry as it would easily be overcome. Her aunt was a retiring type, and any break in her routine or anything unusual tended to upset her nerves. (Nothing's changed, I only thought.) To this response I expressed reluctance at the idea of setting up a meeting, apologising for having initiated some understandable embarrassment, but Angela became alarmed by this back-pedalling, and speaking excitedly she exclaimed, "Don't let me down after all the efforts I've made. I've been speaking with my aunt for four days now, and I know I'll pull her round. She'll appreciate meeting you on the day, and you'll both find it rewarding."

"Alright, but I don't want to call round if it looks like trouble."

"It'll never be that, I promise you," said Angela. "Just phone as soon as you're in Berlin, and I'll arrange all the rest."

On arriving in Berlin I was in no hurry to meet the Renot family until I had become acclimatised to the city of the post-DDR era, and had made contact with other friends. I had visited Berlin on some seven or eight occasions, several times on business, but I had not been in the city for twenty-two years, and it was seventeen years since the Wall had been torn down. I would therefore be experiencing the vitality of a city which for the first time in my life was now politically free in a true sense, if one dated the loss of the city's (and the country's) freedom to the edict of 14th July 1933 establishing the NSDAP as the only legally recognised party under the Third Reich – and that event occurred two years before my birth.

As I stayed with friends whom I had not seen for many years in the quiet idyllic suburb of Schulzendorf, with its handsome villas and lush well-kept gardens, on the northern outsksirts of the city, and as they begged me to prolong my stay, I felt reluctant to push my luck with the Renots and was increasingly apprehensive at the idea of attempting to renew my acquaintance with Dagmar. Hence I felt free to explore the city at leisure, and as it was May, everywhere lilac and horse chestnuts were in bloom.

The city centre was far greener than I had known it, for in the cold winters of the immediate post-War period, and especially during the Berlin airlift of 1949, many trees had been felled for domestic heating, and the newly planted saplings had only attained a modest growth during my earlier visits to the capital. And now these trees had reached a great height, and in small side streets and major thoroughfares alike, they had been allowed to grow to their full potential, unthreatened by the chain-saw of the tree surgeon's lopping or trimming.

A new spirit pervaded a once divided city, and the notorious Wall was fast becoming a memory of the past. It was often hard to distinguish between the former Eastern and Western halves of the city, for heavy investment as well as small-scale entrepreneurship had turned grimy and depressing areas and once-empty streets into colourful and lively centres with pavement cafés and restaurants offering a wide variety of cuisines. Even the old psychological divide between East and West was fast falling away, and it was with some surprise when a West Berliner friend invited me to meet him at the Hackescher Markt, near Alexander Platz, for an evening out.

"The magnetic centre of Berlin is changing from West to East," he exclaimed as we sat with his wife enjoying an Italian meal.

"The Ku'damm's lost something of its old glamour," I remarked.

"The big department stores and the expensive shops are still there," explained my friend, "and at one time it was a centre for the larger cinemas. But now they have moved the multi-screen complexes to the area around Potsdamer Platz – and the restaurants are going too."

"The Wall used to go through Potsdamer Platz, and the area was once a wasteland," I said.

"Next week they're opening a new main line station in Berlin, at the Lehrter Bahnhof," said my friend's wife.

"But that's an old station," I said.

"It's been rebuilt," said my friend. "And the long distance trains will no longer stop at the Zoo station."

"What do the people of Charlottenburg and Wilmersdorf think about that,?" I asked.

"They're upset, *very* upset," answered my friend. "But the centre of Berlin is in the East. All the great museums, the Cathedral, the government buildings, the Humboldt University, are all situated in the East – or rather the East of the post-War period, or what we call the *Mitte*."

One evening I was taken by my hosts to the Reichstag, which behind the handsome 19th century façade had been rebuilt to a design by Sir Norman Foster. We ascended by lift to the roof, and promenade area and restaurant, and then strolled up a gentle walkway within the huge glass dome of the building. A technological wonder comprising a mirror-clad funnel at the dome's centre cast daylight into the parliamentary chamber, and as we walked towards the apex of the dome, so our view of the delegates' seating area was extended to an ever-widening circle. This was the recently restored national parliament of the largest democracy in the EU.

Most notable was the ease and speed of travel within the new Berlin on the S- and U-Bahn local railway networks, for the Berlin of the Communist era necessitated all manner of barriers and lengthy diversions to reach a desired destination. And now on the S-Bahn it was possible to reach destinations in Brandenburg, beyond the limits of Berlin, such as Babelsburg or Potsdam to the west, or Oranienburg in the north, or Königs Wusterhausen to the south east. The trains were clean and comfortable, and the high proportion of stations with disabled access would have put the London underground to shame. I also noted the safety signalling facilities for partially sighted people situated at junctions in all parts of the city. German legislation for the well-being of ordinary people always had been in advance of most other countries in the industrialised world.

In travelling around the capital I soon ascertained that Berlin had become more racially diverse than hitherto – although not to the extent of London. In the Eastern half of the city were many north Vietnamese who had originally been sent by their government during the DDR regime to assist in building projects, and now they were self-employed as street traders and especially as flower sellers, or in opening and managing "Chinese" restaurants. Meanwhile, the Vietnamese in West Berlin were usually "boat people" from the south.

Frequently one saw the occasional schoolchild of Asian or African appearance on an S- or U-Bahn platform, laughing and joking amongst their caucasian peers, but fully integrated as equals amongst their German friends. These were more often children adopted by German couples from Third World countries, and in view of their wretched prospects at birth, and in view of the homogeneity of the German cultural environment, it was heartwarming to anticipate their life chances would be on an equal par with those of any other ethnic German child.

Because of my interest in the recent history of Berlin, my hosts urged me to visit the notorious Stasi prison in Hohenschönhausen, which was now a museum and memorial to the many political prisoners who had suffered torture, persecution and death during the forty-four year rule of the Communist regime. All political suspects in the Berlin area were initially brought to this Special Soviet Camp and remand prison of the Ministry for State Security, but many remained for many years, enclosed in small cells enduring a living death, subjected to brutal punishment on a daily basis. Deprived of a name and given a number, often they were never charged with a crime, and even on release never discovered the circumstances which had led to their arrest.

The prison could only be inspected under the guidance of a group tour leader, and these had been recruited from amongst the ex-inmates themselves. Hence the description of the prison methods was not a second hand account by those who had never suffered as victims of political tyranny, but a living narrative of the immediate experience of day-to-day brutality and the mental and physical torments which had been endured by mind and body in an attempt to destroy the will and last vestiges of personality. We were shown the bunker-like cells in the so-called "Submarine;" the padded interrogation rooms with their double doors; the innocent-looking white vans with their barred interiors in which the hapless victims arrived at the remand centre; the Tiger cages, or exercise yards, which offered the prisoners the only opportunity for a brief glimpse at the sky; and the memorials to those who had not survived the conditions, or had been taken away and executed in Moscow or elsewhere.

As we stood around our guide, Germans and other nationalities alike, captivated by the detailed recital of inflicted humiliation and fear, we were awed by the privilege of meeting such a victim of political oppression, and at the same time humbled by the significance of his courage at having survived such an ordeal. He faced many questions which were answered at length. I asked what "crime" he had committed which led to his arrest.

He explained that as a 25-year old in 1966 he had sent a letter to a newscaster in West Berlin. This had led to six months at the Stasi remand prison followed by a year in a labour camp. At the tour's end we each pressed his hand and thanked him for having shared his thoughts and feelings on his fight for freedom, and an American lady, who had followed the tour through an interpreter at her side, after saying how moved she had been by his account, kissed him on the cheek.

Most surprising were those changes in the lesser known parts of the city I had come to know so well amost fifty years ago. The Eierschale night club in Breitenbach Platz, where I had been with Martin Schutz and his friends, no longer existed. On arriving at the site and enquiring as to its whereabouts from an Indian restaurateur supervising a group of German decorators, he pointed to a door alongside his premises, saying that "down there" such a club had supposedly existed. I descended a flight of stairs into a dark cellar with tables and chairs around a small dance floor, and spoke with an ageing barman with a gold ring in his ear.

"This is a jazz club now," he explained. "The Eierschale packed up about thirty years ago – although there is a restaurant of the same name in Treptow, but it's nothing to do with the old club."

"And where have all the signs gone that were salvaged from the bomb sites and placed on the walls,?" I asked.

"They've all been thrown away for scrap where they should be," he laughed. "No one wants to be reminded of the War any more."

So this is the outcome of the will to forget, I only thought to myself. At this rate, in a few years time the people here will begin to deny that Berlin had ever been bombed in its history!

As for the riotous night club, Remde's St. Pauli Am Zoo, which I had visited with the Krelas on the last day I had been with Dagmar (and I was not to see her the following morning as originally arranged – or indeed in the conceivable future) no one even seemed to know of its existence. It had been situated on Kant Strasse 162, but that was now occupied by a hard core sex cinema and a dozen or so private cubicles for viewing pornographic videos. The staff on the premises, who all seemed to be foreigners, had never heard of Remde's and did not know that a club had ever existed on the site.

Stalin Allee, now returned to its former name of Frankfurter Allee, still existed in all its wedding-cake splendour, and the towers of Strausberger Platz dominated over the indistinctive and more recently built apartment blocks nearby. The Art Shop, which led to that fateful meeting in 1959 was alas no more, and in its place was an insurance office. The café Moscow on the approach to Strausberger Platz from the city centre, with its huge sign on the roof in both Cyrillic and Latin text, and its gargantuan mosaic of Third World peoples being led by a spanner-carrying Russian worker, was now an empty and vandalised ruin.

Of the tramway in Graetz Strasse (now long known as Karl-Kunger-Strasse) no trace remained, and the street no longer led to the Wiener bridge across the Landwehr Kanal which had been a Sector crossing point before the erection of the Wall. Indeed, the Wiener Brücke had been demolished, and the western end of of the former Graetz Strasse now ended in a T-junction along which ran a high hedge on the other side of Lohmühlen Strasse. Between the hedge and the line of the canal, which had been a forbidden area during the period of the Wall, was a hippy encampment, and indeed, many such former no-go strips of land throughout Berlin which had once been planted with landmines, had curiously now been taken over by squatters with their tents and caravans.

The magnificent Görlitzer Bahnhof, originally intended as the terminus of the Berlin-Baghdad railway at the close of the 19th century, had been demolished entirely, and its goods yards and shunting area had been converted into a quiet park and sports area. In Spreewald Platz, which had been taken over predominantly by Turkish grocery stores, I could find no trace of the Pension where I had stayed in 1960. In the other direction where I had often walked with Dagmar to Treptower Park S-Bahn station, the building which had once housed the HQ of the Treptower Volkspolizei in Bouche Strasse remained unchanged, but it had now been taken over by the Bundes Kriminalamt.

The surroundings of Friedrich Strasse station had altered entirely. The pavement café where Dietrich had taken Dagmar on the second occasion of their meeting no longer existed. Whilst the iron and glass structure of the Bahnhof remained as it had always been, the shops and walkways within had been transformed into 21st century modernity; whilst the surrounding buildings comprised contemporary style bronze coloured steel and glass structures, housing banks, finance offices, and shops.

A visit to Werlsee and the former home of the Liebermanns was, I felt, an essential stopping point. I took the S-Bahn to Erkner, and from there by taxi in completing the last two or three kilometres of the journey. As anticipated, Werlsee was situated in idyllic countryside by a peaceful lake, far from the hustle and bustle of Berlin. On making enquiries in searching out the Liebermanns' villa, I discovered it had been demolished towards the close of the 1980s.

After the death of the Lierbermanns, the building had been taken over as a medical practice by a group of doctors for several years, but then the building had been left empty and fallen into decacy – an act of criminal negligence which occurred all-too frequently with historical buildings in the DDR. Then in 1990 the Median Klinik, a convalescent centre for post-operative cases, was constructed on a site nearby, and I felt that this could be taken as a satisfying memorial to the distinguished medical work of Dr. Liebermann.

Having explored the sites associated with the story of Dagmar Renot, I was keen to renew some of the friendships I had made on my first visit to the city in 1959. I wanted to visit Fritz Krela, not because I particularly liked the fellow, but because I was curious as to his fate. He had the type of personality – vulgarly and boastfully workaholic, and hedonistic in his leisure pursuits – which was no longer typical of the German of the 1990s or the 21st century. He was a product of the Erhard years and the "Economic Miracle," and there had been many changes since those early decades of the post-War period.

Germans had become more relaxed and mature in their attitude to work, and some old illusions had been shattered. There were values other than the work ethic, such as family values and the pursuit of cultural interests, and the Germans had become less dynamic in their pursuit of materialism. They enjoyed longer holidays than most other peoples in the industrialised world, and it was the British who seemed to have taken on the mantle of the stressed-out workaholics.

I contacted Anne Krela, and without having exchanged any news over the phone, I was invited to call round that very afternoon. It was still the same flat in Schmargendorf, but the furnishings were different. Gone was the Scandinavian furniture, to be replaced by the reassuring but dark heavy oak in traditional style. Fritz had died suddenly two years previously, due to diabetic complications and a weak heart. He had been seventy-three.

"He was such a dear, really," said his widow, "and he was always such fun. I do miss him. He was always so generous and kind. But he put on weight towards the end."

He always was overweight, I thought to myself.

"He was too fond of his food and beer," continued Anne. "He was supposed to be on a diet, but he never took the doctor's advice. 'If I'm to go I'll go,' he used to say. 'I'm not going to give up pleasure for a few extra years of miserable abstinence. I've worked too hard in my life to deserve such a fate.' It was that which killed him in the end," she added sadly.

Martin Schultz was untraceable in Berlin, and I had to accept the fact it was unlikely we should meet again. I had last met him in London some six months after my second visit to Berlin in 1960. He had formed a close relationship with a British film director – I had not suspected he was that way inclined – and the three of us met in the West End. Martin and I were taken for tea at the Ritz in Piccadilly before seeing a film. After some discussion it was either a choice between Bergman's *Smultronstället*, or Renoir's *Les Quatre Cents Coups*, both films of which the three of us had already seen.

My preference was to see the first, but as Martin's friend had been left cold by the haunting dreams of the ageing professor, Isak Borg, in Bergman's film, we opted for Renoir's moving film about a young truant who fell into petty crime due to the neglect of his parents. Thereafter, Martin and I exchanged several letters, most notably after the erection of the Wall, but then we drifted apart.

At last the time was pressing for a final decision on whether or not to follow my original intention in seeking a meeting with a loved one of almost fifty years earlier. I was filled with trepidation, but as there were only three more days before my return flight to London, I plucked up courage and contacted Angela Kohler as promised some weeks before. She responded with relief at my phone call, saying she had feared I had finally decided against renewing contact with the family. I said I was only too happy to meet her and her aunt, and she invited me to call at her mother's house the following afternoon.

"But don't you want to alert them first," I suggested.

"Don't worry, my aunt hardly ever goes out," said Angela. "If I tell them too soon they'll only get nervous. Everything must be made spontaneous. I'll tell them tomorrow morning. That'll be soon enough."

As I arrived early in Erkner, I strolled around the centre. It had the feel of a holiday resort with its white houses and flowers in window boxes, its wooded park and expansive grass area leading down to the lake, its tourist office with a wide display of leaflets publicising local events and places, and its many yachts moored along the shore. This is a far cry from Treptow, I thought. Dagmar must have come up in the world!

It was three o'clock when I arrived at the house in Erkner, after a short bus ride, and I was surprised by the street and its environment. I had anticipated reaching an area of large apartment blocks, but it was a street of small and pleasant cottages, set in a lightly wooded area, each different from the other, and each surrounded by lush and well-kept gardens. I arrived at a two-storied white house with a steep-pitched red-tiled roof, the eaves of which on either side of the building were a mere four feet from the ground.

On the right side of the house, dividing it from the adjoining property, was a babbling brook in the shade of a willow. At the side of a small wicker gate was a concrete post with separate letter boxes marked "Beck" and "Redler" – the latter being Gisela's married name. I entered and knocked on the door. It was answered by a lively and cheerful woman in her mid-forties, who welcomed me with some excitement, and sat in me a comfortable chair in an over-furnished living room. It was difficult to get a word in edgeways but I wanted to dispense with formalities.

"Please don't address me as Herr Furner," I pleaded. "Call me by my first name."

"That makes things so much easier for an open discussion," agreed Angela Kohler. "You know, it was very difficult to set up this meeting. My aunt didn't want to meet you, but I insisted she should."

"You shouldn't have done that," I responded. "You could have made it embarrassing for us both."

"I hate secrecy – any kind of secrecy. I think people should be open about their lives," said Angela. "My aunt has always been so closed-up and reticent about the past."

"But people have a right to their privacy," I suggested.

"There are many people from the old DDR who are too closed-up. I think it's unhealthy. All their lives they've been on their guard against revealing themselves. It's a legacy from the old regime."

"I can understand that," I said.

"But it's not necessary any more," said Angela. "Today we can say what we like."

Suddenly the front door was pushed open and a thick-set lad of average height bounced into the room with a carefree air. Immediately I noticed there was something familiar about the features and the set of his blue eyes.

"This is my son, Erik," said Angela. "He's sixteen."

"He has a remarkable resemblance to his great-grandfather, Papa Renot," I exclaimed in astonishment.

"I never knew him," said Angela. "He died when I was still a baby."

When I last met Dagmar she was a 23-year old and I was twenty-five, I recollected to myself, and now she's a great aunt to a teenager!

Angela began to speak in broken English, I assumed to show-off in front of her son.

"You can't say that – you speak terrible English," exclaimed her son, and if it was not for his laughing and half-mocking good humour his words would have been taken for rudeness.

"Your mother speaks very good English," I said defensively.

"You don't mean that. You're only being polite," retorted Erik.

"You're being silly now," said his mother awkwardly.

He likes embarrassing people and he's got the Berlin cheek, I thought to myself. He has the personality of his great-grandfather, and some of his mannerisms too. How can that possibly be after four generations,? I asked myself.

"If you want to travel and be free, you have to learn English and speak it properly," continued Erik. "Not stumbling, with all those stupid mistakes like you. No one will take you seriously."

"I didn't have the chances you had," replied his mother. "I spent all my early years in the DDR. We never had a proper choice in life. You weren't born until a year after the Wall came down. You don't know how lucky you are. – He wants to be an environmental scientist," she said turning to me.

"I want to work in Africa," said Erik.

"He's got a lot of studying to do before that," said his mother. "But he'll make it."

"Do you all live in this small cottage,?" I asked glancing around the room.

"No, it's two cottages back to back. My parents live here facing the street, and my aunt and her husband live in the cottage facing the back garden. – There are lots of houses like that in Berlin," added Angela when she saw I looked perplexed. "We share the entrance gate, and the pathway round to the back is a right of way. Normally the front and back gardens would be divided, but as we're a close family, we share all the land around."

"And where do you live,?" I enquired.

"We live in Bohnsdorf – not far from the airport. It's a similar area to this. My husband works in the traffic control tower."

"You must tell me something more about your aunt and her husband before they arrive," I said. "Did she remain a shop assistant all her life?"

"She did nothing else. There's nothing really more to tell about her," said Angela. "Nothing significant has ever happened to her."

"How did she meet her husband,?"

"She married late in life. She married a widower – much older than herself."

"Just like her mother," I put in.

"Mother thought she would never marry. She was thirty-two when she did."

"That's not old," I said.

"It's not old today, but it was then," said Angela.

"What occupation has her husband?"

"He's been retired many years now. He was some kind of government official. I don't know what. We never talk about it. He was just a pen-pusher. Something harmless! Ex-government employees of the DDR never want to talk about their work. They just want to forget."

"Did they ever have children?"

"No, neither wanted children," replied Angela. "As with many couples in the DDR they couldn't reconcile the idea of bringing up children under such a regime. You know what I mean, with children being encouraged to report on their parents, and all that sort of thing."

There was a sound at the front door, and a couple in their late 60s entered the room, the man slim and tall with silver hair and the woman overweight but still with a fresh complexion and large blue eyes.

"These are my parents," said Angela.

"I remember them well," I answered, and rose for the exchange of greetings, and immediately I addressed each by their first names to break through the barrier of formality.

"I'll get the tea and cakes, mother. You sit with Herr Furner," said Angela. "And you, Erik, go and fetch your aunt – and tell her not to delay."

Gisela looked at me with the same friendly curiosity as she had done almost fifty years ago in the family home in Graetz Strasse. At first the conversation was slow and hesitant, as the ageing couple took time to comprehend the fact of this stranger from the past suddenly landing on their doorstep, but with the return of old memories, a warmth began to pervade the atmosphere.

"Do you remember how fascinated you were by my dressing gown that morning as I went into the washroom,?" I said.

"It was such a beautiful silky material. You had such luxurious things," said Gisela. "That's what it seemed like at the time. I remember you had an electric shaver. It was so chic!"

"Gisela was a fashion model in those days," said Franz with a smile. "She liked beautiful clothes."

"I remember the outing we made to the Great Müggel See," I said. "We went for a swim, and then to a restaurant, and afterwards we went for a walk, and Gisela picked some berries in the forest which she gave to us."

"It was to stop you two men talking politics," said Gisela.

"So you *do* remember,!" I said astonished.

"As if it was yesterday," returned Gisela.

"You asked so many questions. You wanted to know everything," said Franz.

"I can't remember that," I said.

"I felt safe talking with you – a Westerner," said Franz.

Again, there was a rustle at the door, and Erik led in an elderly couple. We rose from our seats, and suddenly, my heart lost a beat as a shockwave passed through my body at the scene which confronted us. It was not that she had grown old beyond her years, for she had not, and she was as slim as on the day we had both been last together. It was simply that she had aged at all, a psychological fact I was unable to accept, for she was no longer the 23-year old I had known of almost fifty years ago.

Her face was lined and grey and her eyes were buried beneath heavy brows. Both sisters had taken on the physical characteristics of their father, but in quite different ways. Whilst Gisela had inherited his fat, Dagmar had taken on the dark rings around his eyes. Her husband was clearly a much older man, supported by a stick, but tall with a fine head of grey hair, and evidently he had been handsome in his younger years. Introductions were formal and cold as we shook hands and exchanged bows.

Angela returned to the room and bid us sit round the table, and tea and cakes were served.

"And have you two renewed your acquaintance yet,?" said Angela indicating towards Dagmar and me, as we sat opposite to one another across the table. "I'm sure you both have a lot to say"

"They're tongue-tied and shy of one another," said Erik cheekily.

"You've kept yourself in good condition," said Dagmar in a serious tone to break the silence.

"And so have you," I replied returning the compliment.

"Come on, surely you can say something better than that," said Angela filling our cups.

"You live in a beautiful environment here," I said. "It's so different from Graetz Strasse. And isn't this just the kind of house you said you always wanted to live in?"

"What makes you say that,?" said Dagmar sharply.

"Don't you remember when we were together in Pfaueninsel, and we saw a cottage with which you were enchanted, and I promised that one day I would buy you such a cottage?"

"I don't remember that. It was so long ago."

"How can you forget a thing like that aunty,?" exclaimed Erik. "That was true love speaking straight from the heart."

Dagmar began to ask after the course of my life and career, and as to my children and grandchild, and as to their occupations and prospects.

"You've been lucky in life," she said at last. "You've been free and able to travel. Our lives were blighted. You can't begin to understand what we've had to endure up to seventeen years ago. It's been terrible, terrible!"

She seemed to be expressing some of the reproachful thoughts reminiscent in letters of almost fifty years ago, I thought to myself.

"But now you're free," I said encouragingly.

"It's not always easy for us here in the new Germany," interposed her husband. "Pensions are still not good in the East, and we have to scratch around to make ends meet."

"Yes, it's difficult for the older people, and there's a lot of unemployment, but nothing was as bad as living under the old Communist regime," said Gisela. "At least we have hope and are free to move about. But under the DDR it was just propaganda and mis-information and broken promises, and fear, fear, fear! You could trust no one, and people went missing just like that, and you never knew why."

"And the strange thing is," said Franz, "that no one realised at the time we were living in fear. It had become such a natural and accepted way of life. It was only when the Wall came down, and we regained our freedom, that we began to understand the full horror of the past."

"People simply suppressed their fear," said Dagmar's husband. "They weren't prepared to acknowledge it. And people who'd lived all their lives in the DDR had never experienced freedom. They had to learn from scratch what freedom was."

"Did you ever hear about Dietrich Liebermann again,?" I said tentatively to Dagmar across the table.

"Never," said Dagmar.

"Who's Dietrich Liebermann,?" asked Angela looking around the table.

Gisela and Franz lowered their heads, and I noticed a spasm of irritation pass over the face of Dagmar's husband.

"It's something we never talk about," said Dagmar sharply.

"Was he another sweetheart, aunty,?" asked Angela with a smile. "Now with James's visit, all your secrets are coming out. Tell us all about it."

"It was nothing, nothing," said Dagmar. "Just a silly episode that didn't last."

"We always thought you lived such a dull uneventful life," said Angela. "Now we know different."

"Don't upset your aunt. It'll make her nervous," said Gisela to her daughter.

"It's not that," said Dagmar turning to her sister. "It's just that some things are best forgotten."

"Well, that's not my view," said Angela, "but I won't say any more."

"I think we should talk about our guest," said Dagmar with an ironic look.

"There's nothing more to tell about me. I've told you everything," I responded with a smile.

"You know, I didn't really want to meet you, but my neice is such a curious cat, she insisted on setting up a meeting," said Dagmar provocatively.

"That's because we're all discovering you've got such an interesting past," said Angela to her aunt.

"What about Herr Furner's past,?" said Dagmar with a sly smile. "I think he's had a past we can talk about. I think he's been with lots of women in his time. I didn't think it when I knew him, but I think it now."

"How can you say that? I can assure you you're wrong," I said laughing with embarrassment. "I'm not like that."

"I can see it in your face. Do you think a woman of my age can't read a man's character. Do you think I was born yesterday? What do you think feminine intuition is for?"

"Really, aunty, how can you say such things,?" exclaimed Angela in response to the laughter of us all. "You're as bad as Erik the way you talk."

"You take after your grandmother, Frau Brüning," I exclaimed with a chuckle. "She was always trying to embarrass me when I stayed with the family.

"You were always misunderstanding her," replied Dagmar.

"Let's all try to behave ourselves, shall we,?" said Gisela in mock seriousness. "Franz, put out some glasses and serve the wine. Isn't it wonderful we can talk freely now, and never be afraid of the midnight knock on the door! And Dagmar, you shouldn't be afraid of Herr Furner. What harm can he do you? – Let's look to the future and live for that. If we're to be productive and enjoy life, that's what matters."

"You're right, mother," said Angela. "If life isn't for enjoyment then what value does it hold?"

An hour later I took my leave of the family and left the house. As I walked down the leafy street in the dazzling sunshine of the early evening, I realised my curiosity had been satisfied. Somehow I felt the illusion of a lifetime had been dispelled. I felt the recurring and haunting dreams of the past three decades would return no more. I had seen her in the flesh and acknowledged the ageing which comes inescapably with the passing of the years, and I felt more intensely the reality of time and the prospect of the grim reaper.

Nonetheless, I was saddened by Angela's perception of her aunt as someone who had led a life of uneventfulness. Dagmar had buried all the pain of the past in a grave of forgetfulness. Perhaps that had arisen through the necessity to live and start anew. But didn't she hold the key to a story which demanded re-telling lest we forget the evils and injustice of the past? I pondered on these things, but was reassured by the hope that the family and its progeny were destined for a better future.

———

www.ingramcontent.com/pod-product-compliance
Lightning Source LLC
Chambersburg PA
CBHW061504020726
47502CB00006B/1927

* 9 7 8 1 9 1 4 3 9 0 0 8 1 *